The Trident Series Volume 2
The Trident and the Scepter

Vic Broquard

Published by Broquard eBooks, East Peoria, IL
61611
©2003, 2008, 2012, 2013, 2014 by Vic Broquard
Fifth Printing; ISBN: 978-1-941415-12-2

Art work by Crooked Willows Studio

author@Broquard-eBooks.com
http://Broquard-eBooks.com

For Morgan and L. Ron Hubbard

Table of Contents

Chapter 1 The Call

The hot autumn sun finally set. In its place, a refreshing late-evening breeze swayed the towering oak trees surrounding Jon's Urbana estate. His back leaning against a moss-covered oak, Jon, a budding musician, continued to improvise on his flute — his soft melody floating on the gentle wind. Now that the oppressive heat had diminished, his music had a more restful quality about it as the melancholy maker blended at long last with the world as it was.

For the past few weeks, Jon had been wrestling with his personal problems which surfaced soon after his return from the land of Rochelle. During his adventures there, the supreme god of that land, Ukko, had given him the well-earned title of "Saint Jon Brown." Since his return to his own world, Jon had had time to reflect upon all that had happened to him in the few previous short months. His suppressed anxieties boiled over. Jon was not a religious person, but gods, goddesses, and devils had become painfully real to him; they existed at least in those other realms.

It had all begun when his sole living relative, his grandfather, had died leaving him both a small fortune — for an impoverished college student — and a magical book of pictures. Since he had just graduated from the University of Illinois with a music degree, his inheritance was greatly welcomed. It meant that he could now afford to go to grad school to perfect his musical talents. To be successful, Jon felt that he needed a "home base" and had spent part of the money to buy this stately old home at the edge of Urbana, near Crystal Lake Park, a few miles north of the campus. The property included nearly an acre of grass and tall trees, just the type of retreat to inspire him and create that sense of peace that he so desperately felt he needed.

He had arranged to have all bills paid for the entire year. Additionally, he had given a neighbor boy the large job of keeping the lawn in shape. Now, he had the luxury of complete freedom of action. He could come and go as he liked; his home base would always be waiting for him. "It's my Golden Opportunity to do what I really want to do," he had explained to his friends, Harry and Nick, a philosopher and engineer respectively.

On the other hand, it had been grandpa's magical picture book that had started all of the trouble. That leather bound book with the trident on the cover contained numerous paintings, so real in appearance, that one could imagine oneself actually there. And that was how Jon's adventures had begun. While staring at his favorite picture of Stilmar Pond with its pair of swans, Jon had transported himself to that world!

There, he discovered how to speak to the swans and other animals or at least develop a mutual understanding. Over the next few weeks, Jon found his mental powers growing enormously.

With the aid of three new friends, he became able to do what would appear as miracles to most people. Out of sheer necessity, he found that he could heal wounds. (Actually, he discovered that with intense concentration he could command body cells to do his bidding.) He found that he could transport himself and others from one place to another, even from one world to another. He could read another's mind or thoughts as easily as his own. He could control and dissipate harmful energies directed at him. He could control another's mind, dominating him or her to his will if needed. Indeed, it was as if he had become something of a superman. It had been a gradual evolution to this state of ability, often driven by a necessity to survive.

But it was one thing to be able to do all of this in the realms of Rochelle and Lindy — they were realms full of magic, sorcery, and swords — medieval-like societies. There, his newfound abilities blended rather well. But it was quite disturbing to discover that he could do all of these things here in his own world. They just did not fit with the modern technological society. He didn't fit. That was the real problem. And he had come to just such a conclusion.

But this was only part of his troubles, actually only a small part. Of greater magnitude were his three new friends — the three incredible women.

First, there was Mandy Blackthorn, the Ranger of the goddess Reylona, goddess of the forest, woodlands, meadows, animals, flowers, and fertility. Mandy was the most incredibly beautiful woman he had even seen. She was five feet nine with mischievous, dark brown eyes. She had long, light brown hair with bangs trimmed at her eyebrows. A leather headband with eagle feathers accentuated her high cheeks and pointed chin with the most perfect lips imaginable. Her high leather boots with feathers matched both her hair and tunic as did the pair of leather arm bands that doubled as bow string guard. In a word, Jon found her stunning. Yet, she was a superb swordsman, highly trained and skilled — an outdoors, nature loving, nature protecting woman. She also had some limited mental powers as well, including the ability to read Jon's thoughts. And she even had some mastery of simpler magical spells. Mandy was powerful and dynamic — a rugged individual with her own ideals which she held as the absolute truth. What Mandy wanted to do, she did. Chaotic and unpredictable? Yes, but her actions were always good in nature, never evil. She owned Blackthorn Castle which she inherited from her father. It was located in the Gnarled Oak Woods, so named from all the twisted oak trees that grew there.

A month before Mandy had met Jon, a band of raiders descended upon the northern edge of the Gnarled Oak Woods. They destroyed a section of the woods, carted off the lumber, and took many slaves. The guardian of this section of woods, Drom Talloak, a druid, was powerless to halt such a large party. So she kept close watch on them. She discovered that the strange book the magic user held was indeed some kind of teleportation device. She observed that he had to concentrate on it to get it to function. A plan formed in the druid's mind. The forest-protecting druid shape-changed into an eagle and soared above the raiders, watching them. As she suspected, when they were leaving, the magic user was the last one to go through the portal. And when he began to concentrate to return himself, she attacked with her spell. A finger of death hit him in the back killing him at once. Drom recovered the book and prayed to Reylona for guidance.

Reylona herself came. Apparently, she had heard the cries of agony from her woodland creatures. After hearing

Drom's tale, Reylona asked her to repair the damaged forest. The goddess took the book and came to Blackthorn Castle. Reylona told Mandy about the raid and gave her the book and told her to investigate. She subsequently met Jon at Stilmar Pond in the land of Lindy.

Then, there was Darless, the sexy alu-demon. She was the only child of the desperate Hugo Thornapple, a human mage, and Myleen Dogoroth, a succubus demon, chaotic and evil in nature. Her father had raised her and Darless had a wonderful childhood. However, when her mother had wantonly slain her father, Darless in turn killed her mother. She was half-demon and half-human, cursed by all. To disguise her true semi-demon body, she created the illusion of a beautiful woman. Only Jon had been able to penetrate her magic alteration. To Darless, her true self was degrading, for she wanted more than anything else to be just a normal woman and raise children. But finding a man she could love and be loved by was almost an insurmountable barrier.

Darless was in her twenties with long curly black hair and coal-black eyes that seemed to pierce one to their soul. She always wore the thinnest gauzes of clothing that left nearly nothing for the imagination. Though most people saw her illusion of an extremely beautiful woman, Jon could also see the tiny horns protruding from her head and the tiny bat-like wings on her back. In her true form, she was still remarkably beautiful; her illusion that she created for others to see was merely minus the horns and wings and a lift here and there.

Until Jon came into her life, everyone merely exploited her demon nature for their own purposes. Jon had given her the greatest gift possible — her freedom from such exploitations. Darless now wanted to "mate" with Jon. She was a powerful magic user in-tune with the Abyss and had mental powers similar to Jon and Mandy. She could read his thoughts with great ease. And she did so. Darless, like Jon, was fundamentally neutral between the forces of law and chaos, looking out for oneself was crucial — no one else would do so. But unlike Jon, she was also neutral between the forces of good and evil, raised this way by her father and later on by her friendship with the Lady Ursla Thornapple, the Great Druid of Hollybine Woods. Darless used actions to aid her survival, no matter if evil or not, while Jon always tried to do only things that were fundamentally good in nature.

Yes, Jon had discovered that Lady Ursla was the wife of Darless' father, Huge, though neither woman new about the other. Jon and his companions had freed Darless from a life of servitude to an evil Archmage and they had now become good friends. A bond of trust, mutual respect had been forged during their many subsequent adventures.

Finally, there was the long-haired Alison d'Ambrose. When she was three years old, her family had been slain and their castle destroyed. She had escaped the slaughter because her nanny had grabbed her and fled the castle. Now in her twenties, she had become a powerful mage. Jon was in awe of her magical spells. Magic-use was the central focus of her life. Alison was totally lawful in nature; she always went by the book, so to speak. And Jon felt that she could never even contemplate an evil action. Alison d'Ambrose was twenty-three and five feet eight with blue eyes, dark-brown hair that reached her slim waist. She had a mellow alto voice that enthralled Jon. Beneath her white nondescript robe, she always wore very expensive clothes, yet always in excellent taste. She preferred brown pants with an ermine belt and white silk blouse.

And he had fallen totally in love with her. At their last parting, he had even proposed marriage to her, in spite of the obvious obstacles.

Actually, the magic book of portals that his grandfather had given to him really belonged to Alison — well really to the d'Ambrose family.

A set of eight books was made by the famous Bard Wendell Theodore Zandras, who Jon had met and rescued from the clutches of the evil mage Caleb Durward. Jon learned that when the Bard was a young man, the gods had endowed his magnificent art with magic potential. Jous, the Uncaring God of Magic and the Arcane, and the Arch-devil Dispater decreed that any painting by the Bard that had a tiny trident painted in it would operate as a portal to that place or scene in the painting. Thus, if Bard Wendell painted a church, then one could be magically transported to that church. His skill grew so that if he just imagined a scene and painted it, one could go there; but of course one would discover at once that it was just imaginary for there would be nothing there beyond the scene.

Alison's father had commissioned Bard Wendell to create eight identical picture books, one for each of his children. Later, the fate of the books became obscured after the raid in which the d'Ambrose family was slaughtered. Alison now had the goal to recover her family books and in the process discover the fate of her seven older siblings. After the adventure and with Jon's help, Alison had recovered six of the eight books, counting her own. She assumed that that meant five of her brothers and sisters were surely dead. Still, two remained unaccounted for, and she held onto a faint hope for those two. Her quest was to find the other two books and maybe her surviving siblings. Jon had sworn to help her; Mandy, likewise. And Alison had allowed both to keep a copy of the picture book so they could both visit and help her.

Mandy needed her copy because it was the only way she could get to Alison's world. However, Jon had already discovered that he did not need any aid. If he could mentally picture the place, he could get the idea of "having already arrived and just be there." But it did cost him mental energy to do so.

Jon instinctively knew that the three women formed his core problem. He loved all three, but in different ways — and Alison most of all. However, for some unknown reason, Jon had always found himself embarrassed and tongue-tied around women. The prettier they were, the worse his discomfort. He did not know why this should be, and it caused him tremendous anxiety. Alison, who had no mental powers like the others, accepted him as he was. But Mandy constantly teased him about it, which only made things worse for him.

For a moment, Jon stopped playing and muttered to himself. "Darless wants to mate with me; Mandy wants to make love to me; Alison wants to marry me. I know I want to marry Alison, but I don't know how to handle the situation or the others. Any other guy would probably go after all three, but I — I — I can't." In frustration, he began to play his flute once more, pounding out the rhythm, echoing his mood. He knew that this was the very reason that he had not returned to the magical realms and the women for several weeks now. He had to find a workable solution.

As time passed, his music began to flow, once more reflecting the cool, evening breeze. His mind calmed. His skin sensed the rushing air; his nose, the fragrances of summer. He accepted the fact that he had no solution to his pressing dilemma with his three new friends. *It'll come in time*, he thought. As dusk approached, he stretched out on the lawn and stared up at the tree tops and clouds. In this position, the weight of the giant green emerald about his neck pressed its presence upon him.

He fingered the gem and smiled. It was a present from Lady Ursla of Hollybine Woods. Jon had halted a war and brought justice for the Great Druid of the woods. She had expressed her thanks by giving Jon and the three women identical emeralds. But they were huge! Jon had his mounted on a long chain at a jeweler in Champaign and was astounded to learn that its value exceeded a hundred thousand dollars. But the real value of the gem was not monetary, but rather sentimental. The great green gems linked the foursome together. But they were more than gems as Jon was about to discover.

As the pale sky darkened, Jon began to grow more and more uneasy. Something was wrong somewhere. It was an eerie feeling that continually grew stronger. His instincts insisted that something somewhere was very wrong. He rose to his feet and looked around his tiny estate. All seemed normal. As he headed back inside his home, the feeling swelled. Like a crazed animal, Jon darted about looking, probing for a trace of smoke from an imagined fire. He found nothing. It was a maddening feeling. Then, he felt he heard Alison cry out to him in terror. Although he did not notice it, his emerald began to glow.

Somehow across worlds, Jon had heard Alison's scream for help. He knew that she was in dire trouble. Racing into his front room, Jon grabbed his backpack, which was kept ready to go at a moment's notice. *Thank goodness for foresight!* He thought. Stuffing his flute inside, Jon hoisted his rucksack onto his back and then locked his doors.

He took a deep breath and concentrated on forming an image of the ruins of Castle d'Ambrose, where Alison lived. And he stepped from his room onto the ruins. It was much like taking a step down your driveway, only your foot lands with total certainty on the green grass of another place.

Quickly, he raced for the concealed entrance way to her underground chambers. The sickening feeling grew more and more intense. The destroyed castle lay atop a hill, a massive pile of stone rubble. However, the underground dungeons and passageways were not collapsed and in these tunnels Allison made her home. A secret tunnel normally used in siege situations was the entrance. The hidden doorway was smashed to bits. Heading down the long dark corridor, he blindly stumbled over several strange dead creatures — all were fried by one of Alison's magical fireballs. Their bodies were still smouldering and the stench was retching. His stomach knotted. He gagged but forced himself downwards past more of the dead creatures.

The tunnel now opened into Alison's living room. But there was no light; it was totally black. Awkwardly, Jon called out, "Alison? Alison?" Total silence greeted his senses. He fumbled about for his flashlight carried in his backpack and turned it on. The room held three more of the dead creatures; the entire interior was blackened by the fire. Then, he found a form near the doorway to her bedrooms. It was Alison.

Jon stared at the form. Her clothes had been clawed, ripped away. Her arms and legs were gashed with many deep wounds. Her belly had been sliced open; a massive pool of blood lay about her. From the blood pattern on the floor, her right arm had been groping toward the smooth black stone wall. Turning aside, he puked violently onto the black stone wall; massive convulsions began wracking his body. He knew that he had only seconds of consciousness remaining before shock would come with its welcomed oblivion. With every ounce of mental effort he could muster, Jon formed an image and stepped into it, leaving the hideous scene behind him.

He arrived upon the floor of Lady Ursla's front room floor, realized the fact, and collapsed into unconsciousness. His body continued its convulsions completely out of his control.

"He is the only person in this world, save yourself, Darless, that I could or would ever permit to appear in my home unannounced and uninvited," spoke the Great Druid, in a rather flat tone, setting her tea cup carefully back on the table and wiping her lips carefully on her napkin. "My, but he seems distressed." Though some fifty years old, Lady Ursla still looked elegant, regal, and sophisticated. She had long wavy black hair streaked with grey. Her manner of dress was always immaculate. The numerous jewels she wore were each just the precise shape and size to accentuate her appearance. Few could hope to be so stunning at this age in life. When she spoke, her voice was always smooth and soft, yet full of command!

Darless, face twisted in genuine distress, dashed over to the unconscious, jerking form. "Something is very wrong! But you were right, it is not Jon who is in dire trouble. He's — he's in some kind of seizure maybe?" She knelt over his body, flipping errant strands of her long black hair back over her shoulder. "Oh, please come take a look! You are the expert, my lady. Please." Her eyes pleaded, full of concern; Jon may yet be her man, she hoped.

With an elegant grace normally found with royalty, Lady Ursla rose and walked over to him and knelt beside Darless and Jon. However, her keen, perceptive eyes had not missed the slightest detail from the moment she saw Jon materializing on her rug. She felt his pulse, checked his eyes, and rolled him over onto his side to make sure there were no wounds that she had missed seeing. Confident of her diagnosis, Lady Ursla stated, "Please bring me a pan of water and a towel while I fetch my herb bag." As her eyes caught the wild concern in Darless' eyes, she added, "No, it is not serious — just a traumatic shock of some kind. He'll be fine in a few minutes."

Relieved, Darless ran to fetch water while Lady Ursla went into her study. By the time Lady Ursla had returned with her black bag, Darless had the water beside Jon and a wash rag and towel; she looked anxiously up at Lady Ursla for the next action to take.

"Here, this candle should do the trick. But lilac is going to be needed as well," she announced as if she were instructing a novice druid. She struck her fingers in a loud snap and the candle lit. "See that he does not knock it over," she said as she put it near his head. Soon a calming fragrance permeated the room. Darless felt herself becoming quite at ease, her worries seemed to evaporate. It was having an effect on Jon as well, his convulsions slowly dwindled and then stopped at last. "Ok, now you can bathe his forehead until he comes around. Here, put a few lilac leaves in the water. There now, you can administer to him. I shall finish my tea, my dear." She arose and calmly walked back and took her seat and resumed sipping her tea.

"He's coming around," Darless soon announced. "Now what?"

"Dar. . .Darless! Is Lady . . . ah yes . . . you must help . . . Alison's . . . It's Alison! She's . . . she's dead I think!" The heady fragrance continued to keep Jon calm, but his throat burned with his own stomach acid. Without asking, he took a long drink from the pitcher, ignoring the lilac scent of the water.

Her impatience to know what had happened was intolerable. Darless immediately began looking at the images in Jon's mind. "Oh my god!" shrieked Darless; she jerked away from him instinctively, utterly unprepared for such horrid images. But the herb candle was still burning and her huge reflexive inhales of the herb calmed her at once.

"That'll teach you to read others' minds unbidden, my child," smirked Lady Ursla, placing her now empty tea cup carefully onto its saucer. "Now, Jon, I see you are wearing your emerald I gave you. Very good, my boy. Look Darless, see, his is throbbing as well. They are working perfectly so far. I shall have to compliment Lord Eldaron on his craftsmanship. So, my dear Jon, take a deep breath and tell us what has happened to Alison."

Jon's attention immediately went to his large emerald that hung around his neck in its new golden chain. Instinctively, Darless glanced at hers which was also on a chain around her heck. Both noticed that the two emeralds were throbbing a pale green light. "I'll explain about the amulets later my boy, please tell us about Alison," Lady Ursla commanded.

Under the influence of the fragrant herb and the calm druid, Jon described what he had seen. When Jon had finished a few minutes later, Lady Ursla ordered, "Very well. I shall have to gather a few things that will likely be needed. Darless, you and Jon stay there and keep on breathing the candle fumes. Works marvelously well, doesn't it?"

Without waiting for a reply, she took her bag and went back into her study. When she returned, she had changed into black leather pants lined with a soft white fur; she had the look of an adventurer who traveled with an unmistakable style or flair. She snuffed the candle and blew the wax to solidify it and placed it into her bag. "Now all that remains is to determine how we are to get there."

"I'll get us there with my book," offered Darless.

"Yes, that will be best," Lady Ursla agreed before Jon could protest. "You are currently under the influence of a herb of mine, Jon. No telling what or where you might take me," she playfully jibbed. Jon relaxed, realizing that it was going to take all his strength to confront what was to come.

"Oh, this is silly," Darless proclaimed as she fumbled through the pages searching for the picture of the ruined castle. "Here, just hold hands. I am a wizard, you know!" Without giving anyone a chance to get in a word, Darless spoke a few command words of magic in a tongue Jon did not understand. Instantly, the group arrived at the ruins of Castle d'Ambrose.

"What *are* these creatures?" proclaimed Lady Ursla as she stepped carefully around the somewhat charred bodies of the slain bug-like creatures. Jon was in the lead taking them down the dimly lit entrance tunnel to Alison's converted dungeon home. Jon had dropped his flashlight and from deep within it provided the only illumination.

Darless brought up the rear. None saw the alu-demon's facial expressions as she bent over some of the fallen bugs. But they did hear her curse and announce, "Chasme or fly demons — that's what they are. Nasty creatures from the Abyss."

"Poisonous?" queried Lady Ursla, stepping around another dead bug.

"No, just evil, nasty bugs. Uncontrollable. Good for nothing, foul denizens of the upper layers of the Abyss. I had hoped never to see one again as long as I lived!"

"Here she is," Jon retrieved the flashlight and played it on the fallen Alison.

"We need better lighting," proclaimed Lady Ursla at once.

Darless at once spoke a word of command and a globe of light appeared in her hand. Eyeing a side torch in a bracket, she placed the globe on the torch and adjusted it brighter. "How's this?" The large chamber was now well lighted.

The gruesome scene left everyone speechless. Jon and Darless were still under the calming influence of the druid's herb and Jon did not get violently ill this time. Perhaps it was the fact that he was now not alone; perhaps it was the confidence and presence of Lady Ursla. Jon relaxed a bit and began to confront what he could not do when he had entered here alone before.

He noticed that there was a black sooty residue all down the entrance hall. "Alison must have gotten off one of her fire spells," he muttered.

"A fireball, to be precise," corrected Darless. "She did it right and got a large number of them before they got to her. Chasme travel in a herd, you know. What Allison probably did not know was that, if there were a couple dozen flying in here, there had to be a hundred more outside waiting to get inside."

"Then she had no chance," Jon's voice fell.

"More to the point," interjected Lady Ursla, "she is wearing her emerald as well. See how it also pulses? My, but you children do obey orders! I was hoping you all would be wise enough to bear them about your person at all times. Therefore, she is *not* dead yet, anyway."

"But, but, I, I don't understand!" Jon cried. "Look at her! Blood everywhere, guts ripped out. No pulse. She's dead!" And the suppressed tears finally welled up in his eyes and rolled down his cheeks. Darless' eyes watered, then her right hand grabbed her own stomach. For the *first* time in her life, Darless realized that another person — other than her father and Lady Ursla — actually meant a very great deal to her. The human side of her was no longer suppressed. She sobbed aloud and leaned on Jon, who put his arm around her, steadying both of them.

Lady Ursla, who was kneeling beside the lifeless form of Alison, looked up with a curious look on her face at the two crying children. This Great Druid fully understood what was happening with Darless. And she smiled; she had won a small victory; Darless' human side had been fully reached; there would be now no turning back for her. A soul saved and a small imbalance rectified. She let them cry for a moment; it would do them both a great deal of good. She began a careful examination Alison.

Here in the underground dungeons of what had once been the proud Castle d'Ambrose, a vast quiet pervaded, broken only by the sniffling of the two. However, the stillness was suddenly shattered by a sword being unsheathed and a muffled curse coming from the entrance of the tunnel that lead here into the dungeon home of Alison.

Instinctively, Darless killed the globe of illumination. She took up a defensive posture sliding in front of both Jon and Lady Ursla. She would need no weapons to defeat a swordsman. His blade would likely not even penetrate her skin. Her hands and magical spells would be her weapons.

Damn - I need some kind of weapon! thought Jon. *I'm as helpless as an ass!* He felt very, very small and useless. He heard Lady Ursla muttering, probably readying some druid incantation if needed. He wondered what she might do. *I shall have to rely on my mental blasts.*

In silence, they waited with their ears straining to hear the heavy breathing and footsteps of someone approaching from far down the tunnel. They heard a curse as the approaching figure stumbled over one of the dead bugs. Then, a soft glow suddenly appeared and seemed to move ahead of the intruder. *A magic user too — be wary,* Darless thought to Jon.

In the dark, Jon felt like a caged rat waiting its doom. *This is silly! Why don't I try to sense who is coming — friend or foe?* Straining, Jon could feel no evil intent. However, since he had never tried to do this, he did not know if he could have felt an evil intent anyway. Then he heard a curse.

"Zagroot zounds" echoed faintly down the tunnel. Jon immediately recognized that voice and curse. But caution kept him from yelling. Instead, he closed his eyes and mentally sent, *Mandy? Is that you coming down the tunnel? It's Jon. Darless and Lady Ursla are with me.*

Yes! Was that your light that was extinguished a bit ago? Am I stalking you? came the telepathic reply.

"Yes, careful, Mandy, charred bugs line the tunnel. We will get the lights back on. It's Alison, she's" — his voice faltered.

Darless also recognized the voice of Mandy Blackthorn and quickly spoke her word of command. The globe burst back into light once again illuminating the gruesome scene. She now acknowledged to herself that Mandy had also become a dear, dear friend as well as Alison and Jon. She wondered just how much Lady Ursla had realized about this unlikely foursome: Alison, Mandy, Darless and Jon. How had she known that their lives, their fates were somehow intertwined for all time? She made a mental note to probe Lady Ursla over tea one day in the future.

"Zagroot zounds! What happened here? Is Alison," her voice faltered for a second before the trained ranger side of her kicked in, "Is she dead?" She knelt beside the lifeless form that had been Alison and felt for a pulse. Glancing up at Jon and Darless, she could see their reddish eyes; she could tell that they had been crying. "Yep, dead. Sorry Jon. I wish I could have gotten here sooner; maybe I could have prevented her death." Mandy offered, realizing how much Alison had meant to Jon, valiantly suppressing her own sudden, but not unexpected, grief.

"Good! I see you are also wearing your emerald. See it pulsates as well," the calm, knowing voice of Lady Ursla interrupted. "Children, children, children! You are so quick to pronounce death! But have you seen it? No, don't answer that! Alison is *not* dead, not yet at any rate; we still have several hours."

"Whatever *are* you talking about?" blurted out Mandy, who prided herself on never being at a loss for words. Jon and Darless were speechless. "Will someone *please* fill me in? What has happened here? What *is* going on? She is *not* dead? I *need* a drink!" And she sheathed her bastard sword and looked around this central room.

"Darless, could you manage to boil some water and fix us all a nice cup of oolong tea, please? A dungeon is *such* a dreary, damp place. And this one smells of burned bugs and the odor of death. Where *does* she keep her china?" Lady Ursla commanded.

"The dining room is off that corridor there," replied Mandy. "But be careful what you touch! This is a mage's quarters you are in — no telling what protections she has on things in here." She added as an afterthought and led the way into the dining room kitchen area. *Jon! What is going on here? How can she be so, so, so. Well, you know, so nonchalant about this?*

Somehow, changing rooms into a clean and tidy kitchen and dining room area away from the disaster and going about the mundane tasks of setting a tea relaxed one and all just a bit. Over tea, Lady Ursla began by having Jon relate what he had found when he arrived.

Jon did so but he felt very embarrassed when he got to the point where he had violently reacted on the side of the wall. *I noticed that when I came in,* Mandy teasingly thought to him, watching his red face become even redder as she demurely fingered her cup of tea. Darless caught the wry smile on her lips.

"He was in shock; that's all," interjected Lady Ursla. "You all probably experienced similar reactions in your early adventuring days. Jon here is not a seasoned adventurer. Besides it took him totally by surprise. And he did do the right thing by getting aid as fast as possible. Though, it would be wiser to *knock* on my door, young man, instead of just plopping onto my rug!" She chided in a friendly, teasing manner. Jon stared down at his tea cup, his face felt like it was of fire.

When Mandy had been fully briefed, she said, "Are you sure those are Chasme flies from the Abyss? What in heaven's name are Abyss creatures doing here in this world?"

"Absolutely! But that is an even bigger mystery. Alison might know the answer," suggested Darless.

Seeing the small grimace of pain on Darless' face, Mandy quickly changed the subject knowing that the Abyss was the last thing Darless wanted to talk about at the moment. "So what is with these emeralds? I had mine mounted on a broach pin backing. They are more than just an emerald! I did check mine for magical auras and such. But it appeared to be just an emerald, albeit the largest, most expensive one I have ever seen."

Adjusting her tea cup to just the right angle, which of course got everyone's attention as it was meant to, Lady Ursla began to explain. "Yes, those emeralds are extremely valuable, but not because they are jewels but rather because of what I have had done to them by a master elfish craftsman who was only too glad to finally pay off his obligation to me. Think of them as rather like an Amulet of Life. No, they cannot grant life. Rather, they preserve life. If the wearer should meet an untimely fate while wearing the amulet, the amulet maintains the life of the body for twenty-four hours. It has other properties that I shall let you all discover. However, if one is in grievous danger, the other amulets begin pulsating. The four are attuned to each other as you have observed. And, Mandy, their enchantment is such that even a powerful magic check will reveal no magical properties. That way, they are much safer. The services you four did for me have now been well repaid. I always pay my debts."

"I don't know how to thank you," began Mandy.

"Nor I," added Darless.

"I do," Jon meekly said, and got up and went to her side and gently raised her right hand and gave her a loving kiss on her hand.

Lady Ursla beamed, "Gentlemen, yes that is what this world needs more of. Now if only you were thirty years older, Jon, or I, thirty years younger. Hum, maybe as we are?" She teased him letting her voice trail off. His face reddened as the girls smiled knowingly at each other.

"Well, then the task at hand is how to revive her," Mandy began in her take charge, no-nonsense ranger voice. "I've heard of priests that can raise the dead. But how do we get a dead body that's not quite dead alive again? Is Alison really going to appreciate all those massive scars she's liable to have? How do we sew her up? I suppose we can all take turns trying to heal her somehow. "

"If you knew where such a priest was located, I could teleport us there," added Darless. Then after a bit of a pause, she added softly, "I could use a Wish magic spell if one of you would force me to."

"No!" barked Lady Ursla. "You know as well as I do that every Wish spell you cast prematurely ages your body! You have had enough of that when you were captive. Besides such is not needed. I think that between us all we have the power to work miracles. I am a Druid of the Inner Circle of Seven; I have sufficient power I believe to repair the worst of the damage and get life processes functioning. Then, you three can work on the rest. Between us, I feel we can undo this untimely catastrophe."

She paused, letting the significance of her pronunciation register; Jon had never heard her full title. Then, she continued in a most solemn manner, "Demons from the Abyss do not belong on this plane and need some kind of assistance to get here. Thus, I shall then charge you four with straightening out this gross unbalance of Nature; get to the root of the matter and *terminally* handle it in any manner you see fit. Do you freely *accept* my terms? Alison gets no vote; she will be bound by your decision."

"I, Mandy Blackthorn, do hereby swear by my oath and fealty of Reylona of the Woods to so do!" Her right hand she held over her heart.

Following Mandy's lead, Jon offered, "I, Jon Brown, do here by swear to find the root of the matter and set it straight." He felt a bit funny with no god or goddess in the announcement, and he did not feel the need to place his hand over his chest.

Darless was silent and soon everyone looked her way and saw she was struggling with deep thoughts and emotions. Somehow this matter affected her in a way they did not understand at all. Then, in a small voice Darless uttered, "I, Darless, shall do so or die in the attempt, for to be human is to be blessed with having others to care about that are more dear to one than life itself. I now understand my father more than I ever dreamed possible. If only he were alive so I could tell him so."

Mandy gave her a hug. Jon smiled and as elegantly as he could, kissed her right hand as he had done earlier to Lady Ursla.

The Lady smiled with a twinkle in her eyes and said, "Then, I accept your offers. Now come, there is much work to be done here. You three, clean up this *infernal* bug mess! I will tend to Alison. When I have finished, then you may take turns doing what you may to add to the cure. However, I do give you this stern warning or caution. While we may repair the damage done to her body, give some thought as to her mental state hereafter. That we cannot cure! There is no telling what this experience has done to her mental state."

"You mean that she could be depressed emotionally for the rest of her life," Jon asked. "Or have feelings of unworthiness or have a hardened heart seeking only for revenge? Depression? That sort of thing?" Jon and the two ladies immediately thought of Alison's supreme sacrifice in taking the spear thrown at Jon by Morrigan, Goddess of War, and her subsequent resurrection by the supreme god Ukko and his Air Maidens. This would not be a resurrection by an all-powerful deity. It likely would have all manner of side effects.

"Yes, that sort of thing. Near death — traumatic death — one in which you are totally overwhelmed as she was — can be devastating on a person. We may heal her body, but what of her spirit? What of dear Alison? That we cannot know."

Left with that sobering thought, all began to go into action.

Chapter 2 Grand Central Station

Back in the entrance room, Darless set up another bright globe of light so that Lady Ursla could see to do her druidic incantations. She then joined the others who were standing beside the first of the Chasme carcasses. "Guess we have got to get our hands dirty dragging them outside," complained Mandy. No one relished the idea of physically carting the charred, smelly bug bodies out of the tunnel passage.

Before anyone could respond, the sound of a long, heavy sword being drawn echoed faintly down the long darkened entrance corridor. "Zagroot zounds! Someone's coming!" Mandy cried, drawing her own bastard sword in a blaze of action as she moved ahead of the trio, ready to face the newcomer.

For the second time, Jon felt the uncomfortable concept of having no weapon to draw; he resigned himself to using his mental powers as he could. Not that he wanted a sword. Jon had no illusions about being a swordsman. Something he could use to help keep lethal things away from his body was his idea.

Metallic clanking footsteps echoed their way. A deep, very angry, base voice challenged out. "Vile intruders beware! It is I, Sir Thomas le Bonnaire, Holy Paladin of Ukko. Throw down your weapons and surrender. But if any harm has come to the Lady d'Ambrose, your lives shall be forfeited in the holy name of Ukko!" The clanking, creaking footsteps broke into a trot that quickly progressed into an all-out charge heading down the long tunnel, which in the days of the Castle had been a secret exit.

For a large man heavily encumbered in a suit of full plate mail, Sir Thomas moved exceedingly quickly, deftly stepping over the Chasme carcasses like driftwood. In seconds, he abruptly halted before Mandy whose sword, up and to her right, was ready for a strike. Jon was a safe distance, back and to her left, while Darless hung well back. The paladin's own giant blade, gripped by two powerful hands, was back and to his right. Jon had never seen such a huge sword that could easily slice a man in two. The silver knight eyed each in turn, sizing up the situation.

He was a tall man entirely encased in a suit of highly polished plate armor, head to foot. Light from Darless' globe on the side torch gleamed and brightly reflected off Sir Thomas. Both hands gripped a huge two-handed sword that had a huge red ruby in its pummel.

"I am Jon Brown and this is Ranger Mandy and this is Darless. The Lady Ursla, the great Druid of Hollybine Woods is tending to Alison at the moment. She's dead, well not quite. The Lady is healing her."

Immediately, Jon felt the icy stare of an angry Sir Thomas, although he could only get a faint glimpse of piercing eyes beneath the protective face armor. He felt some form of energy probe coming from the man, but wisely did not interfere. Sir Thomas was at least twice as heavy as Jon without his armor.

"You are not evil," he begrudgingly began. Though still clenching his teeth in anger, he lowered his raised weapon, placing its tip on the floor and leaning slightly on it. "You did not cause this harm to the Lady d'Ambrose? What do you know of these Chasme bugs? You did not bring them?"

"No. Nothing, save Darless says they come from the Abyss. And no." Jon replied dryly. The conversation was not going at all well.

"Accepted. And you do look like a ranger and thus not evil," he growled as he in turn stared at Mandy. After a brief pause, he added "Hmm, you are a beautiful young woman. You would adorn any man's table and make him a fine wife." Jon and Darless both sensed Mandy's ire rising rapidly.

"Sorry, but I'd rather find a "man" to adorn *my* table!" retorted Mandy. If there was one thing that made Mandy go ballistic, it was this kind of attitude that many men had. The conversation was degenerating rapidly.

To make matters worse, Jon now realized Darless had been slowly retreating backward. He had forgotten about the alu-demon. Without trying, he could feel her fear of this man, a fear he had never before sensed in her.

Sir Thomas then turned to face Darless. After a short pause, he bellowed in violent anger "Curses! Demoness! Here is the vile source of the Chasme bugs! Do you not know you are being fooled? She is not a woman! Here is a demon from the very Abyss itself! Prepare to meet thy doom! May the hand of holy Ukko guide my blade!" And he raised his sword menacingly. Jon had to act and act swiftly. The paladin had seen right through Darless' illusion and seen her for what she truly was. No wonder Darless was worried.

With an instinctive inspiration, Jon spoke in a completely bored, nonchalant manner. "Certainly, Darless is half-demon, half human. She is not evil, though. She is a dear friend of Alison. She has aided Alison on numerous occasions. Kindly put down your weapon, please. I had heard that paladins were holy knights. We need all the holiness we can get at this time. Alison is in a very bad way. And for heaven's sake, take off your helmet. I cannot see your face."

Anger defused. Whether it was the emotional tone that he used or his words or his manner, Jon could not tell, but Sir Thomas responded with an audible sigh. At once he sheathed his giant sword, putting it back into its sheath across his back. He then removed his visor and the helmet before speaking. It revealed a face lined with worries. He had a short black beard and short black hair to match. His blue eyes were the kind that penetrated one's soul. Beads of perspiration trickled down the sides of his face.

"Forgive my brashness, but I was terribly concerned for my dear companion, Lady Alison d'Ambrose. I had to be certain. Ah, so you are *the* Saint Jon Brown that I have heard so much about. Sir Thomas le Bonnaire, Holy Paladin of Ukko, at your service!" He bowed stiffly at the waist. "And you are *the* Mandy; please accept my apologies." And he politely kissed her hand. "And you are Darless; thank you for aiding my Alison." Jon could sense some kind of internal turmoil as he mechanically reached for and kissed Darless' hand. But he dared not probe the paladin's mind. Prejudice can be a hard thing to overcome; here was a man dedicated to the elimination of demons.

"Alison has told me a lot about you three. You all have my greatest respect. But what has happened to Alison? I came as fast as I could."

Jon quickly relayed the little they knew. Mandy, having sheathed her weapon, seized the opportunity to have a bit of fun. *He started it; I shall finish it.* She smiled and coyly began to add on additional details none had yet guessed. "But see here how these soot marks align — she got off two fireball spells. If you turn that one over, you will see it is laying in soot — it died in the second blast." With just a wee bit of cockiness in her voice, she added, "She was not taken by total surprise at all. However, alone and against a hundred, the odds were not at all good."

"By golly," exclaimed Jon, "you are right! I never noticed that before. She must have blasted them twice."

"Touché, Mandy!" Sir Thomas chuckled. Turning to Jon, he advised, "Son, if there is one thing I have learned in my adventuring, it is that you can never put anything over on a ranger. Trust a ranger to get you through, I always say. But come, can I see Alison? Where is she?"

"Er, not at the moment, please." Jon continued, "Lady Ursla is doing some kind of major healing process that I do not understand on her. When she is finished, we are all planning to add to those efforts to heal her. But what is your association with Alison?" He had wanted to ask that question from the first moment he had seen this silver paladin. He did not see Mandy watching him carefully from a corner of her eyes.

"The Lady d'Ambrose is our party's mage, simply put. We have grown up together and adventured for years now. Did she not tell you about us?"

Jon's face reddened noticeably, "Er, no, we never really had the time to talk about things much. What do you mean adventured?"

*Now that is a **dumb** question.* Mandy sent mentally to Jon, who felt more out of place than before. Jon quickly added, "Where is the rest of your party?"

***Much** better question,* Mandy replied.

"Son, you certainly do not know our ways. You are indeed a stranger in this land! There are six of us, counting Alison and myself. Bruno the Battler, Tracker Abe, Father Johnas the Holy and Slickster the Trickster — he's really a thief, if you ask me, but then no one listens to me. We accept holy crusades. Why, just last year, Princess Diana was captured by a renegade band of gypsies; our task was to rescue her, which we did. And as to your last question, the others and my five squires are off scouting nearby villages for signs of the Chasme. They may report in here later on. But enough of this talk. We need to get these unholy bug remains out of here and completely destroyed; the place, cleansed of the vile slime. Come, lend a hand." He grabbed a nearby bug and began dragging it outside as if it weighed nothing. "Mandy, find some firewood, we need to totally destroy these carcasses!" Sir Thomas was a take charge man.

"You don't need to ask twice!" Mandy delightfully replied and hastily headed outside in search of wood. She really did not want to get slimy and dirty hauling out the dead Chasme.

"Make you a deal, Jon." Darless spoke quietly with a twinkle in her eye. "You get one of those walking sticks from Alison's bin. I will levitate a bug and you push it outside with the stick."

"Now you are talking!" Jon went to fetch a suitable walking stick. He returned to find the nearest Chasme floating just above the floor. He could see Darless was concentrating and wisely said nothing. Instead, using the corkscrew willow walking stick, he pushed the bug on down the tunnel. He found that once started, he only needed one hand. He grinned as he passed the paladin who was coming back for another. "The easy way!" was all Jon said.

A moment later, he heard Sir Thomas mutter and then laugh loudly, "Ah, a team effort!"

Ten minutes later, a pile of nineteen Chasme bodies lay just outside the entrance. Mandy and Sir Thomas constructed a large bonfire and one by one he tossed the demon bugs into the blaze. Meanwhile, Jon and Darless went back inside to see what they could do about the dirty soot mess. "It'll take days to wash down all these walls." Jon grumbled, "but I guess it has to be done or we'll just track the stuff everywhere." Darless did not answer for a moment. Jon mused. "You know, what we need is like a big wall of water that would just go swish down there. Kind of like the Disney flick."

"Well, I don't know what a Disney is. However, I think I can manage the water but I'll need help moving it down the corridor. Go get Mandy to come help me. You can relieve her on bonfire duty."

A few minutes later, Jon excitedly called to Sir Thomas, "Hey come see this! Darless has a wall of water sweeping the tunnel clean! Mandy's got a staff and seems to be pushing it somehow!"

The paladin strolled to where Jon was near the tunnel entrance for a look. "Mandy's using Alison's staff of power. Yes, handy to have wizards around." And bored the paladin returned to poke at the bonfire, intent on verifying every demon body was totally destroyed.

"Well done indeed!" Jon praised the ladies when they had finished. Mandy and Darless beamed.

"One day, I got to get me one of these wizard staffs!" Mandy declared, "Most useful. Such a feeling of power comes from it! What a feeling! What a sensation! But I could not have managed its use without Darless' instructions though. It is way beyond my skill levels! Thanks Dar."

Just then, Lady Ursla appeared at the tunnel entrance. "Ok everyone. I've done my best. Alison is breathing on her own now. It's time for your assistance. Oh, I *beg* your pardon!" she said noticing the paladin. "I don't believe we have met."

Quickly, Jon interjected, "Lady Ursla, this is Sir Thomas le Bonnaire, Holy Paladin of Ukko. Sir Thomas, this is the Lady Ursla of Hollybine Wood."

"Ah, the pleasure is all mine," spoke the paladin as he stiffly bowed in his shiny armor and kissed her offered hand. "While we may differ philosophically on many most-important matters, I sincerely thank you for saving my lady Alison. Truly. I owe you a great deal for your help. If there is ever a service I can render you, please do not hesitate to call on me. That is, however" he added respectfully, "a service I can ethically provide, you understand."

"Accepted in the manner intended, your holiness," the lady replied, smiling broadly. "Now all of you, come and continue the process."

They followed Lady Ursla back inside. As they walked, Jon sent to Darless, *What was that all about? He's never met her and yet he knows they differ? I don't understand all this.*

Darless replied in Jon's mind. *The Lady is neutral in all matters, preferring the balance of nature over both good and evil and law and chaos. She says you cannot have one without the other. What is good in the absence of evil? Well, the holy paladin is like Alison, only to the extremes, if you ask me. Rather like a goodie two shoes. Goodness gone berserk, in* *my opinion. As soon as you mentioned druid, he knew what her beliefs must be. All druids basically have the same fundamental belief in the balance of nature. But, you see, now, the Lady can at **any time** in the future unqualifiedly call upon Sir Thomas to aid her in some matter of importance. And that is most valuable indeed!*

They found Alison still unconscious but now alive and breathing. Lady Ursla had moved her onto a blanket and had somehow closed the major wounds. Somehow blood had been created and was flowing in her veins once again. But she still looked terrible, but alive. The green gem was no longer pulsating.

"Oh my dearest Alison!" exclaimed Sir Thomas and a tear came to his eyes. "Permit me first!" And he carefully knelt down beside her, clanking sounds echoing as metal met the rock floor.

Mandy sent to Jon, *Holy paladins can heal just by the touch of their hands! Watch, few have seen this.* Jon watched through the tears in his eyes.

"Blessed be the Holy Ukko and in Ukko's name." And the paladin placed his hands onto Alison's body. Jon thought he could see a yellowish glow enveloping both the paladin and Alison. After a couple minutes, he stood up. "That's all I can do for now." There was more color in her face and her body did seem to be breathing better and the wounds, less severe.

Next, Mandy and Jon knelt beside her. *You take the upper part of her body and I will take the lower,* she sent. Jon sniffed clearing his nose and they began. Her face had been violently cut and clawed. Jon went to work on these first. Concentrating on individual cells, he began closing each gash, cell by cell. Neither Mandy nor Jon heard the Lady Ursla motion the others into the kitchen area saying this would take some time.

From their earlier adventures, Darless knew what to expect and without a word went to work in the kitchen putting together some kind of protein rich meal from what she could find. In a wizard's kitchen, one had to be careful what you touched. She could find no proper fireplace to light to cook over. Alison obviously had other means. Darless knew that both Mandy and Jon would not quit their healing process until both had completely used all their possible mental energies.

When they would be done, both would be totally exhausted and ravenously hungry. She had seen that happen numerous times in the past. Jon, she knew, had some kind of wild reserve of enormous mental potential, totally untrained; she knew he would draw on that reserve to his utmost. She would be ready for them when they were done.

Meanwhile, the Lady Ursla explained to Sir Thomas what they were doing and offered him a tea, which he kindly declined stating he needed to tend the bonfire.

An hour passed before Jon knew he had to quit; Mandy had quit more than thirty minutes before, but had stayed at his side, monitoring him. "I guess that is all I can manage for now," Jon finally spoke and with great effort arose; his legs were numb, having long ago fallen asleep. She helped him to his feet and to stumble into the kitchen.

"She's sleeping now. You should see the marvelous job Jon did on her face. I doubt that there will even be a trace of a scar! Zounds! I'm starving! Where's the *food*?" Darless shoved a heaping plate in front of her. Jon was so exhausted that he mechanically took the plate that Darless gave him and stuffed it in without a word. In less than five minutes, both Jon and Mandy lay sleeping on the kitchen floor. Darless covered them with blankets. And she then joined Lady Ursla sitting beside Alison. She dimmed her globes of light and said nothing.

Shortly the clanking of Sir Thomas announced his arrival. He whispered, "Fire has done its work. Demons are gone. I'll take that tea, if your offer still stands." He looked carefully over the sleeping Alison and marveled, "Well, I have never seen such healing handiwork!"

"We all had a hand in it. Life works best when everyone shares the duties and tasks as they are able," Lady Ursla replied as if lecturing to a neophyte, though she doubted she would score any points with the paladin. "Darless is finishing up the process. Tomorrow we shall see." And her voice trailed off as she led Sir Thomas into the kitchen past the soundly sleeping forms of Mandy and Jon.

They conversed in soft voices, though nothing really could have awakened either Jon or Mandy. She said, "After Darless has finished up, can you carry her onto her bed, wherever that is?"

And so it was that the strong arms of the paladin carried the sleeping form of Alison into her bedroom and tucked her into bed. His lips kissed ever so lightly her forehead as he spoke, "Sleep well, dearest Alison. I shall stand guard that nothing shall disturb this sleep."

Lady Ursla slept beside Alison that night, rather uncomfortably in a chair. Darless and the Sir Thomas strolled to the entrance of the tunnel. She brought a dimmed light globe with her. All was absolutely quiet, save the occasional clanking of armor on the stone floor. Outside a cacophony of night sounds greeted their ears. For some time, neither spoke a word.

"My father really wanted a child but his wife could not have children. He was faithful to his vows to his wife; no human would bear his child." Darless softly volunteered as they both stared into the cool evening sky. "Later, my jealous mother killed my father. I killed my mother in turn."

"One less demon to plague the universe," muttered Sir Thomas.

"Yes, but there are nearly an infinite number of them. For many years, I wanted nothing to do with demons or humans. Both can be just plain evil!" She cringed at the memories of her imprisonment at the hand of the evil mage from whose clutches Jon had recently rescued her. "For years, I hid myself from everyone, I did not want to bear a child — to raise another half-breed to face the kind of life I have had. But time heals, tis said. And for the last year or so, I have been trying to mate just to create a child of my own. I — I just wanted the best stud possible — a one night affair with the right man. Then he could be off, none the wiser. But, but something happened to me here today, something really important. Yet, I cannot put it all into words." She was talking not because Sir Thomas was the ideal listener, but more to sort out her own confusing emotions and feelings.

"Do go on," the paladin encouraged her. He never bothered to converse with demons and had only rarely considered half-demons as anything different. Yet, he sensed this alu-demon was different. Quite how, he was uncertain, and that uncertainty piqued his curiosity.

Fighting for the right words to describe a new concept to her, Darless said, "Today I did something . . . something because I cared . . . not because of duty or obligation or any other reason — just because I deeply cared for a human. I feel different somehow. Lady Ursla saved Alison, but not because she cared deeply for her. I — I helped solely and only because I admire and respect her and for no other reason whatsoever. What does that mean? And now I see that I could never deny a child their father! The right man for me would, of necessity, want to love unconditionally his child or he would not be the right man! Like my father to me. What does this all mean?" She did not expect an answer from this biased demon slayer.

Sir Thomas's coal black eyes stared at Darless as if seeing her for the first time. Darless thought he even blushed. He cleared his throat mostly so he could gather his thoughts. "I'm not a philosopher, but one once did explain to me that love, human love, is based solely on a deep admiration and respect for the other person. He demonstrated to me that one might admire someone and yet not respect them at all or that one might respect them but not admire them. I found it a bit confusing at the time. But I am beginning to see his point. When I first met you, I respected you only because of the service you have been to my dear Lady d'Ambrose — I detest demons, and a half-demon represents to me the worst of human nature! The very idea of a human actually *breeding* with a foul creature from the Abyss is totally repulsive to me."

"But this change in your outlook, your deep feelings and commitments, this change is, how do I say it, it represents the higher-held human virtues! Such virtues as I would hope to have. I am finding a bit of admiration for you in me after all, in spite of everything. If you were a human, I would suggest that there is yet hope for your soul! But I do not know how this would apply to a half-demon, I'm afraid. However, I am very curious when these changes began in you. Did they . . . did they start after you met Jon Brown?"

"Now that you mention it, yes. Yes. I have even tried to coerce him into mating with me to create my child." Darless confessed, eyes downcast.

"Fascinating. Perhaps there is something about this 'Saint' Jon thing that I have not seen. I took him to be a bungling, incompetent adventurer — a raw beginner who would be lost at the first sign of trouble. I thought the 'Saint' bit to be merely a title bestowed upon this stranger for services rendered. But now I am not so sure at all! I wonder who he is? What he is? He does not look or act like any god I have ever heard of or met. He does not seem religious or even pious. Long have I wondered how Lady d'Ambrose could be interested in him and not me? What did she see in him that she did not see in me?"

"You're jealous!" exclaimed Darless, in a sudden burst of intuition. Even in the dim light, she could see his face redden instantly.

"Please, please by all that is holy, *never* say a word of this to the Lady d'Ambrose! It is a weakness in me! I am lax on my vows, my honor! Speak not a word of this to a sole!" She had not seen Sir Thomas so animated or concerned since she'd met him.

"You have my word on that. But is . . . " she did not have time to finish her thought, for at that moment, two horse riders galloped into view. Sir Thomas, a man of highly trained instincts, instantly took his fighting stance, whipping out the massive two-handed sword as if it were a feather. Darless did notice that he intentionally, purposefully stepped in front of her — a subtle gesture to protect her from potential harm. She smiled.

As the riders closed the gap between them, one barked out, "Greenfields!" Instantly, the paladin lowered his sword, his great muscles relaxing. He bellowed out the response, "Forever. Welcome Squire John. What news?"

"Stonefist Castle is clear. Jascar Mines was hit about sunset. Three miners were killed. Then, good ol' Slick got rid of them in a hurry. Believe it or not, he read that scroll Alison gave him and blasted ten of them into a fiery grave. He says to thank Alison and ask her for another scroll. Can ya' believe that? Old Slickster pretending to be a magic user! Don't that beat all?" replied Squire John.

"I think he felt insulted because you keep calling him our unneeded thief!" added Squire Francouis. "Oh, yes, he also said he'd join us here in the morning."

"You've done well, squires. Thanks. I've no word from Abe and Squire Frunne yet, but I don't expect to hear from them until the morning; Fountain Head's a fair journey. But the news bothers me. The demons are still within striking distance. They took Alison by surprise. She got nineteen demons before they got her."

The squires gasped, their excitement of the chase replaced by the sudden reality that death could and did strike. Their faces changed from a flush of youthful energy to a pallid seriousness. But Sir Thomas added quickly, "She still lives because of the miraculous arrival of her friends and other companions, Saint Jon Brown, none-the-less. They have somehow kept her alive and have healed her."

Grim despair changed to wonder. In an incredulous voice, Squire Francouis queried, "Not *the* Saint Jon we have heard about? The real one? Is he *really* a saint or just in title as you thought? Can we meet him?"

"Yes, they are all here, including that druid that Alison spoke of, Lady Ursla of Hollybine Woods. The druid really did some kind of major healing process on her and brought her back from the arms of death. Nothing at all like we would expect from Father Johnas. But she lives; Jon, Mandy and Darless then worked miracles on healing. I doubt if she will even have a scar on her face. Absolutely remarkable. You can meet them in the morning. However guys, you can meet Darless." He turned and motioned for Darless to come closer. "Forgive my brash manners, Darless, I was momentarily distracted by the news of the demons. Squires, let me present the Lady Darless." He took her hand and made a formal presentation, though rather stiffly as he still wore the full plate armor.

Although inwardly exceedingly pleased at how Sir Thomas presented her so formally, she did not show any outward sign. It was a new experience to be so honorably introduced. She smiled at each and managed a graceful curtsy. The squires, on the other hand, both barely eighteen, visibly reacted as young men would when meeting a very beautiful woman, clad only in a thin gossamer of a dress. Of course seeing this Sir Thomas hastened to add, "Careful squires, remember she *is* an alu-demon. But do not worry, she is *not* evil and is to be trusted in our councils. Alison owes her life in part to Darless."

"Wow!" exclaimed a shocked and startled Squire Francouis. "Do you really suck the blood of your victims?" he eagerly asked. "I heard such tales as a child," he added.

Darless saw that question coming mostly because her mind was open and she picked up his thoughts and childhood demon stories by the fireside even before he vocalized them. She winked coyly at Sir Thomas and replied most seriously, "Oh no. Never!" And she paused while that sank in and then added, "I actually drain all the life energy from my victims who are always very young men, much like yourself." The shocked look on Squire Francouis's face was so magnificent that it was all Darless could do to manage a straight face.

Sir Thomas could not. He absolutely roared with laughter. In fact, he laughed so long and hard, he finally had to sit down to keep from falling down. It felt so good to laugh, he though, here in the face of serious demon hunting. When he finally regained his composure, he commended Darless, "Thanks Darless, you have taught my squires an important lesson — never believe everything that you hear — boys, you must learn not to be so gullible — seek for the truth. You must learn to sense the truth when you hear it."

Darless added, "I'm sorry about that, Squire Francouis, but I just could not resist that one. No, I have never had nor ever will have 'victims' as you know them. You will be far more comfortable around me if you just think of me as a mage or magic user, rather like Alison."

"My Lady, please forgive my dishonorable, childish outburst. I spoke way out of turn. Curiosity got the better of me," a very red faced Francouis replied, kneeling before her.

"Apology accepted." She smiled coyly at him and then added, "But I will tell you one useful thing so that you may learn something from all this. Should I have been an evil demon as you first assumed I must be and had you attacked me with your weapons, you would have been even more shocked. Your weapons cannot even scratch me, though I likely would be bruised by the force of your blows. And should I retaliate, unleash my magic on you, well, you get the idea. However, I could be killed outright, cut in half, by Sir Thomas' blade. Do you understand?"

"Around a real demon from the Abyss, you must be very, very careful, for your lives and very souls are at stake. Life and death lie on the chaotic whims of a demon. And with that said, I am going to bed for I am exceedingly tired. Good night all." With a subtle swish and flair of her dress, she turned and entered the tunnel entrance.

"Two lessons in one night!" Chuckled Sir Thomas who added after a pause, "Since I am still concerned that these demons may back track during the night, we shall sleep outside here and guard those inside. Go bed down your war horses and retire. I shall take the first watch. John, I shall wake you in three hours. Tomorrow we must take action." Without further words, the two carried out their orders. The night passed uneventfully.

Shortly after ten the next morning, Tracker Abe, Squire Frunne, and Slickster came riding up to the ruins of Castle d'Ambrose. After Abe's report of no demons at Fountain Head off to the southeast, Sir Thomas held a council with his band of adventurers to decide what to do next.

Meanwhile inside, everyone was still sleeping save Lady Ursla. As usual, she met the crack of dawn with a small ceremony. The others were still deep in much needed sleep when Sir Thomas entered the tunnel.

"Top of the morning, Sir Thomas," the Lady greeted him near where the body of Alison had lain the day before. "The others are still not up, I'm afraid."

"Ah then, let them sleep. I've come to say that we are off to track down the demon horde. I expect that they will attack at Mennion, due south of Jascar Mines sometime today. We aim to be there if we can." And he gave detailed instructions to her to relay to the others when they were awake.

However, Lady Ursla refused to let one of his squires remain behind to guard them. "I assure you that no demons have the ability to enter while I am here." And she smiled politely. Sir Thomas realized at once that this elegant, grand old dame, was more than a match for Chasme demons.

"You wield power like a summer rose after a gentle rainfall!" Sir Thomas chuckled as he complimented her.

"You are a wise man," she grinned coyly. "I will relay your message precisely as given. May you find what you desire. After you are gone, I will put up some defenses. Until we meet again, may the days go well for you."

Outside the tunnel in the rolling grasslands about the ruins of Castle d'Ambrose, a lone ground squirrel secretly cheered as the massive horses thundered off into the distance. No one heard its comment, "Good bye and good riddance, ground thunderers!" Likewise, no one heard its exclamation of surprise, "Now how did that enormous hedge get there! I wonder if there are any berries on it?" The tunnel entrance was blocked by a very thick hedge. The ground squirrel scampered over to inspect it for food. All was quiet; it was 11a.m.

"Ieeeeee! Get off me! Ieeeee! Help me!" Frantic alto screams tore through the underground, converted dungeon, reverberating off walls and floors and ceilings destroying the peaceful solitude. Instantly, Jon, Mandy, and Darless awoke, staggered and ran into Alison's room joined by Lady Ursla. That the demons had returned flared in everyone's minds except the druid's.

They burst into Alison's room. She was screaming, flailing her arms about, thwarting off attacks of invisible Chasme. Sweat poured down her face in ringlets, disheveled strands of long brown hair flinging madly about.

"Alison, it's okay. It's us, Jon, Mandy, Darless, Lady Ursla. It's okay, honey. It's all right now." Approaching her, Jon spoke with a voice shaking from concern. Her glazed eyes saw only demons flying about the room. As he got his arms around her to hold her tight, he comforted, "It's all right now, Alison. It's safe. We're here. It's okay."

Mandy and Darless offered similar soft consoling; their voices full of concern. Jon's nose picked up the fragrance of the special candle; the druid was on-duty. When he had a solid hold of her, she ceased fighting and flung her arms around him holding on tightly, nearly crushing him.

Without thinking or forethought, Jon found himself looking at Alison's mental pictures that were flashing by uncontrollably in her mind. He saw the Chasme flying about everywhere, two fireballs exploding, still more demons swooping into the room, charred demons falling to the floor, and still more demons flying straight at her through the sooty haze, completely unaffected by her blaze. Now the demons were all over her, gnashing and tearing at her body, ripping it to shreds. Alison shrieked once more and totally collapsed like dead weight in Jon's arms. Steadily her breathing slowed became more normal; her eyes fluttered, the glaze left them for now.

"Jon? Where . . . I'm . . . dead . . . What . . . "

"There, there, it is all okay now. You are safe. We are all here. You are alive," he softly whispered to her. "And strong as an ox, I might add! Can you relax your grip on me please?"

"Breathe deeply, Alison," spoke the commanding voice of the druid. "It will help calm you. There, that's much better. Now, how is my patient feeling this morning?"

"I . . . was . . . dead . . . I think . . . No, I saw a pale green light . . . no, the world turned green. No, I am so confused!" and she started to cry. Jon patted her on the back as he still held onto her. She sniffled and dried her eyes and sat down on the edge of her bed, Jon sat down beside her. "There, I do feel better, just so weak! I can hardly sit up! What happened?"

Now that the herbal fumes from the candle were in full effect, Lady Ursla began to explain all that had happened to her after Jon had discovered her cut up body the day before. She carefully watched Alison's reactions as she discussed the events, repeating them when necessary, until she was certain that Alison understood all that had happened.

"I — owe you all my life then! How can I ever repay you? How can I ever thank you enough?" and tears flowed again at the hopelessness that the thought gave her.

"Time enough for that later on," commanded the druid. "Now I think it is time to try to get some food in you and then let's get you all cleaned up. A bath is in order I believe." Within minutes, Alison, apparently ravenous, was stuffing food as fast as Darless brought it to the table. "Go slowly, Alison. Easy does it!" sternly commanded the druid.

When Lady Ursla had decided that Alison had eaten all that was wise at this point in her recovery, she then ordered, "Now for a bath. You are still weak and will need some assistance. Mandy, can you help bathe her please?"

Mandy took her arm to steady her and led her off to the bathroom area of the dungeon, while Darless cleaned up the table. Jon was lost in thought. Sipping her tea, Lady Ursla watched Jon; there was a hint of curiosity in her eyes that never missed a thing. After some moments, Jon became aware of her, looked at her and said in a low voice, "What you were saying yesterday — it's — it's going to be a mental recovery that we have to worry about, isn't it?" The druid nodded agreement. Jon remembered reading history books about World War II bombing victims who had shell shock for the rest of their lives.

"Each person is different. Remember that, Jon." She spoke sternly, giving her pronouncement even more weight.

A short while later, Darless brought Jon, who was sitting at the kitchen table staring into space, lost in thought, a cup of mint tea. She too had been lost in thought, though hers were quite different from Jon's. She sat down across from him, sliding the cup toward him. "Oh! Thanks. I guess I was kind of thinking about Alison and all, sorry about that."

"None, needed. I have been giving this demon thing a good deal of thought. Remember what Sir Thomas' message which the Lady relayed to us a while ago said?"

'The demons have struck at Fitzgerald Castle, La Fontaine, Edgeway, here, and then at Jascar Mines. They are obviously on a due south sweep into our lands. I conclude they are now heading south through the Durse Woods and will strike next at Mennion, due south of Jascar Mines at the southern edge of Druse Woods. We are heading there at top speed. Join us there if you are up to it and so desire. Sir Thomas.'

"I'm sorry Darless, but those names mean nothing to me. I should have studied Alison's map of the region long ago. I've been meaning to do so," apologized Jon, more to himself than Darless.

"Sir Thomas has it all wrong," Darless pronounced, a great certainty was in her voice. Counting off the numbers on her fingers, she proclaimed:

"Number 1: Demons, well this kind anyway, cannot get from the planes of the Abyss to here on their own. They need a Gate — a magical portal created by someone both powerful and somehow familiar with this area. Number 2: when traveling to another plane of existence as this one that we are in, they require some major underlying purpose — something they have been commanded to do. Number 3: thus, someone has commanded them to do something here in this world. Number 4: they will not leave until that command has been fulfilled or they are all dead. Number 5: they will not vary from that purpose while on this plane of existence, for they desire only to return to their home planes in the Abyss. No one enjoys being forced to do another's bidding. I can vouch for that one. Number 6: if given half a chance, they would rebel and kill the one who is so commanding them. Finally, Number 7: since they are still around and have been to so many areas, therefore the one commanding them must be powerful indeed."

"Number 8: then, we should be concentrating our efforts on the one who is behind it, who is or who has summoned them from the Abyss!" added Mandy, who had just returned with Alison in tow. They had heard all of Darless' comments. Startled, Jon and Darless looked up at the two who had slipped so quietly into the kitchen while they were intently discussing the problem. Alison did indeed look refreshed. Water still dripped from the ends of her long hair, she had on a white silk blouse and white leather elk skin pants to match. But her facial color was still quite pallid, closely matching her outfit. She still leaned on Mandy.

"Thank you all so very much . . . " Alison began. But immediately Darless interrupted her.

"Alison, that's enough. We know, really we do, how you feel. You would have done as much for anyone of us, including me! I — I do love you! You are like the sister I never had." And to everyone's surprise, Darless gave Alison a long hug and a kiss on her forehead. Then, for a second of time that Alison would never forget for the rest of her life, her eyes and Darless' coal black eyes locked and a total understanding flowed through Alison. For that brief moment, Alison was Darless; Darless was Alison. She understood. Tears rolled down both girls' faces. Mandy and Jon were both choked with emotion as well. There was a bond between these four that transcended time.

"Well, enough of this mutual admiration," scolded Lady Ursla as she entered the kitchen. But everyone knew that she did not mean it. Darless, in particular, knew that she was just envious for it reminded her of what she had had with her long dead husband. "I pronounce Alison physically healed, but it will be some days yet before she regains all of her former strength and perhaps weeks before her endurance is back to what it should be. So, what do you plan to do about Sir Thomas' suggestion that you join him down by Mennion, wherever that is? And *who* shall take me home?" She added that last bit as a subtle clue that she considered her services here completed, that Alison did not need her any longer, and that the rest was up to them.

"Does Alison need to stay here and rest up for some time before we can begin?" asked Jon, who could not conceive that after being nearly dead yesterday, she could be fully well the next.

"She needs to take it easy and let her strength and endurance return. Obviously, she is in no shape to walk, but she could ride a horse. Just do not overdo it with her. You will be able to tell."

"Well, I for one, must return home to get equipped for any adventuring," put in Mandy. "I have access to any number of horses, but it would be hard to get them here."

"Me too," added Jon, "At least I need to get some spare clothes. I guess we shall have to take turns — we don't dare leave Alison here alone!"

"Yes, but first I think we need to decide how to proceed," interjected Darless. "If we know what we are at least planning to do, then we would have a better idea of what to bring along with us."

"Excellent point!" declared Mandy. "My thoughts precisely. So what are we going to do?" And the discussion went back over the message left by Sir Thomas and Darless' observations of demons.

Everyone agreed that there had to be someone behind the summoning or gating of the Chasme, that there had to be some purpose behind it all. It was not just a random event and their path was not necessarily due south, town hopping. Alison laid her map of the surrounding territory in the center of the table and Jon carefully placed now empty tea cups on the map over the towns. It was Jon that saw the first glimpse of a pattern. Darless' insistence on the fact that there had to be some purpose, some motive behind the attacks and appearances, started him reflecting on the little that he knew of this land. Then, he remembered Alison's tale of her father. Though to the others, his request sounded completely off the topic, "Alison, can you tell us all once again of that last adventure your father had just before that disaster befell your family?"

"Sure. But what has that got to do with this?" her look of confusion mirrored the others.

"Maybe nothing. But I know so little about this land. Maybe it will give me an idea. Please?"

"Ok. Dad was a holy cleric of Ukko and an adventurer. I was told that he had been adventuring most of his life, championing the causes of Ukko and doing works for the church. Dad was a very powerful priest, my nanny told me, and his last quest was to recover the long lost holy relic, the Royal Scepter of Ukko, which the legendary priest, d'Argo the Holy, had taken with him when he ventured into the depths of the Abyss during the Holy Retribution Wars, some two hundred years ago. He and his party were lost as was the Royal Scepter. No one ever knew what happened to the relic."

"Nanny explained to me that one day, Dad had come across a scroll that depicted the powers of that relic. It also told of its fate and location in the Abyss. It seems that Metrarch, the Demon Lord who had slain d'Argo, had tried to pick up the Royal Scepter. To his dismay, he suffered eternal, non-healing burns to his hands. In a fit of spite, he hurled the Royal Scepter into a volcano's lava flow hoping to melt it into base metals. But the lava could not melt what the magical smithy had created. So he had it encased in a giant solid block of glass and placed it at the foot of his throne. Anyone requesting audience with him was required to urinate on the block first."

"That infuriated my father according to my nanny. He swore he would recover it from the unholy Abyss. That was the purpose of his last adventure. Nanny said that he left for La Fontaine to pick up some members of his team. From there, they were to push onto Fitzgerald Castle where the last members of his party were located and where they purchased the supplies they intended to take. They were then to go to Baner Towers where the Archmage Coventry Baner lived. It was he who had agreed to open a gate into the Abyss for them to pass. What I never understood was how they intended to get back."

"Some weeks later, they all returned. Gosh I never will forget how tired, exhausted and beat up he looked. Fairly scared a little girl of three! But they all came back via Leeds of all places. It is an empty, desolate, ancient ruins of a temple to an unknown god located on an isolated island in the middle of the Sea of Salt, way west of here and somewhat south. I overheard dad say to mom that they arrived at Leeds about two weeks ago and had stopped at Last Town to desperately resupply and cross the Saline River. They had been waylaid by bandits crossing the Plains of Gorsagatha and had rested a few days in Duncanville before continuing on to Jascar Mines and then here."

"Late the next night, I snuck into my dad's study to see the holy relic, the Royal Scepter of Ukko. Gosh it looked so huge to a girl of three! I can still see it so vividly in my mind! It looked more like a mace, jewel-encrusted and golden, about three feet long. That was the only glimpse I ever had of it, though. Dad caught me and said . . . " she paused as a tear rolled down her face. The others were silent.

In a minute she regained her composure and her alto voice continued. "I wanted to say to dad that I could not sleep and was looking for him, but the words would not come out! I ended up saying that I was really curious to see what it was that he had found. Dad laughed at me and showed it to me. He said that around the Royal Scepter of Ukko, no lie could be told. Then, he told me that he loved me. I hugged him and told him I loved him too. And . . . and that was the last thing I ever said to my Dad." Tears glistened in streaks down the sides of her still pallid cheeks. After a minute she finished up.

"And he tucked me into bed. A short while later I heard horrible noises. Nanny burst into my room, telling me the castle was under attack and to get my precious things together. I grabbed my doll, my picture book and my blanket. Nanny took me down to the dungeon saying that it was the safest place in the castle. I remember hearing sounds of a mighty battle and then terrible explosions. Walls began falling down. Ceilings fell, but Nanny was right, the dungeon was carved under solid bedrock and we were safe, but alone. When the sounds subsided, we tried to go back up, but the way was blocked with fallen stones. So we left through the secret tunnel over there, now my entryway. When we were safely in the woods, we looked back. The entire castle lay in ruins, smoke clouds drifted into the sky. I was just numb."

Though she was done and now silent, the hush continued for several minutes as her companions absorbed her story. "There, Jon, that's the story. I don't see how that has anything to do with the Chasme. When I came back here to make my residence until I can afford to rebuild Castle d'Ambrose, I searched the ruins carefully, salvaging everything I could find. I do have a large supply of dad's walking sticks over yonder. But no trace has anyone ever had of the Royal Scepter of Ukko. It just disappeared, vanished completely. I may have been the last person to actually see even it. So what has all this to do with the demons? Ah ha! I see a pattern here! Is that what you are looking for Jon?"

"Hmm, I thought I had heard mention of those towns before. Look here on the map!" He pointed out the tea cups beside the towns. "Chasme first hit the Baner Towers where your dad began his journey into the Abyss. Then, they hit Fitzgerald where he was just before that, and then La Fontaine and then here. Precisely the path your dad took, only in reverse!"

"Interesting," speculated Mandy, "I think you are on to something. Next came Jascar Mines. Anyone want to wager the Chasme will next hit Duncanville?"

"And then Last Town and then Leeds!" Darless exclaimed!

"Bingo!" said Jon. Then, he had to explain that word to everyone.

Alison excitedly went on, "That's gotta be their route! Somehow all this is tied up with my dad and the Royal Scepter, though I have not got a clue. Sir Thomas is completely wrong! But then he always rushes to judgements; that's why I am so valuable to my party. I never make rush judgements, ever. They always tease me about being the slow poke. But they always follow my decision when I finally reach them."

"Men!" interjected Mandy. "Still, the 'why' makes no sense, That was well over twenty years ago. Perhaps the castle was sacked by someone wanting to get his hands on that holy relic. But you say it was never found. Surely anyone wanting it would have tried to come here and search the ruins before now! It's been twenty years! Why now?"

"Revenge!" softly spoke Darless. When she had their attention, she went on, "If your dad recovered the Royal Scepter of Ukko from Metrarch, the Demon Lord, time would mean nothing to him. If I know demons, he still thinks of nothing but revenge! And to get his hard-won relic back! If he was disfigured by that relic, my gods, would he want it back!"

"But it isn't here! Ukko knows how hard, how thoroughly I have searched these ruins! Every time that my magical powers grew stronger, I have repeated that exhaustive search. It just is *not* here."

"Darless, why would Metrarch wait so long to strike back? Would not he have been behind the initial destruction the castle here?" asked Jon.

"I, I just assumed that one of dad's enemies was behind the raid. No one has ever mentioned seeing demons around here the night of the attack. But the explosions and destruction of the castle could only have been done through the use of some mighty magical spells. One day I aim to know those spells and to know how to defeat them as well!" Grim determination contorted Alison's face.

"Metrarch, the Demon Lord, would more likely have someone in his employ do the dirty work rather than become personally involved, I expect." Darless suggested. "I think the odds are that Metrarch is the one behind these Chasme as well. It makes sense, in a twisted, demonic way."

With a look of determination, Mandy pronounced, "Then, I think all is settled. We go by horseback following in reverse the path Alison's father traveled when he returned from the Abyss. We need horses, food, and supplies. Where is the nearest town around here to get them?"

"Stonefist Castle. I keep my string of horses there. We can get anything we need there. And the best news is that it is in the picture books! See." Alison fetched her book and opened it to show everyone the rustic setting of an ivy-covered, grey castle set near the edge of the mountainous Rolling Hills. "Wow! Look at this! I had completely forgotten. The ruins of Leeds is in the book, here." And she showed them a strange picture of a half-crumbled tower shrouded in mist and surrounded by water.

Staring at the picture, an idea began to form in his mind, but he dared not discuss it in front of Alison. No, not until he had more to go on. He sent to Mandy and Darless,
She never said how her father could return from the Abyss. But suppose he took a picture book with him? I wonder if these books have anything to do with it. And if so, could it

have anything to do with the disappearances of her siblings? We had better keep these thoughts to ourselves for the time being!

"No, Jon. It is always better to be totally up front and square." Mandy spoke. Jon flushed, knowing instinctively she was right.

"Alison, I just had the thought that perhaps your dad knew he could get back from the Abyss any time he wanted to, because, because he took one of the picture books with him." He paused to let the full impact reach her and then added, "And perhaps events now are occurring because Metrarch has somehow gotten a hold of one of the books."

A look of sudden realization and shock flooded over Alison's face. In her weakened condition, she just collapsed onto the table for support. "It, it could be, perhaps one of my brothers or sisters has been captured, tortured into releasing their book!"

"There now, let's not go jumping to conclusions," consoled Mandy. "It's just that such a possibility might be. Not too likely, but then these are most unusual circumstances. I just think you ought to be prepared."

"Right," added Jon and then, "And I'm sorry that I tried to keep something from you. I won't do it again. To any of you!" he added.

Just then, Lady Ursla came in, "Someone is coming. I heard a horse ride up."

Quickly, everyone jumped up and headed for the tunnel. Mandy grabbed her sword, Darless grabbed Alison to help her. Jon again felt embarrassed, he had no weapon to grab. Though he did not know how to use any, he instinctively knew he would feel better if he had even a pole in his hand — just something to deflect sword strikes. He followed on Mandy's heels as she headed down the tunnel, followed by Lady Ursla with Darless and Alison bringing up the distant rear. Everyone halted at the entrance.

"Zagroot zounds! Where'd this come from?" declared Mandy as she stood before a dense wall of hedge that totally obscured the entrance. "Ouch, it has stickers too!"

"My little contribution to Alison's safety," replied the druid. "The password is Hollybine."

"Hollybine!" Mandy spoke in a very determined voice. At once, the hedge parted, opening a wide path through the hedge which was nearly ten feet thick. "Wow."

"Thanks!" declared Alison, as she saw her new protective gate."

"A little something until you can get a new gateway build," smiled the druid. The neighing of a horse broke the stillness. And footsteps could be heard.

"Grand Central Station!" muttered Jon under his breath as they stepped through the hedge to the outside.

"Ho! Is anyone here?" a voice called out, a voice strangely familiar to all, but not quite recognized. They spotted him rummaging through the ruins of Castle d'Ambrose.

"We're here. Who might thee be?" inquired Mandy, sword at the ready, though the stranger bore no weapon that was visible as yet. The man jumped, startled, and turned to face them, a stark, plain, white cross was on the front of his blue tunic. Surprise turned to a broad smile. It was Lonnie, the young squire of the aged Sir Wayne Gilbold, a holy paladin who lived in Rothwood Castle and who had adventured with Jon's deceased grandfather!

"Hail and well met to all of thee!" Lonnie fairly shouted in joy. "Been looking for you all!"

"Hi Lonnie!" Jon responded, suddenly flooded with all of his intentions to visit Sir Wayne and hear all of his tales of adventures with his grandfather. Lonnie rushed forward and formally bowed low to each of the ladies and in turn kissed their hand in a most grand fashion.

When he got to Jon, his hearty hand shake diminished and his face became somber. "I have bad news, Jon. Sir Wayne Gilbold has gone to join Ukko. He died two weeks ago now."

"Damn!" cried Jon, suddenly realizing that he had lost forever the chance to hear tales of his grandpa.

"However, before he died, Sir Wayne knighted me into the Holy Order of Ukko. I am now a fledgling Holy Paladin of Ukko!" The young man who was only about eighteen proudly exclaimed. "Jon, his parting words were as follows."

Seek and find Saint Jon Brown.
Swear fealty and loyalty to him.
Be as a squire and protector to him.

For he can teach you what I am unable to do any longer.

"My sword! Hold on just a moment!" And he embarrassedly ran to his horse and grabbed his sword. In a flash, he knelt before Jon on one knee, sword hilt pointing toward Jon. Well-rehearsed words flowed forth, "I, Lonnie Smith, do hereby swear my loyalty in this life and the next to you, Saint Jon Brown. If my life can aid you, it is yours to command; if my death can serve you, so be it! My life is yours to command, My Lord! Will you accept my pledge?" Eager eyes awaited Jon's reply.

"What?" cried Jon in utter disbelief.

Jon! Careful! This is a very important thing that Lonnie's doing. Mandy sent him.

But I don't want a squire! I don't want the responsibility of having to look after him! I don't know him at all. Help!

"Lonnie," Jon began searching for the right words that would not offend, "I, ah, I am not from your world. I am not familiar with the meaning of your oath. I do not fully know what you would expect of me or I of you. Where I come from, we do not have Lords and Squires anymore, not for some eight hundred years. There, we hold to the principle that all men and women can be on equal footing. Though we do have apprenticeships, where a new person can learn what he can from one who has mastered something." While he was saying this, Jon began to wonder. Did Sir Wayne suggest this as a last final service in the memory of his grandpa? Was there more to this than a simple desire to serve? There had to be, he thought.

"But tell me, Lonnie, did Sir Wayne have more to say about your offering me your service? There was more than just those parting words? Right?"

Lonnie's face reddened slightly followed by a look of amazement. "How did you know that? Well, yes. He said that you would not likely know what I was offering." He stared at the ground and shuffled his feet. In a softer voice he added, "Actually, in truth, he said that I had a lot to learn about truth and life; that if anyone could teach me what I needed to know, it was you. He said that there was more to being a holy paladin of Ukko than chivalry, honor and a righteous, strong sword.

For sooth, there is little that is honorable left in Rothwood Castle!"

"Ah, now that makes more sense. He is right, I am at a loss to know the full intent of your offer. I do know that it is not lightly given on your part. I am not in a position to nor am I really qualified to take on a squire. Nor would I wish to if I were." Lonnie was crestfallen!

"But, I cannot turn down the request of Sir Wayne either." New hope appeared in the young paladin's face. "I have no idea if there is anything I could possibly teach you. Certainly it would not be about the art of combat! Whether or not there is anything you can learn from me I know not either." Lonnie's face fell once again, knowing that rejection was a few words away.

"At the moment, we are involved with some very nasty demons from the Abyss. Probably some very powerful person is behind it. Alison here was nearly killed yesterday battling them. It is not some band of thieves or some renegades that we are going after. We may all die in the attempt." Lonnie grasped instantly that he was being told what might be considered privileged information. His hopes began to grow as he tried to imagine how he might fit into those plans. Death was remote — a foreign concept that only happened to the aged in just time.

"For several weeks we are going to journey by horseback to a place called Leeds. I hear that it may be a wild country. Rather than accept your oath of servitude to me, I make this counteroffer. Assuming that it is acceptable to the others here, you may ride with us and assist us as you may, but as an equal. I offer you neither treasure nor any hope of monetary gain. But while our paths merge for a while, I will do what I can for your education as Sir Wayne wished. If the path actually takes us all the way to Leeds, once there, you are free to go your own way. Likewise, if at any point in the journey, you feel the need to part our company, you must act on that need and do so with no loss of honor or broken vows, with no regrets." Then, he remembered Lady Ursla's words and added, "Your first lesson is this: each person is different. Each has their own personal strengths and weaknesses. My weakness is that I know nothing about fighting and do not really care to know anything about it either. I prefer to use my mind. I really *am* a musician."

That is an understatement! Mandy placed in his mind. Alison wondered why for an instant Jon's face blushed.

"Will you honor us with your presence then as an equal during this several week journey?" Jon finished up.

"Upon my sacred honor as a Holy Paladin of Ukko, I do so swear!" Lonnie beamed happily as a lark, though he had absolutely no idea how this sudden reversal of acceptance had come about.

"Then, so swear in turn to each of us, as we are all equals here." Jon added. Lonnie rapidly did so to each.

Mandy smiled. "Your second lesson for today is a simple one. In this party there are *no* heroics. No one-person grand stands. Always think of the others and what your actions may have on their fate. We always look out for the other person. No rash actions. As Alison says, 'Think before you act.' Try to remember that always. Think first, act when necessary afterwards."

"Your third lesson for the day," put in Darless, for whom this was a totally new experience, "is always trust each of us with your life and without the slightest trace of doubt no matter how grim the circumstances may seem to you. If you can do that, then I welcome your company."

"Most honorable Lady Darless, I shall endeavor to do so always!" was his reply.

She smiled and rebuffed him, "Thanks, but no 'try' — just do so without reservation. And please, call me Darless! We all go by first names here; no formalities, please!"

Alison was already planning. "Lonnie has a horse; I think we should take along one spare that can act as a pack horse unless we need it. Mandy, you certainly can handle a light war horse, right? And how about you, Darless? I know for a fact that Jon cannot." Mandy nodded affirmatively.

"Sorry," Darless replied, "I don't know what one is. Is it just a big horse?"

"They are larger and stronger than normal horses. Both rider and steed have trained for certain fighting actions," explained Lonnie, who rode a medium war horse. "They will not bolt and run off at the slightest provocation. And they will even attack with their front hooves when so commanded by their rider."

"Then, I best ride a normal horse like Jon," she decided.

"Ok. It is a good day's ride from here to Stonefist Castle. I know how to best do this. Jon, if you can transport Lonnie to Stonefist with a shopping list from me, then he can see that it is properly filled and bring the string of horses back here. Meanwhile, you all can return home and get your things ready. And it will give me another couple days to recover," Alison wisely decided.

However, no one would hear of her staying by herself. So it was decided that Jon and Lonnie go first. Darless would take Lady Ursla home. When Jon or Darless returned, Mandy would head home. That way, someone was always with her, just in case.

After they all said their farewells, particularly to Lady Ursla, the druid took Jon aside for a final private word. "Remember that Amulet of Protection that Reginald gave you? Well, you should wear it at all times from now on. There is a reason. Have you ever considered what might happen if someone who had a stronger mental reserve than you have should attack you via your mind? If they held a larger reservoir of power, you may run out of energy before they do. The Amulet provides some defense from that."

"I — I never knew — I never thought — Okay, I will. Thanks!" He swore that he would never again be without it.

So with Alison's list in an envelope with her seal upon it addressed to the castle steward and with a map of his return route in his belt pouch, Lonnie was ready.

Jon planned to take Lonnie to Stonefist Castle using the book of pictures. "These are magical books," he explained as they stood in the kitchen looking at Alison's book on the table opened to the picture of Stonefist Castle. "Do you have an imagination? Well, here take my hand. As I pull you forward, imagine you are stepping onto that grassy way there. Got it?"

Bewildered and confused, Lonnie tried to protest as he felt the tug of Jon's hand on his. He tried to take a step forward, but his mind could not adjust to stepping onto a kitchen table onto a book. He stumbled and found himself lying face down in the grassy area before the castle. He looked up in utter amazement at Jon.

Jon helped him up. As they walked toward the castle's main gate, Jon tried to explain about the books. Lonnie found it all hard to believe, save that he was now here and not in Alison's dungeon any longer.

When they reached the gate, Jon said, "Here's where we part company for a couple days. I have to return home and get my things and get back fast. See you in a couple days."

"Farewell! You can count on me! But wait, where is your book? How are you going to get to your place? Is it in the picture book?"

"No, it is not in the book. My copy is at home. I'll explain if I can later when we have more time. Bye and good luck." Lonnie watched as Jon took a step back in the direction they had been walking. In the middle of the second step, Jon was not there, he had vanished into thin air.

Later, Lonnie confessed that he was glad no one was there to see his expression of complete disbelief. He was utterly convinced that Saint Jon Brown was indeed a god somehow in disguise. Either that, or he had to be a very, very cleverly disguised master mage of great power. However, he knew that magic was Alison's and Darless' realms. So that left him with only one conclusion. And he began to wonder why a god would be here in disguise and what his purpose was. Could he be here to test himself — to prove Lonnie was worthy of paladinhood? No, Lonnie rejected that thought. The world did not revolve around Lonnie Smith. Of that he was absolutely certain.

Chapter 3 Nightmares

Back home in his deserted house in Urbana, Jon's first action was to place his picture book on a chair nearby so he could watch the image of the castle ruins for messages. It was now dark there. Time was not pressing; he had decided to try to arrive there at dawn.

Jon took a much desired bath, allowing himself the luxury of a full tub of hot water and reflection time to make his plans. He forced himself to think only about what he should take with him. He had never really "planned" for an adventure before. Alison's order that Lonnie was filling at Stonefist Castle would handle their food and other mundane needs. So he became practical; what should he take?

He would pack clothes mostly, spare batteries, his Swiss Army knife, a first aid kit, a compass, his flute. On a whim, he added his small portable tape recorder and a couple blank tapes in the sack as well. He added a box of waterproof matches.

Satisfied, Jon put the Amulet of Protection around his neck along with the green Emerald of Life, covering them with his Cardinal's official tee shirt. He wore a pair of heavy jeans and sturdy hiking boots. Then, he rummaged around for a hat. He decided to use his rather rumpled black-felt cowboy hat. It had always kept the sun off of him when he had vacationed in the mountains of Colorado. *After all, we are going by horseback*. He grinned at the thought and wondered how that would go.

He checked the picture book again. The night there was receding so he still had time for a quick bite. Then, as the image of the ruins of Castle d'Ambrose reddened with the morning sun, Jon stepped into the image, sack in hand.

Dew moistened the grass just outside the entrance. He took several deep breaths. *No gasoline fumes!* Chasing a ground squirrel away from the hedge, he parted it and entered the tunnel. Darless' light was still glowing faintly illuminating the long tunnel. This time he noticed numerous leather bags covering the tops of empty torch brackets. He stopped long enough to open the draw string of one. Light beams escaped! Jon realized now that Alison had at least a dozen light globes lining the entrance tunnel. In all of the confusion before, he had not noticed them. Jon made his way toward the kitchen area and the glowing light.

"Morning, Jon." A sleepy-eyed Mandy greeted him. She wore a long gown to ward off the chill of the dungeon; it was one of Alison's he noted. Although her long brown hair was disheveled from sleep, she still looked stunning, maybe more so, Jon thought and just a bit vulnerable.

Acting on instinct and his own feelings, Jon commanded, "Come here, beautiful!" And he gave her a loving hug and a welcome kiss. She reciprocated in kind.

"Been waiting for that for a long time," she teased. "See you are not even red faced about it!" Jon immediately reddened. Mandy laughed. "Come on silly, I'll show you how to at least heat water without getting zapped. Alison has all sorts of magics rigged in here."

Over tea and Mandy's breakfast, she talked with Jon. "Alison's still a bit weak; I have been acting as a support for her when she moves around. I suspect she will sleep in late again today. After I finish up eating, I'm going to change and head home." After a long pause, she, with a frown on her face, added, "Something's been troubling me, Jon. And late last night, when I could not get to sleep, it hit me. Did you notice any singular problem with Alison's tale of this castle's destruction? Think about it a minute, though you might not be familiar enough with this land to notice it."

Jon replayed in his mind all of Alison's tale twice. "Funny, now that you mention it, one thing sticks in my mind. Not sure how to say it. If it were *my* castle and *my* family, I would have not rested until I found out who did it and how and why and had exhausted every avenue to find out what happened to my family."

"Exactly! You see it too. I had not thought about that last though. Certainly a child of three is going to have a hard time finding her family — too much time would have passed before she grew up. However, if the others were alive, why didn't *they* find *her*? I had not thought of that one, Jon. No, it was your first one that has been troubling me. Alison has never been able to find out anything about who raided and destroyed the castle — she just refers to them as 'dad's enemies' whomever they might be. If someone had destroyed my Blackburn Castle, why they would brag about it, tell tales about it. Castles are very hard to conquer. It is no small feat. But to hear absolutely nothing about the perpetrators, why that is unheard of!"

"Maybe the raiders were not from this section of the world?" offered Jon. "Tales might be told in other countries, lands, whatever you call them here."

"Or perhaps not from this plane of existence at all. Maybe from some place like the Abyss? Interesting thought, anyway." Mandy let that line of thought drop, now that someone else shared her point of view. "You know that you have something there about the rest of her family. If I had a large family and something like this happened, I'd spare no expense to find each and every one! It would be my topmost priority! It is probable that her father died trying to defend everyone. That's a given. But what of her mother and all those kids?"

Jon suggested, "If I were all alone in my room and the walls started coming down, where would be the only possible escape route?"

"That's just it. Other than the dungeon's secret entrance, there isn't any!" Mandy proclaimed.

Jon grinned, "Ah yes there is. What did each child have that they considered valuable?"

"The picture book! You don't suppose that her brothers, sisters, and mother used their books to escape the crumbling castle?" she asked excitedly, already knowing his answer.

"Yes, I do. I'd bet that the kids and maybe even her mother got out the only way they could, by stepping into another place, by using the books." Jon added.

"But most of the books are now accounted for." She looked downcast, imagining their fates.

"I'm — I'm not so hasty to make that jump in logic. Just because she has recovered a book does not necessarily mean that the book's owner is dead. Books can get lost, stolen, even left behind. What if some got left behind because, in their panic to escape, they did not hold onto the book to take it with them? See what I mean?"

"Jon! You are such an optimist! You always find a positive side to things! That is one reason I love you so much!" Mandy smiled and laid her hand softly on his. "Don't ever change that nature! Well, I had best change and get going. See you in a short while." Mandy went into the spare bedroom, changed and then used her book to get home.

Jon tidied up the kitchen a bit and sat down and studied Alison's map. Then, he got out his flute and played for nearly an hour — until the screams began once more, promptly at 11:00 a.m.

"Ieeeeee! Get off me! Ieeeee! Help me!" Again, frantic alto screams tore through the underground converted dungeon, reverberating off walls and floors and ceilings. Jon dropped his flute and rushed into Alison's room.

"It's okay! You are safe." He tried to calm her. Again, her eyes had that glassy stare; she did not see him. He put his arms around her and held her tightly. She immediately grabbed him. Jon watched as the images playing through her mind, rather like a motion picture. He could feel her physical reactions to each slice by the Chasme. He waited and, in due time, she got to the end of the horrid scenes and collapsed in his arms and woke up. For a while, she just cried on his shoulder, while he rubbed her back and caressed her hair.

After a time, she sobbed, "What's the *matter* with me anyway? These nightmares are *horrid*! I cannot get *rid* of them. Am I going to have them *every* morning as long as I live? I don't think I can take it!" Alison cried for some time.

All Jon could think of was to walk her around her home. With his arms supporting her, he led her from room to room. As she noticed different objects, she slowly brightened up. Within ten minutes, she was calm and back to her normal self, as much as was possible under the circumstances. "Oh Jon, hold me! Just hold me! I don't ever want you to go." He held her tight and then they embraced long and tenderly.

As he straightened a stray strand of her hair between kisses, he said, "You are so cuddly and beautiful in the morning. I can hardly wait until I can wake up with you beside me in the bed. I don't think I would ever want to get out of bed!" They kissed again.

Then, it was time to eat; she was ravenous once again. After lunch, she seemed much stronger than the day before.

Alison insisted that she needed to pack her gear, so Jon cleaned up the kitchen. Presently, Alison called out, "Jon. Come here a minute. I want to show you some things."

He joined her by the area where she had fallen victim to the Chasme. "See that wall there? Well, it is really my treasury and where I keep my valuables."

"Ah ha! I knew you were trying to reach in that direction when you were attacked. But I just see the rock wall," he replied.

"Just say in a stern tone 'lamb's leaf'. It is the password, the word of power." As soon as he uttered the words, magic flashed. Where there had been only a solid rock wall, an ornate door appeared. "Go ahead. It is safe now. Open it," she said. He did.

Inside was a large room about thirty feet square; it was illuminated by four soft-light globes, evidently magically lit when the door opened. He was speechless. "Welcome to my treasury. Come on in."

Against one wall were bags stacked nearly three feet high. "Those contain gold coins. I have about half of what it will take to rebuild the castle." There was a rack containing numerous scrolls. "Some scrolls here contain magical spells; some contain history and so on. You are welcome to read these at any time. But don't worry, the ones containing the spells will be incomprehensible to you, of that I am certain!" She chuckled knowingly to herself. On a bench to the third side lay numerous articles, including some wands and staffs, obviously her horde of magical items. "While I am sorting out what to take, there is one item you might really have some fun with — that lute over there. It is enchanted. Just say 'play' and a tune's name and it will do so. Course you probably won't know the tune names. So try saying just 'play' and it will pick the tune."

He kissed her, grabbed the lute and headed for the kitchen where his flute had been left earlier. She heard him speak "Play" and the sweet sounds of plucked strings filled the space. Alison was not surprised at all to soon hear the flute join in, trying to match the tune. He was a fast learner when it came to music and soon the two blended. She hummed along with them. Her eyes were bright and her heart was light. Happiness flowed from her like it had not done so in a very long time.

"Do these tunes have words? Can you sing?" Jon yelled inquisitively from the kitchen.

While Alison often sang along when she was by herself, she was way too shy to do so in front of another. But her being in another room felt somehow different. So she started to sing along, although quietly at first. Then, her confidence rose and she really got into the song. When it ended, "Bravo!" resounded off the walls from the kitchen. "This is terrific!" And so the fun-filled hours passed idly by.

Around supper time, Lonnie arrived with the string of horses loaded with their supplies. Alison was feeling strong enough to fix the dinner herself, stating that she did not want men messing with her magical kitchen. Jon, knowing nothing at all about horses, played pack man and carried the goods into the main room, while Lonnie took care of the horses. They were tied in a neat line arrangement close by the entrance way.

They had just sat down to eat when a familiar voice cried, "Did ya miss me?" Mandy strolled into the room, carrying her picture book in one hand and a large sack in the other. "Good timing!" she added and joined them at the table.

They had just started serving up the food when there came a flash of light and a small boom. Small vapors arose from the floor as Darless suddenly appeared, grinning from ear to ear. "Like my entrance? Been working on it!" Seeing the rather startled looks on everyone's face, except Mandy's, she laughed. Mandy had been in on this one; the two girls had timed their arrival together.

Needless to say, it was a very fun filled evening. None wanted to say the obvious, but it might be their last for quite some time.

When it was finally time to retire for the night, Darless gave Lonnie a light globe and taught him how to control it. He intended to spend the night keeping watch over the horses outside and it would be handier than trying to keep a fire going all night.

Alison said, "I think I can manage one spell tonight. I will put an early warning spell around the horses and the entrance. That way, Lonnie can get some sleep." As it turned out, it was not needed and the night passed uneventful.

After breakfast, they set off. Mandy was dressed in her usual brown leather ranger gear, but had a dark cloak draped over her. It seemed to blend in with the land and almost made her seem invisible. (Jon later learned that it was made by elves.) Alison wore her long white robe over her normal clothes, white silk blouse and matching white elk skin pants. Darless wore a dark cloak that hid her gossamer thin dress from view. Lonnie also had a dark cloak thrown over him, covering his shiny suit of chain mail. Jon felt rather out of place dressed in blue jeans and Cardinal's tee shirt, so he gladly accepted Mandy's loan of a dark cloak to ward off the early morning chill.

As they did their last minute preparations, all of the heavy sacks of the day before, one by one disappeared into Mandy's and Alison's portable holes. Both Jon and Lonnie watched in fascination as Mandy explained. "When you open it up this way, inside is a sort of extra-dimensional space, er whatever that is, and you can pile tons of stuff in it and it weights almost nothing at all. This way there is nothing to load down the horse and we can make better time." No one caught the pack horse's sigh of relief.

On the way out, Jon asked, "Alison, can I take along one of your dad's walking sticks? I really do not have any weapon to fend off those bugs if we should meet any. I feel so awkward when everyone else has something."

"I use my nails!" teased Darless. "Alison can clobber them with her staff. Lonnie and Mandy can chop them. But poor Jon is going to beat them with a stick!" Everyone, except Jon, roared with laughter. He was embarrassed for a minute, and then he too saw the humor and joined in. The laugh settled them all down.

"Sure thing. Take anyone you want. But they are not meant to be used as a club. They would probably break," she advised. "They are just dad's old walking sticks."

Jon stood looking at the can that held about a dozen. Some were ornate and fancy. He picked out a plain one, the same one he had used to help push the dead bugs out of the tunnel the day before. It was made from a corkscrew willow branch, carved with a woodland motif and then lacquered. It looked pretty, though rather plain. "I think you will do," he said to it and picked it up and strolled on out with it.

I'm sure I will do. The words appeared in his mind. But Jon was not paying attention, intent on catching up with the others.

And they were off, heading southward toward Jascar Mines. Mandy and Lonnie rode the point with Lonnie leading the spare mare. Alison and Jon came next some distance back, while Darless brought up the rear.

It was a beautiful morning for a ride. The air was crisp and clean, dew still lingered in the grass. Around here, the country was mostly rolling meadows of tall grass. Occasionally, they spotted a herd of animals; sometimes, a herdsman with a flock of sheep. Far off to the left or right the low rolling hills gave way to the craggier mountains of the Verbenloc Range to the west and the Rolling Hills to the east. Alison told them that they would likely reach Jascar Mines just after lunchtime. Since there was nothing dangerous in these parts, they chatted as they rode, passing the time as the sun rose higher in the sky.

It is time. The words appeared in Jon's mind. He looked over at Alison and guessed that it must be nearing 11:00 a.m. "I think we had better stop for a break right now," he commanded. Without waiting for approval, he halted his mare and hopped off. The ground hit him hard. Unused to riding a horse for long periods of time, his legs wobbled as he went over to Alison. Then, he saw her eyes. They were glazing over. Quickly he pulled her off her horse and into his arms leaving her mare to trot off some distance. Jon put his arms around her and held on, fearing the worse. It came.

"Ieeeeee! Get off me! Ieeeee! Help me!" Alison began to scream; the others circled their horses around. Mandy and Lonnie, looking forlorn, retrieved the two mares. Jon held her but this time he did not speak for he knew now that she would not hear him. But he did watch the images in her mind rolling by as if he were watching a movie. In fifteen minutes, it was over; Alison sobbed on his shoulder again.

"Zagroot zounds! This will never do." Mandy began breaking the silence when Alison's fit was finally over. "Excellent job, Jon. If she were riding when that hit her, there is no telling what could have happened! What are we going to do about it?" Darless was silent, fearing the worst. Lonnie finally understood what had happened.

Alison had never felt so completely useless in her entire life. Only now did she fully realize how bad it would be for anyone to take her on a dangerous expedition or even into town! She bawled for a long time.

Darless, Mandy and Lonnie spent several minutes discussing it amongst themselves trying to figure out either a solution or some means around the fits. Mandy, always practical, pointed out the potential disaster should they run into a fight just at the instant she should have a fit. Darless could only offer to the use of her Wish magical spell, though it would physically age her to do so. Lonnie was simply scared. No training he had even had remotely covered this kind of circumstance. He kept interrupting them asking for more explanations of which they had very few.

Jon, on the other hand, said nothing, just held on tightly to Alison and thought. The genus of an idea formed in his mind. At last he spoke, which did get everyone's attention. "Lady Ursla did say not to rush it. And we are in no real hurry at the moment. There is something I want to try, but we need to camp here for a while. How long, I have no idea."

"What can you do? I'm a *hopeless* maniac! I've gone *insane* now! These nightmares come in the middle of the daytime! I'm *useless*. Why don't you all go on without me?" she sobbed again.

Keep guard and don't say anything and don't interfere. I'm going to try something, Jon sent to Mandy and Darless and then to Lonnie. Utter astonishment was the look on the young paladin's face when the words of Jon appeared in his head!

"Alison. Alison, look at me. There now. You do see those horrid images in your mind right?" Falteringly, she nodded affirmative. "Ok. Now I want you to close your eyes and somehow move to the very beginning of the nightmare, right when you first noticed something was about to happen. Tell me when you have found that image, that picture."

She nodded and mumbled "Um hmm," that she had.

"Now I want you to move through the images sort of frame by frame and see everything that is going on. And when you get to the end of it, tell me all about it. I am here and will let nothing interfere with you." Jon carefully monitored her watching as she fumbled about the images. He also noticed the ever so slight presence of Mandy and Darless observing as well.

Bit by bit the scene recorded in her mind played out. Later Mandy would say that it was as if her mind had made a frame by frame picture of all the events including all the pain and terror. When she had viewed it through, he had her tell him about it. (This Lonnie could relate to, but he of course said nothing as he had been told.) Jon was monitoring her bodily reactions and observed that they were not as severe as they had been when he had pulled her off her horse. Nor were they as bad as yesterday morning, nor the morning before. Inspiration struck.

"Very good, Alison. Now let's go back to the very beginning once more and go through the whole thing again. When you are done, tell me all about it." She trusted him totally at this point and did so. This time, she began to yawn considerably and the phantom pains were not so severe, her reactions not as intense. When she told him about it this time, more details began appearing. It had begun when she had heard a funny noise and had gone to inspect it That was why she had been where she was when they broke in.

The tenth time through, Alison was no longer physically reacting to the images; she had yawned and yawned and yawned. But she still was not totally happy or cheerful. Jon was encouraged by her progress though. But something else was interfering. Other images began to crowd in — images of a small child. Suddenly, Jon knew what it was. He asked, "Alison, is there an earlier time when you had something bad like this happen to you?"

"Why yes! I can see me as a little girl. It was when the castle was destroyed!"

"Okay. I want you to move to the very beginning of those images and do the same thing. Look at each image from start to finish and see what is going on. Then tell me about it." She did, but it was slow going. At one point, she let out a high pitch screech as a frightened child of three might do if the ceiling of her house began falling down. The second time through it, no screams occurred. The third time though the images, Alison was yawning heavily.

But on the fourth pass through the mental images, she suddenly started laughing and opened her eyes, "Of course I'd feel completely *helpless*! Completely overwhelmed! I was only *three* and I did indeed try to *levitate* the ceiling of my room backup into place and failed. Haha. It sure would have been something to see a three-year-old levitating tons and tons of rock! How *silly* of me!" And she started laughing. Soon she was laughing so hard she had to sit down. "Me *pushing up* the *ceiling*!" Haha. "I was trying to do it with *one* finger!" Haha. "Not *now*, Nanny, can't you *see* I'm *holding up* the ceiling!" Haha. And on she went for nearly a half an hour, after which she would occasionally let out a chuckle for no apparent reason.

Tears of joy rolled down the other's faces. Even Lonnie was swept up by the emotional release he was witnessing. The black cloud of doom left Alison forever. Since it was lunch time anyway, they made a leisurely time of it. Then, Jon found himself besieged with questions from everyone including Alison. Was this a miracle? Was Ukko behind it? And so on.

Jon tried to explain his new theory and what had happened. "No, no miracle, no intervention by the gods. It was all done by Alison and her willingness and ability to look at her own mental images she had. It's like the mind had made full impression images of the total event and then played them back on cue."

"They were *so* real!" Alison added, "And I could see what I saw then, smell the same smells, feel the same pain! I could even taste that drop of my own blood that got into my mouth as I lay on the floor. God did the floor feel so *cold*!"

"Notice that when she was under the control of the nightmare pictures, she totally acted out the parts. But when she voluntarily examined them with my help, why they sort of erased. Each time through them, their intensity lessened." Everyone nodded that they saw that happening.

"But how did you know that I needed to look at the castle destruction?" asked Alison full of curiosity. "That really did the trick!"

Sheepishly, Jon said, "I was always there watching the images in your mind — right there with you. I kept seeing flashes of a time when you were a little girl. So I asked and you did the rest!"

"That was brilliant, Jon!" exclaimed Mandy. The others wholeheartedly agreed.

The following thought appeared in Jon's mind: *That was indeed remarkable. I accept you.* Jon could not tell from whom it came and so promptly dismissed the errant thought.

"Well, I think that thing is now completely gone!" Alison proclaimed. "And good riddance!" Then, after a long reflectful pause, she added, "You know, if you had not helped me through that, I think that I would have suffered that nightmare over and over for the rest of my life! Thank you from the bottom of my heart!" And she kissed him and hugged him. Then, everyone else took turns hugging everyone else. It took them another half-hour to finally regain their composure and get back on the trail again. But this time they set out without the specter of doom over them.

Everyone continued to discuss the event and its significance and its ramifications as they rode along. In fact, they were so intent on their conversations that they rode right through Jascar Mines without even noticing it!

Only when the trail entered the deep forest and turned now westward did Mandy call a halt. "Whoa, everyone. I'm shirking me duties! We have entered the forest, Druse Woods, I believe, and we are swinging westward. Alison, are these woods safe or should we be on guard?"

"We should be more careful! You never know about these woods. Bands of raiders from the Plains of Gorsagatha do forage in here, mostly here on the far eastern edge. The danger increases as we approach Duncanville, which is at the edge of Druse Woods," she explained. "I don't think we can make Duncanville before nightfall. If you find a good camping place, we can stop while it is still light if you want."

They rode on. But the trail now wandered left and right among the dense oak trees. It was cool and dim. Night would come early and be very dark indeed in these woods. Jon asked, "Does anyone live in these woods? I mean anyone friendly like that would put us up for the night?"

"There are some small hunter's villages, a few hunting lodges. Maybe we can find an empty lodge," she replied.

Quiet! Someone's watching us! Mandy sent to everyone. Lonnie visibly jerked as he realized Mandy had just placed the thought inside his head! This was all so new to him and so completely different from all his training as a paladin. *I will slowly ride ahead of the rest of you.*

Jon strained his ears but heard nothing. Lonnie slowed his pace, placed the reigns over the saddle, and quietly drew his sword. Jon could sense Darless closing the distance between them, just in case. For a time, nothing happened. Birds continued chirping. Nothing seemed amiss to Jon at least.

Don't look, but someone is in the oak tree on our right — the one with the wide bottom branch. As we go by, I'm going to double back from behind. Mandy sent to everyone.

They rode on rather tense as they passed the indicated tree. Just as they passed it by, Mandy appeared on foot at the base of the tree. "All right. I see you up there. We mean you no harm if you mean us no harm." She had her bow pulled back, an arrow pointed upwards.

Branches rustled and the form of a green clad archer snaked down the tree. Here was a gruff looking man about thirty with stubby black beard and long black hair. "Hail and well met." He began once he was on the ground facing Mandy. "I be William d'Groot, First Sergeant of the First Freemen Archers of Duke Richard of Duncanville. And who might thee be, fair, keen-eyed damsel — with a magnificent bow, I might add?"

"Mandy Blackthorn, Ranger of Reylona. These are Darless, Alison d'Ambrose, Saint Jon Brown, and Holy Paladin Lonnie." Mandy did the introductions, putting aside her bow and quiver.

"Well, I'll be! Holy Paladin you say? I can see that. Well, I certainly hope that you are after the devil bugs that went through here!" He turned; looking at Alison, he said, "d'Ambrose, eh? Any relation to the old King Basil d'Ambrose of Verbenloc who died a number years ago?"

"He was my father." Alison softly said.

"Well, I'll be a tree newt! Doesn't that beat all! I knew him when I was just a lad. He stayed at my folks' inn one night. We were all sorry to hear that he got killed."

"What is this about the Chasme demon bugs? Have they passed through here? When? How long ago? Yes, we are on their trail," inquired Mandy.

"That's why the Duke has all of us out on patrol duty. A swarm of the bugs swept down on Duncanville last eve and killed ten townsfolk, including my father. They came right to

the inn, they did! I got two with my magical elfin-made arrows.
I found out that normal arrows just bounce off the bugs. After
I buried my dad, we all hit the trail. The Duke has the entire
First Freemen Archers out on patrol! He even gave us each two
magical arrows!"

"Sorry to hear about your father! But I'm glad to hear
you were able to kill a couple of them vile creatures." Mandy
continued the conversation.

"Well, he was really old and in poor health, so it was a
blessing. Say, are you planning to ride all night into
Duncanville? If not, you are welcome to come stay with some
of my patrol in the Duke's personal hunting lodge. It's a lot
safer than camping outside these days."

"Thanks for the offer. We'd be honored to spend the
night. We were just about to try to find somewhere to camp.
And indeed, a lodge sounds a lot better than out of doors with
these creatures about." She did not add that in all likelihood
the bugs were headed out over the Plains of Gorsagatha about
now. She also smiled because her guess about the demon
horde's next attack had been correct.

He led the way and the others followed; they eventually
departed the main trail moving down a poorly marked side
path. Occasionally, he would stop and whistle to other unseen
archers in the trees. It took another hour to reach the hunting
lodge of the Duke of Duncanville. By then the forest was
becoming quite dark. In Druse Woods, night came well before
sundown. Now Jon noticed that other similar clad archers
were quietly falling in behind them. Evidently, all were
heading for the sanctuary of the lodge and probably the
evening meal. Jon was fascinated by how silent these expert
woodsmen were. They seldom made a sound as they passed.
He marveled at how Mandy had been able to detect William in
the first place.

Presently, bustling noises the friendly crackling of a
fire, and the sounds of voices drifted through the trees. And
there in a man-made clearing stood the hunting lodge.
Probably fifty men were gathering around a large bonfire
outside the building, built from logs made from trees felled to
make the clearing.

Then, it was time for greetings and introductions all
around. Initially, the women got everyone's attention.

Numerous whistles and catcalls echoed through the trees. But William soon put a stop to that. He was their sergeant. However, Lonnie got along terrifically well. This was much more like reality for him. He took care of the horses and blended with the men, discussing fighting tales, tips, and jokes.

However, as Jon tried to dismount, his legs collapsed under him. He was not used to riding. Everyone roared with laughter. "Must be new to a horse!" he heard someone yell. Darless sent him, *Watch me.* He did. She gracefully dismounted as the men watched intently. *I cheated. I levitated during much of the ride — so I am not stiff and sore.* She smiled teasingly his way.

Jon walked stiffly about trying to get his legs to function better. He could sense a change in the group. It was almost as if this band of men now felt more secure because they had a holy paladin and several wizards among them. It was now not just the archers against the demon bugs. They shared the evening meal with the band of archers who convinced them that they had plenty to share. "The forest provides" was the common reply.

The girls went to bed early, mostly so Alison could get needed rest. Jon wandered among the archers for some time, making small talk and listening to everything that was said. Lonnie always seemed to be at the center of attention of small groups. Jon smiled and realized that here Lonnie knew what he was doing. Then, he too realized he really was tired and he joined the others inside the lodge. It was to be their last really peaceful night on the trail for some time.

Dawn came late to those unused to deep forest life. By the time they arose, only a few archers remained. The others had breakfasted and had departed on their assigned patrols. Lonnie was first up and William told him that there would be safe passage from here to Duncanville; the patrols had found no sign of raiders. The sergeant gave Lonnie a green feather to carry as a token of free passage on into Duncanville. He did ask that Lonnie return the feather to the gate keeper as they entered.

However, before the party left the lodge, Mandy, Lonnie and Jon helped cut and stack logs for the coming evening's bonfire. It was a small token of thanks.

The daylong ride was uneventful but not boring. Mandy, knowing that there were occasional concealed archers in the trees, worked on training Lonnie and Jon to be able to detect their presence. By the time they reached the town, the paladin was detecting one in four. Jon had given up; for him, it was a dismal failure — he got only one the whole trip and that was merely a random guess.

The biggest news was the no-event event. In fact the event passed and was not noticed until it was long past. At noon when they halted for lunch, Jon pointed out that Alison had had no reaction what so ever today at 11:00 a.m.! They all celebrated. If Jon had not mentioned it, Alison would have not even recalled it.

By late afternoon, the trees began to thin noticeably. The trail became broader and well-traveled. Now occasional foot traffic came and went. They were getting close to the largest town in this area.

Duncanville lay just at the edge of the woods. Beyond it endless rolling hills went on as far as the eye could see. Home to some 10,000 folks, it was a border town, which meant that all sorts of people came and went. Jon learned that from the north, farmers brought grain to trade. Hunters of Druse Woods would bring forestry products to trade. But the strangest looking lot were the hardy men who dared life on the Plains of Gorsagatha. They were metal workers whose products were scarce and commanded a high price.

They had some discussion about whether to stop and spend some time in town so Jon could satisfy his curiosity or just push on. They decided to ride slowly through town and push on. As they approached the city, Jon saw a low wall, a stone barrier, entirely surrounding the town. The road lead to the largest gates Jon had ever seen. As they approached, many others were entering and leaving. From each, the gate keeper extracted a few copper coins. Jon learned that this was the only tax that the Duke had and it paid for the keep of the Archers, the town's protection.

At the front, Lonnie handed the gate keeper the feather while Mandy tossed him a gold coin, saying "Keep the change. My compliments to the First Freeman Archers." He nodded and tipped his tri-cornered hat.

They had not ridden more than a hundred yards into town when three well-armed men with blue tunics with a yellow crescent moon in the middle, rode up to them hailing them. "You are the paladin party? Please follow us. The Duke wishes to speak to you."

Lonnie sat up straighter in his saddle and replied, "Yes, Lonnie, Holy Paladin of Ukko, at your service. Please lead on. We should not keep his lordship waiting." Then, he bashfully looked at Mandy for approval of his decision. She winked and smiled at him. Jon suspected she mentally told him he had done the proper thing.

Near the center of town, the Duke's residence dwarfed all other buildings. It was a stone structure, three stories tall. All of the stonework in the area was a brownish red color. Not a castle, but with thick walls that could withstand some siege, Jon thought. There were few ground-level windows, and all those that were at ground-level consisted of tiny narrow slits, which Mandy later explained were arrow slits. An archer could fire at will with minimal chance of an enemy reaching him.

Off to the side of the residence was a large stone stable. It was here the riders led them. Jon learned that always one tended to the horses first, then the people. For a horse was a valuable means of transportation especially here on the frontier. Jon really appreciated dismounting. Oh were his legs stiff; this time, he took the walking stick; like an old man, the stick gave him added support. Alison laughed at him, saying "Old before your time, eh? Don't worry, in a few days you will be used to it!"

Jon doubted that very much. Oh, how his thighs ached. He tried to jest that he doubted he would ever get used to horse riding, but found that he said instead, "Yes, I'll probably get used to it in a few days." *Now how come I said that? No matter. This must be the Duke.*

It was. Duke Richard was about forty years old, tall and muscular, evidently a fighter, Jon guessed, for he certainly had the build for it. His dress was immaculate, but it was his rings that gave him away as the Duke. He wore a ring set with a jewel on each finger. Several gold chains dangled over his shirt. His face had a weathered appearance, but his skin was not tanned; evidently, he spent much time indoors these days.

"Hail and well met. Greetings to one and all. I am Duke Richard. Welcome to Duncanville. Please come inside and share some refreshments and rest a spell."

"Lonnie, Holly Paladin of Ukko, at your service," and he bowed low and formally. Then, he passed him by following the path to the front door.

Taking off her cloak, revealing her form and leather clothes, Mandy announced, "Mandy Blackthorn, Ranger of Reylona." She coyly smiled and observed that his eyes opened wide.

"Alison d'Ambrose, mage." She did not take off her robe.

Darless took her cue from Alison. "Darless, mage of Hollybine Wood." Darless had already removed her cloak. The white gossamer thin dress fluttered slightly in the light breeze. She also smiled at the Duke as she passed by. The Duke's eyes covered her form from toes to head.

"Jon Brown, at your service," he said simply.

As he passed, Duke Richard commented to Jon, "Wow! Three beautiful women. I would not mind bedding either of them!" Just as soon as he had said that, his face crimsoned and he hastily added, "Forgive me! I don't know why I said that! My apologies." But he then winked at Jon and added, "Lucky man!" and followed them inside.

Inside, a servant led them into a large meeting room. It was not an elegant room, but comfortable. Duke Richard evidently did not spend money on fancy items, preferring good quality and comfort. The table was made of polished oak and a silver pitcher held wine. There were a number of matching silver cups stacked neatly, ready for use. They had been expected. Duke motioned for them to be seated.

As Mandy reached for the wine, Duke Richard blurted out, "Please, don't drink that wine, it is drugged. I was trying to ensure your cooperation. Here drink this," and he produced another bottle from the side cupboard. His face was very red. "Er, forgive me," he added.

Did you do that? Mandy asked Jon and then Darless. None had.

"Do you mind if I stand a bit? My legs are cramped. I'm not used to horse riding. We are on the trail of the Chasme demon bugs," Jon began.

"Son, you'll soon get over it," the Duke said. "Well, I am thankful for any assistance I can get on this demon problem. They are demons, correct?" He was looking for confirmation.

"Absolutely," Darless replied. "They are called Chasme; they come from the Abyss. You were a wise man to give magical arrows to your troops. And this is a very good wine!"

"Thank you. But why are they here? What do they want? They are gone now, but will they be back? My apologies again. I am usually more conscientious about my guests; I don't know what has come over me today."

"I believe that they are gone now and will not return to Duncanville." Alison began. "We suspect that they are headed now toward Last Town. We are on their trail as are some other friends of mine, Sir Thomas le Bonnaire, Holy Paladin of Ukko. You may expect a visit from him probably in a few days as well. You may tell him we are headed toward Leeds." *Now why did I tell him where we are really headed!*

Alison had said the magic word as far as the Duke was concerned. He relaxed considerably, "Ah Sir Thomas! That is indeed the *best* news I have had to date! If anyone can destroy those foul creatures, he can!"

"Can you tell us that exactly happened when the Chasme came here?" she asked, only too glad to have a way to shift the focus onto the events here.

"Just about sunset, they swarmed down on the town. Some said it was like a locust plague. Must have been hundreds of them, blackened the sky in their path. They buzzed about town for nearly fifteen minutes. That is how come my men were able to arm themselves. It seemed to me that they were searching for something. *Now why did I say that?* I — I guess it is just an old fighter's intuition, a hunch. Then, they all headed in mass to the Boar's Head Inn, Sergeant William d'Groot's parents' tavern on the west side of town. But the archers were ready for them. Cursed demons! The arrows bounced off their thick hides! A few of my trusted men had magical arrows. Those found their marks. Twelve demons died. But I lost a dozen good freemen fighters!"

"They swarmed around the inn and broke in — killed old man d'Groot outright. They were in there maybe five minutes and then they all swarmed outside again. They headed off to the west. After the cleanup was done, I broke out my store of magical arrows to be used in case of a siege and issued them to the entire First Freemen Archers and sent them out to patrol and give us advanced warning. Well, actually, I only issued about half the magical arrows I have in stock." His face once more reddened. "I — I don't know why I am telling you that! No matter, I need some in reserve. Do you honestly think they will not come back? I can recall my men, therefore?" Clearly, the Duke wanted time to regain his composure.

"Absolutely," Jon replied. "I am quite certain that they will not be back here. You see, they are following a pattern." He outlined the various towns that had been previously attacked concluding that Last Town was likely next.

Somehow, putting the attacks into some kind of context, that other towns had been attacked and that they were just unfortunate enough to be in their path, seemed to satisfy the Duke. "I still have another meeting to attend yet today. You are most welcome to spend the night here in my home." Then he added, "Though I would probably try to woo one of you beautiful ladies!" His face was beet red and he cleared his throat.

"Thanks," interjected Alison. "But I should like to spend the evening at the Boar's Head Inn. My father once slept there." *Now why did I tell him that!*

"Tis a fine establishment. Well, then, I must be off. Until our paths cross," he rose and bowed low. He left the room and the party did likewise.

After picking up their horses at the stable and asking directions, they walked the horses down the street toward the inn. No one spoke until they were a good distance from the Duke's residence. "Are we really spending the night at that inn?" inquired Lonnie. "And why did he get so red, so embarrassed so often? He seemed to be speaking the truth! He even admitted that he wanted to drug us into helping. See, he is a good man at heart and could not go through with it."

Jon, he has got to know, Mandy sent to him. She turned to Lonnie, smiled coyly, and asked him straight out, "Wouldn't you like to take me to bed with you tonight?"

"Sure, I er," and his face became beet red! "Oh forgive me, fair lady!"

"Sorry, Lonnie, but I just had to illustrate something. Is that something you would come straight out and ask me, particularly with a person you have never met? Yes, I know there are many men who would do so — but not a chivalrous, honorable man such as you." She was softening the blow a bit; he was, after all, only eighteen. "So think a bit. Such is not something you nor most would interject on a formal first meeting with total strangers, now is it?"

"And who is going to admit they had intended to drug you as they meet you?" interjected Darless.

Not to be left out, Alison explained, "Lonnie, this is frontier country around here. The Duke represents the only 'law and order' these folks have. Without law, anarchy would reign in a town like this. But undoubtedly, the Duke must, of necessity, be forced to weigh good and evil — he probably sits on the fence on that one."

"I take exception to that anarchy bit!" Mandy protested. "The individual is vastly more important than the blind following of some arbitrarily enforced laws! I am not an anarchist, now am I?" Seeing Alison beginning to protest, she playfully added, "And hey, aren't all rules *meant* to be broken anyway?" She tried to turn the conversation toward a less serious note.

Lonnie tried to absorb all this and asked, "Then what you are saying is that the Duke under normal circumstances would not have been so promiscuous with you and he would not have told us about the drugged wine, merely switched decanters? Then, then, that would imply something coerced him into speaking the truth? Is that it?"

"Precisely," chorused the ladies in unison.

An incredulous look flooded over the young man's face. "But who forced him to? How?" He looked at the others.

"I don't think any one of us did," Jon spoke for the first time. "I certainly had no hand in it." *Yes, you did.* Appeared in his mind, but he promptly dismissed it because he could think of no way he could have been responsible for the Duke's actions. Besides, they had arrived at the inn.

Taking charge at once, Mandy ordered, "Here, Lonnie, hold my horse. I will go check us in and make the arrangements. Back in a bit." Without waiting for an acknowledgment, she headed in the door. The Boar's Head Inn was a single-story, sprawling clapboard building that had seen many extensions of growth under the hands of many different designers. None of the newer extensions matched existing ones, rather like a patch-worked quilt. It was an old establishment with its own stables in the rear.

Mandy reappeared and led them around back. "It's all arranged; got us each connecting rooms in the back near the stables, in case we need to make a hasty exit. Hey, Lonnie, the house specialty is Boors' Amber Ale. Wanna try a tankard? I'll treat you all to the first round."

They took care of the horses personally; Lonnie did not trust the stable boy to look after them. And after checking into their rooms, Mandy, Jon and Lonnie headed to the main room for a round of ale. It was not yet supper time and the inn was mostly deserted. It was indeed exceedingly good ale. Time passed quickly. The inn was filled by the time Darless and Alison came down for something to eat.

The food was good but not exceptional. Jon had hoped that the five of them could blend into the background; they could absorb the atmosphere and catch snippets of local gossip. However, the news had spread that a party had arrived at the inn who was going to deal with the demon swarm. And a large percentage of the town dropped in over the course of the next few hours, increasing the inn's business threefold.

Countless times, they were forced to reassure the townsfolk that, yes, the demons did come from the Abyss and that they were on their trail. However, Alison found that by dropping Sir Thomas's name, people automatically felt relieved just knowing that he might be coming as well. Alison explained to the others that her party of adventurers had done several beneficial things for the town over the years. Mandy, of course, pointed out "Notice that it is always Sir Thomas' party they remember and not Alison the mage's party that they remembered. Men! So predictable."

About eight p.m., William d'Groot himself came in; evidently the Duke had recalled the patrols. Over the din, he signaled a barmaid to bring him some dinner and a tankard and strode over to the party, jostling others out of the way. "Welcome again!" he said heartily. "You have done wonders for my business! Many thanks indeed. Why, I'll wager that my business will be brisk for a week after this visit!"

"I see the Duke took our advice and recalled the archers," Mandy inquired.

"Sure did! Glad of it too. Though it is a nice change to be in the woods, the circumstances, you know, with the demons about, made it worrisome. So you think they will not be back, eh?" And they had to explain yet again their theory that Last Town was the likely next target.

After he had eaten and gotten all his questions answered, Alison asked, "Say, can I meet your mother? Perhaps she remembers my dad. If so, I'd sure like to talk with her."

"Sure, she is in her eighties, mighty old indeed. She doesn't get around so well these days — gets all flustered if there are too many folks around. Maybe just a couple of you should come with me." William said. "Oh, yes, she does not know yet that dad was killed."

Jon, walking stick in tow, accompanied Alison and William into the side hallway. They went down several connecting halls toward the western section. The last room facing west was his mother's room. "Mom, you got a couple visitors." He helped her sit up in bed and then introduced them. "This is Alison d'Ambrose, old King Basil's youngest child."

She was indeed old, heavy lines wrinkled her face. Her thin grey hair was pulled back. She was very thin and feeble. But her eyes were bright, Jon observed. "Yes, why yes, I remember King Basil, a good man, if ever there was one!"

After some light talk about how very like her father she looked and so forth, Alison asked her what she really wanted to know. "Can you remember the last time he was here? Probably was twenty years ago. He was with several others." She had no idea how her memory was or if she had even been present on that visit.

"Oh yes, child! I will never forget that night. It was storming something fierce. He and four others came pounding on the inn door about one a.m.. When I opened it, I could see they were desperate, not because of the rain, either! Bloody he was, from head to foot. Now as I remember, only one of them was not banged up in some way. He asked me if we could spare a room for a few days, as well as some food and bandages."

"What struck me so funny was that box! As hurt as those men were, they still struggled to carry some big box inside and into his room. Well, at least I think it was a box.

They had it all covered up with a blanket. I said to him, 'You get in here and get them wet clothes off! I'll see if I can find some spare clothes of Pa that will do til we can get yours washed and dried.' After that, they ate like they were starved! He did say that they had not eaten well for some time. I think he stayed here for about three days. They sure looked better when they left!"

"Did, did anything unusual happen while they were here?" Alison asked.

"Well, yes. He paid for the lodging with a gem — said he was out of coins. But that gem was worth four times the cost! He was the most generous man I have ever met!" Alison smiled, that was what her memories of her dad were like.

Then, after a long pause, the old woman added, "You know, now that you have me thinking back all those years, there was one queer thing — all that pounding and glass-shattering noises. I remember the next day that he asked for directions to a blacksmith shop and came back with some tools. All that afternoon they were in their room just pounding away making all sorts of racket. Then after dark, one of them came out carrying something all wrapped up in that blanket. But it wasn't the box! A little while later he came back in with the blanket, only this time there was nothing in it; it was all folded up."

"This might be important," Alison probed, "When they all left, did you see if they were carrying that box out?"

"Well, no. That was the weird part of it, Basil was still carrying something under his arm all wrapped up in that same blanket, but it wasn't a box! I, well I was curious. So I went into his room expecting to have a big glass mess to clean up. But I found only one sliver of black glass and there wasn't any box in there either. The box just disappeared. Strange."

Alison was now very excited. "Can you describe the package dad was carrying when he was leaving? How big was it?"

"Well, let me think — about so long and maybe this wide." Her arm gestures indicated a length of about three feet and a width of about a half foot. Jon could see that the woman was tiring rapidly. This was probably the most conversation she had had at one time in many years. He nudged Alison who also saw she was tiring.

"Well thank you so much. You have been very helpful indeed," and Alison kissed her hand.

"Well, bless you, my child. Don't know what good all that will do. It has been twenty years ago." They left quietly and rejoined the others.

When Mandy saw the look on Alison's face as they reentered the main room, she knew something was up and announced, "Well, good night all. We have to get some sleep. We want to head out on the trail of the demon swarm at first light." This of course brought another round of cheers and numerous toasts and calls for more ale. In the confusion, the five took their leave.

When they were all safely in Alison's room, Mandy blurted, "Well, out with it! You found something out, didn't you? What was it?" She was impatient to hear. Alison slowly described her conversation with the old woman.

As soon as she finished, Darless spoke forcefully, counting each point on her fingers. "Number 1: King Basil did manage to get the Holy Scepter of Ukko out of the Abyss. Number 2: It must have been a hasty exit for they brought it here still encased in the block of glass. Number 3: the block was very heavy and took the combined efforts of several men to move it. Number 4: they shattered the glass while recuperating here at the inn. Number 5: they then left with the Holy Scepter intact and probably serviceable once again."

Darless paused a moment to think if there was a Number 6. In her mind appeared, *Yes that is correct.* But she was so intent on reviewing her conclusions that she paid it no heed.

"Number 6: the demons the other night were searching this inn for traces of the Holy Scepter," added Mandy, not wanting to be left out.

"Number 7:" Darless continued, though distracted by Mandy, "Matrarch, the Demon Lord, or whoever wants it, still considers the Holy Scepter to be lost."

"And finally, Number 8: he, or someone else, is using the Chasme to actively search for it. There, that about sums it up. So what do we do about it?" asked the alu-demon.

Silence. At last Lonnie spoke, "We catch up with the demon swarm and slay every one of the foul beasts!"

Mandy added, "And then?" More silence. "That's what I thought. Well, let's sleep on it. We've promised an early start. We should not disappoint the locals."

Sleep came quickly to all of them, and the dawn came all too soon for Jon's taste.

Chapter 4 The Plains of Gorsagatha

Though the sun had barely risen, casting its red hues on the already reddish land, many curious eyes were upon them when they mounted and rode westward out of town. "Boy, they sure do get up early around here," commented Lonnie when they had left the eastern gate some distance behind them.

"Creepy feeling being watched like that," Alison added. "I don't like being the center of attention. I guess that's why I let Sir Thomas fill that role." *Now why'd I say that anyway!* She thought to herself and bit her lip into silence.

"I saw all sorts of people peeping from windows, from behind curtains and door cracks," Jon mused.

"No, it was more than idle curiosity. I had a strange feeling that we were being carefully watched! No, not by the townsfolk. I get a sort of tingly sensation down my arms and legs whenever someone or something is spying on me. I'll bet anything that someone there is up to no good!" Mandy proclaimed. "We best be alert at all times. Man, what a dismal countryside!" She added suddenly noting the terrain about them. Gone was the Druse Woods.

The Plains of Gorsagatha consisted of arid, low rolling, reddish hills. Vegetation was sparse; little rain fell here. Alison explained that the desert-like conditions got worse and worse as they approached the Sea of Salt. In fact, Last Town was the last inhabited place before the inland sea. Just beyond Last Town, the land became too salty for anything to grow. This area, the Saline Flats, was a band about twenty miles wide around the Sea of Salt. The only inhabitants of the Saline Flats were the lowly salt miners, desperately poor folks eking out a marginal living by trading salt in Last Town. Salt trading was the only business in Last Town. Caravans that came to pick up salt left as soon as possible. In return, supplies of life were left for the desolate inhabitants. Last Town was about the last place anyone in their right mind would choose to live.

But the further reaches of the plains, though desert-like, were inhabited by nomadic bandits and a few metal workers. Ore and coal veins occasionally surfaced on a hillside, convenient for those hardy enough to take advantage. Alison explained that a hundred years ago, priests of Ukko united and cast all brigands out of the fertile valleys of the north and the forest of the east. They were driven onto these arid plains as the priests of Ukko brought law and order to one and all. "Today, only the frontier towns and villages, such as Duncanville still have to deal with such foul men."

She went on, "Our trail here is following along the Saline River but a safe distance from it. It is a shallow river and full of quicksand traps! No one dares get to close to it. The only safe crossing point is the ferry at Last Town. Sir Thomas once told me about a man who actually went for a swim in the Sea of Salt. He said that they said that they bobbed like a cork! And when he got out, the sun dried the water swiftly encasing him in a layer of white salt. Rather ghastly, if you ask me. Should take us two days to get to Last Town ferry."

As the sun rose, the temperature began to rise higher and higher. Soon all cloaks were removed and stowed. By noon, everyone was drenched in sweat. Jon was thankful he had worn his cowboy hat! No one said much; they just rode on.

By late afternoon, the heat was nearly unbearable to Jon. Everyone was getting grumpy and ill at ease. Mandy made matters worse by announcing, "Zagroot zounds! We have been spotted. Over there, two hilltops to the north. See, there is a rider there watching us. The brigands know we are here." The others watched the lone scout departing to the north.

"Should I go after him and question him?" asked Lonnie.

"No. Where there is one, there's many more. They will find us soon enough I'll wager." Mandy replied. They solemnly rode on.

Darless broke the silence, "Mandy, what do you make of that back over there to the south — behind us there? Like a black cloud in the sky."

Everyone strained in their saddles to peer back and to the right. Sure enough, a small black cloud was several miles behind them. After gazing at it for some time, Mandy cried, "It's moving, probably twenty miles behind us. I think we are going faster than it." They rode on.

Still bothered by the cloud, Darless suddenly halted, which in turn caused Jon and Alison to pause which in turn caused Lonnie and Mandy to pull up to wait on them. "What?" asked Mandy, a bit irritated from the sweltering heat.

"Look at my dress," commanded Darless. Her thin dress moved ever so gently; edges swayed to the west, behind them. "Number 1: The wind, such as it is, is coming out of the east ahead of us. Number 2: That cloud is moving east like us. Number 3: Therefore, it is not a cloud! I don't like this!"

Staring at the distant cloud, Mandy remembered the present Jon had given her some time ago. She dismounted and began unfastening her belt to get at the pouch that contained her portable hole. In a minute, she found what she was looking for, proudly holding up the binoculars. "Jon's Glasses of the Eagles! Now then, how do I work them?" and she fiddled with them. A moment later, "Zagroot zounds! We have found the Chasme swarm! Here, look for yourselves!"

Everyone took a turn looking through the binoculars. It was indeed a swarm of Chasme bugs slowly flying along. "Ladies and gentlemen," Mandy concluded, "we have just gotten our first break. They are evidently slow travelers and, in spite of everything, we have somehow gotten ahead of them. We should make Last Town and Leeds well ahead of them. With luck, we will find out who is behind them!" However, they were not to be lucky.

As the sun began to sink behind the distant rolling hills, talk of finding a campsite ensued. It was interrupted by Mandy's "We've got plenty of company coming!"

Indeed, a few miles away on all sides, riders were closing fast. Their tired horses could not outrun the bandits assuming that they could smash a hole in the encirclement.

"Oh for my lance!" Lonnie exclaimed, "I had to leave it back in Rochelle. I could run a number of them down with that!"

"Ok. Here's what we do," Mandy took command as usual. "Someone has to hold onto the horses at all costs. Without them, here in this desert, we are goners. Jon, you handle the horses! Lonnie, you and I must do everything possible to protect the mages to give them time to do their thing. We are going to be hit from all sides at the same time. So horses and Jon, you are in the center; a mage on either side of them and one of us with each mage. I'll take Alison; you take Darless. Cover an arc 180 degrees. If they should move into my arc, let them go; I will handle. Likewise if one moves into your arc, you get them."

"But how will I know where you arc begins?" Lonnie asked, trying to grasp the hasty orders. Mandy quickly drew two lines in the sandy ground. There — my half — your half. Go get them! If they want to parley first, I'll do the talking." And they waited.

Jon held onto his walking stick and six sets of reigns. *Keep calm!* He sent to the horses and wondered if that did any good at all. Jon had no idea how to keep a horse calm. Alison stood tall and commanding, staff held high, white robes gently billowing in the gentle breeze. Darless stood like a statuette, arms crossed as if she were scolding a small child. Mandy alternated taking long drinks of water with last minute checks that all was as ready as could be. She hated infernal waiting. Lonnie fidgeted; it was his first real combat experience. He recited the creed of the paladin over and over in his mind.

In this rolling hill country, you could see a rider top a distant hill only to disappear as they rode down into the basin and then reappear upon a closer hill top only to disappear yet again as they rode down into the next basin. Mandy had them centrally located in a basin. Though a hilltop might be better, she did not wish to risk not quite making it. Instinctively, Mandy felt it better to be totally prepared than to try to rush things. It would not be long now; most riders had disappeared into the last basin before theirs.

Then, one by one, mounted riders appeared atop the surrounding hills and halted, watching them. "They are just sizing us up and waiting orders. See if you can spot the leader, the one giving the orders. If we get him, the others may scatter." Mandy ordered. "I make about fifty of them."

"They do not have lances or pole arms," called out Lonnie. "If they rush us, it will not be as bad."

"Zounds! Here they come," called out Mandy stating the obvious. "Curses, looks like they got a chicken leader. He's staying back on the ridge!"

The next few minutes were a blur of motion and action. One advantage of their small compact formation was that only a few of the riders could close to combat range at a time. The artillery came first, Jon observed. Well, not really artillery, but it had that impression. The mages both let loose a sleep spell and over a dozen riders veered off and fell off their horses, smacking the ground solidly.

The first bunch to reach them tried to directly take out Lonnie and Mandy. While Mandy easily dodged and parried and struck the last one down, Lonnie was not faring so well with three on him at once. He did fine with two. Just when the third one was about to get around Lonnie's defenses, a volley of magical sparkling arrows struck that bandit; he tumbled to the ground and his horse ran off. Darless was having fun.

Seeing that tactic failing, they then tried a feint and run to get around the fighters to get to the mages and Jon. Mandy was most worried about this maneuver with the untested Lonnie. She parried and kept them at a safe distance until they crossed her lines on the ground. Mentally, she sent to him: *All yours, Lonnie, on your right. Okay. I'm picking up yours on my left now.* Terrific! He trusted her completely and was following orders! Again, Mandy changed tactics and eliminated the last rider retreating from her. Lonnie, who glimpsed her previous action from the first wave, followed suit and proudly eliminated the last one who was retreating from him.

All of the bandits regrouped some distance to what they thought was out of range of the magic users. "All right! Now we are getting somewhere!" Mandy called out. "We've forced the leader to join in."

"What tactics do you suppose they will use next?" queried Lonnie.

"They have just been testing our strength — playing with us. They know we are a strong group. They are likely very worried about the two mages; I sure would be. So my guess is that the leader will now want to fight it out on foot, close-quarters combat. Ah yes. See, he is spreading his men out — placing lots of distance between each man — lowers the numbers that can be affected with magical spells that cover an area. He will try to get them in as fast and close as possible before they dismount. If they dismount, their horses will scatter and that is precisely what we need! Here they come! This is it, their last attempt — all or nothing."

Jon heard both mages chanting strange words, similar words. He watched as the bandits rode in to about fifty feet and then reigned in and hopped off, slapping their horses out of the way. When the horses were clear, two simultaneous balls of fire exploded among the men on foot. A dozen men fell to the ground, never to rise. The rest charged the group in an attempt to totally overwhelm them.

Six surrounded Mandy, preventing her from assisting Alison. Three closed in on Alison. But she used her staff of power, launching continuous volleys of the magical missiles at fighters that got too close to her. She was holding her own. The six horses began getting edgy and Jon desperately tried to hold on to them. He had absolutely no idea how to calm them and resolved just to not let go no matter what. He twisted his head to see how Lonnie was doing.

Lonnie was skillful enough to parry one and fight a second, but six swarmed him. Darless intervened with a volley of magical missiles on the sixth who was trying to isolate him as the others had done to Mandy. Then, she muttered some words and the entire area to Lonnie's left tingled with some form of magical energies. The men in that zone suddenly began moving at a snail's pace, in very slow motion. Lonnie observed the effect and renewed his attacks; now only three could press him at one time as long as he maintained his position.

Then, the third one that was on Lonnie made a fatal decision. Seeing Darless in her gauze of a dress, wholly unprotected by Lonnie, the fighter broke off from Lonnie and charged Darless. She deftly dodged the brunt of his blow; his sword tore her dress but bounced off her skin. Above the din, Jon heard Darless call out, "Is that any way to treat a lady? You tore my dress!" He twisted in time to see a furious Darless reach out with her hand and grasp the fighter on the shoulder. He heard bones snapping and cracking and heard the fighter cry out in startled and massive pain. Another fighter took his place and tried to thrust his blade through her; while the blade did not hurt her, it tore the front of her dress completely. Jon heard her call out, "You beast!" She pointed her right index finger at him and spoke one word. A beam of energy hit the fighter in the head. Jon gasped as the bandit's head totally disappeared, leaving the headless body of a man momentarily standing there. Darless was mad, Jon thought. But now he had worries of his own.

Several others were now making for him, evidently intent on scattering their horses. They were waving their arms trying to frighten the horses. While the light war horses stood by mostly bored, the mares were rearing and reacting. It was all Jon could do to hang onto them. They were pulling, dragging him like a sack of potatoes this way and that. He fought to stay on his feet. Seeing that they were not completely successful, another fighter lowered his sword and charged at Jon. "Can't you see I have my hands full?" Jon called out to him. He could see the man grinning evilly at him. Two more seconds and Jon would be skewered on the man's long sword. Mentally, Jon went into action. He let go of his bodily sensations, concentrated and sent the command. Instantly, the man dropped his weapon. Startled, he was forced to retreat from the weapon as a kicking, jerking horse edged over to where it lay. Three more tried the same stunt and lost their weapons for their efforts.

Alison's tiring! Jon picked up from Mandy. He twisted and pulled the horses toward the mage. Her endurance was shot; she still had not fully recovered physically from the Chasme attack.

Alison, back into me at once! Jon placed the command in her mind. There was little she could do but obey; she just had not the strength. Once Jon got her sufficiently close, a new idea struck him. Darless had used magic to slow down the fighters. Could he do something similar to protect Alison, himself and the horses? Now that he had let go of trying to control the horses with his body and had begun using his mental powers, he saw that he could think far faster than events occurred about him. *Calm, peace and tranquility, that's what I need.* Starting with just the space around his head, Jon mentally created a soothing, cool waterfall filled with the command of 'drop your weapons.' Then he pushed that sphere of influence wider and wider in all directions, millimeter by millimeter. He noticed that the horses calmed down. It was working and that encouraged him to push it further and further out. He saw other men attempting to rush him but he paid them no mind, absolutely certain that they would calm and drop their weapons. They did.

One older fighter, evidently a junior in charge of those that were trying to get at him, watched from a safe distance.

81

Jon smiled at him and sensed the desperateness the man was feeling. He knew what that fighter was going to do at the same moment the fighter had decided what he was going to do. In slow motion, Jon saw the man reach for an axe on his belt, unfasten it, and with expert skill raise it into throwing position. Jon's mind was operating faster than the physical universe was moving. He saw the axe come whirling toward his head. He admired the skill behind the throw; sensed the intention the fighter had of the axe splitting Jon's head open. He commanded his hand to raise the walking stick. With precision, the walking stick deftly deflected the axe just enough. It thudded harmlessly into the ground off to his right. Jon placed a 'Thank you' in the fighter's head. Alison watched the man slowly turn around and walk away from the battle, disappearing over the ridge. Time seemed to stand still, Jon was utterly peaceful.

You can stop now; they are gone. Mandy's thought finally broke into his reverie.

"Huh? Oh! So they are!" Jon shook off the trance-like effect he had been under. Around him only the labored breathing of the others filled the growing dusk. "Anybody hurt?" he asked as reality filtered into him.

"I've got a slice on my leg that could use some tending and a few minor cuts." Mandy said. "Looks worse than it is. Lonnie's left arm is broken, I think. Alison has taken a couple minor hits. Nothing terribly serious."

"Good grief, your leg is really bloody!" A startled Jon knelt down on the ground to examine it. "Let me see what I can do." Since he was still in the proper mode of mental operation, he found it quite easy to command her cells into the proper positions and actions.

"Thanks, Jon! That felt terrific! See what you can do for Lonnie and I will take care of everything else."

He looked up at this take-charge woman and simply smiled and said, "Yes, ma'am." She winked.

Jon found Lonnie lying on the ground. He was in a great deal of pain and held his left arm tight to keep it from moving. *Relax Lonnie. Think of a cool waterfall. Feel the rising damp mist. Yes, hold on to that image.* And he began to probe the arm. He could see the massive amounts of pain waves locking up in the elbow and shoulder and neck.

Inspiration struck. "Close your eyes and see if you can see the images of what happened to your arm. Yes, those. Now look at them from beginning to end and when done, tell me what happened." Simultaneously while monitoring Lonnie's faltering progress with the mental images, he began commanding bone cells.

"I twisted the wrong way. Then, his sword came down. Ow. But the chain mail deflected the edge. Now what?"

"Good. Now find where you first sensed this event starting and examine them again. When you get done, tell me what happened." Jon now felt Darless' hand gently resting on his head. He felt a tingle of renewed energy flowing into him from her mind; she was aiding him, flowing power to him. He smiled and continued on the bone cells.

"I was fighting three and dodged to the right and I slipped and my arm went up to balance myself. I saw the blow coming down and thought there is nothing I can do. Ow! God did that blow hurt! I could hear the bones cracking. But I had the idea that the chain mail would prevent any cuts. Now what?"

"Good. Now let's go back to the beginning once more and examine the images again. When you are done, tell me what happened." Lonnie's body jerked noticeably several times; Jon could see the massive build up of suppressed pain waves beginning to dissipate and flow off from his elbow, shoulders, and neck. *Fascinating!* Darless sent him.

On the tenth pass, Lonnie suddenly started chuckling, "You know, what really happened there? Why right when my arm was up and I saw that blade coming down, right there, I just gave up! Stopped trying. That was stupid! Praise to Ukko! What's happened to my arm? It doesn't hurt anymore? I can move it. It's — it's not broken like it was any more."

"More like it has substantially begun to heal by itself," Jon suggested. "Very well done Lonnie."

Amazing indeed! I am beginning to understand this process, Darless sent him.

"How's everyone doing now?" Jon asked. "Man, am I hungry! No, I am tired." Darless caught him as he slumped onto the ground. She made him comfortable and soon had a blanket over him.

"Council, Mandy!" Darless called. Quickly the girls went over the situation. Jon was asleep but without any food, sleep would not last long; he had overdone it once again. Alison was resting comfortably; no lasting effects that a good sleep would not cure. Lonnie was mostly back in action, though he would favor that arm for several more days. Mandy was nearly exhausted; she needed food and a sleep and needed it very soon. It would be dark in less than a half hour. Dozens of fallen bandits were scattered all around the wide area. "I'll take over from here, Mandy." Darless decided, "You go eat something right now and get some rest. Lonnie and I will take care of things." Mandy did not offer any resistance to the order.

"Lonnie, it's up to us now." Darless said. "We cannot stay here for the night, agreed?"

"Absolutely. But how, where? If we could get into the next basin over, it would help a lot," Lonnie began, his training kicking in.

"Sometimes I think that Mandy is ten steps ahead of the rest of us. I see her strategy clearly now, don't you?" Darless said in a flash of understanding. Without waiting for a reply, "By meeting them in the center of this basin, all we need to do is move one basin away and it will be a totally different space. All the fighting was confined to this one localized area. Had we been on a hilltop, we would have to move at least half again as far!"

The move was handled rather inventively. Darless did not know horses; Lonnie did. Lonnie's arm was on the mend, but he needed to avoid heavy work with it for some days yet. In thirty minutes, a strange caravan began to move slowly westward up the slope of the next hillside. Lonnie had tied the six horses together into a long chain and was leading the long string on foot. Darless had awakened Alison briefly to ask permission to use her staff of power which she now used to illuminate their way and to keep an eye on the semi-sleeping forms of Alison, Jon and Mandy riding along on their horses. Alison had also given Darless a magic scroll to use later on. Jon, she had stuffing himself as he rode along, using this short period when he had awaken to best advantage. They went slowly. In a half hour, Lonnie halted near the center of the next basin; the adrenaline rush had completely gone; he was near exhaustion himself. While waiting for Darless to get each of the sleeping off the horses, he dozed off.

He missed Darless reading the scroll and the flash of magic and the mansion that appeared before her. He vaguely remembered her helping him inside a large door through a dimly lit passage way into a large room. Gratefully, he lay down on the soft rugs on the floor. One by one, Darless had led each into the mansion and laid them out on the heavy rugs on the floor and covered them up. Next, she led each horse inside and tied each to a separate place. At last, she shut the outer doors. In the outside world, the mansion disappeared completely. For a time, the party had vanished completely from the Plains of Gorsagatha.

Then, she ate a large meal herself wondering what to do about the horses. They did not seem right just standing there. *The saddles; they should come off. And they need food and water too! I'll get the hang of this yet.*

In a half hour, she stood back and admired her efforts; the horses seemed contented enough. So she herself laid down on the rugs, pulled a blanket over her body, dimmed the lights even more, smiled, and drifted into sleep.

The cheery alto voice of Alison woke everyone the next morning. "Wake up everyone, rise and shine. Food's ready! Wake up!" Various moans, complaints about it being too early, various aches and pains and I'm starving, greeted her. But soon, everyone was eating and talking at once, wondering where on earth they were to find such a wonderful place to stay!

"This is my Magical Mansion spell," explained Alison, while they ate their breakfast. "When the doors are closed, the mansion becomes invisible and we are safe. It lasts for a couple days if need be. However, only eat and drink what you have brought in because there is no real food in here." Everyone agreed that this was one terrific spell!

Lonnie's arm was examined by everyone; the consensus was that it was healing exceedingly rapidly but that he should avoid any heavy work with it for some time. Jon explained that he had applied the same technique with mental images on Lonnie that he had done on Alison. And it had worked. No one was more amazed than the paladin himself.

Darless had to explain how she and Lonnie had got them all from the field of battle and here into the mansion. A chorus of thank you's arose when she finished.

And that led to Lonnie's query about whether or not they should return to the battle field and properly bury the dead bandits. It was the honorable thing to do, he insisted and Alison tended to agree at first. But it was Mandy that vetoed it.

"It is a question of the greater good, Lonnie." Mandy explained, "We were ahead of the bugs, but now we are almost certainly behind them. We have lost valuable time but we would have had to spend the night anyway. If we are to have any chance to catch up or get ahead, we must press on. I think we must try to make Last Town by nightfall." This made sense; everyone agreed that their best hope of finding the ones in control of the bugs lay in getting there ahead of the bugs.

Another hour passed in preparations. For most, a clean set of clothes was in order; all regretted the lack of bathing facilities. Alison and Darless spent a good deal of time working up their magical spells for the day. Lonnie showed Jon how to rub down the horses. That was the one detail Darless had overlooked the night before.

When everyone was ready, after taking a careful peek through a door window, Alison opened the doors back onto the Plains of Gorsagatha. Out they stepped leading the horses. Full of curiosity, they turned and watched the mansion disappear on Alison's command. But the carrion birds circling in the sky over the battlefield were impossible to miss. Regretfully, there was nothing they could do without jeopardizing their mission. Sobered by the birds, they resumed their westward ride.

Bleak, barren, red hued hills spread endlessly before them as they rode up a hill and down into the next basin only to ride up the next hill, on and on. Even the stunted, twisted, isolated trees began to thin. Though their height had never been much above eight feet, five feet was now about tops. Occasional tufts of hardy grass occasionally lined the red hills, oxides of iron. The early morning chill quickly gave way to the relentless heat they experienced the day before. Also, Mandy set a significantly faster pace than the previous day.

By noon, they had covered many miles. Horses were lathered and panting. People were dripping with sweat. Some were saddle-weary already. No sign of any living creature had been seen. Mandy called for an extended lunch break. That was the only smile many had shown for several hours.

They made a small camp beside a five-foot, gnarled and twisted oak tree on the eastern side of a basin. Shade was minimal under the searing sun. But for Jon, the chance to stretch was heavenly; his legs were stiff and sore. In silence, they ate a little and drank much. Lonnie tended to the horses. Mandy rechecked all the tack for weaknesses. She did not want a girth belt to break or a rein to loosen at a critical point. Her mind was focusing on possible future events that might occur at the end of this day.

Jon, walking stick in hand, said he was going for a stroll to exercise his legs. Alison watched him slowly amble back up the hill they had just ridden down. At the top, she saw him pause and stare off slowly in all directions. She assumed he saw the bleakness that she saw all around. But for Jon, this was a new place, inhospitable of course, but the rich reds and rolling hills he found interesting. Even the unfamiliar stunted trees seemed to speak to him. *Someday, I think I would just like to travel about and see the country sides, with no pressures to have to do something.* A song began to form in his mind that in later months he would call his Hymn to Gorsagatha, a haunting, melancholy melody.

While he was humming, a command appeared in his mind. *Look to the east.* He did so and saw far off the dark cloud that could only be the Chasme flock. Hastily, he began to run back downhill to the others. But the cloud could not be seen from the basin floor. "Hey! We've caught up to the demon swarm, well almost! They are just a ways ahead of us now!" Jon yelled to all pointing off in the direction that he had just seen from the hilltop. A chorus of 'hurrahs' raised everyone's spirits; there was still a good chance for success. But while the others were getting things stowed and ready to continue, Mandy took Jon aside.

"Jon, I've been thinking about Lonnie's arm," she began. "The bones likely have not totally healed. What if we face another heavy battle? What do you think about maybe putting some kind of splint on it, just for protection?"

"Hmm. Probably a wise idea. Another blow would likely just re-break it again," he answered. "I had not thought of that."

Lonnie started to protest, but paused when Mandy explained further as she fastened a piece of armor that was made for her forearm onto his. "This is actually a piece of magically enhanced armor, part of a set I have stored in my portable hole for emergency use. I seldom wear armor, too confining. But this bit here will afford you just a bit more protection if we get into another battle." She stood back a bit and looked at her handiwork. "Hmm. That will never do. Attracts attention to it. There's only one thing to do!" And she got the matching band out and put it on his good sword arm. "There, they match! Much better." The paladin thanked her sincerely and a youthful grin appeared as he twisted his arms around testing the feel of the arm guards.

And then they were off again, riding at a slow trot. In this heat, anything faster would exhaust the horses way too soon. Jon hated the trots more than anything else. He bounded up and down relentlessly adding to his misery. If he could only levitate like Darless!

By mid-afternoon, they had pulled even with the cloud of Chasme who were still closely following the winding shallow river. They were at least a couple miles to their right. Spirits rose as they caught the cloud and began to pull ahead of it once again.

As they started up the western aside of yet another basin, they saw something just at the hilltop ahead of them coming their way on the trail. A solitary figure was leading a donkey cart moving slowly down the trail toward them. The gap between them closed rapidly. She appeared to be a bent, aged woman, wearing filthy, many times patched rags. Her hair was long and knotted. She was way overdue for a bath! Her right hand carried a short pole which she used to help her walk and stand. The other hand held the reigns of the donkey. The cart was full of a white substance; salt, everyone assumed. They were meeting a salt peddler at last.

They halted before the old woman who, in a cracking, whiny voice, inquired, "Need any salt?" Jon could sense waves of pity toward her from Lonnie and Alison. Alison and Lonnie dismounted and went to inspect the salt. "Travelers out here need lots of salt, they do, in this heat," she made conversation. "It's most valuable, but mine is not so expensive — just a few coppers for a bag. Surely you can spare a few coppers for one not as fortunate as yourselves. Go ahead, taste it and see for yourself how good it is."

"Beggars!" Mumbled Mandy quietly to herself, but Jon heard it.

As Lonnie stepped up to the cart to sample it, a voice appeared in Jon's mind. *She is lying. It is sand.* Jon did not stop to think which lady had sent him that warning. He yelled to Lonnie, "Lonnie. Wait — don't put that into your mouth. Let, let one of our mages check it out first. It might not be salt!"

Lonnie had a handful in his hand and was about to put his tongue to it. But he paused, looking questioningly at Jon and the others. Suddenly, the old hag started laughing, sinisterly and mockingly. In an instant of time, she rose up to her full height which was not that of a stooped old woman. The tattered clothes vanished and a grey robe with black trim took their place. The walking pole became a staff, somewhat similar to Alison's magical staff of power. Energy of some kind arced from it into the ground beneath the party's feet.

Jon felt his body go numb. He could not move his body. From the corners of his eyes he saw that the spell had frozen all of them including the horses, frozen them helplessly in their tracks! She cackled evilly, "Saint Jon Brown, you have meddled once too often. This shall be your last day in this world! Ha! Ha! Ha!" Jon watched helplessly as the hag raised her finger pointing it at him, chanting something unintelligible. Mandy struggled violently, but could not move her body. Alison fought to move her arms to cast a spell but could not. Jon tried to think fast, but he found his mind too engrossed in confronting the fact he could not move his body.

Just then from the corner of his eye, he saw Darless leaping high into the air over the horses. Magical energies arced from her right hand tracing a path straight toward the hag. The hag's energies arced out toward Jon and met Darless' counter spell about three feet from Jon's face. When they met, there was a blinding flash; heat seared Jon's face; his eyes saw no more. But his ears picked up further chanting from the hag! Then, he heard the sound of Lonnie's sword being drawn, followed by the chant being replaced by a startled scream and then another flash of magical energies. Then, silence. Then his feet collapsed and he hit the ground in a thud, and for a brief instant panic struck him.

"Help! I cannot see! What's happening?" Jon cried, a bit of terror in his voice.

"It's ok! She's gone! Disappeared in a flash!" Mandy called out. "Everyone except Jon all right? Way to go Darless and Lonnie! You saved our butts!"

Jon sensed that everyone had gathered around him. He sat on the ground. His face burned and he could see nothing but a reddish blackness. Mandy's soothing voice said, "You have a nasty sunburn on your face. I can take the sting out of that." And he felt her gentle probing followed by a cooling sensation as the heat began to flow throughout his body, leaving his face cooler. In a few minutes, he felt much better. But he still could not see a thing.

Now he sensed Darless' hand on his head. After a moment, she said, "Jon, take a look at the images you have of this whole encounter we just had. Look them over from start to finish and then tell me what happened," she commanded him. Jon realized then that he did have mental images and quickly reviewed them. Then, he told her about them. He didn't think it was doing anything on him, though. She persisted just as she had seen him persist on Lonnie the day before.

On the tenth run through, Jon was crying, "I cannot see; I'll never be able to see again!" He felt alone and miserable and utterly helpless. "I'm as helpless as a little baby!" He cried out again.

Darless spoke in a confident soft voice, "Jon, Jon can you see any other similar kinds of mental images that happened earlier, much earlier than this thing today? Can you see them?"

Wait a minute! Jon thought to himself. "Yes, yes there is something else here. I — I cannot quite make them out. Yes, I see a baby. It's dark, must be night. It's all by itself."

Darless softly said, "Ok. Now look at them from start to finish and tell me what happened."

In a couple minutes, Jon started yawning and then began laughing out loud. "You know, I was starving. But I was only about three weeks old. It was the middle of the night. My stomach hurt so bad! I could not see anything! I was completely helpless! Of course a tiny baby is not going to get up and go fix itself a midnight snack! Ha! Ha! Ha! Holy cow, I can see again — well sort of." He was looking up into the sparking, coal black eyes of Darless who was grinning from ear to ear!

He blinked and rubbed his eyes. The world was becoming visible, but red. Everything was unnaturally red. Everyone cheered both Jon and Darless.

With Jon recovering, Darless explained what had happened here. "Number 1: we have finally met one of the people responsible for the Chasme. Number 2: she was an unholy priestess of some unholy god. Number 3: she cast a powerful hold type spell over all of us, except she could not include Lonnie who was back at the cart without getting herself into the area. Number 4: That was her fatal mistake. Number 5: Her magic rolled off of me; I was not affected. But I was at the back and could not get to her fast enough. So I leaped high into the air and tried to counter her spell. I was very nearly not in time; the counter spell collided just too close to Jon's face. He should be all right in time. Momentary loss of vision, I'd guess. Number 6: It was Lonnie who saved the day! Just as the priestess was about to probably blast us to bits, his sword bit deep into her flesh!"

"Number 7," put in Mandy, "she must be a powerful priestess, because I think that she used a spell I have heard about, one that instantly returns her to some 'holy/unholy' place. Thank you, Lonnie!" He beamed with youthful pride feeling he had been of great aid to the others. Then, everyone chattered about the events for several minutes.

Jon profusely thanked Darless for making him confront his past. "You know, I would have never been able to have spotted that childhood thing on my own without your assistance!"

"I'm a fast learner," Darless chuckled. "I've been carefully watching you do it. I think I have the technique figured out. And I rather figured that one cannot delve into one's own painful memories by themselves. Or we all would have done so long ago!"

The donkey cart remained; Lonnie unhooked the poor creature and turned it loose and watched it gratefully amble off over the hilltop, enjoying its freedom.

Then, Lonnie turned to Jon and asked, "Only one thing still puzzles me, Jon. How did you know that it was sand and not salt? How did you see through her disguise? I fell for it completely!" That got everyone's attention, for the others also realized that they had also fallen for the priestess's illusion as well. Mandy was most upset that she had not seen through the illusion.

"I — I don't know. I thought one of you had sent me a mental message. So I yelled it out. Didn't one of you send me that warning?" He looked at the blank faces of the others. All shrugged negatively. "Well, if you didn't, who did?" No one had any answer for that one. Indeed, Darless began looking all around them for some unseen presence. Lonnie did as well. Mandy did not bother; she felt no tingly sensations on her body, so no one was spying on her; she trusted that phenomenon completely.

Finding no one else about, they remounted and continued their journey toward Last Town. In a few minutes, they were once again ahead of the Chasme swam. Now their thoughts turned on how best to defeat that large mass of demon bugs when they swarmed over Last Town, the assumed next target of the Chasme.

It was three in the afternoon when they rode into the outskirts of Last Town. No city walls met them. The trail broadened and numerous other trails coming from northerly directions merged into theirs. At the edge of town, red, adobe brick, single-story, small buildings appeared. The streets were made of the same red soils, hard packed by countless feet and hooves. There were few people out on the street and they looked as forlorn as the old hag, cast outs of civilization, the unwanted, the desperate. It was the most dismal town Jon could imagine. No wonder the caravans stayed only as long as necessary!

Prominent in the center square of town was a large adobe building with one huge sign that read "Salt." Several ragged men were loading a dozen equally forlorn looking horses with heavy bags of salt. Several glanced in the party's direction. Several whistles of admiration greeted the ladies of the party. In the very center of town was the community well. Here was the only fresh water they had yet seen. They dismounted and watered themselves and then the horses.

Jon's eyesight had returned to normal, but he still had traces of a major sunburn on his nose. It was beginning to itch. Walking stick in hand, Jon wandered about the square absorbing the newness of this strange town. He watched as occasional, slow-moving derelicts, that looked much like the old hag, wander in from further east, leading donkeys laden with heavy bags; salt most likely.

He returned to the party in better spirits. His legs had un-cramped, though his butt and thighs ached. His eyesight was now much better as Darless had predicted. Mandy signaled for a council. Though the town was not large, Alison had no idea where her father had stayed when he and his men had passed through some twenty years ago. There did not seem any likely way they could find out either. So it was decided to tackle the demons right here in the large central open square.

They concluded that the best way to destroy the Chasme was by a constant bombardment of fire balls. Though the Chasme, Darless pointed out, had some chance of having each spell bounce harmlessly off of them. If enough spells were cast at them, the law of probability would win out in the end. The last thing they wanted was to be physically swarmed as had happened to Alison.

Next, the horses needed to be rubbed down, watered, fed and stabled some place where they would come to no harm. Lonnie saw to that detail. He returned about an hour later saying that they were being well tended to and that, following Mandy's suggestion, they would remain saddled and ready to go at a moment's notice.

Meanwhile, Alison and Mandy had gone in search of someone in authority to warn them about the eminent attack of the demons. The only 'law' in Last Town was dispensed by Marshal Tucker, an aging, down on his luck, fighter of some skill. They learned that he had been a lieutenant in the Castle Guards some years ago, but a sword wound to his right leg laid him up. Now here in Last Town, he was the man in authority, primarily because of his experience. He had six deputies, if one could call them that. Glorified ruffians, Alison thought was more like it. But after hearing their message, he believed them and did take preventive measures. Within an hour, all the townsfolk had been warned and were indoors, with doors locked. Marshal Tucker would remain in his office and join the fight only if Alison and her party failed to stop them.

"Some Marshal!" commented Alison after they left and were walking back to the town square.

"Would you expect much else is a forlorn place such as this?" added Mandy.

During that hour, Jon and Darless stayed at the well watching for any sign of the approaching demons. Now that Darless had also been able to help another view their painful mental images, the two spent much of that time discussing its significance and use, speculating on how the technique could be more broadly used. Their biggest unanswered question was: could the technique be used by someone who did not already have the mental ability to read another's mind as Darless, Mandy and Jon did?

By four p.m., the heat of the day had passed and everyone had cooled down, all thirsts quenched. But no one was really hungry — too much tension and concern over the eminent approach of the demon swarm. They now had the entire town to themselves. All outside activity had ceased. It appeared totally deserted, except for the five milling around the water well in the central square.

Shortly after four p.m., Mandy spied the vanguard of the Chasme swarm entering the outskirts of the city. They sprang into action. For this occasion, Alison had given Darless a magical wand that could cast fireball spells upon command. She would use her staff. They took up a defensive position. Mandy and Lonnie stood in front of Alison and Darless. Jon acted as rear guard, this time prepared to fend off the bugs with his walking stick. Then the assault began.

Working at the extreme range of the spells, great balls of fire began appearing within the swarm. Just as Darless had predicted, some were not affected. Others were killed and dropped from the sky like the dead weigh that they had become. But overall the strategy was working. By the time the swarm was on top of them, their ranks had dwindled to less than two dozen Chasme. Lost Town would have a big mess of dead bugs to clean up!

When the remainder of the swarm had closed to within striking distance, the fireball spells could no longer be used. Now Mandy and Lonnie could strike at them with swords.

Several died in futile attempts to attack them. Alison thumped those that got to close to her with staff; none went after Darless.

One dove for Jon who dodged and tried to push it out of the way with his walking stick. When the walking stick touched the Chasme, a sizzling sound was heard and the demon dropped dead on the ground. At that point, they swarm made a rapid exit moving at top speed low over the adobe houses heading on westward. Staying so low, the mages dared not unleash another volley of fireball spells for fear of damaging the homes.

"To the horses!" yelled Mandy, and everyone rushed to the stables, Lonnie in the lead. In seconds they were mounted and riding after the remnants of the swarm. They never did see the amazed Marshal Tucker and the townsfolk faces when they ventured outside and disposed of some eighty Chasme carcasses. "They are heading eastwards again. Leeds, it must be! Here we come!" cried Mandy galloping ahead of the others.

Jon held on for dear life as his refreshed mare insisted on not falling behind. He decided he liked galloping better than the infernal trotting. But the speed at which the ground went by worried him. What if the horse stumbled and fell? He would hit the red ground hard! The breeze created by the rushing horses began to chill him as well. He decided he much preferred adventures on foot! He looked over at Alison. In contrast, she was thoroughly enjoying herself! Robes and hair furling in the wind; staff held high in one hand; reins loose in the other, she appeared born to the chase!

Mandy held her sword aloft in one hand and the reins in the other. But Lonnie held his sword aloft with both hands, guiding his light war horse with his knees. "Show off," Jon thought to himself and he gripped the saddle horn with both hands while hanging onto his walking stick which he had not had time to stow. He did not venture a look behind him to see how Darless was doing. That was too risky for him to venture. It might be noted here that she also chose to hang on for dear life.

How long they rode, he could not guess. Ahead the ground turned completely white! Thankfully, Mandy slowed their charge to a walk to inspect the ground. "Saline Flats!" Alison yelled.

"Now what?" asked Jon. "We are miles ahead of the demons now." The horses were panting, but seemed to have enjoyed the run. Jon had not.

"Zagroot zounds! Time is not on our side," Mandy announced. "It will be dark in a few more hours. Should we tackle Leeds at night or spend the night and hope they have not left while we sleep?"

After some discussion and Alison's estimation of the distance yet to travel, they decided to push on. They were too close now; all wanted a crack at that priestess again. Mandy decided to push the horses because they had no plans to travel any further than the ruins at Leeds. And if something did come up, they would be obliged to rest the horses first.

"Look at the ground!" cried Jon. "It looks like it is bleeding!" Indeed, the white salt layer here at the edge of Saline Flats was just a thin coating over the red soil. While milling around, the horses' feet had churned up the salty cover, revealing red oxides below giving the illusion in the late afternoon sun of a bleeding earth.

"That is an ill-omen!" muttered Darless.

They resumed their path across the sea of white salt, but now at a gentler trot that Jon was beginning to detest as he bounced wildly around in the saddle. Occasionally he glanced over his shoulder to see their bloody path across the Saline Flats.

"What was that sizzling sound back at the battle in Last Town? How did you manage to kill that bug?" Darless called out to him now that he was looking in her direction.

"Dunno. I just pushed it away from me with my stick. It just died." Jon hollered back to her. He was as baffled as she was.

A little while later, Lonnie turned around in his saddle and cried out. "Hey, I have just finally remembered the colors of the old hag priestess. She wore the colors of a priestess of Orcus, grey with black! I did not spend as much time as I should have studying heraldry, unfortunately. I wanted to go out drinking with the guys instead." *Now why did I go and say that?* He wondered to himself.

"Now it is making more sense," yelled Mandy back to the others. "A priestess of a demon lord of the Abyss summoning fell creatures of the Abyss for her use. Makes sense!"

"And now I know what has been troubling me!" yelled Darless. "The Chasme died too easy! Those were adolescent Chasme, not adult ones! We are fighting baby demons!"

"What does all this mean?" yelled Jon. No one answered. They trotted on as the sun set behind them.

Chapter 5 The Ruins of Leeds

"There it is!" hollered Mandy, leaning back toward the other riders. The ruins of Leeds steadily grew on the horizon ahead of them. Gradually, the ranger slowed their pace back down to a walk both to give them time to familiarize themselves and to cool the horses. The oblate sun, now ominous blood red, lay directly behind them, giving the ruins the appearance of a mouth with dark jagged teeth.

Leeds had once been a stone tower of some kind; it had crumbled down to approximately thirty feet tall. Bits of wall remained on the eastern side perhaps another five feet up. It lay centered on a small rocky island about thirty feet off the shore of the Sea of Salt. The sea looked shiny black under the setting sun, in stark contrast to the now reddish hue of the white salty flats over which they were ridding. The sea was absolutely calm from this distance. The only sound came from the panting horses and hooves hitting the ground.

Upon reaching the shore of the Sea of Salt, they halted. For several minutes, everyone was silent with their own thoughts, staring at the ruins before them. Who originally built the tower here at Leeds, modern history did not record. As far as anyone now knew, it had always been a ruin.

Then, Mandy stirred, "Stay mounted while I search for signs." She swung gracefully off her light war horse and bent close to the ground searching for signs. There were many to read.

"What a spooky place," commented Darless, whose voice sounded harsh in the total stillness. No living sounds could be heard other than themselves, just absolute quiet from the environment, lifeless, barren.

"There has been a lot of activity around here." Mandy began. "The salt here is perhaps eight inches thick. Looks as if someone has come here to scoop up salt many times. No demon tracks. Nothing out of the ordinary, if anything here could be considered ordinary! Well, anyone have any ideas? What now? How do we get across to the island and ruins?"

"From the tale of my dad's adventures, somehow he and his party must have crossed the water somehow. I don't see any boat that we could borrow. Perhaps we should test the water's depth. If it is not deep, perhaps walk?" Alison offered and dismounted. Since no one else spoke, she walked to the water's edge and inserted the base of her staff probing the depth. "Shallow, so far."

"Wouldn't it be safer for the horses if we rode them across to the island instead of leaving them here in the open?" Lonnie asked. "Over there we can at least tie them to the rocks. I'm a bit worried that they might try to drink from the sea and die from too much salt intake."

"Good point, Lonnie," agreed Mandy. "Cover me." And she mounted and nudged her horse forward into the still waters. Alison stood ready with her staff, intently watching the distant ruins for any sign. None appeared. The water was indeed very shallow here and never reached a depth beyond three feet. Safely across, Mandy dismounted, drew her sword and lightly tied the horse to a rock. "Ok. Come across. I'm covering you." The others splashed across.

Once on the rocky shore, Lonnie quickly took charge of the horses, leading each to a safe area and securely tying them, loosening their girth belts and watering them. The others stood watching and scouting the ruins in the failing light. All except Jon, who stretched and tried to get the stiff soreness out of his calves. Darkness would come within the hour. The moon would not rise for several hours yet.

Mandy found a pathway that led from the shore up to the ruins proper. When Lonnie was finished, he and Mandy led the way up the path that climbed about twenty feet up to the ruins. The island was a jagged, rocky, red granite protrusion; but the path was ancient and well-worn. Soon they stood before the entrance to Leeds.

The tower was constructed from red granite blocks; Alison had no idea where such granite could be found. Its base was still solid. Only the upper walls had failed. Why, not even history said. Here at the base, it was circular, some hundred feet in diameter. But age and the elements had eroded the rock surface, pitting it deeply. It looked dark and foreboding.

The path ended at an enormous set of oaken doors, now off their hinges, lying ajar, dry rotting against the walls.

Here at the base, the walls were three feet thick. No windows could be seen until about twelve feet above ground. Standing silently here at the entrance, their uneasiness grew.

"I don't like this one bit. If we use a light to find our way and explore, anyone here will have the element of surprise on us. If we use no light, we risk falling into untold dangers, such as pits. Either way, we lose. Any ideas?" Mandy whispered. In this complete silence, her whisper seemed harsh.

For a minute no one spoke. "I have something I can try," whispered Jon. "You all keep a sharp eye out for anything and listen for any sounds. Alert me if anything comes up. I'm going to try to see if I can sense the presence of anyone."

"How's he going to do that?" whispered Lonnie to Mandy.

"With his mind. Now sh!" was her hasty, whispered reply.

Jon took a deep breath and leaned on his walking stick. It felt good to have his stick with him. It was coming in most handy. He closed his eyes more for his own peace of mind. After several minutes, he had ceased thinking about his body and cleared his mind of other thoughts. He just faced the tower and pushed his awareness outward. Soon he could feel the presence of the others nearby. He sensed the anxiety coming uniformly from them all.

Confident that he was sensing minds, Jon pushed his awareness further outward, expanding into the tower itself. He remembered how he had once located Darless in just such a manner. He grinned at the recollection. She had been sitting on the toilet in her bathroom. He recalled his utter embarrassment at the time, but it seemed so long ago. *Oops. I'm thinking again. Concentrate.* As he attempted to resume his searching, that momentary loss of concentration caused him to look downward. Thus, as he continued to reach out searching for another mind, his attention actually took on a more downward direction, below the entrance surface.

About fifty feet below the entrance chamber, as they would later estimate, Jon sensed another being. Faint at first, but unmistakable, he had found someone far below them. The life force seemed so remote, so distant, so weak, at first he almost doubted it was real. *Hello.* Jon placed into that mind.

He could sense the other being awakening as if out of a deep slumber; he could feel their mind grasping at the reality. *Hello. I'm Jon Brown. Who are you?* He placed the thought in the other's mind. Then, he thought, *Jon, you stupid fool. Here you are giving away our presence!*

At once a flash of expanding energies swept through Jon's mind. The others watching him saw his body briefly glow in a pale white light. Lonnie stared, eyes wide in wonder. Alison, quite worried about his safety, whispered, "Is, is he all right?" Mandy and Darless merely shrugged "Who knows." Several minutes after the afterglow faded, Jon stood up and stretched and turned back to the others — all were looking at him expectantly.

"An Air Maiden of Ukko is imprisoned inside!" Jon excitedly began, his eye twinkling in excitement. "Oh, I think that the lower areas of the tower itself are empty right now. I accidentally probed below this level; there is some kind of dungeon prison below us. An Air Maiden named Fruella is imprisoned in there. I woke her up. She said she can guide us to the prison entrance. I promised I would free her somehow."

They all started talking at once. "Praise be to Ukko!" cried Lonnie loudest of all.

"How can that be?" puzzled Alison.

"Where the devil are the Chasme summoners anyway?" spat Mandy somewhat taken aback by the wrong news, she fully expected a grueling fight.

"Ah, then she was the source of the glow over Jon just now," put in Darless, "Now that makes sense! Air Maidens are powerful as we all know!"

"Let us charge forward to her rescue!" chimed in Lonnie.

"Wait! We are not charging anywhere. Caution. How can an Air Maiden be imprisoned *anywhere*?" demanded Mandy, still expecting some form of trickery. "Darless, let's have a soft low light. Form lines as before. Lonnie, you are up front with me. Keep your eyes open for traps! Those demon summoners must be around here somewhere!" The take-charge ranger walked up the steps and cautiously entered the ruined tower at Leeds, Lonnie hot on her heels.

Inside was a dusty circular space some hundred feet across. On the far wall, a spiraling stairway built into the side of the wall led up to another level, about fifteen feet above them. Enormous oaken beams supported the ceiling or floor above them and at regular intervals, granite arches held the massive weight of the second floor. The floor was covered in dust at least an inch thick. It did not require the tracking skills of a ranger to see that many sets of foot prints came and went in this room. Junk was scattered all about. Some were obvious remains of the salt miners, who evidently used this room as a shelter. There were even traces of several campfire circles. Rags piles formed what must have been beds for the miners. Flotsam and jetsam lay strewn about.

There was no obvious entrance to any dungeon or any sign that one had ever existed. "How do we get down?" asked Lonnie a bit confused; his idea has been to simply rush in, head down the stairs and rescue the maiden. Jon said also a bit confused, "She said the entrance was behind a couch. But there is obviously no couch!"

"Allow your wizard to assist!" grinned Alison, eyes sparkling. During her many adventures with Sir Thomas, she had developed a knack for finding the un-obvious entrances while the paladin had stumped around poking here and there. Jon watched her closely as she tossed back an errant strand of her long hair and listened to her careful choice of words from some unknown language. As soon as the last syllable barked, a heavy grating sound of metal hinges long unused filled the room. Amazed, Jon watched as a ten-foot section of the floor near the center began slowly to descend, hinges shrieking from centuries of disuse. "There lies the way." Alison added theatrically while smiling at Jon. He could not resist blowing her a playful kiss. She looked so beautiful, so commanding standing there in her white robes and staff held high.

With a rush, everyone moved to the gaping hole in the floor. A rush of damp, moldy, stale air assaulted their nostrils, causing them to momentarily step back. As Darless repositioned her globe providing the illumination closer to the hole, all could see dark steps covered in an undisturbed dust an inch thick leading downward into blackness.

"Have the globe go just ahead of me; I go first, Lonnie second," ordered Mandy. Without waiting for a reply, she carefully began descending the steps, sword held at the ready. On this occasion, she was overly cautious. Each of her sixty-six downward footsteps raised small clouds of dust. The last step ended in a long underground corridor some ten-feet wide extending fifty feet to their right and left. Torch holders formed from the gaping mouths of demonic figures lined the walls at uniform intervals. Some blackish mold grew on the lower portions of the walls. Three doors were uniformly spaced on the long wall behind them while straight ahead of them stood an elaborate pair of rusting iron doors.

A soft, pale greenish glow covered these iron doors. Here was the prison, no doubt. Sitting in special inlay niches carved from the bedrock at the four corners of the doors were four enormous emeralds. Obviously the emeralds were enchanted with magical energies and were the source of the glow over the door. However, stuck between the doors handles and barring it from opening was an ornate broadsword. All, save Lonnie and Darless, had seen swords like this before — this was obviously the weapon of an Air Maiden of Ukko. For a minute, the ladies and Jon just stared at the broadsword, lost in their own memories of their encounters with Ukko's Air Maidens only a month earlier. Jon broke the silence by clearing his throat, "She must be behind these doors."

"Don't touch anything!" barked Mandy and she turned around to face the others. "There is some powerful magic operating here."

"Absolutely, don't touch anything on that door!" the alto voice of Alison broke in. A trace of aching was in her voice. Painful memories only a month old swam through her mind. Vividly she remembered how she had selfishly stepped in front of Jon to take the magical spear of death hurled at Jon by the hand of Morrigan, Goddess of War. She re-experienced her instantaneous death and then her resurrection from the divine hand of Ukko which had subsequently touched her, undoing that untimely death. Still haunting her thoughts was how she could ever repay her god Ukko. Perhaps this was how she could. "Darless and I will see if we can figure this out." She added when the memory flashes had passed.

"Right! The rest of you, come with me, we shall see what lies behind these other three doors." Mandy ordered. Jon felt a bit useless, but trailed behind Mandy and Lonnie as they began the search. They began with the middle door because it was ajar. Here was some kind of vestments or robing room,

Jon decided. Disintegrated fragments of what had once been priestly robes lay on the floor beneath pegs on the walls. There were a table and four chairs. Similar demonic torch holders lined the walls. "We need more light to see what's what," Mandy decided.

"Jon. Here catch!" Darless spoke with a teasing sound. He turned around and saw a globe of light coming his way. Startled, he had no idea how to catch a magical globe of light and instinctively raised his stick to keep it from hitting him squarely in the face. When the globe reached his stick, it seems to connect and latch onto the end. "Good catch!" hollered Darless with a broad grin. She had intended it to latch onto the end of his walking stick in the first place, whether Jon had raised it or not. She enjoyed watching his looks of initial confusion. And he knew that she did and exaggerated it a bit to tease her back.

Even in the sufficient illumination, this robing room held nothing of interest except two keys. They lay on the floor covered in dust; at one time they had been on a leather thong, but time had disintegrated the leather. Jon then made the mistake of attempting to sit on one of the chairs. Damp rotted, the chair collapsed into a pile of scraps, landing Jon soundly on the floor. Red faced, he got up and shook the dust off of himself amid the laughter of the others.

The next two doors they discovered were locked but the keys worked in the latches. However, the metal locking mechanism had long ago rusted and fused. Lonnie had to put his shoulder to them to smash the next door open. Again, the wrenching sounds of hinges long disused broke the otherwise morgue-like silence.

"Zagroot zounds!" exclaimed Mandy as she rushed into the room. "We found the treasury room! Jackpot!" Lonnie had never seen a real treasury room, though the paladin did know of their existence. Jon had only just seen Alison's treasury room. Silver and golden coins lay strewn about the floor where they had fallen when their leather holding bags had rotten and given way to the weight of the metal. Several chests stood open displaying twinkling jewels, necklaces, tiaras, broaches, and pins. Numerous clerical golden chalices, trays and ornate candle holders lay stacked neatly about where they had last been placed centuries before.

"There's, there's a fortune in here!" Jon exclaimed.

"Unbelievable. But perhaps it is all unholy and should be destroyed," Lonnie wondered. The demonic faces of torch brackets glared at him, he thought.

"We'll leave it for now until we can find out if it is cursed or evil," suggested Mandy. "There is still one more door to try." She led the way back down the fifty-foot hallway to the middle where Darless and Alison who were intently studying the magic on the door. Trying not to disturb them, she went on down to the door at the other end of the hallway. This last door was more difficult to open; here the hinges had rusted nearly solid. It took the combined efforts of both Mandy and Lonnie to finally bust it open.

"Armament room!" called out Mandy as soon as she entered. This room held her interest and Lonnie's too. Here were stored the fighting instruments for the defense of the tower. Weapons of various kinds lay stacked neatly on wall racks and mounts. Centuries of disuse and storage in damp conditions had taken their toll on the finely wrought metals. Most of the edged weapons were now useless except for historical purposes. From the remains of the decorations, Lonnie felt sure that they were meant for some demonic group. There were also a number of maces and hammer types on one wall; their wooden handles long ago disintegrated. Jon was fascinated with the wide variety; he had seen only a few swords in his life.

While going from object to object, Jon noticed in one corner a bulge under some rotted tapestry. Using his now trusty walking stick, uncovered an oiled leather roll, whose length was that of a sword. "Hey, look here. This leather is still in decent shape!"

Mandy knelt beside the package. Leather unbound revealed a jeweled scabbard containing a long sword that held a large ruby in its pummel. No sign of rust was on the case.

"Look there! That is the symbol of Ukko! This is a holy blade! What can it be doing here in this demonic place?" cried an animated Lonnie. To come across a holy blade was for a paladin a major event of importance.

"I suspect that it is a magical blade, Lonnie," Mandy suggested, "It has been unaffected by the centuries. I shall have to handle it to tell for sure. Stand watch and be quiet!"

She withdrew the long sword carefully, holding it in her bare hands. Then, she closed her eyes.

Lonnie, moved to the doorway, but could not take his eyes off of Mandy and the blade. "What's she doing?" he whispered to Jon.

"Shh. Dunno. She has some mental powers too." Jon whispered back; he watched as well, fascinated. From the rear squatting down by the sword, he could not fail to notice her long brown hair and well-shaped, tanned skin — both of which blended with the brown leather top, shorts and boots. The eagle feathers in her hair band and those around her legs, arms and waist complimented her looks. *Mandy is one beautiful woman!*

In a few minutes, the ranger stirred and got up and put the blade back into the sheath. *Glad you finally noticed!* She placed that thought in his mind just as she turned around to face them, raising an eyebrow at Jon when their eyes met; she watched as Jon's face turned crimson. Grinning, she had the effect she had desired. Ignoring Jon intentionally, she turned to the young paladin. "Lonnie, I give this sword to you to use until you can return it to its rightful owners. It is named Demon Slayer and is magically enchanted, particularly so against demons from the Abyss. It was last wielded by a paladin of Ukko as you suspected. His name is, er was, Sir Jonathan Blackwood. He was slain battling some demons in this general area a couple hundred years ago. I got the name of Blackwater Creek. Perhaps that is where he came from. The demon who finally killed him tried to pick up this weapon and it burned his hands horribly. They could only transport it in this preservative leather cover."

Kneeling on one knee in formal fashion, Lonnie reached out to receive this holy sword. "I, Lonnie, Holy Paladin of Ukko, swear to honor this holy sword, to do everything in my power to return it to its rightful owners!" Mandy formally presented it to him. As she looked down into the young man's watering eyes, she sensed the depths of his convictions, how important this vow of service was. *Was I ever like this?* She wondered; involuntarily, her mind wandered back some ten years when, as a budding young woman just in her teens, she had begun taking sword fighting lessons from Squire Eldred, steward of Blackthorn Castle. She smiled as she remembered how hard she had to plead, beg, cajole him into training her, how she had put her entire body and mind into that singular task of being worthy of his teaching! *Youth!*

"Well, don't forget to use it until you can find its rightful owners. Perhaps that line is no longer alive. Perhaps, holy Ukko intended it for your service now!" She added that last bit in a subtle attempt to plant the idea in Lonnie's mind that it would be acceptable to use this magical blade in the meantime. *Heavens, why let a magical blade go unused!* "Come on. Let's see how they are doing on that enchanted door."

Darless and Alison were chatting when the others joined them in front of the glowing door. Jon distinctly heard a low pitched humming noise. "Any progress?" he asked cheerfully.

"Well, look at this." Alison spoke a foreign word and the humming increased and some kind of greenish runes, rather like nebulous clouds, appeared on the doors, as if written by some vaporous pen. "Darless can read it."

"It is in an ancient dialect of Hemmel Land in the 66th level of the Abyss allied to Orcus." Darless spoke with authority. "I can barely read it, roughly translated it says":

'By the powers of Orcus, the Unholy,
I, Santos Gubernati, High Priest of Leeds,
Savant of the Marquis de Gritz,
Do hereby ensnare this treasonous Air Maiden,
Now and for all time.'

Dull humming was all that could be heard for several minutes when she finished the translation. After a pause, she added, "Did you notice how many steps led down here? Sixty-six!" Lonnie felt ashamed that he had failed to count them. He had so much to learn.

"Then, this tower of Leeds was a demonic temple of some kind! That fits with all that we have found in the other rooms." Mandy finally spoke. She did not speak of her own inner thoughts that were now filled with fear and foreboding at what they were getting into on this adventure. Mandy was seldom scared, and the twinges of fear that began gnawing at the back of her mind began to shake her confidence. She said nothing further.

Oblivious to the significance of the words, Jon cheerily asked, "Well how do we get her out of there? How do we break this enchantment spell thing?"

"That's just what Alison and I have been discussing. This enchantment is wholly evil in nature. Alison got her fingers burned just trying to touch one of those gems! I can touch them without effect, except feeling that terrible chill of evil that pervades the Abyss! However, we believe that we have it narrowed down to one of three possibilities." Darless went on.

"Number 1: we simultaneously remove the gems and then the blade. Number 2: we remove the blade and then simultaneously the gems. Number 3: we simultaneously remove all. Pick the wrong one and we are all likely to be blasted into oblivion." She added with emphasis.

"Hmm. Nice enchantment!" Jon exclaimed. "So what now?"

"Well," Alison began slowly, "we both agree that the most likely way to break this spell is to perform the reverse sequence of its construction, with Lonnie or me doing the actual removal of the blade."

"Why you or Lonnie? I don't understand why it has to be one of you two?" Jon asked confused. He did not like the idea of Alison being blown to bits.

"Now that *is* a dumb question!" joked Mandy.

"Because Alison and I," interjected Lonnie, who grasped at once what Alison was saying, "stand for the exact opposite of what the evil priest who entombed the Air Maiden!"

"But, but we are all the good guys!" Jon seemed more confused, not enlightened.

"Didn't you once say, Jon, that all rules were meant to be broken?" Alison pointed out, for this was still her major touchy spot about her relationship with Jon.

His face reddened. "Well, yes. But only in the right circumstances when good is going to come from doing so." Jon hastily protested.

"Hogwash!" Mandy could not resist interjecting, "It is not rules that are important, it's people. We need to be free to follow our own paths in life. Individual freedoms are vital to survival of the spirit, not encased in a mantle of silly laws!"

"Well, I don't know if I'd want to go quite that far!" Jon added with a big grin, suddenly catching the totality of the conversation at last. "Okay. Now I understand! These demon creatures are out for themselves and wholly evil. I see what you are driving at. So how do we decide which choice to make?"

"I am willing to gamble that we should remove them in the reverse order they were done." Darless answered. "And how to figure out that one was what we were just discussing when you all came back. In short, we don't know the order of the entrapment spell."

"Oh, then if that is all you need to know, that ought to be a simple task." Jon replied. "I can find that out I think." He went close to the doors, closed his eyes and concentrated, removing all thoughts from his mind. When he was totally receptive, he placed his hands both squarely on the doors. Instantly, he sensed intense heat from somewhere near his fingers; the odor of burning flesh reached his nostrils; then the wave of pain from his own hands reached his mind. *Ah, I see.* He opened up a pathway through his nerves to let the pain flow freely with no resistance at any bodily joint and opened up his blood vessels to allow conduction of the heat rapidly and assisted some cells in his hands to repair the damage. Once done, he focused his attention back on the door itself.

He saw some calloused, blackened hands making motions before the door, strange words were spoken. He saw four other hands in unison placing the green emeralds into their positions and then the original hand slide the blade between the door handles. Blinding flash of an evil greenish light bathed the robed hands. And the image of the door appeared as it was today. He let go and relaxed a moment.

The others merely saw Jon's hands get seared; whiffs of charred flesh assaulted their nostrils. As they watched, a pale yellow glow enveloped Jon's entire body. Shortly, they backed away from him — intense heat radiated from him, like an iron.

When he had recovered, Jon relayed what he had seen. Now they knew what the order would be. Lonnie would remove the sword. But how could the gems be removed without the person suffering massive burns to their hands? Jon pondered this a minute.

"I know. I think I can reach two of them at once. Mandy, you are the next best — use gloves and try to keep up on the healing process as they burn you." Jon ordered.

Jon and Mandy got into their positions, a rather awkward one, reaching both high and low simultaneously. Darless and Alison stepped way back into the end treasure room, safe from any potential blasts, ready to come to their rescue, if needed or even possible. Lonnie waited for Jon's signal. When it came, he ceremoniously withdrew the holy sword from the door. To his amazement, it slid easily out between the handles. Then, Jon and Mandy on a count of three grabbed and pulled the green gems out of their niches in the door frame. A blinding flash of green energy flooded the entire corridors before the doors. The trio stood there violently blinking off the aftereffect.

"You all right?" called out Alison, her voice sounded quite worried and concerned.

"Yes, all okay. Right, you two?" Jon replied. They were fine; but Mandy stood still for another minute repairing her singed finger tips.

"Like sticking your hands in a bonfire!" Mandy explained. "Jeesh, I don't want to do that again! Well, who's going to try to open the doors?" Her take-charge demeanor returned.

Jon grabbed both handles and pulled. They squeaked slightly but did not open.

"Here, let a woman show you how!" Mandy joked; using a swift push from her hips, she shoved Jon out of the way. She gave a mighty pull and the doors creaked and groaned and nearly opened.

"Here, let a real man assist you!" Lonnie added, smiling broadly, finally catching onto Mandy's humor. They each took a handle and together gave a huge pull. Grating and groaning, both doors slowly creaked open!

From Darless' magical globe of light attached to the end of Jon's stick, they looked into a small twenty-foot room, entirely bare except for a bed or block hewn from the bedrock. Sitting on the block was the Air Maiden, Fruella.

Dressed only in rags, she looked horribly thin, like a child near death by starvation. She was so weak she could barely raise her head. But the yellow glow about her body, the holy glow of an Air Maiden of Ukko, was still there. She had kept her faith all these many years of imprisonment.

For a moment, no one spoke; all were stunned by the sight of this unfortunate maiden. Tears rolled down Lonnie's face. Finally, Jon stepped forward a foot and said, "I am, er, Saint Jon Brown. We have broken the spell that has entrapped you. You are free now. Ah, er, what do we do now to help you?"

Speaking with a voice that has not spoken for centuries, the frail maiden could only whisper, "Take me outside, please."

Lonnie rushed forward and gently picked her up. To him, it seemed she was weightless. Jon led the way holding the globe of light on the end of his walking stick high, lighting a path back up the steps into the main floor of the tower and then outside. Lonnie set her down by the side of the ruined tower. When Jon turned around to watch Lonnie gently sit Fruella down, leaning her carefully against the wall, he saw the young man's face clearly. That expression would forever be etched into his memory. His face reflected the joy and supreme tenderness of someone who had just been given the highest honor possible, assisting a holy Air Maiden. Jon knew that this simple event would forever change this young man. He did not know that it also forever changed another, for he could not see the tears streaming down the face of Darless, the alu-demon, standing in the shadows behind him.

Out here in freedom and free from the tomb, the cool night air revived Fruella. Before their eyes, she began to recover; flesh began expanding as muscles renewed themselves. She was, after all, an immortal being. Inside of an hour, she had recovered remarkably. And she began her tale.

"Thank you for rescuing me from that eternal imprisonment!" Then, she described her last days at the Temple of Leeds. "Ukko was besieged with pleas from the local farmers around here. Diabolical and evil deeds were being done at night. Local maidens were stolen from their beds and found the next day lying in the fertile green fields, raped and butchered, evil demonic brands burned into their flesh. Ukko sent me on a spying mission. I pretended to be a local maiden. One night, fell fighters accompanied by a magic user and priest abducted me. We rode over the rolling green hills and finally arrived here at the Temple of Leeds."

"Inside, there must have been several hundred people, all laughing — partying over the sacrifice that I was to shortly become. It was hideous. But as arranged, Father Ukko was watching all from my eyes. Once inside and stripped nearly naked, I was taken to the high altar on what must have been the top floor of this hundred-foot tall tower. There I was to be sacrificed. I was brought forcibly into the altar room."

"Oh how hideous it was, demonic objects adorned the wall; tapestries depicting vile debauchery hung on the walls. And there before me was a black sacrificial altar brought here from the very Abyss itself! And then out walked the high priest and his master both covered in grey robes with black trim. But it was the master's hands that caught my eyes — black hands protruded from his sleeves. Black as night they were! Instantly I recognized that the master of this temple was indeed a demon from the Abyss. He looked at me in instant recognition as well, shrieking, 'This is no maiden! She is a spy! Seize her!' Ukko, looking through my eyes, commanded my voice to speak, 'Behold, the Marquis de Gritz, demon cambion half-breed!' I will never forget the impact those words had on his face. Indeed that look of stark and utter terror has given me many smiles during my imprisonment. The poor high priest just stood there in total non-comprehension!"

"When he recovered from his anger, he shot a spell at me, which, of course, did not affect me, but revealed my true identity to him and caused my holy sword to change from a maiden's waistband back into its true form. But ever was fear in his mind. Father Ukko said to me, 'I have seen enough. Stall them until the legions arrive.' And he slipped out of my mind. I knew then that de Gritz' eminent destruction was coming! He also sensed it, issuing many orders to place the Temple on full combat alert."

"He instructed his high priest to have me taken down into the dungeon. His last words were, 'For you my treacherous maiden, you have all eternity to contemplate the power of Marquis de Gritz!' Hastily, his high priest threw me into that room. When the doors shut me into total and complete darkness, I felt so utterly powerless! When the green flash of magic occurred, I knew my fate was sealed!"

"Later on I heard enormous thunder, the very ground shook. I heard walls above me crashing down. Alas, I could not reach anyone. I could not get any kind of message out. I was imprisoned. Only someone from the outside could get through the barrier, as you did, Saint Jon Brown. Soon I lost all track of time. I was totally alone, in total blackness, totally helpless. I tried everything I could think of to escape, all to no avail."

"How could you possibly ever endure such imprisonment for so many years? I would go stark raving madly!" cried Mandy, deeply moved by her story.

"Faith. I am faith. I am love. I am Truth. I am goodness. I am the wrath of Ukko. I just relaxed and let time pass, just being myself as faith." she answered meekly, knowing they would not understand.

Mandy and the others heard the words. But Fruella knew that they did not know their meaning. She faced blank looks of complete non-comprehension. She thought for a moment and then spoke, "As payment for your freeing me from eternal imprisonment, I shall share you with yourselves. You see, mankind has it all wrong. You no longer think of yourselves as you really are. Actually, each of you is a spirit that is occupying, for a time, these bodies. But you get so wrapped up in the running of these bodies that you have forgotten what and who you really are. You have forgotten what you can do."

One by one, Fruella lightly touched each in turn on their foreheads and simply said "Please float to three feet above your head." For Mandy, the touch flooded her with energy. All thoughts left her mind. She felt like she was floating on air, her awareness expanded in all directions as she involuntarily obeyed the command. Her vision became that of a sphere. It took a bit to acclimate herself to so much sensory perception. Then, she spotted her own body; it seemed so small down there. And there were the bodies of her companions too, small little things. She looked more outward and was momentarily startled. There before her were five other sort of glowing balls, as she would later try to describe them. Shining like a brilliant white beacon in the night was Fruella; not quite so bright was Jon. He was more yellowish in color. She just knew who each was. She realized this was what Jon could do, sense others by feel. There was Alison, though smaller, but still a brilliant white none the less. There, Lonnie, somewhat smaller than Alison and just as white. Darless.

Darless, smaller than Jon, but larger than Alison; she had a tinge of grey in her color. Mandy was serene; certain of who she was. Power. Was there nothing she could not do? *I really am!*

The serene tranquility was interrupted by Fruella's command. "Please move back into your bodies now; danger is approaching." Oh, the *awfulness* of that command! Such serenity *lost*! That was how Mandy later described the action of moving from a state of such freedom back into her normal world. As Mandy re-accustomed herself to being back inside her head, she saw that the others were similarly briefly disoriented. Then, the telltale tingles ran up and down her body; danger was near.

"Danger! Where, Fruella?" Mandy was up with her sword drawn rapidly. The moon was now rising away to the east, casting a pale ghostly light on them.

"Far off yonder," pointed Fruella. "A flying formation of demons is coming this way!"

"Ah, that would be the Chasme cloud we have been after," Mandy declared. "We reduced their numbers by three-quarters yesterday. Now we may eliminate them all together!"

"Wait," cried Alison, "we are really after those who are bringing them into this world! Remember. We thought that they might have been hiding out at this ruins." She explained for Fruella's benefit.

"Why does the ground look so white?" asked Fruella, rather distracted, still curious about her new surroundings. Alison explained about Saline Flats and the Sea of Salt. With a smile, both women agreed on its true origin, the battle between the legions of Ukko and those of the Cambion demon.

The bug cloud would not reach them for another half hour, Mandy estimated. Unfortunately, that would soon prove to be the least of their worries. For at just that moment, the sound of a footstep scuffing the floor on the second floor of the tower startled everyone!

"Zagroot zounds! I thought you said there was no one else here!" Mandy exclaimed as she whirled around and headed for the entrance of the tower.

"There wasn't, well at least I don't think," but no one was listening to Jon. Everyone raced after Mandy who dashed to the entrance way. Jon brought up the rear holding his stick up so the light would illuminate the interior. The first floor was just as empty as before.

"Come on, let's check it out. Everyone, be prepared for the worst! After me!" and Mandy was off moving silently across the floor toward the stone stairs that was built into the side of the tower. Slowly she made her way up the circular stairs. Lonnie and Jon had a good deal of difficulty trying to walk silently. Jon had never considered how such might be done. Both he and Lonnie brought up the rear. It was single file going up the long flight of stairs. Ahead, Jon heard a woman's voice call out.

"Come on in, we've been expecting you!" Mandy, Alison and Darless disappeared onto the second floor; Lonnie and Jon, discarding all further attempts to be silent, raced up to join them. It was a sight Jon would long remember.

To begin with, there was no third floor; only partial walls here were intact. The central section of the floor above them was gone, yet around the edges enough of the third floor remained to provide some shelter. Moonlight provided sufficient light to barely make out shapes until Jon stepped into the room with the globe. Before them, about twenty feet from the exact center of the circular room stood two large men. Each wore some form of black chain mail. Their shields displayed a peculiar heraldry, some form of twisted beast framed by a grey pentagram. Each carried an evil looking sword. But most frightening were their helmets, the same black metal shaped in the form of a demonic head with horns. They appeared to bar their way.

A tall thin man wearing grey robes with black trim stood back at the wall opposite the party. On his head was a felt hat in the form of that same demonic head with horns on it. His right hand held tightly to a tall staff, quite similar to Alison's. He was obviously a mage ready to attack them from a distance.

And to his right some twenty feet and by the disintegrated walls stood a woman dressed in a grey tunic with the same demonic head emblazoned on the tunic's front. She had long black hair held in place with a tiara studded with gems that sparkled even in this dim light. It was the very same priestess that had tricked them earlier. Numerous rings were on her fingers and an amulet was about her neck. She wore very long earrings that touched her shoulders; each appeared to be some demonic creature wrought in silver. Her hand held what had to be a bastardization of a cross, Jon thought, some demonic shape with arms outstretched. It somewhat reminded him of a voodoo doll.

It was she and she alone who spoke. "I am Yandra, High Priestess of Lord Orcus, Supreme Ruler of the Abyss. You have dared to meddle in my affairs. Now the price shall be paid in full. Throw down your weapons and submit to my will or die and submit to eternal torture in Hades. Be it known, there is *no* escape from this tower. Submit now!"

Mandy had not been listening particularly. Rather her combat training had kicked into play. The fighter on her left seemed the strongest. Into Lonnie's mind she placed, *You take the fighter on my right.* She hoped that Lonnie could at least delay the other fighter. To Alison, she sent, *Only one mage to our two; take him out quickly.* To Darless she sent, *Take out that priestess.* And to Jon, *Cover our rear; help where needed. Lonnie's the weak link.*

"Now!" Mandy cried and she charged her opponent. *Heck, there is no point for any conversation anyway*, she thought to herself as she struck the first blow on the fighter, who parried with his shield. Throughout the battle, Jon could only catch glimpses of Mandy's deadly battle; this man was more than a match for her. His strength was far greater than hers; often merely parrying his mighty blows caused her to nearly lose her balance.

Lonnie, simultaneously yelled, "In Ukko's name!" and rushed his fighter. He wisely chose to use the new Demon Slayer sword. Jon saw a bit more of his fight, since his charge was to keep an eye on Lonnie. These two were well matched in strength, but Lonnie's newly mended broken shield arm was his weak link.

The room instantly filled with the clanking of swords in battle. Alison moved off to Jon's right seeking to pull the grey mage and his spells away from the fighters. For several minutes, both mages attempted to launch devastating actions back and forth. Each time just as the glow from magical energy built up to what Jon thought would be the detonation point, the opposite mage's staff seemed to suck up that energy. For several minutes, Alison had a stalemate going. Jon did not know that these staffs could only hold a finite amount of released magical energies.

Meanwhile, Darless moved around the room on the left side, keeping close to the walls, stalking the high priestess. At one point, the priestess unleashed a cube of flames entirely covering Darless. While her thin gauze of a dress totally flamed into ashes leaving her completely naked, Darless was physically unaffected, but not emotionally. The illusion of a new dress appeared over her. Then, as expected, Darless, enraged, returned the favor, creating a large ball of fire centered on the priestess who did not fare as well, shrieking in pain from the burns. Jon assumed that Darless would easily take care of this priestess and he turned his attentions back toward Lonnie.

Had he not done so, he would have seen the disaster as it entered the room. The priestess uttered a word in a tongue Jon had never heard. What he did not see was in the center of the room, black energy formed, blocking all light. For in the very center of the floor was a huge grey pentagram outlined in black. Out of that blackness stepped a demon from the Abyss. Jon heard a startled cry from Mandy and turned to see it.

Standing beside the fighter and Mandy was a creature more than eight feet tall. It had the head of what appeared to be an enormous vulture with a deadly, gaping beak that could tear flesh from bones. Jon did not know that human flesh was precisely its favorite food. It had two long arms with wicked looking claws on them, the kind that could grasp a victim never to release it. Its bird like feet also had enormous claws that could scratch and slice a victim. It said only one word, but Jon found he could understand it. "Food!" and it lunged for Mandy who fell back to focus her attack on this new comer.

In the next second, another black energy wall appeared in the central area. Momentarily another of these creatures appeared, saw Darless and simply said "Food!" and headed her way.

Next, came the cry of Alison as a volley of magical missiles was not absorbed by her staff. A moment later, a lightning bolt arced across the space and nailed the grey mage to the wall. And then another followed along with rolling thunder deafening one and all for a minute. The blue mage lay still and lifeless. Jon's mind was now in high gear, operating faster than his body could in the physical universe.

Crack! The distinct sound of Lonnie's arm re-breaking echoed into Jon's ears. Turning he saw the paladin down on one knee. The other fighter stood over him ready to drive his sword through him. Jon placed a simple command into the fighter's mind. *Drop the sword!* Jon felt the man resisting the direct order, fighting with Jon's suggestion. In the end, the fighter jerked free from Jon's order. But during that instant of delay, Lonnie thrust his sword up and into the other's chest. The fighter fell dead at his feet. But before Jon to get to Lonnie to tend to the arm, yet another black energy field appeared and out stepped a third of these vulture creatures. It paused a second to get its bearings and headed the fallen paladin who was trying to get to his feet. Jon urged his feet, attempting to run to his aid. Over his head arced a huge number of Alison's magical missiles. In slow motion, Jon watched them bounce harmlessly off the creature from the Abyss. It at least delayed the creature which paused to look at Alison.

As Jon reached the side of the paladin, yet again a black energy wall appeared and out stepped a fourth vulture creature which headed toward Alison. And then again another black energy wall appeared and yet again. Now there were six vulture demons or eight of them to the four of them not counting Lonnie. Before Jon could do anything to assist Lonnie, a new comer demon came after Jon. As the creature swung his treacherous claws at him, Jon instinctively used his corkscrew willow walking stick to help deflect the blow. However, the globe of illumination became detached and rolled into the center of the room.

Jon continued to keep his mind free of thoughts, though it took several minutes of concentrated effort on his part to force horror thoughts out. During this time, he and Lonnie were steadily retreating back toward the wall. When his mind finally became free, Jon began to create the combative energy flows he had learned. To his dismay, his heat, cold, and electrical flows — none had the slightest effect on this creature. Then, Lonnie stumbled and in horror, Jon saw the vicious beak tear into Lonnie's chest, ripping him open, only the chain mail preventing his instant death. He heard his own voice far off in the distance screaming "Lonnie's down!" It was surreal.

In that instant, there was a flare of white light, white energy. Instantly, Jon relaxed and felt serene. The Air Maiden! Jon heard her voice, "I will safeguard the paladin." From the corner of his eye, he saw Fruella's blade delve deep into the demon's chest; it collapsed dead onto the floor.

He heard Darless' cry, "Alison's down!" Turning his head in slow motion, he saw Alison, badly wounded lying helplessly on the floor, an ugly vulture poised over her, ready to have its promised feast. Reactively, Jon unleashed a torrent of mental energy, imagining his mental tendrils utterly crushing the very brain of the demonic creature. Instantly, the creature raised its hands to its head screaming a horrid death screech — so violent, wildly uncontrolled and desperate had been Jon's attack. The vulture nearly tore its own head off trying to resist it. Jon now knew how to deal with these creatures.

Quickly he unleashed another massive assault, mocking up crushing the brain of the vulture demon that was on him. It died in a similar fashion. Jon was oblivious to pain and had not noticed that he himself had been badly sliced and torn by the vulture. He only knew that he had the power to deal with these creatures. He turned toward Mandy and Darless, in time to hear Darless' cry, "Mandy's down!"

The overpowering fighter, wounded severely by Mandy, had retreated back from immediate combat. But Mandy was exhausted after the fight with him and was now no match for the demons. Two vultures had jumped her, tearing at her chest and arms. Jon reacted; in seconds, both lay dead beside her fallen body. Jon dragged Mandy out from under the dead creatures; together they lay near the very center of the room. While he was occupied helping Mandy, Jon did not see the high priestess signaling her wounded fighter. He only heard the sound of moaning and of something being dragged toward him. When he whirled around, the fighter had dragged Alison into the center near him and Mandy. There was little the wounded mage could do in protest. Forgetting that this fighter was not a demon, Jon let loose yet another of his mind crushing assaults. To Alison's astonishment, the fighter's head literally exploded, bits went in every direction.

One demon was left. Jon turned toward Darless and her vulture. They were locked into a physical grappling match, each using bare strength to crush the other. Darless was plainly being badly mauled. Jon knew he was getting weaker than he should have been, but he had not yet seen the reason, massive bleeding from the rips delivered by the demon. He tried to focus his remaining mental energies. There was none left. *There must be more! There has to be more! I must strike again! I must! Concentrate! Focus!* Alison saw the blood vessels in Jon's temple enlarge and pulsate, dangerously close to bursting! Then, for the fifth time, a demon's mind disintegrated taking its brain with it.

Darless looked bad but was still on her feet, staggering slowly toward the shrieking priestess, who was absolutely livid with anger at Jon for having destroyed her ultimate weapons. She shrieked, "Jon Brown! You have defiled me for the last time. Go now to meet Hades!" Lying there on the floor in the middle of the grey pentagram with Alison and Mandy beside him, all bleeding profusely, Jon saw four things occurring at the same time. First, some object came hurling across the floor, hastily thrown by Darless who was now very close to the high priestess. Second, the entire central area of the floor began to be outlined in that same black energy they had seen six times earlier. Third, he heard the voice of Sir Thomas crying out as he entered the room "In the name of Ukko!" Fourth, he saw that same telltale streak of energy that he had seen used before in other combats.

Jon knew instantly what spell this priestess of evil had sent his way. She had unleashed her last resort action. From a ring she wore came a beam of disintegration and it was headed straight at his head. Jon was utterly exhausted both mentally and from physical blood loss. He could not move his own body in time to save himself. He had no more mental energy left with which to counter the beam; there was no time to move his body. He had given them all that he had and then some; he had saved them all from death by the demons; yet in the end he could do nothing to save himself. Dazed he watched the beam heading for his head, all in slow motion. He was at peace with himself.

A command entered his mind. *Raise me.* Jon had not the energy to obey. He watched as a spectator might. His arm, still holding onto the walking stick, maneuvered the stick up to deflect the beam. Against a beam of disintegration, the stick should have been eliminated along with Jon's head. The odds of the stick and Jon's body moving it up into position in that slit second was also impossible. Yet the stick met the beam. Further, the beam was reflected in total and streaked back to its originator. Jon saw the look of utter disbelief for a brief instant on the high priestess's face before it was no longer in existence.

He heard Darless scream, "Get out of there — they are gating you into the Abyss! Jon, get out of there! Jon, make me wish! Jon!"

He could not move or speak if he had wanted to, he was only a second from collapsing into total and complete unconsciousness. He was in a sort of limbo, between being aware and not. He felt the tug of Darless' mind entering his trying to assist. Then, his mind and Darless' as well registered the command, *It is ok. Go with this spell.* Relieved that someone had released him, Jon collapsed into a sweet unconscious.

Alison saw Darless literally dive into the center of the room into the black swirling energy, joining them. The gravely wounded mage's last sight was the horror on Sir Thomas's face as he watched Alison and the others disappear forever from the ruined tower at Leeds.

Chapter 6 Five Minutes in the Abyss

From <u>Arcane Lore</u>, by Sage Alistair Fromme, Church of Ukko, Zaire, Mariane, 542:

> **Gate**, definition of: (noun) A gate is an unidirectional teleportation mechanism between two planes of existence. The base of the gate is located in one plane. When the gate is activated, a connection is formed from the base plane to the designated other plane. Once the connection is formed, all material objects located within the gate's radius of effect are transported between the two planes. Only one direction of travel can occur per connection. The duration of the connection is usually short, a few minutes at most. Certain powerful entities have been known to make permanent gates connecting two planar locations. In such cases, a command word causes the connection activation and direction of travel and subsequent matter transferal. The construction of gates is normally the realm of the gods/goddesses of the base plane. However, extremely powerful priests and mages may also construct gates. The duration of time that it takes for matter to be transferred from one plane of existence to another is highly subjective and to this date has not been reliably measured. Reports vary from no time at all to a few minutes, depending upon the person undergoing the transportation.

From <u>Arcane Lore</u>, by Sage Alistair Fromme, Church of Ukko, Zaire, Mariane, 542:

> **The Planes of Existence**, definition of: The land of Mariane is known to be located on a planet revolving about a star system which is called colloquially the Sun. It is known that

other lands exist and that these are not located here on this planet. Some lands are inhabited; some are not. Because it is not known where these other lands are physically located, we say that they lie in their Plane of Existence. To date, the precise location of any other Plane of Existence is unknown. Some speculate that these other Planes are merely other planets revolving around the Sun or other star systems. Others speculate that these Planes are not in this universe. Still others speculate that the Planes of Existence form a circular ring around the Material Plane, which is the name we use to refer to our own Plane of Existence in which we reside. It is known that our Lord Ukko resides on the plane called the Seven Heavens. Travel to other Planes of Existence is usually accomplished by use of a Gate (See Gate, Definition of).

From <u>Arcane Lore</u>, by Sage Alistair Fromme, Church of Ukko, Zaire, Mariane, 542:

The Abyss, definition of: A Plane of Existence (See: The Planes of Existence, definition of) whose citizens (creatures) are both chaotic in nature and perhaps the most evil of all creatures in the known universe. That the Abyss contains 666 layers or levels, each roughly akin to countries or lands in our terms, has been confirmed by numerous sages. The most sentient denizens of the Abyss are called demons (short for demonholme) in our terms and each level is ruled by a Demon Lord.

From <u>Arcane Lore</u>, by Sage Alistair Fromme, Church of Ukko, Zaire, Mariane, 542:

Demon Lords, definition of: The ruler of one of the 666 levels (lands) of the Abyss is known as a Demon Lord. Due to their total chaotic nature, the Demon Lords are continually at war with one another, all vying for power. Some

Demon Lords are worshiped here on the
Material Plane such as the Temple to Orcus.
Demon Lords are extremely powerful beings.
Faith suggests that the Demon Lords were once
powerful beings here on the Material Plane and
that our Lord Ukko banished them to the Abyss.

The four companions were surrounded by various shades of
swirling black energy fields. Though severely wounded,
Darless was the only party member who was still conscious.
She could see the others near her. Up and down did not exist
— no gravity — just the continuous feeling of falling, twisting
and turning. Although Darless had been gated to other planes
before, each occasion had been like this one — against her will.
She hated it. Darless knew that their destination was the
Abyss. How to save her friends was her only thought. Her
mind raced exploring idea after idea.

Bodies can take only so much abuse before they
involuntarily shut down. Alison had passed out from the
severity of her wounds; Mandy, from wounds and intense
physical exhaustion; Jon, from wounds and mental
exhaustion. However, the recent gift from Fruella, the Air
Maiden, proved most valuable indeed.

Less than an hour ago, Fruella had demonstrated to
each that they were a spiritual being. She had separated each
of them from their bodies, exteriorizing the spirit from the
body. The exteriorizing of a spirit commonly occurs at body
death, a bit late for any practical use in that lifetime. Mandy
now floated about one foot above her head and was fascinated
by the swirling black energies moving about her. Alison was
about two feet above her head. Methodical and highly
observant, Alison attempted to absorb the events and correlate
them with her recent experience with Fruella.

Jon was three feet above his body, looking all around.
With Fruella, his exteriorization had been one of complete
serenity of beingness. Now, he recognized that the
phenomenon was the same, but was close to death. He could
see Alison shining brightly to his right. He could see Mandy
and her radiance to his left. And Darless was still inside her
head further to the left. Then, he saw a fifth glow, much
smaller than the others! There was another spiritual presence

here besides themselves! It was located within and around his walking stick. Its glow or radiance was pure white, just like Alison's. *Hello!* Jon thought to it.

No time. Touch the stick to everyone in turn! The stick commanded him.

Jon tried to move his body, but could not. It was, after all, unconscious. *I ... I can't!*

Very well. The stick replied. As a spectator, Jon watched as the stick twisted his body and touched Alison's body. He saw a yellow glow appear over her entire form. Next, his body twisted to the left and the stick touched Mandy whose body also began to glow in a pale yellow light. He watched his body really lean to the left as the stick touched Darless. Finally, the stick touched his own unconscious form. All radiated a yellow ambience. The glow felt good; Jon realized that he was still actually connected to his unconscious body.

Jon! What's happening? Alison's thought suddenly appeared in his mind.

Before Jon could formulate a confused reply, the stick sent to Alison, *Cast a globe of invulnerability about all of us.* Jon next heard the stick command Darless, *Yes, place a sphere of force around all of us; then add in a globe of invulnerability around Alison's globe.* Jon heard familiar chanting and watched fascinated as blue magical energies appeared and swirled around them, mingling with the black energies. (It must be noted here that Alison cast her spell while her body was unconscious, which should have been impossible.)

The spells had only just activated when the swirling gate energies diminished. The utter blackness gave way to a dimly lit world. The sky, if one could call it such, was a uniform grey providing the sole illumination for a bleak land. Jon had never known that there were so many shades of gray and black! The gate deposited them upon a black basaltic platform in the shape of a pentagram some twenty feet across and sixty-six feet above the ground. On all five sides, black basalt steps, sixty-six in number led up to the pentagram platform. Sixty-six torches uniformly spaced around the platform flickered eerily and were supported by iron statuettes depicting various demonic creatures.

Beyond, the land was mountainous; craggy peaks crested within several miles on all sides of the platform. This natural basin was actually part of the sprawling Palace of Matrarch. And the gate itself was part of the Inner Temple of Matrarch. The operator of the gate, Zugblat, the Unholy High Priest of Matrarch, stood near the top of the platform.

Resplendent in his grey robes with black trim, Zugblat's piercing black eyes studied the arrivals. He had long, curly black hair, exceedingly bushy brows and a well-trimmed beard. However, his facial grimace reflected his mental reaction upon discovering four healthy adventurers instead of his expected four near death. At once, he issued orders to two dozen vulture-like demon creatures to encircle the platform. These creatures were similar to those that the party had just fought and who had nearly killed all of them had it not been for Jon.

A party of a half-dozen Palace Elite Guards and two mages stood at the bottom of the platform along with Matrarch himself. All eyes were upon the newcomers. "They've some protections up," dryly reported Zugblat. "I'll give them time to adapt to their new surrounding!" He snickered and laughed in a sneering, belittling manner.

Darless stood, placed her hands defiantly on her waist, surveying her surroundings and the state of her friends, while Mandy was just coming around. While the ranger's clothes were torn and drying blood covered her arms, legs and chest, no actual wounds were present. Alison and Jon, both still unconscious, appeared similarly bloody, but with no visible wounds. *Amazing! How did our wounds get healed during the passage here?* She lent an arm to help Mandy rise and get orientated. Mentally, Darless sent to Mandy, *Retrieve your sword and sheath it. Resistance at this point is useless. Let me do all the talking if possible. Our minds may be monitored; careful what you say and think.*

For once in her life, Mandy had no words to say! A minute ago she was slowly bleeding to death. Now she had no wounds and was physically in the Abyss, surrounded, and with no avenue of escape. Even a curse seemed far to lame to utter. Mechanically, she followed Darless' lead and moved over to assist Alison, while Darless tended to Jon. Both were now coming round.

Soon Jon and Alison were on their feet, trying to comprehend their physical state and their new surroundings. Darless knew Alison would very likely be in physical trouble while on this plane of existence. The Abyss was founded on precisely the exact opposite of everything in which Alison believed! As soon as the young mage realized fully where she was, Alison's body began shaking. The effect that the Abyss had on her was somewhat similar to the Chill of Death that the Arch-devil Dispater had had on her some time ago. But something fundamentally had changed with Alison.

Jon! Jon, I'm burning up! I cannot be here! Alison instinctively placed her thoughts into Jon's mind.

Jon gave her a startled look of genuine surprise, as he steadied himself with his walking stick and leaned on Darless for support. Alison had used mental telepathy to speak to him! Jon had also changed, well, perhaps changed was not quite the right term. As his body revived, Jon remained about a foot above and behind his head. He moved closer to his beloved Alison and replied in her mind, *Like this, honey, don't fight it; face it; help it flow away.*

Always a fast learner, Alison quickly recovered control over her body and its violent shaking. She smiled knowingly at Jon and said aloud, "I see. Yes, it is I that is reacting and not the body. There, I have it under control now. But I have to concentrate on it."

It should also be noted that the four were encased within Darless' sphere of force which in effect encased them within an impenetrable bubble. Nothing from this plane could get inside the sphere while nothing could get out, for that matter. Thus, the air the party was breathing was the air that was brought here during the Gating and not that of the Abyss.

"Well, now that we are all up and going," sneered the priest Zugblat. "Permit me to welcome you to the Abyss and the realm of Inner Temple of Matrarch within the walls of the Palace of Matrarch. I am called Zugblat the Unholy, High Priest of Matrarch and Orcus."

From their viewpoint high atop the temple, they could see a high rock wall snaking its way around the distant peaks, providing a protective barrier from the palace grounds before them. The numerous plants and bushes first caught their attention. In a normal forest, vast shades of green predominate, but here, all of the plants, bushes and more distant trees were colored in vast shades of black and grey.

To their right the towering monstrosity of the Unholy Temple of Orcus rose. The temple had seven distinct levels, each built upon the previous. The style of construction reminded Jon of some archaeological ruins in Southeast Asia. Demon heads ornately carved from stone peered out at the world from every conceivable location. Zugblat commented, "Six thousand, six hundred and sixty-six demon heads, to be precise. Remarkable, is it not?" The High Priest was obviously quite proud of his Unholy Temple. He continued, "Permit me to introduce Matrarch, Supreme Ruler of the 66th Plane of the Abyss!"

From down below, Matrarch himself stepped forward a few feet, bowed to them and then began climbing up the sixty-six steps to the pentagram platform. Metrarch stood nine feet tall and was mostly humanoid in appearance. Mostly, because his face was twisted and deformed, rather like a monster from one of the old black and white horror movies Jon had seen. His legs were long, thick and muscled, but his torso was as thin as Jon's. His arms were about twice as long as Jon's. His body was covered in a black fur; a rich gray robe, skillfully lined with black trim, was draped over his shoulders, clasped at the neck with a huge red ruby. An enormous jewel encrusted Unholy Scepter lay cradled in his arms. But it was his gloves that looked out of place.

Metrarch wore black leathery gloves that came to his elbows. They hid the unhealed state of his hands that had been eternally burned by the Holy Scepter of Ukko so many years before. When he reached the side of Zugblat ten feet from the party, Jon could see vile puss dripping, oozing from the seams around both of Metrarch's hands. Jon sensed the long years of torment this demon had had, sensed the undying rage and anger he had toward that Holy Scepter of Ukko.

"Welcome to *my* realm!" Metrarch began. "So glad of you to drop by. Twas a shame that my High Priestess lost her head back there at Leeds!" He began a long, sneering laugh that was immediately echoed by Zugblat. When he had regained his composure, Metrarch added, "I cannot even resurrect her from the dead now. No matter, she accomplished her mission for me and that is all I asked. Behold my palace!"

About a quarter of a mile to the right and just short of a forest of dark trees lay the Palace of Metrarch, a sprawling, basalt complex at least a half mile across its widest dimension. A stone wall entirely surrounded the palace; there were guard towers rising above the wall about every two hundred feet. The path led to the largest gates Jon had ever seen. Towering thirty feet tall and twenty feet wide, the pair of iron gates each bore a larger than life bronze relief of the head of Metrarch.

In the distance, everyone watched as Chasme demons by the hundreds rose from the forest just beyond his palace. Within a minute, the sky above them darkened visibly as the flying demons circled and hovered overhead. The companions knew now that they had been fighting baby Chasme. These adults were several times larger and more powerful than those sent on the raiding party. Alison grimaced as she thought what might have been had Metrarch sent the adults instead of the children! All were glad that they were encased within several layers of protective spells!

Darless subtly positioned herself just in front of her friends at the edge of her sphere of force and replied, "She did it to herself. I believe she used a magical ring. I am Darless, the Mage of Hollybine Wood. How dare you gate *my* collection of humans here without *my* consent?"

"My, aren't we a sassy lil' demon!" Metrarch roared with laughter once more. After a moment, he stated for the record in a formal fashion among Demon Lords, "I did not know that these were your humans." And he gave the forced nod of acknowledgment such a situation required. However, he then insulted her by saying, "Besides, I would not bother asking permission a lesser demon such as yourself!" Zugblat sneered in delightful laughter over his master's reply while Metrarch smiled, admiring his own words. "But I accept that these humans belong to you. Will you not lower your defenses and accompany me to my palace for a formal discussion? I give you my word that no harm will come to you or your pets for the moment, at least."

Using her telepathic abilities, Darless sent to her friends, *Try to blank out all thoughts from your mind. Concentrate only on the present and what you see and hear. Above all, let me do all of the talking!* She received a mental acknowledgment from all three, including Alison. Startled, for an instant she stared at Alison! Alison attempted to maintain a poker face.

Darless, feigning anger, began talking just as fast as she could, all the while keeping a keen eye on those before her. "This is a base *insult* to demon-kind. In all my years, I have not ever been so *rudely* treated! And by a Demon Lord himself. You should *know* better! Well, as you can see, we have totally *destroyed* all of your summoning party, if that is what they were. I hope you now have a healthy respect for us. You undoubtedly thought that you had the upper hand when you gated us here — just a bunch of nearly dead adventurers. Ha! Guess we have shown *you* a thing or two! Not only are we not dead, we do not even have a *wound*! Though admittedly, our apparel is the worst for wear. We should be *bathed* and properly *attired* for a formal meeting with a Lord of the Abyss instead of appearing like some beggars! What an insult. I have half a mind not to talk to you at all — such rudeness!"

All the while Metrarch bit his tongue, grimacing at the half truths the alu-demon spoke. He was indeed totally shocked that these four were not only not near death but appeared totally healthy and ready for a fight. Things were not going as he had planned. Something was very wrong here. In a way, the Demon Lord appreciated the alu-demon's banter for it gave him time to think of another plan. For a moment, he considered ordering an all-out attack upon them but the alu-demon's words of "we do not even have a *wound*" jolted that thought from his mind. He could easily see that their defenses would be formidable. His mages might not ever break through the sphere or globes of invulnerability. The total loss of his High Priestess was a shock and a setback, but not overly so. Yet, if he should lose Zugblat, then all of his plans would crumble. He concluded that he must not order an all-out attack on them at this time. So he bit his lip.

Darless observed that Metrarch was not interrupting her and that she was giving him something to consider. First, she had to convince him not to attack them and, second, to return them to Leeds. "You must agree this summoning has not followed the Summons Accords of 1721 set down in the Accords of Orcus. Well, it is *obvious* to me anyway that it hasn't. By the Rights of Regress, we are blameless should we choose to eliminate your demons and guards and priest there.

Heck, the Rights should allow us to banish you to a deeper level in the Abyss."

Opps! Thought Darless, *I've gone a bit too far with this!* Metrarch's face twisted in ill-controlled anger. She could sense that he was only barely able to control his desire to smash her to oblivion. So she quickly changed her approach. "But enough of these threats. You gated us here and here we are. That is now behind us and cannot be undone. Be it known that we have not come here to destroy you. Our actions were totally dedicated to the removal of your creatures from our world, where they most certainly do not belong. We accomplished our mission completely. I believe that you should think twice about sending Chasme to our world again. You know, you only needed to communicate with us. You did not have to send all those creatures to their doom just to get our attention. It seems a waste to have sacrificed your High Priestess just to have a word with us. You could have just buzzed me mentally, you know. We are not deaf and you can speak."

Her approach was having the desired effect. Metrarch was bombarded with a continuous stream of truths and half-truths on topic after topic. So fast came her words, that the Demon Lord could not get in a word of rebuttal, even if he had wanted to do so. She continued, "Speaking of which, would you not *stare* at my nude form? Your mage burned all of my clothes off my body back there and I just have not had time to put on some new clothes. What? Am I supposed to be your *harlot*? Don't you know we alu-demons really want to look *pretty* for you lords? How do you expect me or my companions to look *sexy* when you gate us without warning and without giving us time to look presentable? Well, it's no wonder that you have no mistress at this time!" And at this point, Darless became convinced that no attack was eminent from Metrarch. Step One was accomplished; they were not going to be attacked. However, she had no idea how she could accomplish Step Two, getting them all returned to Leeds. She was just about to launch into another tirade of words when another gate opened just to the left of Metrarch.

Metrarch lurched to his right getting well out of the way, while members of his guards charged up the steps toward the magical energy flows off to Darless' right. In a blink the process was over and there stood the now familiar devil. Two horns protruded from his bald head, right above his eyes. He had a goatee and was dressed in rich, blood-red robes with black trim. A soft furry boot was on his right foot. His left leg ended in a cloven hoof, like that of a goat. A small tail protruded from under his robes. He was handsome — extremely so. He carried a staff in his right hand and a rod in his left. He was none other than Dispater, the Arch-devil, and ruler of Dis, the second plane of Hell.

Instantly, Metrarch's guards turned around and hastily retreated back down the steps even faster than they had come up them. Zugblat also moved around to the other side of the platform, putting as much space between himself and Dispater as was prudent. Metrarch crossed his arms and said, "Welcome once more, Dispater. To what do I owe the pleasure of this visit? Come to view my most recent acquisitions?" He pointed to Darless and the others.

Alison and Mandy instantly felt the Chill of Death permeate their bodies, reminding them of their previous encounters with Dispater. This time, however, both concentrated on not reacting to the chill.

"Greetings from Dis, Metrarch. When I saw that Saint Jon and friends were so near to my realm and perhaps very much in *need* of my services, I thought I would *drop* by." He turned to the quartet and bowed, "We meet again, Jon Brown, Alison d'Ambrose, Mandy Blackthorn, and Darless. Hum, it would appear that you do *not* need my services after all. *Most interesting!*" Jon could see the coy smile on his face, hidden from Metrarch.

Jon barely noticed the Chill of Death that emanated from Dispater. In their last encounter with Dispater, Alison and Mandy were paralyzed from his evil chill. Jon noted that this time, Alison just continued to cope and was letting this new evil energy flow off of her. Mandy, though struggling, was also not as adversely effected this time. Jon wondered if Dispater could control how severe his Chill of Death was, but dared not ask.

But Dispater responded, placing simultaneously in all four of their minds, *My, oh my! You have all grown spiritually! You are no longer pawns. How did this happen?* He then bowed before them once more and added, *Good idea.*

Keep your minds blank. He turned to Metrarch. "Since I am here, do you mind if I listen in on your interrogations of them? They are *most* interesting beings!"

Metrarch glared at Dispater for a second but thought better of it and proclaimed, "You are welcome to witness Metrarch in action." He turned to Darless and commanded, "Will you freely follow me to my palace where we may be comfortable? I would like to discuss a few matters with you. Though I fear you will have to cancel your defensive spells to do so."

Darless turned to her friends with a questioning look on her face. Jon and Alison nodded their agreement; they had little choice but to go along with Metrarch. Both mages canceled their protective spells. "You may lead the way." Darless replied to Metrarch. This could be considered a mistake. With the removal of the sphere, the party began to breathe the local air of the Abyss. Jon, Mandy, and Alison immediately began involuntarily gagging, nearly vomiting. The sudden, overwhelming, putrid stench of decaying, rotten, unburied flesh assaulted their olfactory senses. Never had these three experienced such a horrid smell as the air here in the 66th level of the Abyss!

Gasping for air, suppressing violent urges to vomit, the companions found the steps were formidable. Jon and Alison leaned on each other and on Jon's walking stick, while Mandy depended upon Darless for support. By the time they reached the bottom, all four additionally felt intensely thirsty, hungry, weak, and very tired — they really had not yet recovered from the battle at Leeds, and the adrenalin high was completely gone.

Footnote to the reader: the Abyss epitomizes chaos. Indeed, during the next five minutes, total chaos arose. However, the chaos was completely different for each of the participants. Thus, the description of the next five minutes is relayed from five points of view beginning with the viewpoints of Metrarch and Dispater.

Metrarch and Dispater closed ranks and walked briskly down the sixty-six steps. When they reached the bottom, the Palace Guards and the pair of mages, closed in behind them. However, they had to pause when Darless cried out, "Hold on a minute. They are having trouble adjusting to the stench!"

When Metrarch turned around, he began laughing and teased, "So you hearty adventurers don't like my land's beautiful fragrance, eh?" Alison was clinging tightly onto Jon to avoid total collapse; her face was white as snow! Jon was staggering, attempting to keep from vomiting. Only his stick kept them semi-erect as they reached the bottom of the steps. Metrarch and Dispater watched as Jon stumbled as he reached the level path and churned up some ground. Metrarch roared with laughter as Jon instantly began vomiting uncontrollably. Both men saw Mandy, who had been leaning heavily on Darless suddenly jerk to attention, spin around, and make a valiant dash to catch Alison preventing her from actually collapsing on the ground. At the same time, Darless rushed to try to assist Jon.

Dispater said aside to Metrarch, "I *told* you that you should put a little sulfur into your air here. Humans would accept the smell far better that way." Metrarch grumbled agreement.

Mandy turned to Dispater and Metrarch, planted both feet squarely on the ground and glared at Metrarch. Though she uttered not a word, Metrarch felt her total rage directed at him. Then, Alison suddenly seemed to gain new strength and she rose to her full height, no longer leaning on Mandy. She too faced Metrarch but her face and eyes displayed only serenity.

The hovering horde of Chasme demons suddenly swooped down on the two dozen, tall vulture-like, guard demons, the half-dozen Palace Elite Guards, and the two mages who were behind Metrarch. The Chasme attacked indiscriminately in a fit of wild abandon. Bits of wings and other nameless body parts flew off in all directions as mass pandemonium broke out. Dispater and Metrarch received the brunt of the totally unexpected, flying debris.

Dispater quickly surrounded himself with a sphere of force but not before taking several direct splatters. He noticed that Darless had also thrown a dome of force over the others to protect her friends. He saw Jon was still gagging uncontrollably and decided to investigate. This foursome was supposed to have been near death but were not. They had just finished an all-out combat with Metrarch's servants and should be totally exhausted and drained. Yet, the three women were clearly alert and facing him squarely and defiantly. Only Jon was oblivious. His curiosity got the better of him and he entered Jon's mind.

Meanwhile, a furious Metrarch screamed orders to his mages and guards. However, none of them could respond even if they had wanted to do so for they were completely occupied protecting themselves from the horde of berserk Chasme. In the end, Metrarch was forced to bellow out a Demon Lord Command of Power Word that gated his entire horde of berserk Chasme to another layer of the Abyss. In an instant, it was totally quiet save for the sound of someone laughing. Metrarch whirled to see who was making fun of him — a hideous glare in his eyes. But he immediately saw that Jon, still oblivious to what had just occurred, was laughing at something known only to Jon.

Dispater, using the most serious tone of voice that any in the party had ever heard this Arch-devil use before, spoke directly to Metrarch. "I told you that your plan was a *bad* idea. Now I insist that we do this *my* way and *at once* before any other calamities can occur!"

Darless found it fascinating that, here in Metrarch's realm, he should take and follow an order given by Dispater! She began listing out the ramifications of this mentally while counting them on her fingers.

Now, returning to the instant that the protective spells were cancelled, here is what occurred from Alison's point of view. Until she uttered the word that cancelled her protection spell, Alison was located about one foot above and behind her head. She found that her body was so much easier to control from this location; she was not immersed in its sensations. However, just as soon as she breathed the air in the Abyss, the rotting, putrid stench instantly drove her smack into her body. She found herself reeling; suddenly, she was overwhelmed with sensations coming from her body. Exhaustion and fatigue and intense hunger dwarfed the putrid smell. During several of her previous adventures with Sir Thomas, she had encountered rotting flesh. While no one could be immune to such a stench, she could handle it. More significantly, Alison was attempting to ward off Dispater's Chill of Death and the pain of the Abyss. In her exhausted state, she nearly collapsed.

And she depended totally upon Jon to help her stagger down the 66 steps to the ground.

She felt Jon stumble and she looked down trying to keep from falling. She saw his feet had dug up some of the dirt on the path, revealing a swarming mass of white maggots frantically wiggling their way back under the ground. The ground itself was totally rotten. She saw Jon look down at his boots covered with maggots and felt him gag and vomit and begin to collapse. Since she was leaning on him, she began to fall to the ground as well. In desperation she mentally cried to Mandy and Darless, *Help us! We are falling!*

So weak was Alison that she could only watch in slow motion as the ground rose to meet her form. But somehow the strong arm of Mandy caught her; her head was just inches from the ground and the frantic maggots.

I am a total failure. I should just give up. This must be my end, thought Alison as despair flooded into her mind. *I cannot even stand up any more!* Distant memories of her mom holding her involuntarily came comfortingly into her mind. Mandy's strong arm suddenly reminded her of her father. *Dad. Oh Dad!* Then, she had a sudden realization. *Dad was here! He rescued the Holy Scepter of Ukko from this very demon! Well, if Dad could do it, **Alison,** you should be able to do it too. Come on now. If Dad could face this, I can too!* And as she began to just face what was actually present, she relaxed. A newfound, inner peace gradually replaced her despair. She let go of Mandy and straightened up, facing Dispater and Metrarch. And as she did so, she once again found herself backing up and out of her head. She had regained that position of serenity that had been the gift of Fruella, the Air Maiden. For some time, Alison radiated serenity of beingness. No matter what ills would befall her, she was totally at peace with herself and the universe.

She heard Dispater use a most serious tone of voice as he spoke directly to Metrarch. "I told you that your plan was a ***bad*** idea. Now I insist that we do this *my* way and *at once* before any other calamities can occur!"

Now, returning to the instant that the protective spells were cancelled, here is what occurred from Mandy's point of view. From the moment that she regained consciousness here in the Abyss, Mandy felt totally defeated. She was a well-seasoned ranger, a veteran of many campaigns and adventures and situations. Always, she had found a way to triumph. But this time was different. She should have been dead already, but was not. Her body was totally exhausted from the most intense fighting she had ever done. It took all of her remaining strength to ward off the Chill of Death from Dispater. She had been gated into the Abyss. And Mandy knew that there was no way that she could ever get herself or the others back to their world by herself. She was now a helpless pawn of others, evil others. She knew that she would not have any choice what so ever. Whatever Metrarch and Dispater wanted of her, she would have to do if she ever wanted to go home. The defeat that she felt was total and complete. There was nothing left of her will. She graciously leaned upon the strength of Darless to help her stagger down these hard, basalt steps.

Help us! We are falling! The words blasted into her head, like someone screaming at the top of their lungs. It was Alison! Mandy knew that Alison could not do this. But now somehow Alison was mentally communicating with her and not for the first time. *Well, Zagroot zounds! If she can do this at a time like* **this***, Mandy Blackthorn, you darn well better respond!* Mandy is a creature of action. In spite of her exhaustion and total depression, Mandy whirled around and raced into action, catching Alison's falling body only inches from the ground. And that bit of action was all that it took to rekindle Mandy. Holding up Alison, she turned to face Dispater and Metrarch head on. Saying nothing, her whole beingness radiated rage and contempt. *Action, well I'll* **give** *them something to* **think** *about! Chasme — Attack Everyone Now!* She mentally gave the command to the demon bugs, but she gave it with the total certainty that it would be obeyed without any doubts or reservations on her part. She was a ranger and these were animals. Mandy could control animals, even if these were demon animals. **No one** *messes with Mandy Blackthorn!* She continued to face the evil men while watching the Chasme carry out her order as she knew they would. And as she watched the chaos evolve, she too found herself floating up and out the back of her head — serenity flowing over her. She knew that the Chasme attack would cause no real damage to these gods, but they would at least see that she was still her controlling some part of life.

A short time later, she heard Dispater use a serious tone of voice as he spoke to Metrarch. "I told you that your plan was a *bad* idea. Now I insist that we do this *my* way and *at once* before any other calamities can occur!"

Now, returning to the instant that the protective spells were cancelled, here is what occurred from Darless' point of view. Darless had forgotten how much she hated the Abyss. Rage filled her every fiber. From the instant she saw the gate forming back in Leeds, Darless had assumed total responsibility for the survival of her companions, her dearest friends. She knew only too well the danger that they were in. She grimaced as she recalled how she had been a pawn, a servant to Morrigan, the Goddess of War. The feelings of total degradation had been almost impossible for her to bear. And yet it was these very people who had befriended her and rescued her from that life of servitude. In fact Jon had made it impossible for her ever again to be forced into subservience against her will by those who chose to summon a demon. He had given her, and only her, her true name — she now knew her last name, the name of her father. The summoning spells required the true name of the demon being summoned for the spell to work. And now these people who had given her life again were themselves in dire peril, deep within the Abyss, and for unknown reasons. She was determined to get them out of the Abyss somehow.

Initially, her strategy had been to monopolize the conversation so that Metrarch could not act while she sized up the situation and formulated a plan to get everyone safely out of the Abyss. Actually, everyone could have been out of the Abyss and safely back home at once, if only Alison, Mandy or Jon would request her to use her Wish spell. An alu-demon sorcerer could cast this most powerful spell but only if so ordered by another. But Darless knew that her friends would rather die first than see Darless cast it because each use of the spell physically aged her one year. So the alu-demon frantically sought another solution. It never occurred to her that Metrarch actually wanted to communicate with this group of four adventurers.

The arrival of Dispater cast the situation in an entirely new light, as far as Darless was concerned. From personal experience, she knew that devils and demons do not, as a rule, get along well. True, both were unimaginably evil. But all of the devils played by a known set of rules or laws, Dispater exceptionally so. Demons obeyed no law save their own, which constantly changed on their personal whims. *Dispater does not appear unless he has a very good reason, some motive of his own.* She began pondering the significance of the appearance of the Arch-devil, while she assisted Mandy down the 66 steps to the ground. She kept looking back over her shoulder to see how Jon and Alison were faring. Since both were struggling, she was considerably worried. Her mind tested the possibility of one line of action and then another, looking for ways to at least protect these three in her care. *The only ace up my now nonexistent sleeve is that Metrarch cannot use his demon command powers on me as he can command other demons. I'm a free being, thanks to Jon. Metrarch doesn't know that. Somehow, I must make use of that.*

Help us! We are falling! The words blasted into her head, like someone screaming at the top of their lungs. It was Alison! *That's the second time Alison has done this. Somehow Alison has also developed her mental abilities. Now that is also interesting.* She felt Mandy let go of her and move toward the falling form of Alison. *I better get to Jon fast.* So Darless dove for Jon. An alu-demon can move exceedingly fast when she chooses and Darless so chose. She even used her bat-like wings for that extra push. Her arms grabbed Jon and kept him from falling. Still he was convulsing, gagging and vomiting continuously, making it hard to hold on to him.

Jon! What's wrong? She implored in his mind. But he did not reply or seem to even be aware of her query. *Oh, if only Lady Ursla was here. She would know what is wrong with him and what to do! My attention cannot be directed at the outside world to protect them and inwards into another's mind at the same time! What do I do now?* She chose to look into Jon's mind to try to see what was going on with him. If she could determine that, perhaps she could then find a way to help him. This time, it was not hard to do. *He's looking at a mental picture again only this one is so solid, so real that he is totally stuck in it. That's interesting. A person can become totally stuck in a mental picture. Wait! That's it. He's stuck.* And an idea formed. *Jon, move on through the incident until you get to the end and tell me what happened,* ordered Darless using the strongest, most forceful tone she could mentally muster. Unfortunately, she could not see what happened next because a wingless, bleeding Chasme smashed into the side of her head bringing her attention back into the world around her.

Chasme were attacking the guards and vulture-demons. So far they were not coming near the four adventurers. Darless had no idea how or why the Chasme were going berserk, but she had to shield her friends. Quickly she spoke the proper magic command words that brought a dome of force into being over the four of them. Wings and other body parts now bounced off the shield rather like rain on a roof. "Only in the Abyss could it be raining Chasme," muttered Darless in disbelief.

When she turned around to again attend to Jon, she saw Mandy and Alison standing tall facing Dispater and Metrarch. She felt the serenity of Alison and a tear formed in her eyes; whatever would happen next, Darless was proud to be a friend of these women.

Then, she heard the very serious voice of Dispater. "I told you that your plan was a *bad* idea. Now I insist that we do this *my* way and *at once* before any other calamities can occur!" His words rang in her ears. **His** *way? Then, he* **is** *involved just as I thought.* But before she could ponder this further, Jon started laughing and muttering something about being a silly thing for a kid to do. Even without looking at Jon, she knew that Jon had seen and bested that mental barrier. This, of course, started her reflecting upon all sorts of other ramifications of this newfound ability to erase or somehow nullify harmful mental pictures. And just as soon as she started reflecting on this, she became momentarily confused. *Argh. Priorities, Darless. You can look at the impact of that later on. Right now, what's Dispater got to do with all this? Number 1:* And she began to list her observations and suppositions and conclusions regarding the connection between this Arch-devil and the Demon Lord.

Now, returning to the instant that the protective spells were cancelled, here is what occurred from Jon's point of view. Jon still felt a bit disconnected from his body. He did not fully realize that he was still about a foot behind its head. So many unexplained things had happened so fast that his mind was in total confusion. He was not accustomed to combat situations. And the battle back at Leeds and all of the events of rescuing the Air Maiden were spinning in his mind. So many things were unexplained and part of his attention was on these. But when the protective spells were cancelled, the stench that greeted his olfactory senses hit him hard. Such was so totally unexpected that it shocked him, slamming him back into his head, which of course only made the smell that more acute and real. Now he felt the full sensations of his body which were far beyond simple exhaustion. He staggered and nearly fell off the platform. Only his trusty walking stick kept him from a nasty fall down sixty-six basalt steps.

He felt Alison leaning on him so he tried even harder to maintain his balance for both of them. *Take one step down now. Good. Now another step,* he told himself. He and Alison very slowly descended the stairs. However, when he at last reached the ground, his foot stumbled and scuffed up some ground, which appeared at first glance like soft loam. The ground of this level of the Abyss was composed of rotting flesh and his foot churned up a monstrous mass of maggots, wiggling frantically to hide again from the light of the day, such as it was. Jon involuntarily gagged and then vomited. Food! Now the maggots immediately wiggled and crawled their way over to devour the food Jon had just given them. This, of course, only made Jon gag and vomit more and more until he lost all control and panicked.

Jon seemed to be moving in slow motion now, arms flailing wildly about him. No part of his body worked right; no part responded to his desires. More panic arose and still more. Then, darkness came. Calm darkness. Peaceful darkness. Quiet darkness. Oh, it was such a relief to be in the dark. It felt so wonderful. Time stopped and Jon felt at peace and had no desire to do anything else but stay here in the dark.

Jon, move on through the incident until you get to the end and tell me what happened. Jon recognized the voice of Darless.

What do you mean move on through the incident? Jon thought. *I am not looking at any incident. I am in the dark and totally at peace. Huh? Good grief! I'm right smack in the middle of something! And time is moving again. Ah, the sky is lightning up. Morning's coming. Okay. I will move on through this thing.* And he did so.

How long are you going to look at your dead dog anyway? And what are you doing looking at a picture of your dead dog at a time like this? You amaze me even further! Jon recognized the voice of Dispater in his mind. Jon tried to say aloud, though his throat did not cooperate fully, "I was four and found my missing dog. He was dead and full of maggots. I got scared and ran and fell and hit my head on a rock and passed out. It was peaceful until dawn. I decided it is always peaceful at night — in the dark. Haha. Get it? Peaceful in the dark. Haha." And Jon laughed loudly and then vaguely heard Dispater say very seriously. "I told you that your plan was a *bad* idea. Now I insist that we do this *my* way and *at once* before any other calamities can occur!" Jon looked up and was rather startled to see the remains of a major demon battle, Chasme body parts scattered all about, but none on the four adventurers.

Metrarch grumbled something akin to an Okay. Dispater turned to face Alison and the others. "We will gate you back to your world in a second. We intend you no harm. Metrarch has come across one of your brothers, Alison, and wants to trade him to you for a small service. But this is neither the time nor place to discuss this vital matter. Let us return you to your world. We go to Metrarch's servant's fortress called Ravenwash in a land that Mandy knows as the Barren Steppes."

Without waiting for any response from the four adventurers, Metrarch and Dispater both began chanting similar words of power. A gate appeared around the entire group. Soon, that falling sensation enveloped them once again. All the while, the significance of Dispater's words continued to ring in their ears: Metrarch had one of Alison's brothers!

Because Dispater was involved, Darless relaxed for the first time and began to enjoy the gating process. Logic, reason, and law, she felt, are far easier to deal with than utter anarchy. She trusted Dispater, if only for a single reason: for her, trust did not depend on good or evil.

Chapter 7 Ravenwash

Located on a southwestern spur range of the rugged Blank Mountains, the town and castle known as Ravenwash was surrounded on three sides by sheer, three hundred-foot cliffs of reddish black granite. Unless you were one of the thousands of ravens who called these heights their home, the only entrance to Ravenwash lay to the north, through a heavily fortified gate surrounded by two tall guard towers. But it was midnight when the bluish lights from the two gate spells flickered on the walls of the inner sanctum deep within the castle proper.

Sixty-six black and grey candles dimly lit this unholy chamber with its centrally located, ornate pentagram of basalt. Wall brackets depicting demonic creatures from the Abyss held aloft both flickering candles and the now extinguished torches. No one was in this twenty-foot circular chamber to witness the arrival of their cherished deity, Metrarch, and his entourage. First to arrive was Zugblat, the High Priest of Metrarch — his cold eyes glancing about to ensure the safe appearance of his master. *One day; one day*, he thought to himself; he had aspirations of greatness himself. Then, one by one, the others appeared, including Dispater, Alison, Mandy, Jon, Darless, and two trusted mages from the Abyss.

"Welcome to Ravenwash," announced Metrarch using a more formal tone of voice than he had used thus far. Evidently, his demeanor now had something to do with the wishes of the Arch-devil.

But it was Dispater who took charge immediately. "Zugblat, show our guests to their quarters so that they can freshen up and get a good night's sleep." Without so much as a glance at either Zugblat or Metrarch, Dispater turned to the foursome and said, "We will discuss matters in the morning, after you have rested, cleaned up and have eaten all that you desire. Sleep well."

There was such finality in his statement that none thought to raise a single question. At once, Zugblat, accompanied by the mages, lit several torches and beckoned the party to follow him. Though Alison wanted to know all about her missing brother, her exhausted body and overwhelmed mind refused to do anything except fall in line and follow the others down the dark, twisting corridors to their room.

Shortly, they entered a shabby room stinking of mold; a quarter inch of dust covered the meager furnishings. Recognizing at once for whom this room was designed, Mandy complained "This is a disused guard's quarters, not a guest room!"

"It will have to do; all the other rooms are currently occupied at this time," sneered Zugblat. A hint of gross understatement sparkled in his eyes as well, though no one saw it. Handing his torch to Mandy, he turned and left the four to themselves, slamming the door solidly shut as he left. They did not doubt that an armed guard would shortly be posted outside their door.

While the others just stood looking around at the squalid surroundings, Darless went into action. "Alison, can you lend me one of your scrolls so I can conjure us up one of your magical mansions? I, for one, refuse to sleep in such surroundings! Also, do not say or think anything. Undoubtedly, we are being closely monitored. Devils and demons! Who would ever think such disparate types would be working together!"

Alison nodded and brought out her portable hole which she kept somewhere beneath the inner folds of her cloak. After unfolding the hole and rummaging in it, she found her last mansion scroll and handed it to Darless. She was very grateful that she did not have to try to cast another spell; she was too exhausted to concentrate. In a minute, all four staggered through the gates of a shimmering mansion, disappearing from the dusty, unused room.

Once inside, Darless ordered, "Ok. Let's all clean up as best we can, eat some provisions and get some sleep — all just as fast as we can!" No one protested. Like zombies, they obeyed.

For quite some time, Alison lay awake thinking of her brother and what he must be like, having been a prisoner in the Abyss. Thousands of unanswerable questions flooded her mind. *How can I possibly sleep at a time like this?* Then she noticed her body. *Oh, I am asleep!* And she remembered no more until morning.

Jon was running in slow motion. At any moment, he knew his legs would fail him. Behind him a slithering horde of maggots clamored relentlessly, "Food!" Just as his legs faltered, sending him sprawling onto the ground, his nose picked up the smell of freshly cooked bacon. For some reason, the swarm of maggots rushed passed him. Words resonated in his ears, "Food's ready. Get up you lazy adventurers!" The cheery voice of Darless greeted him. Jon woke up.

"Wow! What a bad dream," muttered Jon to Darless. He straightened his hair a bit and sat down at the table, helping himself. "Thanks a million, Darless!" Jon managed to say between mouthfuls. Next, Alison wandered into the table, her hair was in tangles but to Jon, she looked like an angle. "Morning Alison." He paused for a moment. He was going to say, "Morning, my dearest. You look radiant!" But Jon remembered Darless' caution to think and say nothing that might somehow be used against them. So he restrained himself to that simple greeting.

Blushing slightly, Alison instinctively tried to straighten out her hair for a moment. She had already picked up Jon's true intentions which had remained unspoken. She smiled at him and joined him at the table. "Thanks Dar. I don't know what we would do without you!"

"My sentiments exactly!" added Jon.

Now it was Darless' turn to blush. Quickly, she turned around and went to get the simmering tea kettle. Mandy finally walked into the dining area, rubbing the sleep from her eyes. "Thanks, Dar," she lovingly said toward Darless. "I had this bad dream. . ." Then, she stopped abruptly, recalling Darless' orders about being overheard. Hurriedly, she sat down and began eating as well.

As Jon looked at Mandy in her simple white cotton nightgown, he could not help but think, "Here is the sexiest woman I have ever seen!"

Tilting her head toward Jon, her radiating eyes met his. Mandy thought to Jon, *Not now. Remember Darless' caution — we are probably being monitored. Later, I need to talk to you.* Jon blushed as he realized his thoughts were overheard by Mandy. He bent his head down and ate rapidly. All four rushed through their breakfast and then hastily changed clothes and made themselves ready for the day's intriguing activities.

When the four were assembled by the mansion's doors, Darless cautioned, "Okay. Everyone ready? Be prepared for the worst. If someone has been held captive in the Abyss for nearly twenty years, they are likely to be in horrible shape." The alu-demon was trying to prepare Alison for what lay ahead. Many times she had seen the effects that forced imprisonment in the Abyss had had on humans. Such was not good on them, mentally or physically. The four stepped out of the magical mansion. Alison spoke a word and the mansion disappeared; they were back in the long disused guard quarters of Ravenwash.

Their sudden appearance in the empty quarters rather startled Zugblat who had been sent to fetch them for the morning council with his master. Finding the room empty, he had been pondering how he would explain their disappearance to his master. "This way please," he quickly said trying to hide the fact that he had been taken completely by surprise by their appearance. Hastily, Zugblat, the Unholy High Priest of Metrarch, led them down the now bustling corridors toward the Great Hall. Many well-armed soldiers passed them by, some ignoring them, some giving catcalls and whistles toward the women.

The Great Hall was just that, one enormously long room. A huge oak table ran its length capable of seating at least one hundred people. Great tapestries adorned the walls on either side; these depicted various hideous scenes from the Abyss. Earthy colors predominated the decor of the hall. Zugblat brought the party to the far end of the table where Dispater and Metrarch were seated sampling the wine and roasted chicken. Bowing before his lord, Zugblat turned and immediately left the room. Only six people occupied the room. This was obviously going to be a very private meeting.

"I trust that you are all well rested and fed, so let us begin," Metrarch began, using his best manners. After a sideways glance at Dispater, he continued, "I will put this in very simple terms. Alison d'Ambrose, I have recently acquired, or rather rescued, one of your brothers, Lenny is his name, I believe. He is alive and well for now. I will give him to you at once along with the magical picture book found in his possession. In return, you and your friends must perform a small service for me in ten day's time. The duration of said service is not expected to exceed twenty-four hours."

Darless thought that he was being awfully careful with his words. "You realize," she replied formally, "that we follow certain ethical codes — that you cannot ask us to break these codes while performing this service?" Darless thought that she could detect a sneer on his face, but it was gone in an instant, very un-demon like in her opinion.

Clearing his throat, Metrarch continued, "Nothing about said service should in anyway impact your precious 'Ethics.' That is, unless possibly killing one or more evil men goes against such, which I doubt."

Darless interrupted, "Yes, but what exactly is this small service that we need to perform?"

Scowling and gritting his teeth and clenching his fists, Metrarch bellowed, "Prevent my assassination for twenty-four hours at the council!" And he pounded his fist onto the table top, smashing a hole through the thick oaken boards!

Quickly, giving Metrarch time to cool down, Dispater interjected, "You see, I discovered a plot by Lord Jared, another Demon Lord and rival of Metrarch, to have Metrarch assassinated during the upcoming council. Far to the south of here, the Barren Steppes is home to a well-organized band of assassins for hire. During my many travels in search of souls, I accidentally intercepted a letter from the Assassin's Guild acknowledging their acceptance of Lord Jared's offer."

By now, Metrarch had calmed himself down so Dispater dryly continued, "Lord Metrarch, perhaps you could brief them on the council and its importance."

"Hum, well, this is all political in nature. The 66th layer, Ashina as we call our land, is ruled by the Seven Houses of Ashina, political houses, mind you. Every demester — twenty of your years — the Seven Houses holds a Council of Acquirement here on this planet — neutral territory, so to speak — to choose the next Supreme Lord of the Demester. The term of m'Doth expires in ten days; he has wisely chosen not to seek another term." Metrarch chucked as he recalled his conversation with m'Doth a month ago in which m'Doth told him flatly that he did not want to go up against Metrarch.

However, to Metrarch's chagrin, neither would m'Doth ally with him, preferring to be neutral this time.

Then, Metrarch's black eyes reddened noticeably and Jon saw his fists knot. He barked, "That cowardly m'Doth seized the throne from me last demester!" Obviously, time had not softened this blow and Dispater cleverly interjected giving Metrarch time to regain civility.

The Arch-devil explained, "You see Alison, when your father stole the Holy Scepter from the block of obsidian in the court of Metrarch, his force of rule was broken. In the chaos that surrounded the theft, m'Doth quickly seized his opportunity to unilaterally depose Metrarch and elect himself as next Supreme Lord of the Demester. It happened so fast that Metrarch was powerless to avoid the takeover. As you are aware, in the presence of the Holy Scepter of Ukko, no lie can be told. For an entire demester, Metrarch held power because of it. Its sudden theft created a vacuum in which m'Doth made his move to power. But such a move is not without consequences. Today, none of the other Lords will align with m'Doth so there is no way for him to get reelected to another demester." Then, he added if he was lecturing a class of new students, "Remember, there are always unforeseen consequences to actions. For every action there is a reaction."

The upset and pain Metrarch re-experienced had passed; Jon had noted his reactions and wondered. The Demon Lord resumed, "In ten days' time, the Council of Acquirement meets in the southern town called Freetown or Twin's Town as the locals have taken to calling it during the last dozen or so years. Here, each of the seven lords of Ashina will meet. Each lord is allowed to bring seven witnesses to the meeting. It is mostly a ceremonial meeting after which the Games begin. The purpose of this council is for each lord to declare openly their current allegiances — that is, who is going to back whom during the Games. The Games begin at dawn the next day."

Jon frowned and looked puzzled, he queried, "What exactly are these Games you are referring too and why meet here in this world?"

Grinning broadly and with glistening eyes, Metrarch said, "War Games. Each of the seven Lords has amassed an army of followers within the borders of their lands. The people of Ravenwash worship me. So my conquering army resides here in this area. Freetown lies centrally located; it is surrounded by the lands which worship the Seven Lords of Ashina. It is called Freetown because it belongs to none of us — rather like neutral ground, so to speak. Once the allegiances are sworn at the Council of Acquirement, we have until the dawn of the next day to make any last minute preparations. Then, the Games begin. The rules are simple. There are none. The winner is that army which takes possession of Center Well in Freetown and holds it for twenty-four hours. And the Lord behind that army becomes the new Supreme Lord of the Demester. And this time I intend to take back my throne!"

Alison could contain her revulsion no longer. She burst out, "So you mean that all these men get killed, wounded, or maimed just so one of you can be the leader? That is awful! So where do we fit in this horrid scheme? We are *not* going to fight for you, if that is what you had in mind."

Instead of an angry outburst, Metrarch laughed so heartily that a button popped off from his tunic! "No Miss Goodie Two Shoes, you don't fight for me. I only accept worshipers as fighters. No, your job is just to keep me alive during the Council of Acquirement meeting. You shall be four of my seven witnesses. You meet me as I arrive in Freetown and escort me to the meeting, guard me and bear witness during the meeting, and escort me back to the edge of town after the meeting is concluded. That is all."

In a hushed voice, he went on, "You see, my friend Dispater here has informed me of a plot to have me assassinated, most likely sometime while I am in Freetown. Outside of Freetown, I am heavily guarded by my worshipers. The only time that I am vulnerable is when I am in Freetown. No Lord is permitted more than seven witnesses once they enter the town. We suspect Lord Jared is behind the assassination plot. To the southwest of Freetown is a land that worships Morrigan, Goddess of War. And beyond that is the Barren Steppes, home to the assassins. El Hadid is the head of the largest and most powerful band of assassins that I know about!"

Metrarch cleared his throat and said very softly, "I don't know why I am telling you this, but I have made excellent use of El Hadid's services from time to time. He personally guarantees his contracts! But their services tend to be ungodly expensive." And he began laughing once again. "Me, I just send some demons after whom I wish undone! No need for all this sneaking around crap! After all, dead is dead, right Dispater?"

"Well," Dispater smiled cunningly, "I am not so sure about that!" And he chuckled to himself. Jon looked at him and wondered.

Metrarch smiled and nodded his head to himself, "So that about sums it up. Be my personal body guards or witnesses for the time that I am in Freetown and I give you your brother and his picture book."

Mandy had been totally quiet for a longer period of time that she had ever been. Finally, she could contain herself no longer. "So what happens if we fail and the assassin succeeds?"

After another bout of laughter, Metrarch pointed out, "If you agree, I give you your brother now. If you are not successful but have tried, so be it. To be honest about it, I don't ever recall El Hadid's assassins ever failing on a contract. You may all be killed in the process yourselves."

"You are not exactly being honest with them, Metrarch," interrupted Darless. "A Lord of the Abyss cannot be 'killed' while on another plane. Metrarch can only be killed while in the Abyss. If his body is 'killed' here in Freetown, he is transported back to the Abyss and cannot leave the Abyss for a lengthy period of time. So he has nothing to fear if the assassin is successful."

"Wrong, alu-demon! I cannot therefore lead my army to victory and claim the throne!" the demon lord corrected Darless. "Nothing shall stand in my way this time. I want my throne back!"

"Okay, Metrarch, I agree to your terms," Alison said. "When can I get my brother?"

Metrarch drew himself up to his full height and said as formally as he could muster, "With Dispater as my witness, you then agree to meet me ten days from now, at dawn, on the north road into Freetown, protect my life while I am in Freetown, and deliver me safely back to the north edge of Freetown when the meeting is finished?"

"I so do," declared Alison.

"Then, it is sealed. Zugblat! Zugblat!" bellowed Metrarch.

The side door opened and in scurried Zugblat. "Yes, master?"

"Fetch Lenny and his book now and give them to Alison," ordered Metrarch who seemed exceedingly pleased with the events. "And send Captain Rockhard in too." Turning to Alison, he explained, "Captain Rockhard will take you to the stables and get you outfitted for the journey to Freetown, and he will accompany you partway. He can fill you in on any necessary details. I will see you in ten days' time at dawn. Till then," and he bowed to Alison just as Rockhard entered.

"You will come with me please," Captain Rockhard ordered. Evidently, Rockhard already had his orders from Metrarch — the Demon Lord had been that certain that Alison would agree. The four bowed to Metrarch, nodded to Dispater and left the room following the Captain of the Guards.

Captain Rockhard, a tall, lean man in his mid-thirties, bore a deep scar across the left side of his weather-beaten, rough-shaven face. His coal black eyes mirrored his long, unkempt hair; his demeanor paralleled his appearance, no nonsense, serious, yet wild and untamed. Here was a man who was used to giving orders, fully expecting that they would be obeyed without question. He glanced back at the foursome only once to make sure that they were following him. "Stay close. These corridors are a maze and I do not have time to go searching for you. We have a war to fight very soon." Indeed the passage ways twisted and turned with many junctions. Jon knew that he would have to have a map to find his way around this place.

Unlike their previous midnight passage through these corridors, many people were coming and going and no one was "walking." Everyone seemed to have urgent business elsewhere and seemed annoyed when they had to make way for the party. Jon almost had to jog to keep up and was particularly glad to finally walk through an enormous set of gates and arrive in the courtyard of Ravenwash where he could finally get a good view of the castle and grounds. He looked up, eyes wide open, mouth gaping open in awe.

Captain Rockhard halted just outside the gates beside a donkey cart that other men were loading with some provisions.

"This is your transportation to Freetown. I'm sorry but this is all we can spare. Horses are vitally needed in the war effort. There are none to spare." One of the men loading the last of the water gourds onto the cart chuckled to himself. Mandy knew why immediately — a donkey cart was the lowest form of transportation imaginable. Under normal circumstances, this should be considered an insult to the foursome. The Captain then handed Alison a parchment scroll of safe passage through the lands of Ravenwash and gave her specific directions and instructions. He made her repeat these instructions back to him three times until he was convinced she had the orders straight. Mandy also paid close attention to the instructions. This man left nothing to chance. Certain that Alison knew precisely what she must do and when to do it, he visibly relaxed, "Now we wait for Zugblat."

Meanwhile, Jon was gaping at this spectacular castle built at the very end of a canyon. Behind him rose black and red streaked, sheer granite cliffs, towering some four hundred feet above them. A thirty foot tall, barrier wall formed a giant semicircle around this end of the canyon and the gigantic castle rose ever upwards four stories tall. Additionally, though Jon did not know it, immense underground caverns had been carved from the bedrock and were only accessible from secure locations within the basement of the castle. And thousands of ravens had their roosts high on the cliffs. High on top of the various battlements, red flags billowed in the gentle morning breeze, each with the crest of a black raven emblazoned on the red background.

Jon's enthusiasm and admiration for Ravenwash gushed forth in a volley of "Wow!'s" melting the seriousness from Captain Rockhard. He became quite friendly. "Indeed, Ravenwash has no equal anywhere it the world! It is the finest castle in all the lands! I'm proud to be the Captain of King John Ironwood's Castle Guards!" Darless had to agree that this was indeed a showcase castle. Mandy, who owned her own Castle Blackthorn, begrudgingly admitted that Ravenwash was an eye catcher, but added, "Too bad its occupants are all evil men!"

Alison was subdued; her castle was a ruins. Further, she was once again reminded of her tragic loss. So she steeled herself for Zugblat's arrival and her first meeting with any of her relatives in more than twenty years. She did not have long to wait.

"Ah, there you are! All ready for your donkey cart ride, I see," snickered Zugblat. Two men in robes, obviously priestly acolytes, carried her brother. Zugblat continued, handing her a book, "I present you with your picture book, though I do not see what you want with a silly book of pictures. Ah yes, put him in the cart. And here is your brother, or rather what is left of him!" Zugblat roared with snide laughter.

Covered only by a moth eaten, filthy blanket, Lennard d'Ambrose crouched with his knees drawn up to his face, clinging to that blanket for dear life. His eyes stared off into the void of space. Alison struggled to control her shaking hands as she lifted the blanket to see her long-lost, older brother. She said nothing; the shock was too great.

"Zagroot zounds!" exclaimed Mandy as she saw the pitiful creature that once was a human being. Lennard was indeed only a shell of a man. He now weighed only seventy pounds. Festering black spots covered his entire body, rather like leprosy. His teeth were blacked, cracked and rotting. Maggots or lice crawled through his long, filthy, unkempt shoulder length black hair. His beard had never been cut and looked as bad as his hair but with remains of food scattered and stuck in it. He was so weak that he could not move under his own power.

But the physical condition was not the worst of it. He was clearly totally insane. He kept slobbering and mumbling to himself. His words were unintelligible. And he continually rocked to and fro as he mumbled. "He only understands one word anymore," jeered Zugblat. "Mention 'food' and he responds." And Lennard did respond when he heard Zugblat say that word. He got on all fours and began panting like an expectant dog. An acolyte tossed him a moldy piece of bread which he gobbled at once and then resumed his sitting position, mumbling nonsense and rocking back and forth, staring at all and nothing. "Now be off with yea," ordered Zugblat. A broad smile indicated his utter contempt for them. "What fools they are!" he thought as he turned and reentered the doors.

Jon helped Alison into the cart and put his arm around her for support. Mandy took the driver's seat while Darless sat beside her holding the parchment passport. It was a very somber party that slowly rode down the road north toward the giant iron gates leading out of Ravenwash and onto the canyon road. No one said anything as they rode off in dismay. Great tears rolled down Alison's face. Her hands trembled as she tried to touch and comfort her brother while Jon held onto her. No one said a word until they were five miles down the canyon road which now turn in a wide arc toward the south.

"Well, I expected as much," Darless finally broke the silence. "Humans forced to stay in the Abyss do not do well. And he has been there twenty years against his will. It is amazing that he is still alive, actually. He must have a strong will to live."

"You, you expected this?" muttered Alison. "Why didn't you alert me?" Then, she immediately knew the answer to her own question. "I'm sorry Darless. He's — he's just in such a horrid, wretched state!" And her tears flowed so fiercely she could not speak any more.

"Well," Darless' logical mind began racing at top speed, "Number 1, we must at once get his body healed. Number 2, then we can concentrate on his mind. If his body fails him, then we can do nothing for his mind."

Although Jon was comforting Alison, instinctively Jon felt that there was something not quite correct with Darless' two points. But at the moment, he could not say what it was. He filed the observation in the back of his mind.

She went on, "So how do we heal his body? Number 3, he is really suffering from what you might call Abyss Poisoning." She then gave them a brief presentation on how human bodies reacted to the extended diets of food of the Abyss. "So, does anyone know how we can get his body headed up?"

"It's way beyond me!" uttered Mandy who turned and looked back at Jon.

Jon added, "Me too. I've no idea what I could do, but I am willing to try. But in his state, one wrong move could mean his death. Wait! I'll bet Lady Ursla would know or at least she could point us in the right direction."

After a brief discussion, all agreed. They would try the druid first. After a pause, Alison spoke with a firm resolve in her voice, "It's my responsibility; he's my brother. I will take him to Lady Ursla alone. You continue on to Freetown. I will rejoin you as soon as I can."

"But how can you?" pleaded Jon who did not want her to do this alone. It was a huge burden for anyone to bear all by themselves.

But a bit of Darless' cold logic seeped into Alison, stiffening her to what she must do. "I can easily use my teleport spell to get us two to Lady Ursla and I can teleport back as soon as possible. The only tricky thing is knowing where you all are at for the return trip. But I will work that one out somehow. You just keep on going toward Freetown. We don't want Metrarch getting upset because we all disappear on him, like I," she faltered and corrected herself, "we are not going to fulfill my bargin."

"Zagroot zounds!" Mandy interjected, "You know that we all are totally with you on this one! You can count on us! I'll just keep on going at this donkey pace and you catch up to us. Now go!"

"Absolutely!" exclaimed Darless.

Jon gave her a gentle kiss and whispered in her ear, "Remember, I love you!" She blushed, and a renewed hope began flowing through her, steeling her for the task at hand. This had been her darkest hour and her friends had backed her all the way. More tears flowed, but these were tears of joy and gratefulness.

"Thank you all!" she sniffed, wiped her eyes, and began to concentrate. Again, Jon heard a brief series of words he did not understand. In the next second, Alison and Lennard had vanished completely.

The somber trio traveled on down the winding canyon road heading for the main southerly road that would take them to Freetown or Twin's Town as it was now called by the locals. The trio said little fearing that Metrarch may still be monitoring their every move. The sun rose high and continued its daily ground baking. This was still a fairly arid region, though not quite a desert. The road paralleled a dry creek bed that drained the infrequent rains from the canyons behind them. Off on either side, preparations for war could be discerned. A cavalry unit practicing charges raised an ominous dust cloud to their right. Occasional clanking of sword upon sword or shield echoed in the stillness but the combatants could not be seen for the mostly treeless low hills blocked their view.

After an hour of pitifully slow travel, they reached the last sentry post. Six well-armed soldiers in clinking chain mail carefully checked their passport. "Probably take you a couple days to reach Twin's Town at your rate; tis sixty miles yet." He roared with laughter and the others joined readily.

Jon smiled back. "Yes," he chuckled with them, "This has got to be the slowest transport I have ever had the pleasure of riding. It does look very funny — a great big cart pulled by that small donkey! But it beats walking, you have to admit that." Amid their fun, the leader nodded his agreement with that last bit. They continued their slow journey with a "Giddy-Ap" from Mandy.

After another silent hour of travel in which Jon watched the country side slowly move by, he suddenly burst out, "I know. This reminds me of the scrub oak trees of the high plains in Colorado!" Both women jerked out of their reveries. "Yeah, those are oak trees. I'm not too sure that this is a high plains area, though. But what's a Colorado?" asked Mandy. Jon explained and tried to describe his favorite state in which he had taken several camping vacations with his Grandfather. No sooner than he had finished his explanation, than a body appeared a hundred feet in front of them floating about a hundred feet above the ground.

"Alison!" the trio cried in unison. They watched as she floated slowly to the ground. "How'd you do *that*?" cried Jon, eyes wide open.

"I, ah, I sensed your minds, and used that as an arrival point but aimed high and am using a Fly spell," she softly said trying to explain what she had done. It was totally different from any other time she had ever used her teleport spell. She often used the Fly spell but this sensing minds was a totally new thing to her and she decided to say no more about it just now. It was too confusing to her.

When they caught up to Alison's position, they stopped and got off the cart. Her eyes were red and her demeanor and pallid face said more than words to the trio. "Come here, honey," Jon said softly and literally pulled her into his comforting body. He felt her collapse and lean heavily on him. He knew she was utterly emotionally exhausted.

"Put her in the cart, Jon. I'll walk a while and lead the donkey," Mandy ordered.

"Are you all right, really?" asked Darless, dark lines on her face visibly showed her deep concern.

"Yes, just really, really tired." Jon laid her down gently in the cart. He and Darless walked on either side while Mandy lead the donkey. "Emotionally, not physically," Alison added. "I have never felt so drained, so utterly useless."

"Or filthy and dirt!" cried Mandy. "Where we've been and what we've done these last couple days — why, I feel so grimy I could scream! I still smell the Abyss in my nose!"

"What I would give for a *bath*!" laughed Darless. Tensions dissipated all around. Sometimes just stating the obvious relieves a harried mind.

"Is it safe to talk yet?" Alison queried. "I probably better tell you what happened while it is still fresh in my mind, and before I doze off." She yawned several times but felt substantially more alert.

"I don't think we have put sufficient distance between us," Darless stated flatly. "I trust a demon about as far as I can throw one, and that is not very far!"

"Okay. I'll be brief. You should have seen the look on Lady Ursla's face when she saw him. I cried uncontrollably. She believes that she can mend his body, given enough time. His mental state is quite another thing. She . . . she thinks he may never recover any sanity." She paused, fighting back tears, swallowed hard and continued. "Before I left, she said the price is 'Balance' though I have utterly no idea what she is asking of me, or us."

"What did she specifically say? Please be as precise as you can," said Darless in a serious tone of voice. She knew this was very important. Druids demand a service for a service. Certainly healing the shell of a man would be an enormous undertaking. So the alu-demon fully expected the price would be steep. But she did not say a word about that.

"She said 'It has come to my attention via the High Council of the Seven that the Balance is wildly awry in the lands where you are now traveling. For the High Council to act in this manner can only mean that there have been numerous complaints lodged by local Druids. Your task is to restore that

Balance.' I think I got it right. But I really do not know what she is asking of me or us." Alison sighed.

"Search me," said Jon.

"Why? Did you lose something?" queried Mandy.

Jon blushed, "No, it's a figure of speech in my world — means I don't have any idea whatsoever of what she is talking about."

"Well," began Darless, trying to think of a simple way to explain Druidic logic to her friends, "The Balance refers to the balance of Good versus Evil or to the balance of Nature. At this time, we do not know enough about this land to know of what Lady Ursla is talking. We will have to observe and learn first. But we best say no more for now." And she hastily looked all around, as if the black ravens flying overhead had ears.

Alison dozed while the others walked along the dusty trail. At least they were going slightly downhill. Ravenwash was at a fairly high elevation; Freetown was much lower. The sun arced high overhead and boiled one and all. Heat waves distorted the horizon giving the world about them a surrealistic appearance. Sweat and dust clung to their bodies. They ate little for lunch but drank a considerable portion of their water supply. Their silent journey led them through the ever changing hilly landscape. Occasional the trail swerved around large granite boulders but always returned to its due south path. They passed no one, saw no one, heard no one since before Alison had returned. And now it was getting dark. Still, they walked onwards.

For the last hour or so, Mandy kept a sharp eye out for a reasonable camping site, but thus far had found nothing that had even remotely suited her. She knew that they were out of Mansion Spells. At last Jon said the obvious, "Hey, I don't think I can walk much further. I am really pooped."

"I've been looking but so far I've not seen any place that I'd feel secure spending the night out here," Mandy replied downheartedly. "It's just too open — too exposed for my liking especially with the Balance thing supposedly being wildly out around here."

Just then, they heard a clanking sound. All froze instantly. "What's that?" Jon whispered. A rhythmic pattern of metal clanking on metal came from far off in the distance to their left. A faint odor of smoke drifted in the air as well.

Mandy replied frowning, trying to make sense of this circumstance. "It sounds like pounding — like a blacksmith. But there cannot be a blacksmith out here in the total wilderness!"

Darless added, "There are not supposed to be any towns or villages on our route according to the map and what we were told. We could not possibly have reached Twin's Town this soon. It is at least another full day's travel to the south."

"Well, we best go check it out," Mandy decided and led the donkey off the trail toward the sound. Up a hill and down again they went. The sounds increased in volume. It did sound like a hammer hitting an anvil, Jon thought to himself. The dusk was deepening when Mandy suddenly halted, putting a finger in front of her lips, motioning them to silence. "We are being watched," she whispered. "Over behind that big boulder."

Mandy was too tired to play games. "Okay. Come out whoever you are. Friend or foe, we are well armed," she commanded directing her words toward where she suspected the person was hiding.

To everyone's amazement, out stumped a short man, four feet tall, weighing about one hundred fifty pounds. His white beard was nearly a foot long. He was smoking a long stemmed pipe, blowing smoke rings, and looking thoroughly bored. "Nain Azanulbizar, renowned priest and fighter of Silverbeard himself, at your service." And he bowed low, beard nearly touching the ground. Even in the dim light, Jon could see that his face was weather-beaten and well lined. His large hands and muscular build suggested this short person wielded great strength. He wore a sky blue, short-sleeve, loose-fitting shirt and matching trousers. However, the pants showed signs of long wearing, a bit thread bare at the knees. A wide red sash served as a belt. Nain carried no visible weapon.

"I'm Mandy Blackthorn, Ranger of Reylona, at your service," she bowed similarly. "And you are a mountain dwarf, if my eyes do not deceive me." She had added this observation mostly for Jon's sake.

After another puff and while blowing the smoke out, he dryly stated, "Yep, you look like a ranger and act like a ranger, but in these times and places, you will kindly show me your holy symbol, please or permit me my detection spell."

Mandy thought to Jon, *Dwarves are usually friendly, if you don't cross them. Priests can cast a spell that shows him whether we are basically good or evil in nature.*

The ranger moved a bit of cloth to uncover a small golden pin displaying a lady with a bow kneeling beside a doe. Jon had always thought this was just one of Mandy's brooches. But now he realized it was much more than a piece of jewelry.

Nain bowed low once more. "Greetings Ranger of Reylona. A far distance from your forests. But then I am a far distance from my mines as well. And who are these others? And why do you use a donkey cart for travel? Now that is most curious indeed. A donkey cart, of all things."

Mandy did the introductions. "This is Saint Jon Brown and mages Alison d'Ambrose and Darless. It is a long tale and we are tired, dirty and hungry. We were just looking for a suitable camping place when we heard the pounding and came to investigate."

"Ah this way, been expecting you for over an hour now. My sentry spotted you on the road some time ago. Yes, this land does not offer much for camping. I myself, of course, prefer good solid bedrock under my back. I'm, er, doing some mining in the area. Come on this way into the safety of the mine and forge. I'm sure I can provide for your needs, but I require a payment, though I personally do not need money. That payment is a tale. You must tell us all about yourselves and what you are doing out here. We seldom have much human contact, through no fault of dwarves, you see. Humans just do not like to live underground I have observed."

After walking a short distance around the boulder, the dark entrance of a cave or mine could be seen. Another dwarf came strolling out of the entrance; he carried a small lantern. "Ah, they have arrived," he commented. "Hail and well met! Draston Silverthrow, priest of Silverbeard, at your service." He was slightly taller, less muscular, and definitely younger than Nain, but a mountain dwarf nevertheless. He wore matching shirt and pants as well but these were green with a similar red sash. Another round of introductions was made. The dwarves were definitely pleased to have guests in their mine. As they passed into the wide entrance, cart and all, Jon noticed a number of stone blocks off to the side.

"Ah, you have a keen eye there, Mr. Brown," Nain commented, "Yes, if we are threatened, then it takes less than a minute to seal the entrance, that is with all of us pitching in." Jon did not like the image of being trapped inside of a dark mine shaft, though.

Once inside, Jon marveled at the workmanship. The tunnels, though he had to bend over to walk down them, were precisely cut, unlike any mine of which he had ever seen pictures. The pounding noise which had steadily grown louder, now ceased altogether. As they rounded a bend, the tunnel opened up into a spacious foundry area, a blast furnace centrally located cast its reddish glow filling the twenty-five foot square room. "Permit me to introduce another of my assistants. This is Rastinion Rastinorf, also a priest but also a master locksmith. Watch your pockets, though." And Nain laughed heartily. Rastinion bowed low, "At your service."

This dwarf was definitely different. Though just over four feet tall, he did not have that hearty robust build of Nain or Draston. His legs were longer and his beard very short. He also wore matching shirt and pants, but these were brown; a wide red sash served as a belt. Nain spotted Jon comparing Rastinion to Draston and commented, "Hill dwarf. Cousins to mountain dwarves, but they prefer to live out in the open spaces." And yet another round of introductions was made.

"What's all the commotion?" came a voice coming up from a side tunnel off of this main foundry area. "Ah, guests! Sam Sleepstick, Illusionist Extraodinaire, your servant." And he nodded his head. Sam was entirely different, standing only three and a half feet tall and weighing only seventy pounds. He wore a pointy hat with stars dotting it at random positions. He wore a similar red sash, but his shirt was silvery in color that shimmered in the light. His pants were black.

Nain replied, "Ah, yes, and here is our trusty gnome." Another round of introductions was performed. It has been said that dwarves and gnomes revel in introductions. Jon would hereafter always concur with that observation.

After the introductions were finished, Nain ordered, "Sam, you show our guests the latrine and the wash buckets. I am sure they wish to clean up a bit after a day in the sun out there. Draston, rustle up dinner, if you please. Rastinion, how goes the rough shaping?" Nain turned his attention to something in the forge, evidently what was being forged with the pounding noise.

"This way," directed Sam. The wash buckets and latrine were in a small side tunnel, two oil lanterns provided the dim illumination. Then, the gnome blushed, "Er, forgive us, but there is not much call for privacy out here. In fact, you are the first visitors Nain has let inside."

"Don't worry," Mandy said with a big grin, "We won't bite as long as you don't peek!" Then, to the others, "Come on, I for one intend to clean up as much as possible!" Since there were four wash buckets, none needed a second order. However, the latrine, a deep pit carved in the rock floor with a raised rim about a foot above the ground was obviously designed with men in mind.

A few minutes later, the four emerged from the side tunnel to find that a table had been set with the aroma of a home-cooked meal filling the air. Their stomachs growled after the long day's travels. After everyone had taken a place, with Nain at the head of the table, the dwarf tapped his spoon on the side of his ornate cup, calling everyone to attention. "We give thanks to Draston for preparing tonight's feast. Let us take a moment of thankful prayer, each in our own manner." There was indeed a moment of complete silence, save for the dull roar of the forge which burned night and day. The silence felt a bit awkward to Jon who never prayed before meals. Nain broke the silence, "Okay. Now on with the feast and into the tales! What have we tonight, Draston?"

"I call it rabbit-deer stew," came the reply. Whatever it was, Jon thought it was superb and ate two helpings. The mead may have helped his opinion. Nain, it might be noted, had four helpings. When all had eaten their fill, Nain commanded, "Okay, Sam, do your thing."

The short gnome climbed onto his chair so he could see the entire table top and muttered a few words which Jon immediately recognized as similar to the magical chants of Alison and Darless. All of a sudden, two wash buckets floated out of the wash-up tunnel. Then, one by one, each dirty dish rose, floated over to the first bucket, immersed itself in the bucket, rose out of it sparkling clean, dropped into the second bucket for a final rinse, and then neatly stacked itself against the far wall of the room. Sam was immensely proud of his cleaning spell, it showed on his beaming face. Jon was very impressed and told Sam so, who smiled even more broadly; the gnome gave a curt nod to Nain, as if saying "See I told you so!"

And then it was tale time. Jon was soon to discover that dwarves love tales and will listen for hours at a time. Mandy tried to keep the tale simple, revealing as little as possible, but that resistance soon gave way. As soon as the Abyss was mentioned, there was no stopping the dwarves. Nain insisted on having the whole tale from the very beginning with the destruction of the d'Ambrose castle so many years ago. It didn't help that Nain made sure their mead cups were continually full either. Though Jon had no watch on, at least a couple hours had passed with their tale. Many times, Jon saw that Nain was deeply pondering many aspects of their story.

Nain seemed deeply disturbed about the method of destruction of the d'Ambrose castle and had Alison describe it three times. After hearing it for the third time, Nain declared, "I will have to research that. I will get back to you at a later time. Most interesting indeed. Please continue with your tale." Little did Jon know just how significant this promise would be.

Finally, it was the dwarves' turn. Nain clapped his hands twice and the other two dwarves hustled into a side tunnel, returning with their musical instruments, the likes of which Jon had never seen. Jon spent the rest of the evening sitting in front of Draston and Rastinion watching them play. Draston played a stringed instrument which he called a zumbar. It somewhat resembled an eastern sitar. It had ten strings and resonated exceedingly well. Rastinion played rhythmic patterns on a drum with a flared neck which he called a zumbak. Jon thought that the drum resembled a dumbek. Depending upon where on the skin it was tapped, either a low bass note echoed in the chamber or a high metallic sound bounced off the rock walls and anything in between. Both dwarves were master musicians and their instruments were made to be a matched set in tone quality — that is, made to be played together. The music was unlike any that Jon had ever heard before, but he did recognize that they played in the Dorian mode entirely. Jon thought that the sound quality resembled that of a Palestrina Ricercare he once had heard on a recording at Smith Music Hall in Urbana.

With the mood set and the two playing in the background, Nain began his tale of the mighty deeds he had accomplished, of his enormous mines and subsequent fabulous wealth, of his great skill at the forge and of enchantments of magical armor and weapons. Neither Jon nor the ladies had any idea of whether or not any of this was true, but Jon fell in love with the music.

When Nain finished his tale, Jon asked if he could play along with them. Draston insisted that Jon join in and soon, Jon's flute intertwined with the zumbar and zumbak. When the three finally stopped playing, they discovered that everyone else had fallen asleep. The mead and mood had had its effect. Yet, the musicians were totally awake and full of excitement. Draston motioned them to follow him. They went to the tunnel entrance and continued their discussion music for some time, avoiding waking the others in the process. "Just don't get close to the tunnel entrance or you will set off Nain's alarm system," warned Draston. It was nearly one o'clock in the morning before, the three musicians decided to call it a night and headed back into the main room.

Jon made sure each of the girls was well covered with blankets before he himself yawned and laid down on the rock floor. Sleep came quickly but not before he decided what would be his life's work.

Loud rhythmic clanking woke the party at dawn, though here in the mine, dawn was only dim at best. Nain was hard at work at the anvil. The table was set, this time in a self-service mode. Evidently, breakfast consisted of leftovers and whatever you chose to eat. But the party arose stiff and sore from sleeping on the rock floor.

"Man, I didn't know I had so many bones in my body and every one hurts!" exclaimed Jon. He stretched and winced. The ladies were equally moaning but also rubbing their headaches, for they had drunk too much mead the night before.

"Ohhh, that pounding!" muttered Mandy. However, curiosity overcame here stiffness. She moved closer to Nain to see what he was forging. Weapons were her stock and trade. "A broadsword to be?" she inquired curiously.

Nain beamed, "Ah, you recognize it already. You have a keen eye, ranger. Yes, I am forging a highly enchantable broadsword for an elven friend of mine." Their discussion of weapon construction left Jon bored so he returned to the table to eat with the others. Neither Alison nor Darless had any interest in swords. But both women were grateful that Mandy had gotten the infernal pounding noise stopped. A little while later, a very excited Mandy called out from a side chamber, "Hey come over here and have a look at this!"

Nain proudly displayed one of his more recent completed works, a highly ornate broadsword with a huge red ruby in its pummel. Intricate scroll work of intertwined vines ran the length of the blade. It was the prettiest sword that Jon had ever seen.

"He definitely **is** a master craftsman," declared Mandy, awe in her eyes.

"I did say that I was," dryly responded Nain.

"Do you take commissions to make a blade for a person? If you do, I would love to purchase one!" Mandy could not help restraining her enthusiasm.

"I only make weapons for friends or if the commission request is for a blade that is truly worthy of my talents." Nain was not modest.

"Well, I would dearly love to have a very special bastard sword built just for me and my size and skill, one that would give me a stronger edge against heavyset male fighters. That is my weakness; I lose ground in such fights because I have not their strength."

"Hum. A unique bastard sword. I would not have thought so lovely a woman would wield such a power blade," commented Nain, a bit surprised. "I would have predicted a short sword for the females of your species."

"I'll show you my small collection. I grew up wielding bastard swords!" Quickly Mandy retrieved her portable hole from inside her bra and unfolded it and began rummaging around inside. "Here they are. All are magical. This one is enchanted against demons. This one has a magical bonus to combat." Mandy and Nain examined each of her three bastard swords in detail. The others wandered off to the mine's entrance to smell the fresh new day.

"Hum," muttered Nain to Mandy, "Let's duel a round and let me see your style and technique. You say you have trouble with heavier men. I think I can muster something like that." Soon Mandy and Nain began a training round of combat with two of the bastard swords. Immediately, Draston, Rastinion and Sam came to watch their leader. Indeed, Nain's style of combat was heavy thrusts and hacks. *Predictable strong man tactics*, thought Mandy. However, her style illustrated the use speed to deflect power thrusts and gain her position for her swings. Before long, both had worked up a good sweat.

"Yes, I see the problem indeed. Your blade is just a trifle too heavy for your body build. Yes. But we don't want to compromise the length for that is the advantage of the bastard sword. Let me see your two-handed grip. Ah yes, see, your hands are smaller. We could rework the balance point which should yield greater speed." Nain became engrossed in bastard sword designs. "If I use my special alloy — that would lighten the blade while giving it an even greater than normal strength." A few minutes later, the dwarf proclaimed, "Yes, I shall make you a special bastard sword, the only one of its kind in existence!" Mandy was elated and left him a rather large pile of gold coins as a partial payment.

A short while later, the party said their farewells to their new dwarven friends. Each insisted on shaking everyone else's hands, so it took some time. When Nain came to Jon, he lowered his voice so only Jon could hear him, "Jon, may I have a private word with you? Bring your walking stick." Jon obeyed and the two walked back inside the mine to a side tunnel where no one could overhear them.

Nain mysteriously said, "May I examine your walking stick?"

"Sure," Jon replied, "though it is just a handy walking stick I found back at Alison's place."

Nain closely examined every inch of the stick, muttering to himself all the while. At last, he spoke, "Jon, this walking stick cannot be what it appears to be. And yet, it appears to be so. It has the aura of powerful magic about it, though it hides itself well, or my name is not Nain Azanulbizar! Were it in my possession, I would place it upon my holy altar and pray night and day continuously until Silverbeard himself chose to reveal unto me the nature of this walking stick. I know not how you communicate to your god, but if I were you, I would attempt to find out what your stick actually is. Ponder my words, boy, no ordinary piece of wood would have behaved as this one has from your tale last night."

Mystified, though not totally surprised, Jon replied, "It certainly has acted in unusual ways, almost as if it has a mind or beingness of its own. Sometimes I imagine that it talks to me. Imagine that, a talking walking stick!" And Jon chuckled in disbelief.

"Nay, do not laugh, my boy," scolded Nain. "Some of the very greatest weapon smiths and mages have created blades that are alive or rather animated by a beingness or spirit or soul. These are very rare of course. I've never seen one of these personally, but I do know of their existence."

"What do you suggest I do with it?" inquired Jon. "In spite of my title given to me by Ukko, Saint Jon, I do not worship any god. I do not have any altar."

"Hum," Nain pondered this for a minute before replying. "Well, then, you might try communicating with it sometime when you are alone and cannot be overheard. Maybe it will choose to explain itself to you."

"Thanks, I'll give it a try. I guess I'd best be going or this will attract the other's attention." Jon shook his hand once again. "Thanks." He and Nain joked about trivial matters as they rejoined the others. The girls did give Jon a curious glance as if to say "What was that all about?" Jon ignored them and finished saying his farewells. And soon the foursome was back on the road, continuing their northward journey in silence.

Mandy led the way as usual, but her spirits were higher than Jon could have ever imagined. All chose to walk for some time, relieving the stiff muscles. Jon assumed that without the mead the night before, none of them would have been able to sleep on that rock floor.

The only words spoken the rest of the morning were those of Darless. "I think that we should remain silent until we are safely in our rooms at the inn in Twin's Town. Only then do I think that we will be safe from prying ears." The others nodded their agreement, choosing instead to ponder all of their own unanswered questions that had been piled one on top of the other since freeing the imprisoned Air Maiden. Jon watched the country side slowly move by and wondered about music and its effect on life.

Chapter 8 Twin's Town

Slowly the dry rolling hills passed. Several times, far off in the distance Jon swore he could see herds of sheep or perhaps cattle. Occasionally, smoke from chimneys rose drifting to the west in light breeze; farmer's cottages, Jon assumed. By midafternoon of the third day, small homesteads dotted the countryside which now had become somewhat greener and more supportive of life. Twice, they had to halt waiting for a shepherd to usher his flock across the road. They met several travelers in wagons heading north past them. However, the foursome were becoming rather irritable and impatient as the relentless heat continued to bare down on them. Finally, around late afternoon, as they crested another low hill, a mile ahead rose the town, sprawling like an octopus, Twin's Town at long last. They had made very good time.

The town was straddling the Grande, a shallow, yet wide, river whose flow had nearly dried up during the summer months. Snaking from far off to the mountains to the east, it passed to the west and off out of sight. But it was not the river that held Jon's attention, it was the town. Twin's Town was the largest city he had seen in all of his travels, home to perhaps ten thousand people. Though Jon did not know it, Freetown was the largest city for at least five hundred miles in all directions.

It was a sprawling type of city, one that had grown sporadically and in all directions, seemingly at random. The street pattern, as could be partially discerned even from this distance from here atop the northern rim, was random. To Jon, who was used to nicely laid out parallel streets, this seemed particularly confusing. "However does one find one's way around such a city?" he exclaimed, breaking the day long silence.

"With a map," replied Alison rather in disbelief. "Don't they have city maps in your world?"

Blushing, Jon said, "Er, yes. Guess our first order of business is to get us some maps."

"I suggest we find the inn first and get rid of this donkey cart!" Mandy spoke in her take charge tone. "Then, we can explore a bit. This is a large city. Jon, you should find lots of interesting things to see, if I am not mistaken. You can probably get anything you want in a town this size."

By the time they reached the outskirts of the town, people, carts, wagons, riders, and dogs filled the streets. It was near quitting time and folks were heading home or to their local pubs. The narrow streets rapidly filled with people. Jon tried not to stare.

Most buildings were adobe or red brick, the color of the ground. Wood was relatively scarce here. There seemed to Jon's eyes to be several distinct patterns of construction. Most single level buildings were adobe and butted against each other in seemingly random patterns. Scattered between them were two story brick buildings, evidentially housing more wealthy enterprises. At the edge of town, crudely built shanties snuggled up to the adobe homes, but as they got further into the city, the shanties dwindled. The road they were on widened and was now paved in the same red brick of the larger buildings. Evidently, this was one of the main arteries.

The people looked just like people, Jon mused. Cotton or wool shirts, usually of an earthy color predominated, fashioned much like those he had seen at Old English Fairs he had visited back home. Shirts were a simple t-box affair, easy to cut and sew. Pants varied from cotton to leather or deerskin. However, nearly everyone had one or more small leather pouches dangling from cord-like belts. Occasionally, a well-dressed man or woman jostled through the throng of people. "People are people," Jon thought to himself.

Then, store fronts grabbed his attention: Able's Monument, Billy's Smithy, Pete's Tankard, Holly's Homespun, Toot'n Hoot. This last shop attracted his full attention; it was a musician's shop. "Hey, I gotta visit this place. Help me remember where it is, will you?" Jon begged to no one in particular.

"Wow," exclaimed Mandy as she pointed to Sally's Bathhouse, "there is the first order of business once we get our rooms! My treat! A real bath house! You are all in for a royal time." The girls let out a whoop; Jon smiled but did not realize the significance.

Soon they reached the center of town which was a huge open area, octagonal in shape with a ten foot in diameter, rock-walled well right in the middle. "Not much farther," pronounced Mandy, confident of her directions she had memorized along with Alison.

As they passed the well, all four noticed a large bulletin board looking strangely out of place right here in the middle of the octagonal central plaza. It had a sign printed nicely across the top: "Place Requests To The Twins Here." None of the four had any idea what that was. Then, up ahead on the right rose a huge brick building, occupying nearly a city block in size, but not shape, the Grande Inn, their destination. "I'll get us rooms," Alison announced, "Mandy you take care of this cart. Come on, Darless, let's see what it is like inside. It's big. So maybe we can stay in style for a change." Darless and Jon followed close on her heels.

A doorman opened the door for them. "G-day. Enjoy your stay," he drawled rather robotically for the hundredth time that day. "Thanks," Jon muttered as he entered a long dimly light hallway carpeted in red. Jon followed Alison as she strode up to a large desk tended by an elderly woman, conservatively dressed in a brown dress.

From this hallway, other corridors led in all directions. Most people, Jon observed headed to the left or right. Odors of hot food drifted from the right, so he assumed that was the dining area. "Probably a pub to the left," he concluded.

In a few minutes, Alison returned with a ten year old girl also dressed in a conservative brown dress. Alison's eyes were bright; she was smiling broadly. "This is my kind of place! Okay. I have got us three connecting rooms in a suite. That is, all three rooms open into a central area. Just perfect!" Alison began. But before she could say more, Mandy entered, eyes wide, looking about. "Over here," Alison added. "Okay, Susie, lead on. We are all here." Susie nodded politely and led them deeper into the building, then up a set of stairs.

"This is your suite, Number 14. Will that be all?" she asked in a quiet, small voice.

"Yes, thanks," Alison replied, placing a coin in her hand. "Follow me," she cheerfully said and all four entered the luxury suite. They entered into a kind of central living room, with several couches and a table and four chairs centrally located. Oil lanterns adorned the walls and a large wagon wheel hung from the ceiling, six lanterns hung from it. Along the left wall, four doors were ajar. Each would have their own sleeping quarters.

Mandy, of course, immediately checked on the sleeping rooms. "These are well designed. Look here. See they have lots of very tiny windows. Security windows. They are too small for people to enter and rob you while you sleep. Yet, they allow air and light to enter. Well-designed indeed. Looks like our rooms are at the back of the inn. You chose well, Alison." The mage smiled, pleased that Mandy approved.

Darless, who had hardly spoken a word, now broke the silence. "Okay. Let's go get that bath and then something to eat. But first, Alison, can, can I have a private word with you?" Seeing the looks the others immediately gave her, she added quickly, "A girl thing, Jon."

Within a few minutes, the foursome left the inn behind them, heading back toward the bath house. Mandy cautioned Jon, "Jon, we are in a big city. It is likely full of pick-pockets, thieves. So watch yourself, particularly if someone bumps into you. Stay close so we don't get separated in this evening rush hour." Jon looked a bit perplexed, thieves were the last thing on his mind. He was fascinated with the city.

Soon they arrived at the bathhouse. There was only a short line waiting to enter. As they stood impatiently waiting, Mandy proclaimed, "This is *my* treat gang. Whoo hooo. Boy this is going to be great!" Jon looked totally perplexed. "Haven't you been in a bathhouse?" she asked.

"Er, no. I assume we are going to take a bath here," Jon mumbled, his face reddened in his embarrassment.

"Don't you have bathhouses where you come from?" Mandy inquired. "How ever do you get a bath?"

"Each house has at least one bathroom, sometimes two," he replied. Now it was the girls' turn to gasp in amazement, nearly unable to comprehend such wealth that must surely accompany such a thing.

When it was their turn, Mandy made the arrangements and then led them down a long hallway, steam dripping from the brick walls. "I got us the royal bath room! No common bath for us!" she proclaimed. Seeing that Jon had no idea what she was talking about, she explained as they walked. "The common room is usually a huge pool of heated water in which about twenty people can bathe at the same time. For a much higher price, you can get the royal rooms. These are much smaller, more intimate!" and she winked at all of the others, a twinkle in her eye. "Number 6. Ah, here we are. Follow me."

They entered a dimly lighted, nearly bare, brick walled room. Steam rose from the ten foot square recessed pool. Steps led gradually into the pool which was about three feet deep. Red glass lanterns lined the walls providing the only illumination. Jon stood and stared, trying to grasp the situation. The girls began to take off their things as the door opened and a matronly, large breasted, plump woman entered with an armload of towels and several bottles. Jon watched as she poured the contents of one bottle into the pool. Soon a fragrance of lavender filled the room. And just as quickly as she entered, the woman left.

Jon watched as the girls eagerly began disrobing. His face flushed once more. Then, Mandy noticed it. "Look at Jon!" she teased. "Bet you never been in a bath with three gorgeous women before, now have you! Watch out girls, man in the room!" she giggled.

"Sometimes you go too far, Mandy," Alison replied. "You are embarrassing Jon something terrible." Then, turning to Jon, she said quietly, "Come on, join us. It is not as bad as it seems. You can see all of us and we can see all of you. We promise to keep our hands to ourselves." However, her attempt to help him had the opposite effect and he became even more flustered but began undressing anyway.

Eagerly, the women plunged into the slightly scented bath and Jon hesitatingly followed. The bath was designed so that you could sit on the steps and yet still be in the water. The rush of warm water felt soothing, refreshing. Jon's embarrassment soon evaporated. Within a few minutes, each was washing another's backs and chatting. Jon felt the dirt and filth of the last few days drain from him; he relaxed totally for the first time in days — the girls, even more so, particularly Darless.

All three women took turns washing each other's hair. That this was a luxury they seldom had quickly became clear to Jon who merely watched in fascination. Alison and Darless took the longest time to do because of their long hair length.

While they were drying off, Mandy, whose shoulder length hair was the shortest of the three, shook her head sending drops flying in all directions. She was used to quick baths. "Okay, I'll take Jon shopping now. You two finish up here and then do your shopping. Let's meet for supper say in around two hours. How's that sound?"

"Sounds fine to me," replied Alison. "My hair takes some time to dry and de-tangle. We'll meet you back in the rooms. I need to get some new clothes to replace the ones that got destroyed during the demons' attack."

It was near sunset as Jon and Mandy approached the shop that Jon insisted on visiting. The neatly painted sign swinging in the early evening breeze read "Tom's Musike Shoppe — Toot'n Hoot." "This is it," exclaimed Jon, eyes bright with excitement. Mandy nodded, her eyes glancing about as Jon opened the door to enter. She was ever on alert; her instincts told here that this town might be a bit on the roughish side. Inside the twenty foot square room, Jon became even more animated. Instruments of all shapes and sizes were arrayed on tables, hanging from the walls, and on shelves. Dozens of lamp-blackened lanterns provided the indoor lighting.

"Can I help you," drolled a tired, greying man in his fifties. His eyes were bright and black, but his worn, home patched clothes spoke of a man more interested in other things. "Anything in particular? I'm about to close but, if you are really interested in something, why dinner can wait, though the misses will not be pleased. You a musician?"

"Wow, you sure do have a lot of really interesting instruments! Yes, I am a flutist. I'm just looking at the moment, but before I leave in a few days, I want to purchase a varied number of instruments. I just don't know which yet. But certainly the best quality and playability ones," replied Jon eagerly. "Er, you don't mind if we look around for a few minutes. I can come back tomorrow and play on some, if you don't mind."

"Name's Tom, young man," and he offered Jon his hand, his eyes shining not only at the prospect of a big sale, but also at meeting another musician. Jon shook his hand heartily.

"I'm John Brown and this is my friend, Mandy. We are from out of town, just visiting a few days, Jon replied. "Say, are there any concerts coming up soon?" And their conversation continued at length. Mandy felt rather ill at ease. She did not really like being indoors much, let alone a store in which everything was totally foreign to her nature, instruments. But, she contented herself watching Jon, she had never seen him this excited, this animated. She found herself fascinated with him. He was like a kid in a toy shop.

After about a half an hour, Tom begrudgingly said, "I'd best be closing now. The streets are not too safe after dark and it gets dark around here mighty quick when the sun goes down. Desert you know. Say, if you be out of towners, you best be extra careful if you are out at night. Thieves and ruffians. If you get into any trouble, why just post a note on the bulletin board by the well just down there. The Twins may be able to help you out."

"I thought so!" declared Mandy with a vengeance, her suspicions now confirmed.

"Are you going to be safe going home?" inquired Jon, suddenly feeling like a heel for having kept Tom here so late and it was getting dark outside. "We can walk you home, if it is not too far?" Then, to Mandy, he thought, *I assume that we can do that without getting lost ourselves. That okay?*

Sure. Find out what this Twins thing is if you can, thought Mandy back to Jon.

"Well, thank you! I only live a couple blocks from here. Misses would be pleased to know I had companions heading home." Tom smiled in obvious relief, anxiety melted from his face.

After he shut and locked the store, Jon inquired as they began walking, "What's the Twins? Who are they?"

"No one has seen them, er rather their faces. They always dress in black from head to toe. No one knows where they come from; they just appeared many years ago. Saviors in black, we call them. This town's always been full of ruffians and thieves as long as I can remember. Since the Twins arrived, things have changed for the better. Couple years ago, a local gang broke into my store and robbed me of my week's sales. I posted a note on the bulletin board, just like the Misses said I should. Why, that very night, the two black Twins visited our home. The tall one asked us all about it. Then, the next morning, why, my gold sack was sitting right there on my doorstep. Since then, the gang has left my store completely alone! Now isn't that something! Why, the Twins must have taken the entire gang on to get my money back for me! Amazing indeed."

"Wow! That's pretty terrific of them. But didn't you get to thank them?" Jon inquired, completely impressed with Tom's tale.

"Nope, just posted a thank you note on the board is all. No one has ever seen their faces. Like shadows in the night. No one knows where they live or who they are. They only come out at night, like phantoms. Some call them the Shadow Phantoms. Some call them the Black Avengers. They sure have given some of us in this town hope for a better future, that's for sure. But now that the demons are coming, everyone's in an agitated state. What can two do against a horde of demons and the like? The last time they came here, why it must have been more than twenty years ago, they plumb near tore up the town. Took years to rebuild all that got destroyed in a couple days. Misses says we should hide low til they leave. She's probably right. Ah, here's my house. Thanks for seeing me home. Come by tomorrow and look and try out anything you want."

Jon and Mandy shook his hand in farewell and somberly retraced their steps to the main street. When they were safely back on the known street heading towards the inn, Jon muttered, "Well, at least the town knows the demons are coming. But these twins are intriguing indeed. We should try to find out more about them."

"Hum, you are right. It would seem we are right in the middle of something really big and do not know all of the players or the rules of the game! I feel a bit lost, a bit confused to say the least. I wonder if Alison and Darless are back yet. It may not be too safe on these streets. We are being tailed by at least three shadows. Don't look around, though. Keep on walking," Mandy whispered to Jon.

When they reached the central well, they could not help but notice that a pair of lanterns lighted the bulletin board. A couple new messages were posted. Mandy was curious and stopped to read them. "It's just as Tom said, a couple reported thefts with a plea for assistance. Who are these Twins anyway?

The town must be named after them, that at least makes sense now."

Then the inn appeared, brilliantly lighted from many lanterns. Well-dressed people were entering, and a few who had obviously just finished dinner were leaving. It felt warm and welcome compared to their walk down the street, now so menacing at night. They quickly entered and went to their rooms. Darless and Alison were already waiting on them but only for a few minutes.

After Jon and Mandy left the bath house, the two women finished drying their hair somewhat and then left themselves. "As I whispered to you earlier," began Darless as they walked down the street, "from now on, I am no longer going to dress so provocatively. But I really need your assistance in finding the right outfits. You have such excellent taste and style, Alison."

Alison beamed, "Well, you are the first to tell me this!" and they both giggled. "Probably because as a child I lost everything. I decided long ago that only the best will do for me. Kind of making up for my screwed up childhood, I expect. What are your favorite colors? What looks good on you? We need to compliment your eyes and hair if we can, don't you think?"

"I suppose so, I just never thought about it, you know? I am completely ignorant of these things. I just always got the gauziest type, see though clothes that I could find. I'm kind of excited about this," she giggled. "Here we are." They stood before a well-kept store front. Well made, expensive dresses and gowns lined the glass windows. The sign read May's Dress Shoppe. They entered. The strong odor of cotton, linen, and wool overwhelmed their senses. The floor was carpeted in a plush, soft red carpet, though a wooden path led from the door to the main service counter twenty feet back. This main show room was about thirty feet square. Dress forms were everywhere displaying formal ball gowns to everyday wear. The side walls brimmed with cloth of all textures and types and colors.

"May I help you?" inquired a young woman in her late twenties. She wore an expensive, though conservative dress trimmed with white rabbit fur. Her long black hair was pinned up in a bun; numerous pins and needles protruded. She evidently preferred to have her tools within easy reach.

"Yes, I hope so. I'm Alison and this is Darless. We are new in town and well, most of Darless' clothing, er, did not arrive with us. So we need to purchase a number of outfits. Only the best quality, of course," Alison began, easing the way for Darless.

Both of the women felt the probe of the proprietress' eyes. Alison had spoken mostly the truth; it always bothered her when she did not speak totally truthfully. Some of Darless' attitudes were evidently rubbing off on her. But it wasn't every day that an alu-demon wandered into a dress shop in search of clothes.

"I see. Well, you certainly came to the right place. I offer only the best in my shop. My sewing ladies always do excellent work. Now first, let's see your size and what we might have already made that may suit you. Of course, if we do not have it in stock, we can make it for you in a few days' time. I'm assuming that you will be here in Freetown for some time?" The last was more like prying than a question. There was a hint of probing in her voice. She pulled a measuring tape from her waist band and began taking Darless' measurements.

"We plan to be here at least ten days," Alison replied. "I take it you are May?"

Darless blushed as May systematically measured her top to bottom. Never in her life had she been so serviced. She could not figure out why she felt so shy about such a simple thing. She was very glad that she had confided in Alison and sought her aid. On her own, she might have backed out.

"Yes, May. I see. Should be enough time to make some to fit, though events may dictate otherwise. Hum, and do you want those wings tucked into the back of the dress or outside? If they are to be outside, then I'm sure we will have to make extensive alteration, probably a couple days."

Darless' face turned crimson, though May who was sill busy with her measuring did not see her face. Alison did and was caught totally off guard. *I thought no one could see them!* Alison mentally tried to send to Darless using her newfound and untrained mental abilities so recently awoken. Her thoughts came through to Darless rather like a scream, so loud was Alison's intention.

I was hiding them. I've no idea how she can see them! Darless was shocked, taken totally off guard at this unexpected turn of events. She tried to speak but only a squeak came out. She cleared her throat. "Well, I'd like some in and some out. They aren't used for flying, you know," she managed to say somehow.

Thankfully for both girls, May gave no sign of noticing their total lack of composure. She went right on measuring Darless. "Can you hold your hair up so I can get a good bust measurement? Ah, thank you. Hum. Well endowed," May muttered. Alison noticed a touch of envy in her tone; May, like Alison, had an average size, while Darless was noticeably larger, which she had previously always used to her advantage.

Fortunately, the awkward moment passed as rapidly as it had come. May declared, "Well, Darless, you take about a size 10-D on my measuring system. The ready-made outfits in that range are over here. Follow me. Do you have any preference for color schemes or materials or styles?"

Both girls relaxed as they followed May to the back left corner. The plush carpeting felt soothing to their feet, adding to the ambiance. "We want to compliment her black eyes and hair," Alison explained. Soon all three where holding up dress after dress, commenting yes and no, picking and choosing, lost to all cares in the world. They hardly noticed another woman coming out of a back room and lighting several dozen lanterns around the room.

A bit later, they did notice May's six seamstresses leaving. "Golly is it closing time already?" inquired Alison, forgetful of the time. "We can come back tomorrow for more fittings, I'm sure."

"Well, it is quitting time for my assistants. But come, let me get your order written down. Those three there you can take with you." She led them to the central counter and began writing down Darless' order and a receipt for the three outfits the had picked out.

While Darless was paying for them, a side door, that did not appear before to be a door, opened, and in stepped a tall, wiry man also in his late twenties. He had dark eyes but soft facial features and large, fine hands. His black moustache was quite well done; he was a handsome young man indeed. "May — oh excuse me, I thought you were alone."

Both girls caught the sudden tension in May, which left as quickly as it came. "No, Mat. It's okay. We are just finishing up. Be with you in a minute," May hurriedly said to the tall stranger. She evidentially thought an explanation was in order and hastily added to the girls, "Mat is my friend, he owns the locksmith shop right next to mine. He sees me home each evening." It seemed reasonable enough.

And soon the girls laden with three large bundles made their way back to the inn. The streets were getting quite dark now. Darless could barely contain her excitement. "If we get back before they do, I'll surprise them. Which one should I wear first, do you suppose?"

"How about the white one with black rabbit trim. That one looks super on you!" replied Alison, ginning ear to ear, proud of their achievement in so short a time. They were the first back to their rooms, and Darless went to change. Her stomach tingled with excitement. *I wonder what they will think of me now!* She thought to herself.

Soon the others arrived. Jon's face, flush with a reddish glow of excitement, wore the biggest smile Alison had seen. "Looks like you were successful," Alison welcomed him and they hugged.

"You betcha! Instruments everywhere. I'm going back tomorrow and try some out. A finder's paradise!" Jon gushed out.

Mandy laughed. "We all get excited about different things. Personally I was bored. But then if Jon can make music, then it is worth the effort. I *do* like music!" she emphasized. "Say, where's Darless?"

Alison had a twinkle in her eye and a coy smile. "Okay. You two, line up by the couch. There now. Okay, Darless, you can come out now." She stood just in front of the two so that she could watch their every expression.

Darless, wearing her new black trimmed, white billowing dress, sailed into the room and did a twirl before the two. Her face was beaming with happiness and pride. She asked, though she did not need to, "What'd ya think? Like the new look?"

Both Jon and Mandy were speechless. Actually, Alison said Jon's mouth gaped so wide that a trout could have swum into it. "Wow, Darless, you look positively stunning!" Mandy proclaimed.

Jon tried to echo her sentiments, but only a gurgle came out. That brought a spat of hysterical laughing. It didn't help that Jon's face turned beet red once again at him embarrassment.

Amid the laughter, Alison stated, "There you have it, Darless. Men are speechless, breathless over you!" And they all laughed even harder, including Jon.

Jon finally managed to blurt out, "I can see Alison's hand in this one. She has remarkable terrific taste, just the right flair. Darless, you look stunning! Well, done, both of you!" Alison beamed, particularly since she saw that Jon had seen her influence with Darless' choice of color and style. "Shall we all dine? My treat," Jon proclaimed. All were famished and Mandy led the way while Jon walked arm in arm with Alison and Darless, acting as their escort.

The dining room was quite packed when they entered. Although they thought that they would be a bit overdressed for dinner, they were a bit surprised to see other ladies dining in their finery as well and so their attire was not out of place. This inn, the Grand Inn, was the finest in Twins' Town. It was a place to be seen as well as dine. And many an eye covertly noticed the entrance of three remarkably stunning women accompanied by an ordinarily looking young man dress in work jeans. The dining room at the Grand Inn was serving nearly one hundred of the more wealthy city folk.

But what captivated Jon was the musicians in the balcony. A quartet was playing background music. There was a form of string bass, something which sounded rather like a lute, a nasal sounding woodwind and what must have been a recorder played softly with only a short moment between selections. It was a soothing, relaxing sound that occupied much of Jon's attention. The girls chatted endlessly discussing their luck at finding such an excellent dressmaker's shop. Mandy too intended on visiting it the next day as well.

An hour later, the four were back in there sitting room, all holding their stomachs. "I ate too much," moaned Alison. "I feel like a bloated pig! Jon, why didn't you stop me from having a second piece of pie?"

"Because it was delicious, honey. It melted in your mouth. I can see I am going to enjoy the meals at this inn!" Jon declared the obvious.

"Okay. I'd better explain," Darless finally turned their thoughts to more serious and pressing matters. "I have reached the decision that I am no longer going to flaunt my sexuality in men's faces. Those see-through gauze dresses are now a thing of the past. I want a man to want me not my body. There is a difference."

That brought a round of compliments from everyone. Darless was particularly pleased to find that Jon was totally sincere in praise of her decision. Jon's heartfelt proclamation touched them all. "You three women are the sexiest women I have ever met in my life, but your other traits so exceed that aspect that I am nearly speechless. You are three super people! I feel so humble in your presence. I thank my lucky stars that Alison feels toward me the way I do for her."

In normal circumstances, Jon's reference to Alison might have been a social faux pas. But at just that moment, Jon had a clear vision of their future track. He added, "Darless, you are going to have your man, but not just any man, one that is truly worthy of you! And Mandy, you are also about to meet again your other half, one to complete you. I have just seen it! Wow! You know, we are all surviving as individuals, but also we survive as families and groups. We operate in all three arenas. Wow. And you cannot harm one of these areas without damaging the other two. They are inter-related, part of the whole!"

"Hey, don't omit the forest and the woodland creatures in your thinking," Mandy inserted. "They count just as much to some of us and should to all of us!"

"I thought so," a now seriously thinking Darless commented. "Yes, man should operate in all these arenas and when he forsakes one, the others dwindle in power as well. Brilliant, Jon. And can you really see the future?"

"Just for a second there, I kind of spaced out and time sort of jumped. Yes, I am pretty sure I did see a glimpse of our future. I don't know how I did that or how to do it again, though," Jon added.

"Well, I hope Jon is right. We have a lot of things to discuss from the last few days. I'll go first. You an all jump in where you see fit," stated Alison drawing herself up mentally for the task at hand. She had so many unanswered questions that demanded answers, to say nothing of their current task that lay only a few days ahead of them.

She began by asking about what had happened during the battle with the demons in the tower. "I thought I saw Jon somehow disintegrating that high priestess."

Darless replied, "I saw it clearly. She spoke the command words for a disintegration beam directed it at Jon's head. He raised his walking stick there and touched the beam with the stick. The beam bounced back at her head. End of head. But how did you manage that one, Jon? Do you have a way to control that kind of energy? We wizards have a very hard time with defending against that spell even when we know it is coming and can prepare ourselves," she nodded knowingly at Alison.

"Dunno," was Jon's reply. "I was so weak, so totally exhausted that I could not even move. Yes, I saw something coming my way but could not physically move. The stick," he faltered looking for a way to describe it, "it was more like the stick raised itself to protect me. But I thought that you said that that spell would disintegrate whatever it hit? Why isn't the stick history?" They all took turns handling the crooked walking stick. It looked like an ordinary, but well-made walking stick.

"I guess that one remains unanswered," Alison resumed. "What happened when the gate spell began to transport us down to the Abyss? I blacked out there. How did Darless get there? The last I saw of her, she was well out of the gate's area of effect, battling that priestess?"

Darless lowered her head, "I saw the gate open, knew what was about to happen. I refused to abandon you three. I dove headlong from about twenty feet above the floor into the gate just as it was closing. I did see the horror on your holy paladin's face as he watched you, Alison, disappear into the Abyss. Never have I seen such intense pain and frustration of powerlessness in a man's face as I did that day! I'll never forget that look until I die! I never thought I would see that kind of sensitivity in a man. Er, no offense, Jon," she quickly added.

"That's what changed my total opinion of myself, actually," Darless went on. "I've been thinking about that ever since. There are men that are keenly sensitive, perceptive, yet powerful beings. For an instant there, I saw myself diving into the Abyss after you three through his eyes. So I decided that I do have a great respect for myself now, far greater than I ever have had. I intend to live up to my own standards of excellence, or die trying. I want to be worthy of the right man, should he ever come into my life."

Silence. Only the distant crickets outside could be heard faintly. Jon rose and bowed before her and kissed her hand. Tears rolled down his eyes. He kissed her on her forehead and gave her a hug. Then, Mandy and Alison hugged the two — a four way hug of each other.

It was Alison who kept them back on track. "Okay. When we entered the gate, which by my guess should last perhaps a second or two, we three were bleeding to death and mostly unconscious. How is it that we arrived completely wound-less or fully healed and with all of our mental facilities in tact, so much so that we cast protective spells on ourselves even before we arrived at the destination point in the Abyss?"

"A gate between planes of existence as this one was should take about three seconds or thereabouts," proclaimed Darless didactically. "Can anyone explain it? I thought I saw five beings. You know, when we received the gift from the Air Maiden. I saw you all as yourselves, beings, big beings, floating out of your bodies. I saw five of us during the gate ride."

"Now that you mention it, I did too!" exclaimed Alison. "It felt like father Ukko touching me, like he did when I was killed by Morrigan. How can that be?"

Jon looked sheepishly at the floor. "Er, it was my doing. I was semi unconscious, more or less, totally exhausted, more than I have ever been in my life. I saw another being there too and was just following orders. I was commanded to touch the walking stick to each of you, which I did. We all recovered shortly thereafter. I, I, my body just followed this other being's orders mechanically, like I was not there. It was weird being so out of control." Everyone stared at the walking stick once more.

"What is *with* this stick?" exclaimed Alison. "I have cast detect magic on all those stick and nearly everything else around my ruins countless times. There has never been the slightest hint of magic about it. But I will try once more." The others watched intently as Alison muttered a command word. They saw nothing at all. That is, except for two gold rings on Alison's hand seemed to have a bluish glow about them as well as one on Mandy's index finger. "Well, the spell is working," Alison dryly stated. "Here's my invisibility ring and another magical ring of mine. I see you are wearing your invisibility ring too, Mandy." She grinned but did not answer.

"Here, let me try," interjected Darless. She spoke a similar word of command but her spell had exactly the same effect as Alison's spell. "It would seem to be just a walking stick. It does not radiate magic. Nearly all magically enchanted items glow under the detection spells."

"Well," Jon interrupted. "I guess I gotta tell you what Nain said to me as we were leaving." All eyes turned to Jon. "He said that if this walking stick were his, he would place it on his holy altar and pray for divine guidance in its nature or some such thing. I do not know what he is talking about. I do not have a god to pray to for that matter. Nor an altar. Nor do I want one, whatever one is. It sounds heavy."

"Ah ha!" declared Mandy, who had been quiet throughout the proceedings thus far. She knew only a tiny bit of magical incantations at this point. She fully appreciated the dedication and effort that the two mages had had to achieve their phenomenal level of magical skills. However, this was in her realm of experience. "Why didn't you say so in the first place? It is starting to make sense." The others stared at her with gaping mouths.

"Nain is a high priest! Not a magician. Perhaps, he was telling you that this walking stick is not magically endowed but priestly endowed — a priest's thing. When I need guidance from Reylona, I pray at my altar to her. She answers my prayers, endows me with priestly spells to assist those in need. Jon, specifically what Nain was suggesting is the usual thing a priest would do. If they wish a priestly object of suspected power to be revealed to them, they bless the item and place it on their altar and begin a vigilant prayer time. They do nothing but pray hour by hour, day by day, I've heard, until their god deem them sufficiently worthy to enlighten. Nain thought you were a priest, Jon, that's what he was trying to tell you."

"Can you do that here?" wondered Jon, "since you are a priestess and all that."

"I can give it a try tonight, Jon." Mandy replied, unsure of just how long such might take. Everyone encouraged her to give it a try.

That line of inquiry settled, or taken as far as they could, Alison resumed, "Okay. Back to the gate period. Something happened to me there. As you have discovered, I who previously had not one tiny trace of ability to telepathically communicate to you three, have somehow been awakened. At least that is the only way I can describe it."

"Yes, you were positively shouting at me back there at the seamstress's shop!" Darless proclaimed. "How did it all of a sudden appear? This is most unusual. In fact, I have never heard of this happening ever before. You are either born with the gift or not. It is not something you learn or develop, as far as I know. Demons are well disciplined in the use of the mental powers, so I do know of what I speak."

"Dittos from my point of view," added Mandy, who had also been trained when she was just a young girl in its use. She remembered the day when her dad had discovered she had the ability to read other's thoughts and had at once sent for Old Herman to teach her in how to use her gift.

"Oh my god!" exclaimed Jon, who had just realized what had happened to Alison as well as himself. Everyone stared at him instantly. And just as instantly his face reddened as he felt the total attention of the three women on him and him alone. "Oh my god!" he exclaimed a second time, but for an entirely other reason. They waited impatiently for him to say more.

"I just realized why Alison and I have late in life by your standards suddenly developed this mental ability. It is not a mental thing at all! It is part of the capabilities and potentials of a spiritual being! And we both have only recently become totally aware of ourselves as being spiritual beings and not just a body with a mind! Alison received the gift of seeing who and what she really is from the Air Maiden Fruella. That revelation has opened the door, so to speak for Alison, if you want my evaluation of it all. If I am not correct, Alison, forgive me for evaluating it for you. I do not intend to make less of you or your abilities."

"No, Jon. You are right. It is a spiritual thing with me. For such a long time I thought it was a mental thing you three were doing," Alison explained. "I tried so hard to do it too, but with absolutely no effect what so ever. I resigned myself to being dead in me head, so to speak. Then, when I saw that I am me and me's not this body, why it's me wanting to talk to you. It's me trying to place an idea or though into your head." She blushed, "I'm sorry, Darless, I didn't mean to yell. I have not yet got the hang of it properly. I suspect you and Mandy are partially right, I need to practice doing things so I get them done right."

"Hum," Mandy thought, "Jon, you might have something with this. Come to think of it, I have always known I am me, Mandy, not my body. Probably cause dad wanted a son so badly and all he got was me. I had to be me and not that son. I have been acutely aware of me all my life as a result."

"Jon, you may be on to something major," added a thoughtful Darless. "I too have always been aware of me — very different from my body. Gods knows how hard it has been for me to exist in this alu-demon body! I've ever considered my mental powers as being spiritual in nature. But if they are as you are suggesting, then we all should be able to increase them. Hum, now I wonder the best approach to take to accomplishing that?" And she drifted off in intense thought.

"Okay," Alison continued with her questions. "Then, when we arrived on his gate platform, chaos reigned. I could not understand or follow everything that went on — it happened way too fast for me to comprehend."

Jon commented dryly, "Dispater is using Metrarch for some purpose of his own. He is not willingly assisting a Demon Lord, of that you can count on. Am I right, Darless?"

That brought her out of her reverie. "Yes, Jon's right on that point. Whatever assistance Dispater is providing has nothing to do with anything in which Metrarch is interested. He's being used, though he cannot see it."

Darless explained, "When we arrived, I knew I had to thwart what are the usual greetings to newcomers, a pitched battle. So I tried to jam Metrarch's communications by a continuous stream of chatter. It worked pretty darn well, if I so say so myself." They all chuckled as they recalled her endless chatter and the Demon Lord's major confusion and difficulty in getting a word in edgewise.

"I was burning up," Alison continued her line of questioning. "The abyss and I are in total opposition. When Dispater arrived, I had the Chill of Death to also deal with, which last time nearly did me in. When Jon nearly fell and began vomiting, I thought that this was the utter end. Then, I remembered Dad was here and retrieved the Mighty Scepter from Metrarch. I decided that if Dad could do it, surely I could do it. Serenity came over me and I backed out of my head as I was shown I could do by Fruella. And I was in command come what may. But then all heck broke loose with those demon bugs attacking everywhere."

Mandy grinned sheepishly, "Er, that was me. When I was there, that was the lowest emotional point of my entire life! I felt utterly useless to help you all. I felt like a total pawn under the power of demons and devils. I was moaning in self-pity when you screamed telepathically in my head, Alison. That is what did the trick. Zagroot zounds, I said to myself. If Alison can learn to do telepathy at a time like this, I darn well better do something. I am a person of action. So I gave them action. I commanded the Chasme to attack and gave that command with the total certainty it would be carried out, no doubts or reservations, period. They obeyed. Er, sorry for the mess it made. But I enjoyed the effect," she grinned broadly.

The others let out a whoop and cheers and hugged Mandy. A bit taken aback by their warm response, she added, "Never get a Mandy ticked off!" Everyone roared with laughter.

Alison again brought them back to the topic at hand. "I vaguely remember Dispater saying something like we all have grown spiritually since he last saw us."

It was Darless who replied, "Yes, he did; and yes we have. I was trying to keep us all going, but the arrival of Dispater rather changed things. Did you notice that a Lord of Hell actually commanded a Demon Lord in the Demon Lord's own palace? Fascinating and very significant, but I don't yet know its importance. Well, when Alison telepathically screamed in my head for help as Jon vomited and began falling into the maggots, I reached a decision. Either I could try to have my attention outward protecting us or I could dive in and help Jon mentally overcome his situation. I chose to help Jon. I used our newly developed technique."

"Yes, but how did you know that I needed help, that I was stuck in that picture?" Jon asked and then added for the other's benefit, "I was totally stuck or plastered into a mental picture I had that I lost complete touch with reality — that thing was more real than reality itself, bizarre to say the least."

"Honestly, Jon, you looked stupid, staring at the mental picture. It was like you were wearing it. You were totally awash in it. So I just had you start recounting it to me. We got quite a bit of it sorted out before the Chasme hit," Darless commented.

"Yes, I lost my dog when I was four. After looking for it, I found it late one night and hugged it and so on. But it was dead and when morning came, it was full of maggots — I was hugging maggots all night!" Jon explained.

"Yes, but Jon, did you notice that Dispater was also there watching our recounting procedure! He was more than a little interested in the technique!" Darless stated.

"Hum, yes. I am sure we are on to something of major significance, though I am just not sure of it all yet," Jon replied. "But gosh, I am tired. What time is it getting to be anyway?"

It was very late indeed. So they decided to resume their discussions in the morning. True to her word, when Mandy was in her bedroom, she got her small altar out of her portable hole. She prayed before it, cast her bless upon the stick, placed Jon's walking stick upon the altar, and retired for the night. During the night, she had a vision of a holy scepter waving in a battle, but thought nothing of the dream by morning.

Chapter 9 The Twins

Everyone rose rather late the next morning, around nine a.m. Jon's cry brought howls of laughter from the ladies. "Where's the bathroom around here; I really gotta go!" he cried in dismay.

As soon as she stopped laughing, Mandy called out from her room, "Use the chamber pot by your bed!"

"Ah ha!" was Jon's reply which was followed by additional laughter from the women. Within a few minutes, the foursome went down for breakfast in the large dining room. What a contrast from the evening before. This late in the morning, the place was nearly deserted. Only late risers, such as themselves, were here — two older couples who were nearly done. Only one waitress, who introduced herself as Sally, was on duty. They all ate a rather large breakfast. "I could get used to this," commented Jon as he pushed himself back from the table after finishing another helping of pancakes.

"Ah, but think of the pounds you'd put on!" Alison chuckled. After a pause to sip some juice, she inquired, "You know, I've been thinking that perhaps we should warn these Twins about the Demon Council meeting and all that. Perhaps they do not know the details that we do. It would seem that these Twins are looking out for others."

"Caution is the word," urged Mandy frowning, "we do not really know what their actual purposes are. This is a pretty rowdy town, a bit rough at the edges, a thief's paradise, perhaps. But how do we go about contacting them? Put up a message on the board out there?"

Just then, Sally came by bringing a refill of steaming tea. "Say, Sally," Jon interrupted her, "we are new to this town, just visiting and all. And we were wondering about these 'Twins' and how one can contact them."

Sally was a young girl, perhaps seventeen, with long blonde hair tied this morning in a ponytail. Her bright blue eyes were full of life. "Oh that's easy. You don't. They don't talk to anyone. You just leave them a message out there on the board and, if they choose, they take care of an injustice for you."

"Okay, but what do they look like?" Jon continued pressing her for more information.

"Oh, that's easy too. No one has actually ever seen them. Several folks swear that they saw them, but they were all dressed in black. Even their faces were completely hidden by black masks. Now I have not really seen them personally, you know, but some friends of mine swear that they saw them walking the streets late at night, all dressed in black, very hard to see," she paused for breath.

"But they always help folks out, right?" Alison jumped in quickly.

"Sure. This town's full of ruffians, bullies, and thieves. Some say the mayor's the biggest thief. But I say old Butterbottom is too fat to be a thief! He pretty much lets the Twins do whatever they want to do. A couple years ago, someone stole the money bag from this very inn after a busy Friday night. Next day, the manager posted a note and, within three days, he found a large sack with the money in it on one of these very tables when he opened up at five am! Imagine that!" Sally finally ended.

Seeing that Sally really could offer them no additional clues, Jon changed the subject. "Say, Sally, where is the best tailor around here? I've got to keep up with the ladies; they are all buying terrific new outfits. I now look rather out of place."

"Hah, hah, yes you do. Your shirt does look a bit strange. I've never seen anything like it. Nor your pants, for that matter," Sally added.

"T-shirt and jeans, they are called where I come from," Jon pointed out.

"Well, I'm not too conversant with men's tailors, of course, but I think it all depends on how much money you want to spend," she replied thoughtfully. "There is Radagar's place, a few blocks further south, but I've heard that he is expensive. Where do you come from?"

"Thanks. Urbana," Jon replied without giving it much thought, but quickly added when he saw her confused expression, "a town very distant from here. Say," inspiration struck, "have you heard of a town called Edgeway, or La Fontaine or perhaps Duncanville?"

Dismay filled her face. "No sir, I've never heard of them. Are they far from here?"

"Yes," Jon replied, putting her at ease, "so far that we are not sure just how far we have come or have to go, actually." Noticing that the ladies were getting a bit impatient with his line of questioning, Jon asked, "Say, can we take the tea and cups up to our rooms?"

"Sure, just leave them in the room and the chambermaid will return them later on. I've got to tend to the Sharnhorsts. See you later on," and Sally headed toward another elderly couple just sitting down for breakfast.

Back in their rooms with the tea, it was down to business. Alison began the discussion, "Well, since I got us all into this mess, I guess I'd better get us started on figuring out what to do next and how we are going to stop an assassin."

"Number 1," began Darless in her methodical manner, "the meeting is definitely a closed meeting. Once all of the participants are present, there should be no others present. Number 2, only perhaps inn staff will be likely allowed in bringing refreshments, if at all. Number 3, this means that the assassin must use some kind of disguise. Number 4, since he cannot count on even the inn staff being allowed into a closed meeting, he must find another way. Even though I have run into many really evil people in my days, I've never run into an assassin that I know of, so can anyone add a Number 5?"

"Well, I know of them," Mandy added, "they are a lot like thieves but kill for hire not rob, but that's about all I know, except I've heard that assassins have a sort of closed society and are very nasty men!"

"Hum," Jon muttered, "are they always men?" No one answered him. It would be a very long time before he had an answer to that question.

After a long pause, Alison commented, "You know, in the adventuring party that I used to go with, you know, led by Sir Thomas, our Paladin, one of our members, Slikster, got his name because I swear he is a thief, though he never has admitted it. He is always slinking off somewhere to get secret training and such. When a lock needs to be picked, or a trap scouted out, he is always taking care of it. Sir Thomas always looks the other way because the lock had to be opened or the trap defused, you know. Now, if he were here, perhaps we could press him for more details. Though I don't suppose you could openly go about asking to talk to a thief."

"Then, somehow we are going to have to get more information, that is the only answer," Darless concluded. "Why don't we try to get in touch with the Twins and see if anything comes from such a meeting?" The others solemnly agreed that that was the next likely step. So the next order of business was what the posted letter should actually say. Around noon, Jon tacked a message to the public board. The wording was carefully chosen to prick the Twin's interest. It read as follows.

Twins: We four are from very out of town. We have news of the impending Demon Council and War Games we wish to share. Can we meet? Saint Jon Brown.

The rest of the afternoon passed relatively uneventful. Jon and Alison went in search of the expensive tailor that Sally suggested. Jon had little concept of what "expensive" actually meant in terms of these gold and silver coins; Alison did. And Jon depended upon her exquisite taste. He purchased four coordinated outfits, ranging from a heavy canvass-like work set of clothes to a fancy dinner suit that blended superbly with Alison's new gown. Together, they looked like a matched pair. When Jon so stated this, she winked and gave him a loving hug and kiss.

Mandy and Darless returned to the dressmaker, Darless for more fittings and Mandy to acquire some new clothes as well. Later on, they switched partners and Mandy assisted Jon at the music store. He purchased seven instruments, including a drum, a couple flute-like instruments, and various stringed instruments, none of which were at all familiar to him but they sounded beautiful. Mandy felt rather like a pack horse carrying them back to the inn.

Meanwhile, Alison and Darless went looking for maps, to scout out the town, and to learn what they could about its defenses and government.

It was around five p.m. when they all rendezvoused back at the inn. Jon proudly demonstrated to all of them his newly acquired instruments. He reached into his pocked to find a bone pick to use to play the oversized guitar. "Say, what's this?" he pulled out a small piece of paper.

"Wow. Look at this!" he cried. Everyone crowed around. It read:

Be in the square by the board around midnight tonight. Twins.

"Where'd you get that?" Mandy inquired.

"I've no idea! It is just here — in my pocket!" an amazed Jon excitedly replied. "You are right about the pickpockets, Mandy. I don't even know when or how someone put it there. Incredible!"

"They are good, that's for sure. We'd best be very careful around these two, whoever they are!" Mandy cautioned. After a pause, she queried, "Did you notice anyone bumping into to you while we were on the street? Or perhaps when we were in a shop?"

Jon looked forlorn. "No. Well, I got jostled a couple times in the busy street. I didn't think anything of it though. I guess it could have been just about anyone. Some adventurer I am!" and he laughed.

"Don't be so hard on yourself, Jon," Alison consoled, "because a thief would not be much of a thief if his victims saw him doing the pilfering, now would he?" Jon had to agree with that.

Just then, a knock on their door was followed by "Maid Service." Alison let her in. "Will you folks be needing anything further tonight?" inquired a matronly older woman dressed in a drab, yet functional dress, various rags and cleaning items protruded from a dozen pockets.

"No thank you. We are fine," Alison relied, "This is a very excellent inn, and I have been to quite a few!"

"Thank you," and she curtsied and added, "Are you all going to the ball this evening?"

"No, what ball," Jon replied, thinking at once that here would be an opportunity for all of them to have a bit of fun. Of course, he was keenly interested to hear the music.

"In the ballroom starting around seven. It is the late summer Festival Ball, a very formal ball. Very dress up, you know. Everyone who is anyone in this town goes to it." The maid nodded knowingly at the three women.

"Thanks. We will for sure go!" Jon acknowledged. The maid left and he turned to the girls and said, "Will you three accompany me to the ball tonight? I would be honored with your presences!" Sure, came the chorus; Mandy pinched him on his rear; Darless gave him a formal curtsey; and Alison gave him a hug. Then, it was off to dinner and then back to change for the ball.

Jon and Alison looked terrific in their matching white linen garb with black ermine trim, as if two peas from a pod. Alison let her hair flow down over the back of her billowing dress, low cut in front, and teasing gentlemen's eyes. Mandy, who always favored the touch of leather on her skin, wore her new soft, green leather dress and matching shoes. (Note, she carried a long dagger in a sheath strapped to her inner thigh, well out of sight, but easily accessible.) Her dress was more like velvet to the touch, sensuous. Darless wore one of her new dresses as well, a yellow cotton chiffon that also billowed wide at her feet. Her black hair and eyes matched her wide belt and new shoes.

The ballroom accommodated nearly three hundred dancers entertained by a dozen musicians located in a small loft about five feet above the main floor. To Jon's utter delight, the music sounded very reminiscent of Renaissance dance tunes with which he was familiar. Of course, the girls knew how to dance, and Jon didn't. But he was a fast learner and danced with all three.

Since most of the party attendees came in pairs, only a few young men flirted with the three women, who did enjoy the extra attention. The glow on their faces and sparkle in their eyes, bespoke just how much the women appreciated this respite from their cares. When the dance ended shortly after 10 p.m., all four were tired and glad to return to their rooms to relax and change for their late night rendezvous with the Twins.

"Well, I'm ready," Mandy commented mostly to herself after she had changed back into her usual leather adventuring attire. "While I do enjoy the occasional dance, I do get a bit bored with it. I'm really keen on meeting these Twins tonight, Jon. How about you?" They were lounging in the sofa in the common room adjoining their bedrooms. Jon had changed quickly and was relaxing with a cup of tea he had managed to commandeer on their way back from the dance room.

"Dunno, it could go many different ways. I'm more worried about the assassin. I do not want any of us getting killed because of a darn demon lord!" Jon replied emphatically. After a pause, he added, "And I really don't know what Lady Ursla meant by the balance being off in this area. Do you suppose that she means that there are no good people around these parts — a den of thieves and all that?"

"All towns have their fair share of pickpockets and thieves. Isn't that true in your homelands?" Mandy asked rhetorically. "But it would seem that in all directions lie lands controlled or worshiping the Demon Lords. You know, 'Birds of a Feather Nest Together' or do you have such a saying where you come from?"

"Flock together, we say," corrected Jon. "So where does that leave this balance thing? Beats me. Maybe Darless is more attuned to this sort of thing and can help us decipher the Lady's meaning." Just then, the other two appeared from their rooms, dressed for adventure once again. Jon noted that Alison wore her magician's magical robe. Darless wore a black leather pants suit but now had one of Alison's magical wands stuck in her belt.

"We're armed and taking no chances," announced Alison. "I gave a wand that shoots magical arrows to Darless. I figure that, here in town, we best not launch violent, loud spells that can draw undue attention to ourselves. So now we wait, right?"

They spent an hour discussing the balance factor that Lady Ursla commanded them to set to rights. In the end, they were no closer to knowing what the Great Druid was talking about than before they started. It was frustrating.

Midnight found the four leaving the inn walking slowly toward the central well in the open, octagonal plaza. At this time of night, the streets were deserted. They caught the occasional distant dog bark or cat cry. The street was very dark. The first quarter moon had long ago set, Mandy duly noted. Some patchy high clouds obscured the starry heavens above. Cautiously, they walked to the well. Looking around, they saw no one and so prepared to wait.

"I hope they show up soon," Jon leaned heavily on his trusty walking stick. "I'm falling asleep. Must be all that dancing," he whispered.

Mandy's voice sounded distant and harsh. "Fight it Jon. We are being attacked with some kind of magical spells!"

Whoosh. Her meaning struck home. Jon blinked and immediately shrugged off the unnatural sleepiness which was gone faster than it had come upon him. Now he was alert, glancing in all directions in the dark. So were the girls, whispering among themselves. No one could spot their attackers or the direction from which the sleep spell had come. Alison had her staff at hand; Darless held on to her wand; Mandy had her hand on her bastard sword. So Jon just relaxed and looked about.

Suddenly Jon cried out, "Look out; here come some really hideous beasts, belching fire!" He saw three large dog-like creatures breathing fire from their mouths darting toward him.

"No, there must be at least a thousand vile, nasty rats about to swarm us!" cried Alison. Mandy looked in all directions and saw nothing but a huge twenty foot tall demon lord with six arms each waving a sword which were twice the length of her sword; and this demon was coming straight for her.

Darless spoke soothingly, yet commandingly, "It is all an illusion. Fight it. Don't believe what you are seeing. Close your eyes and you will still be seeing it, which cannot be!"

"Wow. It sure looked convincing!" Jon muttered, wiping his eyes with his hands. "That was pretty amazing."

"You sure this demon is not real?" Mandy said, not quite believing Darless.

"Close your eyes. You still see him as if your eyes were wide open, right?" Darless replied in a soft voice.

"Zagroot zounds! I was spoofed!" Mandy cried out. Then, she yelled challengingly, "Hey you, come out and fight like a man!" Everyone was looking in all directions at the same time, yet seeing nothing but the dark shadows of dark things on a dark night.

"This'll never do." Jon muttered to himself. *I'll bet I can find our attacker mentally. They gotta be around here somewhere.* He closed his eyes and mentally began to expand his space. Quickly he felt the presence of his three close friends and soon saw their glow of beingness. He slowly expanded his awareness outward in an ever growing circle.

"Hey, someone's over that way, maybe two hundred feet," Jon whispered as his mind contacted another mind. "He's drawing a sword out now."

"Terrific!" exclaimed Mandy.

"How'd you do that," whispered Darless, "Can you teach me that trick someday real soon?"

"Say, can I learn how to do that too?" added Alison, upon just realizing how vital such a skill could be to her.

"Sure," Jon whispered distractedly. "I'm searching for more."

"Right," Darless commented, "Spell casters do not use swords; they cannot be a master of both arts! There are most likely more of them. Keep searching." Jon continued his sweep.

"Okay, Mister Swordsman, let's see just how good you are!" taunted Mandy loudly in the direction Jon had indicated. The distinct slithering, scraping sound of a blade, sliding from its sheath across her back, broke the stillness. Mandy could not effectively wield a two-handed sword; she had neither the stature nor the physique. However, the slightly shorter and less heavy bastard sword was her favorite. In one well-practiced motion, the ranger drew the blade from its sheath across her back. Slowly she paced cautiously forward into the darkness toward the menacing stranger, ready for action. *Zagroot zounds! I do love this action!* "Come on, show yourself!" She ignored the whispered, pleading words of caution given by Alison and Darless.

Her keen eyes, used to combat in the dark, spotted a movement in the shadows maybe a hundred feet in front of her, just under the archway of a building. She caught the dim shape of a tall, thin man and the distinctive, tell-tale glint of steel. A ray from a star flashed off his blade and that was enough for this experienced ranger. She relaxed for she knew now the nature of the threat before her, a short sword and perhaps here in the city, a dagger in the other hand. No match for a well-wielded bastard sword. Perhaps her opponent was thinking the same thing for he seemed to hesitate a moment.

In a blur of motion, a man dressed wholly in black set upon her. Indeed, Mandy had surmised correctly; she faced a short sword and dagger combination, speed and thrust came her way. The man wore black leather pants, black shirt, black boots, swirling black cloak. His face was entirely hidden by a black mask; only eyes, nose, and mouth were visible. And he was quick, very quick. With a loud clank of steel upon steel, combat was joined. Mandy had some practice in street fighting, though she neither cared for it nor was good at it. Instinctively, she kept both hands on her raised bastard sword. Both of her opponent's blades hit her blade and locked in a vice grip. Just as soon as she felt the pinching contact of the pair, her blade was forced to fly in a counterclockwise arc. Had she only been using one hand, she would have been forced to let go of the blade or break her arm trying to hold on to it. But with two hands, she could follow the motion. Trusting her training, she followed on through with the disarming motion her skilled opponent was using on her. At the bottom of the long arc, she thrust upwards, continuing the same motion, rather like cutting circles of air before her.

Her black garbed opponent, instead of disarming her, found himself having to choose to become disarmed or knocked off his feet. He held onto the blades as long as he could, falling in slow motion to her left. As he fell, he planted his left foot between Mandy's feet. Thus, when he chose to let go of the blades and hit the ground, the momentum of his fall instantly tripped Mandy. Taken completely by surprise by this unexpected movement she had never experienced before, she fell over backwards, catching her fall by using one arm. The two lay on the ground; their feet were about three feet from the other's. The entire encounter had taken five seconds.

"Nice move!" Mandy commented as she got back onto her feet, nursing a sore buttocks. Her opponent did an unusual flip and hop motion to regain his feet seconds before she did. He was amazingly agile and fast. He made no motion to regain his short sword and dagger, preferring a martial arts style stance.

"Nice move yourself," the stranger whispered in a low voice. She saw him making some kind of finger motions, rather like a sign language. She had seen those finger flicks before, but could not place it. Now she was facing an unarmed man. She had no desire to swing a large sword at a defenseless person. However, his startling speed and dexterity made her overly cautious for she realized that he probably could dart in close with his fists or feet before she could wield the heavy blade to counter. Thus, she kept the blade vertical between her and him. They stared at each other for a time, he slowly circling around her like a tiger on the prowl, seeking the right opening to lunge.

Meanwhile, the other women strained their eyes in all directions trying to find the obvious other opponents, to no avail. Yet another spell of some type totally foreign to Alison hit the area where they stood. For a fleeting instant, she felt as if she were in a total confusion; but Darless quickly dispelled its effect, having seen that magic before, she had acted nearly instantaneously to counter it. Both were totally perplexed, because normally, when an invisible wizard attacked someone, their cloak of invisibility diminished. But not so for some strange reason neither mage understood. "Back to back," commanded Alison, "I still cannot figure out from where the attack is coming!" The two did so, eyes probing the darkness searching for their opponent.

Jon was still remembering the intriguing dance music from earlier in the evening. Neither their supposed rendezvous nor this sudden unexpected attack could quell his merry mood. He was still humming one of the melodies as he expanded his sensory probe for the hidden other opponents. Alison and Darless both turned to look at each other with an expression of "How can you possibly hum at a time like this?" when Jon suddenly froze.

"Mandy. Don't hurt him. He is one of the Twins! Whatever you do, for heaven's sake don't hurt him!" Jon cried out loudly. Then, he pointed over to a dark entrance way to a closed shop. "She's over there. There are only two and they are The Twins. Okay. We are here. We must talk, if you please. I'm Jon Brown."

"How'd you find her?" blurted out Alison.

"How do you know it is a her? I thought they were supposed to be twins?" Darless commented dryly, relaxing her guard.

"I won't hurt him, if he doesn't hurt me or us!" Mandy commented slowly backing away from her opponent, who took the opportunity to retrieve his weapons. She noted that while doing so, he never took his eyes off of her. It was like he could sense where his weapons lay without seeing them!

"Quiet!" the man in black said. "Okay, come with us," he ordered, then added, "Please." After a glance in the direction of the other twin, who remained utterly invisible to everyone except Jon, he whispered, "And be very, very quiet about it. We do not want prying eyes. Secrecy is vital. Speak nothing until we tell you to. And that **is** an order, if you please, or else this meeting is ended."

As quietly as they could, the four moved toward the entrance way where Jon had said the other twin was located. None of them seriously believed that the twins would end the meeting over a little noise, though. There were simply too many unanswered questions for one and all.

When the four, followed by the twin in black who kept glancing about looking for spies in the shadows, reached the entrance way, another twin dressed identical to the first was barely visible in front of the shop's door. Mandy again saw the new twin's fingers making deft motions, a signal of some kind. "Follow quietly!" the twin behind them spoke almost as if in response to the sign.

The silent twin led them cautiously down a dark alley into other alleys. They moved slowly and cautiously. No sound could be heard from either twin. Jon was becoming annoyed with the sounds of his own footfalls on the cobblestones. In the stillness of the late night, his footsteps sounded like gongs heralding his arrival. He notice that Mandy made no sound either but that Alison and Darless, by virtue of their soft shoes, made very little noise. In the near total darkness of the alleys, Jon soon lost all sense of direction. He was completely lost. But he had a hunch that Mandy would not be so easily fooled. It was so dark that he bumped into Alison in front of him before he realized that they had halted. "Sorry," he whispered. "Shh," came the replies from somewhere in front of him and behind him.

Alison took hold of his hand, motioning him to grab Mandy's who was behind him. Evidently, she was following orders from the twin leading them. A tug from Alison got him moving, pulling Mandy with him. They were entering a building. They went inside from the dark alleyway into an even darker room, then across its space, around a corner, through another door. It was pitch black. However, Darless who was leading Alison had no problems. She could see the heat given off by the twin leading her and followed easily, pulling the others in tow. Thump and the door they had entered shut; they heard a lock click and then two sighs of relief. "Okay. Light the lamps; the wards are in place," a voice familiar to all three girls commanded.

All four blinked as six lanterns were uncovered by one of the black cloaked twins. They were in a twenty foot square, windowless room whose stone walls were wet with dampness. The air held a twinge of mold. Before them was a rough-hewn table with six chairs. On its top sat six pewter mugs and a large pitcher of ale. It was obvious now that the Twins had intended to bring them here by any means possible.

Both twins stood now side by side. To a quick glance, they appeared totally identical, identical in clothes, height, and build. With only their eyes and mouths visible, to any untrained eye, they would appear as twins. But Jon could see the difference between the two at once; to him, the eyes and the lips gave the Twins' secret away; the twin on the right was a woman. The silence lasted but a moment before the woman spoke. It reminded him of Alison in a way.

"Thank you for meeting with us. Please excuse our feeble attempts. We meant you no harm. It is imperative that no one see or hear or follow us or find us. We want no one to know that we have even met. We are called the Twins around here." Then as one, both twins removed their cloaks and masks.

"You are the seamstress, May, right? And you are the locksmith, Mat?" Jon stated the obvious.

"And you four are among only a handful of people in this town of some twenty-thousand that know this!" May began. "And we trust that you will keep our secret."

"Absolutely," Jon replied. Then, his thoughts formed in Alison's mind. *Trust me. Be prepared. You are in for a wonderful welcome surprise!* "Allow me to introduce ourselves," Jon continued. This is Mandy Blackthorn, a ranger of the goddess Reylona." Mandy nodded her head. "You already know our mage Darless; yes, she is an alu-demon, but is one of us; we trust her with our lives and have done so on a number of occasions." Darless smiled; Jon detected a red flush appear for a moment on the alu-demon's face.

Thanks! Appeared in his mind. To be so totally accepted as one of them had been her goal and to have him so state that to others had made Darless flush. "I've already said that I am Jon Brown." Instantly, three mental nudges hit him. He had just committed a social faux pas by not introducing Alison before himself.

"And this is Alison d'Ambrose, our other mage." Jon's eyes were squarely on May's as he uttered this last introduction. The other's watched in disbelief as both twins' jaws dropped. They looked like they had just seen a ghost. Their eyes opened wide, and then tears welled up in May's eyes. She nearly fainted; Mat staggered himself, but managed somehow to steady is sister.

Alison, Mandy, and Darless were dumbfounded with this totally unexpected reaction. The silence in the room tore at their ears. Jon then continued with the introductions. "Alison, let me present to you your long lost sister and brother, May and Mat. Am I not correct?" It was all May could do to nod her head in agreement. She clung to Mat to avoid collapsing. Jon watched as Alison's mouth fell, eyes grow wide, and tears swell up. He was right at her side as her body suddenly went limp, catching her just as Mat had done for May.

There are instants of time that are timeless, precious, precious beyond belief. This was one of those moments that the six of them would always remember. "Is, is, is it really you, Alison?" May managed to mumble, "baby Alison? All grown up?"

"It's me," wept Alison. "I've spent years and years looking for you! Is it really my big teasing twins?" Memories of all the little jokes they had played on her as a three year old, flooded into her mind.

However, Mat, ever protective of May, cautioned, "May, we better make really sure of who she says she is. It's been twenty or so years; she was only three when we last saw her." Turning to Alison, he said, "Okay, if you are really our little sister, then you know where May always put the locket that mom gave her when she went to bed at night."

The warm memories flooding through her mind abruptly halted with this challenge. He was right, what if these two were not really her long lost brother and sister. "On Teddy, she always hung it on the little stuffed bear that she would never let me play with," replied Alison with total certainty. May let out a cry interpreted by everyone that meant she was right. "And what did you do to me every night just before I went to bed, Mat?" she challenged him.

"Oh, that's easy. I'd read you bed time stories to try to scare you, Runtling!" he replied without hesitation, realizing the she really was his little sister. He had not used that term in over twenty years. And as he said "Runtling" he began to cry as profusely as Alison and May. The three joined in a tight three-way hug, long overdue.

Jon's face was wet with his own tears. He turned to look at Mandy and Darless. Both had streams of tears flowing out of control as well. They hugged each other too. All six huddled into one big hug, full of sobs of total joy.

After several minutes, they calmed down a bit. Alison turned to Jon, wiping the tears on her sleeve, she gave him a warm kiss and said, "Thank you for such a priceless gift!" Then, she turned to the twins and introduced Jon properly. "Jon here is my fiancé. He is actually called Saint Jon Brown, by Father Ukko personally, though he is so modest that he never uses the title so bestowed on him." Mat and May's eyebrows rose noticeably and both took another long look at Jon, who again became red-faced, and stared at the floor.

Seeing Jon's discomfort, Mandy asked the obvious, "How in the world did you know that these two were her family, Jon?" A chorus of "yes how's" came from all directions. Jon welcomed the shift of attention.

The question set off a chain reaction with everyone trying to speak at once. But May got hers asked first, "And how did you find me in the first place and how did you know that I was a woman anyway? It was pitch dark out there and I was also invisible by clothing and spell."

"The answers are all related. When we were standing around the well out there, I nearly fell asleep," Jon began.

"I know, I tried to put you all asleep so we could get you here quietly and without anyone seeing anything," May could not help interjecting.

"Well, we just came from that dance. I'm a musician, you see," he added trying to explain why falling asleep was so unnatural at that time. Seeing the looks of total disbelief, he added, "Yes, I am a flutist, a musician. I am not a fighter — Mandy does that; I am not a magician — Darless and Alison are. I'm just a musician, really, honestly!"

It took confirmation from Alison for the twins to finally believe him. Jon continued, "I was enthralled with the music.

And these three even taught me to dance. There was no way I could be sleepy, the tunes were ringing in my head. So it was obvious to us all that we had just been attacked by some magic. It was so dark that we could not see anything. So I closed my eyes and began searching for you and your minds. I found Mat's here as he was preparing to fight Mandy. As I widened my circle of probing, I found you, May. I sensed your mind. I sort of read minds, you know. And I heard you chanting a spell or two there, sort of like Alison and Darless do when they are performing magic. Hum, but not the same," he mused for a moment. "When you did your magic on us again, I began to look at your mind and your images. I sensed your body." Then, Jon stopped abruptly; his face turned beet red.

Darless, Mandy, and Alison glanced at him, saw his face, and then roared with laughter. Jon's face turned even more crimson. Finally, Alison explained to the bewildered twins, "Jon gets embarrassed easily around women, especially since he once 'dropped in' on Darless once when she was using the bathroom. I think he detected your bosom, sis."

"Or was it something a bit lower?" interjected Mandy letting out another howl of laughter. Even May blushed as she grasped to what Mandy was alluding. Jon's embarrassment grew once more, as Mandy knew it would.

"Okay, okay. We've embarrassed him enough," Alison finally took pity on Jon. "So you were telling us you detected some female anatomy. Then what?"

Jon was only too glad to get back to his explanation. "Er, yes. That startled me, you know. I did not expect that. I thought what on earth could a woman be doing here? You know, everyone talks about the Twins, so I naturally thought you would be, er the same sex. So without thinking about it, I just looked at your mental pictures. I saw Castle d'Ambrose as it must have been before that terrible night. I recognized the shape and the lands about it. And I remembered Alison's description of her twin brother and sister. I sensed you must be about the right ages. When you turned on the lanterns in here, I could tell by your eyes and lips that you were a woman. But I was not totally certain until I saw your faces. There is such a similarity there, you know. You three all have the same eyes! The same as your other brother we just rescued, Lennard."

In unison, Mat and May gasped! "Lenny? You found Lenny?" they said in disbelief.

"He's in a really bad way," Alison began to break the sad news to the twins. "He has been held prisoner in the Abyss all of this time. He is still alive, barely, a rotting shell of a man, and basically insane. Lady Ursla is right now trying to heal his body, but she has warned me that his mind may never recover. He acts like a dog." And the tears flowed once more from her eyes. The twins, so elated over finally finding one of their family members, sobered. They looked at the others for confirmation of what Alison had said. They nodded solemnly.

"Take heart," Darless took the opportunity comfort them and Alison. "Lady Ursla of Hollybine Woods, the Great Druid, will very likely be able to cure his body of the Abyss diseases. And Jon, here, and I, have discovered some pretty amazing things about spiritual beings and minds. I have hope that we can apply what we know to Lenny to erase the insanity that his long imprisonment in the foul Abyss has created. I'm sure our new techniques will help him recover." She spoke with such authority, such certainty, that hope began to grow deep down in Alison's heart, where no hope had been.

"However," Darless continued after a pause, "we have accepted a task to perform. And we definitely need some information, if not help. But it is a long story." She added that last as she realized how awkward this must all be sounding. The Twins would have no idea of what she was talking about.

Alison had drunk half a glass of the ale, mellowing her out a bit. "I'll tell you my tale first, or at least the highlights. When the castle was crumbling, Nanny grabbed me and we headed into the dungeons. That was what saved us. Only the dungeons survived the castle collapse. And with the castle gone, everyone else abandoned the outlying areas, so Nanny had to raise me in town. Although we looked and looked, we could find no trace of anyone else. As I grew up, I swore I would devote my life to finding out what happened to everyone, to try to get what's left of our family back together somehow and to rebuild Castle d'Ambrose. But that needed money. I became an apprentice mage and with some friends, began to adventure, taking on deeds that needed to be done. Sir Thomas le Bonnaire, our holy paladin, has been my tutor and has saved by hide on several occasions. I am now a rather powerful wizard in my own right and have nearly amassed sufficient funds to begin the castle construction."

"Then, I heard that someone was appearing in Brunsway Village by using one of our picture books, you know with the tridents on them made by Bard Wendell. By the way, I actually met the Bard. We here saved his bottom, but I'm getting ahead of myself. So I donned my ring of invisibility and staked out the village, hoping to catch the book thief. Well, it turned out to be Jon and Mandy; they each had a book. Jon is not from our world. One of our older brothers was being chased by the Hounds of Hell and he gave his book to Jon's Grandfather just before he died. No, I don't know who it was yet. When Jon's Grandfather, Jon's only remaining relative died, Jon inherited the book and discovered how to step into the pictures."

The twins were fascinated by her tale and listened eagerly as Alison took another long drink and continued. "Jon has immense mental powers, psi powers some call them, but he is totally untrained, undisciplined in its use. Anyway, he used his abilities to save a dying maiden by Stilmar Pond. Now concurrently with all this, raiders using another of our books decimated part of Mandy's forest area. Her goddess, Reylona, gave her the captured book and requested her to get to the bottom of the evil that was destroying the forest. Mandy ran into Jon and then they ran into me spying on them." She went on to describe their many adventures trying to solve the puzzle and how they had met Darless, who was commanded by Morrigan to serve an evil mage.

The twins really enjoyed the description of their little sister's grand adventure. They had her repeat several times how Jon could seem to step into any where he wanted. Jon tried to describe it to them, "All you do is just get the idea you have arrived and then just arrive. That's all there is to it really." But they just stared at him in disbelief.

Alison described how they had rescued Darless, how in finding the special tree for the Lady Ursla, Jon had uncovered Darless' true name. Once she was informed of her true name, the alu-demon could no longer be summoned by anyone anymore and forced to do their bidding. But when she told them about the confrontation with Dispater and Morrigan, their gasps were heartfelt! When Alison described how she and

Jon had fell in love and how, realizing that she truly loved Jon, had jumped in front of Jon to take the Spear of Death hurled by Morrigan, they gasped in unison! "Yes, I was dead, but only for a short time. Jon took us all to Ukko's realm — he actually took Morrigan there along with my dead body. Don't ask me how he can transport a goddess!" Jon blushed and stared at the floor as Alison finished up by telling what she had been told of how Father Ukko raised her from death and pronounced that Jon would hereafter be known as Saint Jon Brown. Jon's face was very red at this point and he drank an entire glass of ale, hoping no one would notice him.

The twins stared at him in awe. Jon protested, "I'm only a musician, really just a musician." But no one believed him; he burped.

Alison continued, "After everything was settled, Jon proposed to me and I agreed. Only we have to see if it works out, you know, we are from such different worlds and all. Jon left to take care of some things back in his world. And while he was gone, a horde of Chasme demons attacked me one night and nearly killed me!"

"Wow! Exclaimed May, "we have seen some of them creatures around here from time to time. They are very nasty things indeed. But what do you mean nearly killed?"

Alison went on, "Well, the Lady Ursla gave us each one of these green emeralds enchanted with some powers of which we do not fully understand. I was killed, I think. They say my belly was opened and my guts on the floor, just awful. My life force, no me, now that I think of it, was somehow kept barely alive by this emerald. Jon heard my screams for aid across the vastness of space between our worlds and came and found me and got Darless and Lady Ursla and Mandy to help. Between them and my paladin, who also arrived while I was deadish, they healed me up. Don't ask me how, I have no clue." She purposely did not tell them about her subsequent "nightmares."

"We discovered that the horde of Chasme was flying in the reverse route that Dad took when he went on his last adventure to rescue the Holy Scepter of Ukko. So we went charging after them to do battle and warn folks. Well, it all led to the ruined tower of Leeds. You know, it's in our picture book. Well, there, Jon discovered a hidden chamber beneath the ruins and you'll never guess who was imprisoned there? An Air Maiden! Fruella. We rescued her and she gave us a gift of knowing what we really are, spiritual beings, but that's really hard to describe. And then the real battle began."

"As it turns out, Metrarch, Demon Lord of the 66th level of the Abyss had sent the Chasme Horde. We had a pitched battle with many demons gated from the Abyss and his henchmen and high priestess right there among the ruins of Leeds. We were out gunned and out manned. But Jon here managed to find a way to mentally explode the heads of those enormous bird-like demons; pretty impressive and he even deflected the priestess's Disintegration beam she aimed at his head, reflected it back to her and annihilated her totally! He still has no explanation for how he could do that trick!" Jon's face reddened once more and he consumed another glass of ale, and was feeling rather mellow now.

"Just as we were all just about dead once again, Metrarch opened a gate from the Abyss and sucked us all down to his realm. Darless here did a swan dive, uninvited, into the gate to help us survive the Abyss. But once again, Jon here somehow healed all of us fully before we arrived at the other terminal of the gate in the Abyss. That not only shocked all of us, but also Metrarch who transported four nearly dead adventurers only to have them arrive in perfect health." Alison went on to describe the total chaos that the next five minutes brought. Mat and May were startled to hear that Dispater once again entered the picture. Alison then described the bargain that they had made for the return of another book and Lenny.

"So you see, we must somehow prevent Metrarch from being assassinated here during the council meeting, which is in just a few more days' time." She did not mention that they were also under the obligation to restore the "balance" for she still had no idea what that meant.

"Hum," Jon finally broke in, "Er, I need to use your restroom. You know, too much ale." Mat showed him the way using a lantern. Jon staggered after him, just a bit light headed and swaying.

When he had returned, the others were also heading for the restroom. May had brought out some food. When all had returned, they ate a late night snack, answering the odd question here and there that May and May had. It was quite a lot for them to grasp in so short a time.

Finally, May took a drink and began, "Well, now it's our turn. I'm afraid, little Runtling, our tale is not quite so adventurous as yours, rather mundane indeed. Let's see, when the castle came under attack that dreadful night, a portion of our bedroom archway collapsed, trapping us inside. We could find no way out. Then, we remembered the picture books. Mat held his opened so we could step through and I took mine with us. We intended to get back as soon as it was safe. We came here in the middle of the night. Can you imagine two scared children arriving penniless in a town of thieves? The page with our home went all black and stayed that way for about a month. When we finally saw the desolated ruins reappear on that page, our hearts sunk about as low as they ever have. I think that was the lowest point of our lives!"

"The only way we survived at first was by begging a handout here and there. Then, we were forced to take to a bit of petty thievery ourselves just to stay alive. We lived in the sewers below the streets. There is a huge maze down there, quite impressive, but unbelievably smelly! After we saw that there would be no going home, we sold my book to get some funds on which to live. Mat has always been looking after me and I, him. Us two, against this den of thieves. We are not proud of becoming thieves, but we did excel at it, if we do say so ourselves. We did it just to survive, taking no more than we needed. But every time we were forced to steal to live, we felt so guilty, that finally we decided to try to do something about all the inequities in this town! We became the Twins, bringing a small measure of justice back into Freetown."

"One day, I helped an Illusionist recover his purse from a pickpocket. In return, he taught me my first spell. I quickly discovered that if I became powerful enough of an illusionist, it would help us in our quest to set things right in this town. To make a long story shorter, I am now even more experienced as an illusionist wizard than I am a thief!" She looked very pleased.

Then, without the slightest pause, Mat continued, "And one day I helped out a stranger in town. He ran into a street gang of thieves. He carried no weapons, so I jumped in to help him out, fearing the worst might happen to him. Well, it turns out that he needed no weapons; he is a marital arts monk. I was so enthralled at the incredible moves he had, that I just had to learn how to do that as well. So now I am Brother Mat, Master of the Silver Moon. I really don't need to use any weapons anymore."

And without the slightest pause, May continued, "As the Twins, we have been putting in law and order or at least justice back into this town for nearly a dozen years. We hear that outsiders are even calling this Twins Town now. We assembled some funds and slowly have built up respectable businesses, our disguise. By day, I make clothing and"

"I am a locksmith of some renown." added Mat without interrupting May, who then continued, "But by night, we don the cloak of black and set right the affairs that we are able to."

"So you see, compared to your tale, we have done nothing at all! However, I'm sure we can help you out in this demon matter. We tend to know everything of importance that is going on in this town. Er, well that is a bit of an exaggeration," May added, quite unsure of why she added that last bit. (Jon's walking stick was lying on the floor.)

Jon, who had recovered from a case of too much ale, yawned heavily. "Perhaps, we should meet tomorrow, I'm about to fall asleep, oops make that later today," he smiled. Everyone agreed. He had no sense of time because of the windowless room. But it had to be the wee hours of the morning.

"Let us walk you back to the inn. The streets are really not safe at night," May offered. Jon looked about; everyone was feeling the lack of sleep. He did not like the idea of spending another half hour getting back to the inn. So he said, "Here, I'll show you how it's done. We'll drop by your shops later today." Alison, too drained from the evening's excitement, simple took his hand. A sleepy Mandy did likewise and Darless held on to Mandy's other hand.

Mandy had the last word, "Now watch this carefully!" Tired though she was, the ranger still had that twinkle of mischief in her eyes. She knew what the effect would be as Jon simply stepped them all into their common room in the inn. Mat and May watched as all four just disappeared, poof, right before their eyes. Both blinked in disbelief. "Saint Jon," May mused as she headed for bed, followed by Mat, who added, "Brown."

Chapter 10 The Conference

Once again, everyone rose rather late the next morning; the effects of the late night took its toll on one and all. After brunch, Alison, who was so excited about finding her twins, just had to go visit them. It would not do for all of them to appear at May's dress shop, after all, Jon would be quite out of place. So Mandy accompanied Alison to May's while Darless accompanied Jon on a stroll about the town but not until Jon received stern warnings about pickpockets from Mandy and Alison. He appeased them by saying he would take nothing of value except his trusty walking stick which no one would want.

When Alison and Mandy arrived at May's, they found the small store packed with women, well dressed women, all after one thing, dresses. After listening to conversations and asking a few leading questions, they discovered that many were fearful that wonton destruction by the warring armies was about to befall the town and they wanted to stock up on May's excellent clothing should doom befall May and her shop. Others were planning on leaving the town; there was talk of a caravan to the west leaving fairly soon.

May was a bit frazzled with all of this sudden, rather unexpected business. She was more than a little alarmed when no one would place an order for future business, even buying dresses that clearly did not fit. Alarm was spreading. May had only a few minutes to spend with Alison. Together, they decided that May and Mat would meet them for dinner at the inn.

They left May who trying to convince a large busted woman that the dress she had picked out was at least two sizes too small. Instead, they went next door to visit Mat and his shop, "Locks Galore." While May's shop was quite large, Mat's was just the opposite. His entire operation appeared to occupy a room about thirty feet in length and twenty wide. Back against one end was a large worktable full of small bits and pieces of metal lock parts. One wall displayed iron locks of various shapes and sizes. But what caught the women's eyes was one large table displaying numerous jewelry style boxes.

Some were made of mahogany, some of boxwood. But the black teakwood boxes were fabulous. All were exquisitely made. Mat was certainly a master craftsman.

"May I help you," Mat smiled as he saw that special look in both women's eyes as they examined each and every box. It was the "I just *have* to have one of these boxes!" look. He had seen it many times before. He teased his little sister, "So, you just have to have one of these don't you?"

"Absolutely!" cried Alison, without even thinking. Then realizing what she had said, she began to laugh. "You sure do a terrific job. These really are excellent indeed!" She teased back, "A woman's got to have a safe place to store all of her jewelry, doesn't she?" Mandy laughed as Mat smiled. Neither woman wore much jewelry ever, but both had visions of other items in these boxes. "I do have a lot of magical rings that could do with some organizing. These would be perfect." After a pause, she asked, "I don't know if you can answer this or not, Mat. But are these locks of sufficiently high quality so as to take a magical enchantment?"

"Yes. May's experimented with them. They have her seal of approval, though no one else knows that, you see. Keep quiet on that detail, Runtling," Mat explained.

Meanwhile, a number of men came in to purchase a rather large number of locks. The two women overheard some mutterings about protection from the thieving armies. No sooner had Mat taken care of them, than a number of women came in laden with bulging packages to purchase some boxes. Quickly Alison and Mandy grabbed as many of the boxes as they could hold and took them to Mat. "We'll take these!" Alison panted.

Mat laughed, "Seems there is a run on my boxes today." But the tone in his voice showed deep concern and worry. There was definitely a level of suppressed panic among many in his store.

As the women were leaving, Alison tried an experiment. She concentrated on Mat and placed a thought into his mind, *Bye, see you later for dinner at the inn.*

The startled, surprised look on Mat's face told her all that she needed to know. It had worked! And she had spooked Mat for a change, a small payback for all those scary bedtime stories he had told her so long ago. Grinning from ear to ear, she and Mandy walked out heavily laden with all the boxes.

"What'd you do back there to Mat? He seemed very surprised about something." Mandy asked when they were a block from the store and after a careful glance to make sure no pickpockets were close to them.

I placed a good-bye thought into his mind like I am doing to you now. Alison concentrated, placing it into Mandy's mind.

Wow! You are getting the hang of this! came the reply in her mind from Mandy. Both girls laughed for nearly a block.

Darless and Jon stopped beside the well, pondering the city maps they had acquired the day before. "I think we should stick to the major roads; it is likely safer, less riskier, if the town is really full of thieves," Darless pronounced.

"Okay," Jon agreed but added, "I still think a big city is neat. All of these unusual shops, the people, the ancient trades and skills. It is like a trip back into time for me."

Her eyebrows curled downward, Darless said, "Don't you have shops in your Urbana? I don't understand you sometimes."

Jon grimaced, he knew he had stuck his foot into his mouth this time. He tried to think of a way to explain it to her. But he could not find any effective means to communicate it. "I've an idea," he finally said. "Look at my mental pictures. I am going to walk you through a typical day in Urbana." Her eyes brightened; though Jon did not realize it, he was giving her a tremendously valuable present, the kind that she had only dreamed her lover, her mate, would one day share with her.

Jon strolled down the busy Urbana Green street. The numerous cars took Darless by surprise. *Horseless carriages,* Jon sent her, *people going to work or to the stores or on errands.* He remembered his last trip to the grocery store and brought those images back into his mind for her to view. Darless watched fascinated, surprised, but determined to burn those images into her memory for further study and reflection.

Can I see your house and Crystal Park you told us about? she thought to him. Immediately, Jon recalled one early evening stroll to the park and lagoon and then the walk home, past the huge oak trees that bordered his house.

Without thinking, he recalled the last time he was there lounging on the lawn at dusk, pining for Alison. *Wow! You have a beautiful castle or house or mansion. I do love that park! Thank you for sharing that with me, Jon. This is a present beyond my wildest imaginations.*

"So can you see how this looks to me?" Jon asked her when he finished showing her his memories.

"Ah yes. You have the meat all cut up and nicely packaged and stored in those ice chests. You do not have to buy today's meat from the butcher who has just cut up the animal. Yes, I see. But are there no horses in your world?" she asked.

"Well, yes, mostly for sport or fun. We have car machines called tractors that do the plow horse work cheaper and more efficiently," he tried to explain, unsure how much of this she was grasping.

"Okay, I believe I understand your view point of this city now. Primitive, right?" Darless inquired. Jon nodded agreement. She went on, "You know, you have just done for me what I have always dreamed my lover would do — that we would share our minds, our memories, our dreams." She felt a bit self-conscious and looked down at the cobble stones. Then she hastily added, "I know, it is just my fantasy."

"No don't make less of your dreams and desires, Darless. I feel strongly that a marriage is indeed as you have said, a union of the two, a total sharing of each other. You are absolutely right in wanting that. Please, do not ever settle for less than that with a man. Promise me that you will not settle for anything less," Jon implored her. "Just because your immediate body is different, that does not make you less. You are not your body; don't ever forget what the Air Maiden has shown us!"

Her eyes glowed; she kissed him on the cheek. "I won't!" she promised. "Come on, let's see the sights." And they strolled arm in arm down the busy street, looking at the colorful shops, the people, the buildings and trees.

Jon continuously failed to watch where he was walking and repeatedly stepped into manure piles. Darless just smiled. Neither were paying too close attention to where they were going and did not notice that the street they were on had become rather narrow.

They had entered a residential area of cheap, rundown houses. Children of all ages in worn out clothes were playing in the street. Suddenly out of nowhere a heavyset teenager rushed up to them, stuck a dagger up against Darless' throat and said, "Give me your purse or your lady gets stuck!" His dirty, unshaven face snarled. The stench of his unwashed hair assaulted their nostrils. While his clothes looked beyond repair, he sported very new and stylish shoes.

Don't worry, Jon, his dagger cannot even scratch me. Darless immediately sent to Jon.

This must be one of those ruffians that May was referring too last night. I'm going to see what I can see. Play along, Jon sent back to her. Then, he took a look at the mental pictures their opponent was looking at. Suddenly Jon had a realization. *He has lost his self-respect! Do you see that one back when he was a child?*

Where? Oh, yes. Nasty thing to do to your mother, though, Darless replied. *How can we get him to see it?* Darless knew instinctively what Jon had in mind to try.

Inspiration struck. Jon said to the boy, "Tell me about that last girl you stuck!" So forceful, so unexpected was his utterance, so full of total command, the boy instantly complied.

"I, uh, well I just saw her walking alone, rather stupid thing to do, and she had her purse just dangling there. So I stuck her and grabbed the purse and ran. Women deserved to be stuck, don't you know."

"Thank you. Now is there an earlier time that you stuck a woman?" Jon acknowledged and asked that key question.

The lad had no choice but to look and reply, for he was really stuck in these memories. After a slight hesitation, he replied, "Yes, last week. This dandy was out for a stroll with his woman friend and that's how I got my new shoes here. I stuck my dagger to her throat just like I got yours here and demanded his shoes or I'd stick her. After I got his shoes, I stuck her anyway. Women deserve to be stuck!"

"Very good. Now, is there an earlier time when you did something similar?" Jon persisted. After a longer pause, the lad told him about another one. And then another and another. He had done this so many times that Jon lost count.

The ruffian did start to yawn and fidget, so Jon felt he was on the right track and persisted patiently.

At long last, and not too soon for Darless who was getting sick of seeing all these women getting "stuck," the lad said, "Yeh, when I was maybe three years old something happened." And he yawned and yawned. "But I cannot see what it is."

"Tell me about it from beginning to end," Jon requested.

The lad did so. "Something about me mommy. Dunno. She got hurt somehow. That's all," he struggled to say, perplexed that that was all he could remember.

"Okay. Now go back over it again and see if you can see what else is going on at that time," Jon commanded.

After three more times through the incident, Jon discovered that the boy had accidentally raised a knife to help his mom cut the potatoes. But she had moved downward to pick up the knife just as he raised it up and had gotten stuck by the knife in her neck. Suddenly, the teenager started laughing, "You know, after that, I decided that I could never ever trust myself again. And I never did. That's crazy; women don't deserve to be stuck with a knife." And he laughed some more.

"Very well done, young lad. Now take some responsibility for life and make things go more right for you and your friends," Jon replied.

"Say, who are you anyway and what was that that you just did?" he asked, realizing that something of great importance to his life had just happened totally unexpectedly.

Darless spoke for Jon, "He is Saint Jon Brown. And you my lad have just been given the gift of life, a second chance for life. Don't blow it this time!" Turning to Jon, she said, "Come on, it's getting late; we'd better be heading back." Jon let Darless lead him back the way that they had come. He felt elated, but tired. Doing this took a deal of mental energy and he was somewhat tired.

When they were back on the major roadway once more, Darless was excited, "Do you realize what you did back there? Do you realize the importance of that experiment?"

"Well, I just got him to look at what he had done is all," he replied, not quite getting what her point was.

"The lad was a ruffian, evil — lord knows how many helpless women he has stabbed. But the root of that evil, that criminality, lay in losing his own self-respect. Don't you see how critical that really is? I sure do. I've been there. When you lose your self-respect, what's left? You cannot trust yourself! See how he twisted that accidental stabbing of his mother around to make himself right in stabbing other women? It all fits! Now how do we do this on *any* individual, *that* is the real question!"

Jon muttered, "Hum, yes, I see. I had only seen that the kid was stuck in that childhood accident incident. But now I see what you are driving at. Self-respect. That's a heavy thought. Lose self-respect and what is left? Golly, nothing! I had not thought this through."

They walked on; a bit later he added, "You know, it was so hard to do because I could see that basic time there with his mother, but I wanted him to see it. Did you notice at first he could only barely remember that something happened when he was three? It was only after going over it several times that he finally saw it as it was. That is why I knew we had to sort of go down that chain of later stabbing incidents to get to it. Now if there was only a way to do this without me having to see it all first and guide them."

Darless was extraordinarily cheerful, "Yes, that is what we need to work out. If we can do that, think of what we can do for people! Incredible, just incredible. Oops, we are back. Guess we better go inside and see if Mandy and Alison are back yet." They nodded to the doorman and entered.

"Hi, you two! Mat and May will be here for dinner." Alison cheerily welcomed Jon and Darless as they entered the common room of their suite. "Guess what, Darless? We have a present for you. Come look," she bubbled with excitement. Mandy had a dozen of the ebony jewelry boxes spread out on the table.

"Mat's work," Alison explained as she watched Darless' eyes open wide. "He is a master craftsman. I think these are all enchantable. You can have your pick of any of these here. Mandy and I want those on the right.

Jon left the women discussing the boxes and went to rest a bit before the evening dinner. He was still a bit tired, yet something Darless had said intertwined his thoughts. As he lay staring up at the ceiling, he pondered how the loss of self-respect doomed a person. Yet, if a person could spot how that respect was actually lost, he could possibly recover. Did that apply to all men? How about demons? And devils? He mused, *Is Dispater the way he is because he has lost his self-respect?* And what would happen if a demon could recall such a terrible incident? Would it blow off as it had done with that young lad? He had more questions than answers. *I'm no philosopher!* He fell asleep.

In his dream, he was being kissed, passionately. He was aroused and returned the kiss with equal emotion. Suddenly the bliss ended, "Wake up love," it was Alison and she had kissed him. Her eyes glowed and her face was radiant. "Come on, get dressed. It's nearly time to meet the twins.

"Thanks, love. Say how long was I asleep?" Jon mused as he got up and scrounged around for some clean clothes.

"Only an hour or so. Darless explained what you did with that young hooligan. That was an awfully nice thing to do. I'm proud of you," she replied. "But do hurry up. I don't want to be late. I cannot wait to talk with my family. It's the first time I've had this chance since I was three!"

The four were seated at a larger table than normal when the twins arrived. The tired, worn look on their faces spoke for them — brisk business, but for all the wrong reasons. However, in unison, their faces broke into broad smiles as they spotted little Runtkin. "Hi, sis!" they spoke in unison and joined the foursome.

The twins described their day while they ordered and then ate a leisurely dinner. Since Alison was treating them, she insisted that they eat something they always wanted to try but thought might be too expensive or extravagant. After all, this was rather like a homecoming dinner. It is noted here that Mat had the very aged steak while May tried the exotic mushroom salad. Jon, however, insisted on trying six different types of tea. He was becoming very addicted to the drink. All in all, it was a very enjoyable dinner for everyone. After dinner, they headed up to their common room to talk, Jon once again bringing the teapot and cups.

"Well," May began, "it is really starting to happen again. We went through the Demon Lord's Games once before when we were younger, before we became the Twins. It was awful. After one set of soldiers, if you can call them that, captured the well and declared victory, the men broke up and practically dismantled the town!"

"Well, not totally," Mat corrected her. "It just seemed that way to our young eyes. Looting and raping was rampant. However, we did discover that various underhanded people paid some of these 'soldiers' to loot and wreck certain establishments or homes of those with which they wanted to get even. I'm certain that a lot of that sort of thing went on and still does."

"Many businesses were wrecked, lives destroyed, that sort of thing. The beasts!" May continued passionately. "And it is happening again. We tried to bring some order to this chaotic town and I think we were succeeding, bit by bit. But now I've heard that some folks are planning to leave. They are forming a caravan and heading west away from the mountains. We were even asked to join them! It's the more respectable folks who are abandoning the town; many are those we have helped as the Twins."

"But I would really be worried about a caravan heading west. With many armies out there and with the lands of the Morrigan worshipers just beyond and all of it a vast desert, I would not give them much chance of getting away without losing everything they own!" Mat warned. "But there is no reasoning with them. I tried. 'Stay here and get ruined or worse or try to make a new start' was all that I got from them. Sometimes I wonder if we should not just pack up and go with them!" There was a note of surrender in his voice.

The room was quiet for a spell. Thrusting his hair back, he pronounced, "Ah well. But I did find out something about the assassins that you might find useful." He had everyone's instant attention. "I did some discrete checking in the Thieves Guild. The Assassi lie to the south and a bit west of here. They are assassins of great renown, and rightly so if all the tales of their deeds be true. What I find interesting is the price of an assassination. Given the nature of your particular 'mark' as they call the proposed victim, the price must be upwards of 500,000 gold coins! Further, they guarantee their work or your money back. Imagine the arrogance of those evil men!"

"What have we gotten ourselves into this time?" muttered Mandy.

May picked up the conversation, "I looked into their modus operandi. These are really nasty fellows. They usually use various desert poisons on their weapons to make doubly sure of their score. And what I find particularly diabolical is that they employ magical spells to assist their dirty work. It is said that they can change form and shape and even species! One person I talked to even said that he'd heard that they can be transformed into a fly. Imagine that. A little fly lands on you. Who'd think this was an assassin? Why you'd be stabbed and poisoned before you had any clue you were being attacked! What have you gotten yourself into little sister?" May sounded very worried indeed.

Alison's face looked forlorn. "I'm sorry I got you all into this!" She looked at her three friends apologetically.

"Pay it no mind! That's what friends are for," Mandy replied. "But I do prefer a fight to all this sneaking around stuff!"

"We are here for you, just as you were there for us," spoke the alu-demon with a tone of certainty in her voice.

Jon, who had not said a word thus far, interjected, "We've got one thing in our favor." All eyes turned to him. "We know who the mark is to be and roughly when it must occur. Who and time and place, so we have an edge that others might not have."

"You have a point, Jon," May nodded. She then discussed various ways an assassin might use to complete his mission, back stabbing, neck cutting with a poisoned blade, and so on. She told of bludgeoning attacks, garroting, poisoning food, and snake bites. The list seemed endless. No one heard Jon's comment, "Are they always men?"

After discussing this situation for nearly an hour and really reaching no conclusions, May then changed the topic. "Perhaps you can help us with this one. We really do not know how to respond, for once." Everyone welcomed a change of subject matter. Amid a chorus of "Please go on's" she explained. "Today, this message was posted on the board for the Twins. Here, Mat, you read it; I cannot do so without crying." And she handed the paper to Mat.

He cleared his voice and spoke, "Dear Twins, My name is Pattie and I am thirteen years old. I have heard about the coming War Games. My friends have told me all of the horrid things these bad men do to young women and all. I don't want that to happen to me. I don't want my parents to get hurt either or have daddy's livery stables destroyed. My boyfriend is trying to get me to come away with him on the Westward Caravan. My parents cannot decide whether to stay it out or go. They are very afraid for me. But daddy says the caravan is not safe either. Please help me. What should I do? Yours respectfully, Pattie Harrigan"

May broke down and started crying and Mat moved over to comfort her, but Alison beat him, cradling her in her arms. For once, he was deeply thankful that he did not have to support May. He could barely support himself. Obviously, he was deeply touched as well.

It was Darless of all people who responded, filling the awkward void, counting the following off on her fingers for emphasis. "Number 1: you have the knowledge and wisdom to help people. Number 2: you have assumed that responsibility. Number 3: others now recognize that and are depending upon you. Number 4: with that responsibility and knowledge also comes the ability to control. Number 5: you are to be highly commended for all that you have done. Number 6: all that you lack at this point is sufficient knowledge and wisdom to answer her. Thus, Number 7: we must help you acquire the additional certainty you need to be able to help her and the others under your care. It's that simple."

Both Mat and May looked at Darless not fully understanding what she was saying. "Yes, she always talks like that on serious matters," Jon joked and winked and smiled at Darless. "She had a coldly calculating, brilliant mind. She is seldom, if ever, wrong." Darless blushed, pleased.

Mandy interjected, "So what you are saying, Darless, is that they just need more facts upon which to base their reply, right? Or have I missed the whole point?" Mandy definitely knew that she did indeed sometimes miss the whole point when it came to intellectual matters. And she was not afraid to so admit. The alu-demon nodded in agreement. "Then, all we need to do is get them more facts. There, that is simple." She finally had it down to her level of thought.

"Well, once the council meeting is done, the Games begin in twenty-four hours. That gives a tiny bit more time for a response," Alison offered. Then inspiration struck her. "Say, you know I am intending to rebuild Castle d'Ambrose. Maybe some of these good folk may want to help start that project or build a village around the new castle. Then they would have an ultimate destination for their travel and a purpose, well a better purpose than just trying to run for their lives."

"Ah but think it through, Alison," Mandy interjected. This was something she understood only too well. "Think about it for a minute. From the maps we glimpsed back at Ravenwash, to the west lies at least two or three armies heading pell-mell in this direction and beyond that lies a land of Morrigan worshipers. Also, a caravan of folks with all their worldly possessions would attract every raider between here and your place. The poor folks would be sitting ducks! It would take an *army* to guarantee their safety. And another army we are lacking." A sobering silence followed.

"Mandy's right, you know," Darless broke the silence. "We could escort a few wagons safely, maybe. Between us, we can generate enough fire-power to defend a small number. But not a caravan, I'm afraid. Advising someone to do that is tantamount to giving them a death sentence. It is a certainty that they would be robbed of everything of value."

"However, rats swarm off of a sinking ship," Jon stuck his thoughts into the conversation. "There is probably no argument you can make to those that are going. For them, to stay is a guaranteed destruction, while to go at least offers them some small hope for the future. Like rats, they will leap at that chance. Because if they don't, they end up in a terrible apathy! Ruined as a person. I think that a person is as alive as he can envision a future for himself."

Mat and May looked forlorn. The others were just confirming what they already had considered between themselves. Darless saw their dejection and countered, "But, as I said, we need more information, more knowledge, which we have not yet acquired. You see, suppose that a gate could be built that would transport the caravan wagons one by one to say a location three hundred miles away. That would nearly resolve the dilemma."

"Wow! You are right," Jon exclaimed; a burst of insight flashed in his mind. "We are facing a problem. To be a problem, both opposing sides must be of comparable force, equal significance, so that it cannot be resolved. If you make one side or the other way bigger or totally remove one of the pressures or forces, poof, the problem vanishes! That's brilliant, Darless. I see now where you are heading us. We need more information so that we can make one side go poof."

She grinned. "You give me more credit than is due; I had not quite thought of it that way. But yes, we could sit here and see what all we could invent, such as a gate. We could try mass teleportations. But still, knowledge is the answer and then can come responsibility to use that knowledge properly. So allow me."

"Mat and May, Number 1: could this town be roused to defend itself and put a total stop to these invading armies? Number 2: how many armed men are planning to go on the caravan trip? Enough to provide decent protection? Number 3: this War Game contest thing has been going on apparently for a very long time. So what was the town's defenses say a hundred years ago? Number 4: has this cycle of destruction by the game participants always occurred during all of the previous contests? Number 5: how many powerful mages and fighters are there in this city? Enough to make a difference if they were roused to action? Number 6: has something happened to this town in the past to cause its citizens to lose their self-respect on a broad scale? Number 7: if a safe passage caravan could be arranged, how many of the townsfolk would go? There is a difference between ten going and one thousand going. Number 8: are there hiding places where people could go and not be discovered, like maybe in the sewers? We need answers to those questions for starters. I'm sure I can think of some more," she chuckled.

"Impressive, Darless! Now I really see what you meant by more knowledge," Jon cried. "Answers to those would give us something with which to think and plan. But of course, the answers probably would lead to further questions," and he and everyone else began laughing, all imagining an endless sea of questions and answers.

"We follow you," smiled May and Mat in unison. "But it will take some time to get them. I've nearly emptied my shop of clothing, so I can really just close up shop for the time being," May commented. "Me too," added Mat, "All the boxes are gone; an entire year's worth of production sold off in one day! Unreal indeed."

"We can help too," Alison added. "Does the town have a library where I can study something of the town's history and the like? Maybe I will find out something that way."

"I'd like a better feel for whether or not the town could even be defended," Mandy put in. "Mat, can you take me on a guided tour. Let's just see what kind of defenses there are or could be used in such a manner."

"Sure thing," Mat replied eagerly. "It's been a while since I was not always going around on business, you know. It is sort of like having a vacation, only an unpleasant one."

"We really need to get fully informed about this caravan thing," May added. "I want to know who is organizing it; who is going, and so forth. I think a little Twins' effort tonight will have those answers by morning. Mat and I have work to do tonight. Tomorrow morning, er late morning, I'll take some of you to the library and Mat can show the others the city." Everyone agreed.

May's eyes were bright; a smile was on her face. She suddenly realized that hope had returned to her. "I feel like a really heavy burden has been lifted from me! I don't know what you all did, but I feel really hopeful somehow. Thank you all." She looked at all the smiling faces and added, "I'm beginning to feel like you *all* are my family! That is a feeling that I have not had since that dark night so very long ago when I was a child. I'm so happy, I could cry!" And tears of unrestrained joy trickled down her cheeks. No one saw Mat wipe his eyes.

It was about nine in the evening when Mat and May said farewell. It was time for the Twins to discover information under the cloak of darkness. "Boy, this is a tricky problem," Darless commented after the twins had left. "We could perhaps erect a huge force dome over the well blocking any army from acquiring their goal. But undoubtedly Demon Lords and their henchmen would eventually find a way to dispel such a spell."

"Yes, on StarTrek they erected huge protection domes over cities — nothing undesired is allowed in or out. But that is just SciFi," Jon mused and then spent five minutes trying to explain what science fiction and StarTrek was all about.

When the others finally understood his comments, Alison responded. "You know around here the Gods can do just that, erect huge force fields to protect their worshipers. But here it seems rather like this town is nothing but a pawn in the hands of the Demon Lords. In the meantime, let's see what we can propose to do about this assassination attempt."

They discussed plans at length. By ten o'clock, they had made some progress. They decided that their biggest strength lay in their ability to instantly communicate mentally. At the first hint of an assassin's presence, all four would know at once. Next came a unified attack plan. Since a great deal of magic would necessarily have to be employed by said assassin just to get into that fortified room and next to Metrarch, Alison and Darless would first concentrate on dispelling any and all magical effects possible as their first action. Mandy and her blade offered their biggest chance for a direct intervention halting the attack or at least delaying or deflecting it. So Mandy's job was to attack the assassin directly as her first action. This meant that the three women would be visible the whole time of the meeting. Over Jon's protests, they would surround Metrarch acting as a human barrier of sorts. Jon, who had proven he could detect the presence of others, was to remain invisible the whole time, standing in some out of the way place where he could fully concentrate on the entire space and do his thing, alerting the women as soon as he detected the assassin's presence. Jon decided that his next action would be to attempt to control the assassin either mentally or control his body directly, if that were somehow possible. They thought that they had a fighting chance against the unknown assassin.

"I'm really thirsty after all that talking," declared Mandy. "Anyone care to join me for ale downstairs at the pub area?"

"I'll go with you, Mandy. I am always game to try different stouts and ales," Jon declared. But the Alison and Darless decided to turn in for the night. Both were tired. "We won't be very long," Jon added.

And so it was that Mandy and Jon were in the pub portion of the inn late that night. They had a table in the back of the smoke filled room from which they could watch most all of the other people and the bar and the entrance. The inn's pub still had about twenty customers, many smoking pipes, all chatting and drinking and occasionally bursting into a boisterous song followed by laughter. Jon could not figure out if they were being laughed at or with, as the singers sounded very drunk.

Jon had Wilkenson Ale while Mandy had the House Extra Strong Ale. Each shared theirs with the other. They both were excellent, Jon declared. Mandy was describing the local pubs around her castle for Jon when a tall man covered in a dark cloak entered the pub and walked slowly up to the bar. They were close enough to overhear this stranger.

"Perchance we can make a deal, barkeep. I am a traveler in need of a meager room to stay for a few days at most. In return, I offer my services. I am an excellent baker," said the stranger.

Mandy stopped talking mid-sentence. She thought that she recognized that voice; she motioned for Jon to listen too. "I swear I know that voice from somewhere!"

"Ya mean you're broke and want to barter a room out of us, eh?" drolled the barkeeper, drying a mug in his hands. "How do I know you can bake anything? I give you a room tonight and come tomorrow I'll find out that all you can do is make a mess, I'll wager. I think you are just trying to con me out of a room for the night, that's what I think!" He was not about to be swindled out of a night's lodging.

The stranger's back was to them so they could not see his face. But his brown cloak looked well-worn, his tall boots covered in dust. "Well, you have a point there. How about if you give me a room for this evening; tomorrow I bake a number of batches of breads or whatever you like. If they do not meet with your expectations, then I will pay you for the night. I believe I can manage paying for one night, if need be."

The barkeeper thought for a moment and replied, "Sounds fair enough, except what if come tomorrow you no longer have your money and cannot pay? What then? Are you willing to do any kind of labor to work off your bill, if baking fails?"

"Absolutely, though I'm sure you will be more than satisfied with my skills," the stranger replied. There was a hint of extreme fatigue in his voice.

Suddenly Mandy put it together, the voice and baker. She rose mindless of everything and yelled out, "William, William Conners? Is that you?" Jon caught her ale mug just as it was about to tip over. He saw the startled stranger jerk upright and spin around on one heel, eyes darting about the unfamiliar room in bewilderment. The barkeep looked straight at Mandy. "Over here," waved Mandy, excitement in her voice. The stranger's eyes found Mandy; Jon watch the unshaven man flush. He obviously recognized her. After a "pardon me" spoken hurriedly to the barkeeper, he strode over to the table, attempting to be as formal as he could muster.

"My Liege Lady," William bowed low after quickly removing his woolen cap, letting his disheveled hair fall in tangles on his cheeks. "You most humble servant, William Conners, ma'am." His face, though journey worn and in need of a wash, flushed; Jon noticed his feet shuffled. He was evidently not so comfortable at this unexpected meeting.

"Well, zagroot zounds! It is you, William, and in this place no less! Amazing!" Mandy added. She yelled over to the barkeeper, "Give him any room he wants; put it on my tab; and bring three more house ales over here real fast, please." She glanced at William, balancing first on one foot and then the other. "Have a seat, man. Boy do you need a bath!" The man sat down very carefully, as if he was in the presence of a goddess, unsure of himself.

"Oh," Mandy realized she had forgotten the introductions. "Jon, this is one of the villagers that my castle protects, William Conners. He is our local baker. And a finer baker you will never find! William, this is Jon Brown; you know the one I've been talking about."

William's discomfort rose another notch. "You, you are *the* Saint Jon Brown?" he managed to mutter. When Jon acknowledged it so, his brown eyes opened wider. He was saved by the barkeeper sliding three mugs of ale across the table.

"William here is the best baker I have ever seen. He is my official Blackthorn Castle baker, believe it or not. You would be wise to let him bake whatever he wants," Mandy defended him.

"Well, you get him cleaned up and have him report to the Chief Cook tomorrow and they can make an informed decision. We have a quality reputation around here to live up to, if you take my meaning." And he hurried off answering another call for more ale.

"You are most kind, my Liege Lady," William thanked her for the compliment.

"Oh do stop being so, so formal," Mandy retorted. Since Jon had that confused look on his face, she explained further, "Our society does not have a proper title for a woman head of a castle, you see. Normally, they would call their leader and protector, 'My Lord.' But that is totally male-ish you see. And 'My Lady' does not carry any weight at all; you know, women are seen but not heard in castle matters. So they call me 'My Liege Lady.'"

Flustered, Jon asked, "But you don't actually own him do you?" He was really uncertain just how this aspect of these societies operated. From his meager history courses, he had vague ideas that somehow the lord of a castle owned his serfs, if that was the right term for William.

"Not exactly. He owes me his allegiance and I owe him protection. It's a rather symbiotic relationship," she explained. "Whatever I ask, he will do. And should anyone or thing trouble my villagers, I am duty-bound to intervene at once. Without the villagers, the castle folk would starve. We both need each other to survive well." Turning to William, she added, "Please address me as just Mandy around here. We are not in our usual settings. There is absolutely no need for formality."

"Yes, My Liege Lady, er, Mandy," William muttered. He took a long thirsty drink of ale. "My, this is good ale. Could I have another please, Mandy? I used up most all of my funds just getting to this place. I'll work out what I owe you when I get back to the village, if that's okay with you, ma'am." The ale was having its effect, William's tenseness started to melt.

"Certainly," and she signaled the barkeeper. "But tell me, William, whatever brings you here? You are the last person I expected to see in this town! How did you get here? How do you know of this place? I have no idea how to get here from Blackthorn." Jon watched his face grimace; he could see the young man fighting an internal battle of some kind.

At long last and after taking a big gulp of the ale, he mumbled, "I'm on a secret mission."

Mandy's eye brows raised and she was instantly alert. That was the absolute last thing she expected to hear from her village baker. That he was visiting some distant sick relative was what she was expecting to hear. She could contain her curiosity no longer, "Okay, William, out with it. What secret mission? For whom? Perhaps I or we can help you out." Jon watched as the poor man became even more frustrated. Jon could not resist temptation and tried to peer into William's mind. He saw nothing but a genuine confusion and embarrassment concerning how to explain this all. Notably absent were all mental pictures. This Jon found very strange and became keenly interested in this village baker.

Play it cool, Mandy, Jon thought to her, *he is trying to find a way to tell you.*

"Yes, that is it, I really am trying to find a way to tell you," William said.

Both Jon and Mandy did an immediate double blink; their mouth's opened but nothing came out. *Did he read our minds just then?* Mandy sent to Jon.

"Oh darn, now I have put my foot in my mouth," William commented to himself. "Let's see you get out of this one, Billy Boy!"

"Zagroot zounds! Men. Why don't you just begin at the beginning and move through the middle and end up at the end? Hey barkeep, I need another ale here! How about you Jon?" Mandy retorted. Jon shook his head; his mug was still half full.

William struggled a bit more, downed the rest of his ale, signaled for another two rounds, hick-upped, and finally spoke in a low voice, leaning over the table so only Jon and Mandy could hear. "You must promise me two things, My Liege Lady, er Mandy." She glared at him, but nodded; Jon nodded affirmative as well.

"Okay then. You see I am actually a servant of Reylona. Yes, I know, all of her priestesses are women. But many years ago, she came to me and bought a ten loaves of my almond bread. I didn't realize she was the goddess then. But she introduced herself and all. She said that I was to be her servant; that my gift was going to waste and that I needed to use it to help others no matter my personal sacrifice. Well, I knew all along what I should be doing, and I told her that too. She said that she also knew that and that she had come to help me make the decision to use my gift." He paused a moment to make sure that they were not laughing at him. They weren't, just keenly interested.

"Well, she told me that she would visit me whenever there was a situation in which I should use my gifts for mankind. I told her that that would be perfect, because I never could figure out when was the right time to use it. She also said that her priestesses needed a sign that would let them know without question that I was one of her chosen. She blinked and this mark appeared on my arm." He slid his loose fitting sleeve up. There on his forearm was the unmistakable symbol of Reylona, the same design of a deer that was on Mandy's holy symbol.

"You know I am one of her priestesses, don't you, William?" Mandy whispered back.

"Yes, ma'am. So I figured that if I showed you this mark, you would know I am telling the truth." He pulled his sleeve back down and took another long drink. "Now that I know you know I am not fibbing, I'll tell you more. About two months ago, she appeared to me again and told me to go to a town called Freetown. Be there by the second full moon. She etched directions in my mind and I've made it with a few days to spare."

"Yes, so what are you to do here?" Mandy quickly interrupted, trying to hurry him up.

"I am to join a caravan of wagons heading westward. There will be a time shortly after that when I need to use my abilities. Then, I may return home again. There you have it," and he took another long drink.

Exasperated, Mandy retorted, "But you have not told us what you are to do! You are not a fighter — that I can vouch for. You do not cast healing spells — none that I have ever heard about. You are not a magician. So what is it you are to do? Zagroot zounds! Men, honestly!"

The young man cringed. "I calm men," he muttered.

"Huh?" Mandy replied completely missing any point he was making.

"I can make fighters put down their weapons and go home. Haven't you ever wondered why there are never any fights in our village, My Liege Lady, er Mandy?" he replied.

"Now that you mention it, no, I cannot recall ever having to resolve a fight. That is unusual. You'd think there would be the usual petty fist fights and the like. But as the Lord or Liege Lady, I have never had to settle any village matters. How is this possible?" Mandy asked, genuinely surprised and feeling rather stupid for never having discovered this fact before now.

"If a fight breaks out, I calm the participants who leave. Matters get settled peacefully, if I am around," he explained.

"Wait a minute, William," Jon interrupted. "You mean you use your mental powers to sort of force others to your will? How close to them do you have to be? How many can you calm at one time? This interests me very much indeed!"

"Er, it has nothing to do with my mind. I do it. I've always been able to do it even as a young kid growing up. Came in handy cause I could always avoid any fights. I don't force them; they just always calm down and leave for home. That is all they ever do. I only have to be able to see them; distance does not even matter, just so I can see them. I've never counted how many I can get, but I once ended a rather large barroom brawl; must have been fifty or more. You believe me when I tell you I can do this?" he asked in disbelief.

"Of course," Jon replied. "Why should I doubt you?"

Relief flooded across his whole body. Tensions evaporated, he relaxed totally. Jon suddenly realized that this was William's big concern, not being believed. Jon stated the obvious, "So this was what was holding you back from telling us all about your mission? You thought we would not believe you?"

"Yes, I thought you would make fun of me or think I was imagining it. I just cannot handle people not believing me when I say something this important to me," he replied. "I am not a fancy adventurer like you folks; I am just a humble baker. All I want to do is bake, to have others enjoy good bread. I know tis a small thing. But from small things done well come larger things, is my belief."

"Wow. William, you and I have a lot in common here. I am no adventurer either; I am a musician, not sure how humble I am, but just a musician. I love to make music. However, I do have some powerful abilities that others do not seem to equally have. So I am using them to help out, much like you. If I did not have Mandy here protecting me every step of the way, I'd been killed a long time ago." It was William's eyes that bulged; his mouth gaped. It dawned on him that he might not be the only one in such circumstances. Jon continued, "At first I thought, as did everyone else, that my abilities came from my mind somehow, something they were calling psi power. But recently, an Air Maiden showed me that I am a being, a spiritual being. And now I am not so sure that what I do is a mental thing. I am beginning to suspect that I do it."

"You mean you did not know that you are? That you are a spiritual being residing behind your head?" William asked in utter disbelief.

"Wait a minute," interrupted Mandy. "No, none of us had any real certainty of what we really are, not until the gift from the Air Maiden. Now we all know who and what we are. And what do you mean residing behind your head?"

"Er, I am always behind my body's head, maybe two feet or so. Isn't everyone?" William asked in complete disbelief. "I never thought to ask anyone about it. I just took it for granted everyone is located thereabouts."

"I've got news for you, William, no one I have ever encountered, excepting gods of course, knows that they are a spiritual being. And they are all plastered inside their heads! Only now I can move out of it, thanks to the Air Maiden," Mandy explained.

"Oh good grief!" exclaimed the baker. "I never thought," his voice trailed into silence and he never completed his sentence.

Mandy changed the subject. "So you have been traveling for nearly six weeks to get here?"

"Yes, mostly by mule. I cannot afford a horse and a mule gets me there. This time the journey has been exceedingly long, but I did make it in time. You don't know the whereabouts of said caravan perchance do you?" William inquired.

"Yes we do. But not the full details yet. I'll let you know when I know more for sure," Mandy volunteered. "Have you done this sort of thing often, William?"

"Well, I think this is the tenth time I had gone to do the wishes of Reylona," he answered. And then he stated, "No I don't read minds. I just know what a person is going to say or is thinking before they say it sometimes. Not always, just sometimes."

Mandy flushed as she realized he had just now known what she was about to ask and had answered it before she had asked it. "That's pretty darn good, William. I never would have guessed you were so, so interesting," she replied. William blushed. "But it is getting late. We'd better get you to your room so you can clean up and all that." In her take charge mode, she got the key to his room and led the way, Jon bringing up the rear. William was staggering slightly from the rather large volume of ale he'd consumed. She showed him the rooms she was staying and then led him on down the hall to his room. She opened his door, motioning for him to enter.

He protested slightly when he saw the high quality of the room. "Ah this is a bit too fancy for me, terribly expensive I expect."

"It's on me, no strings attached. You need some minor rewards for helping Reylona. Night William, see you in the morning," Mandy whispered. Jon noticed a twinkle in her eye. He picked up her errant thought, *He would look handsome if he were cleaned up.*

The others had gone to bed when Mandy and Jon entered the common area of their quarters. So they hugged and headed to bed as well.

Since the twins would likely be out late gathering information about those who were planning an exodus from Freetown, everyone assumed that they could afford the luxury of sleeping in once more. And they all did.

Over brunch, Mandy related to Darless and Alison her chance meeting with her village baker, William Conners. They were just as surprised to hear that he had some form of calming abilities that her own goddess was using as was Mandy the night before. Neither of these mages could offer any ideas on exactly what his ability actually was. They were as baffled as Mandy and Jon. Mandy ended with, "Well, I certainly have no idea what he does, that's for sure. However, I can tell he is working in the kitchen. Can you smell that aroma? We are in for a treat later today. He's baking and that means the finest eating you have ever had, come dinnertime."

"Hi Runtling! We thought we'd find you here," teased May. The twins just entered the dining area in search of Alison and her friends. "What's this about good eating?"

Mandy had to explain about William Conners, her baker, once again. Like the others, the twins had no idea of what he did or could do. "However, it is going to be needed," Mat replied. "We were successful last night. A man named Far Gone Art is leading the caravan; he is an excellent tracker and has actually been to many towns in the far west. He seems like a reasonable fellow."

May continued seamlessly, "So far there are at least twenty-five wagons in the caravan, probably a whole lot more Folks are being secretive about who is actually leaving town for good, and rightly so. However, from what we can tell thus far, many of those who are leaving we have helped. Mat and I believe that they are in search of a 'better life' elsewhere."

Mat picked up the report as May paused to order a tea. "However, they are not traveling light. I heard that some are taking all of their belongings, valuables and all. So we are indeed now becoming very worried about their ultimate safety. There is just no reasoning with them. I think that if Alison actually makes them an offer of a new town, many would jump at the chance. Probably more would decide to make the trip. I think that making that offer just now would be dangerous for them indeed. But we don't know everything like the gods do. So perhaps, Reylona has foreseen this venture and has sent William to help, though I don't know what one person alone can do."

Over tea and biscuits, the girls talked of the superb dresses that May created. Mat was a bit embarrassed over the lavish praise they had for his boxes. Then, they split up into two groups. Mat took Jon and Mandy for an inspection or appraisal of the town's potential defenses. May took Alison and Darless in search of historical information.

The girls first visited the Guild of the Mages. Since May did not belong to this guild, she left them there and spent some time in her guild nearby, the Illusionist's Dreams. Just after noon, she returned and met the others and together, the three headed for the town's library. Only a town as large as Freetown actually had an official library. What is completely inexplicable is that while on their way to the library, they passed the decaying Church of Ukko, the only remaining one in town. Alison insisted that they check it out, since it was on their way. The three entered through the large, creaking oak doors.

Meanwhile, Mat led Jon and Mandy to the edge of town. From there, they slowly circled round the entire city. Mandy estimated that the circumference was likely six miles which meant that the town was about two miles in diameter. The town was roughly split into two halves by the large very shallow, but broad, river Grande. At least six wooden bridges carried the main arteries of the town across it. The desert like lands around the town had low rolling hills, offering little or no protection. Far off in the east, the distant mountains could be seen, the southern reaches of the Blank Range. A strip about a half mile wide of green lay on either side of the river which flowed from the distant mountains through Freetown and on off to the west.

The major road that the four had used to get here from Ravenwash continued its southward direction from the opposite side of the town from which they had entered. Another large road ran east and west, though the eastward portion, toward the mountains, was noticeably narrower and less well-traveled. Unfortunately, from Mandy's point of view, the town had no barrier walls; rather it had just grown outward, slowly encroaching on the more arid lands. It would take a large force to effectively defend this town, Mandy lamented.

As they strolled through town, Mandy observed a number of men dressed in red leather armor carrying broadswords. Mat explained that these were the Red Guards who provided the town's security. Mat estimated that the Red Guards boasted at least five hundred fighters. Membership in the Guards was for life. However, many were rather unscrupulous and could easily be bribed. But for all their shortcomings, the Red Guards did provide a measure of security, even if it was for a price. "Theoretically, the Mayor controls the Red Guards," Mat explained, but added, "However, I know for a fact that they really take crucial orders only from a secret Council of Ten. What these ten want, the guards provide. As far as we can tell, the Council of Ten is composed of the ten most powerful and wealthiest men in town. We have been tracking them down one by one and have identified all but one member of that secret group."

"Say, did you notice that wall-like construction we just passed?" Mandy interrupted. They were walking along the busy North-South Road that went past their inn and were about half way from the northern entrance to the city and its center. She noticed what appeared to be a wall about ten feet tall ran behind the buildings on both sides of the road. The top was about three feet wide. "That sure looks like a barrier wall," she added.

"Oh that. We call it the Tramway. It may have been the outer wall of the city eons ago. Most all buildings adjacent to it use it as a back wall. It is very solid. Notice the flower pots on top over there? Folks use it for all sorts of things, including a deck and sunbathing in the winter months when it is not so hot." He chuckled and added in a hushed voice, "It is said that the Twins use it for fast secret getaways; it bypasses all the crowds." Mandy and Jon smiled; they understood his true meaning.

"Well that's more like it. The founding fathers did know how to design a city. You need a wall for basic protections. It's a shame that in outgrowing the wall's dimensions, the town did not build another one. We might have used it," Mandy commented mostly to herself.

"I noticed that most of these wide streets run straight. I've only strayed from them a bit yesterday. Is the town laid out on a square gird?" Jon asked. "The side streets are a maze."

"Yes, but the narrower streets do a bit of winding around the smaller hills. Only in the wealthiest part of town are the streets really arcs. They bend around all of the mansions and grounds. Do you want to see that part of town?" Mat asked. Both nodded, so he turned right onto Dries Lane. "The rich live in the southwest sector of town. Dries Lane runs right into Cactus Boulevard, which is the main entrance into that part."

They had gone perhaps a half mile when a crumbling, three story church on their right caught Jon's attention. "Say, isn't that a Church of Ukko? Those markings on the entrance arch look like those we saw in Zaire."

"Yes, but you can see it is really in bad shape. There are not many Ukko worshipers in this town. Actually, there is not a common religion in this town, just a little of this and that. These days, the churches of the Demon Lords tend to have the larger Sunday attendees. The Twins already ascertained that detail," Mat explained. "This one is the last Church of Ukko in town."

You must go inside the church. A thought appeared in Jon's mind. He assumed that Mandy had placed it there. "Come on," he reacted, "let's go inside and see what it looks like. I loved that highly ornate church in Zaire." Fond memories flooded Jon's mind, memories of his flute concert for all of the priests, the huge flower gardens, Bard Wendell, and the Air Maidens.

Mat thought this was a waste of time, but accompanied them up the broad but crumbling steps to the main doorway, two oak carved doors. Though old, and partly rotten, you could still see the scene of a trio of Air Maidens descending to a flock of warriors whose arms were upraised in praise of Father Ukko. "Should we knock or just go in," Jon asked as they reached the doors.

Mandy opened the creaking door and stepped inside, "Go in silly; it is a church." The others followed her into a hallway shaped like a T. Ahead lay the central portion of the church. Evidently, church offices lay to the left and right. Jon walked straight ahead into the high vaulted ceiling chapel. The smell of dust and mold greeted their noses. The stained glass windows high on either side provided the only dim illumination. Jon stared in awe at the magnificent window art. They slowly walked toward the altar, past rows and rows of benches covered in dust. "Jeesh," Jon uttered and the sound echoed in the vast space overhead. Embarrassed, he said no more but continued ambling forward.

"Well, it is not all bad," Mandy observed. The front two rows of benches were clean and appeared to be well cared for. There are at least some worshipers here at some times; she pointed to the pews. When they reached the altar, seven large-based candles burned emitting a faint iris odor. They heard a distant door slam followed by the patter of hurriedly shuffling feet. From their left, a chubby elderly man came rushing their way, hastily donning his priestly garments.

"Strangers. Well, welcome to the Church of Ukko. I am Bishop Franco. How may I be of service?" He was nearly out of breath. Jon guessed his age as nearly seventy.

When later asked, Jon could not explain why he next said what he said. "I am Saint Jon Brown, lately from the Church of Ukko in Zaire. I've come to see your church." *Now why did I say that?* Jon wondered.

"Oh my!" The expression of total surprise on the priest's age-lined face gave way rapidly to wonderment, followed by one of deep concern, then fear, and finally awe. His mouth wagged but no sound came out. He tried to speak, but kept opening and shutting his mouth. "You, you, you be wanting to see our Holy Paladin, Sir Henry. Oh my. Oh my. Just wait right here. I'll bring him," and he dashed back the way he had entered before anyone could say anything.

"Zagroot zounds! What was or is this all about? What did you say to him, Jon? Did you see those looks on his face?" Mandy urgently whispered to Jon. He did not get a chance to reply. Suddenly, the main doors they had entered creaked. Someone else was entering. They turned around to see Alison, Darless, and May entering.

"Jon! What are you doing here?" Alison blurted out in total surprise.

"Well, we were passing by and I saw this Church of Ukko. I dunno, something told me to enter. Say, what are you girls doing here?" Jon suddenly realized that they were supposed to be at the guilds and library.

"Dunno, either," Alison muttered as she walked down the aisle to the altar. "We were just on the way to the library and somehow I had to come inside. Did you call?"

"Er, no. This is getting weird. We were just greeted by a really old priest, Franco, yes, Bishop Franco. I told him who I was and he just freaked out!" Jon said dismayed.

"Yes, but what did you say?" Mandy continued. "You said 'I am Saint Jon Brown lately from the Church of Ukko in Zaire.' You have never called yourself Saint Jon that I can recall; everyone else has to call you that," she grinned, unable to resist teasing him a bit. "And then the Bishop spooked. You should have seen his face! His mouth refused to work; it opened and shut but nothing came out!"

"Yes, and there was a streak of fear in there too," Mat added. "He acted as if he had seen a god or something!"

"I thought he might be having a heart attack, or something," Jon muttered, then immediately wondered if they knew what that was. So he quickly added, "You know, maybe his heart stopped beating or something."

"Incredible," Alison responded. "Boy this church is in need of a thorough cleaning!"

"And major structural repairs," May added. "I've heard rumors that it may be torn down if it isn't repaired soon. Pity, these glass windows are splendid!"

Just then, a panting Bishop Franco came rushing in leading another man. "See I told you. There he is, the man in those strange blue pants." When he neared Jon, Bishop Franco hastily bowed as much as his arthritis plagued body would allow. Jon had no idea why this priest should bow to him and stood there rather befuddled not knowing what to do or say. Behind the priest strolled a tall, muscular man, about fifty, sporting a nearly trimmed beard and moustache, both black as black as his eyes and shoulder length hair. He wore a blue tunic with a white cross on the front and back. He had the build of a skilled fighter. "Let me present Sir Henry le'Boldaire, Holy Paladin of Ukko," the Bishop hastily introduced his companion.

The paladin stepped in front of the bishop, stood squarely before Jon and extended his hand. "Welcome to our humble church," he said dryly, eyeing Jon from head to toe to walking stick. His stern look did not abate as he then routinely glanced at the others.

Jon cleared his throat; it was going to be up to him to do the introductions this time. "Let me present Alison d'Ambrose and her brother and sister May and Mat."

"I'm familiar with those twins," he commented.

So Jon continued. "This is Mandy Blackthorn, a Ranger of Reylona and this is Darless, a mage." Jon fervently hoped that this paladin would not recognize that she was an alu-demon as had Sir Thomas. He did not want another big argument.

"You do have strange companions. I believe this is the first time a demon has been in our Church of Ukko. But if she is with you, then there must be a good reason for her presence.

You are speaking the truth. You must forgive the childish actions of the Holy Father here, he believes too much in his omens and visions."

"Oh my god!" Mandy exclaimed out loud. She had been dutifully placing Jon's walking stick upon her small portable altar just before she went to bed, praying for guidance. She kept having the same dream night after night. But each morning, it was gone. But now, the dream returned full force. Instantly all eyes were upon her. "Jon, hold the walking stick out and say 'In the name of Ukko!'"

Jon had no idea what she was talking about, but was so startled by her order, that he did so. Holding the plain walking stick out before him, though he felt a twinge of foolishness flow over him, he spoke, "In the name of Ukko." Poof. The walking stick instantly changed form into a scepter, a highly ornate, beautiful work of art, jewel encrusted and golden in color. Everyone gasped in unison!

The paladin's eyes opened wider than Jon could imagine anyone's eyes opening; his mouth gaped. The bishop nearly fainted and only remained on his feet by grabbing onto the side of the altar. Alison cried out, "The Holy Scepter of Ukko! Jon you have had it all along!" Instantly, Sir Henry dropped to his knees clasping his hands together in prayer, yet never moving his eyes from the jewel scepter. Jon swallowed hard, staring at this incredible thing of beauty in his hands.

"Oh Jon, you've done it. It is even more beautiful than my memories of it!" Tears of joy and childhood memories, both good and bad, flooded through Alison's minds.

"That's the thing that destroyed our family!" cried May in disgust. "Dad and mom were killed because of that thing! Our home destroyed," and she broke down in uncontrollable sobs. Mat was not long behind her. May spoke for him, together they cried out years of suppressed grief.

"I've got to pay more attention to my dreams!" Mandy declared, realizing that she had been given this gift nights ago but that she had not recognized her dream for what it actually had been. Now she had really gone and done it. Mat and May were in hysterics when the occasion called for immense joy and praise. She felt a bit guilty for having just blurted it out. She had no idea why she had chosen this exact moment to reveal her dream. She sighed.

Alison tried to console her sister and brother, but neither even heard her words. She held on to them and looked forlornly at Jon.

Darless coldly sized up the situation. She sent to Jon, *Which one do you want to help? I'll take the other.*

Her words jostled Jon back into the present. "Here, hold this," he commanded of Sir Henry. He took May's hands in his and confronted her squarely. With pure intention, he said to her, "May, remember the night of the attack on your home. I want you to go back and look at your mental pictures of that night. Go to the very beginning of that time. Then, go through it all and tell me what happened as it occurred."

Just as soon as Jon reached for May, Darless likewise took hold of the moaning Mat. Mustering her full attention onto him, she repeated what Jon had said to May. For Darless, this was a very fascinating time. These two twins were so close, their minds so linked, that they spoke, thought, and acted as one. She immediately theorized that they would confront their past together. She was correct, but it was shocking. Both protested that they couldn't face it again. So strong were their protests, that Jon and Darless had to repeat their orders.

Finally, May said, "Dad's back. I wanted him to play with us."

Mat continued, "We want him to tell us a story — to tell us of his grand adventure."

Both cried as May blurted out, "But he said no that there would be time enough for that tomorrow. But tomorrow never came!" And they both cried hysterically.

"And then what happened," Jon asked calmly and soothingly. Darless did likewise to Mat.

"We cannot see!" cried May and Mat together and wailed uncontrollably.

Suddenly, Jon understood. *It is what they were feeling at that time!* Jon sent to Darless. He heard her 'a-ha' of recognition. Jon asked, "I understand. And what else were you feeling at that time?" Darless followed suit.

"Oh," a startled Mat uttered, "we were terrified. We heard all these hideous noises of a battle and crumbling stone. We are in our room. It's dark. We cannot see anything. The dark is terrifying and yet comforting at the same time."

"We clutch each other," May went on. "We tried to go out the door but heard a horrible crashing noise. Stuff hit us in the face!"

"I got brave and fumbled for the lantern," Mat continued. Their uncontrollable sobbing gave way to stark terror; both were physically shaking wildly. "We can see what's left of our room. The doorway has caved in!"

"We cannot get out!" May cried. "We try but cannot move the stones. More crashing sounds. The whole castle is falling on us. We gotta get out or be crushed."

"We remember our picture books. I grab them. May places hers in her lap. I hold onto mine. May says to hold her hand and we go together. I bring my book so we can get back. More crumbling noises. A huge crack appears in the wall behind us. Not much time. Let's do it," Mat described.

"It's night here in Freetown. Very late. It's dark. No moon. We are scared. We cling to each other," May went on.

"I lead us down an alley. We huddle behind some big pile of garbage. We tremble and cry and fall asleep. Sun comes up. We hear voices. We get up and act like we are out for a walk. We walk and walk. Find a park. We huddle close and look at the picture book. Our home picture is totally black," May continued.

"We cry awhile. We are hungry. We set off in search of a place to stay and eat. We have no money, no clothes, no nothing. We are terrified. By evening, we begin begging for a handout. We finally get enough to afford to get something cheap to eat. We find an open sewer drain. Darkness is comforting. No one will bother us down there. We climb into the sewers for the night. We like the comfort of the night. The sewers become our new home. And that is about all of it," Mat finished.

"Thank you," Jon said softly, "Now, go back to the very beginning of it and go through it again and tell me what happens as you go along." Darless likewise commanded Mat.

This time the uncontrolled wailing was less in volume and the violent shaking terror was less in intensity; they both yawned a bit, which Jon took as a very promising sign. Jon and Darless put their twin through the incident four more times, each time the emotions lessened in intensity accompanied by heavier and heavier yawns. On the fifth pass through, both twins suddenly began laughing, "No wonder we love the dark night! No wonder we always feel like the night gives us comfort! We decided the dark was our only friend! And so it has been all these years!" And they continued laughing just as uncontrollably for the next ten minutes.

When Jon and Darless had begun, Alison and Mandy sat down on the nearest pew. Sir Henry, holding the precious scepter, and the Bishop were both speechless and utterly confused by the sudden appearance of the most sacred item in their world accompanied by total hysterics. They also sat beside the two women. They watched and tried to comprehend what on earth was going on. It soon became apparent that what the twins' connection to the Holy Scepter had been.

"Pray for their souls," lamented the Bishop, "for their wounds there is no cure. Pray, Sir Henry, for they are lost souls," and he began praying for all he was worth.

The paladin was curious. "What is Saint Jon and the demon lady doing?" he whispered to Alison.

"I do not fully understand it, but it works miracles. Watch, be patient, and observe," she replied. Her heart ached for her brother and sister. She knew what they were going through. She had been through it before, but Jon had salvaged her from her mind's effects. She prayed to Father Ukko that Jon could do the same for her family.

The sudden, unexpected laughter and total release from all of that pain and suffering and terror took the others by surprise. Several minutes passed before Sir Henry realized what he had witnessed and the ultimate result. When it finally dawned on him what he had just seen, he stood up and loudly proclaimed, "Behold, Saint Jon the Redeemer!" Jon's face turned beet red once again as the paladin gingerly handed the Holy Scepter back to Jon.

"It's a miracle; it's a divine miracle!" cried the Bishop. "All praise to Father Ukko!"

"Please, no, I am no redeemer. I am just a musician," protested Jon. "And here, doesn't this belong to you folks," as he tried to hand the Holy Scepter back to the paladin.

"Oh no! I am truly not worthy of even holding such a holy artifact! Had I not lost my senses for a moment there, I would not have accepted it when you handed it to me. I am totally unfit to even touch it!" the dismayed Sir Henry protested.

"See, I told you Saint Jon the Redeemer would come to save Freetown! I told you," gleefully teased the aged Bishop, who had for once proven he was right to the paladin who had evidently never believed him.

Jon looked at Mandy. "Okay, how do I get this thing back to being my walking stick? I cannot go around like this!" Jon was feeling very disturbed holding on to this incredible artifact. He vainly hoped that all that would go away as soon as it was just his trusty walking stick once more.

Mandy looked sheepishly at the floor. "Er, that was not part of my prayers or dream. I have no idea at all. Ah, sorry Jon," she mumbled, perplexed that she had not thought of that aspect.

"You had better try something," added Darless, "you cannot go about town carrying that!"

Jon looked at the jeweled scepter. "In the name of Father Ukko, please go back to being my walking stick again," he said pleadingly. *Oh, all right,* appeared in his mind. Poof. He held his favorite walking stick once more. "It, it spoke to me!" cried Jon. "Ah, ha. It has been speaking to me on several occasions, but I did not realize it. Well, I'll be."

"Of course it can send thoughts to you," stated the paladin. "It *is* the Holy Scepter of Ukko! It has intelligence of its own."

"Wait a minute!" Mandy interjected suddenly realizing something that had been bothering her for many days. It had always been in the back of her mind; one of those things you just cannot seem to express in words. "It is a being like us. I distinctly saw five beings, including myself when we were in the gate spell heading for the Abyss, Jon. But we are only four! It is a being, it has life."

A chorus of "Oh, yes" echoed from the others as they too also realized what they had seen but what had never registered with their conscious minds.

"What's this about the Abyss?" Sir Henry was instantly keenly interested. But as soon as he uttered his question, he immediately remembered his manners. "Come, this is not the place for talk. Let us offer you some refreshments in the holy sanctuary. Bishop, will you lead the way?"

"Oh yes. Please forgive us. The events have made us loose our senses. This way," and the old man led them to the left and down a long hall into his sanctuary. Old tapestries adorned the small room's walls. A dozen golden candelabra provided the illumination. All of the furniture, though very old, still showed the signs of elegance of a by-gone day when this church had held some prominence in this town. The Bishop produced a bottle of "holy wine" and a loaf of bread. The paladin opened a corner cabinet and brought out eight golden goblets, obviously only used on very special occasions.

So over wine and bread, they told the eager ears of Sir Henry and the Bishop their tale from the beginning. This time, though, some of the little details suddenly made sense to the foursome; Jon had been bearing the Holy Scepter of Ukko all along. The paladin and priest interrupted with the occasional "Praise be to Father Ukko." And they asked many questions, some of which could not be answered.

When they had finished relating all that they now knew, the Bishop proclaimed that he would spread the word the Saint Jon had arrived and that the town would be saved from the ravages of the demon-led armies. Before Jon could protest, the paladin asked sternly, "And how do you propose to save the town, if I might be so bold to ask?" It was clearly a loaded question. The paladin obviously had not even the faintest hope that anything at all could be done. In previous years, he always had more than he could do just to defend this church from the ravages of the soldiers.

Jon's red face told the paladin that he was indeed right. "Honestly, Sir Henry, I did not come here to save your town. I came to try to prevent the assassination of Metrarch so as to fulfill our bargain that won the release of Alison's other brother. I have no idea at all how to protect the town." The Bishop looked crestfallen; the paladin, smiled. He had guessed right; he was still a good judge of men and their intentions. He did not believe in the fantasies of feeble old men.

"However, we are all working on it," he added. "In fact, that is what we all were doing before we entered this church." He purposely did not mention that he had been out for a walk around the town, looking it over. It seemed such a minuscule action in light of what was going to be needed. "I think that we probably should get back to it, though. We should get together later on and discuss plans and such," Jon added, looking for a way out of this situation.

Sir Henry, like Mandy, was a take charge, man of action. "Yes, by all means. We will only tell a few trusted people of your coming at this time. When you have some ideas or if we can be of any service, no matter how small, let us know at once. I am your humble servant," and he slid off his chair onto one knee and bowed humbly before Jon.

Images of the fledgling paladin Lonnie begging Jon to accept his services flooded into his mind. He also recalled Mandy's cautions she had sent him. "Thank you," he said as formally and solemnly as he could. "We will get back to you just as soon as possible."

That ended the encounter. The paladin rose to see them out the main church doors, bidding them farewell and the best of luck. All were glad to be out of doors once again.

"How on earth did you know we were in here? And how did you know precisely when to come?" Jon immediately asked Alison as they walked down the steps to the street.

She gave him a kiss and whispered, "I love you. Maybe we are becoming as Mat and May, you know, thinking and feeling as one?" Then, she said aloud, "Seriously, I we were just on our way to the library and I saw this church and something pulled me into it. That's all. No divine guidance, just dumb luck."

"Oh, I don't know about that!" interjected May. "Jon, thank you and Darless for what you did for us in there. I don't know what you did, but I have never felt so alive, so alert and so full of life in our entire lives!" And she gave him a hug and kiss on his cheek. Mat, however, was content to just give him a hug.

Alison teased her sister, "Cool it May, he's mine!" Everyone roared with laughter. Then, they split up to continue their separate quests for more information on the town and its history. It was now mid-afternoon.

It might be noted here, that as the afternoon passed, every now and then, Mat would let out a chuckle for no apparent reason as he walked along giving Mandy and Jon their tour of Freetown.

Chapter 11 Of Plans and Sewers and Chaos

When Jon and Mandy got back to their room in the inn, Alison and Darless were already there waiting for them. Both girls had a sheepish grin on their faces. "Look what came for you, Mandy!" Alison teased. She handed the ranger a box of flowers with a card attached. This was about the last thing Mandy had expected. Her curiosity instantly rose, as she opened the box to reveal a dozen red roses. She blinked. "Open the card!" insisted Alison who was dying to know who had sent Mandy flowers.

Mandy opened the card and blushed; then she read it out loud. "Not as pretty as you, though. Please join me for dinner. William." Both girls giggled.

"He's got a crush on you," teased Alison. All three women laughed. Mandy asked Alison to put them in some water somehow while she went to clean up for dinner. Mat and May would, of course, join them within a half an hour. Mandy changed into one of her new dresses; the smell of fresh leather would encase her tonight. It was her favorite flagrance. When she appeared and before the others could tease her further, she said while twirling around, "Well, what do you thing?"

"I think you look terrific!" Jon proclaimed. The girls giggled.

"You always do," Mandy taunted him back.

"You look like a million," Alison replied, just a bit envious of her figure. But leather would have been her last choice for clothing.

"Ah, you need this," Darless answered and pinned one of the roses onto her dress. "There, that does it. Knock him dead!" she teased.

Shortly, the twins arrived; all six headed down to the dining room. As soon as they got near, the heady aroma of freshly baked yeast breads filled the air. "Ah ha. You are now in for a royal treat indeed," declared Mandy. "There are no finer breads in the world than those made by William. Prepare your selves," she cautioned. But her cheeks were faintly reddish in color as they entered. William, who had been waiting patiently for them, waved from a large table in one corner, so they all headed over to his table. Mandy's cheeks flush even more. There was something about this man, but she could not figure out the what.

"You look positively stunning, My Liege," William started to say but quickly caught himself, adding "Mandy." He rose and pulled the chair next to his out for her. As she sat down, he slid it in for her. "I'm so glad you could join me. I wanted to repay the favor from last night."

As the others seated themselves, William looked totally different. He had had a bath and was wearing a clean set of clothes. "As you can smell, I have now come into a bit of money," he grinned. "I suggest you try the pumpernickel and the pear-almond breads. They now want to hire me permanently," he chuckled.

Indeed, the breads were superb. While dinner progressed, they all chatted gaily. And the time passed swiftly. When they were finished eating the leisurely meal, William asked Mandy, "Would you cared to go for a stroll outside? A breath of fresh air after our delicious meal?"

"Sure, William. Oops, I forgot, we all need to hold a council first. Can I come get you when we are done?" she replied. He beamed with pleasure. And the six headed back up to their room while William went to the pub for a smoke on his pipe.

Mandy just knew that the girls would tease her about her handsome young beau, and so they did, all the way back to their room. In a way, Mandy rather enjoyed all of this unexpected attention. And William did look quite handsome now that he had washed off the grim of his long journey.

Once in their lounge area, it was back to business. Mandy began by summarizing her findings. "Well, there once was a ten foot wall around the town, but the town has long since expanded more than double its radius. It is now of no use whatsoever in providing any protection. As I see it, this town cannot possibly fend off an attack from one army, let along seven. Their position is utterly hopeless. There are some Red Guards that serve to keep a resemblance of law and order, but they are likely no match for even a portion of one of the armies."

"I noticed an unusually large amount of people purchasing goods in nearly every quarter of the city. Stock piling necessities, I suspect," Mat added. "The last time these games were held, we were still children, but as we remember, there was a lot of confusion and shortages once the armies left. Those that had supplies made a tidy profit from those that didn't."

Jon added, "Well, at least at one time in the distant past, there were people who thought enough of Ukko to raise a pretty impressive church in his name. But it would appear Father Ukko has few followers remaining today. What happened to all of them? Did their children and children's children lose faith?"

"Jon, you have put your finger on it," Alison replied. "We have found, after diligent research, mind you, that this town was indeed founded by a people who worshiped Father Ukko. About four hundred years ago, a legendary high priest called Bishop Allen d'Free founded this town. So it was named after him, naturally. The legends state that this would be a free town amidst the heathen worshipers of the surrounding lands. And so it was for many years."

"Apparently, these War Games have been going on ever since the town's founding," explained Darless. "Evidently, d'Free erected some kind of magical barrier that could be raised to protect the city. Thus, whenever they were threatened, the Barrier of Light, as it was called, would rise and keep all intruders outside the town's limits. About two hundred years ago, some vile treachery occurred. The ancient scrolls are very sketchy on the details. But it sounds just like something that Demon Lords would dream up for revenge. As near as we can piece together, the Demon Lords hired some assassins to capture all of the priests of the Church of Ukko. There is mention of a nighttime raid on the church. Nearly all of the priests of Ukko disappeared from Freetown never to be seen again."

"And it was evidently these priests who were in charge of the magical Barrier of Light," Alison continued. "With these men gone, by the time of the next War Games, there was no one to turn on the Barrier of Light. You can imagine what happened after that. Pretty grim."

"Yes, the records are almost non-existent from that time period," May put in. "To this day, no one knows what that Barrier of Light was. But a magical device of that power must be located somewhere. It very likely works like a machine, I would guess. You know, some kind of command word to turn it on; another to turn it off. But all details, it would seem, have been lost centuries ago."

Silence reigned for several minutes, each lost in his or her own version of feelings of helplessness. It was Darless who broke in on their moodiness. "But there is one thing that keeps gnawing at me. Remember all of those sketches and drawings we saw of the town's early layout? Always that octagonal central plaza with the community water well was there. The maps are always centered about that well. Now, I find that just the least bit unusual."

"Why?" muttered Jon. The other nodded their bewilderment as well. It seemed so insignificant.

"Number 1. The earliest sketch of the town showed the well centered on the map, but the actual buildings now lay mostly to the north. The Church of Ukko marked the easterly edge of the initial town. There was a huge space across the bottom right of the map. That is not how I would draw such a map. Number 2. A map made some fifty years later, showed the establishment of the wall you spoke about. Again, the well was at the center. Though the town has grown considerably to the north and east, only a small growth has happened west and south of the well and wall. Number 3. If you look at the current map of the city we bought a few days ago, notice that the town is now drawn centered upon the page and the well is located in the bottom left quadrant, very different from the old maps. The town has expanded in all directions. So, Number 4. Why would all of the map drafters prior to the Assassination of the town's priest draw the map centered on the well? By all common sense, they should have drafted it much like today's maps. I ask you, would you draw a map and leave the most of the bottom portion entirely blank?" Darless paused for a breath.

A chorus of "No's" echoed through the room. "Well, I guess it is obvious now that you pointed it out to us," May replied. "I just did not see that detail. How did you see it?"

"Always take the time to observe and reflect," she replied. "It was such an odd thing. I observed it, but, I must admit, until we were all talking a minute ago, it did not register with me either."

"Then, that well must somehow be important to this riddle," May conjectured.

"I wonder what's down in that well," Jon questioned aloud. "Mat, does anyone ever go down it to clean it or make repairs or whatever? I am totally unfamiliar with wells."

A look of dismay filled Mat's face, "You mean you don't have wells from where you come? How does your town get its water?"

Jon had done it again. Quickly he tried to explain, "We have wells but not like these. Er, we drill tiny holes hundreds of feet down and pump the water out with giant pumps. It is then sent under pressure to all of our houses. So we all have running water, just turn on the spigot."

Individual running water in every home certainly impressed Mat. He then answered Jon's original question. "Yes, occasionally, a well-master does go down to repair stones and perhaps clean it out a bit. We could try to find out when he last did it and if he noticed anything unusual about it."

"I think you are all barking up the wrong tree, so to speak," Alison broke in, "Can you imagine high priests climbing down into a well to turn on their protection device? Not very likely."

"No, but suppose that something were down there. Would not they likely have some kind of underground service entrance," Darless countered.

"Well, there certainly are a maze of sewer tunnels running under the entire town," May offered. "Perhaps there is some secret entrance down there lost to the ages."

"Now we are getting somewhere," Jon exclaimed full of excitement. This seemed the most reasonable idea yet. "I'll bet anything that there is an entrance to the sewers at the Church of Ukko we were at today. It would only take a priest a few minutes to navigate to the secret entrance and activate the protection device. It makes perfect sense. Now all we need to do is locate it and see if we can make it work again. Even if it only protects the original town's size, we can move those who want protection inside the perimeter. Great plan!"

Smiling faces beamed at one another as hope renewed in all of them. At least until Darless spoke, "We have only three or four days to find this secret entrance, if it exists, to figure out how to activate it, and to work out how to save the town. Not much time, if it still exists and can be made functional after all these centuries. That is an awful lot of 'ifs'," she said dryly.

"Well, then we need to get on it as soon as possible, then," stated May.

"Are you suggesting that we do some exploration now, at night, when it is dark?" Jon wondered.

Grimacing, Mat cautioned, "Yes and no. Do you realize the dangers in exploring the sewer system? Yes, there are filthy rats down there as you would expect, but a species of giant rats nearly two feet tall roam the tunnels. And there are the various vipers that call the system their home along with scorpions and other nasty critters — to say nothing of the smell and filth. The town sewers are not a place to go for fun. It's dangerous."

"On the other hand," May continued without interrupting Mat, "if we explore by night, we risk only running into the occasional thief who is using it as their sneak route. But then we cannot see at all well. It would not do to have a lot of light showing up through the openings on the streets, for example. If we go in the day, we can see what we are doing as well as the creatures that live down there and not be taken by surprise. But then we rise being spotted by passers by on the streets above."

"We grew up in the sewers, so we know pretty much what's what and where," Mat went on. "We have done quite a lot of exploring. There are many secret entrances into the sewers; some are likely escape routes, long unused. Others, well, there are all sorts of dirty dealings going on in this town, out of sight, if you get my meaning. The Twins have long made use of the sewers to accomplish their goals." His broad smile and twinkling eyes told the story.

"Ah. Perchance, do you have a map or sketch of the system?" asked Darless. "This would be most useful, especially if we can coordinate it with the street maps we have. It would likely narrow the search area considerably."

"Well, not exactly. The Office of City Affairs does have the 'Official' map of the sewer system under lock and key. We could 'borrow' it for a while later tonight, as long as it was returned by morning, no one would be the wiser. If only there was a way to copy the map really fast," May replied.

"Hum," muttered Alison, who had been rather quiet for some time, imagining how awful it must be to have to go into the sewers and how horrid a childhood her twins must have had. "If you can give me say about an hour or so and provide me with some paper the same size, I believe I can manage to make the copy fairly rapidly."

"You're on, Sis," Mat grinned, excited about another clandestine, nighttime operation. "We'll go 'borrow' the map now. Be back when we can as fast as we can."

"Need any help?" Mandy asked, feeling rather left out of things at the moment. She already knew what the answer would be.

"No, this is a job for the Twins," May replied, "We need stealth and secrecy and total quiet and some lock picking skills. But thanks for offering."

"Well, then," Mandy concluded, "I'll go get William and go for a short walk with him. Don't worry, we will not go far and will stick to the main streets." And she bounded out of the room in search of William without waiting for a reply or the usual "Be carefuls."

Mat and May left hastily, Alison retired to her bedroom to study her large spell books. "Darless, my dear, would you care to go for a walk?" Jon teased, formally offering her his arm.

"My, what a fine idea. It is such a nice evening, now that the heat has lifted," Darless teased back as she took his arm. Out the door they strolled.

Outside, the first quarter moon basked the street in a romantic glow. Other couples strolled by; Jon nodded to them. "If we stay on this main street here, we surely cannot run into much trouble," Darless commented. "And it is such a lovely evening. I'm afraid that there won't be very more like this. Very soon now, we must counter an assassin and do what we can for the town and/or the caravan. A handful against armies is not good odds. So let's enjoy our time together." They strolled along with no thought of where they were headed.

Perhaps fifteen minutes later, they found themselves standing beside the well in the plaza. "Say, here we are at the well," Jon noticed absentmindedly, "the object of our knowledge quest. As long as we are here, we might as well take a closer look at it. What do you think?"

"In this darkness, I'm not sure we will be able to see much, but since we are here," her voice trailed off into silence. They casually strolled around its circumference. "Twenty-five feet around, more or less," she whispered to Jon.

Jon dropped a small pebble into the well and listened for the 'kerplunk.' When it came, he whispered back, "Water is not far down there either. How can we tell how deep the water is?"

She playfully poked him and said, "I could throw you into the well and you can swim down to the bottom and report back!" They both chuckled softly to themselves. "Wait a minute, I have an idea. Why didn't we think of this in the first place? Use the bucket that's right here. Jon, you go find a substantial rock to use as a weight. I'll untie the rope. We can lower the weight and see just how deep it is. Then retie the rope back to the bucket." Jon was off at once. He was gone for a couple minutes.

He brought back one of the street's loose cobblestones. Darless quickly fashioned the rope securely around it and lowered it into the dark depths. Jon kept a lookout, but no one came close. As others strolled by, he pretended to drink from the bucket. "Okay. Here put the stone back while I figure this out," Darless commented and began carefully measuring the wet rope.

When he returned, she whispered, "It's about twenty feet down to the water. The water is about ten feet deep. I wonder where its water comes from? You know that might be a clue too," she added.

"How so?" muttered Jon, not quite following her, wishing he had paid more attention to his mandatory science class at the university. He had never been much interested in science, though. "You mean like a spring or something?"

"Let's talk on the way back. We've been gone quite a while now," she responded. And arm in arm, they strolled back toward the inn. "This is a fairly arid land. So I think we can rule out artesian springs. Maybe the water table is fairly high at this point so natural seepage fills it up," she theorized.

"How do you know so much about these things?" Jon asked, only too aware of his own ignorance.

"Silly, it's what I do. I am interested in many, many things, and how they all work," she said. "I think I got that from my dad, you know. I've just always been interested in how things work. Haven't you?"

"No, not really. Just music. That is my passion. One day soon now I want to start in on my big project of recording all of the local music I can find wherever I can find people making music. That's my life's goal."

"Understand. The reason I say the water source may be important is that where the water comes from may impact how the magical mechanism is setup, where the entrance is located and similar things," she explained.

Jon let out a small laugh, "Here I am gazing at the nearly unfamiliar star patterns, the glowing moonlight, the fresh smell of the out of doors, even if it has the town odor, and you are still right there thinking about the real problem we all need to solve. You are a pretty amazing person, Darless. You put me to shame." And her gave her a hug and gentle loving kiss. She reciprocated. "That's your reward for staying the course and working on our problem while I goofed off," he added with a big grin.

"Hum, maybe I should do this more often," she teased back and they entered the inn once more. They did not see the two shadows that had followed them partway to the inn, followed them on the rooftops of the buildings they passed.

While Darless headed up to their rooms, Jon stopped to get a large pot of tea and a number of cups. "Tea anyone?" he announced when he entered their rooms. Mandy had returned just before Jon got there, returned with a glowing complexion and a sparkle in her eyes. "You look like you enjoyed your walk," Jon added to Mandy.

"Don't mind if we do, thank you," answered Mat. The Twins appeared out of nowhere in the room. Jon was so surprised by their sudden appearance, he dropped an empty cup. Everyone was startled by their appearance. They had been following Jon and Darless back to the inn from the nearby roofs and had just come in through a window somehow. This, of course, was just the reaction the Twins had intended. "We followed you two back from the roofs above you, Jon, and you didn't even notice us!"

"Pretty impressive," Mandy exclaimed, only too glad to have the attention directed onto someone else. She was starting to care a great deal for William, but was not totally sure how to handle it.

"Here's the map," May said, handing a rolled parchment tied with a blue ribbon. "I took the liberty of including a couple similar sized blank pages for the copies."

Alison opened the roll and laid the map on the table and placed a blank page beside it. "Okay, everyone be quiet so I can concentrate." She began chanting softly to herself. Jon knew that she was casting some kind of spell. Normally, her spells were useful in combat or rescue situations. But how she could use a magical spell to copy a map this detailed he could not begin to imagine. He watched in fascination, as did the others.

When her chanting ceased, a quill appeared mid-air, moved to one corner of the blank page. Another quill appeared and moved to the corresponding map corner. Alison moved the pen to a starting point of her choice. Instantly, the other pen moved to the same relative position. Then, she said "Trace and draw." Evidently this was some form of command. The pen over the map began to follow the lines while the other pen actually drew a copy of the lines on the blank page. After a few minutes, Alison muttered softly, "Based on how fast this is going, I think it will take about thirty minutes. Jon, can you hand me a tea cup? I'll sip as I concentrate." He quickly poured her a cup and handed it to her. Everyone sipped tea and watched this interesting map copying spell do its work. Within twenty-five minutes, it had finished. They now had a copy of the official sewer system in great detail.

"If it is okay with you, we will return the original at once," May suggested as soon as Alison had cancelled her spell and the pens had vanished. Within a minute, the Twins, still dressed in black, disappeared out the window onto the rooftops.

The four crowed around the table and began to study the map in earnest. Darless laid her city map out beside the sewer map and tried to correlate the two. After a few minutes, she pointed out one line. "This tunnel seems to go in a nearly direct line from somewhere near the Church of Ukko toward the area of the well. And here, just beyond, joins up with this other larger line. This is where I would begin the search."

A short while later, the Twins returned. Upon hearing the map analysis, May volunteered, "If we go into the sewers, we need to be prepared. Wear old clothes, be well armed."

"Above all," Mat continued without interrupting May, "be very alert for danger at all times. We should probably go in the morning. Shining lights down there at night might raise an alarm. We have found many secret points of egress over the years. But this one, if it exists, has eluded us. Any ideas on how we are to find it?" Everyone began tossing out ideas, but Jon was not listening.

Something does not feel right about this, he thought and slowly paced around the room; the voices of the others faded into the distance. He imagined himself a high priest of Freetown who had just been given the order to activate the magical device. He imagined himself in priestly robes, torch in hand, rushing down the dank, dark, danger-filled sewers to fulfill his holy obligations. *I can't; this isn't right!*

From the corner of her eyes, Alison saw Jon way across the room, pacing slowly back and forth, deep in thought. His facial muscles tense, contorting is face. Intuitively, she touched him as she might the pedal of an iris in spring, *What's the matter, my Love?*

It doesn't add up, he angrily shot back without thinking. She did not flinch when his anger came back upon her; perhaps she rather sensed his turmoil. Instead, she maintained her soft, loving flow towards him. Then, he realized it was Alison; instantly, Jon pulled out of his melancholia mood and returned her loving flow. Physically, he smiled and blew her a kiss across the room. *Thanks, my dearest.*

Alison broke in on the conversation, "Hold on a minute, Jon has something important to say about all this." Heads turned this way and that, trying to locate him. The others had not realized he had left their close circle around the table.

"Well, er, I ah," Jon began breaking the sudden silence, "This just cannot be right." He floundered for a way to explain his feelings. "Damn, a picture is worth a thousand words," he muttered. Then, inspiration struck. "Close your eyes, all of you. Watch this." Jon concentrated. Mentally, he created the illusion of a high priest of the Church of Ukko, dressed in the finest robes befitting this man's highest position. The illusion he placed into everyone's minds. Then, he added action to his creation. An acolyte came running in suggesting the sudden urgent need for the town's protection. He had this high priest quickly grab a torch. Next, the priest was dashing down the sewers, at least how Jon imagined the sewers to be.

Then, he saw May's images of the sewer and altered his to appear more like hers. He heard her suddenly gasp, knowing that she now saw it as well. Jon had the priest hold his nose from the stench, had the priest wade through vile refuse water up to his knees, ruining the robes. He had snakes slithering out the way of the rushing priest, and rats scuttling about. Then, he had the priest halt before an otherwise bare wall and poof a door appeared and the priest entered. Then, Jon ended his illusion. "Okay. Open you eyes. You see what is bothering me?"

"How did you do that?" cried May. "That was fantastic! What an illusion! So real; I could see it with clarity! Are you sure you are not an illusionist?"

"I am just a musician, I keep telling you. We are all spiritual beings; we can make our own illusions if we try," Jon replied humbly.

"Jon," Darless added, "that was pretty incredible. The images were so real. I'm going to have to learn how to do that!"

"Yes, but do you see what I mean? It cannot be right," Jon protested.

"Well, yes," Alison replied. "If I were that priest, how incredibly icky, ucky. Just thinking about walking in that slop with my best clothes on — no way! I hate rats and slithering snakes. Just no way would I want to do that, well, unless the safety of the town depended upon it," she added as an afterthought, realizing that she would do it if it really was needed to save the people from the ravages of demons and murderous men.

"Hum," muttered Darless, "that is a good way to put it. It doesn't feel right. You might be on to something there. Are we looking in the wrong place?"

Mat added, "Well, I'd do it if I were a thief trying to make a quick get-away or if my home was under attack and I wished to flee to safety or perhaps just hide from my enemies," he winked a knowing glance at May. Both recalled many times they had done just that, hide out in the sewers.

"Right," Jon went on. "Surely the high priest had other more direct means to activate the magical device."

"A secret tunnel is the way I'd do it," Alison interrupted Jon. "I'd have made a secret tunnel that led directly to it."

"But where would that entrance be located?" May asked, catching on to Alison's idea.

"The Church!" said May, Mat, Darless, and Alison in unison.

"Right!" said Mandy, catching on quickly.

"It is the only logical answer," Darless went on to say. "They must have build a secret tunnel from the Church of Ukko to the chamber where their device was housed — a tunnel known only to a select few, the chosen ones. That would also explain why the knowledge was lost when the demon lords eliminated all of the high priests. Secrets have a liability; they can get lost."

"I wonder just how much that Bishop we met really knows about his church grounds?" Alison wondered aloud. "I'm sure he wouldn't mind us nosing about, if we explain what we are trying to accomplish." She sounded hopeful. "It sure beats going into the sewers!"

"I hate to be a pessimist," Darless pointed out, "but we are running out of days. We cannot go looking for it tonight; anyway it is getting very late. We should probably go searching there first thing in the morning." Everyone agreed on all points. Hastily the Twins gave Alison a hug and said their farewells, promising to return around eight next morning.

The day dawned bright and sunny, quite usual for this semiarid area. It would be another hot day, but with little humidity. "This is more like it," Mandy commented as they awaited the Twin's arrival. They had arisen early and breakfasted hastily. She had put on her adventuring leathers and strapped her bastard sword across her back and was just finishing lashing a couple daggers to her leggings.

"Surely we are not going to need all that; we are just going to look for a secret tunnel," Jon exclaimed a bit worried.

"Yes we will!" came the voice of Mat as the Twins opened the door and entered. They also looked ready for action, wearing leather pants and tunics. Both had short swords strapped to their belts and a dagger on each leg. Their faces were grim indeed. "You won't believe what's happening out there!"

"The town's going nuts!" May exclaimed. The serious tone of her voice was in stark contrast to the cheerfulness of the night before. "Half the town is out buying up everything in sight, or stealing it. The Red Guards are going to have a really bad day, that's for sure! A panic has set in, I think."

"As near as we can tell, some strange mercenaries came to town last night spreading terrible rumors of the vastness of the approaching armies. Word has spread like wildfire," Mat explained.

"They are probably afraid is all; trying to ensure their survival somehow," Jon mused. "I know I would be worried, I suppose. Is it dangerous for us to go to the church?"

"We are now a fairly large, well-armed party. If we stick close and do not provoke anyone, we should be safe. But be alert and on guard," Mat explained.

As they left the safety of the inn, the doorman cautioned them, "Please be careful outside today. It is an unusual day. I'd stay in the inn if I were you." They thanked him for his concern.

Outside, it was mayhem. Throngs of people crowed the streets. Some were laden with as much as they could carry; others hastened from shop to shop. Some stores were closed with signs that proclaimed all their merchandise was sold. Several provisions shops had long lines of people waiting just to get into the store. They had to push and shove their way along the main street and witnessed several altercations and attempted thefts. At least three young men had wounds indicating they had lost some scrimmage.

It didn't get any better when they turned and headed east on the secondary road that led to the Church of Ukko. Indeed, it got worse since the street was substantially narrower. Suddenly, eight young men bearing swords accosted them, demanding their money. "Protect May," Mat shouted. Mandy's bastard sword sprang into action as she deftly squared off to face those at the front. Mat took the left flank while Darless, the right. May and Alison were in the middle with Jon, as usual, bringing up the real with his trusty walking stick. From his vantage point, Jon could see all the action, what little there was to see. He heard May chanting softly and knew that a spell was coming. He watched expecting to see a blast of fire or lightning or missiles or something equally exciting.

Jon watched fascinated as nothing appeared to happen at all. Then, one by one, their attackers screamed, dropped their swords, grabbed at their heads, turned and ran away as if the devil himself was after them. "Let's get going now," Mat urged, "before the Red Guards come to investigate." Mandy pushed on forward, but kept her huge sword raised. Seeing her coming, now the townsfolk began to give her a wide berth. Her threat cut a path for them to move forward.

As soon as they were moving again, Jon bursting with curiosity, asked, "May, what on earth did your spell do back there? I was expecting fire or sparks or something dramatic."

"Oh, just a little one of my illusions," May teased him and winked at him. "Okay. They saw in their minds that of which they are the most afraid. I certainly don't know precisely what each saw, only the nature of it. Pretty effective, don't you think? And no one got hurt." She was quite proud of her action.

"Impressive!" Jon replied very sincerely.

What should have been a leisurely half an hour walk to the church took nearly an hour because of the throngs on the streets. It was a sobering scene. "These people have lost all of their self-respect," observed Jon as they approached the church at long last. "How does one give back an entire town its self-respect?" he wondered out loud. Darless and Alison in front of him just shrugged. They had no idea.

Sir Henry, stalwart with long sword drawn and wearing chain mail and a blue tunic with the white cross, stood beside the opened front doors of the Church of Ukko, guarding the church from the crowds. "Hail and well met! Some day isn't it?" He bellowed above the noise of the bustling crowd of people on the street. "Come on in and get out of this madness." One by one, they passed by him, hastily entering the church.

The Bishop, just inside the entrance, was praying and wringing his hands. Clearly, he thought the whole situation utterly hopeless. He had seen it several times before in his long life. "It is always the same. Panic before the armies arrive; total chaos while they are here; devastation when they are gone. It never changes." Deepest apathy accompanied his long hopeless sigh.

"Hey, where there is life there is hope," Jon consoled him as he passed by the knight and entered. Mat was right behind him along with Mandy forming a rear guard. Jon then heard Mat speak to the holy paladin.

Mat whispered, "Keep a look out for a young lady who is likely bringing her family here to the church for protection. The Twins suggested she come and seek your keeping."

"By my life, I shall not fail the young maiden," Sir Henry whispered back. Jon smiled to himself. Amidst chaos there is a spark of greatness, thought Jon to himself.

Everyone was inside but milling around, unsure just how to explain what they wanted. "Er, Sir Henry, can you come inside for a minute? We need to briefly explain something which may be very important," Jon called out, realizing that since this was his idea, he needed to get their permission to search.

Jon hastily told them of their historical findings and what they proposed to do. "My son, you are free to search anywhere within the church," the Bishop replied, "But my predecessors have already thoroughly searched and researched to no avail. There is no such magical device; it is the stuff of legends that we tell our children."

In stark contrast, Sir Henry was encouraging, "Ah, but Saint Jon here possesses the Holy Scepter! That may be a sign that Father Ukko is looking down upon us. Go and make your search. I will guard the entrance. All other entrances are currently bolted shut."

"I'll join you," Mandy announced. "I'm no good at finding secret doors and the like. Instead, I'll make sure no one interrupts all of you."

"Gosh, where do we even begin," Alison wondered aloud. "Maybe we should split up in several teams to search."

Alison and May began a search of the first floor robing rooms behind the central chapel while Mat and Darless thoroughly searched the chapel and the high altar. Jon chatted with the Bishop because he had absolutely no idea whatsoever of what to do to look for secret doors. So to fend off boredom, Jon had the Bishop give him a guided tour of the entire church. But it was a slow tour because he did not want to tire the elderly priest unduly. Occasional thumping and tapping sounds echoed throughout the spacious church.

An hour later, Mat produced a small find. Located in a secret compartment behind the main altar was a small walnut box. It held a string of pearls. "Well I'll be. Those are Angel's Holy Pearls," exclaimed the Bishop as Mat showed him his find. "They have been lost for nearly a hundred years! It is said that an Air Maiden presented them to Angel d'Free for all of her contributions to this Church. You have indeed found a very Holy Relic of ours, my lad. Thank you. Thank you. Thank you." Then, as an afterthought, he asked, "Can you show me how that secret compartment works? It seems to be a very secure place for these extremely valuable pearls!" Mat spent a few minutes showing the Bishop how to work the hidden push-driven latch.

The others admired the pearls as well. And their discovery raised everyone's hopes considerably, because that was the only thing found after the hour's search. Darless decided that the only way to be sure they were not missing something was to carefully measure the dimensions of each room and correlate them, looking for an unexpected gap. She and Mat spend the next hour carefully taping out the entire first floor of the church. By noon, they still found nothing amiss anywhere on the main level. No one bothered searching the upper side rooms for obvious reasons.

The Bishop and Sir Henry invited them to share their noon-time meal down in the kitchen area. Everyone followed them into the basement which sprawled beneath the huge church. This lower area was about twelve feet below the surface and was always cool, refreshingly so on hot summer days. Here was the main living quarters for the staff. In better times, the Bishop explained some twenty priests and assistants lived here. Today, only Sir Henry and the Bishop lived here in the church. But he did explain that he had several assistant priests that volunteered their time and services periodically. They entered a huge kitchen area filled with three stoves and three ovens, all fueled by charcoal. In a side room, Jon noticed a huge quantity of charcoal. The pantry was a large room brimming with supplies of all kinds.

"We are now prepared for the circumstances," explained the Bishop as Sir Henry actually set about cooking their lunch. "We expect to provide sanctuary for perhaps a hundred people once the demons begin their assault in a few days." He showed them the linen closet equally full of blankets, sheets, towels and similar items.

However, it was the bathroom area that got everyone's attention. The latrines opened directly into the sewers, though only a rat could get through the openings. Likewise the wash basins emptied into the sewers. "This may prove a fruitful area to search after lunch," pronounced Jon.

"Here is our humble library." There was a note of pride in the old man's voice as they entered. Plush red carpeting covered the floors. One wall was lined with shelves brimming with scrolls and books of all kinds. Oaken tables and chairs were centrally located and the room was well-lit by nearly twenty oil lanterns.

"It is a nice study," Jon commented as they all left to Sir Henry's call to dine.

"Sir Henry, perhaps we should open one of the vintage wines for today's meal," suggested the Bishop, noting that only water goblets were set on the table.

"A wine cellar! This I have to see," Jon exclaimed and he followed the paladin to another side room that was slightly lower still in elevation. It was a very dark room. The paladin lit a lantern and handed it to Jon, cautioning him to watch his step. "Ah, there is a raised area here, strange," mused Jon. The extensive wine racks stood neatly upon a raised dais area about twenty feet square. They stepped up about a foot and closely examined the many bottles.

"Ah, this one will do," commented Sir Henry, "it was a good year. Over on the other side there are the kegs of new wine and the fermenters. At the moment, we have about a hundred gallons fermenting. You know — holy wine for services and such occasions."

Over lunch, the paladin and the Bishop were entertained with an account of some of their adventures in Zaire and the beauty of the Church of Ukko there. When they finished, Mandy washed up the dishes with Jon's aid while the others returned to their searching activities, now centered in this sprawling basement area. The Bishop took his afternoon nap. All was quiet save the tap-tap noises of the ongoing search.

One hour passed, then two, then three. The searchers were getting quite irritable at this point and had mostly given up and were sitting in at the lunch table, downcast and frustrated. Jon said, "It just has to be down here somewhere, this is the most logical place for it!"

"Well, no one can find a way into that section over there," grumbled Darless. "My measurements show that there is a twelve foot gap between the library room and this wall here. But it does seem to be solid stone all around. I've been over it a hundred times!"

Alison was just as irritable, "Okay, Jon," she said at last. "You claim it should be down here somewhere. Then by golly I'll find it!" And she began chanting a magical incantation. Everyone looked at her wondering what she was about to do. She finished by barking a word that sounded much like "Open!" Suddenly every door in this portion of the basement flew wide open. Loud banging noises echoed throughout the entire basement.

"What on earth is going on?" cried the startled Bishop.

Alison's face turned crimson. "I just used a magical spell to force open any door in this portion of the basement, including any secret doors. Well everyone, go have a look and see if you can find our elusive door."

"Brilliant!" exclaimed Darless. "Good thinking!" Everyone rushed about the basement area looking for a new door. With everyone running about looking at all of the opened doors, it only took a minute for the discouraging news of "nothing new." But Darless stalked around this singular area which her measurements just did not add up. She saw nothing, so she entered the library. "Wow!" came her cry. "Everyone, in here. We've found something!" Everyone rushed into the library. On one side, the stone wall had pivoted revealing her missing room. Only about ten feet wide and perhaps fifteen feet long, the room was entirely surrounded by stone walls making it pitch black inside. "Better bring some lanterns!"

When six lanterns illuminated the secret study, for that is exactly what the room had been, it was gruesome. Dust an inch thick covered everything. Shelves with books and scrolls lined the upper portions of the side walls. A small, ornately carved table with three chairs was positioned against one wall. A workbench or writing or study carousel nestled against the back wall. And a mummified corpse was sitting in the chair, one arm still holding a quill over a parchment on the bench. "Oh my, oh my," was all that the Bishop could utter as he stood at the entrance staring inside this room.

After a staring at the scene for a couple minutes, the high priest finally suggested, "Well, I think it best if you can bring his remains out here. I'll fetch a blanket. He should be searched for anything important, such as who he was, and then given a proper burial."

Jon and Mat volunteered to do the deed. Jon carefully removed the quill from the dried leathery hand. Bones cracked slightly as the two of them lifted the incredibly light weight body onto the blanket. Still, an arm and a leg broke off as they laid him down. Once they had the body out into the well-lit library, the Bishop performed a thorough, diligent search, which yielded only a set of keys to the church; he carried no identification.

Meanwhile, Jon and the others searched the room. A small chest yielded a fortune in gold and silver coins, which would be a welcome addition to the now meager funds of the Church of Ukko. The scrolls and books were all of a religious nature, Jon supposed. He could not read any of their writings. However, what caught and maintained his interest was the parchment with the last writings of the priest. Even this he could not read.

Though yellowed with age and exceedingly brittle, the black ink was still legible but the script showed signs that it had taken the last living effort of the priest to write. Much of the surface was covered in brownish and cracked splotches, dried blood. However, Alison was able to read the words for it was in a special language with which she and the priest both were familiar. Solemnly she read his last words.

"Demons have come; killed us all. I am Father Samuel d'Free, grandson of our city's founder. I am slowly bleeding to death; my time to join Father Ukko has come. For those who come after me, remember to get the wine and say In the Name of Father Ukko. May the demons get their just rewards."

"Well, we know who he is. He can finally have a proper burial," Alison said softly. The somber search of the room continued. The Bishop was in awe at all of the lost religious treasures now found, for that was what all of the written materials actually were. Nowhere did anyone find any other passage to the theorized magical device tunnel. However, Mat figured out how the secret door operated and demonstrated its usage to the Bishop. It cleverly utilized pressure upon the wall itself to open. It was in perfect balance and very well made indeed.

The glum faced searchers finally halted their day's search at supper time. The girls decided to fix supper for everyone and set about the task. Jon volunteered to set the table and be a gopher for the women. Mat went for a stroll outside the church along with Sir Henry.

Over dinner, the Bishop said apologetically, "Well I did say that this church has been ever so thoroughly searched over hundreds of years. Though you did not find this supposed tunnel, I am very thankful that you found the lost study. The religious value of those materials is priceless. Thank you all very much."

His cheerfulness did nothing to part the glum the others felt. Jon muttered, "I had it all worked out. It just had to be right. But it sure isn't."

"There must be some other way that the High Priest would use to get to the magical device," consoled Darless, "though at the moment I really am fresh out of ideas."

"Word of Recall," offered the Bishop. "Some very able, highly trained priests of Ukko are granted a secret word. When they say that word, they are instantly transported from wherever they are to their personal altar room, wherever that may be. Perhaps, the High Priest used that as a way to travel to this place legends speak of." But then his face fell, "It has a fatal flaw, though. How would the priest get back here?" Gloom settled in once again.

"We could all do with a little holy wine," the Bishop said in hopes of lessening their disappointment. "Why don't you go into the cellar over there and pick us out a really good bottle, Sir Henry?"

The paladin got up to go fetch another of his favorite vintage. Jon joined him. "Your wine cellar is most impressive," he said, his spirits rising. "I've never seen so many bottles in one place outside of a store ever before." Together they strode into the wine cellar room.

"Careful, watch your step. Remember it is a raised platform," the paladin cautioned Jon as they entered. He was holding the sole lantern. The room was thus very poorly illuminated. Jon stepped carefully upon the raised section of floor. It seemed utterly peculiar to have a raised floor section here. Then the parting words of the dead priest echoed in his mind. "Get the wine and say In the Name of Father Ukko." Jon picked up a wine bottle from the stack and said out loud, "In the Name of Father Ukko." In the next instant, everything went totally, completely dark; totally silent.

"What's that you say," Sir Henry turned around towards Jon. He had just retrieved another bottle of wine. To his utter amazement, Jon was nowhere in sight. "Hey, help! Jon's has disappeared! He's vanished into thin air. Look out for Demons!" he cried as loudly as he could. The sounds of steel being drawn struck his ears; lanterns hastily approached, lighting up the wine cellar. Everyone crowded into the cellar.

"Zagroot zounds!" exclaimed Mandy. Jon has been abducted right out from under our noses! How could we let this happen?" Extreme worry lined Alison's face, though she was not yet ready to believe that demons had abducted Jon.

Darless frowned. "What happened in here, Sir Henry?" she asked coldly and calculatingly.

"I don't know exactly. I was over here getting this wine bottle when he said something. I didn't quite catch it and turned to ask him to repeat it. And he was gone, completely gone!" the amazed and worried paladin explained.

"Where was he standing when you last saw him?" Darless pressed him.

"Right over there," he pointed to a spot about five feet from where he was standing. Everyone followed his gesture and looked there, and poof there was a worried looking Jon standing there.

"Jon!" several gasped at the same time.

"Er, hi all. I got a bit of a scare there. Good. You all got lanterns, we are going to need them," he said.

"What on earth happened to you? You gave us a fight!" Alison signed with relief and inwardly grinned that she was right, he had not been abducted. She felt that she would somehow sense or know if anything really bad ever happened to him, her man.

"I've found something, though I have no idea what. It was right there in d'Free's letter. You stand here upon this raised stone and say those words. You are instantly someplace else. It is totally dark there, though. Not even the slightest trace of light. Pitch black. For a minute I panicked; I froze; I dare not move. Nothing happened to me. But I could not see a thing. Where is a wizard when you need one?" Jon joked. "Of course I knew I could just step my way back here, and then I relaxed. I figured that if those words got me there, wherever there is, they may also get me back. They did and here I am." Jon finished his brief tale.

Instantly, the four women chanted the same words. And four bright globes of light appeared on their fingertips. "Wow! Now that **is** light!" Jon laughed. "Okay, bring them lights with you. Come up here by me and just say 'In the Name of Father Ukko.'" Poof, instantly Jon was gone again. One by one the others quickly followed suit. When the light came, Jon could finally see what he had stumbled into.

They were in an underground room, square, about thirty feet across. Bedrock formed all four sides and the floor. There were no other entrances, no seams between the floor and the walls. This room had been carved out of solid rock.

In the center of the room on a stone Diaz was a machine about five feet tall. Some kind of glass or lense was at the very top of the device. Only one lever could be seen at its base. The roof of the room, some twelve feet above them appeared to be made of black glass, which later Jon surmised was actually a basaltic volcanic glass, very highly polished. Not a speck of dust was in the room. It was hermetically sealed. Several large chests stood in one corner. Otherwise the room was totally empty. For several minutes, no one said a word; they just stared in complete disbelief and wonder.

"Oh my! Oh my!" squeaked the Bishop, his voice failing altogether.

"Praise be to Ukko!" cried Sir Henry who fell onto his knees and began praying. A miracle beyond words he had witnessed was his view point.

"Amazing," was all that Jon said as he looked over this incredible room and its construction. "How unusual."

"Jon, you did it!" exclaimed Alison, and she gave him a loving hug and kiss.

"Congratulations, one and all. We all played our part," corrected Darless.

"What a strange room! I sure would not want to be cooped up in here for very long," drolled Mandy. "I feel like I am in a cage!"

"Unbelievable, Jon. You are amazing," Mat insisted on shaking his hand, making Jon a bit embarrassed from all of the attention. May gave him a kiss of thanks further adding to his blushing face.

"Wonder what's in those chests?" Jon diverted their attention to the only other items in the underground chamber. It was just enough of a diversion.

Mat cautioned, "Hold a minute; let me inspect it first. There could be traps for the hasty." After a thorough search, he announced, "It appears to be safe. Who would like the honor of opening these chests?"

"Why don't you do it, just in case," May replied. The others consented.

"What kind of traps could be in or on a chest? And why? And who would do such a thing?" asked Jon completely baffled by the idea of a booby-trapped chest. Such a thought had never occurred to him before.

"Well, if you had something of great value and wanted to protect it from petty thievery, you could have various kinds of booby-traps installed, such as poisoned needles that strike the fingers as they manipulate the lock, for example," May carefully explained. "And then there are the explosive devices that go off when the chest is opened. Those can be deadly or just knock out gas and anything in between. The list is endless." She halted with a gasp for Mat had opened the lid of the first chest to reveal a huge stash of gems. The others gasped and stared in disbelief. Here was a fortune in gems, about a cubic foot of solid gem stones, diamonds, emeralds, rubies, and many others. The other box's contents were more mundane: six sacks of gold coins and an equal number of silver.

"Well, your church is not going to want for the lack of funds any longer," Mat pointed out cheerfully.

"We can afford to get the long overdue maintenance done on the church and then just think of all the things we can do for the town," the Bishop acknowledged, his voice had returned. "Never in my wildest dreams did I think I would live to see such wonders as I have in the last few days. It is a Holy Miracle, a portent of better things to come!"

Sir Henry took a more practical stance, "Well, if this much of the ancient legends or history is true, then the rest of the children's tales we have told about the magical device protecting the city from the demon armies may also be true. If so, the ravaging of Freetown may be at an end for good! If only we can figure out how to use it and what it actually does and if it still works. I'd say that that is still a lot of if's!" He did not sound overly optimistic.

"It doesn't look all that complex to me," put in Mandy. "Only one lever and it can only go downwards. So it is probably an on-off lever. Not much to its operation, I'll wager."

"As to its effects, I think we should research that a bit before we just pull the lever," Darless cautioned. "Does the Church have any documents that discuss its operation or usage?"

"Tomorrow I will collect all of my priests together and we will see what we can find out," the Bishop replied. A new value and purpose had begun to grow and expand in this servant of Ukko. "Sir Henry, you must go at once and contact each of them and tell them of these momentous events!"

"Your wish is my command," the noble paladin replied. But to Mandy and Mat, he added, "I'd feel a lot better running off like this if you would not mind staying around the front door. You know, to prevent any undo action. The crowds were getting pretty unruly earlier today. We cannot afford to have anything bad happen just as we are about to make history."

"Sure. You can rest assured that nothing bad will happen while you are away," Mandy replied. It had been many years since she had done simple guard duty, but at least it was some action. Mat nodded his agreement as well.

Everyone then returned back into the wine cellar. Sir Henry left to deliver the news while Mat and Mandy took up positions just outside the front doors. Mat also did a quick inspection around the building's perimeter just to make doubly sure all was still well. It was, of course.

The Bishop excused himself and went into the library and began searching through its many volumes and scrolls. The remaining four fixed themselves a cup of tea and chatted about the day's events. Jon grew bored and went up into the main chapel area. Sitting on the bench nearest the high altar, he took out his flute and began to play tunes appropriate for a stately old church. The soft sounds of his flute echoed through the entire church and the other three women soon crept up and into the chapel just to listen to him. Jon heard May whisper excitedly to Alison, "He really *is* a musician! I did not really believe it until now!"

When Jon was playing, time disappeared. There was only the music ebbing and flowing. How long he played, he could not say. When he finished, he felt whole and calm and totally at peace. It was excellent timing for Sir Henry had just returned and had heard part of the last piece. "You *are* a musician!" he commented as Jon finished and began putting his flute away.

"Yes," said Jon, "Just a musician." And he smiled. The party said their farewells and the six headed back toward the inn.

It was now about 9 p.m. and the street traffic had nearly disappeared. The heat of the day had given way to the chill of the arid evening. They had a very pleasant stroll back to the inn, completely uneventful.

Chapter 12 The Day Before — an Unexpected Guest

"Well, one day to go," Darless pronounced with an air of resignment. The four were eating breakfast along with Mat and May who had joined them. "It's not hard to tell something is up. Just look at all of the seedy characters in here this morning!" Several groups of ill-looking mercenaries had chosen this inn for their morning breakfast. Unkempt, long hair, untrimmed beards, road-stained clothes, muddy boots, and a variety of weapons — all spoke of their recent arrival and purposes.

To make matters worse, their waitress told them that due to circumstances, the dining areas and pubs would be closed all day tomorrow but would reopen after dark. She did not elaborate and none thought it prudent to ask further questions. It was a sober meal; they ate quickly and returned with a couple tea pots to their spacious quarters.

When they were all back in the living room area, May quietly asked "Alison, are you really serious about rebuilding the castle? Serious about building a town around it and needing tradespeople to populate it?"

"Oh absolutely. I think I now have saved up about enough to get the job done right. When this mess is over, I'll get the process started, though I am not totally sure just how best to go about it yet. But that's just a detail to be worked out. Why?" she replied.

"Well, Mat and I have decided that we definitely want to return with you and help rebuild it too. We want to build a family home. We want to be surrounded by honorable townsfolk. We are tired of living in a thieves den. Some others we know might also be interested in moving. From what we can tell at this stage, many of those joining the caravan would be good prospects to help settle a new town. That is, if you wouldn't mind," May said reservedly.

"Sis, if you think they are okay, then that is fine with me. I trust your judgement," Alison emphatically declared, setting her sister's mind at ease a bit. "But how are we going to move all of your things, your possessions and all?"

"We don't have a lot of stuff really. We've been investing our funds in gems. They are small, lightweight, and easily transportable and convertible by any money changer. However, if we travel overland, it is such a far distance that we would need to take a small wagon mostly with trip supplies. And with the exodus at hand, wagons are going for a premium price. And we will need some time to prepare," May explained. She had evidently thought this out carefully.

"Well, I had not thought much about timing. Tomorrow is the big council meeting. If we survive the assassin, then the War Games do not begin until the next day. I cannot imagine that the armies will get to the town here much before the third day hence. But we have to try to help the Church learn to use their protection device and all that that entails. I don't know exactly what that is going to involve. I'd feel awful just abandoning the Church of Ukko here in their hour of need," she explained.

"We either," May agreed with her. "However, there is just no delaying the caravan folks; they want to leave before the council tomorrow. There is talk of leaving at dusk tonight. I fear for their safety. But we don't know what we can do about it." Her voice betrayed her deep concern for the departing fellow townspeople.

"Please promise me that you two will not go off with the caravan without waiting for us!" exclaimed Alison, suddenly getting a vision of her twins leaving on the suicide journey with out her. "I don't want anything to happen to you two!"

May smiled, "Don't fret, Runtkins, the Twins are not foolhardy. Cold and calculating maybe, but never foolhardy!"

"The best thing for the caravan," Jon offered his opinion, "would be to not leave until this whole thing has blown over, say in a couple of weeks. That's what I think. But I don't expect they would remotely see it that way. People are terrified, and rightly so. But if that ancient machine still works, the town is going to be the safest place in this whole countryside, if it works."

"That's a big if," Darless added. But Jon wasn't listening. An idea had just formed.

"Say, May. Just how trustworthy are these caravan people? Can they keep a secret for twelve hours?" he inquired.

She thought a moment, looked at Mat who flashed some finger signs. Then she answered, "Most are honorable. But we don't know about the secret keeping. Just no way to predict that one. But what's your idea? We are very interested in at least hearing it."

Jon thought a moment longer and then said, "Suppose that around midnight, when most people are totally asleep, they saw the legendary magical device working, doing its thing. Would that be enough to convince them to stay a little longer? But most importantly, not to tell anyone else about it?"

"Hum, I would certainly think it would convince many," May replied. "But there are other eyes in the night as well. Unfriendly eyes. The secret would be out of the bag."

"Yes, that is what keeps troubling me. If the Demon Lords discover that the Church of Ukko is back in the business of Freetown protection, they could just re-raid the Church once again. Only this time only a single paladin and an aged priest are there. All would be lost in an instant," Jon said downcast. "Yet, sometime we have to test this thing. But hopefully not until after the council meeting is finished and the Demon Lords have gone. Yet, time-wise, that is going to be too late for the caravan people. I'm sure the Bishop would not jeopardize the entire operation and perhaps the survival of the town just to try to keep the foolish from doing foolish actions."

"Oh it is a simple matter," Mandy interjected. She had been listening intently to all of this and saw the solution at once. "No matter when the caravan leaves, they will be making only a few miles an hour. Even with a couple days head start, they cannot get far. On a set of good light war horses, why we could catch them in a day or two at most. So why not have someone in the caravan drive your wagon when they leave, fill it with provisions and such. Assuming we can get a hold of six good horses, why we can catch up with them in no time after it is all over with here."

"That might work," Mat responded. "If nothing bad happens to the caravan during that time, we could easily join up with them. Of course, if ill befalls them, we might find there is nothing to join up with. But any ill is going to befall them no matter what we do. And if they can manage to stay out of trouble for just a couple days, it might work out. But there are only two problems with this, Mandy. First, the horses are going to be hard to acquire just at this moment and second, neither of us have ever been on a horse."

Just then there was an urgent knock on their door. Darless opened it to let a worried William inside. "I've a message for my Lady, er, Mandy," he explained. Darless motioned for him to join them.

"Oh, here, I be forgetting my manners," he said to her apologetically and handed her two freshly baked loaves of bread still warm and fresh out of the ovens. "For you all to enjoy," he added. "Er, Mandy, can I have a private word with you please?"

"Sure William," Mandy led him into her bedroom. "What is up?"

"I have a message for you from Reylona. She came to my dreams last night and instructed me to tell you this. 'When it is time, ride like the wind!' I don't know what that means or when or where or anything. Just that," he looked very worried as if she would not believe him.

She gave him a warm kiss and said, "Thanks! I will follow that to the letter when the time comes." After a short pause, she teased, "Say, how come she comes to you and not to me?" There was a hint of jealousy in her voice as well as a bit of playfulness.

"Maybe she likes me," he teased her back and gave her a loving kiss back. "I've gotta go now. They've got a rather large order of way-bread to fill; I think some caravan folks are buying up all the bread they can find. See you later on if possible. I believe these are the people I am to protect, so I may have to leave in a big hurry. I'll let you know when I do, if I can."

"You'd darn well better!" she exclaimed, real concern was in her voice. He smiled and left at once to see to the bread making but waved goodbye to the others as he left.

"Well, what did he say?" Darless teased Mandy, thinking it may have been a bit romantic.

"Actually, he had a message for me from Reylona. She said that when the time comes, I am to ride like the wind. That has me more convinced than ever that we are going to have to catch up with that caravan after the town is taken care of, don't you think so too?"

Everyone agreed that that was a strong omen that Mandy's plan was the right one. So Mat and May left to get their affairs handled, a wagon purchased, supplied and ready to go. The others decided to visit the Church and see if anything else was needed. Mandy needed to get acquire six good horses. It was going to be a busy day.

When the foursome hit the streets, they knew things were different. Yes, throngs of town people filled the streets, but today hundreds of soldiers displaying various banners joined the hustle and bustle. And they were neither polite nor courteous, preferring to bash their way through anyone and anything. Interestingly enough, the Red Guards were nowhere to be seen.

Mandy took the point holding her bastard sword threateningly before her. Few dared to challenge such a large blade directly and moved out of her way. Jon brought up the rear walking stick in hand. Law and order were diminishing by the day, he noted. This time, both Alison and Darless carried wizard staffs; they walked and looked like powerful mages not to be trifled with. And so they out-bullied the bullies of the street, arriving without mishap at the Church of Ukko.

What a change from the day before. Six well-armed guards each with a blue tunic and white cross barred the entrance to the church. As they walked up the steps, one of them challenged them, "Hold. What business do you have with the Church?"

"It's us, Jon Brown and Alison d'Ambrose and Darless and Mandy to see Sir Henry and the Bishop," Jon replied before the others had a chance. But he was not expecting quite the response for which he was looking.

"The Saint Jon Brown?" came the incredulous reply.

"Er, none other," he said.

Instantly all six men got down on one knee, clasping their hands together in prayer. "Forgive me for not recognizing you, Your Supreme Holiness. We are your humble servants. How can we ever repay you for all that you have done for us?"

Be careful what you say! Mandy placed into Jon's mind.

"Two things. Remember always, that the women here did far more than I; in fact, without them, I would be dead several times over. Secondly, always continue to help others who ask for aid," Jon replied straining hard to maintain a solemn air about him.

"We will, Your Holiness," said several in unison.

"Oh yes, and third, just call me Jon, please," he added as an afterthought.

"Yes, your — Jon. Please enter. We will defend the church with our lives if need be," the leader pronounced. They entered quickly and went in search of Sir Henry and the Bishop. Once inside the church, a young man in acolyte robes greeted them. He had overheard the guards and did not make the same mistakes.

"They are in the library doing research. Please follow me," said the young man who could not have been even twenty years old. He formally led them down and into the library and even announced them, "Saint Jon and party, Your Eminence." He bowed low and returned to the chapel.

"Ah, there you are. Good morning to you all. We have a little more help today," said the Bishop cheerfully. Jon noticed that much of his apathy had evaporated. The man seemed much younger than his years this morning.

"More are coming soon," Sir Henry called out from behind a stack of books. "I have a dozen armed guards about the place at the moment. However, I expect about fifty will report in within a day. All of the dozen part-time priests are also on duty along with their families. There is a growing crowd of townsfolk here now seeking protection. Oh yes, please tell Mat that the young girl he spoke to me about has brought her whole family here. The rooms over yonder are filling up." He grinned broadly, very pleased with how things were now progressing.

"Yes, and I have made sure that the 'secret' will not be so easily suppressed this time," added the Bishop. "Not only do all my priests know about how the gate operates, but also several of the trusted guards. The Demon Lords will not succeed in stamping us out a second time! If only we can figure out how it works and what it actually does. I really don't want to promise something that we cannot deliver."

"Have you made any progress in figuring out what it actually does do?" asked Darless full of curiosity.

"Yes and no," he replied with s sigh. "Yes, it is the legendary device; yes, the lever does control it. But no, we still have no idea what it actually does, save the legends of keeping the Demon Armies from the city." He added confidently, "But I am sure we will get it figured out. Have you come to help?"

"Well yes and no," grinned Mandy. "First, I need some assistance from Sir Henry. I need to get six light war horses or perhaps two lights and four swift, sound mares. And yes, with full riding gear. And I don't know where the best place to go to acquire them."

"Ah, that is a bit of a problem," Sir Henry replied. "On an ordinary day, such would be an easy request to fill. But under present circumstances, it will take a bit of doing. Let me see," he paused a moment thinking rapidly. "Yes, it's time I called in that favor Longbottom Jones owes me. Bishop, if you can spare me an hour, I will assist her."

"Certainly, be off at once," the old man chuckled. "I'll put these others to work."

So Mandy and Sir Henry quickly left, leaving Alison, Darless and Jon to help the Bishop and two assistants in their research. He soon had them pouring over scrolls looking for all references that might be useful.

Time passed. They found many references to its use and results, but none said actually what it did do. Mandy and Sir Henry returned and joined in the search. Later a young priest called them into the kitchen for lunch. Then, it was back to the search once more. However, by late afternoon, they had finally examined every book and every scroll in the entire church to no avail. Not one described what it did. Their spirits sank and they all sat there looking solemnly at each other.

Just then, a young girl about ten years old came meekly into the room. She fidgeted with her cotton dress hem a bit, getting up the courage to speak. She addressed Jon, "Are you the ones that are going to save our town from the bad men?" Jon look up into her blue eyes and blonde hair tied in two pony tails. Her look, the innocent face, the eyes so full of trust, moved him deeply. He knew he had to do something. "Yes, honey. And tonight late, you get your parents to let you stay up, all of you, look to the south, to the central well. And for a brief instant only you will see what Father Ukko has given to this church. It's only going to be visible for a brief time, mind you. But then tomorrow night, it will be visible for several days in a row."

"But what do you have in mind?" quickly interrupted the Bishop.

"We have to know more about it. It is a risk we are going to have to take. At the stroke of midnight, turn it on for only one minute. We'll get as many us strategically placed outside and that should give us enough time to see firsthand. Let as many of your most trusted people know about it as well; let them witness it too. It's time to start rebuilding faith in this town, faith in good not evil!" declared Jon. She giggled and ran to tell her parents the news.

Jon then explained that with all of the new guards about the place, the device was likely safe, since the Demon Lords did not yet know of its rediscovery. Further, even if spies saw the midnight display, whatever it turned out to be, certainly none would know what it meant; none would have been alive when the device was last used several hundred years ago. So the secret would be safe for a little while longer. All agreed with his reasoning.

The next half hour was filled with various opinions on what the device might actually do. Everyone had the chance to voice their thoughts and opinions. On these matters, Jon was completely silent. He had no frame of reference by which to even imagine magical devices. Finally, they began discussing who and where and what needed to be observed when the device was activated. Everyone agreed that the Twins should be here to assist them, because Jon wanted to have some people actually out and about in the city, live and on the scene.

"How are we going to contact them and let them know to be here appropriately dressed?" the Bishop asked, alluding to the fact that he knew about their secret identity. "I can send Sir Henry off to search for them."

Jon relied, "Well, it might be hard for him to find them. They had quite a few errands to take care of today." He did not want to actually blurt out that they were planning to leave the city. It would be best for the Twins to tell him personally. Jon did not know what relationship they had with the church leader. "I know, I will contact May. Give me a couple minutes."

And he closed his eyes and calmed his mind. He concentrated on May and began to thrust out his awareness in search of her.

"What's he doing," whispered the Bishop with a puzzled look on his face.

"He's using his mind, his powers to try to contact her and tell her to come here," whispered Darless back to him. The Bishop's eyes opened wide and he stared at Jon, certain that he was witnessing yet another miracle.

Jon's awareness swept across the city in a widening circle, feeling for Alison's sister. He felt the presence of thousands of minds, many black or dark grey in color. These gave him a very uncomfortable feeling which he ignored. After some time he felt the warmth and caring he associated with May. *May? It's Jon. Oops. Sorry. I'll get back to you in a couple minutes.* He felt the blood rush to his face and hands. He knew that he was very red. He heard Mandy's whisper and all three girls giggling, "Look. I'll bet he's done it again!" He heard the Bishop's urgent whisper, "Done what?" And he heard her reply, "Nothing important. You don't want to know," which was followed by more giggles. Jon tried his best to totally ignore them and counted out the time until he thought it was safe to try again.

He made contact again. *Is it safe now? Okay. We need you and Mat here at the Church of Ukko dressed in your Twins outfits about an hour after dark.*

"How do I reply?" a distressed May spoke aloud; she was in the back of her shop packing some small items for the caravan.

You only need to think your answer. You don't have to say anything. I'm reading you loud and clear. Jon sent back to her.

Okay. We'll be there. What's going on? she strained to think with all her might. She had never experienced this kind of communication before.

We are going to active the device and try to see what it does. We need your help. Thanks, he sent to her. *Bye and sorry for intruding so abruptly on you.*

She said "Bye," without realizing she didn't need to speak the thought.

"Okay, the Twins will be here about an hour after dark. That should give us plenty of time to get into positions. So the next step is to figure out what those positions should be. Any ideas?" Jon asked only too eager to get the subject changed. He had once again intruded on a woman who had chosen that moment to make use of the bathroom.

Darless took the pressure off of Jon by offering, "Someone should be near the central well, that's for sure." And right on cue, everyone began offering ideas of what and where to look until supper was announced.

The evening meal was held in stages because of the large number of refugees in the church. After eating hastily, they returned to the study once more to try to decide just where to observe the effects of the device. However, Mandy, who had not said much up to now, made an important suggestion. "You know, I've been thinking on this some time now. And I think I have a suggestion." She saw that she had everyone's attention and so continued, "The other day, Mat was showing us the city. I was looking it over for natural defenses and such. I did notice that there used to be a barrier wall around the town. It's still there, but the town has expanded several fold since the wall's construction. My professional opinion is that that wall, which is too low to provide any real obstacle to an invader, may be connected to the device. Why else make a wall that is only ten feet tall and just a few feet thick? From what I have seen, there are few, if any, wild animals to keep out. No barbicans, no guard towers. So what's the point of such a wall if not somehow connected to this protection device?"

"Does that old wall still exist?" wondered the Bishop. "I guess it does, but it has been incorporated into many buildings as I recall."

Darless was the first to realize its impact on the town. "Wait a minute," and she got out her map and spread it open on a table. "Here's the town layout. But the wall is not shown directly on the map. Can anyone show me its outline? I think we have a more serious problem."

"We can," came a familiar voice from behind them, as in walked Mat and May, dressed head to foot in their black Twins' nighttime clothing.

"We didn't hear you come in," said the Bishop startled.

"You weren't supposed to," chuckled May. "We'll keep the masks on because of all the townsfolk who are here. Just call us the Twins." Mat took a piece of charcoal and drew a nearly circular line on the map defining just where the old wall was located.

"It is as I thought. It is circular," said Darless. "We do have a problem if this turns out to be connected to the device." She stared at the other's uncomprehending faces.

"Oh, I'm beginning to see," said Sir Henry. "Look Bishop, if this wall forms the outer defense line, protecting those within the walls, what happens to all those who reside beyond its boundary? Speaking only of area of coverage, let's see, the town's roughly circular and the wall is circular."

"That means area-wise, 4 to 1," Darless finished the calculation. "Yes, for every home within the protection barrier, there are going to be four homes outside our protection."

Mat and May began laughing, "That means all of the wealthiest folks, all of the secret council members' homes and shops are outside the wall! What an irony!"

"Oh my! Oh my!" the Bishop commented grasping the severity of the situation at last. "Whatever are we to do now?"

"You sir and this church are about to become the real power of the town, to regain all that was lost two centuries ago," commented Jon. "After the council has disbanded and the demon parties have left town, up goes the barrier, assuming of course it still works properly. Then, when the word has spread, those on the outside can take shelter within the protection zone. I'm sure most will avail themselves of the safety."

"And we, by virtue of providing the only real security for the town, will become the true holders of power and authority in Freetown," Sir Henry delivered his observation. "We must be ready to assume that mantle of power and responsibility. There is much to do, once we see that the device actually does still work."

"I've only got one small question," May asked. "If the device is turned on for only a minute with all of us out there in various places, how will we observers know when that minute will begin?" Suddenly Jon realized that they had no watches in this society. "Are you going to use some kind of lantern signal? Will we be in a position to even see it?" Silence.

"Hum, I think I can handle that part. I will go with the Bishop to the device. I can maintain mental contact with each party and will know when everyone is in position. I will let you know the exact moment when it is activated," Jon volunteered.

"How can you do that?" queried Sir Henry in disbelief.

"Jon has telepathic powers, Sir Henry," Darless exaggerated. She sent to Jon, Alison and Mandy, *This explanation will make sense to him; go along with it.*

"Oh I see," he said, totally accepting that explanation. "Then, let's divide up into observation teams and get this experiment going." May took Mandy and Alison to the central well and then left on her own to be near the south wall entrance. Mat and Darless went to that section of the wall nearest the wealthy estates that lay just outside the wall. Sir Henry took a couple of his men to the eastern wall edge. Jon, the Bishop and two other priests went to operate the device.

Carrying lanterns, the priests and Jon headed down to the wine cellar. Then, speaking the words, they reached the underground chamber. Jon then sat down on the floor and made himself comfortable while the priests examined the mechanism. "I'll tell you when to pull the lever down," Jon said and then relaxed his body and mind. Slowly he let his beingness and awareness expand outwards in a circular pattern. He easily spotted Alison and his close friends. It took some doing to find the paladin though. For a minute Jon thought that he might not be able to spot him as he realized that he really needed to be familiar with the other person to be able to locate them. Just as he was about resigned to having not found the holy warrior, Jon made contact, startling Sir Henry who had never experienced this form of communication. "Now, activate it please," Jon whispered. The Bishop pulled on the lever. It slid downwards with ease after two centuries of abandonment.

A flash of blue energy shot upwards from the lense, up and through the basaltic glass ceiling. The chamber was filled with a low humming sound, almost a throbbing. Jon had never seen such a pure blue light before. Serenity flowed through his every fiber reminding him of how he had felt when he was in Ukko's realm with Dispater and Morrigan. Like some distant shadow, Jon heard the priest muttering prayers to Father Ukko. "Off," he heard his harsh voice break in on this wonderful humming, vibrating sound. The Bishop complied. His head filled with yells of astonishment and success from the observers; he clasped his hands to his ears to block the overwhelming sound. It had, of course, no effect. He muttered to the Bishop, "They report it worked. Let's get back to the study." Jon was staggering still holding his ears, so one of the acolytes held on to him and helped him get back into the study.

Another brought Jon a glass of wine which seemed to revive him. "What happened to you? Are you alright? You gave us a bit of a scare back there," asked the Bishop.

"What an experience. I had too close a contact with everyone. In their excitement, they fairly yelled to me. It was like being at the center of a yelling crowd, and covering your ears didn't help a bit," Jon laughed at it now. "It took me by surprise, that's all. I should have expected it. Ah well, no harm done."

Within a half an hour, everyone was safely back inside the study of the Church of Ukko, excitedly telling everyone else what they had seen. Alison began by saying, "It began as a Holy Blue Light streaking up from the center of the well, up to several hundred feet. Then, like a fireball, it exploded into a hemisphere falling to earth." The others described how that falling curtain of blue made contact with the old wall forming a dome over the center of the city.

May had an additional observation. "I, we, tried to walk through the gap where the street opening is at. It was the most holy feeling we have ever experienced — all of that blue energy was flowing over my body! We'll never forget that as long as we live!"

Mat nodded his total agreement with her statement and added, "And I saw one of those mercenaries try to walk through it; he was walking down the street when it activated. He was repulsed by it and could not penetrate it. So we are convinced that the barrier of energy repels those of an evil nature. What an incredible gift from Father Ukko. The town's founders must have been extremely important to have warranted such a Holy Gift!"

"This calls for a celebration!" And Sir Henry brought out wine for everyone. An hour later, the six headed back to the inn to get ready for the next day, the day of the Demon Lords' council. The women chatted excitedly with May about how it felt being surrounded in the blue energy field. Jon just listened; he was just totally mellow. He knew what she had felt. He had felt it up close in person and had simultaneously received Twin's sensations because he had been totally attuned to her and Matt and the others. In effect, Jon had received a triple dose of the energy.

The Twins saw them safely to the door of the inn and parted, wishing them the best of luck for the coming day and to holler if they needed anything at all. Jon did detect a note of anxiety and worry about Alison being hurt by the assassin.

The four ambled up to their suite. As they approached the door, Mandy became instantly alert. "Something's not right here," she whispered and drew her sword out very quietly. Their gaiety vanished in an instant. The mages prepared some quick spells just in case. Jon clutched his trusty walking stick and opened the door when Mandy indicated to do so.

"Come in quickly. I've been expecting you," came a cold voice which they instantly recognized. Metrarch was in their room sitting in the dark. He snapped his fingers and a ball of light appeared on his fingers illuminating the room. "Come in quickly. I did say twenty-four hours of protection, didn't I?" he smiled as he saw them recall that fact as they entered and shut the door.

"But, but, I thought you'd come tomorrow," Alison managed to say. "Grand Procession and all."

"Yes, everyone is to think that. Zugblat is taking my place, just in case. I am already here. That should throw off the assassin just a bit. Clever, don't you think?" Metrarch said coldly and with a hint of pride. "I'll sleep out here, don't worry about sleeping arrangements," he added with a grin. "I wouldn't think of interfering with you and your women, Jon."

"Well, make yourself at home," Darless said just as dryly and coldly has he had spoken to them.

"Thank you, I have," he replied with a grin. "Jon, may I have a private word with you?"

"Er, this way, into my bedroom," Jon said, shrugging his shoulders to the girls indicating he had no idea what this was about.

Once inside and the door shut, Metrarch began using a very soft voice that had a hint of humanity in it. "Remember what you whispered to me at our last meeting?" Jon nodded. "I have given it considerable thought. "I will agree to any and all of your terms, if you will go along with me when the time comes, just play along with my lead. You will know when that is. It will violate none of your principles and will actually benefit everyone."

Jon agreed, "Okay. To do this, you must allow me to view your mental images as you look at them and follow my commands." Metrarch consented. Jon closed his eyes and reached out to Metrarch who was easy to find; his mind was very, very black indeed. Then, Jon felt the tiniest presence of Mandy, Darless, and even Alison. They were observing from an extreme distance, being very careful to not make their awareness known. They were not about to let anything happen to Jon. He ignored them and continued his process on Metrarch. "Tell me how you acquired the Holy Scepter of Ukko." And the images began to reveal themselves as Metrarch recounted the truth for the very first time ever.

Gruesome images from a bloody battlefield of slaughter filled Metrarch's mind. He had watched as another Demon Lord delivered the fatal blow to the scepter's wielder only to be slain in the process. With nearly everyone on the field of war lying dead, maimed or unconscious, Metrarch stole out from his hiding place and snatched up the scepter and claimed it for his own. Instead the scepter burned his hands in such a way that they would never heal. Jon had him go over the event many times, each time, some forgotten detail revealed itself to Metrarch. However, the pain in his hands only grew worse.

Jon felt a touch of panic, what if this process didn't work on Demon Lords? What if it only worked on human beings? He had promised. He wavered a moment in uncertainty. *No, it cannot be different. There must be something earlier hanging this up.* "Okay. Now is there an earlier time something like this occurred?" Jon asked the key question.

Metrarch looked for a while, searching his past memories. "Why, yes there is indeed, maybe three years before this." And they were off re-experiencing another event in the Demon Lord's life. And after going through this one several times, another appeared. And then another, and another. Three hours later, Jon was nearing exhaustion when Metrarch suddenly sat up, opened his eyes and began laughing. Not a demonic laugh, not a glee of insanity laugh, but a real genuine belly laugh. And it did not stop. The Lord tried to say coherent sentences to explain it to Jon, but could not. He would utter a word or two and then continue laughing so hard that he could not go on.

Jon smiled, "I think we are done for tonight. That's it."

"Thank you," came the reply between fits of laughter. The Demon Lord opened the door to leave, saw the concerned women, and laughed even harder. The joviality was contagious. No matter what they had thought of this despicable being, his genuine laughter forced them to smile as well. "Night you three," and he roared even harder.

"Jon, are you okay?" whispered Alison.

"I'm drained, pooped beyond belief. Need sleep." And he collapsed onto his bed. She tucked him in. Since there was not much else the women could do, they retired to their rooms. All three found it hard to get to sleep because of Metrarch's occasional fits of continuous laughter.

They awoke the next morning in a panic as they suddenly realized that the Demon Lord himself had spent the night in their common area. But when they opened their doors, the smell of roast duck and freshly baked bread assailed their senses. Metrarch had ordered breakfast for them ahead of time. "Good morning lovely ladies," Metrarch said calmly, between mouthfuls. "Come and partake of this excellent cuisine." Hesitantly, they obeyed. He seemed somehow different this morning. They did not understand nor grasp its significance, but they ate not knowing when the next meal would come during this eventful day. Whether they liked it or not, they were his bodyguard for another twelve hours.

After they had eaten, Alison roused Jon from a very deep slumber. He staggered out to eat what was left. Only after eating did Jon finally fully wake.

Meanwhile, when Darless had finished, Metrarch took her to one side of the room. "May I have a private word with you? It is of the utmost importance for everyone concerned." She nodded and, as Jon had done, led him into her bedroom.

"My pretty little demon lady, do not speak a word out loud. Hear me, say the words mentally. Commit these words to memory." And he formed a pattern of words in his native Abyss tongue into her mind. He insisted that she repeat them mentally many times, coaching her on getting just the right inflections. "Now, promise me that the instant that I am dead or dying or seem dead or at death's door, you come here to this room and speak aloud those words. Promise me this and only great good as you define it shall come from so doing. Swear this to me, My Lady."

Darless did not have any idea what the purpose of the words were nor what would happen. She did not trust any demon. But some instinct deep within her nudged her. "Okay, I so swear."

"Thank you. And not a word of this to anyone until such time as you need to say the words. Remember, come here to this room and say it in a very timely fashion. It is of the utmost importance. When the occasion presents itself, time is *vitally* important." She looked so utterly baffled that he added, "After you utter those words and see what occurs, all will become clear to you; you will understand perfectly. You will have to explain what occurs to the others for they will not understand, but you will." And he left her pondering this new mystery.

"Okay, Alison, my beautiful body guard, it is show time. Get your equipment or whatever's, and fall in to line. We go to greet the incoming Grand Parade; we go to meet me gallantly riding into town. — well, Zugblat posing as me anyway, assuming he has not been assassinated already." Alison and Darless carried two magical staffs of power and walked on either side of Metrarch. Mandy with bastard sword drawn led the procession. Jon carried his trusty walking stick and trailed immediately behind the Demon Lord.

Metrarch was dressed in his finest clothes and strode confidently forward seemingly without a care in the world. They paused outside the entrance of the inn and waited. A large crowd of the mercenaries had also gathered here lining both sides of the street. Many and varied weapons were drawn, each guard allegedly ready to protect the Demon Lord that they served. They did not have long to wait for soon the Lords on Parade began to arrive from different directions. Some came from the north while some came from the south and east and west.

Chapter 13 The Assassination

m'Doth and party were the first to arrive. His trumpeters announced his arrival. He sat boldly astride a huge war horse which was covered in shiny chain mail with ribbons of red tied to its mane and tail. This demon was huge, fully eight feet tall, very muscular build, but rather overweight. His face looked rather like a gorilla's but with several differences. He had two enormous fangs for tearing his meat. He had two huge conical horns protruding from his head. And his face shaped or contorted into an eternal contemptuous sneer. "Ah, I see you have already arrived, Metrarch," he bellowed in a very deep bass voice.

Metrarch smiled at the usurper of his throne. "Not really, I am yet to get here." He left m'Doth trying to grasp his meaning. Seven huge guards immediately surrounded m'Doth and stood alertly at attention. "Ah here comes another, d'Raul, if my eyes do not deceive me."

Indeed, from the other direction came a fine coach decorated in shades of green, d'Raul's parade colors. The coach stopped before the inn to cheers from portions of the crowd. A number of guards positioned themselves in front of the door. And out stepped d'Raul. This Demon Lord had a similar body to that of m'Doth. He stood perhaps an inch taller, but lacked the potbelly. Also his face sported a grimace of anger and viciousness, as if he wanted to crush everything in sight and was using all his self-control to not instantly tear into the crowd around him. "m'Doth. Metrarch," he bowed as was the custom between the Demon Lords. He said not another word as he and his guards took up a position near the entrance to the inn. His coach moved on down the street.

f'Tarch arrived next riding a two wheeled cart-like affair pulled by several enormous black skinned slaves chained to the affair. His build was similar to the other two, except that he spouted a well-kept goatee and had black hair and black clothes. His face had an evil grin embossed upon it, so that one could never be sure if he spoke the truth or not. When the cart halted, another slave got down on his hands and knees to be used as a stepping stone as f'Tarch got out of the cart, black robes flaring in the light breeze. "Ah, Metrarch, you are here already, I see. And you still live. That is, shall we say, encouraging. m'Doth, m'Raul." He bowed in a like manner as the others had done. A small group of black skinned warriors took up positions around him as he took his place before the inn.

Next, a group of beautiful white stallions came trotting down the street, accompanied by some cheering. Each horse bore light blue tack — saddle and harness. "El Grad, I do believe," Metrarch, announced mostly for his body guards' benefit. El Grad's body was nearly nine feet tall, but extremely thin. His legs and arms were extremely long and emaciated looking. Yet, looks can be deceiving. He wielded enormous strength yet had the agility of a bird. His hair was very long and straight, black in color, matching his piercing eyes. His gaunt face reminded Jon of the Goddess Morrigan, skin tightly stretched over bone. Jon watched in amazement as El Grad nearly floated gracefully off his steed, landing on the ground, almost as a bird might. "Greetings, Metrarch. I see you are still with us. That is good. It would set a bad precedent for a Demon Lord to be assassinated. m'Doth, m'Raul, m'Tarch." And he bowed low. Quickly, a number of his men took up their positions around him as El Grad fell into line with the other Lords.

A flock of orange birds appeared in the distance, coming towards the inn. Metrarch commented to his guards, "Here comes Junanon; he fancies himself as a bird." Indeed as the flock got closer, Jon could see that these were not birds but flying demons dressed in orange robes that flared in the wind. They gracefully landed before the crowd which clapped and cheered for them. Quickly several of the bird like demons surrounded the larger one, Junanon, and together they walked up to the inn. This Demon Lord had large wings that folded across his back. He was the smallest of any of the Lords, standing only six feet tall. His hands sported six long spindly fingers each with extremely long, razor sharp nails. His feet also had six toes all of equal length and nearly twice the size of Jon's fingers. They had many joints and could curl around a branch just as easily as their long nails could tear the flesh off of any body in an instant. His face looked bird-like with an elongated nose. His mouth was narrow and protruded much like a bird's beak. But unlike any bird, this demon had dozens of razor sharp teeth, gleaming white in the sun. His voice was high pitched, bordering on a squeak. "My dear Metrarch, so good of you to come. I thought the assassination plot might keep you away from the council! m'Doth, m'Raul, m'Tarch, El Grad." And he bowed low as had the others. Jon was noticing a pecking order; they all greeted Metrarch first, followed by their current council head, m'Doth. He wondered if there was any significance to it.

Jon did not have much time to ponder this before the rhythmic sound of beating drums could be heard far off in the distance. "Ah here comes Jarred; watch out for this one," Metrarch commented to his body guards. They watched as the ominous sounding drums came closer and closer. Soon marching waves of demons appeared marching down the street. Dressed in robes of yellow, a row of drummers pounded out the enchanting rhythm came along with a drum major holding aloft the yellow flag emblem of Jarred. Behind them marching in perfect unison came fifty human foot soldiers with Jarred leading them. This demon was the most human-like of the bunch, but towered over Jon at seven feet. His build was that of a warrior and his manners were that as well. The absolute precision of the marching brought yells and cheers from the crowd. His was the loudest welcome of the seven lords, a fact that Jon noticed did not go unnoticed among the other Lords nearby him. Jarred had long blond hair gently flying in the light breeze. He wore leather armor, carried a shield with a sunburst in the center and a spear in his other hand. The group marched up to the inn in perfect order and halted in an instant. It was quite a remarkable display of precision marching or drilling, Jon thought.

"Well, well, I see Metrarch has managed to stay alive a little longer. m'Doth, m'Raul, m'Tarch, El Grad, Junanon. I see that we are all here. Shall we enter?" he ordered as if he was the total authority here.

Metrarch chuckled, "Not so fast. I have not yet arrived. See here I come." He pointed out an approaching carriage. Several elegant carriages, with ornate ironwork flaring the grey banners of Metrarch trotted up to the inn. "Ah, here comes Metrarch," Metrarch joked. Jon noticed that the other Demon

Lords said nothing. He could not tell if they were speechless by this unexpected turn of events or were merely being polite and following a rigidly adhered to ceremony. The lead carriage halted before the inn and out stepped Metrarch, dressed in his finest grey. Jon looked at Metrarch. So did all of the other Lords and half of the crowd. The second Metrarch regally stepped out, grey-gloved hands gingerly touching the sides for support as if his hands ached from even the slightest contact. Jon listened as Metrarch's voice coming from this second Metrarch said, "Ah, Metrarch, I see you have survived. m'Doth, m'Raul, m'Tarch, El Grad, Junanon, Jarred. I see that we are all here. Shall we enter?"

"What the blazes is going on here?" demanded their current leader whose term expired at the end of the day, m'Doth. The tenseness and violent, suppressed anger was so thick Jon swore he could cut it with a knife. Only the pretense of a ceremony kept a brawl from occurring.

Metrarch roared with laughter and cancelled his spell. The second Metrarch suddenly turned into his faithful servant, Zugblat, who also was roaring with laughter. "Just avoiding being assassinated on the way to the Council," Metrarch explained and said, "Now we are all here. Shall we enter?" Jon could not help from chuckling as well. Demon Lords were no dummies, in spite of their looks, he realized.

m'Doth merely grunted something unintelligible and turned to enter followed by his seven hand-picked observers. One by one the others entered likewise. They all went into the spacious dining room which for today held the Council of the Seven.

The huge room was now divided into seven equal-sized areas set in a circle about the center of the room. Each of the seven tables had the color banners of one of the houses and behind each table rested seven chairs. All the other tables had been pushed back against the side walls and were filled with various kinds of food items and pitchers of drink.

One by one each group made their way to their specific table. Jon noted that Metrarch's table was closest to the entrance doors. Going clockwise from Metrarch's table were m'Tarch, m'Raul, m'Doth, Jarred, Junanon, with El Grad on Metrarch's right. Jon watched as various members helped themselves to drinks and a little food as they passed by and took their assigned places.

Each Demon Lord sat in the middle of the table's side with three trusted henchmen on either side. Metrarch's layout was noticeably different. While he sat at the center, Mandy was on his right, Darless on his left, Zugblat even more left. Alison sat directly behind him and Jon took his position as ordered way back against the wall near the food tables, about twenty-five feet behind Metrarch. Jon was also fairly close to the door, so that he would be instantly alerted to anyone's entrance.

When everyone was seated, m'Doth rose and spoke solemnly, "It is time to bar the door; cast your lock spells in sequence." He muttered a command phrase and a reddish glow appeared surrounding the door. One by one, the other Demon Lords cast their spells and Jon watched in fascination as the different colors blended around the door. He assumed that no one could go in or out until the Demon Lords so chose.

m'Doth continued, "I do hereby state that the Seven Ruling Houses of Ashina of the 66th level of the Abyss are in attendance. I formally open this Council of the Seven. I so state that I am accompanied by six of my men. They are to be dutifully recognized."

The other Demon Lords responded in unison, "We so state."

Then one by one, following in the same order as they had casting the lock spells upon the door, the others similarly announced themselves and their men. Metrarch was last and was very different. "I so state that I am accompanied by one of my men and four of my protectors. I ask that they be treated as my men for the duration of this council."

"This is highly irregular! I protest," sneered Jarred. The others mumbled audibly.

Before m'Doth could make any ruling, Metratch dryly stated, "There is nothing in the charter that defines who we may chose as our witnesses, Jarred. I have chosen wisely. So shut up." Jarred fumed and smashed his fists on the table nearly breaking it.

"He has a valid point, Jarred," m'Doth ruled. "There is nothing that defines who we may have as our witnesses. Thus, we accept your unusual witnesses. I declare that this Council of Seven is now in session. The first order of business is the

House population and supporters summarization reports. As the head of the council, I will begin."

And m'Doth boringly began rattling off figures and facts of the goings on within his House during the last twenty years. Evidently this had something to do with choosing a new leader, but the what eluded Jon. Besides, he had to be on guard duty.

He relaxed and let all thoughts leave his mind. He was just there, just being and observing. He closed his eyes and expanded his awareness. Their plan was for Jon to be aware of all minds in the room so that he could tell when and if the assassin arrived and so warn the others. Jon located his friends at once. Then he located the eight corners of the room and one by one located each of the other persons. He counted them, seven, seven, seven, seven, seven, seven, six. No assassin, he concluded. He sent a brief message to that effect to Alison, Mandy and Darless. Now all they had to do was wait.

The speeches were long, tedious and boring. To Mandy, they seemed utterly useless and pointless. "Oops," she realized that she was reacting and forced herself to relax and concentrate on the guard duty. *Perhaps the assassin is masquerading as one of the other Demon Lord's men.* They had not considered this approach, so she quickly placed her concern into her friend's minds. Alison and Darless began studying carefully each of the Demon Lord's men. But after a half hour examination, they could tell nothing more than when they started looking and gave it up. If the assassin was disguised as one of them, they would have to wait for an overt move on the assassin's part.

Upon receiving Mandy's thought, Jon decided to see if he could feel each person's emotions. He gave that up quickly; they all were filled with hatred for each other group. Only the degree of hatred varied.

Finally after two hours, they broke for lunch. One by one, each Demon Lord cancelled his locking spell upon the door. And after m'Doth cancelled his, the door opened and inn workers entered with trays of replacement food and more drinks. Tensions relaxed just a bit as everyone milled around the food tables. Metrarch carefully abstained from eating any food. Jarred teased him about trying to avoid being poisoned. After that, Jon and the others decided to not eat anything either. However, it was very difficult to keep Metrarch under constant protection. They thought that this would be an ideal time for the assassin to strike. But no attack came.

An hour later, much to the relief of the four, m'Doth again called the meeting back to order. They watched as the Demon Lords once again cast their locking spells in order upon the only entrance to the room. Jon relaxed in the back of the room once again. It certainly was easier guarding Metrarch during the actual meeting, he mused. He slowly became totally aware of the room and its occupants once more.

"It is now time for the candidates for this office to announce themselves. Be it known officially that I do not seek another term. Who wishes to occupy the Head of the Council position for the next decacentenial? Speak now or hold your tongue."

Jarred rose instantly before any other Lord could. "I, Jarred, leader of my House will be the next Head of the Council!" He ranted and raved about how well he was suited for the position, about how badly m'Doth had run it. And then he let loose a horrendous tirade against how Metrarch had previously conducted their business. He cursed Metrarch for having forced them to meet standing over the accursed Holy Scepter of Ukko. His tongue lashing went on endlessly. How Metrarch could sit there calmly and not react was beyond Jon's imagination. But the Lord did just that. He was evidently used to such invalidations.

When he finally had vented every conceivable argument for his righteous ascendancy to the leadership position, he sat down. Junanon then rose to state that he wanted to lead the council as well. The bird-like man talked far more quietly than Jarred, but with equally stinging comments about m'Doth's leadership. He made only small references to Metrarch's rule before m'Doth's reign.

Finally, Metrarch rose to stake his claim to the throne. He began softly and pointed out all of the wonderful benefits that the Council had had during his previous reign, particularly emphasizing the fact that while in the presence of the Holy Scepter of Ukko, none of the other Lords could get away with an outright lie. He pointed out how smoothly things had been run during his tenure and ended by asking everyone to support him for another term. Never once did he raise his voice nor did he make less of either of his opponents.

When he sat down, Jarred jumped up crying, "His hands! Look at those gloves. Poor man cannot even wield a sword anymore much less a fork! Do not place your support on a crippled old Demon!" And he sat down, knowing he had scored many points with the other Lords. This point had been discussed among them in private on many, many occasions.

m'Doth rose, "And now it is time for the other Lords to openly state their allegiances as of this moment. Bear in mind that these can at the moment of battle and often do change."

El Grad rose and stated, "I support Metrarch; my army is poised to slice into Jarred's." He sat down as quickly as he had gotten up.

m'Raul rose and bellowed, "I support Jarred. It is time for a change. My army will slice into Metrarch's."

m'Tarch stood up and yelled, "I support Jarred and my army is poised to smash into Metrarch's."

Since Jon was now in such close contact with all of the room's occupants, he began to see the overall strategy Jarred had worked out. From his prior close contact with Metrarch, he had seen the demon's strategic map of this entire area. Based upon the lands the followers of each of these Demon Lords held and from which the army would march forth. Metrarch's army marching forth from Ravenwash would be cut off from either side by Jarred and m'Tarch leaving d'Raul to pinch off any that escaped their pincer movement. Jon could not help but see mental images of the various Lord's battle plans. He was fascinated by all of these moves and counter-moves.

But then he remembered that he had forgotten to count heads when the afternoon session began. So he quickly began counting spiritual beings within the room. Seven, seven, seven, seven, seven, seven, seven. *Wait a minute! We're only six!* Instantly he sounded the alarm; he fairly screamed into the other's minds, *The assassin is probably in the room. There is one extra being near our table.* The next set of events took less than a minute to occur.

Mandy jumped up, her broadsword flashed faster than Jon had ever seen it drawn. *Where is he?* she sent to Jon.

Likewise, Alison and Darless rose ready to do battle with the unseen enemy. *Where Jon?* they screamed into his mind.

Right behind Metrarch! Jon screamed back to them. *He's right behind him.* No one saw anything behind Metrarch, who had turned slightly to see what was going on.

Without thinking further, Alison shot a Dispel Magic spell over the back of Metrarch. In the next instant, Mandy swung her blade knocking a striking scorpion off Metrarch neck. No one could tell whether or not the scorpion had time to attack Metrarch or not.

The scorpion seemed unharmed by Mandy's blow, so she stomped on it with all her might, intending to smash it to bits. Her foot bounced off the scorpion. Seeing this, Darless cast another Dispel Magic spell on the scorpion. Instantly, the scorpion grew to over six feet long and three feet tall. "Zagroot zounds!" cried Mandy, "Now this *is* a target!" And she began chopping at it. Her blows began to have some effect, though they did not chop it in half as everyone thought when they watched her blade strike. "What is this?" yelled Mandy and continued hacking at the scorpion which now lunged at her, its stinger rose trying to strike her.

Just as the stinger found an opening, Darless blasted the tail with some kind of pushing spell that forced it to miss its mark. Mandy's blade struck this giant scorpion once again causing some bruising to appear in its side but no real damage. A volley of magical arrows suddenly shot from Alison's fingers and bounced harmlessly off of the creature. The scorpion again lunged at Mandy, catching her feet in its giant claws. Darless bashed the tail once again with her staff unleashing a powerful force that spun the creature around. It held onto Mandy's legs and so just spun in a semicircle.

Meanwhile, Jon entered this foreign mind. It was human. He saw numerous mental pictures of similar assassinations. He tried to enforce his will over this mind but met a resistance so strong that he failed utterly. Alison heard Jon say, "Damn!" She had no idea what he meant. Mandy tried to strike the moving creature but missed and gouged the wooden floor instead. Jon saw that there was only one avenue left that he could try.

He calmed his mind and floated out of his head over to the scorpion. He latched onto the scorpion's body and forced all of its muscles to seize up; he immobilized its body. But the owner of this body did not give up without a fight. The being struggled with Jon for control over his body. Jon held on tenaciously, imagining he was a crocodile and this was his dinner.

The others saw that the scorpion was now motionless for no apparent reason. Mandy began hacking away at its body, while Darless and Alison began whacking it with their staffs. Then, less than a minute after it began, the scorpion succumbed. Jon felt the body expire and let go. He also sensed the tremendous fear that the body's owner suddenly had. Stark terror. This assassination had not gone as planned. The being now had no body and felt utterly lost and helpless and fled the area as fast as it could move.

Jon floated back into his head, discovering that it now ached tremendously. He had greatly over extended himself this time. However, as girls recovered, they turned to Metrarch only to see him body fall corpse-like onto the floor, hitting it with a thud. They rushed over to him. "What happened to him? Why is he so stiff?" Mandy called out. Indeed, she tried to lift his arm to feel a pulse but it was very rigid. He seemed lifeless.

It is duly noted here that during this brief attack, none of the remaining forty-three persons in the room did not so much as lift a finger in assistance, including Zugblat, who merely moved out of harm's way.

Jon forced his aching body to rush over to Metrarch. He reached out to Metrarch and found him pleasantly still in his body. *Play along with me, Jon.* Metrarch placed into Jon's aching head. Jon kneeled down beside him feeling the very stiff body.

"How could that scorpion have done this?" Mandy cried and looked over at the fallen creature. "Zagroot zounds! Look!" she cried.

All heads turned to the dead scorpion. It was not now a scorpion, but a desert dwelling human, dressed in light leather armor, a rusty yellow color. His lifeless hand clutched some kind of a pointed stick with something unknown at the pointed end. It looked like a feather. His other hand still clutched a dagger dripping some oily substance onto the floor.

Darless rose and solemnly stated to the crowd, "The assassin was successful: a poisoned blade and Cockatrice feather, a deadly combination. Metrarch is stiff as a stone. Zugblat now assumes Metrarch's position as head of this house. Please open the door so we may remove his body and that of the assassin."

The total elapsed time had been but two minutes. Never had an assassination been attempted during a Council Meeting. While the other men were completely speechless, the Demon Lords were fuming. They all had prior knowledge that a contract had been placed on Metrarch, but none dreamed it would be done under their very noses — not with all of the pains they went to secure this room. Meekly they lowered their door locking spells.

Zugblat, though taken completely by surprise and still in shock from having just witnessed his master's death, rose and struggled to find the words he had dreamed of saying for his entire life, "I, Zugblat, do rightfully assume the position as head of this house. Nothing has changed except that I am obligated to attempt to secure the throne." He continued in this vein.

Meanwhile the four lifted up the rigid, yet very heavy, Metrarch and carried him out of the room, laying him down just outside the doors. Then, they went back for the assassin. Darless urged them to use extreme caution and touch as little of this body as possible. Fortunately, the corpse's hands held a death grip on both weapons. Compared to Metrarch, he was light as a feather.

Just as soon as they got the assassin out of the room, the doors slammed shut. They knew that the locking spells were back in place. Outside of the dining room, Jon saw a half dozen inn staff. He asked, "Can you help us carry this man up to our room. He has been injured and we may yet be able to revive him." Though terrified of demons, six stronger men volunteered, and Jon led the way up to their room. Darless went with Jon but not before she requested that Mandy and Alison get a hold of the Twins and have the Twins do a thorough search the dead assassin.

They looked at each other. "How do we do that?" asked Mandy. "That's what Jon does."

"Hey Jon, get a hold of Mat and get them here at once," yelled Alison toward her disappearing fiancé. "Let's see if we can drag him out of the way," she said to Mandy. They grabbed his legs and found that they could move him, albeit slowly. Following a suggestion of a maid, they pulled him into an unused side room. Then, they waited for the Twins. Both were very glum. They had failed to stop the assassination. Though neither felt any remorse for the Demon Lord's death, they did feel badly that they had failed. Neither had ever totally failed before. Both were lost in their own thoughts.

Once the men had the stiff body of Metrarch placed inside the common area of their quarters and left, Darless and Jon began to examine him for wounds. To their utter amazement, an eye twitched, blinked and then opened. Then he spoke, "Is it safe to get up now? Are we alone?"

Jon's mouth quavered, "But, but, but."

Darless controlled her surprise. "Are you okay?" she said dryly. "That was not a very nice thing to do, scaring us like that. We thought you were dead and have transferred your house's power to Zugblat!"

He slowly stretched and then stiffly got up. "It was necessary. Seize the opportunity; seize the day. Life is within us today." He pulled his gloves off to reveal perfectly healed hands; all traces of the infernal burning were gone. "I must be off. I am now officially dead. Remember what I told you to do in such a circumstance. Do it as soon as I leave. Mind if I go out through your window? Good bye, Saint Jon Brown, the Redeemer. Remember, my little alu-demon, life is within you today, so seize the day!" And he crawled up to the narrow windows, changed into an eagle and flew off into the sky.

"But, but, but" as all that Jon could say.

"Just a minute, Jon," Darless said, "I have something he demanded that I do. It is supposed to be useful." She concentrated bringing back into full recall his demonic words in the common tongue of the demons that her mother had taught her. She spoke them just as he had instructed taking particular care to enunciate the syllables as he had so insisted. When the last deep, guttural sound was uttered, a great flash of magical energies filled the room. Three huge boxes appeared floating in the air above her at arm's reach. "Oh my goodness! What is this?" she exclaimed. Then, suddenly she realized what they were. "Quickly, Jon, help me open these boxes and dump the contents onto the floor!"

She fiddled with the first box until she found the proper combination to open it. "Two twists to the right, one to the left," she called out. When the door opened, she gasped in total disbelief. Inside were stacked neatly thousands of golden coins. In trying to remove them, she discovered that you could easily tip the suspended boxes over, coins flooded onto the floor everywhere.

"I got mine opened. Holy cow! Look at all these gems!" cried Jon.

"Get them out fast," Darless ordered. "I do not know how long these boxes will stay here on this plane." Jon saw Darless tip the middle box's contents onto the floor, so he did likewise, gems rolled in all directions.

Five minutes after the boxes appeared, they vanished as they had come. Poof. Jon kept saying, "But, but, I don't get it. What's going on? Where did all this come from?"

Darless laughed, "Now I get it. He wasn't kidding; this is his treasury or part of it. But what is going on with him?"

Suddenly, everything fell into place in Jon's mind, "I believe I understand. It begins when we were in the Abyss. I saw into his mind for an instant and realized why his hands never healed. As we were leaving, I mentioned to him that I thought I might be able to assist him in healing his hands. I thought that it might give us some extra measure of survival if we needed it."

"That's what you did last night with him in your room, isn't it. We were watching from a distance. Hope you don't mind. Alison was very worried about you, you know. We all were," she said.

"I know, I sensed you. It worked, but better than I realized. You know how we seem to need to get to the first incident in order to relieve the difficulty? Well, I think Metrarch removed his demon-hood, if that is possible. I believe that he staged his death as a demon so he could quietly leave and start a new life somewhere else other than the Abyss," Jon finished his summation.

"That fits with what he told me. Those words he had me memorize were his retrieval gate spell that brought some or all of his treasury here. It's probably only a small portion or else Zugblat would get very suspicious. We are to recompense all those that suffered because of his attempts to summon us. All this may help ease the burden of those who lost someone during the Chasme horde attacks. It doesn't replace the lives he took, but it does make amends to those still living. That is one very un-demon-like action! I do believe he has changed," she observed.

"We'd better get the others up here and explain all this to them," Jon suddenly remembered Alison and Mandy. "Good grief, how on earth can we carry this much gold? I'm surprised the floor doesn't give way!" The two left the room but not before Darless cast a locking spell of her own on the door.

When they finally found Alison and Mandy in the side room, Mat and May had just arrived. "Gosh, I sure am glad you all are okay. We were very, very worried," May exclaimed, a deep concern in his tone. He added, "Are you sure you are fine, Sis?" Meantime, May looked her little sister over carefully.

"Yes, yes, we are all fine. Mandy took the brunt of the assassin's attack," Alison replied.

Seeing his worst fears had not come to pass, the dark cloud of worry was quickly replaced by an enthusiastic curiosity. "Okay, then tell us what happened! Nowhere in his experience had he ever heard of a master assassin being killed. He was eager to hear the details.

Alison quickly related the highlights of the brief encounter. "It was over in less than two minutes, really," she continued.

"Number 1," added Darless using her formal tone of voice that indicated importance, "he used a combination of magical effects. Number 2, either via a spell or a potion, he transmuted his body form into that of a scorpion. Number 3, using either a spell or potion, he altered his scorpion size to barely one inch in size. Number 4, using either a spell or a potion, he toughened his skin to repel any blade attacks, which is why your sword did not cut into his flesh at first. Number 5, considering his audacious plot and that he intended to eliminate a Demon Lord, he must be carrying items that are sufficiently lethal to do that job, which is why we need you Twins. We need his remains thoroughly searched without endangering our lives by a wrong move. Can you assist us?"

"Well, that explains a lot!" interjected Mandy. "I've never fought an opponent and had my sword do nothing at all. It was frustrating!"

"Sure," said May and Mat in unison.

"Thanks. Be careful of the two items frozen in his hands; they must be very potent as those must be the items with which he intended to kill Metrarch," cautioned Darless. "I'm sure that is poison dripping from that dagger. But the other item we are not sure about, perhaps a Cockatrice feather?"

Trying to be helpful, Alison added, "I am experienced a bit in unraveling magical items of vanquished opponents for my old party of adventurers. What I usually have them do is put all of the deceased's items into a pile and I can then search for magical items on the entire group."

"Makes sense," May replied. "Now all of you stand way back, just in case. Considering who this person was, I suspect all manner of deviousness. Things may not be as they seem." She and Mat then began a careful inspection.

"Ah, the buckle is rigged," muttered Mat.

"Yes, I see it. Clever. Can you disarm it?" May replied.

Mat fiddled with it. "There, I think it is now harmless. If you had taken off his belt, the mechanism would have fired some kind of gas into your face. Toxic, I'll wager." They continued their search. "Here is another nasty surprise. If you try to take his small back pack off, another mechanism sprays some liquid on you. It probably would not be good for you," he chuckled as he disarmed that one.

"What do you make of this rod that he is holding, with the feather like thing in the end," May asked of her brother. "I think I have seen a picture of some feather that looks sort of like this, but I can't remember."

"Dunno," he replied totally engrossed in the removal of the poisoned dagger from the assassin's other hand. "Here's a real nasty one. See, I am using my knife to pry it loose. Watch what happens when the dagger is freed." He gave it a final push and the dagger fell out of the death grip onto the floor. Instantly, three needles popped out on the hilt and on the pummel. Only a quarter of an inch long, they were hollow and some greenish liquid oozed out of their tips.

"You were very right in getting us to help," May commented to the others. "This guy is a walking booby trap. You might have been killed three times so far." She went back to her work. She carefully removed his boots which looked very fancy with no trace of wear. They were made of leather. "Here, Mat. Check this out." Two more daggers were strapped to either leg. Mat carefully removed them. Next, they got his back pack removed and undid his belt. They removed his leather armor very carefully with no surprises. The man had on a thin cotton shirt and underwear.

"Ah ha. Throwing daggers," commented Mat. Taped to his arms in an unusual contraption were six perfectly balanced throwing daggers. "I'll be this carrying device is some kind of quick draw mechanism allowing a dagger to quickly appear in each hand." He removed them and placed them in the growing pile of items.

"What's that black thing on his chest?" May inquired. Mat rolled the body over a bit.

"Looks like a portable hole from over here," Mandy replied, trying to sound helpful. It did look very much like hers.

May pealed the small black item off his under shirt and placed it in the pile. They continued their search. When nothing more appeared, they then stripped him of all his clothes and even searched his hair and mouth for concealed weapons or traps. They found none. "Man, look at his body! You all must have really smashed him up good! I'd say he has severely crushed ribs, while massive internal bleeding probably caused his death," May pronounced. Mandy smiled; she had hit him pretty darn hard; so had Alison and Darless, for that matter; their staffs hits undoubtedly broke many of his ribs.

Just then there was a knock on the door to this side room. "Yes, who is it?" asked Mandy who was closest to the door.

A voice she'd never heard before replied, "The Undertaker. I hear that you have some work for me." She opened the door.

"Good timing," Mandy smiled. "Word must spread pretty fast in this town."

"Well, it is not every day that a Demon Lord is killed in Freetown," he replied totally bored. "Where are the two bodies? I assume you want pauper's graves, no funerals? And who will pay for his burial?"

Jon tossed him a gold coin that he had picked up when Metrarch's treasury had spilled into their room. "Only one body. That ought to cover it; keep the change. Other body has already been disposed of." He really had no idea if a single gold coin was ample payment or not. But from the gleam in the Undertaker's eyes, he assumed that is was more than enough. "There it is, please dispose of it."

The Undertaker flashed a signal to his assistant who had remained just outside the door. He rushed in and the two of them lifted up the body and carried him out. That was the last they ever saw of that assassin.

"Okay, now for the really hard part," announced Mat. "We have to open the pack and the portable hole. This can be very dangerous."

"Wait!" cried Alison, suddenly coming to life. As Mat moved the pack around, she recognized a greenish dot near the opening flap. "The green spot — it is a guard and ward spell. Let me defuse it." The twins stood back while Alison, holding onto her staff spoke a command word. Jon saw an energy connection between her staff and her activate. A flash around the pack indicated it was successful; the green spot was gone.

"Alison, did your staff do that? I saw some energy flowing between it and you. Most curious," Jon asked.

Alison smiled, "Good eyes. Yes, I used stored magical energy from the staff to power that spell. I don't usually cast that spell very often; it is more convenient to use the staff." But while she acknowledged this, an inquisitive look appeared on her face, "But only a magician can detect that; most curious that you should see it. We'll have to do some experimenting when we get home. Maybe I'll make a wizard out of you after all!" she laughed and teased.

"Needle trap on the opening flap; disarmed," called out Mat. Then, he gently opened the pack and dumped its contents on to the floor. All sorts of items scattered about the floor. Nothing exploded.

May carefully unfolded the portable hole until it was its full size, a three-foot circle of extra-dimensional black space lying on the floor. May spoke a command word and a globe of light appeared on her index finger, she poked it into the hole and peered inside. Once she considered it safe, she began bringing out all sorts of things, laying them in the every growing pile. In a few minutes all of the assassin's possessions lay spread out on the floor.

Alison and Darless both cast spells over the entire area, detecting what was magical and what was not, conferring over each item together. Satisfied, they then described their findings.

Alison explained in detail. "The six throwing daggers are indeed magically enchanted. There is a great enchantment on the main poisoned dagger that was in his hand. This small money pouch is magical in some way. The three rings in that small pouch are also magical. We have three vials of magical potions of some kind. The leather armor itself has a small enchantment about it. But the really strange thing is that rod with the feather. The rod is not magical in any way that we can tell; however, that feather is inherently magical in some manner that we cannot tell just yet. We need to research it further. It undoubtedly was carried around in that long, narrow leather bag. All the rest is ordinary as far as we can tell." To be on the safe side, she very carefully placed the rod into its leather bag. She then added, "If we are right and this is a feather from a Cockatrice bird, then one touch from it and you are turned to stone. Hence, extra caution for now."

May then counted the various coins and announced, "He carried the equivalent of two hundred gold coins."

Mat, on the other hand, was inspecting the gems from another small pouch. "Here was the real wealth. I'd wager these gems are worth at least ten thousand gold coins. See, Jon, gems are much more transportable than carrying gold coins, vastly lighter and more compact."

"Mat, what do you make of this?" May queried her brother. She handed him a small blank piece of paper. It was six inches wide and eight inches long, blank on both sides.

"Dunno," was his reply. He handed it to Alison.

"Now why would he be carrying around one piece of blank paper?" Alison wondered. "He had no writing quills or ink or even charcoals. Most strange."

Jon laughed. "Maybe it is a message written in invisible ink!" Jon teased. It reminded him of spy movies he had seen on late night TV shows.

Darless took the paper from Alison. "You laugh, Jon. But you know you may have hit upon it. Maybe there is some kind of secret writing on it. We shall have to study it more carefully indeed."

"Maybe I can help," Mat offered. "I've a jeweler's lense that permits close inspection of tiny things. Maybe I can find a clue. May I take it with me? My lense is at home." Darless gave the paper to him nodding her thanks.

Meanwhile, May and Mandy tided up the pile, throwing the unwanted items into a trash bin in the corner.

"Oh my gosh, I nearly forgot!" exclaimed Jon. Everyone stopped and looked at him.

"Forgot what?" led Alison.

"To tell you why Darless and I rushed down here to find you all," he said getting very excited.

But Darless hushed him. In a quiet, yet most commanding tone, she said, "This is not the place; doors have ears. Let's all go up to our room right now!" And she began to lead the way which was her method of convincing the others that this was very important without actually saying a word.

Carrying the assassin's magical items and money, they went up to their third floor room.

"What's this? A guard and ward on our door?" demanded Alison, as they reached the main door.

"Darless' doing," whispered Jon secretively, while the alu-demon disarmed her ward so they could enter. "Oh yes," he warned, "please make no sound until the door is shut!" They entered and gasped. Darless reactivated her ward the instant the door closed.

"Where's Metrarch's body? And what is all this money, gems all over here? This is a fortune!" exclaimed Alison before anyone else could speak.

"He's gone. We'd better explain all this Darless. He is not dead, not even hurt. It was all a ruse. He only pretended to be killed," Jon said completely confusing everyone.

"But that was a real assassin!" protested Alison.

"Let me explain," said Darless, "I think I have it all worked out now. You see it all began when we were in the

Abyss. Jon somehow saw why Metrarch's hands had never healed. Basically the Holy Scepter burned him badly because he is or was totally evil. But afterwards, he fabricated a big lie by telling everyone that he had slain the Holy Priest and taken the Scepter from him. Thus, the burns never healed; he was living a lie. Jon told him as we left that he thought he could help him heal his hands. Evidently Metrarch believed Jon could do it and that's in part why he was here late last night. Jon did heal him, but he got more than he bargained for. We, Jon and I, think that in erasing the source of the non-healing burns, somehow Metrarch also discovered the real reason he was acting so evil. With the source of the evil that was driving him eliminated, he decided to start a new life somewhere else, presumably no longer doing such massive evil actions, at least we hope so."

"This assassination plot gave him his chance. He pretended to be killed until we had him brought into this room. At which point he startled both of us out by becoming alive. Let's see, what did he say exactly?" She paused and recalled the event and said, "I quote him:

"It was necessary. Seize the opportunity; seize the day. Life is within us today. I must be off. I am now officially dead. Remember what I told you to do in such a circumstance. Do it as soon as I leave. Mind if I go out through your window? Good bye, Saint Jon Brown, the Redeemer. Remember, my little alu-demon, life is within you today, so seize the day!"

"There are his gloves. His hands were perfectly normal! And he crawled up to the window there, changed into an eagle and flew off into the sky."

"Now, he also instructed me to do something in the event of his death. He claimed that I should use it to help make amends for the deaths he caused by the flying Chasme when he summoned our aid. I didn't realize what it was until after I performed the deed. The words gated part of his Treasury here. Three boxes full of coins and gems. They were here floating for about five minutes before they returned to the Abyss."

"Since I agreed to this, I hereby accept the responsibility to visit all of the relatives and so on of those who lost their lives to the Chasme or were wounded and offer some monetary assistance. While money cannot replace life, it can assist those in need; a small amends," she finished up her long speech.

"Bravo!" cried Mandy. "What a really good thing to do! You know, he must have changed somehow. There is a huge fortune on our floor!"

Everyone congratulated Darless and Jon. And then they all began to collect and count the incredible pile of coins and gems which lay scattered over the entire floor. They placed most of the coins into the assassin's portable hole, because inside it the coins weighed almost nothing. Jon was still fearful that the floor would collapse under all that weight.

While they were picking up the loot, Alison commented to Jon, "You know, I cannot help thinking about Metrarch's parting words, Saint Jon Brown, the Redeemer. That title certainly fits you and what you do. And I love you for it!" And she gave him a long, loving kiss. His face reddened as the others catcalled in the background.

It took the six of them the next three hours to clean up, stack and count the pile. There were about sixty thousand gold coins weighing about four thousand pounds; thirty thousand silver coins which Jon estimated weighed two thousand pounds. Mat gave a rough estimate that all of the various gems stones would probably bring around another five hundred thousand gold coins. This was indeed a Demon Lord's Treasury.

However, as Jon pointed out, transportation of this vast weight was going to be a major problem. The portable hole could only hold about one third of the coins, but he had not factored in the presence of the two mages.

Alison realized that this vast a sum would attract thieves like honey does a bear. "Darless, check on the amount of charge still left in that staff I lent you while I check mine." She obeyed while the others looked totally baffled. Both still held about half of their original charge. "Okay, Mandy. You and I empty out our portable holes. We fill them with the money. Darless and I teleport all three holes back to my treasury room and then we teleport back. We'll be gone only a couple of minutes."

"Brilliant!" exclaimed Jon. But then he worried, remembering Alison's explanations about teleportation and arriving only to find you miscalculated and are now deep inside the earth and quite dead. "Are you sure it is safe?"

"There is always a risk, that's why I always aim high and use my ring here." She was slipping a ring onto her finger. "A ring that allows me to fly or levitate," she added for May's benefit, followed by the dumping of the two women's portable holes. A vast array of magical items, scrolls, potions, wands and other magical gear came out of Alison's hole along with the new dresses she had bought from May, other clothing, some emergency rations, lanterns, rope, and two of her magical picture books. "Here, you two can look at the picture books while we are away. Maybe you can see us arrive at the ruins," she added as an afterthought.

Mandy dumped the contents of her hole out onto the floor. Here was a vast array of weapons, her bow and three quivers of arrows, her other two bastard swords, several other swords that Jon had never seen her use, daggers, bits and pieces of what he assumed was a form of armor. Also the new dresses she had purchased along with other clothes were in the hole and a stash of money and numerous pouches containing he knew not what.

Quickly, the six stuffed the rest of the coins into the holes. The gems they placed into various bags. These they could safely carry. And then holding onto their staffs, they each spoke a single command word and poof, they were gone. "Look! There they are!" cried out May. In the picture book page showing the ruins of Castle d'Ambrose, down floated the two mages still holding onto the bags and the staffs. The women quickly disappeared into the ground.

Jon explained to the twins about the underground entrance, but they remembered it from childhood. And a few minutes later, the two women knocked on the door, asking Darless to lower her guard and ward. They had arrived back outside the inn so they could arrive high and float down. Neither had wanted to risk arriving in the middle of the inn room; it was too risky.

A few minutes later, both had all of their gear back into their portable holes. They placed all of the assassin's items into the remaining portable hole, folded it up, and gave it to Jon for safe keeping. He stuck it into his pocket.

By now they were all starving. They had abstained from lunch for fear that the food might have been poisoned. It was now late afternoon and all were very hungry indeed. However, if they were going to get any food here at the inn, they knew that they would have to wait until the demons ended their council and departed. "Let's go over to my place and get something to eat," May offered. "I've got plenty of leftovers we can eat. It should hold us over until tonight." She didn't have to ask a second time. Everyone headed out the door at once.

"Thank you May!" said Jon, his stomach was more than growling.

Once outside of the protection of the inn, Jon was a bit dismayed. Throngs of thugs, mercenaries or fighters, he could not tell which, milled around in the street. Already some of the shops had been damaged — goods outright stolen. Jon felt a pang of guilt knowing that he had sent for the twins and they had had to pass through this crowd. Mandy took point, broadsword drawn. Mat was to her left, his short sword also drawn. The women got many catcall choruses and whistles, which they totally ignored. It was scary, for at any moment, these men might lose their self-restraint. But five blocks later, the streets were nearly deserted and they all breathed a sigh of relief.

"I'm sorry I had you two come to the inn through that gauntlet of thugs," Jon apologized, feeling badly about it.

May smiled, "Accepted, but really, it was only a small matter, for the Twins, if you follow me. Here we are. Come on in," and she unlocked the back door to her shop. They made themselves comfortable while May played hostess and rummaged for left overs. Jon observed many piles of stuff about the shop. May was packing. She noticed Jon noticing, "Nearly done. I'm giving the shop to one of my assistants. She has been faithful all these years and I think she can carry on the tradition of high quality dress making."

They ate bread, cheese, dried meat and fish and a bean and peas dish which was more like a soup. Mat produced several mugs of ale from his shop next door. The food and drink tasted like heaven to everyone; none ate slowly.

When everyone was done, Jon asked, "Now what do we do? Should we go back to the inn and wait for the demons to leave? Or should we perhaps check in with Sir Henry? I believe that I have had enough demons for one day — heck for one lifetime for that matter!"

"It is our responsibility to see that the demons leave so that we can then get on with the town defense activities," Alison sternly stated, "though I too have had enough demons for one day."

"Follow me," Mandy jested and they all left May's shop retracing their steps back to the inn. Unfortunately, getting back took more doing. The ruffians, also tired of standing around and also getting very hungry, were far more rowdy, boisterous and challenging. They had gotten to three blocks from the inn when one particularly nasty bunch accosted them, demanding sexual favors from the women. The man waving his sword at Mandy and making the most obscene gestures lost his hand and sword with one swift swing from Mandy's bastard sword. Three more which had closed in upon the others, found that their ribs were broken by the blinding swift kicks of Mat. Ten more that chose to come from the rear lay sleeping soundly on the ground, compliments of Darless, while another half dozen ran off screaming in terror as May smiled at their flight.

This action, of course, drew the instant attention of all of the other fighters milling around. Hundreds began closing in on the six, mostly to see what was going on — what the commotion was all about. Jon had visions of an all-out battle here in the streets. But just then, as if by some magic, the crowd parted in front of them. William came walking down the street toward them. When he saw them, he waved to get their attention.

"Ah here you are!" William said. "Been sent to look for you. The demons' meeting is about done. One of them Lord fellows wants a word with you. Sent me to fetch you."

"Thanks, William," Mandy smiled at him. They then followed William back to the inn. As they walked forward, the large crowd automatically opened up before them and then promptly closed behind them. How very weird, thought Jon, who wondered if the others were noticing the effect. It had to be William's doing.

When they arrived at the inn, the various Demon Lords and their companions were leaving the inn, much as they had come. Their various transportation vehicles were lined up on the street, dutifully guarded by an army of followers. "Ah there you all are," Jon heard the now familiar voice of Lord Jarred call out.

The Demon Lord pushed his way through various milling men to confront Jon and the others. "I just wanted to thank you for failing in your mission to prevent Metrarch's timely demise. It has guaranteed my successful bid for Head of the Council! Also, I would advise you and your women to leave this town before nightfall. When I return, I will personally kill you but I shall enjoy raping your women before I kill them too. I promise you a most hideous death, one that you will long remember!"

That ticked Jon off. He was very tired from this long day and had had little sleep the night before because of Metrarch. Now the likely new ruler of the Abyss was threatening him and more importantly those he loved, to say nothing of giving them the largest insult imaginable. They were not his women; they were his equals, if not superior to him. "Jarred, Demon Lord of the Abyss, I will say this only once." He spoke very, very slowly, very deliberately, and very full of anger. "Things are not always as they seem." Then he raised his voice so that all the other Lords in the vicinity could not help but hear. "You will never ever hold another Council meeting in this town. You will never again be able to win the game by occupying the central well. And if you ever harm even so much as one hair on their heads, I will turn your entire body into an un-healing mass of burned flesh as was Metrarch's hands. I have spoken." All the time he spoke, he stared straight into Jarred's eyes, unflinchingly. Then, he slowly turned and entered the inn, leaving Lord Jarred fuming as well as totally confused about the meaning of his words.

He did not, however, take his awareness off of Jarred. He was in Jarred's mind, saw and heard him begin a devastating spell, knew that Jarred intended to disintegrate the back of his head. *Grab onto me now!* Jon placed into the other six companion's minds. Without waiting for them to obey, he forcefully moved their hands to touch his body. And he calmly began to step up the steps of the Church of Ukko, while behind him, he heard the command word spoken. But they were no longer in that place. Later, when they returned to the inn, they would discover a huge chuck of a wall was missing. It had received the disintegration spell, not Jon's head.

"What the?" cried out William as he stumbled onto the steps of the church. One second he was staring at the Demon Lord wishing with all his might Jon had kept his mouth shut and the next instant he was tripping up the steps of some church. He vaguely remembered his arms, of their own accord, reaching out to touch Jon.

He was not the only confused person. May also fell up the steps, banging her elbow in the process, totally disoriented. Mat fell, but his training kicked in and he regained his balance, though he was just as disoriented.

"I'm sorry, everyone. I just got really pissed off back there and lost my temper. I had to get you all out of the way really fast. He was about to disintegrate us, I think," Jon apologized, watching the others stagger and fall up the unexpected steps. "I should have avoided the steps, sorry about that. God am I tired!" And he promptly slumped to the steps, sound asleep.

"What happened? Would someone explain to me what just happened? Are we safe?" May pleaded, looking at Alison and Darless.

Alison got up and brushed herself off, "Jon's usually not this inaccurate. Well, I think that he provoked Lord Jarred beyond that demon's self-control. From what Jon suggested, I think that he was casting a disintegrate spell, right Darless?" The alu-demon, nodded in agreement while straightening out her robes, as she too was taken off guard and had stumbled unseemly up the steps. "So Jon used his mental powers or spiritual being powers, I now suspect, to transport us all to safety in the nick of time. He has to be touching whatever he intends to bring with him when he does this, though. But doing so always tends to tire him out. He is sleeping it off at the moment. When he wakes, if I know him, he will be starving, right Mandy?" Mandy nodded her agreement, nursing a bruise on her elbow which had hit the steps rather hard.

May looked very confused. "You mean he used a teleport spell? I thought you said he was not a wizard?"

"He's not. That was not a teleport spell. No one could bring six people with them using only a single such magical spell — too much weight. It is a mental or spiritual thing that he does. None of us can do it. It is a fascinating way to travel, you will have to admit. He says that it is easy to do; 'just get the idea of having already arrived' is how he puts it," she explained.

"Are you sure he isn't a god in disguise?" muttered William in disbelief.

"Pretty sure," she smiled. "He is a musician, as he says. However, he is one powerful spiritual being who does not even realize or know that fact."

"Well, then, we'd best get him inside," William replied, and he lifted Jon up. Aided by Mat, they carried the soundly sleeping Jon up the steps. Mandy knocked on the doors and the guards opened the doors hastily, apologizing for their tardiness; they were eating their evening meal.

While Jon slept, the others brought Sir Henry, the Bishop and their companions up to date on the events. They merely said that Metrarch's body had left of its own accord. Most would assume that it had automatically been gated back to the Abyss.

William took Mandy aside and said, "My Lady, I have my duties to perform. I must get back to the inn." She mistook his meaning figuring he had more baking to do. He said very softly, "Until we meet again. If I may be so bold," and he gave her a loving kiss. She let him and responded by hugging him close to her. And then he was off. She had no idea what he was really about to do.

The large group then began discussing what they should do next and when. However, they made no final decision. They all wanted to consult Jon before they acted, if that was possible. Jon was, however, in a much needed, deep sleep.

Chapter 14 The Legend Awakens

It was dusk; the heat of the day had passed along with the Demon Lords and their faithful. Soon the night chill of the desert would seep its way into Freetown. At the western edge of town, carts and wagons began assembling, forming a line, waiting for the signal to depart Freetown forever. These were the people whose patience with the periodic death and destruction of the demons and the despotic whims of the city's leaders had finally collapsed. Taking all that was valuable to them, these folk intended to depart and take their chances out in the open arid plains to the west.

Yes, they were aware that none of the Demon Lord's lands lay directly west of Freetown. True, to the northwest lay lands worshiping Lord Jarred and to the southwest, those of d'Raul, but once beyond say the first thirty miles or so, the vast Lost Steppes of Vyderland. This semi-desert region offered no sanctuary, for this was the land of the marauders of Morrigan, a savage race of fighters who knew no mercy nor displayed it. It was their hope, their dream that somehow they could get past Vyderland, past these arid steppes, into a more promising land. None in the caravan, however, had any idea what actually lay beyond Vyderland.

These were not idle dreamers; these were not fighters. They all knew their prospects were slim; their survival changes, grim. No, one was a blacksmith and his extended family; another was a barrel maker; another, a seamstress; all were skilled tradesfolk. The elected caravan guides were themselves traders but who had a good deal of experience traveling in the relatively nearby lands selling their wares. But each and every one of these hardy folk shared one thing in common; they had a tenacity for life and a hatred, a loathing of chaos and evil. These were normally a conservative people who rarely took a risk. But all had lost a loved one, a business partner, or a shop during the last War Game some twenty years ago. Change, it had to come now; they felt determined to make it or die trying. It was their self-determined choice, their own personal integrity.

The trail blazer, a title bestowed upon him by the caravan folk, was fifty year old, retired Red Guard captain, Raul d'Freeze, who had spent his career as a forward scout. He knew the lands for fifty miles about Freetown like the back of his hand. And he made no secret that their first goal, their immediate goal, was to get to Beached Rock some twenty-five miles directly west. He knew many side trails that he hoped would get them safely there, out of harm's way as the Demon Lord's armies swarmed down upon Freetown. From there, it was anyone's guess.

Raul rode up and down the streets forming the wagons and carts into a semblance of order, counting them, and double checking with each family to make sure they had the necessary supplies. When they received his "Okay," they placed a lantern upon a post at the side of their wagon to light their way. When he had finished, his count of two hundred twenty-five wagons tallied with his manifest. He did not bother to count the several hundred whose only mode of transportation was a horse or mule. He was just about to give the order to move out, when another mule rider hastily appeared.

"Sorry I am a bit late," William apologized. "Hard time getting away from the demons and that entire fracas."

"You cut it close, friend," he said. Then, he yelled out, "Okay. We move out. Remember stay in line. Follow the lantern in front of you." He galloped up to the front to lead the first wagon. Twenty-five riders joined in behind him; these were the best fighters he could find, handpicked for the caravan. A twenty-sixth joined them, William.

It was dark now and still Jon slept soundly. Alison debated with herself about whether or not to wake him. In the end, she decided to let him sleep. She left his side and joined the others who were crammed into the basement library.

"Hi sis. How's Jon?" May asked her. "They had decided to turn on the device at nine, in just a few minutes."

"He's still sleeping like a baby. He's cute when he is totally out like this," she replied with a smile.

May smiled, then handed her a paper. "They are going to plaster these notices up all over the town later tonight and in the morning." It read:

Thanks to the work of Saint Jon Brown, his associates and our own Twins, the power of the Church of Ukko has been restored. The Ukko Protective Sphere is once again in full operation to protect the town within the Old Wall. So bring your valuables and supplies and spend the next few days with relatives and friends who live within the Old Wall. For those who have nowhere else to go, come to the Church of Ukko on Center Street.

Bishop Franco

"Ah, I see that I am now an associate," she laughed. "Men!" May laughed along with her.

"Seriously, the plan is to leave the protective sphere up for three hours and then take it down so folks can move into the inner city and safety. Some of Sir Henry's men will ride out of the town and watch for the vanguard of the approaching armies. Just as soon as they are spotted, all will be recalled and the Sphere raised indefinitely," May explained.

"Hum, you know, it is going to get quite crowded in here. By Darless' estimate, four in five live outside the Old Wall. How are they going to manage to get so many people in this safe zone?" wondered Alison. She had not really thought this completely through before now; so many other things had been more urgent.

"There are a lot of shops, such as mine. I have donated its use for families who have nowhere to turn. I believe that the Church will put out a plea for others to donate the use of their empty businesses tomorrow, once everyone suddenly sees the reality of the situation," she replied.

"Hi, Alison," Darless interrupted, "Yes, it sure is going to get cramped around here. I bet this church is going to have more people coming here than have had in the last hundred years! I hope it all works out fine for them. But I bet it will be more like mass pandemonium!"

On that point, everyone agreed. Then, her tone changed to extreme concern, "No one has yet to consider what is very likely to happen when the Demon Lords discover that they cannot get into the town. Nearly eighty percent of the town by area lies outside the protective sphere! They do not know demons like I know demons. They are as likely as not to go into a destruction frenzy, destroying all of the town that they can get their hands on! Devastation of that magnitude would have an enormous impact on this town!"

"Zagroot zounds! You are right!" cried Mandy who had moved over to her friends and had overheard Darless' dire prediction. "Destroying eighty percent of the town makes the looting and destruction of the previous War Games look like a trifle not to be bothered with! I think that we may be have made a horrible blunder. What does Jon think about this?"

"He's still out like a light, unfortunately," said Alison worriedly. "Do you think I should try to wake him?"

"Let him get all the sleep he needs," Darless decided, "I think that he will need all of his abilities soon enough, though I wonder if he has thought this thing through."

"Thought what through?" interrupted Sir Henry who had just arrived. Quickly, in a hushed voice, she described her deductions.

"Yes, I have thought about that. It can go one of two ways. If the total numbers of the enemy are not great, it is my hope that many of the stronger men, those with some fighting skills, will rally and charge out to attack them in small forays. That would be the honest, noble thing to do. On the other hand, if the enemy's numbers are too great, then such would be suicide. So I just do not know really what can be done. But certainly reactivating the Sphere of Ukko is the honorable thing to do. He did not give it to this town for no reason. It must be used, regardless of the consequences, right Alison?" He looked to her for agreement.

"Well, yes," she replied thoughtfully. "A gift of this magnitude from Father Ukko should not be cast aside." And after a pause, she replied. "But still, how can the town survive if eighty percent of it is destroyed? Would not the eighty percent be so offended that they would overrun us and destroy the Church, viewing it as having caused their huge losses? I do not see how they would not, especially since most all of them do not even worship Father Ukko!"

"Actually, neither do I," said the glum paladin. "Neither do I." And he left the conversation drop, preferring to handle other pressing business.

"Where there is life, there is hope," Darless muttered mostly to herself. "Come on demon, think this one out." Her mind began mocking up the imagined worst case scenario. In her mind's images she saw the central part of town capped in the blue dome of Ukko's protective energies. Beyond the Old Wall, hordes of men and demons rallied and cursed at them. And then out of pure malice, pure spite, pure hate for anything other than themselves, they began looting and systematically burning down all the buildings that they could get to. It was a horrible scene she had imagined. She stood there silently studying it, wondering what she could do to counter it.

Hi. It's me. Body's sleeping like a rock. I'm bored. So I am experimenting. I'm right behind your head. What is this you are looking at? Jon placed his thoughts into her mind. Startled, she nearly dropped the teacup she still held.

How do you do that? Is it easy to get out when you want too? She thought back.

Dunno. I just sat up and got up and realized the body was still lying down sleeping. So I just moved on in here to see what's going on, he sent back. *What is this conflagration you are looking at anyway?*

She explained her deductions. *Considering just how mad Jarred got today, such an outcome is highly likely, don't you think?* He agreed and they both stared at her images of the city ablaze in wonton destruction by enraged demon armies.

Then, Jon had an idea. He added a little thing to her pictures. Darless saw several little figures rise high above the dome, bathed in the energies flowing from the central well under which the apparatus was located. From the little figures enormous magical spells blasted demons and men right and left. Terrified and helpless to counter these mages, the armies fled the town, at least that's what Jon added to her images.

"Terrific idea, Jon!" she exclaimed out loud, startling Alison, Mandy and May.

"What's the matter?" inquired Alison, wondering what was going on with Darless.

"Jon's here behind me and has given us a great idea," she replied, her face full of life, the glumness totally gone.

"Where?" exclaimed Alison and Mandy, who were looking right and left, totally perplexed. "Is he invisible for some reason?"

"Oops. No, he is here but his body is still sleeping. Come on Jon, show them too, please. I don't want them to think I have lost my mind!" the alu-demon stated flatly.

Jon floated over behind Alison and created the sensation of a soft loving kiss on her neck and put into her mind, *It's me, my love. Out of my body. Bored really.* And then he did the same to Mandy, saying *It's me, beautiful. Out of my body. This is a pretty cool thing to do don't you think?* Both girls had the strangest, loving, kissing sensation upon their necks, one that they would never forget. Both beamed, their faces glowing. Then, he placed into all three, *Say I think my body's stirring. I'd better get back to it. See you in a bit.*

"So what's the great idea?" implored Mandy.

Darless thought for a second, "Can you two see my mental pictures like Jon can?" Alison started to protest that she did not have these kinds of mental abilities, but Darless cut their protests off. "Close your eyes, and look at what I am showing you." She made her images and Jon's alteration as vivid and real and as solid as she could. The wow's coming from Alison and Mandy told her she succeeded. "See a picture is worth a thousand words."

When they had viewed them, she said, "Number 1, how do we get so elevated? Number 2, we need a massive amount of long range, area effecting, destructive spells, a rather unlimited amount of them. Any ideas?"

"Sorry, Darless, I am only a fledgling mage. I am a ranger basically and I only know a few simple spells, like how to make light and such. I don't know how to make balls of fire and bolts of lightning. That's way, way beyond me!" implored Mandy, downhearted. "I'd love to be up there blasting away at them demons, though!"

"Ah, but you could if you had a Wizard's Staff," interrupted Alison. "Ladies, come on, let's find a quiet spot. We have some planning to do. I wonder how many mages are in this town anyhow." And the three grabbed May and headed for a quieter location, waving briefly at a sleepy eyed Jon who was just going to the restroom. He waved back mostly.

After relieving himself, Jon wandered into the kitchen to find himself a snack; he was starving. He'd used a bit more energy of late than he was accustomed. Actually, he had relied on the body instead of just doing it himself. *Cause I was angry,* he justified to himself. He found some remains of what looked to be a chicken and filled himself a mug of ale and headed off to find the girls and some company.

Just then, an acolyte came rushing through the area crying, "Now it the appointed time. If you want to see the Sphere of Protection go up, head outside at once." He rushed from room to room with the same message.

"Over here, Jon" yelled Alison over the commotion of people rushing out of their assigned rooms, all heading up the stairs and through the Church proper and out the front doors. Mat was now with the women and Jon hastily joined them, holding on to his food and mug, trying not to spill his ale. At least a hundred people rushed out on to the street in front of the Church of Ukko; all heads staring up at the sky, waiting excitedly.

"Don't stop here," Alison cried. "We have got to get close to the Old Wall. Come on, keep up, Jon!" They were running down the street, led by Mat and May who knew the shortest route to a section of the Old Wall. He tried to keep up but managed to spill half of his ale on himself in the process.

In five blocks, Mat halted. They could see sections of the Old Wall on either side of the street. "What is going on?" Jon asked when they all stopped right here in the middle of the street. "Is this a better place to see it?"

"No silly. We are about to test your theory," Alison replied. Jon did not get the chance to ask her what theory, for at that moment the Ukko's Holy Sphere of Protection energized once more. A pale blue energy shot up like a geyser from the central well, rising high in the sky, then bursting like fireworks into a ball that descended over the town. It was a dome that rested upon the top of the Old Wall. Where streets passed through the wall, the sheet of energy reached all the way to the ground. It was spectacular and intensely beautiful and serene. All stood transfixed by the sight.

After a couple minutes, Alison finally broke the incredible peaceful aura, "Okay, let's test the theory. Mandy, you ready?" The ranger nodded, unable to speak. "Then on the count of three. One. Two. Three. And three mages began chanting their prearranged spells. Within seconds of each other, all three went off. Mandy shot several magical arrow bolts arcing up and through the blue energy. They passed through the field as if it was not there. Darless sent a bolt of lightning high up into the sky, streaking its blinding light and peal of thunder. Alison launched a big fire ball that burst into a huge ball at least fifty feet in diameter and two hundred feet in the air. All three spells had gone right through the blue energy field unscathed.

"They all made it!" cried May and Mat in unison.

"Spectacular!" cried Jon. "Like the 4th of July back home. Oh I do love fireworks! Thanks for the wonderful show, my love!"

"Er, sorry to disappoint you, Jon," said Alison meekly. "That was not what we are doing. We have demonstrated that we can cast spells out of the Sphere from within the Sphere. Just like your images suggested to Darless."

"Oh. Still it made a wonderful display. Can you launch another one? Just for fun? And can you make this one burst into green colors instead of red?" Jon asked totally excited, like a little kid.

She glared at him. "Jon, magic is a serious business. We don't waste spells! We might need them. Oh what the heck." His bubbling enthusiasm was just too much for her and this was such a momentous occasion. So she launched another ball of fire, and had this one turn green instead of red.

Jon let out a "Wow!" and then "Thanks! It was terrific!" And from nearby several bystanders began clapping. They turned around to see a small crowd of people had gathered on the street gaping at the display.

Jon called out to them, "Ukko's Sphere of Protection. It is working again! Isn't it terrific? You can even stand in the energy flow! Feels like nothing you ever felt!"

But no one ventured close enough to try it. The locals were just awestruck. For them, the legend that they had been told as a children's tale had come true right before their eyes. They stared and stared and stared. No one spoke for quite some time.

After about five minutes of staring at the majestic sight, a small girl about seven years old came shyly up to Jon. "Will that light protect me and mommy from the bad men?"

Jon looked down at the wide open, innocent blue eyes and blond hair. "Yes, it sure will, just as long as you and your mommy are here inside the Old Wall. No bad guys can touch you. That's Father Ukko's promise." She smiled and rushed back to tell her mother the news. And the six turned and headed back towards the church.

Along the way, hundreds of people were out on the street; many wearing their night gowns, all staring at the blue dome high over the town. They spoke in soft hushed tones of the awesome sight before them. This would be one night that this town would never forget. It was a night that would become a legend in its own time. Jon felt totally serene, totally calm. How could he not? He was basking in the pure energy flows of Ukko himself, a touch of the energy that pervaded Ukko's realm.

The six got back to the church and sat down on the steps. All of the others were out in the street talking and watching the sight. "Magnificent, isn't it?" Jon said and he relaxed and felt total serenity flowing over and through him. He moved outside his body to better feel it.

One by one, Jon sent to the other five, *Be a couple feet back of your head and watch from there.* Darless, Mandy and Alison backed out at once; it was as easy to do as when Fruella, the Air Maiden had helped them out bad at the Tower of Leeds.

Mat and May, though totally at peace and serene, had no idea what Jon was asking them to do. But it didn't matter. May rested her head on Mat's shoulder as she often did. They felt relaxed and comforted. Jon saw then what he had only guessed at. Mat and May were very, very similar and very close. They appeared to have a thin connection of some kind between their beings, a brotherly-sisterly bond of love and devotion to each other. Unseen, this bond had always connected them together.

Jon pointed this detail out to Alison. *Yes, I see it too. I wonder if we can develop such a strong bond of love, my dear. Seeing this makes me want to try with all my might!* Jon, the spiritual being, snuggled in close with Alison, the spiritual being. Both knew they were on the way towards making such a bond between themselves. The three hours that the Sphere was to be activated seemed like only a very few minutes to these six.

When the blue light faded at last, all six moved their bodies out of the way of the many people heading back into the safety of the church. There were cries for a celebration. Break out the Holy Wine! But the six still retained their serenity and remained long sitting on the steps.

"I, we, wish this feeling would never go away. We are so serene, so calm, so tranquil. The world seems so beautiful, so peaceful. We never want this to go away," said Mat.

"I think that Father Ukko would say that that peace comes from within you. You make your own peace," said Mandy dreamily. "I feel so incredibly huge, I cannot describe how big I feel. I could touch a star! Well, maybe not that far. Zagroot zounds! William has off and gone away with the caravan folks!"

"What?" cried Alison. "How do you know that?"

"Well, the caravan was supposed to leave tonight; remember, we told you that yesterday," said May.

"I, I, I just touched him. I was feeling so big, I was reaching out in all directions, and I just touched him, felt him. I saw through his eyes. There is this huge line of lantern lights moving out across the steppes," she tried to explain what she had just inadvertently done.

"Well, then, flow some love toward him," Jon suggested. "Blow him a kiss, that'd be romantic." Alison leaned over and gave him a kiss and a thought *That's your reward.*

"Oh. I can do that," said Mandy. At once, all her concern for William evaporated and she was serene once more and smiling.

Together the six sat on the steps of the Church of Ukko for another hour at least. Finally it was time for bed. The night guards insisted on shutting and locking the door. So they had to come inside.

They were met by the Bishop none the less. "Say, I have been looking for you. Can you lend a hand? We are trying to make a thousand copies of the notice to be distributed later tonight and in the morning. I'm afraid that my scribes are never going to get that many copies in time. They are all displaying writer's cramps and we've only got a couple hundred done so far. I'm asking everyone who can read and write to lend a hand. Will you help us out?"

"Well why didn't you say so sooner," exclaimed Alison. "You have two perfectly capable wizards here you know. Come on Darless. Let's show these priests what a simple Copy spell will actually do!" Darless chuckled and they both headed to the library.

The room was filled to capacity by people writing furiously with quills carefully scratching out copies of the important notice. "Okay. Everyone out. Thank you for your efforts. But we need to get a thousand of these done lickety split." The people looked at the Bishop, who nodded his assent. So they gratefully left, though many chose to stay by the door to watch the women. Alison got out her large spell book from her portable hole and rummaged through the pages. "Ah here we are. You can read over my shoulder, Darless. Let's get two of these going." They both chanted a few magical phrases and suddenly several quills floated into the air and began furiously scratching out the message.

Once the spell was going properly, Darless calculated the rate of production. "Hum, I think we need another set going." So both mages repeated the spells. Soon a dozen quills were writing like mad. As soon as the message was copied, the paper floated over to the completed pile and a fresh page floated down and under the quill which immediately began scratching out the message once more. "That ought to do it. 1,000 copies in about an hour I estimate." There was a note of pride in her voice. Everyone who was watching was dutifully impressed. This labor intensive operation was totally handled and sooner than expected. So now the Bishop had to scurry around getting the message deliverers ready to go hours ahead of schedule.

Stating that the quills would stop when either they ran out of paper, or ink, or had reached the 1,000[th] copy, the ladies then went off to bed. One of the acolytes had prepared a room for the six of them to sleep. They were grateful for that. All were really tired and fell asleep at once, sleeping a restful sleep unhindered by any bad dreams. The energy of Ukko still resonated within them.

The next day brought the first of many changes to Freetown. The priests of Ukko knew that four out of five residents of the town resided outside the Old Wall or had their business establishments beyond the wall. A large percentage of those people were expected to pay a visit to the Church of Ukko in search of assistance, in search of someone to blame or curse, yet perhaps a few to offer some help. Sir Henry was hoping against all hope for the latter. He knew their limitations; an aged Bishop and a dozen part-time acolytes could not hope to handle even a tiny fraction of the concerned citizens who suddenly, without warning, found themselves in the situation of being on the wrong side of a wall.

One item of physical interest lay in the fact that there were many larger business establishments with the Old Wall. As with many towns, the new buildings, new homes, are constructed at the edge of town which thus expands outwards. And this was true of Freetown; the older portions of the city now contained large spaces that could house a fair number of people for a short while. The challenge was getting access to them in time.

Jon woke refreshed; the peacefulness of the night before still lingered, as it did with the other companions. They ate a leisurely breakfast and then stepped outside the church to watch. Three large tables had been situated far apart from each other. Numerous signs were plastered about giving directions. Behind each table sat those who were ready to help the people. The largest table with the most helpers was labeled "Those in need of shelter within the Old Wall area." This table had six workers and already six long lines had formed behind them, stretching off down the street. Another table manned by three helpers carried a sign stating "Information Only." Finally, a lone man sat at the third table with its sign, "Those who have accommodations to offer." Currently that third table had no one else around it.

Naturally, a lot of anger was directed at the middle informational table. "How dare you?" "What's the meaning of this?" "By whose authority?" "What are you going to do if they destroy all of our homes and businesses?" "Who's going to pay for all the damage?" Some were just angry businessmen, some appeared to be the affluent. What was unnerving was their anger and frustration tended to upset all of the others in the huge lines frantically trying to get some place for their families and themselves to stay. Jon watched the peaceful mood evaporate from his companions. The ill emotion was contagious. Then, he had an idea.

Sitting on the top step of the church off to one side and out of the way, he took out his flute and began to play cheery pieces, uplifting songs and melodies. Soon, others began to echo his mood instead of the anger. Within a few minutes, a lean fellow dressed in mismatched leather shirt and pants came up to Jon. "Mind if I join you? You could use a bit of percussion."

"Sure, have at it," Jon replied. "I'm Jon, by the way."

"Name's Fred. Didn't I see you at the dance at the inn a couple nights ago?" he replied, setting up several different sized drums between his legs as he sat.

"Oh yes, now I recognize you," exclaimed Jon. "You were one of the musicians. You were great! Fabulous sounds. Loved it. Wished it wasn't over so soon," Jon said. The young man beamed and began tapping out rhythms on the pair of drums, one of which looked to Jon like a dumbec in nature. Soon they were playing well together.

Not long after that, a man named Greenfield joined them playing what looked to Jon to be an eight stringed guitar. Within an hour, the musicians had grown in number. Eight were playing all sorts of lively dance tunes, none of which Jon had ever heard. But he improvised right along with them.

Needless to say, the effect worked magic. Gaiety drowned anger. What had been a scary, somber, frightening experience for those in the ever growing long lines, had now become something akin to a party or dance; it was enjoyable. And the musicians were well rewarded for their assistance, it could be said that their ale mugs and dinner plates never ran empty all that day. What Jon found interesting was the interchangeability of the musicians. From time to time, one would take a break, having other matters to handle. Another musician would appear from the crowd, as if on cue, and take his position, usually bringing a different instrument with him. Thus, the overall sound varied throughout the day. Jon was in heaven. All these instruments, all these tunes, if only he had a tape recorder with him.

All was not rosy, though. Three singularly important events occurred that day. About midday after the musicians were well established. Mandy spotted a mass of red approaching from way down the street. She was "on self-appointed guard duty," she said later. Mat identified them as being a bunch of the Red Guards led by several of the Council of Ten members. Big trouble was heading their way. Someone went to fetch Sir Henry right away.

The three leaders, all very much overweight, but dressed impeccably, carried an air of complete authority.

Indeed when they approached, the musicians ceased playing instantly, mid tune. The noisy crowds hushed. Mat whispered to the others, "That's Renfeld on the left; Cottersbeam in the center; and Wakeley on the right. They are the top leaders of the secret council we told you about. All three are not to be trusted!" About two hundred Red Guards, all bearing swords, stood ready to back them up. They halted before the steps.

Renfeld sneered, "We demand to see who's in charge of this fiasco. We are taking this whole operation over. There will be no further usage of that blue magical light."

"I beg your pardon, Renfeld," stated dryly, but forcefully, Sir Henry who stretched up to his full stature. "You will do no such thing. The Holy Sphere of Protection has and always be the province of this Church of Ukko."

"Perhaps I have not made myself clear in this matter. You see them?" he indicated the couple hundred Red Guards behind him. "I said we are taking over. Move out of the way or there will be bloodshed. Your handful cannot match our might. We will gratefully allow you to just leave the church now!" his face had a covert, evil aura about it.

At this point, the Bishop, who had been watching from just inside the door, stepped out. "For two hundred years now, you and your council members have grown fat off the blood and sweat of these poor townsfolk. In return, you have done nothing to protect them from the ravages of the demons and their armies. Some even say you are in league with them; but I won't go so far as that. You don't appear to have horns. But now Father Ukko has returned to bless the folks of this town once more. You may join us in helping to save and restore this town if you want. Your help would be accepted. But we have and will always control the Holy Sphere of Protection."

"Foolish old man," cried Renfeld. "Have it your way then. Okay, men. Force your way in; you have my permission to slay any who resist you!"

Jon piped up in a calm voice though rather annoyed that all the wonderful music had stopped because of this ill-mannered man. "I think not, sir! This is a Holy Church protected by Ukko and his followers. You have only two choices and you must decide now. Leave in total disgrace or join us in helping to save this town. It is your choice; make it now."

"I've made my choice," he shrieked. "Take them now!" he cried to the Red Guards. To his utter amazement and to the amazement of the Red Guards who stood in the front line, none moved. The feet of those in the front row seemed to have grown roots. They could not move their feet. As others behind them tried to force their way over and around them to get to the church steps, their feet too began to grow roots. "What vile trickery is this?" he screamed and grabbed a sword from one of the struggling guards. He tried to rush up the steps and put an end to this at once.

Jon heard the faint chant of May in the background. She had many years of practice and could easily launch a spell drawing absolutely no attention to herself. He smiled and let her continue.

Renfeld took one step toward Jon before he shrieked in utter terror. In his mind he saw something terrible standing at the top of the stairs. His own excrement trickled down both his pant legs. The sword clanked on the stone steps. He turned and ran, ran as if all of the demons of the Abyss were chasing him. May looked over at the other two. Now they too shrieked in stark terror and instantly fled the other direction.

It was actually rather funny to see three dignified, yet evil, men running away. Jon relaxed his total control over the front line of bodies facing him and started laughing. "They are running away like rabbits," he managed to say between fits of laughter. It was catching. The huge lines of townsfolk who had been frozen in line, also began chuckling. Then, the chuckles turned into roaring laughter, an unstoppable laughter.

Here and there within the ranks of the Red Guards, a chuckle was heard, followed by outright laughs. About half of the men simply said nothing, but turned around and left just as quickly as they could. The others joined in the hearty laughter of their fellow townsmen. *Recruit them*, Jon placed into Sir Henry's mind. Five minutes later, the musicians stopped laughing enough to begin playing once more. And Jon took a restroom break and went inside with the others.

"Pretty impressive spell, May," Jon congratulated her when they were outside the sight of the crowd. She smiled appreciatively.

"But how come those guards couldn't move? Who did that and how?" she asked.

Alison and Darless shrugged their shoulders, "Not us; we were readying other spells."

Everyone then looked at Jon. His face reddened slightly. "Okay, I did it. I was upset that they caused the terrific music to stop. I am still feeling expansive today. I just took over total control of a dozen or so body's feet. A trifle. That's all. No one got injured in the slightest. Besides, I think we maybe can recruit another hundred men to help out the town."

"What may be a trifle to you is pretty darn impressive to the rest of us, Jon," Alison retorted. And everyone laughed and headed on down into the basement.

The second major event occurred around mid-afternoon. It also was totally unexpected. The lines asking for a place to stay had become enormous. Three additional tables had to be setup to handle them. Unfortunately, they had long since run out of places for people to stay and were mostly taking names and addresses and the number of people in the group; they promised to get back to them just as fast as space for them could be found. Only the music kept the crowd civil at this point. The lines at the information table remained fairly constant; for these inquiries could be quickly dispatched. The event occurred at the vacant third table, where those that wanted to help by providing spaces for people to stay could volunteer.

A party of ten men walked up towards the church. These were very different men. "Say isn't that Father Dommfeld?" said May to Mat. "And that one is Brother Marcus, right?" He replied affirmatively. Each man wore the robes of his office, priestly office. Jon marveled at the very different styles of priestly garments they wore. Some were a bit gaudy, he thought; others way too plain and mundane. But these men walked with a surety of gait that defined their sense of holiness in their various religions. They paused and read the direction signs; they did not need to because they had already passed many similar signs plastered half way down the block. As a group, they walked up to the vacant third table. The huge crowd at the other table hushed in the presence of so many of their holy men in one place at one time.

The poor acolyte who manned that table was utterly speechless; May intervened discreetly. "Greetings your

Reverence or rather your Reverences," she said as politely as she could muster.

Brother Marcus, a monk in plain brown robes, spoke for the group. "We have come to offer our assistance. Pray let us speak with the Bishop."

"I'll get him at once!" May replied and turned, intending to rush off to find him. But he had already been informed of his fellow priest's arrival and had come to meet them personally.

"Greetings, welcome brothers. Your assistance is more than welcome," said the humble Bishop. "Indeed, I have prayed for your aid. We face a force so huge that we must all stand together, united as one to survive. We must somehow find food and shelter for eighty percent of our town and we only have hours in which to do it. I'm sure that I can speak for the entire town when I say, 'Thank you for coming.'" They all bowed in respect as did the Bishop.

As these spiritual leaders climbed the steps, they paused and turned to the folks in the long lines. Each one, in their own custom, blessed the crowd. And they responded with cheers and clapping and whistling. The musicians struck up a cheerful tune and the holy men entered the Church of Ukko to make plans as they could.

"The town is pulling together," Jon commented to Alison, who smiled and nodded her complete agreement.

The third event occurred late in the afternoon. The various priests had all left except one, Brother Marcus, who stayed to chat with Jon. While they were talking, a middle aged man with a long black beard streaked with bits of grey, coal black eyes, and wavy graying hair suddenly materialized in front of the church right before Jon and Brother Marcus. He was dressed in swirling robes and carried a large diameter twisted staff. He spoke slowly and carefully, pronouncing each word distinctly, "I am looking for Alison d'Ambrose. Can you direct me to her, please."

"Sure, this way. She's inside doing something. Excuse me a minute, Brother Marcus," Jon replied. He led the obvious mage into the church. They found Alison and Darless in the study pouring over the city map, formulating plans of some kind. "Alison, someone here to see you."

She looked up, a surprised look appeared on her face. "Gatekeeper. I didn't expect you to come here. Welcome. Here have a seat. We were just working on some possible plans."

The man nodded and sat down across from the two women. With a wave of his hand, he bid Jon be off, though he did not speak a word. Jon shrugged and left to talk further with Brother Marcus who was trying to convince Jon that a sound, fit, martial arts program was spiritually uplifting. Jon, impressed by Mat's skill, was most curious to find out more.

The Gatekeeper spoke softly and distinctly as before, "I could trust this message to no one. So I can myself. Here," and he handed her a small pouch. "Six rings. That's the most I could get on such short notice. In direct response to your request, there are five plus myself that are both able and willing to assist in this endeavor. Again on such short notice, I have been able to acquire but five staffs. Others are charging them fully while I am here. They should be ready to go by midnight. If they are needed before then, they can be used, but not for as long a period. I have the five diligently studying the spells at the moment. They will be ready."

"Thank you very much," Alison replied. "As I said before, I have two myself but have not had time to fully recharge them yet. I'll get to that tonight. We don't think that the armies will be here that soon. But you never know. Lord Jarred was pretty angry the other day and determined to be the next ruler."

He nodded and said, "Have you determined the required height?"

"Darless has done some calculations. We believe that the height required should be two hundred feet," she explained. That seemed to fit with his own calculations.

"Alright then, I must get back to the Guild. Here, take this token," he handed her what appeared to be a small marble. "When it is time for the mages to join you at the well, simply throw this onto the ground hard, so that it shatters. It is a small notification spell I have perfected." Alison carefully took the marble and placed it cautiously into one of her pockets inside her robe.

She turned to thank the Gatekeeper, but he was not there. He had vanished just as he had come. "Bit unnerving when they come and go like that," she commented to Darless, who smiled.

"Their six and our two is eight. That should really make some difference; sparks will really fly!" And both women laughed at the irony.

Jon stuck his head back in. "Safe to come in?" Marcus had gone and his curiosity got the better of him. They nodded and he came inside the study. "Who was that guy? Where'd he go? What'd he want?"

"Nosey aren't we?" teased Alison. "He is called the Gatekeeper for reasons that I cannot tell you — Magician's Guild secrets, you know. He replied to my summons for aid. We can expect six more mages to assist defending the rest of the city that is outside the Old Wall."

"Great! We are going to need all the help we can get. I'll bet they are six really powerful wizards too," Jon added.

"Well, because of my plan, they must be. Also, not every wizard is willing to stick their body out on a limb to safeguard the city," she explained.

"But," added Darless, "if we are successful in this endeavor, then those six will be looked upon as heroes of the town and the Magician's Guild will have earned significant respect with the ordinary townsfolk. I don't think the Gatekeeper could afford not to at least make some attempt to help us. The risks to them are minimal and they stand to gain enormously if it works."

"If what works?" asked Jon.

"Our surprise for the demon armies; and that's all I will say at the moment. Now leave us, we have lots of magic work to perform at the moment," and she gave him a kiss. Jon left feeling better about things. She teased Darless, "See, give a man a kiss, and he does what you want him to do." Both women laughed and then set to work on the two staffs. Both needed recharging.

The rest of the afternoon was uneventful and rather boring for Jon, who had nothing really to do. He wandered here and there, bored. The evening meal was run in shifts because the church now served close to six hundred meals. Jon was glad to see an army of women tending the kitchen. Sure enough, the meal, though simple, was delicious; a chicken stew that could easily be served with minimal dishes. The women were intensely practical. Jon wondered where and how they had learned the skill for making such a huge batch of food at one time. But they were so busy, he refrained from asking.

After dinner, he sipped a mug of ale on the church steps. The lines were now much shorter indeed. And the streets were full of people laden with goods heading into the central portion of town and their assigned locations. At dusk, some returning scouts reported no signs of the approaching armies. However, around nine o'clock, the Holy Sphere of Protection was again activated for the night as a precaution.

After it was up, Alison got her friends together and asked, "Okay. Darless and I need to go to the central well to experiment. Want to come along?" She knew they would without needing to ask. So the six headed through the now crowed street, filled with people of all ages staring at the magnificent blue energy dome over their part of the city.

As they approached the well, Mat commented, "Have you noticed a change?"

May immediately said, "Absolutely!"

"No, what?" inquired Jon, wondering what Mat was talking about.

"Normally, the streets are unsafe to travel any distance at night. But tonight, everyone is out in the streets and it is peaceful and safe. Big change, don't you think?"

"Now that you point it out, yes, it certainly is!" Jon replied wondering how he failed to spot this change himself.

At the well, the two mages took out a pair of matched rings and placed them on their index fingers. Then, holding onto their staffs, they spoke a command word. The others watched as both wizards began to rise into the air. They maneuvered themselves into the skyward shooting, blue energy flow and continued to rise high above the city. They stopped about two hundred feet above the ground, well below the top of the energy dome. Jon noticed that they were looking off into the distance and taking to each other pointing out locations in the distance. Apparently, they were satisfied and then came down.

"Yes, this will work!" Alison exclaimed eagerly. "Quite a view up there. We can see all over the rest of the town. I think my plan will work."

"What plan?" Jon inquired.

She explained her ideas as they slowly walked back to the church. If the armies attempted to loot the unprotected part of the town, then eight wizards would launch spells from up there where they could see the enemy all around the town. "Only certain spells will be useful in this situation. We do not want to burn the town down with fire balls. And the spell has to have a long range of effect. We are quite some distance away, you see."

Jon did not see, but then he was not a wizard. He gave her a reassuring hug. "Thanks," he said. The rest of the evening was calm and peaceful and quite. They all went to bed early that night. They enemy was expected to arrive the next day.

Chapter 15 The Battle for Freetown

The next morning brought a great deal of activity within the Old Wall section of Freetown. People clogged the streets with one way traffic. Most of the residents did indeed live outside the original protective town wall. Every soul in the town knew that the demon armies were about to descend upon Freetown just as they had done every twenty years for the last two hundred years, bringing devastation and destruction with their uncontrollable armies. This time promised to be different; an artifact from the town's distant past had miraculously reappeared promising to protect their lives, but unfortunately not their homes and businesses — if and only if they got themselves and families within the Old Wall portion of town. Most had braved the long lines in front of the Church of Ukko yesterday to get an assigned location, a place to stay for the short while the armies would besiege the town. Now, with the threat of the approaching armies at hand, they hastened to first get safely within the Old Wall and second to find their temporary quarters.

Jon and his companions watched from the steps of the Church of Ukko. He noted that there was no panic or pandemonium, just worried and concerned people moving to safety as fast as they could. Because of the large numbers, this was not as fast as most would have preferred. Jon was concerned that the demon armies would arrive before all those who wanted to get to safety had made it. But he need not have.

Around mid-morning, the first signs of the approaching armies were seen high in the sky over Freetown. From the south came huge flocks of crows cawing and circling the town. Mandy explained that they were undoubtedly the "eyes of the enemies" spying on the town and the other demon armies. Shortly thereafter, a large number of ravens swooped down from the north. Jon surmised Zugblat was behind their appearance. *Anytime now*, he thought, *anytime*. He sighed.

About noon, one of Sir Henry's lookouts came galloping down the street up to the church, crying, "They are coming! They are coming!" Sir Henry hastily got a report from his excited, young scout. "They are about two miles away and closing fast on horseback. Cavalry charge, I think."

"Okay. Thanks, son. You've done well," said the paladin. The fifty-year old, seasoned paladin turned to Darless, "Okay, please send the recall signal." She nodded and spoke a command word. A huge streak of light soared from her fingers to high overhead. Several hundred feet up it burst into an enormous ball of fire, much like the huge aerial fireworks that Jon loved to watch on the 4th of July.

"Nice one, Darless. Beautiful," he commented.

"Yes, but normally I am trying to fry nasty opponents with this," she mused. "But it makes a signal that all of the outlying scouts can see," she replied. "Well, now I guess it begins."

Sir Henry counted the galloping, incoming riders carefully. As soon as the twelfth one arrived, he gave the signal to raise the Holy Sphere of Protection. His order was relayed to the Bishop who activated the lever. Interestingly, ten of the other holy church leaders who had offered their assistance the day before were with him. This time, the secret of the town's protection was not going to be lost with the capture or killing of the priests of Ukko. All of the holy men would be able to operate it.

Jon felt a little out of place. Alison and Darless, both dressed in mages robes were handling last minute details with their staffs and rings. Mandy finished buckling on some of the various bits and pieces of armor Jon had rarely seen her wear. "Extra defensive measures," she explained while attaching a quiver and her bow across her back. She had two bastard swords slung also across her back, drawable from either side. Mat and May were dressed in their Twins black. Each had their short swords ready and May also carried some kind of magical wand. Jon also noticed she wore a couple of rings that he had not seen before; he presumed they were magical in nature. It was obvious that they were ready to do battle with the enemy.

Jon looked at his trusty walking stick and shrugged. "Guess I'm ready." To his surprise, a voice replied in his mind, *So am I.* Startled, he looked down at his walking stick wondering what it meant by that remark.

Just then, Sir Henry stepped out of the church joining the six, followed by two dozen of his men. Encased entirely in a suit of plate armor, to Jon he looked like something out of the middle ages. He, as well, carried several swords. Through his open vision, he said to Mandy, "Okay. You have the central well and the southern main entrance. As planned, I'll take the north entrance. Some of these others will watch the eastern side. Both of us can also watch the western approaches as need be. May Ukko guide our lives today."

"Right, we are all set to head out now," Mandy replied. Turning to her friends she said, "Okay, let's do it. To the well." And they began their short walk down the nearly empty streets from the Church of Ukko to the Central Well. But hearing horses behind them, they turned to watch the Light Cavalry of Freetown mount up and ride off in the other direction. "Twenty-five against seven armies; not good odds," Mandy commented somberly. As they walked, they were surprised to see perhaps two hundred ex-Red Guards and other fighters on foot heading to the eastern entrances of the Old Walled portion of the city.

"What are those long things many of them are carrying? Like long spears?" Jon asked.

"Pole-arms, Jon," explained Mandy. "They do respectable damage to the enemy while keeping the wielder slightly out of range." Then, she added a bit more explanation for his benefit, "Slow and heavy though. When set, they can stop a cavalry charge too."

They walked on. It was a beautiful day, sunny and bright, hardly a cloud in the sky. It was a typical late summer's day in Freetown. Except for the blue sphere and the two strange flocks of circling birds, it seemed a normal hot, dry day. No one else was around the Central Well when they arrived. They did not expect to find anyone there though.

"I'm going up for a peek," Alison explained. Just as she had practiced, she spoke a command word. The mage floating up and into the surging blue energy rising from the apparatus located below the well. From her vantage point some two hundred feet above the city, she could see for miles in all directions. She pointed out the encroaching armies and yelled to those on the ground, "About a mile that way coming toward us." Then she turned to spy in Sir Henry's direction. "Couple miles away over there. Nothing to the west or east as yet." Then, she floated back to the ground.

"Zounds, I do hate all this waiting," proclaimed Mandy, pacing in circles around the well.

"I think that we are going to have a lot of waiting to do before this one is over," Jon commented. "Perhaps if we are lucky, they will get here and just turn around and go home."

"Wishful thinking, Jon," interjected Darless. "Somehow I don't think Lord Jarred is just going to go home empty handed."

"Say Jon," Mat suddenly spoke up, "I'd nearly forgotten to tell you. I think I have managed to read that blank piece of paper we found on the assassin. It isn't really blank. The writer used a special ink that is visible only when the paper is back-lighted. I found the letters but we cannot read it. We're not sure what language it is written in."

"Let's see it, we have time to kill," Jon said, only too glad to have something to think about. Mat got out the paper and showed everyone what he had discovered. By holding the otherwise blank paper up toward the sun, placing the sun behind the paper, lettering appeared. "Looks like Chinese to me," Jon said and then found himself explaining that that meant he had no idea what language it was.

Dareless took one look and pronounced, "That's Demon's Scrawl, the secret language of the Lords of the Abyss, usually ceremonial in nature."

"Can you read it?" Jon asked.

She studied it for a few minutes. "Not entirely. Just bits and pieces. It's from Jarred to this assassin whose name is Jeng. Something about 250,000 in gems having been deposited at some bank in the named account. Looks like a general description of what a Council meeting consists of, when the breaks usually occur, just like we saw. I cannot quite make this out, but it looks like Jarred wanted this assassination to be completed before the end of the council meeting. There is even a sketch of the inn and the dining room is X'ed. Conclusion: I think we know who hired the assassin: Jarred!"

"Wow," exclaimed Jon. "That does make sense. Let me hang on to that for a while." And Jon put the paper into his pocket.

Meanwhile, Darless sat down and got out her portable hole and brought out a large basket. Then, she spread a white sheet and produced some mugs and silverware and plates. "Picnic time! We don't know how long this is going to last, so I took the liberty of bringing along enough food to last us until nightfall." Everyone gave her a cheer and a round of thanks. While no one was yet hungry, the pot of hot tea was readily received by all. Time passed very slowly.

Close to noon, they were startled from their respite by the sounds of hooves clattering upon the stone streets. The advance cavalry of Lord Jarred had entered the town. Quickly Alison and Darless, using their magical rings, floated up to watch and report.

Jarred was no fool. He was leading his cavalry personally allowing his henchmen to march the foot soldiers up behind them. He was about three miles from town when he saw with his own eyes what he had seen earlier through the crow's eyes that he had sent on ahead to spy on the town and on the other armies. He swore several curses, for he, and he alone amongst all of his henchmen and followers had seen that accursed blue light before. *How long had it been?* he wondered, *two hundred and some odd years now?*

He slowed his column of cavalry to a walk giving him time to think. One thing was absolutely certain to Jarred, as long as that blue energy field was active, neither he nor any of his men could penetrate it to get to the Central Well. He issued orders to his seven mages to begin thinking up ways to counter this obstacle, though he knew full well they would be unable to do so. Jarred just could not think properly, he was fuming. A rage filled his every fiber of existence. Ten years of careful planning, even more years of behind the scenes work, and even his skillful assassination of his strongest opponent, Metrarch, had been now totally thwarted by this human upstart, Saint Jon Brown. No one had ever insulted Jarred like Jon had and then lived to tell the tale! All night long, the Demon Lord lay awake, envisioning the best way he was going to torture his upstart, to torment him, to make him pay more than he could ever imagine! Jarred intended to make Jon beg and plead for death and not give it to him! Oh was he going to pay! But now, even this was impossible as long as Jon stayed within the blue sphere of protection. Jarred's hatred swelled unrequited. Where had he come from anyway? It was all Metrarch's doing. Jarred saw an image of Metrarch laughing at him from his grave. Jarred was mad, too mad to think clearly. He had to calm himself. So he called for a complete halt. "Grab some lunch," he growled and walked some distance ahead of his army to think.

Jarred took a deep breath, held it for several minutes and slowly exhaled. I must put his into perspective. *What's the most important goal? Obtaining the position as Head of the Council. Alright then, the unsettled business with Jon must wait. Holding the Central Well is no longer workable. What did we do in the distant past? Think man!* And he searched his memories of the distant past. *Ah, yes, we used to surround the town and hold that position. Well, so much for the old ways of choosing the Head of the Council! That is completely impossible for any of us to do now — the town has grown enormously in size. That is just not workable unless we quadruple the size of our armies. That I got here first will have to do. Now what was that signal we all agreed to that forces the other Lords to come to a summit?*

"Okay, mount up, we enter the town now," Lord Jarred barked his order. "We will enter the town and wait for the rest to join us." Within five minutes, their horses clattered on the cobblestones of the streets of Freetown, coming up the main street from the south. However, they halted just inside the town proper.

Alison described their position and the fact that some of the men were looting a pub, rolling ale barrels into the streets. "It looks like they are stopping there just inside the city. Maybe they won't come any closer," she said optimistically. It was at this point that Jarred launched his summoning spell. A streak of lightning shot skyward and exploded, revealing a huge flaming torch with a shaft some two hundred feet long and yellow flames extending another fifty feet beyond that. It was an impressive display.

"What is that?" Jon asked the obvious. No one had any answer.

After a minute, Alison ventured, "Well, it appears to be a harmless spell."

"Hold on; it looks like all of the seven Demon Lords are now standing beside Jarred. My bet is they are holding a meeting to decide what to do next," Darless responded. She was imagining the worst. Whatever the Demon Lords were doing didn't last long. From their distant viewpoint, they appeared to be arguing amongst themselves. All save Jarred, made a hasty exit in less than five minutes.

The hot afternoon sun baked the city. It was frustrating not knowing what the demons intended to do. Time passed slowly for the six adventurers. Occasionally one or more of Jarred's mages would come up to the energy barrier and cast a spell into it. They discovered that nothing harmful could penetrate the protective sphere. Several horsemen rode entirely around the city verifying that there was no way to penetrate it, no openings.

During this time, several of the pubs that had stayed open brought out kegs of ale for the troops who simply milled around the outskirts of the town. Jon wondered if the owners actually got paid for their goods; he doubted it.

By two o'clock, Zugblat's forces had fully arrived and took up positions on the northern sections of town where Sir Henry was watching. Evidently, no other Demon Lord chose to challenge the Sphere of Protection. Zugblat was too young to have firsthand knowledge of the sphere; however, the other Demon Lords knew only too well its purpose, capabilities and significance though none had ever actually seen it before. As Sir Henry observed Zugblat's forces, he realized that Zugblat had no intention of challenging Jarred's claim to have captured the town. Instead, he was studying the protective energy field itself, gaining firsthand knowledge for his future use.

"Hey everyone, heads up! Here comes Lord Jarred himself carrying a white flag!" yelled Alison from her floating perch. She slowly descended accompanied by Darless. Together, the six walked south down the empty street toward the edge of the Old Wall to meet the demon.

Jon instinctively realized that Jarred was likely after him and not the others. "I think he wants to parley with me. So let me do the talking. Send me mental messages instead, especially if you have any bright ideas. I think we may need them." The others readily agreed.

It was an eerie conference. Jon stood facing Jarred, separated by about five feet with the sheet of blue energy streaming upwards between them. Jon knew with certainty that only this energy field protected him from facing the full wrath of the Demon Lord. He could feel the intense anger Jarred radiated from every sinew in his large body. Jarred spoke first.

"Saint Jon, the Meddler. I have a proposition for you," he began through clenched teeth. Jon nodded and the demon continued his rehearsed speech. "Lower the barrier, give us control over the mechanism, and surrender yourself to me. I will spare your women, they can become my concubines. If you choose not to do so, then I will totally destroy the remainder of the town, which I may point out, is eighty percent of the entire town. I will burn it to ashes and smash all buildings into total rubble before your eyes!" He laughed long and hard, a rather sickening, gleeful laugh.

Jon knew that it had come down to this decision. He had suspected this would be the situation days ago. If he tried to protect the people, the demon army would destroy the remainder of the town, which would totally devastate Freetown. The town might not even survive such destruction. Certainly the backlash on the Church of Ukko and himself would be enormous if not annihilation. How could they hope to fend off an entire army hell-bent on the town's destruction? Jon pondered his few options for a minute before replying.

When he finally spoke, he spoke with a calmness he did not know he possessed, "Jarred, listen carefully to what I am about to say. It is for our ears alone." Jarred reacted but withheld his sudden surge of rage primarily out of curiosity. *What is this human up to?* Jon went on, "I have in my possession a certain piece of paper. I got it off of the now deceased assassin, Jeng. It was written by the person who hired the assassin." Jon paused, studying Jarred's every facial expression to see what reaction this brought. He watched the look of anger change to that of concern. "It is written in a secret ink so that it can be viewed only in a special way, which we have done. The writing is also in a very particular dialect known to only a very few, such as yourself. It has some very interesting information in it concerning the Council of Seven meeting that just transpired. It is signed by a certain person that we both know," Jon grinned staring Jarred in the eyes. He saw that he had the Demon Lord's full attention.

"So here is my order directly to you, Jarred. If anything should every happen to me, I have arranged to have six copies of this letter sent immediately to the other six Houses of your plane in the Abyss. I think that they would find that letter intensely interesting, don't you?" Jarred grimaced noticeably; his teeth made a horrible grinding noise; his face became fiery red as he fought to control his rage and anger toward Jon. "So you see, from now on, my life is your life. If I die, then you are very likely to meet a similar end yourself, but not from my hands."

"Show me proof you have such a paper, assuming that it exists," Jarred fairly screamed back at Jon, nearly losing what remained of his self-control. Without the constant flow of serenity coming from such close proximity to the energy flows of Ukko, Jon knew that he would never ever have had the courage to calmly speak to this demon. Jon carefully produced the letter from his jean's pocket and held it up for the demon to see. Jarred did recognize it; the ground shook from his stamping rage; words that no one present understood echoed in their ears. After a minute, Jarred suddenly calmed down; an idea had struck him. A wicked smile pursed his lips.

"You could not possibly have had the time to set up all of the requisite spells. So I will destroy the town and besiege it until the fools lower this accursed magic. Then I will take the paper from you and give you the most agonizing, painful death that I can dream up!" He paused watching Jon's heart sink a bit. "On the remote, offhand chance that such does not occur, that you somehow leave this town alive, which is totally inconceivable, then I shall honor your word because I believe that you would indeed do this to me!" He roared with diabolical laughter at his own brilliant counter to this pesky human. He could see nothing that would now stop him from enforcing his will on the town. It would just take a very short time to turn the entire population of Freetown against this thorn in his plans of dominance. "Behold the total destruction of Freetown!" And he turned and walked back toward his generals and his large army. He did not see Alison throw a small marble onto the ground; he did not see it disintegrate into a puff of blue smoke. He did not see the arrival of six of Freetown's most accomplished wizards at the Central Well. Nor would he have cared had he seen this.

The six rushed back to the well. "What have I done?" moaned Jon, now seriously doubting everything he had done since arriving in Freetown.

"You have done the right thing!" insisted Alison. "Always remember that, no matter what happens now. You did the only honorable, right thing! I will fight to the death to protect this town." Darless spoke a single word in a language none understood, but the sound of the word did not sound hopeful. Mandy could think of nothing to say and so kept quiet.

When they reached the well, Alison handed out more of the magical rings to the waiting wizards, each of which carried a staff similar to that carried by Alison and Darless. Jon assumed that these were the staffs of power she had talked about. The men seemed extraordinarily quiet and calm, Jon thought, evidently resigned to the fate that awaited them all. When each had put the ring on, Darless gave a final set of orders. "When we rise up to take our positions, remember the plan. Each of us takes a sector of town to protect. Holler if you need additional firepower in your zone. Remember, when you have exhausted your firepower, get out of here as fast as you can!" Jon's heart sank further as he caught her words. He knew that each of these wizards had a finite number of spells that they could cast. Compared to the enormous number of men they faced, an entire army, it seemed futile indeed. It would only be a matter of time before these brave souls would have done all that they could.

Just then the sound of hooves upon cobblestones echoed in the otherwise silent town behind them. Sir Henry and fifty mounted cavalry halted at the well. "We are ready," he said calmly but loudly so Alison could hear from above. "Just direct us when needed." She waved and nodded.

"Excuse me, Sir Henry," Jon asked with a confused look upon his face, "what exactly are you planning to do? Somehow I have missed out on this detail. And it seems your force has doubled in size."

"Oh, it is just a little something Alison and I have worked up," he explained. "When the mages spy a mass of men that they cannot easily handle with their spells, I intend to make a foray out of the sphere and attack them; then retreat quickly back into the protected zone. A quick hit and withdraw tactic. It should be of some help in thwarting the enemy's plans. But to tell you the truth, I am more worried about a massive fire. Look there, they have started a huge bonfire. Soon they will undoubtedly set much of the town ablaze."

"Not if I can help it," retorted Mandy. "I guess now is as good a time as any for a good, old-fashioned downpour."

"But it hardly ever rains that hard here," protested Sir Henry.

"It will in a few minutes," Mandy replied as she stepped away from the group, grabbed her small holy symbol of Reylona tightly and began her prayer. Fascinated, Jon watched her every movement. He had never seen her so solemn, so reverent, so intent on prayer. It was a side of her that he had not really ever seen, Mandy was very private in her actual devotions to Reylona. For the next two minutes, the ranger was totally oblivious to the world, so intent was her prayer. Then, Jon noticed some high clouds forming in the otherwise clear, sunny day. He found this incredible and began staring at the sky.

Back on the University campus about a year ago, Jon had caught a Friday night flick made by a Canadian photographer who used a time lapsed method of speeding up an entire day's worth of cloud buildup, ending with a storm. He had watched fascinated as clouds ebbed and swirled and swarmed and formed a thunder head. Now before his eyes, he saw a similar swift buildup of one massive thunder head centered over the town. A huge bolt of lightning struck a stunted oak tree just outside of the town; one second later, the entire ground shook from the massive shock of thunder. Mandy ended her prayers and looked up at the now very dark skies. "That ought to do it, unless I overdid it. I've never actually done this before. Well, let it rain, rain, rain!"

"Holy," Jon cried out loud, but his second word was completely drowned out by another thunderous blast. And then the rains came, torrential rains. A massive downpour drenched everyone and everything. The mounted troops had an awful time controlling their startled beasts. Chaos had erupted.

Mandy heard several cheers from Alison and the mages high above her. There was no place to take cover from the sheets of water; everyone was thoroughly drenched within two minutes. But no complaint was heard, only cheers and, of course, the "this is incredible!" Alison and Darless saw an enormous cloud of steam rising from the bonfire. A few more minutes of this torrent and it sputtered and went out. A side note, the next day the boundary of the actual freak storm was clearly visible to everyone. For about a mile around the town, a tremendous quantity of plant life appeared overnight. For the next week, lush fields of blossoming greenery entirely surrounded the town.

Undaunted and further enraged, Jarred ordered the total destruction of the town. Fighting the pummeling torrential downpour, his men began to fan out into the town, smashing whatever they could as they moved down the streets. The noise of their destructions could be heard clearly between thunder peals, but the mages could not see well enough to cast any spells. However, just as suddenly as the rains came, they dissipated. Now Alison could see the Jarred's marauders and the real action commenced.

As bands of around twenty-five men marched down a side street, one of the mages launched a huge bolt of lightning spell at them. When it struck the men, their bodies were thrown helter-skelter, many never to rise again. However, only the eight levitating magicians could actually see the direct effects of their spells. Those on the ground only saw spell after spell being launched with the resultant thunder blast. Jon estimated that each of the six town's wizards launched about twelve spells before they simply vanished from the air. For a time, he tried to look through Alison's eyes, but he found that it distracted her, so he immediately stopped. But he has seen two dozen men get stuck by a bolt and sent sprawling. He did a quick calculation and was surprised to estimate that at least fifteen hundred men had been hit.

Jarred's rage only escalated. He ordered more and more garrisons into the streets. Soon, only Alison and Darless remained floating high over the Central Well. By plan, they had held back their spells until the end. She yelled down, "Okay, it's now hand to hand. We'll use our bolts to provide you with cover. Three streets down and two over to the left, Sir Henry. Go get them!"

Instantly, the cavalry dashed down the main street to the blue energy wall and dashed on through it. Jon watched and counted three streets down and then watched the charging horsemen disappear to the left. He felt totally useless. But his feeling only increased as Mat whispered, "Okay, Wish us good luck, we are off."

"Huh?" replied Jon, not grasping what Mat had said.

"May and I are going to disappear into the streets and do our thing. Darless will be guiding us and covering our rears. See you later on," he hastily explained.

"Great luck!" encouraged Jon. "Be careful you don't get hurt!" And he watched as the two black figures quietly disappeared in the growing shadows of the street. He turned to Mandy. "Well, it is just the two of us. I feel quite useless. I wish I had a horse or something so I could do something!"

"Yes, I know. But what would you do anyway? Never mind. I have an idea." Her eyes had that mischievous, almost teasing, look Jon had seen before. He knew she was up to something. He watched her closely and blinked and rubbed his eyes. There standing before him was a beautiful Pegasus mare. *Hop on and hang on tight. I may have to do some wild maneuvering,* she placed into his mind. Jon did not need a second invitation. He hopped on and then in his enthusiasm, cried "In the Name of Ukko!" and his walking stick transformed into the Holy Scepter of Ukko. Only this time, the scepter radiated an intense white light, nearly blinding anyone who looked at it directly. Jon had no time to wonder why he did this action. Perhaps the scepter did it of its own accord. He knew it had a mind of its own.

Mandy took a fast gallop and leaped into the air, her huge wings unfolded and flapping as she rose high into the air, circling the Central Well, gaining altitude. "Wow what an incredible view!" Jon exclaimed.

You betcha! came her reply. *Be on the lookout for some that we can attack somehow.*

From this high view point, Jon could see the cavalry of Sir Henry engaging in a swift attack on several dozen men. They literally cut a path through them, turned and charged once again through what was left of that small band. Then, they charged off in another direction, evidently following Alison's orders.

After watching the action for a few minutes, Jon asked Mandy, "How are we going to attack these men down there?

Won't we have to swoop down and get really close? Isn't that going to be dangerous?"

Let's not swoop too low too often. I don't want archers using me as a target very often. Why not just blast an area with energy? It certainly won't really harm anyone seriously, but it may likely stun them for some time. Mandy did not wait for Jon to answer. Instead she began a dive that took them through the blue energy field down toward a couple dozen men who were smashing up a blacksmith shop.

The men looked up and saw a Pegasus swooping down upon them carrying a rider who held a blazing, burning white torch. The next instant their minds were flooded with a crushing flow of energy. Most just collapsed in shock, shielding their eyes as they fell. Mandy swooped upwards to regain altitude just as fast as she could. Jon saw a belated volley of arrows suddenly arcing skyward their way. But none even came close this time.

"How long can you keep this up, Mandy?" Jon asked, elated that he was at long last able to make a slight contribution.

Dunno, maybe an hour at most, unless I get hit by the archers, she replied in his mind.

Then, a strange thing occurred. The command *Let's take out Jarred* appeared in her mind and in Jon's simultaneously. She did not question the order and swerved to her left taking aim at where she had last seen him near the edge of town. Soon she spied him standing on a rooftop bellowing orders to his lead officers below. Six mages surrounded him. *Dive now and get close enough to kick him!* appeared in her mind. She dove, heedless of the potentially lethal volley of spells those mages were likely to launch her way. She had the element of surprise. Neither Jarred nor his wizards expected a direct attack on his person. No one was that foolhardy they thought. They looked up in surprise to see a diving Pegasus bearing Jon holding a blinding light in his right hand.

Jon could see the mages reacting instantly, chanting feverishly spells that foretold doom for Mandy and himself. Suddenly a lightning bolt arced past them striking near the wizards. One ceased chanting and sucked the bolt of lightning into his wizard's staff. But another bolt whizzed by Jon's head.

This one detonated in the middle of the wizards, throwing them to the rooftop.

Mandy swooped down on a cursing Jarred. Another force took control of Jon's body, a force coming from the scepter itself. Jon watched as his body leaned over and his arm swung the Holy Scepter of Ukko at Lord Jarred. He felt it connect with the side of his head; he felt the flow of a searing energy; he heard the terror scream of intense pain coming from behind him as they swooped up from the Demon Lord, frantically trying to gain altitude before the wizards got to their feet and began blasting away at them.

Lord Jarred's mages were highly skilled. They rebounded onto their feet at once and began chanting another volley of spells. Mandy flapped her wings as hard as she could and had risen to two hundred feet before the volley went off. Six lightning bolts struck Jon and Mandy simultaneously. Jon felt his body and Mandy's violently jerking, muscles expanding and contracting involuntarily from the supercharged blast of energies. He felt Mandy's body go limp beneath him as the entire world suddenly went totally black on him. His body no longer followed his orders. He did feel the sensation of falling.

He felt his right arm drop down. The scepter on its own accord touched Mandy whose huge frame responded with a lurch of life, followed by frantic wing flapping as she narrowly avoided crashing through the roof of a building. Then, his arm curled up and the scepter touched his head. White energy surged through Jon's body. The first thing he noticed was that his eyes began to work once more. The blackness lifted revealing a swirling, dizzying series of images of a near collision with a roof top.

Remain low and get back into the Sphere of Protection, appeared in Mandy's mind. She was only too glad to obey this order, realizing the wisdom in the command. The mages would not have a direct line of sight to blast them again. A minute later, Mandy landed beside the Central Well and instantly transformed herself and collapsed onto the ground, gasping for air. Jon tumbled to the ground and managed to right himself into a sitting position.

"You two all right?" came an urgent cry from both Alison and Darless. "Need any help?"

Jon managed to wave an Okay sign to the women above him. He could not speak just yet. His confused mind was not operating fully. Neither was Mandy's for that matter.

He will bear my mark for all eternity! appeared in both Mandy and Jon's minds. Now they understood. This had all been the work of the life force within the Holy Scepter of Ukko. Jon immediately recalled the festering, never healing burns that Metrarch had had. They realized that the burns on the right half of Jarred's face likely would never heal, just as they had not on Metrarch's hands.

A few minutes later, Sir Henry and his cavalry, now down to forty men, came riding up to the well. They looked utterly exhausted; blood of all kinds was splattered over horse and man. But this glow in their eyes and faces left no doubt of their successes. Alison had floated down to check on Jon and Mandy. She exclaimed, "That was one incredible blast you two took. Do you realize you took six lightning bolts at the same time and survived it? I thought you both were goners!"

Jon replied sheepishly, "We had a little help from the scepter; otherwise, I think we both would have been dead before we even crashed." She looked both of them over carefully for wounds and burns, but could not find a scratch on either.

Satisfied that her lover and dear friend were really fine, she yelled up to Darless, "Yes, they really are okay. Not a scratch on them! Incredible! Unbelievable!" She gave him a hug and a kiss and then went back up to join Darless.

Jon watched as Sir Henry and his men dismounted and took long drinks from the well and tried to tend to their wounds. "Permit me, Sir Henry. I've been neglecting my duties," Jon hastily said and struggled to his feet, still a bit unsteady. The tired paladin looked at him but had no idea what he was talking about. Jon simply touched the still radiating Holy Scepter of Ukko to Sir Henry and watched as the scepter did its job.

The wounds of the paladin disappeared at once. Recognition of what Jon had done flashed in his mind. "All praise be to Father Ukko. Thank you Jon!"

But Jon had already moved on to the next man and had touched him. One by one during the next two minutes, Jon managed to touch each of the forty men. The scepter fully healed each man in turn. And while the men grasped what had actually just happened to their wounds, Alison and Darless both descended to join them.

"The Twins are now back within the sphere. We've shot all of our spells, drained every ounce of power from our staffs," explained Darless. She added, "Jon, the Twins could use some of your help as well. They are limping slowly down the street that goes by the Church of Ukko. Are you up to perhaps riding to them to help them out?"

Before he could reply, Sir Henry lifted him onto a nearby horse as if he weighed just a pound and then mounted his war horse. Jon noticed that he had removed a good deal of his armor. Obviously exhaustion had set in and rightly so. "Thanks!" Jon managed to say. "Let's go get them." And they were off at a trot that bounced Jon senseless until he got the hang of riding once more.

They found the Twins leaning on each other and slowly making their way step by step down the street three blocks distant from the church. Jon slid off the horse, landing with a jarring jolt on the stones. He quickly touched the scepter to both Twins. He could see that each had taken many wounds to their arms and chests and thighs. Their clothes were in tatters from all of the slashes. But their eyes shone with wildfire. Jon knew that their opponents were not so lucky.

A minute later, both Twins were talking at once, examining every part of their bodies in complete disbelief. Neither now bore any wound or scar, just the blood soaked remnants of their black clothes. "What, what did you do?" May asked when she finally found her voice. "We were nearly done in."

"The Holy Scepter of Ukko did it; it has the ability to heal wounds," Jon explained. "All I did was get here and touch you with it. It did the rest. How do you feel now? Can you make it back to the Well? We can let you ride if you want to?"

"Thank you Jon, Sir Henry. We really did need help," May replied. "I honestly didn't think we'd make it back to the Well this time. I think I'd prefer trying to walk, if you don't mind going a bit slowly. Not too sure of how my body is doing at the moment." And the four began walking slowly back to the Well.

Then May suddenly stopped. "Jon, you are alive! The last we saw of you, you and that flying horse got devastated with six lightning bolts and fell from the sky. How on earth did you survive it?"

Jon meekly waved the scepter. "It was Mandy. She can shape change into things. The Pegasus is her favorite. But the attack on Jarred was totally the idea of the Scepter here; its doing. And it managed to pull it off. I think I can safely say no matter what else happens today, Lord Jarred will never forget that brief encounter with the Holy Scepter of Ukko!"

"Good gods! Are you two all right?" said a shocked Alison when she saw the condition of her brother and sister's clothing when they arrived at the Well.

Jon smiled and said "They were a little worse for all the wear, but yes, they are perfectly fine now, right?"

Both Mat and May convinced Alison that now they were indeed in perfect condition, just very tired and exhausted. May was also totally out of spells. And their clothes were now basically rags.

However, Darless spoke what none were willing to say. "Well, we've done our best. We've exacted the toll. Not much more can we now do, except watch and wait. We've nothing left with which to stop Lord Jarred from destroying the town as he pleased." Her words mirrored all of the somber faces.

Alison had not given up all hope yet. "Say, I still have a few magical wands. We can use them to help support Sir Henry and the cavalry for a little while yet. They shoot smaller, less damaging spells. But we will need to be fairly close to the targets to use them."

"What have you got?" May cheered up. "I'll blast them with whatever wand you can lend me." Darless echoed her sentiments. So Alison retrieved her portable hole and began rummaging in it looking for anything that could be pressed into service.

Meanwhile, Sir Henry asked in a humble, low voice, "Mandy, do you have an enchanted long sword or broadsword that I could borrow? My trusty blade shattered and I've been using just a regular old long sword. I know you favor bastard swords, but those are too heavy to wield effectively from horseback."

She laughed and said, "Sure thing. I have a couple of long swords, no broadswords, though. I don't like them." And she began rummaging in her portable hole as well. "Ah, here it is. She's a beauty!" She handed it to Sir Henry who thanked her generously and began testing it.

"Whoa, yes, this one is very good indeed! Thanks, I promise to make good use of it!" he replied. When she had finished re-folding the hole and inserting it close to her bosom, she saw that the three mages now were testing small magical wands Alison had found. "Looks like we are about ready for combat once more." Then, she heard a large number of footsteps approaching and whirled around. "Hey everyone, we have company."

The small group looked back toward the center of town. Their eyes opened wide. This wide north-south street was filled with an enormous crowd of men heading their way. Townsfolk for the most part, carrying every imaginable kind of weapon from swords to blacksmith hammers and pitchforks. When the front of the wall of men drew near, one of them shouted, "Hey, it's our town too. We all want to help defend our homes as well!"

Beaming with joy, Sir Henry yelled, "Welcome one and all! Thank you! We need all the help we can get." Then he paused a bit surprised by the sheer number in the crowd. "How many strong are you?"

Alison floated up fifty feet and tried to estimate their unexpected helpers. She yelled, "There must be several hundred of them!" and floated back down. Quickly, Sir Henry began to organize the townsfolk. Jon marveled at the leadership skills Sir Henry possessed. One minute, this paladin was preparing to meet his doom defending the town. The next minute, the balance had changed and he shifted instantly to organizing mode.

Meanwhile, Alison and Darless once again took their spying positions several hundred feet in the air trying to ascertain what forces Jarred had were and what they were up to at the moment. His forces had suffered extremely heavy casualties thus far and it took his force of will to keep them from routing and even more force to re-assemble some form of battle lines. Yes, his crows overhead had alerted him to the unexpected reinforcements of this pitiful town. His mind raced seeking the means to put an end to this uprising once and for all.

Within a half hour, Sir Henry had the rag-tag group, who numbered well over a thousand men and a few women, into fifty attack groups, all marching down various streets, stopping at the edge of the Sphere of Protection energy wall, ready for the command to charge into Jarred's forces. Mandy chose to ride a medium war horse and lead the right flank into battle. May, Alison and Darless got behind the cavalry lines, ready to support Sir Henry with their close range magical wands. Jon and Mat provided foot soldier protection for the three mages and volunteered to try to assist the wounded. Sir Henry surveyed his unexpected army and felt a surge of pride in his fellow townsmen. While they probably would not prevail over the demon army, it was the first time in two hundred years that these people openly defended their town. That was what was significant to this paladin.

Viewing these arrangements through the eyes of his spying crows, Jarred cursed knowing that his own forces were close to the breaking point. He had to do something and do it fast. He called his high priests together issuing orders. The four priests and Jarred stood on the points of a hastily drawn pentagram and chanted a power spell opening a gate to the Abyss. Within a minute, the ugly bird like headed giant vulture demons appeared in the center of the pentagram, looked about, and moved out onto the surrounding streets. His demoralized troops began cheering; their ultimate weapons had finally arrived!

"Zagroot zounds!" cried Mandy as she saw the giant head of one of these creatures of the Abyss appear, strolling down the street. Sir Henry gasped; he had never faced these powerful demon creatures before. While he estimated he might be able to defeat one of these large creatures, he knew full well that the townsfolk could not hope to even scratch its skin! Hope faded as rapidly as it had come.

"Oh no, not again!" cried Jon when he spied these creatures. These were the very same kind that had nearly killed them all during their battle in the ruined Tower of Leeds. He yelled to Sir Henry, "I can kill several of these demons, so let me at them first. When I am too exhausted to fight any more, you take over." He tried to estimate how many he could get, six maybe. He held no expectations that Jarred would summon only six of these powerful creatures. Perhaps it was as Darless suggested, the bitter end of their struggle.

Jon watched terror begin to filter through the townsfolk. It was one thing for them to get up the courage to fight the human army from up north, but it was folly for them to try to attack actual vulture demon creatures from the Abyss itself! An unearthly silence fell upon the city. Jon could hear Jarred's hideous laughter off in the distance, reveling in his now certain victory.

And then the totally unexpected happened. Above the town and the glowing Sphere of Protection, a huge white cumulus cloud suddenly appeared. Out of it floated eight Air Maidens, armed to the teeth with weapons. All heads stared skyward; mouths fell open or fumbled for air. Total silence fell upon the entire town.

Four people instantly recognized the lead Air Maiden who descended near Lord Jarred. It was Fruella, now fully recovered from her centuries of imprisonment. She glowed with an energy that was blazing to behold. Her golden armor threw beams of blinding sunlight in all directions. Her broadsword held high, she was in total command of the situation. "Jarred, Lord of the 66th Level of the Abyss, you are in defiance of Ukko. This town, as you well know, has invoked his absolute protection. I give you one minute to reverse your gate and send all of your foul creatures back to the Abyss. I give your men five minutes to leave this town. After that, you face the total and complete wrath of Ukko." She paused, letting her message sink into his mind, displacing his rage. Then, she added, "On a personally, I do hope you continue to defy Father Ukko; I long for a glorious battle; I have not had one for far too many centuries. So please don't do as Ukko commands, I want a fun fight!"

The remnants of the human army Lord Jarred had led did not need any further encouragement. En-mass, they turned and began running from the town. Many were so filled with terror, that they dropped their weapons and packs so that they could run faster. In an instant, thousands of men began running back the direction that they had come, running as fast as they could.

Even from this distance, Jon could see the utter rage within Lord Jarred. His temple blood vessels expanded to huge dimensions as if his very head would explode. But he did mentally command his demon horde back through the gate. The Demon Lord could not speak even if he desired to do so, so great a volume of hatred flowed through his body. He just stood there fists clenched so tightly together that the pummel of his sword crumbled into iron particles. His terrified priests still stood at the pentagram corners but Jon could see their bodies were shaking, but their own force of will kept them functional to the very end. Just as soon as the last vulture demon stepped into the center of the pentagram and had disappeared, the four high priests and Jarred did likewise and disappeared from view, gated back into the Abyss. Jon heard Fruella comment, "Darn, and I had such high hopes for a battle today. Ah well."

She turned to the gaping townsfolk and commanded, "Today, you have asked for the protection of Father Ukko and he has granted it. Do not forget this day!" Then, following a hand signal from Fruella, the other Air Maidens floated down. One landed beside Alison, Darless, Mandy, Mat, May, Sir Henry, and Jon. "Behold this day the ancient Holy Scepter of Ukko has once again appeared in battle, wielded by Saint Jon Brown, the Redeemer. We go now to personally return the artifact to Father Ukko. Your town is now safe. We will be watching in case of treachery."

Each of the Air Maidens took hold of the left hand of one of the seven and together they rose into the cloud, Alison, Mandy, Darless, Jon, Mat, May and Sir Henry. Fruella floated close to Jon and said softly so only her four friends could hear, "Congratulations. I see that you four have made good use of my gift."

Jon replied meekly, "You realize you just saved our butts! We were totally doomed back there. The vulture demons would have carried the day for Jarred. Thank you from us and the entire town as well."

"You earned it," she replied. "And besides, Jarred just broke some serious laws gating in those creatures. And he knows it. But I see that you have given him something by which to remember this day, or rather, I suspect, the Holy Scepter of Ukko did."

"Yes," Jon replied, "That was totally its doing. In time, he may learn from it. Metrarch did so, I believe." Fruella smiled at him; she was fully aware of what had happened with Metrarch.

The cloud floated into Ukko's realm. Alison, Mandy and Jon had been here before, but under entirely different circumstances. Darless, Mat, May and Sir Henry only stared in amazement, their mouths hanging open, unable to speak. Their eyes, however, took in everything.

Jon felt a total serenity flowing over him; he knew he was in the presence of Ukko himself. Here was a being whose very presence impacted those around him. Father Ukko formed a material body out of the cloud material, appearing as an elderly man with full white beard and long hair, dressed in white robes. When he spoke, the body seemed to mouth the words, but the words really appeared directly in their minds. "Welcome to my realm."

Holding the Holy Scepter out before him, Jon said, "I believe this belongs to you. Alison found it and kept it safe all these years. I, er, rather used it quite a lot. It has saved us on several occasions." His hand reached out and accepted it from Jon.

"You have become rather fond of it I see," he observed. "I know that you do not like the fact that this scepter can control you and sometimes force you to do its bidding. It was never meant to be wielded by you, Jon. He for whom it was constructed made a fatal mistake; he began to depend upon it instead of just using it. I was afraid that would occur and so it did."

"For your assistance and for your deeds in my name, I present you with another walking stick, one more suited to your needs." Fruella handed Jon another walking stick that looked identical to the one Jan had been carrying, the Holy Scepter in disguise. She also handed him a small book. "This is the owner's manual, Jon. You are a musician and have a musician's mind that demands order. So I give you the owner's manual; the stick does only what it says in the manual. No surprises."

Jon accepted the two from Fruella; he knew not what to say, but managed, "Thanks a lot. I was regretting this day because I really liked the walking stick form of the Holy Scepter."

"I understand completely. And no, you do not need to worship me, Jon," Ukko replied, answering the gnawing question Jon had had for some time now which had just popped into his mind once again. "Many believe that they must pray to worship me. While that feeds the ego of some beings, I do not feed on such. I look at actions — at what a being actually does. Go now and hence forth be known as Saint Jon Brown, the Redeemer. I know what you have done for Metrarch; I see what you will do for others in time. The title is most apt." Jon bowed and stepped back.

"Darless, step forward." She involuntarily did so. "This is the first time an alu-demon has ever set foot in my realm. But I also know that you are not a demon. A being is not his body — many are not aware of this fact. From this time forward, be it known that you Darless Thornapple are a true Holy Paladin of Ukko with all the rights and benefits so accorded one of that rank. And no, you do not need to worship me, for you, like Jon, demonstrate what it means to be a Holy Paladin. It is not prayer and devotion; it is what you do in the world. Please accept my mantle."

Fruella appeared carrying a blue tunic cover with a simple white cross on its front and back. She placed it over Darless' head so that the cross appeared from her front and rear. Tears of joy flowed down her cheeks, she managed somehow to say "Thank you."

"Oh yes," he added smiling at her, "I do approve of what you have planned for your college." She blushed, knowing that Ukko had seen what her plans for her future contained.

He then continued his presentations. "Mandy Blackthorn, Ranger of Reylona, step forward." Mandy was once again in total awe; here she was in the presence of a legendary god but not her goddess. She felt more than a little out of place. Somehow her feet managed to move her forward a couple of very cautious steps.

"Hum, you feel less because you are in the presence of someone you consider is vastly more powerful than yourself," Ukko observed, hitting the mark dead center. Instantly, her eyes met his.

He is right on that account, she thought to herself. She just then realized that was what drove her to launch the bug assault when she was in the Abyss. He also saw her memories as she saw them.

"Ah, I see what you did in Metrarch's realm!" and he roared with laughter. "Most interesting effect, was it not?" She nodded and a small smile pursed her lips. The others grinned as they now understood what Ukko was discussing. "But we digress. I did not bring you to my realm just to observe. Rather, I reward those deeds that further my cause. What Reylona chooses to do with her follower is her business. I will not interfere. But I will give you a gift to show my appreciation, one that is most appropriate for you for whom personal independence of action is all important." He placed his hand upon her head. In her mind she heard and saw, *I show you the way. Look and train yourself to see, see through time and see through distance.* Mandy would later describe Ukko's action as sort of lowering a veil she held tightly over her senses. Once pierced, she could see, see by knowing that she could see, could perceive. The view was at once immense and vast and not the least overwhelming, but she realized that was why she had the veil in place in the first place. Never again would the veil be so tightly bound to her. Her feet moved her back, but she found that she had to move herself back with her body. The others just saw a radiance of serenity upon her face. This gift of Ukko, this unlocking of a skill she possessed, would prove of the utmost value in the not so distant future.

Ukko then continued. "Alison d'Ambrose." She bowed low and stepped forward to meet her god for whom she had often felt unworthy. Her eyes avoided his. "Daughter, as you well know, few are worthy to be in my presence. That you are here twice should remove your doubts, but I see it has not." He paused looking her over carefully. "Hum, I see just how much Fruella's gift has changed you. That is indeed interesting! And in a wizard; doubly so. This factor changes everything! I must think first." For a second, he appeared deep in thought.

Alison's mind raced trying to grasp what he had said. *I am a powerful wizard; but now I am using my powers just like Jon, Darless and Mandy, though I have not got it all figured out yet. They keep telling me I am screaming into their minds. But these so called mental powers are not magic.*

Magic and mental are two separate things. Or are they? Are they related? Suddenly, she understood something and that something that startled her. Her eyes met Ukko's. *I see,* she sent him.

I know, he sent back. *This is of the utmost importance which is why I am thinking it through.* The entire thought process took only a couple of seconds, during which time the others saw that both Alison and Ukko appeared deep in thought as if wresting with some immensely significant concept. Then he spoke, "Yes, we continue as planned. Alison, I present you with more knowledge, knowledge that you seek to further your career in the mystic arts." Fruella stepped forward with a large spell book, handing it to Alison.

"In this tome lies much of which you seek. Learn them and cast them wisely for the good of mankind. The book will only open by your touch, and to no one else. On the green page is that spell for which you have been searching for so many years. Read and learn before you build your new castle," he pronounced.

He then went on, "Yes, on your return trip you will find what you need for your castle's construction. Once home, you will discover the means by which it may be accomplished. Build an unassailable bastion for good in my name." As Fruella then placed another white mantle with a blue cross on it over Alison, he proclaimed, "Be it known from now on, Alison d'Ambrose is to be called the Holy Mage of Ukko."

Then, he added, "Continue the search for your family. More are still alive and in need of your aid, but I do not have details, unfortunately. I, like you all, do have limits." All three d'Ambrose children's eyes opened wide. Hope flowed where none had been.

But Ukko was not finished. "Finally, in the matter of the mystic arts and mental powers, continue along the lines that you have just realized. See where that takes you. I am keenly interested in the results. Expect my Maidens to one day bring you to me another time to discuss the results, good or ill."

"Thank you! I will on all accounts!" And a beaming Alison stepped back with the others. She had much to ponder, much to learn, much to do. It was all a bit overwhelming.

Then Ukko called, "May and Mat, step forward together as it is impossible to separate you two." He grinned broadly, as did their friends, who had not actually vocalized this observation. Both felt very self-conscious and hesitant. Never in their wildest imaginations did they see themselves standing before a god, let alone on another plane of existence or world.

"You two are special to me. I have been following your actions all these many years, right from the very moment when you arrived in the town of thieves. I had high hopes for you two and you succeeded beyond my wildest expectations. But before I go on, please note that I do not directly interfere in the lives and actions of people. The choices you make, the actions you take are all of your own choosing. I am not an 'all-seeing' god; none of us are. Let's say that I am observant. Through all these years, you maintained your sense of dignity, honesty, integrity, and righteousness. Using any means at your disposal, you began to reverse two hundred years of decline in the people of Freetown. And today, you have seen the culmination of that achievement. You two have demonstrated the best qualities of beingness. I feel rather like a proud father at this moment. Henceforth, be it known throughout the lands that May and Mat d'Ambrose are the Holy Children of Ukko." While the rest of their friends had no real idea of what this designation actually meant, the Air Maidens all clapped loudly and cheered. It was obviously a coveted honor that had just been bestowed upon them.

"While it is within my power to grant you both special clerical powers as befitting a high priest of the Church of Ukko, I will not do so for I and you both know that you pride yourselves on what you achieve by your own hands and efforts. Instead, following the wisdom of Fruella who has taught me a bit of wisdom — yes, an Air Maiden has indeed taught me something." All eyes momentarily shifted to the Air Maiden, who smiled and lowered her eyes. "My first gift is to let you see exactly what you are, opening the blinders you had constructed about yourselves. Mind you, what, if anything, you choose to do about it afterwards is your own choice. But if you choose to explore, I suggest you work with Jon or Darless who have found the beginning of the path, the way. If you choose to explore the path, you will certainly find that ability that you have always greatly desired, the one thing you cannot do yet desire above all others to be able to do." Their eyes opened wide in awe but the rest of their friends began wondering what this was all about. Ukko said no more about it; this was between him and them.

"My second gift to you is two-fold. Yes, your work in Freetown is done. You have earned the right to return home and to start a new life full of joy and happiness. Go with my blessing and eternal thanks. However, I will tell you the answer to one burning question you have talked about at length and in secrecy. Since this is meant for you two alone and is highly personal, I will simply place my thoughts directly into your minds." The Twins stood rooted to the spot wondering what would happen next.

In their minds they heard Ukko speaking. *Yes, you will both find love and marriage and have many fine children and soon. The connection, the bond you two share, is indeed very rare. But take heart; there are others like you in the world of men, seeking love just as you are. On your return trip to your homeland, be observant and you may find what you seek.* All that the others saw was a pair of very embarrassed Twins, their faces turned crimson. But both wore a huge smile and their eyes were very bright.

"Fruella, will you please take them aside and open their eyes?" Ukko requested. She did not hesitate for even a moment.

"Come with me," and she took their hands and led them off to one side where they could share a private moment together. Jon, Darless, Mandy and Alison all knew what they were about to discover about themselves. It was precious and perhaps the most valuable gift that could be given another being. May and Mat found themselves floating about three feet above and back of their heads; she had accomplished what Jon had asked them to do on the steps of the Church of Ukko last night when they were basking in the blue energy field. The Air Maiden said softly, "Welcome to you, Mat and May. Behold, you are spiritual beings, you are not bodies."

Recognition came to the twins. In unison, they realized, "I do not have a soul. I am a soul!" The afterglow in their eyes did not diminish for a very long time.

Meanwhile, Ukko continued, "Finally, last but not least, Sir Henry, Holy Paladin of Ukko, step forward." The paladin had also never ever dreamed that he would ever directly meet his god let alone be brought to his realm. Just being here was reward enough. But holding himself erect, proud and tall as befitting a knight of Ukko, he stepped forward.

"You have lived through some of the grimmest times any Holy Paladin of Ukko has ever had to endure, almost hopeless at times. Never did your faith or courage depart. While other paladins have charged forth into the world performing great deeds in the name of Ukko, you chose to defend the integrity of an entire town against overwhelming odds for so many long years. You have never once wavered from that course. Had it not been for your efforts, the Church of Ukko in Freetown would not have been present when the current events needed it. Thus, be it known that your actions far surpass those of many, many other holy paladins. Be it known from this time forward that you are now Sir Henry, Holy Paladin of the First Grade, the Guardian of Freetown. Your prayers to me will never go unnoticed or unanswered." Another Air Maiden stepped forward and pinned a huge broach upon his tunic. It had a central red ruby surrounded by seven smaller rubies set in a golden rose pedal base. The broach denoted that this man had reached the pinnacle of paladinhood in service of his god, his lord. Tears streamed down his face. Only with great effort did he manage to say a proper thank-you and bow.

Fruella led the Twins back into the group. Jon immediately saw both were floating about three feet behind their heads, a look of utter serenity upon their faces. He knew what they were experiencing. He felt the weight of responsibility fall on his shoulders; they would soon be bombarding him with questions for which he only had the vaguest answers.

"And now my fellow beings, it is time that you returned for I know you have pressing matters to which you must attend. Go now with my eternal thanks. Oh yes, one small detail. Alison, you will find that your staffs are fully recharged. A small token I know, but one you may find useful." They watched as the elderly body of Ukko seemed to grow thin and disappear. When he was gone, the Air Maidens took each one by the hand and off they went. The cloud like realm vanished; soon they could see Freetown far below them as they descended. The blue energy field was clearly visible even from this height. Tiny figures could be discerned on the streets, people were coming out of hiding. They floated down toward the Church of Ukko. When they were several hundred feet above it, they could see the Bishop and the acolytes and others standing on the steps.

Fruella spoke as they touched the ground. "Behold, I present Saint Jon Brown, the Redeemer. Here is Darless, Holy Paladin of Ukko. Here are your Twins, the Holy Children of Ukko. And Sir Henry, Holy Paladin of the First Grade, the Guardian of Freetown." Jon observed the incredible awe in the townsfolk's eyes. He knew that this day would become legendary in the town.

Then, one by one, they began clapping and cheering, breaking the silence. At this point, the Air Maidens rose, waved, and departed, but not before Jon yelled, "Thanks, Fruella!" She smiled down at him and blew him a kiss.

For the next ten minutes, the six were forced to wave to the crowd which grew larger and larger, pressing in around the church. Finally, the Bishop graciously ushered them inside the church. "Thanks," Jon heartily said. "We are starving! And I hate all this attention." The Bishop chuckled, "Tis the price of fame, my son. But come, you must tell me all about it while you eat." He led the way to the basement kitchen. "You were gone only for a couple of minutes. I barely had time to get outside to witness your arrival!"

The delicious odors of the evening meal assaulted their nostrils and turned on ravenous appetites, as Jon knew it would. He was only too grateful to let Sir Henry give the account of their meeting with Father Ukko. Of course, the hundreds of people who were in the church seeking sanctuary crowed as close to the kitchen area as possible to hear the tale firsthand. Sir Henry had to repeat various portions several times. Jon knew that Sir Henry was now doomed to have to retell this encounter over and over for the rest of his life. He was most glad that he would be leaving soon.

When they had eaten their fill, which was a rather large amount indeed, they looked at one and other and began laughing. Sir Henry, Mandy, Jon and the Twins were covered in dried blood. The Twins clothing was tattered beyond repair. Everyone needed a bath. And so the next half hour was spent cleaning up. Of course it was a communal bath, and Jon was, as usual, rather embarrassed bathing with four beautiful women. For them, communal baths was routine and they, of course, teased Jon about it. Needless to say, there was a lot of horseplay during that bath. The tensions of the day washed off with the filth and dirt, leaving all six recharged, feeling terrific, though tired.

Once everyone had dried off, they all sat around a table drinking a cup of tea; the girls were drying their hair, getting the snags out. "I could sleep a week!" declared Jon.

"Me too," added Alison.

"Well, perhaps not that long," added Mandy. "I would get too bored." Then, she recalled something William had said. Her radiant smile was replaced by a very worried, concerned look. "Zagroot zounds! I almost forgot. Reylona told me when the battle was done that I was to 'Ride like wind!' The caravan! We've forgotten the caravan! They must be in dire trouble by now. Come on, everyone. We must go, and go at once as fast as we can go!"

Instantly, the cheerful mood vanished completely. Alison suddenly realized the impact of Ukko's parting words. "No wonder Ukko recharged my staffs. Darless, you take one of them. Otherwise we have no spells left to use. May, you can carry all of the wands. Let's get moving!"

"Sir Henry," Mandy asked, "Can you send someone to fetch our horses? We must leave at once! The caravan is in dire straits!" He nodded and immediately ran out of the room to see to it personally. The six had little packing to do. The Twins possessions were already in their wagon in the caravan. Within five minutes, they were ready.

The Bishop thanked them over and over for everything they had done, begged them to come back for a visit when it was all over. The Twins did promise to return someday. A hearty round of hand shaking followed. Everyone wanted to shake the hands of the saviors of the town, of the new legends.

Soon, Sir Henry returned. Outside the church, the six horses were saddled and ready. Another round of farewells followed, with the paladin hugging tightly each of the Twins.

All three had tears in their eyes at this parting. Only their promise to return one day kept the spirits up a bit.

Mandy mounted her medium warhorse. "Hey, this stallion is spirited! Great choice, Sir Henry. Alison hopped into the saddle of her light war horse; she carried her staff in one hand and held the reigns in the other.

Jon helped Darless onto her riding mare; she found it awkward to hold onto the staff. "How on earth do you hang onto the saddle and the staff at the same time?" she queried. So Jon had to fasten the staff across her back with some rawhide straps. Darless felt much better when she could hang on to the saddle horn with one hand.

"Er, what about us?" asked Mat and May. "We have never ridden a horse before. What do we do?" Mandy tried to explain while Jon helped each timid Twin get onto their horse. He knew full well what they were experiencing; he'd been through this same thing earlier. Finally, Jon tied his new walking stick across his back and climbed aboard his mare. And waving, Mandy led the way, the other horses followed behind hers.

She felt frustrated at the slow pace they were making through the streets clogged with people. After an eternity, which was just a half hour, they finally left the last home behind, heading west. "We've got at least two more hours of sunlight," Mandy declared. "And look everyone. See there is the caravan's trail." There was no missing the trail of the hundreds of wagons paralleling the winding, nearly dry river bed down the dusty road. The sudden rush of rain run-off had already passed on downstream ahead of them. Now clear of the town, with open road ahead of them, Mandy called out, "Now let's ride like the wind! Hang on everybody!" And she kicked her stallion into a full gallop. The light warhorse bearing Alison followed instantly. The remaining riding mares took a little coaxing but also began flying along. Mat and May hung on to the saddle horns for dear life, petrified. Darless followed Alison and Jon brought up the rear, keeping an eye on the Twins.

Jon watched Alison's long hair flowing back toward him, her robes fluttering, her staff held at the ready. *God, you are impressive and beautiful!* he placed in her mind. She blushed, but no one saw it.

Chapter 16 The Ride Like the Wind

The reddening sun cast long shadows across the semiarid plains. Mandy had the horses cantering at the fastest speed she figured was safe for the totally inexperienced Twins. They were traveling along the bank of the mostly dry riverbed. Scrub bushes flew by. "The caravan of hundreds of wagons has left a trail that a blind man could follow," she muttered to herself. Off to her left grassy steppes waved in a slight evening breeze. She figured that they had a couple more hours of light remaining. However, the moon was nearly full, so she resolved to push on by moonlight.

Alison followed right behind matching her pace and trying to observe what Mandy observed when the ranger glanced down at the trail. Tracking was never Alison's forte; she took this opportunity to learn from what she considered a master tracker. Darless, concentrating on staying in the saddle on her galloping horse, came next. The Twins followed next. Though this was their first time on horseback, much of their initial panic had subsided as they fell into the rhythm of the canter. Each tightly gripped their mares with their legs while both hands firmly gripped the saddle horn and reigns. Jon brought up the rear keeping a wary eye on the Twins.

The breeze generated by their run felt refreshing; the reddish hues, romantic. Under normal circumstances, Jon would have taken enormous pleasure from the evening ride. Instead he fretted; was the caravan still safe? Had they come under attack? Would they only find dead bodies on their arrival? Poor William, he thought, what a tough situation for him.

The longer they rode, the more worried Mandy became. *I'm supposed to "Ride like the Wind, but we aren't, just a canter. I could push for a flat out run, but the horses could only sustain that for a short time. And I have no idea how far ahead the caravan is. Has he continued to lead them along this road beside the river? If I could only see ahead, see the caravan, see their plight, see what I must do. Oh William.*

How are we doing? suddenly appeared in her mind from Jon. *The Twins are relaxing a bit. Are we going fast enough?*

That's good. And not really. I do wish we could go faster, but the horses could only do a run for a short time, Mandy placed into Jon's mind.

I know you need to go just as fast as possible, Reylona's orders and all. Have you tried to see the caravan? he sent back.

No. They are not in sight. I would not think that they would still be so close to the town; they've got quite a head start, albeit they do travel very slowly. Let me think a minute. Mandy replied and began to form an estimate. She made the assumption that the caravan spend a total of twenty-four hours actual travel time; any more and they would be endangering the horses for such a long haul. If they made say three miles an hour, that would place them about seventy-five miles ahead of them. The cantering horses had already covered about five of those miles, she estimated. But soon she would be forced to walk them and do at the very most two miles an hour. Pitiful. Certainly by traveling all night, they should catch up with the caravan later the next day, assuming the caravan stopped for the night. She sent to Jon, *This will never do! If we are lucky, we might meet up with them by tomorrow night!*

Jon thought for a minute and then suggested, *Mandy, why not try to see through William's eyes? Ukko did say that you should be able to see far now. I can do that sort of thing but only via someone with whom I have a good reality and affection. Perhaps, you can use William to help you see where they are at and what's going on.*

How do I do that? she frantically replied.

Calm down, relax. Then, see if you can see ahead a little farther than your eyes see, he suggested.

Mandy took a deep breath and slowly exhaled, determined to relax as much as possible. She was thankful for the relatively smooth, flat ground under hooves. She looked as far into the distance as she could. Then she tried to see further and got totally confused. *Jon, I can't do it; I think I am imagining it all.*

Okay. Mandy, look one foot beyond where your eyes can see, Jon ordered.

After a pause, Mandy replied excitedly, *Okay, I think so.*

Good. Now look ten feet beyond.

Yes, I believe I am. Now what? Mandy returned.

Alright. Now look a hundred feet beyond, Jon requested.

Oh I get it! I can do this, Jon. Hang on, I'm going way ahead. Keep an eye on things here for me. She realized that she could see without the use of her eyes. Things appeared somewhat different though, and would take some getting used to, she considered. But she was doing it. She pushed a mile ahead, then two, then three. After a couple minutes, she saw the caravan, but had lost track of the distance that they were ahead of her. It confirmed her worst suspicions.

The caravan was under siege. All of the wagons were close together, bunched into an enormous tight formation. They were not moving and were in a small river basin area. The low hills rose on all sides except to the front and rear. Many horsemen were silhouetted against the evening sky on all sides, ringing the wagons. As she watched, a few riders charged down the hill toward the wagons. She saw William stand up and raise his arms. She watched as the riders dropped their weapons and turned around and trot away.

Mandy faintly sensed the presence of Jon in her mind. *Can you see what I am seeing?*

Yes, I'm with you. It looks bad. Look someone is giving William something. Looks like a cup of coffee. I'll try to sense how he is doing. Jon reached out to touch William via Mandy's perception of him. Jon felt an immense tiredness flow over him. *They are trying to keep him awake; I think he is very short of sleep.*

Now what do we do? We simply must get there now! implored Mandy.

Maintain your contact with the caravan and let me think a minute, Jon replied. He knew that if they did not get there very soon, the caravan would very likely not be there when they did arrive. Sooner or later, William would fall asleep. And the riders could charge en mass. *Think, Jon, think like you never have before!* he told himself — if they could only just appear there. It was just like he always did when he stepped from one place to another. Only now there were six and galloping horses to consider. If they just suddenly appeared near the caravan, all six and the horses would be totally startled and likely stumble and fall, spilling the riders. At this speed, it would be catastrophic. But he knew that if he asked Mandy to slow down so that they could avoid falling off, she might lose her contact with the caravan. *Let me prepare the others,* he sent to Mandy.

Darless, we are going to shortly find ourselves riding into the caravan. They are besieged. I'm going to try to make us all arrive there between gallops. Do not be startled.

How? Okay. No wait, I am startled already! she sent back, but braced herself.

Alison, the caravan is besieged. Mandy is watching the caravan at this moment, thanks to Ukko's gift. I am going to step us all there between gallops. Let lose a huge fireball at the riders you will see on the hilltops.

Alright! I'm ready! Say that is pretty cool that she can see that far ahead. I sure cannot, Alison replied.

Mat, May, the caravan is besieged. I am going to get us there in an instant. Here's how it will seem to you. We are galloping along. One step we are here on this road and the next instant we will be close to the caravan. Hang on. Let the reigns lay loose so that the horses can adjust. I'll try to help the horses adjust if I can. Jon found it fascinating to talk to the Twins this way. The two beings were so close together, it was almost as if they were one.

He felt their rising panic and sent out a calming flow their way. Then he had a better idea. *I'm going to take temporary control over your bodies and the horses. Don't fight me, please. Try to relax.*

We don't understand. But — oh we see. We just relax. Okay we are ready, they thought in their minds and Jon, who was now controlling theirs as well as his own body, knew what they were thinking.

Now Jon felt for the horses. It was easy to pick up their rhythm, their footsteps. In a minute, he felt he had the horses under his control as well, so he sent to Mandy, *Okay, here we go. You just keep on looking at the caravan. I will make us arrive on the grassy flat area to the left side.*

Jon, you can do this. Just get everyone together. Ah, now this step is here and this step is here.

From Alison's viewpoint, they were cantering along at a fast, smooth clip as the sun was about to set. In the next instant, hills rose around here. A large number of wagons were packed tightly together in the river bed. Many dark riders rimmed the hills ahead of her. He horse momentarily broke stride but caught itself and continued rushing ahead. She spoke her command word and a beam of magical energy arced up the hill toward the riders. As she watched the streaking energy flow, she decided that it would be best if the fireball covered ten times its usual area of effect but not harm the horses. She watched her spell detonate in its usual red ball of fire. But the ball continued to expand and grow. Normally, it produced a ball thirty feet in diameter. This time, it swept out to three hundred feet, flaming over thirty riders. But most peculiarly, the ball's shape distorted and did not touch a single horse. "Did I do that?" Alison commented to herself.

From Darless' eyes, first she was flying along the dry road bed beside the river. In the next instant she was flying by hundreds of parked wagons, heading slightly up towards some low hills. She could see many riders' silhouettes against the skyline. Since Jon had forewarned her, she had readied a fire ball spell of her own. However, it meant that she needed access to her staff which was strapped across her back. The alu-demon formed her own plan. Just as her eyes took in this entire startling new vista, she levitated up out of the saddle, twisted around so she could touch the staff with one hand and spoke the command word. She saw the enormous ball of fire Alison created; then hers detonated but only in the usual thirty foot diameter. "Hum, what's going on here," she said aloud, and launched a couple more fire balls at the distant riders. She watched her horse gallop on after Alison's and slowly lowered herself to the ground.

From Mandy's viewpoint, she was watching the caravan, yet in one instant suddenly her eyes now perceived what she was seeing. "This is more like it!" she cried, whipping her bastard sword off of her back in a quick draw motion. She urged her stallion into a full running gallop up the hill toward the black riders. She watched the great ball of fire explode ahead of her, but she only smiled. Her war horse was well trained and it did not flinch either and continued its charge into battle.

In less than a minute, she reached the line of bandits; her blade sliced to the left and then to the right as her legs maneuvered her stallion weaving in and out of the line. When she had passed through the line, she turned around and cut another path as she descended back toward the caravan. Ten men fell from their saddles in her wake.

Mat and May blinked. In that instant their eyes now saw a totally different place. To their right lay the wagons; to their left, a huge ball of fire demanded their attention, followed by several smaller balls. They saw Mandy charge up the hill slicing into the line of horsemen, turn and slice through once again as she galloped back toward them. Then, they noticed their horses were not moving, just panting heavily after that long run. Both rubbed their eyes in disbelief several times before turning around to look at Jon who was asleep in the saddle.

It took every ounce of concentration Jon could muster to control so many at the same time and not interfere. Vaguely he saw the fireballs explode; he was more intent on stopping the Twins and his horse. He felt their legs moving and slowed their motions gradually. Only when the ground below his finally was motionless, did he pause to look around to get his bearings, and saw Mandy galloping down the hill toward them. He had done it! He could relax now; and he did so. His eyes shut. The next thing he saw was the light of the morning sun warming his face.

From the startled viewpoint of those in the caravan who were preparing for the worst case scenario when William finally fell asleep, suddenly out of nowhere beside them came the thunderous cantering of a large war horse whose female rider bore an enormous sword. Involuntarily, all eyes followed the horse and rider as she rapidly closed upon the line of bandits on the left ridge top. Another war horse galloped from thin air right behind the mysterious warrior. This female rider, robes and long hair flowing in the draft bore a wooden staff in one hand. Their eyes caught the huge ball of fire erupting amongst the ranks of the bandits. Then another smaller horse thundered from thin air bearing yet another woman with a staff across her back. Shortly afterwards, several smaller balls of fire erupted amongst the bandit lines. Then a pair of riders, pale faced and clinging tightly to the saddle horns, appeared from nowhere followed by yet another rider. The last three slowed almost at once and stopped just beyond the lead wagon.

The caravan's nominated leader, Raul d'Freeze, an experienced scout for the Red Guards, now retired, was the first to grasp the situation. He had been stoking a small fire, keeping the coffee pot boiling attempting to do anything necessary to keep William awake. "In all my born days, I've never seen the likes of this!" he bellowed in his deep bass voice. He drew his sword, just to be on the safe side. All he could see was the back sides of the three nearest riders. "In all my born days," he repeated himself three more times. Then, he added, "I think that help has arrived and none too soon!"

"Say, that's Mandy leading the charge!" cried William, "Mandy Blackthorn, my Liege Lady! Yes, help most definitely has arrived! Boy am I ever glad to see her; I thought that I would never see her again." He threw his hat high into the air and began cheering. Soon the hundreds of fellow travelers joined in, waving and yelling encouragement. Mandy joined up with Alison and Darless and trotted back to Jon and the Twins and the caravan. They could not help smiling at the very warm welcome they were receiving.

When they got close to the Twins, the pair forced a smile on their pallid faces. Although they were no longer moving, except the heavy panting from their horses, their hands still held onto the saddle horn in a vice grip. Neither dared to move a muscle. When Mandy was close, May whispered, "Now what do we do? And I think something might be wrong with Jon."

At once Mandy took charge, "Alison, you and Darless see what's with Jon. I'll take care of the Twins. Okay, you can relax your grip now." And she took the two pairs of reigns from them, holding the horses and had them dismount. "No, not that side. Always mount and dismount from the horse's right side. You'll spook them if you go off on their left." Both Twins hit the ground unexpectedly hard.

"Ouch, my legs aren't working properly anymore," exclaimed May crumbling to the ground.

Chuckling, Mandy explained, "You'll get used to riding in a couple days. They are stiff and sore mainly because you were gripping the horse too hard and you kept your legs tense. Try walking around a bit. That'll loosen them up."

"Jon's asleep in the saddle!" proclaimed Alison. "I think he is otherwise all right."

"I concur," Darless added. "He's just exhausted from the effort to pull us all ahead here to the caravan. That was some trick he pulled off! Pretty amazing indeed! Looks like we are just in time too."

By this time, Raul and William had closed the several hundred feet from the caravan wagons to where the six stood. "Boy am I ever glad to see you, Mandy!" William cried giving her a warm hug! "I thought that I would never get the chance to see you again; it did look pretty bad here."

"Hail and well met indeed!" Raul added. "You have saved the day. Look there on the ridge line, the bandits are pulling out. Finally we can get on our way again."

Everyone turned to look. Indeed, most of the riders had already departed. And the few that remained were just in the process of turning around and leaving as well. "I was at my wit's end. Do you think it is safe to have the caravan move out now, Mandy? Or should we stay put? How did you get here? What's happened back in Freetown?" asked Raul.

Throwing back her hair, she laughed, "Which one do you want answered first?" Then, she sobered up and became serious, "I don't know what's been going on here, so it is hard to advise. But this location is a most indefensible one. How on earth did you get boxed in here in this gully?"

He stared at the ground wiggling his feet, "We got ambushed; basically, the bandit raiders drove us into this gully and blocked our forward progress. I got every wagon close together to avoid being picked off one by one. You know, make the best of it somehow."

"Hey, before you get into it, we have to get Jon someplace to sleep before he falls off his horse!" interrupted Alison.

"Let's take him to our wagon," suggested May who had been staggering in small circles getting her legs to cooperate. Mat had done the same and was now stretching. "Only I have no idea where it is."

Raul help them locate their wagon and Mat and Mandy carried the soundly sleeping Jon to the Twin's wagon and tucked him into the makeshift bed. Then, Raul and Mandy held a brief conference, with the others paying close attention. Mandy had Raul explain what had happened since they left the town.

The leader explained that all went well for one day. Then, various scouts began following them along the low distant hills. About thirty-six hours ago, this large band of bandit swarmed down upon them. William explained that he stepped forward and faced the oncoming riders and forced them to turn tail and head home, giving up the fight. As far as Raul was concerned, William had performed a miracle. Quickly he had the wagons form a tight formation, ten abreast, and they kept on moving for a short time. After that initial encounter, the bandits dogged them from the nearby hills. When the caravan rounded the last bend, they found nearly a hundred riders blocking any further forward progress. So Raul had gotten all of the wagons into this tight formation and took up a defensive posture.

Eventually, more riders attempted to close on the caravan. When they got sufficiently close, William had them decide to give up the fight and go home as he had done before. This, of course, brought cheers from the travelers and left the raiders in total mystery about what was happening to their men. After a few more hours of experimenting, the bandits figured out that some magic must be coming from William and that they would just wait until he fell asleep. "We've been forcing coffee down him ever since keeping him awake."

"But I'm so tired, I could fall asleep on my feet like Jon did," interjected William. "If you don't need me for a while, I am going to get some sleep!" Mandy gave him a good night kiss and walked him to his makeshift bed beside Jon in the Twin's wagon.

"I know you would prefer to sleep on the ground in your bedroll, but if we decide to travel on a bit more tonight, we'd have to wake you. This way you can get your much needed rest. See you in the morning," said Mandy and she gave him another big kiss. As she did so, she felt his muscles relax. She left him smiling contentedly, dreaming about her.

She slowly walked back to Raul and the others. By the time she had returned, she had her plan worked out. "Raul, I think the best thing to do is to get the wagons moving for a while at least. I will ride ahead and Alison and Darless can ride the flanks. We will look for a more defensible place to camp for the night. The horses and mules are well rested, so we can push them a bit. I know everyone else is overly tired from this ordeal, but I think the worst is yet to come." After a brief pause, she added, "And let everyone know that when we finally camp for the night, we will all gather in a circle and we'll tell them what has happened back in Freetown. For now, just know that the town is totally safe from the demons. They will not again be waging their war games in Freetown." That brought a smile to the veteran and he began moving amongst the groups explaining what they were going to do.

May, also very tired, crowed into her wagon along with Jon and William for some sleep; Mat took over the driving of their wagon. Within a few minutes, Mandy led the caravan out of the low spot and back onto the road beside the stream which still ran eastward. This time, she had the wagons formed into twenty rows each with ten columns in close formation. Alison and Darless took up their positions on the ridges to either side. Raul insisted that a couple other of his men ride with each of them. And they slowly moved on down the dry, dusty, road as the sun set before them in the west. The nearly full moon had risen in the east behind them and provided all the illumination Mandy would need.

However, for the adventurers, this new pace travel seemed excruciatingly slow and boring. The rush of the long day's events gave way to boredom. Mandy felt the telltale signs of fatigue setting in, but forced herself to stay alert and look for a more defensible location to camp for the night. Soon she realized that this was going to be a difficult task indeed. Supporting only scrub brush, the semi-arid terrain of low undulating hills offered little in the way of overall protection. "I'll just have to make the best of it and find something fairly soon before we fall asleep in the saddle like Jon," she muttered to herself.

They had covered about four miles when Mandy found a hill that was just slightly taller than those around it. Here she decided to make camp and rode back to inform Raul who agreed with her choice of location. Raul quickly set about the task of directing the incoming wagons into a proper defensible formation. Mandy watched and aided where she could. The wagon drivers needed a lot of explanations. They were, for the most part, inexperienced drovers. The camp formation consisted of tethering all of the horses and mules at the top of the hill which was also at the center of all the wagons. Wood was a scarce commodity and several charcoal pits were strategically positioned beyond the rows of animals. In one smaller area, a couple of men dug several latrines.

The wagons were formed first like spokes radiating outward from the top of the hill, just beyond the common area and the animals. To loose animals on this trip was a death sentence; they were now highly prized and well protected at all times. Then, at the ends of the "spokes" the remaining wagons were pulled in tightly into a circle with no outside entrance. This formed a solid barrier. Enemies could not ride into this camp. The diameter of the tight circle of wagons was two hundred feet making the circumference of the outer wall of wagons nearly a quarter of a mile around. More than half of the wagons had no top, only tarpaulins covered its contents. There were several carriages pressed into duty but these made sleeping very difficult. Most folks bedded down on the ground beneath their wagons.

Mandy next looked after their six horses, trusting no one else with their well-being. Alison and Darless were most grateful for this because both were nearly asleep on their feet. The ranger also observed that nearly all of the other folks were dead tired as well.

After the camp was established and everyone began gathering in the central common area, Mandy decided to keep this short. She elected herself as spokesperson. She explained that Freetown was now safe, giving a very brief account of the action. She did not mention their trip to Ukko's realm. "I am very tired and so are you all. Let's call it a night and tomorrow over breakfast, we will tell you all about the events." Everyone agreed with that and hastily returned to their wagons and some most needed sleep.

Raul took care of posting ten guards strategically around their encampment. He left strict orders for them to wake him and Mandy if anything suspicious occurred. The first ten would be relieved in two hours by another ten, and they in another two hours and so on until morning. Finally he too turned in having been awake for nearly the last forty hours. No one rose early the next morning, except those on guard duty. The night passed totally uneventful.

By the time the late risers had finished breakfast and cleaned up the camp and were ready for the day's travel, three hours of daylight had passed. Mandy had everyone gather around the central commons and the six began relating the events of the freeing of Freetown. Alison did most of the talking, describing the actions that had occurred. Mat and May were introduced as the famous black garbed protectors of Freetown, the Twins. With all that had occurred, the twins knew that there was no escaping being unmasked. And since they were now officially leaving the town, it was at long last safe for their secret to be exposed. They received a huge round of applause and choruses of thank you's. Their faces flushed slightly at all of this attention, but they beamed with pride.

When the folks learned that all six had been taken to Ukko's realm and their Twins had been given the honor of being Holy Children of Ukko, the noise and cheering was absolutely deafening. It took nearly an hour to present all of the events and answer myriad questions.

Next, Alison also took the time to explain what her lands looked like and what they would find, green grassy hills, dense forests, much game and plenty of rainfall. "It's heaven!" someone shouted, and everyone laughed. No one asked the key questions of how far away was it and how many days travel would it take to get there, fortunately. For these, no one had any answer.

At long last, as far as Mandy was concerned, the hitching of the wagons began. Confusion was avoided by first moving the outer circle of wagons slightly apart and hitching them. The wagons forming the spokes were made ready next. And those who were to ride saddled up last.

Mandy took this interlude time to discuss travel plans with Raul. "If you don't mind, Raul, I am assuming command of this caravan, but you are second in command." She half expected an argument. After all, he was a seasoned veteran and a man.

"After yesterday, my prayers have been answered. I was way out of my league. You have no idea how your words are music to my ears!" He added hastily, "But please don't tell my men that." She nodded and smiled her agreement.

Raul then explained that he was sure that there was a small village ahead and that they should pass it later this day. What lay beyond, he had no idea, only vague rumors. No one had any real maps of these Lost Steppes, for there was nothing here of any interest to place upon a map. Mandy felt a bit sick at her stomach as he told her this.

Mandy subsequently took Alison aside for a hasty conference. "Okay, Alison, we simply must have some idea of where we are at, what lies ahead, how far, and so on. Otherwise we are traveling totally blind. Yes, I know if we just keep going west, we will eventually get to your lands. But will we all starve to death before then or run out of charcoal or fodder for the horses? I am really concerned with this ill-planned venture. There is so much that could go very wrong, to say nothing of these bandits and the like."

"So if we had a map, no matter how sketchy, that would help you plan this better, right?" the young mage asked. "I can levitate way up there and see for miles in this land; perhaps I can see the village Raul told you about. That would give you something to go on for now."

"Yes, that would help for a short while," the frustrated ranger replied.

"Okay, I will first try to spy out the lands before us. Then, I will teleport back to my home and see if I can find some kind of map. I should be back before nightfall," Alison replied. She did not mention how she would be able to find the caravan after they had been traveling all day in order to safely return. She went to find Jon to tell him what she was planning and to give him a good bye hug and kiss.

"Oh don't fret so, Jon," she said after Jon protested her leaving. "You are going to have your hands full helping the Twins. You know that they are going to have many, many questions for you. You are going to have to sort of train them a bit, you know." He agreed and gave her a long hug and kiss.

"Say, wait a minute," Jon hold on to her arm as she was about to leave. "It just occurred to me, how are you going to know where we are at in order to teleport back? That is what was causing all my worrying, love."

She smiled, "I've already figured that one out. I'll come to you, love. I can sense you now, rather like you do me. I just hope I don't seem to be screaming when I send you a message. That's rather embarrassing, you know," she teased, but it was truthful. She did feel embarrassed that she had not yet mastered this skill.

"Hey, if it is a map of this area you want, I have an idea. Please bring back some paper I can draw on," he requested. She agreed.

Alison proceeded to float up high into the sky to survey the land ahead of them. She saw a sea of endless, low rolling hills, but there was indeed a small wooded area still many miles ahead. Small swirls of smoke rose from within it; the village, she assumed. When she landed, she described it to Mandy and finally holding her staff in one hand, she disappeared from view, arriving above the hilly remains of Castle d'Ambrose and her home beneath it in what used to be the dungeon.

No one was about, as was expected. She ducked through the wall of thorn bushes that Lady Ursla had grown for her which hid the entrance. Quickly she set about the task of finding a map form amongst all those that she had accumulated. "Here are Verbenloc and my ruins," she said to herself, spreading out her map of her lands. "I know I am at the southern edge of the vast green prairie land, the Green Way." She spread out another map. "Yes, here are the northern and western sections of Green Way. Yes, there is Banner's Tower at the very edge beside Banner. Now to find out what's further west." She then spent an hour searching through every map she had accumulated, all to no avail. "Okay, now what shall I do?"

She fixed herself a cup of tea and pondered her situation. They had to know just what course to steer to get her to her lands and what distances were involved and where supplies could be acquired. She had never been to Banner, though the deserted tower was in her picture book. Until now, there had never been any reason to venture to the westernmost edge of the known lands. "Well, it is plainly obvious to me. I shall have to go to Banner and seek a map there. Why didn't I think of that before! Silly me." Alison gathered together a few supplies, stowing them in her portable hole and then left her dungeon home.

Once outside the thorn bush barrier, she surveyed the long rolling green hills. They looked so lush compared to the Lost Steppes. If only she could get these people here, she was sure they would love the new environment. Life would be so much easier than it was back in Freetown. For a minute she dreamed of what this area would look like with an impressive castle standing guard over a newly built village with extensive farms stretching off into the distance. She imagined villagers happily going about their tasks, children playing in the dirt roads. *Children, Jon has never mentioned them.* She wondered what he thought about starting a family. "Stop imagining things, Alison. First, you have to get the people safely here and that means you have to find the way." She concentrated and muttered her familiar chant.

She vanished from the green meadows and appeared above a large town nearly the same size as Freetown. From her vantage point high above the city, she surveyed its layout, seeking some reference points to guide her. It seemed a bewildering array of streets bustling with folks going in all directions. She lowered herself to the ground on a side street avoiding calling much attention to herself. Quickly she made her way to the wide street which she calculated would be a main thoroughfare.

She began asking passersby for directions to a map shop. The tenth person was able to give her some good directions and she set off at a brisk pace. In fifteen minutes, she entered Blake's Maps. The distinctive smell of scrolls and parchments greeted her nostrils. She found it a pleasant odor. An elderly gentleman greeted her; she was the sole customer. "Welcome stranger. How can I help you this fine day?" He had greying hair, his face was clean shaven but pronounced age lines bespoke his age.

"I am after maps that show what lay to the east, far to the east. Have you ever heard of a town out on the Lost Steppes called Freetown?" She asked, hoping that he might have heard of the town.

"Well, I certainly do have a map of the lands to the east of here up to Hell's Gate in the Desolation Range." He went to one large cabinet. There were twelve drawers in it, each three feet square but only three inches high. All were filled with maps of various kinds. He pulled out one and laid it across the cabinet top for her to see.

Alison looked at it wondering where Banner was. The map maker spied her hesitation and said, "You are new in town, I take it. Here is Banner," he pointed to the city on the extreme left edge near the middle of that side. On the far right, a mountain range ran from top to bottom, labeled Desolation. A narrow passage cutting west to east through its middle was labeled Hell's Gate. A thin wavy line ran from Banner across the map and up to the mountains. There was some kind of pass there; she saw that Hell's Gate had Deadman's Pass in parenthesis below it. Far north and east of Banner was a dot labeled Tannersville. No other towns were labeled.

He watched her study the map and guessed at her motives. "You would not want to go that way, my dear child. Oh no. Certainly you don't want to go to the Hell's Gate. The Desolation range is full of nasty giants. Why do you suppose it's called Deadman's Pass?" he said rhetorically. This, of course, pricked her interest. Alison spent twenty minutes pumping the shopkeeper for information. Most of it she figured was rumor and exaggerated tales of travelers. But it would give her some idea of what lay there.

She asked for any maps of what lay beyond. "Not much call for that," was his reply. But he looked. After a couple minutes, he found a crude map made by one Rugby Jones, Adventurer Extrodinarie, or so stated his signature. On the other side of Deadman's Pass lay the Ghost Marshes with an annotation of "Ghostly Eyes Follow You" written in the center of the marsh. Some distance to the south lay a land called Vyderland which Alison recognized from the maps at Ravenwash as belonging to people worshiping the evil Morrigan. She shuttered at the thought. Further east lay an area labeled Dead Sea. From there, she saw the familiar river waving its east-west course all the way to Freetown and the Blank Mountains to the east of Freetown. She knew she had just the needed maps. She paid him a little extra for the maps and asked directions to the nearest park area.

It took her another ten minutes to get to the park, having lost her way a couple times. But finally she found it, an oasis of green lawn and trees. Numerous children were playing tag and kick ball. She found an isolated, quiet spot and sat down on the lawn, leaning against a tall oak tree. Concentrating, she cleared her mind of all thoughts. She tried to sense or perceive Jon. Her plan was to sense him and teleport there. Unfortunately, she had never done this sort of thing before and she failed to find him. "Perhaps the distance is too great," she rationalized. "How will I ever get back to the caravan?" she wondered. Before panic set in, an idea formed. "They could not have gone far. I just go back to where I originally left them, going high into the sky and spy them off in the distance. Then, it is just a short hop to get there." She smiled at her cleverness. And then she executed it with flair. Actually, she arrived above where she had departed late in the morning, found the caravan as a small dot in the distance, transported high above them, spotted Jon's wagon, and then materialized sitting beside him.

Jon jumped nearly six inches off the seat, dropping the reigns in the process. Alison and the Twins who were sitting in the back of the wagon began laughing at him. "You startled me," he muttered. "Now how do I get the reigns back?" They were now trailing on the ground beneath the wagon. She smiled coyly and muttered a chant. Jon watched as the reigns slowly rose up and placed themselves back into his outstretched hands.

"Like that," she replied, stifling a laugh. The Twins roared.

"Hey, that is pretty cool! How did you do that? And welcome back, Love," he queried.

"I am a wizard, you know," she teased and gave him a kiss. "How's everything going here?"

"Quiet as a door mouse," Jon said, but then he added seriously, "We are being followed discretely from a long distance. See way over there on the distant hilltop. You can occasionally see a rider or two trailing along with us. The bandits have not given up totally, that's for sure. Probably biding their time. Were you successful?"

"Darn, I'd hoped they would have given up. Yes, got two maps. But we are in for a long trip, probably dangerous too. It may be a thousand miles that we have to travel, all of it looks pretty dismal. I'll see what Mandy thinks about it all. We are getting close to a village I think. Are we stopping there do you know?"

"Mandy was talking like we would," Jon sounded hopeful. Riding in a slow moving wagon was not much fun.

"Here, I'll drive for a while," and she grabbed the reins from him. "Can you please play me a tune? I'm beginning to miss a little music." Jon grinned and poked around for his flute. It was a little jerky trying to play from a bumpy wagon, but he managed to pick out several tunes. He realized he missed the discipline of daily practices and resolved to find a way to get them going again, once all this was settled. The time passed idly for both.

Around mid-afternoon, the dark green patch on the horizon had grown steadily in size until everyone recognized a large grove of trees. A village lay beneath its boughs for tendrils of a bluish smoke wafted up into the sky from within the trees. The caravan continued to follow the dirt trail which led straight to the trees. Spirits rose among the travelers as they neared the village. When they reached the edge of the trees, a side road branched to the right into the trees and village while the main road continued on its westerly course. Here at the junction the caravan halted. Mandy rode back to confer with Raul and the others.

A couple minutes later, Mandy, Alison, Darless, Jon, May and Mat rode off down the side road to check out the village. Raul felt it safer with this large a caravan to not get boxed-in in any way. He and twenty of his guards took up positions around the wagons. As the six rode toward the village, Alison quickly told everyone what she had found out from the maps she'd acquired, particularly rough distance estimate, terrain and lack of towns along their way.

"That is very useful information. Thanks for getting it," she replied with a stern tone in her voice. "I was afraid these people were ill prepared for this journey. Now I am convinced and very worried. We are going to need supplies and a lot of them, probably more than any one village could spare. Let's see what we can get here. Whoa," she called out to her horse. A large sign hung from a tree branch announcing the name of the village, Hope's Lost. "Zounds, what a dismal name for a village!" The others echoed her sentiment. They continued walking their horses into the village which opened up before them.

A dozen children were playing hoop ball in the large common central open area of the village which consisted of about twenty thatched huts laid out more or less in a circle. Blue smoke rose from the blacksmith shop along with the clanking of hammer on steel. As soon as they rode into the village, the kids stopped their game. Several rushed excitedly toward them, while many of the littler ones scampered home as fast as they could run. Strangers were rare in Hope's Lost. "Hi ho," said the tallest boy, "You want John the blacksmith? He's over there. Most everyone that comes here wants him," he went on trying to be helpful.

"Sure, that's as good a place to begin as any," Mandy replied smiling. She dismounted and the others followed suit.

"Are you mighty warriors?" asked the same lad, spying her huge bastard sword across her back.

"You'll have to excuse Robert," said a middle aged woman who had just come up to greet them. By now, dozens of adults were coming out of their houses to see the new-comers.

"Oh that's all right. Yes, Robert, I am Mandy Blackthorn, Lord of my castle far away, and a mighty warrior of Reylona, goddess of the forests and meadows. I'm leading a rather large ill-prepared caravan from Freetown heading far, far to the west. We've come basically looking for some supplies, if you have any to spare."

"Freetown, my, you are far from home that's for sure. We don't get many visitors out here," she replied. "John's the man to see for equipment and such. Do you need food supplies?"

"Well, actually, yes, we do — stuff that can sustain folks and not spoil on a long trip. But I don't expect to find much here. You probably have a hard enough time as it is. This village is a long way from anywhere," Mandy stated the obvious.

The villagers all laughed heartily, but the six adventurers did not understand the joke and look mystified. Finally, one older man with two teeth missing, explained, "We like it that way. This is Hope's Lost after all. The sheriffs of Morrigan to the south just leave us alone cause here Hope's

Lost. But actually it is just the opposite," he winked while the others laughed even harder.

"Quiet you fools, you are confusing our guests," said a deep bass voice. The blacksmith, John, wearing his leather apron, had just come to see what was going on. His arms were well tanned from the sun and the heat of his blast furnace. "Pay them no mind. Come on over to my shop. Martha, you fetch them some mugs of ale. Come on kids, make way for our guests." He turned and led the way to his blacksmith hut. They tied their horses to the hitching posts and sat down on the long bench in front of his hut whose front half was open on three sides. The blast furnace was in the center of this area.

The villagers followed them and sat outside on the ground straining their ears so as to not miss any word that was said. Mandy again explained their needs. "I'd like to buy a wagon and team if one is available and selling it would not pose a hardship on the village."

"You are in luck. I have a brand new one that I finished up about a week ago. As far as the team goes, Rupert picked up some strays recently. We can sell you them, they are not draft horses, mind you, nor are they trained to pull wagons. But they can be I expect," John explained. Martha and two other women arrived with mugs and a large pitcher of ale. Two teenaged girls brought a couple of baskets with oval breads and a bottle of honey.

"Hum, this sure is good bread and ale!" exclaimed Jon, which brought smiles from the women. Over the snack, they learned a bit more about Hope's Lost. These were pioneer families, all of them. Many years ago they discovered this oasis here in the steppes. Essentially, an artesian spring surfaced here and the bountiful desert region flourished nearby. They raised or grew nearly everything they needed. A rich iron ore vein was exposed on the bank of the mostly dry river bed. The only thing they really needed was more farm animals.

Alison picked up on this at once, "So really, you would rather be paid in chickens and ducks and the like, not in gold?"

"Well, yes, as a matter of fact," John replied; she detected a bit of hope in his demeanor.

She smiled, "You are in luck. I just came from Banner and passed more chickens than you could shake a stick at. Why don't you make up a list of what you really need, and

Darless and I will go get it for you. That way you will be helping us out and we will be helping you out; a great trade all around." That caused quite a stir among all of the listening villagers. "Great's" and "wow's" echoed behind the six along with "is they really wizards, mama?" and "I told you so's."

"This is our luck day!" exclaimed John, "You got a deal! Let's get down to business. Come out back, I'll show you the wagon. Martha, you see to what way food we got to spare. Come on, it's this way." He led Mandy, Jon, and Mat off to see the wagon, while the others accompanied Martha to see about food supplies.

Within a short while, the deal was struck. With his list of needed animals safely tucked in one of her robe's pockets, Alison was ready to go back to Banner. With a big smile on her face, she thought to Darless, *Let's give the kids a magic show as we leave.* She and Darless both holding their staffs in their hand stood in the center of town. Alison also held onto Darless' hand. "Okay, kids, the Great Wizards are off to fetch the chickens. Watch closely." She muttered her command word, concentrated on arriving high above Banner once more. Poof. She and Darless found themselves right on target, a hundred feet above the city of Banner, floating gently to the ground, compliments of Alison's magical ring. Back at Hope's Lost, the kids shrieked when they suddenly vanished before their eyes. The littler ones blinked and rubbed their eyes in complete disbelief. Many were asking their mommies how they did that and if they could learn to do that.

Meanwhile, Mat rode back to let Raul know what was occurring and for him to lead the caravan onwards. The others would catch up in a short while. Mat went with them, confident that if something ill should occur he could somehow let May know.

Jon played his flute for the children to help pass the time and liven things up a bit. Shortly, an older man brought out his fiddle and joined him and then a young girl joined in with her guitar like instrument. Many of the children played rhythm on pairs of wooden spoons. All the while, Mandy and the others helped prepare the wagon and team and load the precious supplies that they villagers could spare.

A half an hour later, there was another poof of magic accompanied by much clucking a squawking as the wizards returned floating down holding onto numerous wooden crates. They had brought several dozen chickens, two roosters, four ducks, four geese, four lambs, and several smaller animals, including two kittens for the kids. For these hardy pioneers, these were priceless commodities worth far more than golden coins. It offered future survival.

They said their farewells and thank yous and left with Mandy driving the nearly full wagon. The two horses were riding horses unused to pulling a heavy wagon and she did not trust anyone else to their initial training. All of the children followed them to the edge of the village. Once they were back on the main road, Mandy said, "Well that was a refreshing change, Hope's Lost is really Hope's Gain. Thanks for getting the animals, you two. That was brilliant thinking."

"Yes," replied Alison from her light war horse, "it was actually fun too. They are really fine people. I hope they continue to thrive and prosper. But is certainly is a harsh existence way out here in the middle of nowhere, surrounded by nasty bandit peoples on all sides. I can see why they do not want any money. Nothing for bandits to steal."

"Safer that way," added Darless.

"And they have music, too," Jon inserted, "did you notice?" They all laughed.

In another half hour, they joined with the caravan. Mandy had an experienced drover take charge of their wagon, while she got back on her medium war horse and rode off to take over the point position way out in front of the caravan. Onwards moved the caravan. And the day light hours passed slowly and uneventfully.

Mandy found that the hills were getting a bit higher and once more they camped at the top of the tallest hill around their location. They used the same defensive setup and the travelers seemed to get the hang of how to orderly go about parking their wagons. They were learning and learning quickly, which was a good omen, Mandy felt.

The six adventurers shared the two wagons and had them parked side by side in one of the spokes radiating outward from the tethered horses. The Twins had had the foresight to bring along sufficient rations for the six of them and May volunteered to play chef while Jon volunteered to do the dishes. That left the others free to visit with fellow travelers, which is just what Mandy wanted to do.

She held a quick conference with the others. "I want to visit all of the wagons. We need to know just how many days of rations each has got and how many days of fodder for the animals they have. Explain to them that we are trying to see how we are going to make it. Tell them we face at least forty days' worth of travel. I doubt that any of them brought that much with them. So let's try to see where we all stand. Got the idea?" The others nodded. And they divided up the caravan into fifths and set about the task, being as gracious as they could when asking for these details. Incidentally, Jon also asked if any had any musical instruments. He had an idea to form up a caravan band if possible to lighten hearts around the evening meals.

They returned to the two wagons about the same time as May had their dinner prepared. So while they ate, each gave their reports to Mandy, who made marks on the ground, tallying up the quantities. "Zagroot zounds!" she uttered when the last report had been given. Everyone knew this was not a good sign and waited for her to explain. "One week at best and we'll be out of food."

"Say," William interrupted, "did I see several sacks of grain in your new wagon? If so, we can stay in one spot for a day, I can bake up a huge quantity of bread that will stay edible for maybe a week."

"Terrific, William. And while you bake, some of the rest of us will go hunting. A couple of large deer will extend it a couple of days, if we cook it all first. We don't have enough salt to preserve it properly for any lengthy duration," Mandy added. "I'll keep my eyes open for signs of any grazing herds."

Jon washed up the dishes and then continued visiting all of the other wagons in search of musicians. In the end, he found a fiddle player and a guitar player. And the three of them agreed to strike up a band the next evening, for now it was getting dark.

Meanwhile, the others studied the maps that Alison had brought back. The estimate was that the caravan was now a little over one hundred miles from Freetown. Another four days and they should make the Dead Sea, whatever that was. When Jon finally joined them, she showed him her maps.

"Ah ha," he exclaimed with relief, "now I can put locations in their proper perspective. You see, with all of that mental contact I had with the demon lords' minds, I saw many partial maps of this area. I do believe I can add some details to this rather sketchy one." And he began to draw in some additional details.

On their far eastern side, the high red granite Blank Mountains angled from the north towards the southeast. Freetown was centrally located uniformly about seventy miles from each of the seven demon lord's main castles. In fact, Jon pointed out that these seven castles were perfectly aligned, forming a seven-sided figure, but he did not know what you call a seven-sided shape. They had been at Metrarch's Ravenwash Castle which was the northernmost cradled in a spur of the Blank Mountains. Southeast and also in a long valley of the mountain range lay Stone Blight Castle of f'Tarch followers, while their arch enemy, Lord Jarred held sway in the Castle Arroyo just to the southwest of Ravenwash. That meant, there was absolutely nothing for leagues to the west and north of the lands of Jarred. Jon wondered just how far that demon's influence extended. He would discover this information, but not for some weeks yet.

Slicing nearly due east-west across the entire Lost Steppes lay the river Grande whose origins lay in the Blank Mountains east of Freetown in the realm of South Reach Castle under Lord Junanon's influence. Jon pointed out that at least they had a straight as a arrow line to follow across this wasteland so they could not get lost if they followed the dry riverbed.

Directly south of Freetown some seventy miles lay El Pointe Castle, home of El Grad followers. This castle was at the northern-most point of the low Red Hills which expanded both eastward and westward from El Pointe, forming a natural barrier separating the Lost Steppes from the Barren Steppes — home of the assassins. Jon sketched in a town perhaps forty miles due south of El Pointe just beyond the end of the Red Hills. It was called Assassi, the home of El Hadid, the assassin leader.

Further, about seventy miles southwest of Freetown lay the Last Oasis, home of d'Raul followers. Here, the Dry Wash, which began new El Pointe, ended its northwesterly flow.

Similarly, to the southeast lay Muscat, home of m'Doth followers.

Jon sketched in the roads that connected these castles and nearby towns as best he could from his memory. William drew a line from Muscat on down southeastwardly. He told Mandy, "I came up this road from Castle Blackthorn. It was a very long distance." So now Mandy knew two key items. One, she knew for sure her world, her lands, were connected eventually to those of Alison. Two, she knew there was a way home for her, albeit a nasty road to travel. However, she did not know what she really wanted to know which was "Is there a more direct and safe route to Alison's lands?" She would not learn that information for quite some time yet.

However, all were much more interested in the details Jon could add to the west where the caravan was heading. Jon indicated the scale of their undertaking. If you took the total distance from Ravenwash in the north to El Pointe in the south, the far distant Desolation Range which they must cross lay about two and one half times that distance from Freetown.

Mandy did some rough calculations. They were as far as Hope's Lost. If Jon's estimates were correct, they had some three hundred miles of exceedingly arid steppes to cross. Given an optimistic daily travel rate of twenty miles, it would take all of two weeks to reach the mountains. They had supplies enough for one week. It did not look at all well as far as she were concerned.

Just before sundown, Mandy and Alison walked the short distance down the hill to explore the nearly dry river bed. "Caution," Mandy observed, "See those tracks, looks like a snake. I sure don't like the looks of this. Mostly dry sand, hardly a river I'd say." They stepped carefully down onto the sandy bottom of the river. The soft sand gave way to their steps. "Quicksand is very likely when there is water in here," observed the ranger, though none appeared visible to their eyes.

They stopped a few feet from the water itself, which was barely three feet wide in the center-most and deepest channel of this long shallow river. The water looked a bit yellowish. She tasted it and quickly spat it out. "Brackish! Now we have an even bigger problem, Alison, water, or rather the lack of it."

"I guessed this would happen," Alison replied with a big grin on her face. "I don't know about you, but I feel sticky and grungy, long overdue for a bath. But when I was back at my place, I took the liberty of bringing my decanter back with me. It can supply a rather large amount of fresh water."

"You are a genius!" Mandy shook her hand. "You have saved the day and as yet no one even knows that you have! Water is going to be a very scarce commodity. Most all of the travelers have a water barrel in each wagon holding about fifty-five gallons; I'd guess it is at least half gone already."

Alison smiled appreciatively, "I wanted you to be able to just concentrate on getting us a safe passage and perhaps some fresh game. You know, spread the responsibilities amongst ourselves as much as possible. If we really get desperate for food, Darless and I go to Banner and bring back a fair amount using our portable holes."

"You are a treasure! Okay, I'll worry about the path and game; you take the water and supplies," agreed Mandy. Alison did not miss the look of relief on her face. "I'm going to also keep an eye out for a possible watering hole where we all could take a bath. Probably won't find one for some time, though, as this heat tends to dry everything up." The two made their way back to camp.

It was dusk as they arrived back at their wagons. Jon also had just returned, one big smile on his face. "Guess what?" he asked, and without waiting for a reply added, "I've just formed up a small band. Tomorrow evening there will be music floating on the breeze, assuming there is a wind."

"Great, that should relieve any tensions. I know these townsfolk are getting a bit edgy. Most have never been on such a long trip as and we have only begun," Mandy replied, as another unspoken concern of hers just evaporated.

"How about an evening walk, Alison?" Jon then asked, putting his arm lovingly around her waist. She put hers around his and together began to stroll slowly around the hillside among the wagons. They did not see William approach Mandy and lead her off on a walk as well. The two ended up sitting on the ground back to back staring up at the stars and the Milky Way.

"Jon, I've been thinking," she said dreamily. "Do you want any children?" Alison asked the question that had occupied the back of her mind all this day.

"I'd love a bunch of kids! Maybe I'd have my own band!" he teased. "Seriously, I have not asked you about this because they would need a house in which to grow up. I have a big one back in my lands, but that would make you move and I am not even sure I want to live there, you know, permanently. If I did, I guess I'd have to get a job; I certainly want to support you and all the kids." Suddenly, he sat upright. "What on earth am I saying? We got all the money we could ever need. I love it here; my life is where you are at, just being with you is all I want." She gave him a long, loving kiss.

"When we get back, I am going to have a strong castle fortress built for us, my family, and all my villagers. I intend to be able to provide real security for all of us. That's my immediate goal," she stated. "But to have children running and playing at my feet would be a real treasure. But I am terribly afraid that that would be the end of my adventuring days."

Jon saw the dilemma at once. "You can always do your magical research at your castle. And I certainly do not see why you cannot go off on adventures, though with a family, we'd all be fretting and worrying while you are gone."

A tear formed in her eye, "You hit the mark." She sniffled, "Being a woman, this is terribly hard for me. I have my own interests — my magic and helping others in need, though you and others call them adventures. Yet, I want a family, children, want to be home and raise them, to love them, to take care of them. With a man, it is so easy. You can just take off, come and go as you please."

"Now wait a minute," Jon argued. "A father must be there to play with and help raise his kids as well. Alison, my love, you are a being, a beautiful one at that. We both have goals and purposes in life and many that overlap. If you intend to give up your magical career and your unhesitating assistance to others in need just to be married and raise children, I will not marry you. I will not be a party to the enslavement of another being! For that's what I think that would be! We share and share alike. A union is just that, something bigger than either one of us alone. We each help the other expand and accomplish the things we set out to do.

When I said I wanted to join with you, I meant it — you and all you do, your life. We just have to make some slight alterations to fit changing circumstances. You know, no gallivanting off when you are very pregnant. We need to find a good nanny to help us when we do want and need to go on some mission."

Big tears of joy and relief flowed down her cheeks. She hugged him so tightly, he could hardly breathe, and he held on to her. Both said nothing for quite some time. After a long loving kiss, she asked, "Do you want sons or daughters?"

He did not hesitate. "Can I have some of both? Maybe lots of both!" Both spontaneously began laughing.

"Just what do you think I am? A cow?" she teased and both laughed and then hugged each other some more. Just then, Mandy and William, arm in arm, came up to them.

"Ah there you are," she said. Jon detected an urgent tone in her voice. "We've been looking for you two. The camp is being spied upon; I can feel it in my bones."

Both were on their feet instantly. "Where? How many?" asked Jon.

"William and I have caught glimpses of riders, we think, on the far hills to the south. At least we think we saw riders, perhaps just shadows," the ranger replied.

"Sneak attack in the night?" asked Alison, "do you suppose?" Her question was ill formed as she was thinking faster than her words could form.

Mandy thought a bit, she still clung to William, and he, her. "If they were only bandits, I'd say that would be likely since they have been soundly defeated in direct daylight assaults. On the other hand, as Jon pointed out, we are near the lands whose inhabitants worship Morrigan. She prides herself on daylight, open battles, where great deeds can be seen."

"Well then, we will find out soon which we are facing," Jon added. "I'll put my walking stick to work tonight. I've been studying my manual and if I place it in the ground beside me, it will alert me to any approaching danger when such gets to within five hundred feet of me. That should give all of us plenty of advance warning of s sneak attack that gets by the guards."

"Great! What all can the stick do, Jon?" asked Mandy, who was not quite curious about its abilities.

"Dunno all of them yet. Only got to read a bit of the manual today. I'll let you know when I figure them all out. It does do a lot of healing, I do know that," Jon added. They all headed back to their wagons and to warn the guards, some of whom were turning in, to be on the alert for a sneak attack in the middle of the night.

Jon and Alison snuggled together beneath the wagon with Jon's stick firmly stuck in the ground at the side of the wagon. They kissed passionately for some time before falling asleep in each other's arms. Mandy and William also slept beneath a nearby wagon, snuggling as well. No sneak attack came that night, but several guards swore that they saw some movement on the distant hills to the south.

Two more hot, dry days came and went. Hygiene problems only grew in size since no one had been able to clean up for nearly a week. Alison began using her water decanter to refill each water basin in turn during the morning meal time. Jon and his band brought welcome relief each evening; many other folks began singing along when they played local tunes.

They had gone another fifty miles and the terrain looked exactly as it had when they first left Freetown. Only their general fatigue accounted for the distance. Mandy had still seen no game herds, though she did expect to find some for she occasionally spotted evidence of their existence.

The distant riders continued to follow their movements, but always at an extreme distance, well over a mile away. Mandy and Jon both felt that this meant they were followers of Morrigan and not mere bandits. At noon on the seventh day, their suspicions were confirmed beyond all doubt.

As the caravan reached the bottom of a rolling hill, thundering hoof beats broke the relative calm. All eyes turned to the left as wave after wave of charging cavalry bore down upon them from the crest of the distant hill top about a mile away.

"Battle positions!" cried Mandy at the top of her lungs as she galloped from the point over to face the enemy on their left flank. "Lead wagons halt. The rest pull up to the others in very tight formation! Guards fall in behind me. Wizards, behind a wagon."

Frantically, the wagon drivers closed ranks with the wagon directly in front of them. Orderly chaos ensued for the next two minutes as most, hanging on to the reigns, got their family and themselves safely beneath the wagon for cover. Alison, who was on the left flank, dismounted and took a position behind her wagon; Jon held onto the reigns of her horse. The Twins and William soon joined Jon and Alison.

Darless, wearing her tunic of blue with its white cross, rode instead to the side of Mandy. "You forget, only a magical blade can even scratch me. I intend to cause some damage today!" The alu-demon's coal black eyes radiated a fierce determination, bordering on hatred. She held her staff but muttered another spell innate to her species.

Alison, only vaguely aware that Jon took her reigns, concentrated on the approaching cavalry. She could see the banner of legions of Morrigan followers fluttering in the flying air. The men rode medium war horses covered in ornamental cloth hangings. Each man was tightly enmeshed in a silver chain mail. Two ox horns protruded from their helms. Each held a long lance currently pointed in the advance position, high in the air. Jon noted that the caravan's flank was at least a hundred feet long with the wagons positioned so close together.

The lead riders bore down straight toward Alison, or so she thought. Alison changed her mind and spoke a command word and then concentrated on mentally enhancing the magic. She was about to experiment with magic and mental abilities.

A slender bolt of lightning arced forth from her staff straight toward the leading men. They lowered their lances to attack formation and her bolt began to fork and then it detonated, electrocuting the first ten men in their saddles, their bodies blown from their saddles. Behind them, a ball of fire erupted compliments of Darless.

Steel determination was the lot of these battle hardened cavalry, some of the best of Vyderland. While the riderless horses veered off of the charge, those behind bore onwards. Another bolt of lightning took another ten men down, while another ball of fire erupted in their ranks. Still they charged onwards, heedless of life or death.

"Zagroot zounds!" exclaimed Mandy. She knew that she must issue some kind of orders to the guards. Being motionless, they would be slaughtered when the lances struck home. "Flank right!" She cried aloud and began galloping toward the front of the caravan; Raul and the others followed her to relative safety although he wondered what she was doing. This left only Darless astride her riding horse standing before the onslaught.

When Mandy had gotten her men a distance away, she wheeled around and forming the men into a line. As they arced their horses in a wide turn to ride back the way they had come, all witnessed the viciousness of Darless. She had conjured an invisible barrier, a wall of force, just before her. As the charging cavalry approached her, she expanded its dimensions covering the length of the caravan. *No spells for a moment,* she placed into Alison's mind, *force wall.*

Oh my gods, thought Alison! The cavalry, charging at top speed, did not see the slight shimmering indicator of the force field. Others later described the effect as seeing a charging horse suddenly run into a rock wall. The effect was terrible to behold, grim beyond words, as blood and bits and pieces of horse and rider splattered and bounced back onto other riders, who themselves in a second became more blood and bits flying back upon others. Darless poured every ounce of magical energy she could into maintaining her barrier against the tons of force smashing into it. Still she could only hold it for less than a minute before the tremendous forces disintegrated her wall of force. The recoil from the collapsing wall sent her flying backwards off her horse and into the side of a wagon. The blow to her head stunned her, though it did not, of course, cause any physical damage.

But she had had her effect. Fifty men and beasts were totally destroyed. The charge was halted. The remaining fifty riders, many wounded, frantically dropped their lances and reigned in their galloping steeds.

"Now," Mandy yelled, "Charge!" She did not wait for the others to follow her. Bastard sword raised high, poised to strike, she charged into the momentarily stunned cavalry, whose horses were spinning this way and that, as riders fought to regain control and determine how to respond. Her passage through their chaos, left several men short an arm and others seriously wounded. Only their armor saved their lives.

But before Raul could get his guards to follow the path cut by Mandy, William stepped forward. Alison and Jon watched as the remaining men dropped their partly drawn swords and turned around and began trotting off in the direction that they had come, all that remained of the initial charging forces. William now looked quite tired and leaned on Jon.

Simultaneously, Mat, who looked as if he were praying, laid his hands upon William. Jon found it fascinating. For a moment, he could see the energy present in the contact between the two men. The exhaustion of mental energy was like a vacuum sucking energy from Mat, who seemed to channel it from elsewhere into William. Nothing, of course, was visible to the human eye. But Jon was not looking with his body's eyes; these were still looking at his and Alison's horses which he was trying to hold still.

May was the first to reach the semi-conscious Darless. Likewise, she seemed to be deep in prayer as she too laid her hands upon Darless. In a moment, Darless opened her eyes and blinked; she was no longer dazed. Even the large bump on her forehead began to recede as Alison, who had now gotten over to her friend, watched in amazement.

Mandy whirled around for a repeat charge only to find the riders trotting off leaving a bloody pile of dead behind them. Confused, she trotted back toward Jon. "What the heck happened? I turned my back for an instant and they are all gone!"

"William's work," Jon hollered, watching the amazed expression form on the ranger's face as she grasped the significance of William's action.

"Zounds, what a mess!" Mandy commented next as she stood beside the scene, holding in check her panting war horse who was prancing and dancing, unready to give up the fight. "Way to go Darless!"

Now Raul and his riders arrived beside the scene as well. Their pale faces bespoke their total shock; the last two minutes was nearly beyond their comprehension. Likewise the others began to crawl up from underneath the wagons, staring in utter disbelief at the carnage they had just witnessed. Finally, Raul spoke with a tone of reverence they had never heard from him, "My gods, you folks are more powerful than anything I have ever witnessed or heard tell of! If I had not seen this, I would never have believed it! I am forever your most humble servant," and he tried to bow from his saddle only he was not sure to whom he should bow. So he nodded to each of the party in turn.

When he got to Darless, he added, "Remind me never to get on the wrong side on you! That was indeed spectacular."

She smiled and replied simply, "Sorry, but I just got a little angry that medium cavalry would charge a defenseless caravan of simple wagons! I attempted to teach them a lesson in manners." Everyone roared with laughter.

As the shock of the slaughter they had just witnessed wore off, more than a few of the simple townsfolk lost the contents of their stomachs. Seeing this, Mandy urged the caravan to move out at once. Raul also saw the urgent need to get these people as far as possible from the bloody scene and expedited her orders. One by one the wagons began to roll forward once again, though two wagons did not, Jon's and the Twin's.

"Thanks," Darless said to May, "I was really stunned there by the back flow of my own spell. I think I went flying backwards."

"You sure did!" exclaimed May. "I expected to find your head smashed to pieces, yet you only seemed to have a bump. Thanks for letting me try out my new gift from Ukko."

"Thanks for doing it," she replied. "I don't even have a headache now. I thought for sure that my head would ache for days after a bump such as that one! You know what kind of a body I have," she lowered her voice so only May could hear. "In this realm, only a highly magically enchanted blade can actually hurt me." May's eyes opened wide as she grasped significance of what Darless had just told her.

Mandy dismounted and went to check on William. "My heartiest thanks, William. What you did was absolutely amazing indeed! No wonder Reylona has chosen you!" He blushed beet red and muttered "You're welcome. Twas the least I could do to help you out."

Alison was still methodically reviewing all the actions that had occurred. "Darless, that was actually a brilliant piece of thinking, a wall of force. Pretty gruesome in its effect, but it did stop their charge. It was far more effective than my lightning bolts!"

She smiled and replied, "It makes up for me not seeing that they all wore chain mail making fire balls far less effective than electricity. And how did you manage to fork it like that? you got at least ten at one shot?"

Alison would only say, "We'll have to talk about that enhancement a bit later on. It was something that I added after the spell was cast, actually. Maybe you too can do it." She sounded hopeful.

"Well, I am very impressed with all of you," Jon added. "All I got to do was hold the horses as usual. But this time, I did hold onto them," he chuckled, proud that this time he managed to keep them relatively still. Everyone but the Twins and William, laughed. So they had to explain to the twins how Jon always seemed to get to hold their horses during their battles.

"I did feel a bit useless," confessed May with Mat concurring. "We are at home in town conflicts, but out here in all this openness, we are afraid that we are not of much use."

"Nonsense, sis," Alison replied, "I was counting on you two to handle any that got by the front line. I figured between Mat's punches and your illusions, they would quickly be rendered harmless. It's just that Darless and William saw to it that none got by this time. Pretty amazing. We sure do work well together."

"You can say that again," Mandy pronounced.

"We are a team," Jon declared. "You all notice how this time we did not have to do much communicating at all to handle the situation? I think that is really terrific!"

"Say, did any of you notice that they headed straight for me?" queried Alison. The significance of her initial perception surfaced in her mind.

"Well, I thought they were heading for me," Darless commented.

"Well, both of you were close and a good tactic is to take out the wizards as soon as possible," Mandy explained. "At least that is what I would attempt to do."

"Hum," Jon muttered, "I was standing behind both of them." But they did not respond to his thought. He resolved to test his theory should there be a next time.

"Okay, enough of this mutual commendation, we need to search them, confiscate any salvageable weapons, armor and the like. Going to be pretty gruesome task, though," Mandy took charge once again. "We need to move swiftly and so we can catch back up in case they counter attack while we are back here."

"Say," a sudden thought struck Jon. "Do you want the stray horses? Are they useful to us?"

"Sure, but look they are scattered all over the place. We would have to spend far too much time trying to round them up, I'm afraid."

William and Mat, followed Mandy onto the field of carnage and following her orders began searching for useful items. They pitched them over to Alison and May who piled them into the wagons.

Jon, however, walked apart from them and relaxed his mind. He had found that he was becoming rather fond of horses after all. He expanded his awareness outward and began to contact the strolling, grazing horses scattered about the hills around them. One by one, he convinced them to come to him. He did all this with his eyes closed. The others, spying the strays walking their way, turned to watch as the medium war horses, one by one, walked up to Jon and nuzzled him. In the end, when Jon opened his eyes, he found twenty horses standing silently around him.

"Well, if that doesn't take the cake! Jon, do you have a connection with horses that we have not been aware of? Way to go!" Mandy praised him.

"Please, Mandy, come and help me!" Jon whispered, "I got them here but I don't know what to do with them now that they are here!" Quickly Alison, Mandy and William came to his rescue, showing him how to take their reigns, loosen saddle girths and tie them into a chain behind the two wagons.

The seven joined up with the caravan an hour later bringing the new horses and a huge pile of gear with them. Among the items were over fifty money pouches and numerous weapons and twenty intact suits of chain mail. Later the mail was distributed to the guards of Raul for they currently wore only thin leather protection pieces or none at all. From this point forward, they were far better protected in their duties as guards. And their spirits rose accordingly. Even though this time they had not gotten a chance to actually fight, they had followed all orders and done so quickly against overwhelming odds. And that was important in their own eyes as well as in Mandy's.

The rest of the day passed completely uneventful. Still Mandy found no herds of game nor did she find any watering hole where the caravan could pause and bathe. She, along with many others, were incredibly dirty, a mix of dried perspiration mingled with the blood of battle smeared with the dusty sand of the roadway. Her hair was oily and matting, just the opposite of her desires. It annoyed her and distracted her from her duties. And she knew if she felt this way, certainly the others did even more so. She needed to find a large water hole and soon.

That night around the dinner table, she held a conference looking for ideas. The only suggestion came from Alison who volunteered to teleport four people at a time back to her place where they could bathe properly, and bring them back. She estimated that she could manage two round trips a day. Darless added that she could manage one such trip a day. Mandy vetoed it out of hand, fearing the loss of their crucial wizards' protection while they were gone.

Jon piped up, "Well, you really don't need me as such. I could step them there perhaps ten at a time. Then, they could also see where they were ultimately heading. That might also be a morale booster. But then again, in a wizard's home, there's no telling what mischief they could get into by touching the wrong thing," he teased.

"I'd have to re-setup my decanter of water first; otherwise there is no running water down there," Alison replied.

"I think we are going to need that water here for the animals and us," Mandy countered. "This is nearly a desert region which goes on for a good distance yet. I think it is going to be baths from a water bowl all around. Boy, what I wouldn't give for that great bathhouse back in Freetown now!" The others echoed her sentiments.

"On a more serious note," Alison changed the topic, if only to get her mind off of their grubby state, "have we concluded that the attackers are definitely from Vyderland?"

"I'd bet anything on it," concluded Mandy. "We have been most fortunate that they have not deployed their own wizards against us. I wonder why not? Can I see you maps again?" Alison brought out the maps and spread them on the ground for all to examine.

"The only town that is shown is Vyndoc which must be the main city in the area," Alison pointed out. "And it seems to be a very long way to the south of us, perhaps several hundred or so. Mandy, where do you think we are now, approximately?"

The ranger pointed to a spot directly west of Freetown. "I think we are two days travel from this Dead Sea place, whatever it is. But look, we've been followed by these people ever since we left Hope's Lost. And that puts these men a very long distance from home, if their home is indeed Vyndoc. That is strange."

"Well, maybe not," Darless commented, "If this dirt rut called a road is the only road in this entire area large enough to appear on a map, then it would only make sense to have one's bandit groups stationed along the route, especially positioned far from any other towns or villages where victims might find help."

She thought for a minute and then asked, "Mandy, suppose those cavalry men were stationed in Vyndoc. If they attacked us today near midday, how long would they likely have been traveling if they had originally left Vyndoc to come attack us?"

"Good question. They arrived fresh as far as I could tell in the brief encounter," she began her thought process. "From the map, that means they must have traveled some five hundred miles to intercept us. We are about one hundred-seventy miles out of Freetown. If we were to travel that distance, you could estimate that the caravan would need about twenty days. But they came by medium war horse. With good hard riding and not overly taxing the steeds, they could do it in maybe seven days."

"You know, that is kind of what I was feeling. If you track that back, then they left Vyndoc about the same time as the caravan left Freetown," Alison observed. "And what does that suggest?"

"They knew about the caravan and even its departure time!" cried May, suddenly grasping what Alison had been thinking all along. "They had spies in Freetown. That would be a very reasonable assumption."

"Number 1," began Darless, sizing up the situation, "what are they really after? Number 2, how long will it take for those in charge to realize what happened to their cavalry charge? Number 3, how long will they take to formulate a backup plan? And Number 4, how long will they take to catch us to put it into effect? Which, of course, gives us a better idea of where to expect further trouble."

"Well, I would expect that any wizard worth his or her robes would have been spying on the cavalry and already know the outcome," Alison answered the second question. "I'd assume that they have already decided on their next move, to answer your third question. If they come by horse, then allow another seven days to intercept, which tells me that we are very likely safe until a few days beyond the Dead Sea. But what are they after?"

"Booty, probably," put in Mat. "If your assumptions about spies in Freetown are correct, they probably know that this caravan is transporting entire families with all of their amassed wealth, most likely in gems, as we have done. I would hazard a guess that there is a substantial amount of valuable items in this caravan, far, far more than any normal caravan. Just ripe for the pickings."

"Then you think that they are materialistically oriented?" Alison asked. He nodded. But she was not convinced totally. It did seem like a reasonable explanation.

Jon, who had not said much because he did not know much about any of these matters, had been listening and learning. He finally cautioned, "You know, I am not so sure that riches is the motive. These are Morrigan worshipers that we are dealing with here. And if I am not entirely mistaken, Morrigan may hold a deep grudge against me and you all — from when we interfered in her plans for a major war."

"Hum, Jon does have a valid point," Darless commented, "Morrigan could well be holding a grudge against Jon and urging her followers here to exact revenge. They did charge only the area where Jon was at."

"Yes, but we were there too," protested Alison. "If I were attacking, I'd want to take out the opposing wizards as fast as possible. We can argue this both ways. So I really don't think we can really draw any solid conclusions that she is after us." That ended the speculations.

"You know," Jon reflected, "one thing still has me puzzled. I think we have all overlooked this point." All eyes turned to him; each person rapidly checking over all that had happened but finding nothing amiss. He paused and then said, "What is Dispater's involvement in all this?" Indeed, from the surprised looks on the others faces, he knew that they had really forgotten about him completely. Jon had not. He had grown used to the diabolical trickery these gods and goddesses played upon one another. "The Arch-devil does not go joining forces with a Demon Lord, as I understand it, right Darless? They are very much opposites, except in their passion for evil actions." She nodded affirmatively, but was deep in thought, her mind racing down various avenues.

"Maybe it was just some old score he was settling; honestly, there is no way we can figure him out too!" protested Alison. She hated dealing with total uncertainties, the imponderables.

Ignoring her protest, Jon added, "The last time we dealt with Dispater, we became the instruments of his revenge on Morrigan. Is it so farfetched that somehow even now we are playing a part in some scheme of his? On his behalf, though, I must say that he keeps a low profile. We have not seen or heard from him since that meeting back in Ravenwash. Maybe I am just being paranoid."

"As much as I love you," Alison replied, "I think you just worry too much. How could there be any possible connection? I think they are just after the riches the people are carrying with them, that's all. But even if you are right, what could we possibly do about it? Nothing."

Most agreed with her; they absolutely no clue about Dispater's motives. If speculating about the bandits of Vyderland was tenuous, speculation about Dispater was vaporous. Only Darless continued to trace that line of thought and she said nothing.

About this time, a young girl in her late teens with a long pony tail came boldly up to Jon. "Excuse me, my name is Althea. I heard from Albert that you are starting up a camp band. I don't play any instrument, but I do sing pretty well. Do you want a singer in your band?"

"Wow! I totally forgot voice. Sure, that would be great. But I probably don't know any songs you know. But the others do. It's time we got together to play anyway. Come on and let's see what we four can work out," he replied excitedly, forgetting the concerns of the day. "You all get ready for some good old fashioned campfire fun, excepting we don't have the campfire." And he grabbed his flute from the wagon and together the two went in search of Albert and Josh.

Within ten minutes, the camp was treated to a rousing rendition of "A Song of Vainamoin" followed by another half hour of various songs and dances. Spirits rose and for a short while; everything in camp seemed like a normal warm, late summer's evening. Cares evaporated everywhere.

Chapter 17 The Dead Sea

The next few days passed without incident. Monotonously, by day the caravan edged slowly along the dirt road, always heading west. The terrain of low undulating arid hills never varied, like a never-ending sea. Only the Wayward Minstrels, Jon's camp band's adopted name, kept spirits high with their evening blend of familiar songs and dances. Indeed, nearly everyone looked forward all day long to the music of the evening.

This was the sixteenth day since the caravan had left Freetown, early September. Their food supplies were now nearly exhausted. But Alison's decanter of water kept them well supplied on water, even providing enough extra water that the several hundred people could afford to waste some with basin baths, as Jon called them. All of the extra food that they had acquired from the generous folks in Hope's Lost had been doled out to those whose supplies had run out. Only the many sacks of wheat remained.

Mandy had kept her eyes open for water holes and for game herds, but so far had only found evidence that such did exist. She knew that if she would sooner or later be forced to lead some men off on a hunting foray, leaving the caravan to fend for itself. This she was putting off as long as she could for fear of attacks.

On the positive front, Mandy could detect no spies observing them from the distant hills. It was as if the bandits of Vyderland had given up leaving them to their fates. However appealing and widespread this thought was, Mandy did not believe it for a minute. The "pickings" of this caravan were just too tempting. She remained ever vigilant, ever on guard, only relaxing in William's arms during the evening music festivities. This became her private hour and she found herself looking forward to it more and more as the days went by.

The first sign that Mandy had of their approach to the Dead Sea was birds, lots of birds. She saw several flocks flying in wide arcs over the hills. As she crested yet another hill, far off in the distance a large dark green patch obscured the hills for several miles. This, she figured, was a good sign. Quickly, she, accompanied by several of Raul's guards, Alison and Darless, went to see what lay ahead.

The first indication of the unusual nature of this sea came from the stunted trees that grew around the Dead Sea; none were more than eight-feet tall, with twisted, gnarled limbs. This narrow band of deciduous trees grew out to about a one mile from the edge of the sea itself, thinning as the distance from the water grew. The trees were home to a variety of hardy bird species which took flight as they rode into the trees. Interestingly enough, the road bypassed the Dead Sea altogether passing it on its southern edge.

As they rode toward the sea, several wart hogs grunted, startled from their diligent rooting. One of the guards managed to spear one followed by other guards' cat-calls of a pig roast that evening. When they reached the Dead Sea, they paused and looked out over its vastness. From here at the southern edge, the brackish, pale blue, totally still waters stretched northward for twenty miles. The sea was about ten miles wide at the widest portion.

As they peered out over the sea from horseback, an eerie feeling seeped into each person; all felt just a little uneasy. Mandy searched in vain for the source, always trusting her instincts. Raul's voice broke the stillness, "This place is creepy!" He spoke what the others felt. There were no other signs of life and certainly no obvious villages.

"Well, it is not an oasis in the middle of the desert, that's for sure," Mandy declared. She dismounted and approached the water's edge to examine it closer. She scooped up a taste of the water. All watched the swirls ripple over the still surface out toward the far distant center. "Ack!" she cried spitting it out. "Salty, we certainly cannot drink the water, it is far too brackish. But we can all have a bath I expect. That'll be welcome enough."

Raul sent riders back to bring the caravan to the shore and pitch camp. He sent other riders on a scouting mission on either side. When they returned in a couple hours, they reported nothing at all, just more of the same trees and sea. The place seemed utterly void of human encounter. Meanwhile, the caravan arrived and a camp was setup early this day. Everyone's spirits rose upon seeing trees, however weirdly shaped, and a vast sea of water. None of the Freetown people had ever seen a body of water this large.

The Dead Sea was very shallow at its banks and one had to wade out nearly a quarter of a mile to get in over your head. So it was deemed safe for bathing and the children all dashed straight out into the water. Soon the sound of laughing children filled the air, bringing warmth to one and all that had almost entirely disappeared during the trip thus far.

There was enough dead wood lying about to have a proper fire and a giant pig roast began. Of course, another couple of wart hogs had to be obtained. Fresh meat was most welcome that evening and for several to come. Mandy decided to take an extended rest stop here beside the sea. And many people wandered around exploring this new territory.

Three finds proved most useful to the caravan. The first one was discovered by the blacksmith. While wandering around the edge of the trees where the caravan had halted on the southern edge, he found an exposed coal seam. Nearly everyone's supply of charcoal was gone. A dozen men began mining the coal to be used for cooking in place of the charcoal.

The second find was by one of the children who while swimming around a cove found a beach full of white sands. It turned out to be a salt flat. Everyone took the opportunity to replenish their supply of salt.

The third find was by Mandy, who did her own reconnoitering of the area. She found that many deer herds periodically came to the sea edge, presumably for the salt. One entire day was spent butchering a large number and preserving them with the salt. Thus, every wagon now carried sufficient dried meat to last several weeks.

The caravan thus paused in its long eastward journey for three days by the shores of the Dead Sea. It was the evening of the first day that they discovered something was most peculiar with this body of water. After the sun had set and Jon's musical interlude had finished and most people turned in for the night, Jon and Alison, accompanied by May and Mat and by Mandy and William, took a leisurely stroll along the bank of the sea.

"Look at that!" cried Jon. "Do you see those weird lights far out there in the middle of the water?" Everyone stared at the dark waters. There was no moon yet and it was very dark. From perhaps a quarter mile from the banks, strange ghostly lights appeared in or over the still, black waters. The specter lights grew in number, expanding to cover a circular area nearly a mile across. They wove and bobbed this way and that as if they had a mind of their own, ghostly lights. At first, no one said anything. They just stood and stared, wondering what they could be.

Mandy grew even more uneasy. She had never seen anything like this before, not even remotely. But the newness was not the same as her ill feeling. "What are they?" No one answered. "It's almost as if the lights are alive, the way they move about. Spooky. I have a bad feeling about this."

Mandy continued to stare which did nothing to relieve her growing anxiety. She remembered something Ukko had said, something about seeing far. So she relaxed, exhaling a long, slow breath and gazed out over the sea. She let herself expand; her awareness grew and pushed out forward, reaching toward these ghostly lights. She made contact and shrieked. "Zounds! They are ghosts! Real ghosts, spirits!" That got everyone's immediate attention and they all stared hard at these lights.

"How can you tell?" murmured Alison, who now felt very ill-at-ease. "Are they dangerous?"

"Dunno," was her reply. "I was practicing my new seeing far thing and I reached them. They are thin, filmy, translucent ghosts!" Then she added, "This seeing far thing has the unwanted side effect of letting you see something you might not want to see!" And everyone laughed along with her. Sometimes a little ability goes a bit too far, she thought.

"Well, as long as they stay way out there, I think we are safe," Darless commented. "They have not made any movements toward us. How do you fight a ghost anyway? And what is a ghost? I've never seen one. I thought that was just fairy tales for children."

"Well I don't know what else to call them," Mandy replied. "I still feel really nervous with them around. Maybe they are why I have felt uneasy since I first laid eyes on this sea." They watched the eerie lights for another hour. Other than moving around in eddies and swirls, the lights never moved any closer to the shore. Eventually, the three couples also retired for the night.

The next day, one small girl made a discovery that shed some light upon the ghostly inhabitants of the Dead Sea. While swimming, she found a rusty helm on the bottom and brought it back to show her mother. Quickly, Mandy and the others were informed and they hastened there to study the ancient artifact. No one here could identify its style. The blacksmith thought it was made of bronze and copper perhaps, but it was pretty well rotted at this point.

Now other children went looking for "artifacts" while pretending to swim in the sea. Several brought human skulls ashore. That ended the swimming. No one wanted to go swimming in a sea that contained skulls. No telling what else lay below the pale blue waters. Incidentally, the parents threw the skulls back into the sea. But the discovery of the skulls gave Jon an idea.

Later that night, he and Alison walked to the bank just after dark. Sure enough, once it was quite dark out, the ghostly lights appeared on cue. "If they are really ghosts or spirits, one should be able to communicate with them," Jon explained. "I'm going to give it a try. You watch over me here."

Alison wanted to protest, but realized Jon was intent upon finding out. So she took up a guard position. "Do be careful!" She urged.

Jon relaxed and expanded his awareness outward toward the ghostly lights. He made contact with a mind and sent it a "hello." The ghost instantly stopped moving about, startled by this totally unexpected event. It took a second "hello" for it to grasp what was going on. Then, it sent back an avalanche of communication, words spoken in a language Jon did not understand. He did get vague mental images of scenes of battle, but could not make heads or tails of it all.

He broke contact and began to tell Alison what he had discovered. "There really is a person or spirit out there, they have a mind. They are talking fast and furious to me, but I don't understand a word they are saying. It's some foreign language." Alison asked a few questions trying to better understand Jon.

"Hum. Okay, Jon, I think I have just the magic you need."

"What do you mean?" he asked baffled.

She ignored him and did a short chant and touched him when she was finished. "Okay, I just put a spell on you that will work like a translator. You should be able to understand and speak whatever language they are using. Can I listen in, too?" Her curiosity was fully peaked.

Jon nodded and he again let his awareness, his personal space, expand outward toward the lights. He felt Alison's attention or presence in the back of his mind. She kept a very low profile; she was basically telepathically eaves dropping. He made contact once more with the same mind.

Hello. I am Saint Jon Brown. Who are you? he placed in its mind. Jon sensed total surprise coming back from the spirit — the amazement it had on hearing words spoken in his own language.

I am General Edrahir Lithondel, Lord of the Tinagon clan of Dark Elves, or rather was Lord. The whole tribe is gone now, due to our greed and mistakes. We are all here, doomed eternally to rest in the Dead Sea, dead but not dead, the spirit thought back to Jon.

Jon, who was always inquisitive, immediately sent back, *Please, General, tell me your whole story! I'm fascinated.* Jon also felt the excitement of Alison as well. Both were not disappointed.

"I was the leader of a mighty army of Dark Elves back in the land of our forefathers, of which I am not at liberty to identify. There are still some secrets that remain even in death. There, more and more I fought with our political leaders, the Grand Council of the Wise. My own gallant victories on the battlefield ignited my own ego exalting my own sense of worth, until I thought I was wiser than the politicians. In my folly, I resolved to leave our homeland, desert the unscrupulous leaders, and bring forth my clan and army here to Vyderland. In my folly, I intended to create a new civilization here governed solely and only by my great wisdom."

"To that end, I stole the ancient artifact, the Crown of Egladhir, the legendary founder of our people, he who brought the Dark Elves true glory. I was going to wear that crown on my new throne here in Vyderland. I brought forth with me a thousand warriors and their families to conquer this land and establish my new city. That was about one thousand years ago now as you humans reckon time."

"In my thirst for total, absolute power, I took what I wanted with no thought to consequences. That was my downfall; I've had a thousand years to discover and accept what I did. In essence, we stole this whole land as far as you can see in all directions from the Vydersee Lords who ruled this vast steppe. We stole materials for construction from the dwarves of Hell's Gate in the Desolation Range, the mountain range that lies to the west. We even raided the stone giant's quarries. I believed that I was untouchable, I was a god, so great was my ego."

"When the end came, it came so fast that there was nothing I could do about it. One day the cavalry of the Vydersee Lords, two thousand strong, swooped down upon our encampment here at the edge of the sea. Joining them were five hundred stout dwarven foot soldiers encased in plate armor with two hundred dwarven archers. A hundred stone giants smashed our defenses to rubble. Even a hundred Dark Elves from our homeland were present, including many powerful mages. They sought, of course, the recovery of the Crown of Egladhir. The four races banded together to annihilate us."

"We had no chance whatsoever. The battle was lost before it even begun. The Dark Elves cursed this sea, turning it into a briny pond, utterly unable to sustain life. A powerful curse has doomed us to forever remain here in this realm, this sea, unable to live again or to die, only to dance upon the surface of the waters by night. The only consolation we have is that we still retain the Crown. They never found it."

"Wow!" was all that Jon could say. "But haven't you tried to break the curse? Cannot beings just float up and away?"

"Nay. We are cursed to be here until the day that we redeem our transgressions. And there is utterly no way for us ever to do that, and so here we be for all time." Jon felt an immense sadness that was utterly overwhelming, until he realized that he was now sensing the combined loss generated by the thousands of other Dark Elven spirits around their leader.

Surely there is a way out of this, there has to be. I just do not see how a being can be trapped like this, thought Jon to himself and accidentally to Alison.

Alison sent his a nudge, *Ask him for the exact wording of the curse.* Jon did so.

You are doomed to float by night above the sea and rest by day beneath the waters you so covet until the day of amends is met. You see we are eternally doomed, the General replied in apathy so great it seemed to swallow Jon and Alison. Jon finally managed to end the conversation by saying that he would see what he could do to help. It gave the General no hope at all. A human could do nothing, of that he was as certain as he was that he was cursed.

Slowly, the intense apathy still affecting them, Jon and Alison walked back to their wagon. It took a half hour for the sticky hopelessness to fade from them. Darless was pivotal in bringing them both out of it. She immediately saw that something was very wrong with both of them and kept asking them "what happened" and "go through it again and tell me what happened." This alu-demon demonstrated her complete mastery of Jon's accidental discovery.

When the last traces of the apathy had gone, the six adventurers and William were very excited. Mandy felt reassured that her initial sense that something was amiss here had been proven correct. None of them had ever had any contact with a Dark Elf. But Mandy did know that they existed somewhere and were basically nasty, evil, dark-skinned elves never to be trusted. That was the sum total of all of their knowledge of these people. And of course, no one had any clues about how to break the curse. But the next day, the entire company of travelers was informed of the sea's inhabitants. After that, no one went for a swim and wary eyes were always kept on the water.

The dawn of the fourth day here, supplies of coal had been mined and loaded into wagons. Some deadwood had been stowed as well. Fresh deer meat was about dried out preserved with a great deal of the salt. That morning, plans were being made for their departure on the next leg of their long journey. This next stretch would take them up to the Hell's Gate in the Desolation Range and at long last out of these dry steppes. All were now eager to get on the road again.

Mandy led the caravan back out of the confines of the stunted trees to the east-west dirt road they had left four days ago. Unfortunately, that is as far as they got. When they cleared the obscuring trees, there before them, in a vast line across the distant hilltops in a huge surrounding arc more than two miles long, were legions of mounted cavalry, tiny banners waving in the slight breeze. They were motionless, riders and steeds, all facing Mandy and the point where the caravan met the road. Her "Zagroot zounds" fell off into a whisper as the magnitude of the army facing her registered in her mind. Everyone halted their horses and stood equally motionless, staring at the overwhelming distant army before them.

Far off, a lone rider slowly made its way down a hill toward them and disappeared in the dip. No one moved; they just stared as all hope began to seep and slip away. Presently, the rider reappeared atop the hill directly before them. Even at this distance, they could see he carried a white banner. He was coming for a parley. Mandy jerked to attention, breaking the mesmerizing effect. "Okay, Alison, Darless to the front. Wagons, spread out among the trees. That will make them harder targets for the charging cavalry. Raul, get your men assembled into a compact group. Jon, May, Mat — your job is to protect the two wizards with your lives; keep them alive as long as possible."

Her tone of command pulled the others out of the spell of doom. Wagons scattered, Jon and the Twins came running to the front, forming a circle around Alison and Darless who had dismounted and tied up their horses to a nearby tree. Both got their staffs ready for action and were conferring on the best wide-area of effect spells to cast. Both knew that their job was to remove as many cavalry from the battle in as little time as possible or the scant fighters would be utterly overwhelmed by sheer numbers alone.

The lone horseman arrived walking his medium war horse, as if he had all the time in the world. He and his horse were covered in shiny, silver chain mail. He wore the black tunic of they had seen on the previous cavalry. He currently wore no helm. Instead a crown of gold set with emeralds held his long black hair out of his eyes. His weather-beaten face held a stern countenance. His brown eyes radiated supreme confidence and power. He spoke first in a deep, commanding bass voice.

"I am Lord Olaf Petersen, Second General of Vyndoc, commander of all the southern legions. I have five hundred seasoned heavy cavalry poised on yonder hilltops awaiting my orders to attack; they will show no mercy when they do," he spoke slowly and with authority and sureness.

"So why the parley?" retorted Mandy, "I'm." She did not get to finish her thought, for Olaf interrupted loudly.

"I know who you are," he bellowed, and looking at the others, "All of you. We know what you have done. We know where you are heading. We know what you are carrying. We know all." He paused a second, letting that sink into their minds. "Why the parley? Simple. I am not a butcher. Morrigan rewards great deeds on the battlefield; there is nothing to be gained in a slaughter, no glory. So I, out of the goodness of my heart, came to offer you a deal. Surrender this Saint Jon fellow to me to deal with as I choose. Surrender yourselves and I will find a suitable place for you women in my tents, after you are suitably humbled and are taught your place. The pitiful people of Freetown will be awarded slave status and allowed to live out the rest of their natural lives in our servitude. It's a simple choice. The alternative is to resist and be utterly and mercilessly slaughtered by my men. Your choice. Either way the head of Saint Jon Brown will be presented to Morrigan this day and we will have your riches."

"You egotistical fool!" Mandy had not gotten past his "suitably humble." "We will not submit to your whims. If you persist in attacking us, many, many of your seasoned men's lives will be terminated this day. Have you not heard of the results of your last attempt? We may all be slain, but we will most definitely take a great many of you along with us. I promise to personally take you out and show you your place! Men!" She suddenly realized that men of power and command had a great deal of difficulty relating to women who were also in command. They violated their preconceived notions of womanhood. Thus, these men continually blundered.

Alison spoke up, glaring at Lord Olaf, "You underestimate your strength. You have a good distance to cover. It will be a slaughter all right, a slaughter of your men before they can reach us. I am a great wizard and I promise to demonstrate that fact here today!"

Darless added her comments, "And it is very likely that I, Mage Darless, Holy Paladin of Ukko, may be the very last person of our group still standing when the battle finishes. But I promise you that before I leave, I will personally pluck out your eyes and rip your testicles off and feed them to the carrion birds that come. You cannot kill me, you fool. You only sign your own death warrant!"

Jon sensed the complete bewilderment and confusion that had momentarily come over Lord Olaf. He had never, ever faced three women in battle before, and they, not this Jon fellow, were in total command. He stared in disbelief as if his ears were playing tricks on him. Jon saw him mentally superimpose images of fierce male warriors in place of the women his eyes saw. Then, his anger burst forth. "So be it! Prepare to be slaughtered to the last man, woman and child! I will personally cut off each of your heads," he declared, looking at the three women in turn. He whirled his horse around and cantered off into the distance.

Mandy turned around, "Since this does not look good at all, let me say that I love you all. You are the greatest friends a person could ever have!" A tear formed in her eye. The others echoed her words.

Alison whispered to Darless, "If you are the last one alive, please do as you said, pluck that bastard's eyes out and let him live the rest of his life damned."

"It will be my pleasure," she replied with a fierce, grim determination that Jon had ever seen. He was glad that he was not in Lord Olaf's shoes.

Raul gathered all of the defenseless members of the caravan into one central area to better protect them with their meager forces. Mandy got out all three of her bastard swords and her short bow and a supply of arrows. May and Mat also got out all of their hand-to-hand arms. She also got out several magical wand, deciding to use those first while the cavalry were at a distance. No one had time for self-pity or worry that this was to be their last minutes of life, all were too busy rapidly preparing for the onslaught.

Jon wondered what he could do to help. He had nothing that could stop an army. He dealt with individuals,

usually at close range. While he might be able to take control
of several men's bodies, he could not control hundreds. He
laughed and said jokingly, "Where's our army when we need
it?" That brought a round of laughter from everyone, breaking
their pent-up tensions. Many others repeated it in jest, as well.

"I can cast a spell that creates an illusory army of
perhaps a dozen men," interjected May. "They fight and act as
if they were real. They can cause death to their victims if the
victim believes that he has been mortally wounded. Will that
help?"

"Sure thing! Cast away," Alison replied, "we need all
the illusory help we can muster."

"My god! That's it!" cried Jon. "Alison, quick, cast that
speaking spell on me again. Hurry up!"

She had no idea what Jon had in mind, there was no
time to query it either. She did as he asked. Jon then grabbed
the nearest horse, it was, in fact, Mandy's medium war horse,
and he cantered off through the trees heading for the Dead
Sea. Part way there, Jon realized his mistake — this horse was
way too much horse for him! Fortunately for Jon, the horse
chose to stop at the edge of the sea, dumping him headlong
into the waters. Spurting and spluttering, Jon stood up. He
knew what he had to do.

Mandy and the others were now ready. Far off in the
distance they heard a trumpet sound. A multitude of other
horns sounded in reply. A waving tide of cavalry began
galloping down the distant hills heading their way. Neither
Mandy, Alison, Darless, nor Jon saw their green emeralds of
Lady Ursla begin to glow.

Just as soon as the riders appeared atop the hills
immediately in front of them, the fireworks began. And
fireworks it was, literally. Both Alison and Darless launched
fire ball spell after fire ball spell. It was deafening and had a
significant impact upon the advancing legions. With each
detonation, many men and beasts fell to the ground, clothing
and harness in flames. However, these were indeed seasoned
fighters. None of those on fire attempted to flee, but
determinedly began rolling on the blackened ground in an
attempt to put out the flames beneath their chain mail. Many
died there on the ground.

May had not been idle. She had cast several of her spells. Thirty passable warriors stood in a battle line before her and began marching out toward the oncoming charging riders. Now she took up a wand in each hand, ready for closer combat.

Mandy stood tall at the point of their defense. She would be the first to directly draw blood of the charging riders. When they were finally in bow shot range, she launched a volley of arrows downing four. Dropping the bow, she took a bastard sword in each hand, whirling them around, sensing their balance. She was ready for the fight of her life.

The lead riders bore down on her. This time, they carried no lances. Their long swords were aimed at her as they charged. Two swerved right at her, intending to pass her on either side. As they swung their swords, she ducked and thrust. Both bastard swords found their mark and propelled with the oncoming momentum of the riders, poked all the way through their bodies as they fell lifeless to the ground. She whipped the third bastard sword out in an instant, ducking and missing a third rider.

Then the mass of cavalry was on her, surrounding her on all sides. Her blade struck this way and that, parrying here and there. More than one rider fell of their horse, dead before they hit the ground. However, some of their slices found their marks and Mandy began bleeding from several wounds. Mentally, she controlled the blood loss and continued her fierce attack with minimal defensive moves. The death toll around her grew as bodies became stacked upon bodies.

Mat, May, and Darless formed a circle around Alison, protecting her. Alison now switched spells because the enemy was at close quarters. She launched volleys of magical arrows that devastated each man she hit. Mat held nothing back in his martial arts kicks, breaking arms, legs and necks of those who ventured too close. May waved her wands in all directions, firing off magical missiles which had a lesser effect than those of Alison. Darless, now low on spells, resorted to the brute strength which alu-demons possess. When an enemy closed to strike her with his blade, she grabbed that man, wrenched him from the saddle and literally broke his neck and cast the lifeless body aside. Her eyes, normally coal black, now glowed fiercely red. Soon, her clothes were in tatters; she was like a vicious wild animal, tearing into men. Only a magical blade could scratch her and even then she did not feel those occasional scratches.

Mandy was now bleeding profusely in spite of her attempts to quell it. She was weakening and knew the end would not be far off. She heard Alison curse, "Damn! I'm out of spells!" Alison never cursed so Mandy knew that the end now was near, but she fought on, though missing her targets most of the time now so weakened was she.

Alison realized she had drained all magical charges from her staff and had shot every spell she had ready for the day. There was nothing left but hand to hand combat which she detested. *Think, Alison, think,* she told herself. She would later try to describe what happened next to Darless and Mandy. She began to correlate the magic discipline with the actual capabilities she had as a spiritual being and found a nexus, a junction. That thought process took at least a half an hour to bring together into a unified whole, but only one second of real time elapsed. She began launching even more powerful magical missiles — a single missile killed its target and she launched three with each spell. The spells came from her, not from her magic discipline. Alison d'Ambrose would not go down without a fight, but she realized she could not kill all of them before they got to her.

Then, May went down followed shortly by Mat. Alison herself now began to feel wounds, she knew her body was getting the worst of it. But she, she carried on the attack heedless of her body which seemed so distant, so insignificant.

Just when all was about lost, suddenly something strange happened. A deadly chill filled the air. The entire battlefield turned black, black as a midnight with no moon. A frigid coldness that seeped instantly to the bone was felt by every human that still lived on this bloody battlefield, friend or foe. Strange ghostly shapes appeared in the darkness, the spirits of the Dark Elves. Each carried rusted, twisted weapons and wore remnants of mostly rotten armor.

These phantoms could kill, and kill they did. Swooping with great speed, the specters attacked the helpless cavalry men. Horses spooked and bolted from the field, often spilling their riders. The cavalry men swung their blades at and through these ghostly warriors, but to no effect, they were spirits, not Dark Elves. Waves of panic spread like wildfire. No battle seasoning could have prepared them for combat against a foe they could not harm, yet one that easily killed them. Frantically, tripping and falling over themselves and their fallen comrades, they fled the battlefield rushing this way and that way in the absolute darkness. It was terrifying to behold, seasoned fighters in an utter route, helplessly clawing their way through the magically enforced darkness.

Out of the five hundred and forty two men that began the charge that day, only twenty-five lived to tell the tale. One of those was Lord Olaf who was missing his eyes. (A carrion bird gratefully ate them where Darless had left them for the bird.)

How long the field lay in this total darkness, no one could say exactly. No one said a word. The shock was too great. Many of the Freetown folks just fainted. Alison watched as the pale spectral forms bobbed this way and that, stabbing occasionally at something on the ground. She, of course, could not see what they were stabbing. It is noted here that none of the twenty-five survivors were within the area of total blackness.

And then the sun reappeared once more, blinding everyone with its brilliance. Dead bodies of men and beasts lay strewn everywhere, many piled one upon another. Jon's stomach was wrenching as he walked through the mess to get to his friends. He nearly had not been in time. He held his new walking stick firmly in his hand and went to each of his friends as fast as he could step over the fallen. He touched Alison first, saying, "In the name of Ukko." He saw a beautiful yellow energy flow come from the stick and encompass her bleeding body. She smiled at him as her wounds simply vanished.

"Thanks, we better rescue the others really fast," she said. Jon did the same to May and Mat. The Twins were most impressed by the healing and recognized the hand of Ukko. Both got to their feet and began to seek out others to help. Next, Jon maneuvered himself over huge piles of the dead to get to Mandy. She was still alive, but barely. He touched her and all of her wounds vanished.

"Wow. Now that is most useful. I was figuring I'd need a month of healing to get back into shape. Thanks," she said. Then, she stood up and looked at the carnage.

"Say, where's Darless?" Jon asked, looking about. She was not where she was supposed to be.

"Over here," called Alison, she was over by Raul and his men who had tried to keep the enemy from the helpless towns people. Jon got there as quickly as he could, but the ground was very slippery, blood was everywhere.

He found Raul lying on the ground with many wounds to his arms and legs, but somehow he had escaped any direct hits to his chest. May and Mat were right behind him. "Let us help him, he is not at death's door," May implored. Together, chanting a short prayer to Ukko, they laid their hands upon Raul and healed many of his wounds.

Meanwhile, Jon and his stick helped three of the most seriously wounded men. Two, however, were beyond his help. After healing the third man, the stick ceased operations. "I guess it's reached its limits," Jon acknowledged. "Thank you Ukko!" he exclaimed, looking up at the sky for he did not know where else to look for Ukko. So Jon resorted to his normal methods of commanding cells to heal on the others who did not have the life-threatening wounds. Mat and May and Mandy joined him and treated the remaining twenty or so men.

Jon kept asking everyone if they had seen Darless. None had after the blackness fell. He became more and more worried. Finally, Mandy volunteered to go looking for her. She did not get far before she saw the alu-demon, clothes tattered and torn, flying toward them. She was coming from the direction from which the cavalry had originally come. Miraculously, her blue tunic with white cross was unscathed.

She landed and cancelled her spell. "Well, I did not expect to see any of you alive when I got back!"

"Jon's work, the stick," Mandy told her, trying not to give away too much information to the wrong ears. "We are all alive and okay. Two of Raul's guards didn't make it though."

"That's more than I even hoped for!" the alu-demon replied.

"Where did you go?" asked Mandy, curiosity getting the better of her.

Darless did not directly answer her. "Why is it that loudmouthed generals are often nowhere to be seen upon the battlefield? Well, I was just keeping my promise to him."

"You didn't!" gasped Mandy, recalling Darless' final words.

"He still has his manliness. I just could not be that barbaric. But he'll never command again," was all that she said. She was distracted by the sight of the battlefield. "What a horrid waste! Men!" she added disgustedly. Both returned to assist Jon, Mat, May, and Alison, who were tending the wounds of the guards.

Alison could only play nurse, for healing was one area about which she had no knowledge. Mat and May were elated. While working on binding wounds, they related how much they had longed for this new ability that Ukko had helped them attain. To actually heal and help the wounded had been a goal of theirs since they had arrived in Freetown so many years ago. And now they had many to tend.

While they were busy going from fighter to fighter, Althea Westfold, the young woman who sang in Jon's band, cautiously came over to them. "Excuse me, can I help somehow?" All six were startled, as they suddenly remembered the hundreds of townsfolk. They had not yet even checked upon how they had faired.

"Sure, help me tear up this old petticoat into strips to use as bandages," Alison replied. The teenager grinned and enthusiastically set to work. The others looked at the huddled mass of the townsfolk. They had followed orders and all six hundred and some had formed into one small dense compact group, protected by Raul and the guards. And the guards had done their task flawlessly. Not a single towns person had been wounded.

One glance at the tightly bunched people, told all. The poor townsfolk, save this one teen, were in total shock. Many were unconscious on the ground. Those that were not just stared off into space like zombies. "Oh my!" uttered Jon. "What's happened to all of them?"

"Shock, I suspect," Mandy observed. "I've seen it before. You have to admit this battle was pretty horrible to view. The utter carnage they've witnessed along with the utter hopelessness that grew until the Dark Elves saved us was more than they could experience. Their minds just shut down."

"How do we help them?" he wondered aloud. Alison shrugged that she didn't know.

"Given enough time, many will recover. But I've seen some poor folks that never recovered from such awful sights," Mandy answered.

"Hum," Darless thought aloud, "then it is a mental effect. The answer is simple, Jon. We use your technique on each one of them!"

"Brilliant!" he exclaimed, feeling rather silly that he did not think of it.

She continued in her methodical manner, "Only there are six hundred plus of them and only two of us. Let's see, if each one takes an average of an hour to handle, that's three hundred hours for each of us. And at say ten hours a day, we need an entire month just to help out each one of them."

"Can I help?" inquired the young teenager. She had no idea what Darless meant, but she certainly wanted to help in any way she could. This simple request stirred something within Darless.

"Well, yes. You know, Jon," said Darless thoughtfully, "this technique is actually very easy to do. I suspect that we could train her and all of the others to do our mental assist thing. If there were seven of us doing it, why it would take only maybe four days. And most of these guards are going to need at least that much time to recover sufficiently to ride."

"It'll take that long to bury all these men," Alison added. "We aren't barbarians. They were people after all and should at least be buried and not be food to the scavengers."

Mandy again took charge. "All right, there are at this point there are ten of us able to carry on. Wait a minute, what happened to William? Has anyone seen him?" Suddenly she had a sickening feeling in her stomach. What if he had been slain or lay wounded bleeding to death before she even remembered him!

Alison now took charge, "Mandy, you take Jon, Raul and Darless and go looking for him. We will continue tending these others." Mandy did not need any further encouragement and began systematically dashing about the area looking for him. The other three joined her and they quickly found him.

William had remained close by the townsfolk that he had been charged to protect. Unfortunately, he had taken a knock on the head and fallen unconscious fairly early in the battle. They found his legs protruding from a pile of fallen raiders. "William, William, are you all right?" Mandy pleaded once they had him extricated from the dead bodies.

Slowly he came around, moaning about his head. Mandy did a thorough exploration and concluded that he had a concussion, but no other wounds. She, joined by Jon and Darless began to heal his head wound. He regained consciousness, "Mandy? You survive? Are we in heaven? How? Oh! My head!"

"Yes, we all survived. You have a concussion, you got your head busted. But we have you mostly fixed up," she said lovingly. "But you will probably have quite a headache for days." He forced a smiled and shut his eyes, relaxing. If he did not move, his head hurt far less, but they insisted on carrying him back to where Alison had setup a nursing station of sorts. He complained every step of the way.

"As I was saying," Mandy resumed her take charge attitude, "Raul, you and your two guards set to work moving the wagons back to the sea shore camping area. Setup the camp. We will finish up binding the guards' wounds and the work on reviving the townsfolk. We will remain here for several days." Raul and his two men set to work on gathering up their loose horses, and leading them back to their previous camping area.

By the time that Raul was ready to begin moving the wagons back to the camp site, the others had finished binding all of the wounded. The twenty-two wounded guards were helped into several wagons and were taken back to the camp.

All this took only a few minutes, and now several of the hundreds who were in shock began to come around. They looked around disoriented, confused. Mandy kept saying in a low soft voice, "It's okay, we won. Let's go back to our old camp for a while. She and the others helped the dazed people find their wagons and get into them. At least one hundred remained unconscious and had to be carried into their wagons. In less than an hour, everyone was back at the original camping area they had left just a short time ago. And the surge of energy of combat had drained away, leaving exhaustion in its wake. Although Jon's stick had healed wounds, compliments of Ukko, the fatigue of their exertions and the mental stress of the battle's slaughter sapped their strength and wills. They all needed time to sleep and eat.

But Mandy knew that time was a luxury that they did not had to spare. Time would play into the hands of the steppes clean-up crews, the scavengers. If they did not act, soon roving bands of hyenas and such would descend upon them, along with multitudes of carrion birds. Raul also knew the danger of their present situation. He took Mandy aside.

"You know what we have to do, don't you?" he whispered.

"Yes, either we all just leave this field behind or we clean it up, bury the dead. And soon," she whispered back. "I just don't have any strength left at the moment. We cannot leave, that is an understatement. They are in shock. You look like you can hardly stand yourself."

"Aye, that's true, but tis us that's gotta do something or there'll be hell to pay in a few hours," he replied.

Alison and Jon walked up, "William is sleeping now, Mandy. He's going to be all right," she said very slowly. Indeed Alison looked like she was about ready to drop and was leaning on Jon for support. "You know we've got to bury those men somehow, don't you?"

"Yes, Raul and I were just discussing it. It's just that we don't know how we are going to manage it. We are all ready to drop!" Mandy sighed.

"Well, there are two of us that are in good shape," Jon broke in. "Darless and I are still going strong. I rather missed the whole affair. Just tell us what needs to be done and we'll do it while you all get some rest." He had no idea what he was getting himself into, yet had he known the full extent, he would have still volunteered.

Mandy explained their peril and the minimum that needed to be accomplished and quickly. Jon agreed to take care of it and commanded them to go get some rest. He left the entire camp in Althea's care and she wore a huge smile for several days. Jon found Darless and the two of them walked just out of earshot. He explained what they had to do; Darless grimaced. "Come on, then. Let's go see the magnitude of this," she said. They walked slowly back to the field of battle less than a half mile away.

"Good god! Where did all those flies come from?" exclaimed Jon as they reached the perimeter of destruction.

Flies swarmed everywhere adding to the disgusting, revolting scene.

Darless knew and said only, "Men! Only men could do this kind of destruction, Jon. Okay. Here's the situation. Number 1, we cannot dig six hundred graves. Number 2, hundreds of their horses are roaming all over the lands out there. Number 3, we should salvage all that is usable or valuable. Number 4, the bodies must be disposed of and fairly soon or it will not be just pesky files that we have to fend off."

"But if we cannot dig the graves," Jon protested, "how can we dispose of them so the jackals don't come? Dig one huge pit?"

"Well, I could use a spell to dig a pit. But I am not good with the horses. I think Mandy would want us to obtain as many of them as possible. So I tell you what. You go get the horses and bring them back to camp. I will take care of the dead here. If you get done before I do, come help me out."

"You got it. Holler if you need anything," Jon was only too glad to be able to avoid the burial detail. "Thanks, I just don't have the stomach for this, you know."

"Yes, I know. I detest it, but I can face it and handle it. I grew up with demons, you know," she replied grim faced. This was not a part of her past that of which she was fond, rather a part that she tried to forget. Jon gave her a thank you kiss and set off to try to retrieve the abandoned horses.

In the western movies, Jon recalled how the cowboys would ride out and rope or herd the strays back to camp. He quickly discarded that notion. He could barely ride. "Guess I'll just have to talk to them, convince them to follow me." He figured he could do that and he strolled out onto the steppes, stepping around the tufts of tough grasses that grew at irregular intervals on the parched ground. After walking about a mile and catching six of these larger medium war horses, he came up with a better plan. He sat down and began asking the horses to go off and tell strays that he spotted to come here and join up with him. He promised them plenty of food, water, and far better care than they had had. Only an eagle soaring high in the sky observed this roundup. And it was so fascinated it circled and watched. Horses trotted away from this human and up to another distant horse. Then both trotted back the human. Then both would trot off in other directions after other horses. After an hour, two hundred horses were grazing at this human's feet. The eagle thought this was a most curious behavior; it flew home to tell its mate what it had seen.

Darless, though totally out of spells for the day, still had some spells written on scrolls tucked away in her portable hole. She rummaged through her collection and brought out two. She read the magical words and instantly a large shovel appeared. She commanded it to dig an enormous hole near the densest section of dead bodies. That way she would have the least to move. Then she set to work systematically removing all objects of any possible value from each of the deceased, casting them into an ever growing pile of stuff.

Once the hole had been dug, she used the other magical scroll, which allowed her to levitate objects. Each of the stripped victims was levitated and pushed into the pit. She had only handled one-tenth of the bodies when Jon returned leading his herd of horses. "I can use a hand," she called out. "At this rate, it will take me far into the night to get this done." Her voice was a little cranky, Jon noted, not unexpectedly though. It was a loathsome task that she had to perform. He hurried as quickly as he could and left Althea with the task of unsaddling and tethering the new horses. She enjoyed the task; handling horses was something she knew how to do.

Jon joined Darless, but he put a handkerchief over his nose and mouth, partly to keep the flies out. "You strip them, throw whatever might be useful or valuable in that huge pile there and I will take the body to the pit," she ordered. He set to the grim, awful work.

Two more hours passed. Jon's hands ached from the toil. Overhead, carrion birds began flocking. They were now only about half finished with the immense task. But help came. Mandy and Raul and the other two guards that had been healed walked up wearing handkerchief masks as well. "We got three hours sleep, recovered a enough to help out," Mandy announced.

"Thanks!" echoed both Jon and Darless, who personally was greatly relieved because after three hours at this, they still had half to go. With five working on the project, in another hour, the gruesome task was finally finished. They stood silently watching as Darless' shovel mounded the remaining dirt and sand on top of the huge pit. Beside the huge mound were two very small ones, of the two guards who had given their lives to protect the caravan's people.

Even this much exertion tired out Mandy and the others, so they left the pile of chain mail, swords and other items where they lay in one enormous heap. Darless knew that somewhere in that mess were several magical blades that had cut her. She resolved to find them tomorrow. They all slowly walked back to camp.

Jon was amazed to see that the shock had worn off of many of the folks. Here and there were signs of normal camp life, small fires, smells of cooking food, and chatting. As they walked into camp, several of the men came up to them. One acted as spokesperson for the others, "We all want to thank you all for saving our lives yet again. We thought it was certain doom this time. Is there anything we can do for you all now? We'd like to help if we can." He was sincere, Jon noted.

Mandy was too tired to worry much, "Yes, there is actually. Back on the battlefield we left a huge pile of chain mail, swords, money and such. I'd appreciate it if that pile was brought here close to the edge of the sea so we can sort through it all tomorrow. We've buried all of the dead, so the area is mostly cleaned up." Jon watched smiles appear on their faces upon finding out that they could contribute. They rushed off to examine the pile and figure out the best way to get it all back to camp. The five adventurers wandered to their wagons, crawled under and fell asleep.

The next thing Jon knew it was supper time. Camp noises woke him along with the aroma of food cooking. The others rose as well. Jon was surprised to find that eighty percent of the people were now up and about doing their daily chores as if nothing had happened. The other hundred people were at least awake, though docile. Althea motioned to a number of nearby wives, who at once brought all of the adventurers a hot meal. "This sure hits the spot, Althea! Thanks to all of you," Jon exclaimed and he meant it. The others also expressed their thanks as they ate. And eat they did, a rather large amount.

While they were eating, Althea brought them up to date, "All of the injured are doing well. Most all of those that were in shock are coming out of it. All of the new horses have been rubbed down and fed. They seem to like it here, I think.

The guys brought in four wagon loads of stuff; it's over by the sea edge as you requested. Everyone's just so grateful for you all saving our lives again. It's like another miracle. They are all saying that if there is anything, anything at all that we all can do to help you, just ask."

"You've done good, Althea," Jon acknowledged, "really good."

"Thea. My friends just call me Thea," she smiled at him.

"Well, there is one thing that you all can do," Mandy said between mouths full, "this is delicious. How about having the women cook our meals for us six, no seven counting William? I hate to cook, really." The women who were standing nearby grinned and agreed to that task.

The food revitalized everyone. And after dinner, Darless called the others together for a council and even invited Thea, who beamed with pride as she sat beside her heroes. Darless began to explain what she wanted to attempt. "Today every one of the Freetown folks witnessed an extraordinarily savage, brutal attack with no thought of survival. Yet we survived. All but Thea here was shocked, some more than others. We've fended off doom twice before this day and the accumulated shock on their minds and bodies is getting worse each time. What I propose is that we use Jon's technique on each person, one at a time. Thea, Jon's technique helps a person get rid of adverse mental effects of life. Now I have not told you all yet, but when we get back and this episode is finished, I intend to build a college to train others to be able to do this, helping all people become better. So I guess it is time to put it to the test. I propose to train all of you in just how to do this and then, together, all seven of us will assist all of the others. We will reserve Raul and his guards for Jon and me as well as the hundred or so who are displaying the most serious symptoms." This was a very long speech for her, perhaps the longest one she had delivered. She looked at everyone now for their reaction.

"Do we have to see into their minds for this to work?" inquired Mandy.

"I don't think so. I think we can keep it very, very simple. At least that is what I am hoping. I've got it narrowed down to a very easy to do action, I think. Are you willing to give it a go?" Darless asked, anxiously awaiting the results.

"I think that this is an unbelievably terrific thing to attempt! Darless, you are a genius," exclaimed Alison. "If you want to build the college around my place, I'll donate the land even."

Everyone agreed to give it a try, though Thea had no idea what she was agreeing to do. "All right, then here is the simple procedure. Ask them to remember the events of the day, to recall them to mind and to run though their mental pictures of the day's events telling you what is happening as they go along. When they have finished, why, have them go back to the beginning of the events and run through it again telling you what is occurring. Do it over and over. Then, one of two things will occur. They may start laughing and become totally cheerful and the events will be found to no longer be troubling them. Or the events get heavier and do not seem to be lessening or perhaps even worsening. In that case, you just ask them if they experienced something like this at an earlier time. Give them some time, and they will find the earlier event that is similar. Have them run through it telling you all about it as they go along. And you just keep going over it until its effect on them is gone or you need to ask if there was an even earlier time that experienced something like this. See, it is really simple to do, I think. Just don't say or ask anything else. Don't be surprised or even comment on what they answer. Just be a good listener."

"But what if we run into trouble?" asked Alison, who was imagining all sorts of unexpected things occurring.

"If anything goes wrong or you have trouble, signal us, and Jon or I will step in and help out," Darless replied. "So, Alison, you are up first. You do it on Thea here. That way she will have some idea of impact this is going to have on people."

"Are you sure?" asked Alison, rather unsure of herself. This stuff was Jon's thing, not hers. She looked at Thea who looked eager to get on with it, so she shrugged and agreed to do it. She and Thea went over to her wagon to get a bit of privacy and then Alison began.

While she knew this technique had blown her horrid nightmares caused by the Chasme Bugs, she hope that she could do it half as well as Jon had done it on her. "Okay Thea here we go. Can you remember when the events started this morning?" Thea nodded excitedly. "All right then. I want you to go through the events and tell me what is going on as you go through it." And Thea was off. Alison noticed that by the second recounting, Thea was expressing a good deal of apathy, she'd resigned herself that this was the end of her life as the battle began. After several passed over the day's events, Thea began crying about it, so Alison asked if there was something like it that had occurred earlier in time. Thea then went through the battle at Hope's Lost several times, but the grief did not abate. Again, Alison asked her if there wasn't something like this earlier. Thea now went through the original first attack just outside Freetown. On the third pass over those events, she started laughing, "I said 'Where's the darn hero when you really need him?'" What a silly thing to say. Alison was beaming when she brought the laughing Thea back to the others. It had worked perfectly and Alison had done it. Both women we happy.

"Yes!" exclaimed Darless. "It works, it can be taught! Now let's all go do the others." And they began their systematic assistance therapy. Before dark, Jon helped three of those that were the most traumatized by the day's events. Darless did another two of those, while keeping an eye out for the others ,in case they needed help. Mandy, May, Mat, Alison, and Thea each helped two that night.

The next day the seven began making their way through the caravan, wagon by wagon, family by family, averaging seventy assists per day. When they had finished and had therefore given each member of the caravan an assist, ten days had passed. However, the last five of those days, the assists had been delivered while the caravan was back on the road slowly making its was westward. News of the assists and the incredible benefits spread like wildfire throughout the folks and everyone was very eager to be next.

It became obvious to everyone that there was indeed something vital to this technique, for they saw just how rapidly the twenty-two wounded guards recovered. It was amazing. Darless also observed an unexpected side-effect. The entire caravan's level of communication had increased three-fold. Folks were talking to each other and to their leaders far more than they had in the past. New friendships were forming. They had bonded as a group. Hopes for the future grew by leaps and bounds. And the overall spirits of the townsfolk was amazing, considering everything that they had been through. Darless had much to ponder, much to analyze. She was certain that Jon had discovered something of major importance.

The next four days of healing passed without further attacks. Indeed had the enemy known just how weak the caravan was at this point, any concerted attack may have succeeded, for seven could not hope to defend well over six hundred people. But they did not know just how significant a blow the annihilation of the Sixth Cavalry was to Vyderland.

As the healing progressed and as the mental assists worked, there was no shortage of volunteers. Before, the caravan people kept mostly to themselves. But now, men, women and children cheerily chatted with them, constantly asked for chores they could do to help out. It was quite a change. There were two blacksmiths in the party and they assumed responsibility for sorting out the huge pile of armor and weapons. Able estimated that each suit of mail was of high craftsmanship and was worth around twenty-five gold pieces. After sorting and cleaning, they now had some five hundred complete sets, representing a small fortune.

When they men had all of the mail and weapons cleaned and arranged in uniform rows, Alison and Darless examined each for the presence of any magical enhancements. They were very pleased to find ten sets of magical chain mail. These they gave to Raul to distribute among his guards as he thought best.

The weapons were very uniform. Around five hundred fifty long swords, all of the same design, tested non-magical and were worth fifteen gold coins each. Three hundred short swords of excellent design would fetch eight gold pieces. The five hundred knives, another two gold pieces each. The ten prize swords were very carefully studied by Mandy as well. Each of these tested positive for magical enhancement; half were highly enhanced; all were long swords. The best one was worth about ten thousand gold pieces, if one could find a buyer. In all, these magical blades could easily have sold for another thirty-six thousand gold coins. Thus, the armaments that they confiscated was worth well over seventy thousand gold coins.

In a fitting ceremony after dinner at sunset, Mandy presented the best magical long sword to Raul as a token of their appreciation for his efforts. The remaining nine were bestowed on members of his guards at the same time. It was smiles and thank you's all around as the caravan folks cheered.

Mandy observed other war horses still lingering in the area in these following days. And on the third day, she and Jon rode out to try to retrieve them. Jon used his techniques while Mandy preferred her own methods. In the end, they managed to bring back another hundred more medium war horses, bringing the total to just about three hundred of these strong, highly trained horses. When Jon asked how much one was worth, he nearly fell out of his saddle. A well trained medium war horse would bring well over two hundred gold pieces each! Thus, the worth of the horses they managed to capture nearly equaled the combined total of all of the weapons and armor! Jon found a new appreciation for these large beasts.

Alison and Darless personally took charge of the analysis of all of the more personal possessions from the giant pile. These had been warriors, but there was still some jewelry and rings and cash among the booty they had collected. The sum total of all of the cash amounted to about a thousand gold coins. The jewelry was appraised by a jeweler in the caravan to be worth perhaps ten thousand all told. Six special rings were found to be magical in nature and would require further study to determine their exact nature.

On the fourth day, while walking back to his wagon for lunch after giving another assist, Jon suddenly remembered something that the Lord of the Dark Elves had said as he left to charge the enemy cavalry. "Alison, I forgot something that is likely very important."

She was all smiles too because she had just finished giving her patient a successful assist. "Well, out with it, silly. You should try to remember things that are important," and she chuckled.

"He said that in the exact center of the sea, count down to the tenth step. The step slides to the left. We may have the contents of the secret vault," Jon explained. "In the aftermath of the battle and all, I just forgot about it. I have no idea how we are to find the center of the sea, get there, or dive under water or retrieve whatever he was talking about."

"Hum, probably treasure. We are going to need all the cash we can lay out hands on if we are to rebuild Castle d'Ambrose and a village to go with it. I say, we need to get it. The question remains how. Let me discuss it with Darless."

Later that afternoon, she and Darless stripped down to their underwear — neither had a swimming suit. Their appearance as they walked through the camp to the sea's bank caused quite a stir. Dangling from their waists were numerous sacks and a couple of daggers. "Treasure seeking," they repeated over and over as they passed gaping onlookers. By the time that they reached the shore, the entire camp was right behind them. This was not going to be an event to miss.

First, both spoke a short command word and began to fly up into the sky above the sea. They headed out towards its center and rather high up. They gained sufficient altitude so that they could better fix the center point. At the center area, or as near as they could estimate, they appeared as mere specks in the sky as the crowd covered their eyes from the sun's glare and stared. As the wizards flew down to the water's surface, each caused a globe of light to appear on their left hands and they streaked down into the water and disappeared from sight.

Periodically, the globes of light would pierce the surface followed by the wizards as they flew up into the sky only to repeat their dives, searching for the steps. On the sixth try, only Alison surfaced, this time to speak another chant and then dove underwater once more. Neither surfaced for well over ten minutes, causing everyone to speculate that perhaps they might had drowned. Jon and Mandy kept constant mental contact with both of them and reassured the crowed that both were well and hard at work.

When they surfaced this time, the lights were gone and they flew low to the water's surface and exceedingly slow, taking nearly a half hour to return. As they got closer, the sacks at their waists were bulging. They had been successful and the crowd cheered long before either mage could possibly have heard them.

When they got closer, the reason for the low, slow flight became apparent. Each carried a significant weight. They had the treasure. They landed amid yells of delight and cheers. Alison, beaming with pride, took this opportunity, even dressed as she was in her underwear for she normally would not have been caught dead in public wearing such, to address the crowd. "The spirits of the sea have given us their ancient treasure. We now have far more than enough money to not only rebuild Castle d'Ambrose but to build all of you an excellent, high class town!" The crowd screamed and cheered for ten minutes while the others helped them undo the heavy bags.

Alison opened several sacks to display piles of rubies, emeralds, diamonds, golden jewelry, and even some coinage. One sack she did not open or show, but just handed it to Jon, placing in his mind, *The Legendary Crown of the Dark Elves is in here. Take it and don't reveal that we have it for now. We need to examine it and figure out what to do with it.* Jon did as he was told.

But he did place in her mind a little tease, *I do like your appearance in your undies, pretty sexy.*

She replied in his mind, *If you say one more word about this, I'll drop this heavy bundle of treasure on your head and not give you an assist!* She also blushed and lowered her eyes. She wanted to snuggle with him really, but thought better of it just now.

Shortly after she had dried off and changed back into her working clothes, Althea approached her wagon between giving others assists. "Lady Alison, may I have a word with you?" She was most polite.

"Sure," grinned Alison, patting her hair dry. It was always a job drying such long hair.

"I've given this considerable thought. I want to become a wizard just like you. Can you please teach me? I don't have any idea how to become one. I promise to work hard and do everything you tell me," she pleaded. Her eyes were as begging as much as her voice. Alison stared hard at this teenager.

"Althea, are you sure? It is lots of book work, reading and studying. It's not all just fun and adventure. Spells can go wrong and you can get hurt. And besides, in a battle, the wizards are always the first target the enemy attempt to kill," she was looking for any and all means to try to discourage here. It had no effect.

"Please, just call me Thea, all my friends do. I know it is hard, I've been watching you and Darless all the time. I'll study really hard, honest I will," she continued pleading.

Alison remembered how badly she had wanted to become a mage when she was a child. The memory softened her heart. "Okay, Thea, but can you read and write?" She hoped that this would dissuade Thea. But it didn't.

"A little. I worked as a clerk for a money changer. He taught me but I there are a lot of big words that I don't know yet. But I can learn," she added hastily.

"Alright then, we'll give it a try. Realize that we cannot do much out here; we've not got a proper study, no tables, no chairs, no desks, no writing supplies and so on," she consented.

"Yippie!" cried Thea, her enthusiasm exploded, and she could not stand still from the excitement. "What do I do first?"

"You need a beginning spell book, but there is no way to make one out here," Alison replied, damping her enthusiasm a bit. "But tomorrow, I'll bring back my very first spell book that I was given when I became an apprentice wizard. I'll let you use it until we can make you your very own book. Now go on with your assist giving, I've fallen behind schedule. We really must help out everyone." Thea thanked her over and over and over and rushed off to her next appointment. *Was I ever like that,* she thought to herself and her memories of being accepted into the wizard's guild as an apprentice came unbidden. She smiled, *Guess so!* And she went in search of her next appointment.

Later that night the six adventurers examined the royal crown that had caused the downfall of an entire race. It detected highly magical and Mandy determined that it also radiated very evil energies. It was an evil artifact of the ancients. For the moment, none had any idea what it was or did or what they should do with it. So they kept it in the sack. The next day, as the caravan was departing, Alison teleported the valuables to her dungeon treasury room and returned to the caravan in time to watch it leave the trees and join the east-west dirt road once more.

A number of men in the caravan were traders by training and they created drag sleds from some of the dead wood. The medium war horses were put into service hauling the fifty sleds carrying the armor and swords. Each wagon also trailed several war horses behind it, securely tied to the wagon. "If only they had brought spare wagons or could buy some," bemused Alison.

The next five days they continued their westward journey up one hill and down the next, in the same monotonous manner as had been their lot every day of this journey thus far. Each of the seven gave more assists during these five days and finally had helped everyone in the entire caravan.

Half of the guards had recovered sufficiently to at least ride a horse. Mandy had them stay close to the flanks of the caravan. Raul and the two that had been fully healed by Jon rode in front. Mandy, as usual rode far out in front with Darless and Alison far off on either flank. There was no one to spare guarding the far rear, but she calculated that that was the least of their worries. She had seen no signs of any distant spies as they had earlier, this reassured her somewhat. However, she felt strongly that they had not seen the last of the Vyderland cavalry.

The evening of their fifth day out from the Dead Sea, Alison and Thea left the others to begin the apprentice training. Alison gave Thea her original little book of beginning spells and together, they studied one very useful spell. Alison had Thea go over and over the words of the spell until she felt Thea had them down pat. "Okay, now try it. Here's a piece of dried grass to practice on," she said.

Thea took a deep breath, concentrated hard on the grass and spoke the words of the spell. A small flame appeared between her thumb and forefinger and shot out into the grass, catching it on fire. She got so excited that she forgot to drop the grass and got her fingers slightly burned. Thea had just cast her first useful spell. Alison was also happy because in a pinch, there was now someone else who could start a fire, when flint and tinder should fail in a rainstorm, though a rainstorm here in the desert was highly unlikely. She could not know just how valuable this single spell would later become. When they had finished, Thea rushed over to her parent's wagon to tell them all about it and to try it in their fire pit.

Later on, her parents both came over to Alison. Her father spoke, "We both would like to thank you for taking Thea under your wing, so to speak. We always knew that she was different, but we never had the money to send her to the guild."

Her mother added, "She showed us that she can light our campfire. And for that I am very grateful. It is a very practical skill and valuable. Thank you."

"Yes, she is a very bright young woman. You should both be very proud of her. I promise to take very good care of her. Please don't worry about any danger. I am only teaching her small useful spells that one can use around the house, so to speak," she replied.

Alison observed a bit of tension in them evaporate. As an afterthought, she asked, "Say, do you have any clothes that need mending?"

"Er, sure, there is always mending to do. But I've never been able to get Thea to sit down long enough to mend anything," her mother chided.

"Well, that will be tomorrow's lesson. You may expect all of your mending to get done rapidly after tomorrow." And both women laughed. "If ever you have any concerns or worries about Thea, why don't hesitate to ask me right away. Night." And they smiled and returned to their wagon, arm in arm.

During their long stay in the Dead Sea camp, William had not been idle. Once his headache went away, he set to work making a temporary oven. With the aid of several millers in the caravan, he had gotten a lot of the wheat they had gotten from Hope's Lost ground in to flower. He began baking mountains of way bread, tasty, nourishing and a bread that would not spoil for days even in this heat.

This evening, he brought out a special loaf he had made just for Mandy. He wined and dined her that evening. Well, it was tea and dinner, to be more precise, for there was no wine to be had in this caravan. He had turned the end of the wagon into a table covered with a white sheet. He had found a yellow wild flower during the day and it was in a cup that served as a vase. The unexpected dinner took Mandy by surprise, and she thoroughly enjoyed every minute of it. Later, they took a long walk, arm in arm, around the camp.

On the sixth day out from the Dead Sea around noon, the terrain changed ever so subtly. Mandy was the first to spot it. As she crested yet another hill, in the distance, a dark jagged line stretched all across the horizon. The Hell's Gate and the Desolation Range was finally visible. She paused and studied the panorama. As the wagons caught up to her, she heard cheering rise from the caravan folks as they too spotted the line of craggy peaks far off in the distance. The endless steppes finally were ending and none too soon for everyone. It also meant they were at long last leaving Vyderland and their continuous threats.

Chapter 18 Of Giants and Dwarves and Sulfur

The eighth day out from the Dead Sea brought many changes, some unwelcome. The hills became taller and more frequent. A hardy grass covered the hills which made walking off the dirt road difficult. The hot dry arid region began to give way to a more humid climate. Tiny groves of oak and aspen trees began to dot the hillsides. Indeed, the mostly dry river bed that they had been following broadened and shallow waters trickled along hosting numerous end-of-season wild flowers. Each day the craggy, tall mountains grew larger on the distant horizon, foreboding peaks devoid of trees, black and grey sheets of rock thrusting skyward.

Alison riding on their left flank one hill over from the caravan was the first to spy the distant spies once again. Several riders were again paralleling the caravan from several miles away. She alerted Mandy by placing her thoughts in the ranger's mind. *They are back. Riders two hills over from me, about two miles distant. Shadowing us. This is sure a terrific way to alert everyone!*

I assumed that they would be back. Thanks for the alert. Yes, you have got the hang of sending us messages now, very good. It is so intimate a way to communicate, so personal, isn't it? Mandy sent back. After a pause, she sent, *I'll relay this to the others, thanks. Keep a sharp watch on them. And be careful. I am very surprised that they have sent no wizards of their own to do us in thus far. So stay alert.* Alison did keep a close eye on the hills to her left, but the out riders did nothing more that follow their passage.

With this not really unexpected news, Mandy grew very worried about their safety once more. They were still days from the mountains where she hoped that they would leave the Vyderland cavalry behind forever. One tactic she had not yet used, pushing the caravan at faster speeds for longer durations to speed their passage, now presented itself as a possibility. With all of the sturdy new horses to assist, it was a feasible tactic. Though she knew that the war horses were not trained to pull wagons, she figured something could be worked out. Of course, she knew that if she speeded up their progress that would only force the cavalry to speed up theirs. The Vyderland riders were running out of steppes and would be forced to act fairly soon.

Worse, though, was the total lack of knowledge of what lay ahead. It was conceivable that they could escape one peril only to find themselves in a worse predicament. She needed knowledge of what lay ahead. *I could just fly up ahead, but I don't dare leave them for a day or so. I should practice my new gift and see far ahead*, she thought to herself. But she decided against this as well. She would have her full attention far ahead of her location leaving her defenseless should the raiders choose this moment to strike again. *Tonight we should hold a conference and go over everything in our arsenal; we must be better prepared this time. Maybe we should drill some defensive actions*, she mused. She sent word to her friends to meet after dinner to discuss all of their options.

Instead of taking a lunch hour's respite, Mandy kept the caravan moving, forcing an eat on the move situation. The presence of the spies once more had not gone unnoticed by the townsfolk who were more than eager to forgo a lunch stop. however, many did hop out of the wagons and walk along for a time to stretch their legs.

Mandy halted for the day beside a little glen of trees that nestled up to the ever widening river. The children, cooped up on the wagons all day ran off to play, while the parents made camp and began cooking the evening meal. Mandy had just seen to the care of her horse when she heard some kids crying for help. She dashed toward them beside the river. She was the first to reach them. A dozen children were pointing to one boy who was up to his neck in quicksand. "He's stuck and sinking," exclaimed one six-year old girl.

"It's quicksand," she yelled. "You kids stand back from the bank." She looked around for something to use to reach the panicking boy. He could not even get his arms up any longer. He rocked his head back gasping for air as he sunk further into the mire. Only his mouth and nose remained above the sand. She had to act fast but there was no way to reach him from solid ground.

She concentrated and shape-changed into a very large eagle and flew up and out over the boy. Her claws sunk down into the muck and latched onto his shoulders. Then, she flapped her wings as hard as she could, raising him up very, very slowly. She had his whole head above the mire now. A number of other people had now reached the back and were met with a chaos of children all speaking at once. "It's Mandy. She's pulling him out. It's quicksand. Johnny's stuck. Johnny fell in." Several men ran for ropes. Try as she might, Mandy could not pull him out, only keep him from sinking all the way.

One of the men tied the rope to a tree and then waded out into the quicksand. He put a long arm under the boy's arms and grabbed him tight. Mandy then let go and flew back to the back and changed back. She lay on the ground panting for breath, totally exhausted from the strenuous effort. Other men pulled both the rescuer and the boy on out of the mire. Once they verified the terrified boy was otherwise all right, it was kudos all around, especially for Mandy who had saved him. By now the entire camp had come to see what was going on and soon the tale of the rescue spread throughout the camp.

"You all right?" Jon asked as he finally reached her side, helping her up.

Between pants, she answered, "Yes, but that was work!" And together, they walked back to Mandy's wagon. Raul quickly had his men put up warning sticks to mark the closest anyone should approach the river.

The dinner for the seven went quickly and soberly. All were anxious to discuss their situation. But just as they were ready to start, Thea came by for her evening lessons in the magical arts. "She is a fledgling wizard," Alison began, "so we might as well include her. She can help out if I train her." The others agreed; they needed all the help they could muster. Thea beamed with excitement; she was embarking on a whole new career and was accepted as a member of her band of heroes. She could hardly sit still!

"I thought we should discuss options," Mandy began, not too sure how to present her concerns. "So far, we have been phenomenally lucky or resourceful. First, we arrive just in the nick of time to relieve William. They raise the stakes with a small cavalry charge but a surprise use of a force field by Darless saves the day. Next, they go all out with a massive cavalry assault but Jon gets ghosts to fight for us to end their own curse. And still they trail us! I have no doubts that they will make another attempt before we disappear into the mountains ahead. I just don't know when or where yet. I'd like to be a bit better prepared next time because I think that they will pull out all of the stops. It's likely their last chance at us. And we are not up to full strength. Twenty-two of the guards are still on the mend with broken bones and wounds. I cannot ask them to defend the caravan in their current condition. So we need to devise some better advance plans, just in case. There, I said it all," she paused and then grinning, "well not all, I intend to get some sword practice time in with Raul later tonight. I believe that I can improve my speed of execution and get in two swipes to their one."

"Wow, two?" Alison cried truly impressed. "I think the Sir Thomas, my paladin friend, can do that. You are becoming an expert swordswoman! Congratulations indeed!" After Mandy acknowledged similar appreciations from the others, Alison continued. "Mandy, how many days until we are safely in the mountains?"

"Ah, you are using a word there that I would not — safely. I am not so sure that the mountains are going to be any safer. It is just my gut feeling from observing them from afar. Nothing specific," she commented. "Can I see your maps again?" Alison got them out and everyone looked over her shoulders. No one said anything.

So Thea asked, "So where are we now? Looks like vast nothingnesses everywhere."

Jon laughed, "My sentiments exactly, Thea. In my world, there are so many roads going every which a way, that our problem would be which road to take and which of hundreds of towns to visit on the way! Where are we anyway?"

Mandy estimated and pointed to a likely spot. "If, and this is a big if, the road passage does not change, I guess we might make the mountains in three or four days. But it is changing. Have you noticed that every time we climb a hill, when we go down again, we do not go down quite as far as the previous hill? We are slowly gaining elevation."

"But isn't that normal?" inquired Alison. "We should be gaining as we reach the foothills of the mountains."

"Look at the map. We are getting closer to that thing labeled as the Misty Marshes. The river is getting swampier by the mile. Quicksand has appeared. Taking heavily loaded wagons through a marsh is tricky, *if* you already know all about the marsh. We have no data on it at all. Worst case scenario, the wagons all sink in quicksand and we have to abandon them. I doubt that it will be that extreme, but it could," the ranger cautioned.

"Couldn't you just go on ahead and check it all out?" Darless suggested.

"I thought of that this morning, but rejected it," she sighed. "I would be gone for quite some time, perhaps even a day or so. What if you were attacked while I was off exploring? I just could not leave you in that kind of peril."

"Is there any other route we could detour and take?" May interjected, thinking that perhaps they could head much farther north and cross nearer the city labeled Hoar Frost.

"No marked roads or passage through the mountains are on the map. It could be that there is another way through but we could waste weeks searching and trying all sorts of dead ends. And it is getting closer to winter. I suspect that it comes early in these high mountains. We are not equipped for winter mountain travel, that's for sure. I'd rather not take that risk," Mandy cautioned.

"Well we certainly can't go south and skirt the whole thing," added Mat, "that would mean going right by Vyndoc itself! I'd just as soon stay as far from their main city as possible."

"What's all these tiny little dots?" asked Thea who continued to examine the map. "See they are all over the place in the mountains proper." No one had the slightest idea. Had they known, they might have been even more worried.

"So you see, it all boils down to us trying to become as prepared for anything as we possibly can in the next couple of days," Mandy concluded. "I will get Raul and the two others that are fit along with me into the best fighting form manageable. If it is any comfort, Reylona has granted me even more priestly spells. I can now even cure diseases and dispel magic like you all do!" She beamed with well-deserved pride.

Alison then said seriously, "I did receive a book of advanced spells from Ukko. I have had no time to even look at them. I know that I should be able to use several more spells a day than I have been. I should be able to use some upper grade ones. I hope there are some of that power level in that new spell book. Darless, you are in the same situation, right?"

"Yes, I should be able to cast at that level as well, but as yet I have not come across any. There just has not been any time to spend researching spells. I think that we should study your book and see what we can devise," Darless offered.

"Say, sis, I am way overdue for spell research as well," interjected May. "Although I use many different kinds of spells than you do, preferring those of an illusionary nature which work best in a town setting, I can learn some attacking spells. I should be able to use many middle grade spells. Would you mind if I searched through your books as well?"

"No, be my guest! If you can also cast some attack spells, we will be in even better shape," said Alison. "And while Thea here is only just beginning, I think that she can easily handle some of my wands and add to our firepower."

"Yes, but she is just beginning. One counter attack of force and she is toast," protested Mandy. "So we need to find some magical ways to protect her. See what all you can come up with. If nothing else, I do have some magical protection bits and pieces that will help her some."

"I will also look after her safety," Mat, who had been mostly silent, said. He added very humbly, "During that last battle, I perfected a number of my skills. While I congratulate you, Mandy, on finally equaling my former speed, I am now even faster. I have reached the Master of Winter skill levels. Though before I can claim that title, I must find and defeat the current Master of Winter. I have not said anything about this before, but in that last battle when I was so badly wounded that I was about to collapse, my last action was to experiment with vibrations of death. And I was successful."

"You're teasing me," May cried in protest.

"No sis, I have been withholding that from you. I was not totally sure that that is what I did do. But I have been studying a bit before bed since then. And I am now pretty sure about it. Sorry about not saying anything sooner, I just was not sure," he said almost tearfully; he never held anything back from May.

"I understand," she said softly. "If you can do that, that is awesome indeed."

"Do what?" asked Jon baffled.

May replied, "One of the most powerful actions a monk can do, and only the very highest monks can do it, is to set up vibrations in a victim's body and then command that body's death! It is the ultimate control. Mat dreamed of gaining such ability, for we could then really enforce law in Freetown."

"You mean that he could just touch my body and then tell it to die and it would?" asked Jon utterly amazed. "How?"

"Yes, but I would only use such in dire circumstances," Mat whispered, a little afraid of his own power. "How you ask? I could tell you but you would not understand any more than I understand how Mandy got it to rain or how you got all the horses to do your bidding or how Alison got those lightning bolts to split or fork onto so many men at the same time."

"You are right, of course. I have no idea about anything magical," Jon added. "And I really am not that interested. Each of us follows our own path to enlightenment."

"On that we totally agree," Mat said with a broad grin and he bowed to Jon, honoring him.

William, who had been totally silent, for what could a baker possibly have to suggest that these heroes could use, finally spoke, clearing his throat. "Hem, ah, my skills are useful only so long as I am not knocked on the head like last time. I'm not a fighter; I prevent fights. But I would be more useful if you could somehow keep me from being knocked out in the early going of a battle."

"He's right!" Mandy replied. "We can make you invisible if you like. And I have some bits and pieces of stuff which, when worn, makes you far harder to hit.

"I'm sorry everyone," Alison broke in unexpectedly. "I am your main wizard and I have been shirking my duties. Up to this point, I have been taking every offensive attack spells I possibly can, forsaking all others. I have one spell that I should have been taking and using on you. It makes your skin appear as if it were stone so that any combat strikes on your body will have no effect. Of course, it only stops a limited number of actual hits. But if it would deflect the first five hits you would otherwise have taken, it will keep you alive and going strong longer. I am sorry about not suggesting it sooner."

"Hey, no apologies needed! We needed every bit of firepower you could muster!" exclaimed Mandy. "But mark my words, this time they are going to throw everything at us. Think about their position. First they send a small band of raiders to take out a nearly defenseless caravan which fails. So then they send in a cavalry regiment which should do it but fails utterly. So then they send in a general and an entire cavalry division which should be enough force to wipe out most towns and only a few return to tell of its devastation. It would not surprise me in the least to next find ourselves facing their high priests and top wizards and maybe an entire army if they can get it here fast enough."

"I get it," Jon exclaimed. "You want us to be prepared for all sorts of spells and such and not just more cavalry. It makes perfect sense to me now. Why didn't you say so in the first place?"

"She did, silly," taunted Alison playfully. Everyone laughed.

"So when you decide what spells to utilize, just remember that you can now count on me for a couple of magic dispelling spells from Reylona. I will also pray for a lot of healing spells as well. But the real problem has been and still is just how to protect the six hundred or so in our care. It is pointless if we survive and they all die."

"Point well taken; let's get to work everyone. Ladies, let's study spells!" Alison proclaimed and the four spell casters began to set up a work area at the back of the wagon. Alison pulled out all of her spell books and Darless did likewise. Darless had just the right book for Thea, "Workings of the Wand" by Mage Alister the Great. The fledgling wizard spent the rest of the evening studying its pages.

May rummaged through Alison's main spell book. Occasionally she let out a little yell of surprise and excitement as she found a new spell she understood and could learn to use. Carefully, she began marking their pages. In an hour she was done going through all of the spell books that she could read. "Sis, I believe I can now teleport like you do! And I can create one of those walls of force that Darless used!"

"Great! That will really help out. Three walls of force, now that is something with which to work out a plan," exclaimed Alison.

"Plus, I can easily learn to cast a ball of fire and a lightning bolt. I've just never figured them out before. They are pretty useless in town," she added. May then set to work transcribing over a half dozen of the more critical spells into her own book.

Meanwhile, Darless and Alison began a thorough search of the new book Ukko had given to Alison. Occasionally they both let out a whoop of joy. While both wizards could now use a high grade spell, Alison could also use additional lower grade spells because she still was more skilled in the magic arts than Darless, though the alu-demon was rapidly catching up with her. They both declared, "We can now actually cast the fancy mansion spell! Jon and Mandy will love that!"

A short while later, they both cried, "Wow, the finger of death!" Then, "Stun!" Then "No errors in teleporting, wow!" This was followed by "Teleport Objects, now that *is* useful indeed!" And finally, "Disintegrate! That is what the high priestess shot at Jon back at the Tower of Leeds and had reflected back at her."

"Thank you, Father Ukko! This is one incredible spell book you have given me," said Alison reverently. Quickly, the two mages set to work copying these into their own spell books. Though the hour was getting late, Alison then rummaged through all of the items she had in her portable hole, looking for anything that would help sustain Thea and William. Darless already knew that she had nothing to offer because she never collected such since she had no use for them.

In the end, Alison decided upon two small items. She presented her apprentice with a ring and a cloak. "Wear this ring at all times. It makes you harder to hit in the first place and give you some aid in dodging the effects of enemy spells. When we go into a battle, put on the cloak as well. It offers similar protections. Between them, you will be much harder to hit and will be able to avoid enemy spells significantly better. But remember, you will be burned toast, if you take the full effects of a ball of fire." Thea was in total awe and handled these precious gifts as if they had come from a god. It was all that she could do to muster a "Thank you."

"And now for an offensive wand. You can have this one. It shoots magical missiles. It is nearly out of charges so use it sparingly. If we get into another pitched battle, I'll give you a second wand of fire balls. It is a bit more difficult to use, so we'll wait until we need the firepower. Your wand is activated by the phrase 'Blast them.' You point at the target and say the words. I think you can still do it another ten times." Alison next went over all of the important points from the book on wand care and usage. She was pleasantly surprised to find that Thea had understood nearly all of them. Perhaps Thea would make a good mage after all. It was encouraging.

Jon came by. He had just finished the evening band concert for the caravan audience. This had been their first concert since the big battle. All of the previous evenings he had spent performing assists on those that still needed revitalization. "Hi Love, how's it going?" he asked. He was in a cheerful mood; he always was after a concert.

"Terrific, Jon. Actually better than I ever hoped for. I can now cast those fancy mansion spells and a bunch of other really powerful ones. I can even shoot a disintegrate beam like the one that nearly got you back in Leeds."

"Isn't that a bit dangerous?" Jon asked looking a bit worried about her safety. He recalled how the high priestess had literally vanished when hit by her own beam. "I sure don't want anything bad to happen to you!"

She hugged him and gave him a kiss. "Don't worry. I promise to very rarely use that one. It is not my style. It's more an act of desperation, if you ask me. But it adds to my arsenal of possibilities."

"Okay. Say, did you come across anything that can lighten the wagons or make them go faster?" he asked. All this chain mail they were now toting along with them seemed to slow them down in his opinion.

"Well actually, we have. I can move about seven hundred pounds of stuff in one spell, moving it from here into my place back home — all without lifting a finger, just by standing here beside the stuff. Pretty neat, don't you think?" she asked.

"Wow! Now that is really useful. Maybe we can dump all of the stuff and lighten the load on everyone," he suggested.

"I'm already on it," she teased. "Darless can now do it as well, though not quite as much as I. We will be able to unload all of the armor and weapons tomorrow. Then, the war horses can be used to help pull the wagons somehow." She added, "Look to May for more help. She will be able to shoot some offensive area spells tomorrow. And now between us, we can utilize three walls of force."

This Jon found fascinating. "Do you suppose that if we could get all of the wagons and people in really close, that they could be completely covered by those walls?"

"I see what you are suggesting. We will have to see about that. I would think that if the people all got sufficiently close together, we could manage it," she replied. "But come on, let's take our nightly stroll. There goes William and Mandy." And the two began their nightly walk, arm in arm.

The next morning, Alison grabbed Jon and Mandy just after breakfast. "Okay, I did the estimations. Three of us can build walls of force and join them However, you are going to have to pack the wagons in very tight, say into no more than twelve feet by twenty-five feet per wagon. The durations will vary from mine at thirty minutes down to May's at half of that. That would likely protect them from the main brunt of the attack, since such is hardly likely to last a half hour. The other possibility, which is far riskier, is that I can create mansions now, bigger than the ones I got from the scrolls. However, if everyone piled in, they would have only about three feet between each other — way too cramped! There is chance that Darless could also cast one which would nearly double the space per person. But the liability is they might be trapped in there forever if the caster of the spell perishes; there would be no way out for them."

No one really liked the idea of the mansion just because of the extreme risk to the people. So it was tabled as a last resort. Mandy observed, "We probably can get all the wagons that close, but that would leave the three hundred valuable medium war horses outside the protective sphere. I'd sure hate to lose them."

"Say, Mandy, what exactly do these types of horses do?" Jon asked. He had not really seen a cavalry attack, just the foiled ones.

"If the rider closes to combat distance, the horse kicks out with each hoof and can also bite," she replied. "The kicks can cause some damage if they do several."

Jon had the beginnings of an idea. "When the battle comes, can all of the war horses be turned loose with no bridles or anything, just the plain horse? I may be able to do something with them."

"Sure, it is probably the best thing to do with them. I'd really hate to see them get hurt," she replied. "But what can you do with them?"

"Not sure yet. I'm going to experiment with them today. I'll let you know," he answered, already deep in thought.

And so the ninth day out from the Dead Sea began. The mages were now well prepared with spells because the successful defense of the caravan now rested squarely on their shoulders. The first thing they accomplished was the moving of all the heavy chain mail and unneeded weapons from here into the hallway of Alison's dungeon entrance. She and Darless both cast one of their new spells to accomplish this vanishment. This greatly aided one and all because the three hundred war horses now only had to be haltered and led along.

While the mages were getting rid of the weighty items, Mat approached Alison. "Excuse me Runtkins, but can I ask a very big favor?"

"Sure Big Brother," she smiled remembering all the playful times he called her that.

"Can I borrow one of your rings of invisibility?" he asked.

"Sure," she replied without thinking. While fetching it from an inner pocket, her curiosity rose. "What are you planning, Big Brother? Something mischievous?"

"I'm going to contribute in my own way. We are just so naked out here in the wide open spaces! We are not really equipped or trained really to be effective outside a town. Do you realize that this is farther than we have ever traveled?" he replied.

"Yes, but you did not answer my question, Big Brother," she teased, unwilling to take a non-answer answer from him just now.

"I can move cross open country like this as fast as the wind. Actually, sis, I probably can out run your horse over short distances," he explained.

"That is incredible! But you still are avoiding my question," she chuckled and he grinned, knowing that he could not elude her further.

"Okay. I am going to go infiltrate the enemy and try to learn their plans. There you have it. With your ring, I should have no problems at all doing so," he blurted it out and then quickly added, "And you are not going to tell me I cannot do it."

"No, I certainly would not try to prevent you from trying it. But do be careful, please! I'd feel horrible if anything bad happened to you." And she hugged him tightly. Very surprised by her acceptance, he thanked her and slipped on the ring and disappeared. She felt him move off southward toward where the enemy spies were last seen the day before.

She quickly alerted the others to what Mat was doing. Jon promised to keep his senses alert for Mat. And then the wagons pulled out, heading westwards as they had done daily for well over a month now. This time, however, Mandy had Raul keep the wagons bunched more closely together than ever before so less time would be needed to form a tight grouping for defense.

As usual, Mandy rode point and was nearly a half mile ahead of the slow moving wagons. She halted and twisted in her saddle to view Alison and Darless who were riding on either side of the caravan, but about a half mile south and north, respectively. She was highly doubtful that they would be attacked from their right flank because the enemy forces would have to cut across the trail either behind them and then catch up or in front of them. She'd seen no signs of any passage across the trail. In fact, she'd seen scant signs that the trail they were on had much use recently. All tracks were so old they were nearly wiped out by nature's winds. No, the two previous attacks she had witnessed came from the left flank, closest to Vyndoc, the side Alison was patrolling.

Watching Alison slowly keeping pace with the caravan, Mandy worried about her friend. She certainly would not have put her strongest mage out there in the most vulnerable position. She had visions of hordes suddenly attacking the lone wizard. Blinking, Mandy wiped those fantasies from her mind. There was no other choice except Alison and she knew it. Alison was the only expert horseman here besides Raul and he was needed to actually command the wagons. She nudged her horse forward, resuming her advanced scouting.

Based upon her tracking skills, this east-west road was not used much. That was a good sign in many ways, not the least making her job easier. She didn't have to sort out tracks and try to figure out what had passed by. As she crested another hill, a glint of sunlight caught her eye. She looked to the southern hills and caught sight of several horsemen paralleling the caravan. Only this time, they were more brazen about their activities, making no pains to hide themselves from view. Mandy thought that this was an ominous, bold sign. "Zounds! I do hate all this sneaking around stuff!" she muttered to herself.

However, on the other side of the hill, the terrain changed. Trees grew more dense, though it was still not classifiable as a forest from Mandy's point of view, the trees were perhaps ten feet apart with good grasslands in between. And up ahead was a cross road, the first cross road they had encountered. As she pulled up at the junction, she looked both ways. As far as she could tell, the north-south road paralleled these foothills of the mountains.

A quick glance at the ground told this ranger much. Many, many horses had passed here within the last twenty-four hours, all heading north. This was a scary thought, for that meant the enemy could be planning to attack the caravan from both sides now. Quickly, she mentally sent a message to Darless who was patrolling their northern flank. *We are at a cross roads. A large number of cavalry has ridden on north of us within the last twenty-four hours. Be alert for a sudden assault on your side.*

Darless responded and indicated she had not even seen an out rider as yet. It was totally quite on her side. That gave Mandy pause to consider what was going on here. She dismounted and began to study the tracks very carefully. From the depth of the newly trodden ruts and the pulverized dirt and the voluminous number of hoof prints, she concluded that an entire regiment of cavalry had passed by here, very likely similar in size to the group that had recently attacked them, perhaps six hundred strong. From the individual depth of the prints, she concluded that they were medium war horses heavily laden, most likely with supplies. She also spotted the tell-tale tracks of three supply wagons that cut deep trails in the now powdery dirt of the roadbed.

She was just finishing up her inspection when something unusual caught her attention. She found one unmistakable footprint in the dirt near the center of the intersection. It was a bare footprint of huge dimensions, nearly twice that of her own foot. And it was made last, for it covered a bit of the wagon ruts and hoof marks.

"Zagroot zounds! What have we here?" she muttered. She heard the sounds of the approaching wagons now catching up to her. She quickly signaled Raul to halt the wagons well before the cross road. Shortly he came riding up.

"A crossroads. This is not on the maps, is it? Looks like it is well traveled and recently," he commented.

"Yes, within the last day, I'd say," she replied. "Keep everyone well back of here for now, I am still studying these trails. Also, keep a sharp look out. Riders are on the southern hills watching us now. They are getting bolder, so maybe an attack is eminent."

He trotted back the hundred feet to the lead wagon and began issuing orders. This time, he had every wagon pull up very close to each other into a small, dense formation. Since everyone wanted to know what was going on, he found himself repeating his observations at the cross road.

Jon walked up to Mandy, but stayed well back of the tracks. He knew better than to walk out into the scene before him and mess up the ground. Since she was concentrating hard, staring at the ground and moving about, he remained quiet and observed her. Presently May joined him also standing silently looking about. Alison and Darless edged in closer to the halted caravan to see what was happening. Both could see the cross road and the intersection.

Mandy looked up and saw the others watching her and smiled. "Thanks, there are lots of tracks that still need explaining here." Then, she signaled Alison who quickly rode up and dismounted tying her horse to a nearby tree.

"What's up? Looks like an army went through here," she said. The tracks were unmistakable even to a non-tracker such as herself.

"Come here a minute," she said with a serious note in her voice. "What do you make of this footprint," she pointed to the large, bare foot print. "And there is another here and another way over here."

Alison carefully walked over to the spot Mandy had pointed to first. "Wow, what a large foot! Bare, right?"

"Yes, and it looks like the person walked from just ahead out here to the middle of the road, paused a bit, and then walked back," Mandy suggested. Seeing a blank look on Alison's face, she elaborated, "Look which way the toes point here and then here. Look how deep the heel print is over here compared to that one in the middle of the road. See the difference? Here the person is walking and there they are standing — no heel dig in."

"Ah, yes, I see it now that you point it out," she replied. "It is rather obvious, isn't it, if you know what to look for."

Mandy smiled and then went on, "And here is another print. I think we have a left one here and a right one there. Now I make that stride about eight feet."

The mage curled her lips and frowned. "Wait a minute, no one can have an eight foot stride! Not even if they are running. To do that, why their legs would have to be really long!" Suddenly she realized what she was looking at; Mandy did as well. They looked at each other and said in unison, "Giant."

"Giant what," hollered Jon bursting with curiosity, but still unwilling to trample over the clues on the ground.

"Giant giant," replied Mandy. "Alison, you go explain it all to the others. It's probably a good time to grab some lunch. It'll give me more time to explore this situation." The mage did so.

"Hi May, Jon. There are people, rare people though, that have really large bodies compared to us, giants who stand maybe twelve feet tall or more. There are whole races of them, some good and some evil, just like humans. Mandy's found giant tracks here and is studying them," she explained.

"Wow, I thought that giants only lived in fairy-tales, like Jack and the Beanstalk," Jon replied.

"What's Jack and the plant?" asked Alison who had no idea what he was talking about.

Jon had to explain the children's story to her and May. Then, Alison continued, "I've only heard of giants, not actually seen one. I think that Sir Thomas, our paladin, has met one once some years ago. I've heard that they throw boulders at people, so I really don't want to run into any."

May then added her ideas, "Well, a grey skinned giant once came into Freetown about three years ago. He stirred up quite a sensation, everyone was gawking at him and following him around. Seems he wanted to convert a huge pile of gems into bars of gold. He carried several hundred pounds of gold off with him in a huge sack, carried it like we carry a nap sack!"

"Boo! Hi all," said Mat, taking off the ring of invisibility and suddenly appearing in their midst starling everyone.

"Don't do that again!" said Alison sternly, "you nearly scared me into casting a nasty spell on you!" Then she smiled at him and gave him a hug. May knew he was coming and had expected his trick but had not said anything. She enjoyed a little fun too.

"What's all this about a giant?" Mat wanted to know. "I sort of came in at the end of the conversation." Alison told him of Mandy's findings.

Jon, Alison, pretend idle conversation and walk slowly over to me right now! Mandy placed in their minds. She also told Mat and May to continue chatting where they were at. All four instantly glanced at Mandy, but she pretended only to look at the ground. She was now across the road and standing beside the first tree closest to the road. *We are being watched!*

Jon and Alison ambled over to Mandy, trying to avoid looking all around for the unseen spy. Jon found that this took self-control for he naturally wanted to look all over for this person. But he managed to mumble on about fairy tales. When they stood beside her, she sent, *It is a male probably, over there behind that huge boulder. I was following the trail back and picked up giant foot steps heading that way. The trail came originally out from behind that rock, paused in the middle of the intersection, and then went back on this side of the boulder. Careful, if he is a giant, he may throw huge boulders on us! What should we do?*

Alison thought quickly and carefully sent both, *Spread out so one boulder will not get us all then let's confront him.*

I have an idea. Let me try, Jon replied back mentally. *You stay out of the way because I can easily dodge any flying rocks.* While they did not know how he could duck flying boulders, they fanned out. *Let's not make any threatening moves,* he added as an afterthought.

Jon then strolled around the area, slowly meandering toward the location Mandy indicated. He expanded his awareness searching for another being and mind. He soon made contact. It was a very foreign mind, but he felt only the emotion of curiosity emanating from him. So he wandered even closer and moved around the boulder. "Oh, hello," he said as calmly and friendly as possible; he narrowly avoided bumping into a huge sized leg. He looked up to see a man dressed in a loin cloth standing nearly twelve feet tall. His body had no hair on it whatsoever and was very grey in color. The giant's leg was larger around than Jon's chest. "My name is Jon Brown. May I help you or be of some service to you?" He wondered if the giant would even understand his language.

Relief came as the giant spoke, "Hello small fry, Jon." He bent to look down at the small man. "I be Rolf. You not be Vyndocian?" From the serious tone in his deep voice, Jon knew this must be somehow important.

"No, the Vyndocians have attacked our caravan three times now. Each time we defeated them and drove them off. Nasty people, these Vyndocians." Jon wondered at the name, but he used Rolf's term. The giant's face was very elongated making facial expressions appear greatly exaggerated from Jon's view point. He swore Rolf was reacting to his last comment by manifesting some strong emotions or feelings, but what they were, surprise, excitement, impressed, he was not sure.

"Me hate Vyndocians too," Rolf answered. "Me been spying on them. Vyndocian army passed by here not long ago. Me worried. What they up to now? Me need help. Me hungry too. Me looking for treasures for me bag."

"Well, traveler, we have just stopped for lunch. I don't know what you eat, but if any of our food will do, you are most welcome to come and share it with us. Over lunch, you can tell us what kind of help you need and what kind of treasure you are looking for. I am looking for music and songs, personally, though no one else in our caravan is looking for that," Jon smiled.

"Okay. Me hungry. Me eats most anything," Rolf replied eagerly. And he followed Jon back around the boulder joining Alison and Mandy. "Pretty womens, thee be," he added as he saw the two.

"This is our trail leader, Mandy Blackthorn and our wizard, Alison d'Ambrose," Jon performed the introductions.

"And this is Rolf." He bowed slightly. Both girls smiled and tried not to stare too much.

"Me watch you from behind boulder; you pretty," he complimented them.

Mandy decided to say the obvious, "Well, Rolf, you are the first giant that I have ever seen. I hope you don't mind if I stare at you. In fact none of us here have seen many giants, so we will all probably be staring at you, if you don't mind, that is."

He let out a bellowing laugh, "No, me not mind cause me not seen you either. Me stare at you." As he said that, he remembered something; his expression changed. Mandy spied a tear forming in his left eye.

"What's wrong?" she instinctively asked.

"You remind Rolf of Tessa, she me woman-wife. She gone. She captured by Vyndocians a moon ago," he said with a great sadness exaggerated by his elongated face.

"Well, you will have to tell us all about it over lunch," she replied. "Maybe we can help." She added that last out of politeness; she had no idea how she could help a captured giant. Almost at once, they reached the location where Mat and May stood, waiting patiently. This was the second giant that they had seen, so they did not stare as much as everyone else did. Jon introduced the Twins, and they headed toward the closely bunched wagons. The smells of food drifted on the slight breeze.

Then came more introductions. And Mandy was right, the entire camp strained for a closer look at their first giant. Rolf stared at them as well. He saw lots of pretty womens, from his point of view. Once more several women brought lunch for their leaders; they felt terrific that they could do something to help out. But they got a wee bit more than they expected with their new guest. Rolf consumed ten men's portions before he was satisfied. It became obvious that either giants had large appetites or he had not eaten for a while.

After satiating his hunger, they found the latter closer the mark. He told them his tale. Because of his language and thought patterns, the entire story was not clear until he had completely finished. Rolf was the leader of the Shaggy Rock Clan of Stone Giants. These mountains were home to many such clans and had been so for a very long time.

The Vyndocians had for many years been attacking these giants. In defense, they built huge stone semicircles around their cave entrances and had been successful at fending off the horsemen. Recently, though, the attackers used vile magic on them. Just as the raiders attacked, their stone walls made of solid boulders just melted into mud, leaving an opening through which the raiders charged.

A month ago, while Rolf was out hunting deer, which was their favorite delicacy, the Vyndocians attacked his cave. They subdued his wife, Tessa, and his son, Tog, and took them away. When he returned to find them gone, he started out after them. He caught up with the raiders many miles from here. They had his family locked up in great cages on wheels pulled by many horses. There were no boulders around that he could use for attacking and there were too many of them for him to defeat all by himself. So he just followed them. They went all the way to the Vyndoc city.

Late one night, he snuck into the city and found them securely locked in cages. Try as he might, he could not bust them free. Tessa said that they were all right and being fed and for him to get away and get help. Unfortunately, Rolf had found no help as yet. But on his way back here, two armies of horsemen passed him by while he hid. One went towards the mountains to attack yet another giant cave clan. The other rode north but evidentially had turned around and had just passed through here yesterday heading north toward the dwarven towns. Their passage had spooked all of the deer herds and he had not eaten in two days.

Rolf's story was vitally important from a number of angles. First, Alison nearly choked when she heard how their stone walls turned to mud. It was a sudden revelation. That was how the evil ones had destroyed Castle d'Ambrose! She finally had figured out what had brought the castle to its ruin. Mat and May gasped as she quickly explained her theory. Then, she had to explain to Rolf what had happened to her family and castle. He was very sympathetic.

"That ties in well with what I have found out," Mat explained. "I really got an earful while spying on them. First, it was the Sixth Phalanx Division that we defeated. There were only a handful of survivors. It seems the motto that all of the cavalrymen follow is 'Live or Die by Glorious Combat in the

Eyes of Morrigan.' They are all nuts on this goal. I think that there are or were just six of these cavalry divisions left. One is on guard duty at Vyndoc city. Two are on guard duty far to the east and to the extreme south. One is raiding the giants; one is headed for the dwarven cities. Evidently one or more of them lie fairly close to the pass that we need to use. From what I can tell, they are first trying to cut off any assistance we might get from the dwarves. In three days, both groups are to come at us in a pincer attack, one from each flank simultaneously. I think the division that passed through here is called the Hare's Back Phalanx and the ones going after the giants is Mare's Head Elite. They also have three of the Royal Family with them. I'm not sure what that means except that they are apparently spell casters of some renown." He finished, satisfied he had told everything he had picked up.

Alison and Mandy sat speechless for a minute. Then Alison blurted out, "How on earth did you find all that out?"

Mat and May smiled, there was a twinkle in their eyes. He said teasingly, "We are the Twins, you know. It is our business to find out the goings on in towns."

"Yes, but there is no towns here," she protested.

"Ah, but there are outriders with big mouths," he laughed. "You'd be surprised what all they talk about to pass the time on patrol duty watching us moving like a predictable snail. They are awfully bored men."

"Gang, we gotta help Rolf out," Jon pronounced. "We have time, three days." That turned the conversation onto the most pressing matter for the giant. He was grateful.

Of course, Mandy raised the big question, "How do you propose to help him, Jon? We don't exactly have an army to send to Vyndoc. And if we go, then who's going to protect the helpless caravan?"

"That is the catch," Jon had to admit. He explained their plight to Rolf. "So if we go to Vyndoc, our people here need protecting."

"Hides 'em, me says," was Rolf's immediate answer.

"Where?" was Mandy's immediate counter. "This is pretty open spaces around here and we are being tailed. And even if we lose the spies, the ruts left by the passage of all of our wagons will lead a blind man to where we are hiding."

That killed the conversation for a minute. At last, Rolf spoke up, "Hides 'em in me cave. It's plenty big. Me mess up wagon ruts. Go at night. No moon til sun comes back."

"Say, that's an intriguing idea," Alison replied. "If we could somehow lose the spies for a time and get the caravan hidden safely in caves, not only will that allow us time to rescue his family, but it will also totally confuse the enemy. I'm for giving it a try. Anything to confuse those Vyndocians!" On that, everyone agreed. The sudden disappearance of the caravan would perhaps cause them to make some errors. At least it may throw their pincer attack plans overboard.

"May and I can see to it that the nearby spies are knocked out for the night," Mat declared with complete confidence. "We've done this sort of thing many times before." Alison now had no doubts about that. So next, the details of how best to move the caravan and where exactly Rolf's cave hideout was located were discussed. In actual fact, he lived in a mountainous spur that jutted out eastward. They could reach it during the night he was certain, especially if they continued on the east-west road for the rest of the day.

So after lunch the caravan moved out once more, heading westward as normal. Mandy noted that the spies followed suit.

Jon, on the other hand, continued chatting with the giant, trying to figure out a way to rescue his family. He found it frustrating. "You know a picture is worth a thousand words," he said in disgust.

Rolf nodded his agreement, "Me not so good with words either."

"I know, Rolf. You just get a good picture of Tessa and Tog in your mind and I will look at it."

"How you do that?" he asked baffled completely.

"Don't worry. You won't feel a thing," he encouraged. It worked perfectly and Jon saw what they looked like. "Say, she is a pretty woman too," he added mostly out of courtesy. He saw a twelve foot woman also dressed only in a loin cloth. Tog, on the other hand, appeared to be about the size of Jon. Next, Jon had him remember images of what Vyndoc looked like. "Wow!" was all he said for he recognized the city from one of the pages in Alison's magical picture books.

Jon then sent to Alison who was a half mile off riding on the flank once more, *Vyndoc is in your picture book! We can use the book to get there. Tomorrow night, you and Mandy and I are going giant rescuing!*

She sent back, *Terrific! I'll be ready!* And she meant it.

The plan to hide out for a few days in the relative safety of the giant's cave and perhaps escape yet another attack along with an attempt to deceive the spies echoed throughout the caravan. Only a few expressed the slight worry about whether or not the giants could be trusted. Indeed Jon observed a good deal of enthusiasm all that afternoon from in those in their wagons about him.

As they rolled onwards, the terrain changed just as soon as they passed the north-south intersection. Huge boulders lay strewn about as if some gods had played a game of ball. The track now wove this way and that around these large obstacles and rose ever higher in elevation with each passing mile. Groves of aspen and oaks dotted the hillsides between the rock out-crops. These travelers welcomed a change from the steppes, for most, it was scenery they had never seen before. Excited children ran alongside of the wagons darting among the trees and around the boulders.

By evening, Mandy picked what their spies would also concur was an agreeable place to camp for the night. Her site lay just south of the road near a bubbling creek that fed the main river which still was on their right. To the unseen eyes of the spies, nothing looked different from any previous evening. Jon's band even played popular tunes for an hour just after sunset.

When it was full dark, May and Mat, dressed in their Twins black clothing, prepared for their foray to the enemy's camp. Jon remarked that the only thing visible were their eyes! He watched them melt into the night. Based on Mat's observations earlier today, he had a good idea where to find their camp. They had grown bolder and were only a mile away in a sheltered glen. They even had the hot coals of a campfire providing dim illumination. All six men were bedded down for the night with one poking the coals and smoking a cigar.

Mat crept up quietly behind him and thumped him on the head; he went down like a rock. Now it was a simple task to knock the sleeping men out cold. They then tied the men securely using some rope from one of the guards saddle bags. They also left a knife where the men could struggle to reach and eventually free themselves. Then, the two led the six horses back to the caravan. It was the easiest time they had at overpowering ruffians. They had been gone less than an hour.

Just as soon as they got back to the caravan, Mandy gave the orders to harness up and move out. In actual fact, the drovers had not really untacked all of their horses. So in less than an hour the caravan was moving out, single file now. Each wagon followed closely behind the one in front. Since Mandy did not want to risk any lights, it was a bit of tricky driving indeed. Soon they were heading south following Rolf's guidance. Periodically, he and Mandy went to the rear of the long line, leaving Alison to lead the forward wagon. There they proceeded to hide all traces of their passage. In the dark it was hard to do. Mandy vowed to return in the morning and do a better job of it.

Excitement kept all of the drivers alert far into the night, for alert they needed to be to keep from ramming into the wagon in front. They could not really see the ground and so had to simply follow the leader and hope for the best. The late night air became very chilly, horses panting exhales cast a shower of misty fog but was not seen. The chill also kept the men alert.

Dawn brought them more worries. They had not yet reached Rolf's cave complex. They had climbed above the timberline. All around them lay grey boulders and rocky surfaces covered with lichens. It was a stark, barren land they had entered. To either side of the narrow track the mountain side slopped steeply down. There could be no possibility of passing a broken down wagon. And any miscue to their left would send wagons and horses plummeting down for at least five hundred feet into that boulder filled terrain with oak and aspen groves they had left behind. The dangerousness of their position now kept the drivers on edge; there could be no mistakes.

Finally, around nine, the trail turned a corner and entered a canyon. Up ahead a huge stone fortification could be easily seen, the remains of the outer works of Rolf's protection wall around his cave complex. A dozen grey giant heads peered around and over the barrier wall at the incoming wagons, led by Rolf. For them, this was a new experience for never before had any humans been welcomed into their clan cave. And as the wagons slowly pulled inside the wall, everyone was talking excitedly at once, Rolf was explaining and gesturing over the din. And so amid chaotic discussions and plenty of staring from both parties, the caravan was safely led inside the caverns of the giants.

Now as Alison had approached the actual giant built fortifications, she could see what had happened. They had formed a thick barrier wall of various stonework, a patchwork quilt of available stone. Much of it was the grey rock of the mountain they had traversed. But several sections had most unusual black stone blocks which contained a silverish spirals within it. It was obvious where the Vyndocians had breeched the fortifications. A gaping hole in the wall through which the wagons made their way had a long dry mud flow cascading down the mountain side, the remains of the stone to mud spell.

This interested Alison. She dismounted and closely examined the mud flow and what remained of the stone wall. It was now very obvious to her just what spell had been cast. Darless concurred with her observations. A mage or possibly a high priest had caused a key section of the rock to change form into mud and flow off down the mountain, leaving a breech. Alison's keen eye for detail noticed that in no place in the breech and mud flow had any of the black stones with the silver speckles in it been so altered. Chunks of this stone remained protruding from the grey mud all around them.

Later that day when she got an opportunity to question Rolf about it, he said, "Me see blacky's not melted. Me wonder why, too."

"Where does that black rock come from?" she queried.

"We gets it from far over yonder in a sacred quarry. Only giants ever go there. Whole mountain side of blackys there. Me show you what me do with it. Come you see." He led her inside the cave. The cave was actually a complex of five adjoining caverns, greatly enlarged by the handiwork of the giants. The ceilings, while roughhewn, were usually fifteen feet overhead. The wagons and horses and humans were making camp in the chamber closest to the entrance, just to one's left as you entered the caverns. The chamber to the right was they giant's communal play room. It was here Rolf led her. Numerous torches affixed to the walls burned and crackled and illuminated the room which was about a hundred feet in diameter. All of the furniture was huge in dimensions to fit the owners. But all were hand carved from giant blocks of stone. All were from this blacky stone.

Each chair and table was highly polished. The silverish swirls sparkled in the light, breathtaking in their beauty! "Wow!" exclaimed Alison. "They are spectacularly beautiful. Did you make them?"

He beamed with pride, "Me and Tessa and some others. Make them ourselves. Tessa loves them. Real pretty. Me like do nice things for Tessa." Alison just had to show her friends this magnificent stonework.

Rolf and several others were very pleased with the compliments the others also gave their handiwork. Darless was so impressed that she asked, "Rolf, do you take commissions to make blacky things for others? If so, I would like to order some things made just like these, though not so large, of course."

"What you mean commission?" Me not know that word," he faltered a bit embarrassed.

"I mean I give you something you want in return you make some blacky things for me," she tried to explain.

"You mean you gives Rolf some treasures and me makes blacky things for you?" he queried, a look of hopefulness appearing in his eyes.

"Yes, that's it exactly. What kind of treasures do you want?" she continued, eager to establish a trade. She had never seen stone work so beautiful, the sparkling swirls were just magnificent.

"Me wants soft gold. Not much gold around here. Hard to find. Nice to work. Tessa likes it. You give Rolf gold and Rolf gives you blacky things." He was very eager to strike up a trade. But at the mention of the word gold, several other giants suddenly became very interested. And soon several others who had crafted some of these stone items wanted to trade with her as well. In the end, she agreed to make deals with all of them. This was one trade that left both sides elated!

When Mandy came riding into the caves several hours later after having back tracked and made some touch ups further hiding their passage, she found Alison once again studying the dried mud flow. The mage's concentration was so intense, that she did not even hear the ranger approach or dismount. Mandy had to touch her on the shoulder to get her attention. "What's going on?" she asked now also full of curiosity.

"Oh, excuse me, I was studying these marvelous black stones. See they were a small part of the barrier that the enemy transformed by spells into mud. But the blacky's, as Rolf's people call them, were not affected at all. See they still are in their original positions as near as I can make out."

"Cool looking rock, basalt I think. Good hard stone. Good for castles, even. Say what is this sparkling stuff within the rock?" Mandy asked.

"You should see what these rocks look like when polished! Rolf's people have made all of their furniture out of this rock, highly polished. It's just spectacular! You must see them. But just what this silver actually is, I am not certain. I have a wild notion, though. Do you recognize it?" asked Alison. Darless walked up and joined them, catching the end of their conversation. She examined the stone more closely along with Mandy.

Mandy drew her knife and tried to scratch a portion of the silver where it was more dense. He knife tip failed to scratch it and instead its point became quite dulled! "Well, it is not silver, that's for sure. Look what it did to my knife point! Now I will have to spend an hour working that dent out." After a pause, she muttered to herself, "What's silver and is not silver? Beats me," she gave up and led her horse on into the caverns and went to inspect how the caravan people were faring.

Darless was just as intrigued. "We cannot even get a flake of the silver to analyze. It is much harder than Mandy's toughened steel. This is indeed a mystery. But they will make just about anything we desire in trade for gold. I intend to have them make me some cool items, like a chair with a very high back. It should be spectacular indeed!"

Alison agreed that this was indeed the find of the year. And she searched and found a smaller sample and stuck it in one of the many pockets in her clothes. Then the two went inside to join the others. The mystery would remain a mystery for now.

By noon, everyone was asleep. After the all-night journey, sleep, even on a stone floor, came fast to everyone. Mandy still thought it prudent to maintain a watch. So several guards took turns watching the sleeping people throughout the day.

By dusk, the sounds of smashing boulders woke them. At first, Mandy fretted that they were under attack. But Rolf quickly explained that some of his clan were playing a game of Stones. He led several of the more curious outside to observe the game in progress. They saw six giants lobbing rounded boulders that must have weighed twenty pounds at least down a narrow corridor. At the other end some two hundred feet away ten crude stone man-like figures stood in a triangular formation. The objective, Rolf explained, was to knock all ten down with one toss. A seventh giant was repositioning the stone men between tosses. The winner was the first giant to get all ten down with one toss three times total. As they watched, a giant named Alfo just won the game with a good deal of bravado accompanying his win.

After eating dinner, Jon took his friends aside. "Okay, I think that the time to go is around midnight. That should have most of the city dwellers asleep. Here's my plan." And he briefly outlined what he had in mind. Darless and Alison and May all took an hour to prepare the needed spells. And at midnight, May, Mat, Darless, Mandy, Alison and Jon stood beside a table in the common room looking at a page in one of Alison's picture book. There before them was a city of unusual architecture. Tall spiraling structures with many minarets dominated the scene. It reminded Jon somewhat of pictures of old Russia that he had seen in a National Geographic magazine. Each of the buildings was decorated in vibrant bright colors. All colors were represented, most likely they were painted structures. "Welcome to Vyndoc," Jon announced.

After some comments, Mandy decided to stay behind just in case of trouble either here or in Vyndoc. Via the book she could reach them if needed. They just could not leave the entire caravan unguarded by at least one of them. When they were ready to head out, Jon had everyone hold hands and hold onto his. "Now just begin to walk forward, and here we are." One instant they were in the cavern common room and the next instant, as they stepped forward, their feet landed on the ground just outside the city walls. Mat and May, disoriented, stumbled and fell flat on the ground.

Mandy managed to catch herself with only a slight stumble. "I'll never get used to that," she muttered.

"We still don't know how you do that!" exclaimed the twins in unison as they got up and dusted off their black clothes. Mat asked, "Why did we land here outside the walls? How are we going to get inside?"

"I am being overly cautious," Jon explained. "It seems quiet enough. What do you think, Alison?"

She listened for a time and whispered back, "I think they are not expecting us and all is quiet as I would expect at midnight. I think it is a go for the next step."

"Okay, hold hands again, we are going inside and near where Rolf last saw Tessa and Tog," Jon whispered. When everyone was ready, he whispered, "Step forward now and here we are." They were now inside the city standing in the middle of what could be described as a town square.

It was dark, very dark indeed within the city. No moon, no streetlights, only the starlight. Jon and the others stood very still, straining their other senses, alert for danger. "This is our terrain," whispered May. "All's quiet. Why don't you stay here out of sight and let us see what we can find."

"I can see heat, if that will help," Darless said in a low voice. "There are no bodies in any direction that I can see, not even giants."

"They must have moved them; we'll go find them; you stay put here," Mat ordered. Without waiting for a reply, he and May were off heading down the street. Jon was only too thankful for their suggestion; he had no idea how to find the giants. He could only barely see his hands in front of his face.

Alison tugged him over to the side near an alley way out of sight of any late night passersby. *Darless' will keep watch for us,* she placed into his mind. And then added, *This sure is a good use of this ability, silent communication. They* waited patiently for at least an hour. Jon sat down on the ground and dozed slightly. Alison finally joined him, relying on Darless who stood statue-like, her eyes methodically scanning the street in both directions, roof tops, and windows. If anything, she was methodical.

Here they come, Darless at long last sent to both her friends. Jon looked in all directions but saw nothing until the twins were almost in front of him. He marveled at just how well they blended invisible into the night.

"We found the giants, all dozen of them," May whispered. "Follow us and be as quiet as you can."

"What do you mean all dozen of them?" Jon had to ask, there were only supposed to be two. He got no answer as they were already slinking down the street. He had to hurry to keep up with them and still be as quiet as possible.

This street was quite wide, probably a main artery Jon concluded. Only the tall dark silhouettes of the unusual looking buildings could be seen. At a side street, the Twins hastily pushed all of them back against a wooden store wall. Ahead, the bobbing of a hand held lantern came their way. The light paused before each shop on the opposite side of the street from where they were hiding. In a couple minutes, the city guardsman was directly across from them checking on the stores. Evidentially there was some security in the town. And in a few more minutes, the light disappeared around a distant corner. The twins waited a bit longer to make sure that he did not return before leading the group back onto the main street.

Another five minutes walking and two side streets later, the street opened into a large market square. Dozens of small stands shuttered for the night lined one side of the approximately hundred foot across plaza. On the opposite side, a dozen steel cages on wheels were lined up in a row and chained together. Even in the dim light, Jon could see the massive shapes of sleeping giants inside lying on the floors. "We did not disturb them," May whispered. "You take it from here."

Jon walked up to the nearest cage and began whispering "Tessa, Tog." The giant inside the first cage gave a grunt and stirred but did not get up. He opened his eyes and looked into Jon's. Jon whispered, "We're here to rescue you, all of you, especially Tessa and Tog. Rolf sent us. Which ones are they?" The giant pointed to the next cage. Jon moved over there and repeated his call.

She got up rubbing her eyes, "Tog!" she whispered. Jon saw the smaller form of the young son get up in the third cage.

"Rolf sent us. We are here to rescue all of you. Wake up and be prepared," Jon whispered. Jon then examined the cages, "Locked," he whispered. "Rats."

He felt a gentle touch on his left shoulder accompanied by a whisper, "Leave the locks to us." It was May. She and Mat took something, Jon could not see what, out of their pockets and set to work on the locks. In less than a minute, he heard a clink come from the lock Mat was opening. Shortly afterwards, Tessa's lock clinked open. When all twelve were open, the score was Mat eight, May four. But then, he was a locksmith, Jon recalled. Quickly the giants climbed out of the confining cages, free at last, stretching their cramped muscles.

"Now what?" asked Alison who realized that Jon's plan was to transport two giants home, not twelve. She added being helpful, "May can take Mat back with a teleport spell. Darless and I can each take perhaps two giants with us. Can you manage eight? They are awfully heavy, Jon."

Jon was thinking rapidly. Eight times perhaps four hundred pounds was well over a ton. He'd never tried to move anything like that heavy a weight. He had his doubts. Then, he realized doubts would cause it to fail. "No, I cannot. Four perhaps. Let me make two trips. Only I am worried that I cannot see you to know where to come back to. Let me think a second." Always before, there was some kind of light by which to see, if only torch light. This was another matter. He wondered if he could home in using other senses.

"Jon, when you are ready to step back here, contact me and look through my eyes," Darless whispered. "I can see very well in this light. You will see." Jon agreed and took hold of a hand of Tessa and Tog. He told them to hold hands with one other giant. When they whispered they had, Jon whispered, "Okay, when I say 'now,' simply walk forward about three feet and we will land in your common room. Here we go. Now." And he stepped forward and arrived in the common room fairly pulling the heavy giants along with him. They were so startled that they fell forward onto the floor, scaring the heck out of Mandy.

"Zagroot zounds!" she cried stepping back from the table and a crashing giant who nearly landed on her. "Ah, welcome back, Jon. Say where's the rest? Troubles?"

"No, just a whole lot more giants than we bargained for. A dozen to be exact. I gotta go back for more." She remained quiet letting him get going as fast as possible. Jon concentrated letting his awareness expand outward searching for Darless. In about two minutes he located her. *I'm ready. Are you ready?* he sent her.

Sure, just look out my eyes, she sent to him. Jon made the decision to view from her eyes, and sure enough he saw the shapes of the other giants and the Twins still standing where he had left them. The images were very strange looking. *Heat,* the alu-demon sent him. Jon stepped toward here and landed at her side. *This is very intimate, you know,* she then sent him. He blushed but only Darless could see it.

"Okay, now let's all go together this trip," Jon suggested.

Mat and May were just putting on a pair of rings that Alison loaned them. Since this was May's first actual teleport, Alison was giving her a lot of guidance and some wisdom. "Remember to aim high and the rings will activate and lower you safely to the ground. It has never failed me. Jon, I'd feel better about this if we let them go first and I can make sure they get off okay. Then, we can go together."

Jon watched while May began her short chant. Even though he did not know or understand the words she used, he did recognize them. He'd heard Alison chant them many times. Then, poof May and Mat were gone. Now Jon took hold of another pair of giants who in turn took hold of another pair. Alison and Darless took hold of another a pair themselves. He waited for their chanting to finish. Just as they disappeared, Jon said "Now," and he and the four giants took a step forward and landed in the common room. This time, Mandy and the others were prepared. In the couple minutes he was gone, all of the stone furniture had been hastily moved to the back wall. Sure enough all four giants' reality were so shaken to find their foot falls landing in the common room after stepping forward in Vyndoc that they too stumbled and fell flat on the floor with a loud thump. They took Jon with him and he hit his head solidly on the floor and remembered nothing else.

The commotion and confusion was of giant proportions with the giants' unexpected rescue, finding themselves home at last. Rolf was talking like mad, trying to explain things. Mandy dragged Jon out of the way; she did not want the disoriented giants stepping on him. She saw the swelling on his head and went to work healing it. About two minutes later, the others walked in from the outside. All three wizards landed outside where the chances for error were greatly lessened. None of the giants arriving via the wizard's spells were disoriented. But they had a huge number of questions and poor Rolf repeated his explanation once more while Tog just held onto his right leg as tightly as he could. Tessa had her arm around Rolf.

"Wizard's arrived perfectly," Alison announced to Mandy. "Oh no, what's happened to Jon?" Her excitement rapidly changed to worry and concern as she saw his lifeless form with Mandy working over him.

"Giants fell and he hit his head on the floor. I think he is okay. I've got the swelling going down now. He'll probably have a giant headache when he wakes up," she teased and the others laughed at her pun.

Jon stirred, "Oh my aching head! What happened? I remember now. We fell." He tried to sit up and that only made it hurt worse.

"Me thanks you," Rolf began shaking his hand so hard that Jon's head seemed to split.

"Ooh, not so hard," Jon moaned. "My head hurts."

"You no got giant's head," laughed Rolf. And one by one all of the other giants had to shake his hand to thank him. Each one also shook the other adventurer's hands as well. "We all in your debt," Rolf explained. "You need something, you just ask Rolf."

"And us too, don't forget us," several of the rescued added. As it turned out, seven of the other giants were from nearby clans. Like Rolf, they pledged their eternal gratitude. Further, they also thanked Rolf profusely for having arranged their rescue. Indeed, in the ensuing days, Rolf and his clan rose in stature among the surrounding stone giant clans.

"What were they doing to you? Why did they take you in the first place?" Alison asked the question she had wanted answered since the moment she heard of their capture.

One of the taller giants named Heft explained, "Put me in cage. Make me work in mine or no eat."

"I see," Alison muttered. "What kind of mine?"

"Smelly mine. Dig out yellow powder stuff, smelly like bad eagle egg," he answered.

"Me dig other stuff," volunteered another giant. He did not know quite what the other stuff was but described it.

"Mommy, can me tell what me see?" Tog asked. She nodded.

Excited and very happy that he could contribute something as well, Tog explained how he had seen a man wearing robes put part of the yellow powder and some of the other stuff into a metal tube. Then he touched it with a torch and there was a loud noise, lots of smoke and an iron ball bounced off of a distant wall, knocking a hole in the bricks.

"Gun powder!" cried Jon. "The bastard is inventing gun powder!" Everyone turned to stare at him. Quickly, Jon explained in simple terms what this invention actually meant. When he was through, you could hear a pin drop in the room. The immensity of the effect of the gun powder reflected in everyone's face, including the giants.

"We have to stop them," Alison said defiantly. "If they succeed with this, they will overrun the entire world. There would be no stopping an army like that. Why it would be like having an army composed entirely of fire ball casting wizards. And no castle anywhere, no defensive walls anywhere would be safe."

Though it was nearly two in the morning, Alison insisted on finding out all she could about these mines. Only when the giants had told her everything they could think of did they all decide to get some much needed sleep.

It was an ill sleep for Alison and for Jon in particular. He knew only too well where inventions of this nature would lead. Alison also had a very good grasp of the seriousness. She had nightmares of hordes charging her newly built castle, blasting it into rubble. She woke with a start. It was pitch black and she laid back down beside Jon and tried to get back to sleep.

When Jon woke in the morning, Alison was laying in his arms. As he stirred, she did too. Their eyes met. In unison, as if speaking with one voice, they said to each other, "We have got to stop them somehow." They laughed as they realized they both had the same thought at the same time. A warm, loving embrace followed.

Over breakfast, they discussed the problem but had no solution. Darless joined them, wiping sleep from her eyes. Tossing back her hair, she began eating. But she listened to their discussion. When Jon and Alison had all but given up, she threw her opinion into the mix. "Number one. They are still trying to perfect it. Number 2. The yellow stuff is probably sulfur as Jon says. Number 3. To stop them, it is only necessary to remove part of the combustible mix. Number 4. From the giant's information, it seems that they only have that one sulfur mine."

"Yes, that's it. Remove the sulfur mine and no more threat," cried Jon, catching onto her line of thinking. "And a little fire would certainly do that! Sulfur burns very nicely. I remember from by chemistry class. A bit smelly though."

"Great! How do we find the mine and how do we light such a large fire that it destroys the sulfur?" asked Alison. "Won't they just clear away any rubble and dig deeper into the ground to expose more of the sulfur seam?"

"Not if you had an illusion to accompany it," May broke in as she came to eat breakfast, "an illusion that convinced them that it is utter folly to ever again mess with this sulfur stuff."

Beginning to follow her train of thought, Jon added, "So we light a huge fire and they see something along with it that scares the heck out of them."

"Yes, like the first thing you do with a fire is throw water on it. So when they do that, a massive fireball erupts cast by Runtling here. Only they see the effect as though throwing water on the fire caused the explosion. The flames appear twenty times larger than they really are, a roaring inferno," she added. "I'm sure if you give me a little time, I can think of some other wonderful things to add to it to make it really believable and scary. We can, in effect, make the majority completely believe that this is a dangerous thing indeed, overruling those who are doing the experimenting."

"Brilliant, all of you!" exclaimed Jon. "We'll teach them not to experiment. Looks like we gotta go back there tonight." And over tea, they hatched out the details of their plan for tonight's surprise visit. Jon explained that he could easily take them to the mine using the images that the giants had of the place. Certainly they would not be expecting such a form of retaliation.

During the morning, Alison explained to Rolf how she thought he could rebuild his barrier wall to make them impervious to the rock to mud spells. He and ten other men immediately set about the task of removing all of the grey stone. Midday, Alison and Jon accompanied them on a short trip to fetch more of the blacky stone from Rolf's secret place. As it turned out, the location was only about a three hour walk from the cave.

Hidden in a valley shaped like an immense bowl lay an exposed seam of the black stone. Other than the precarious path that Rolf led them on, there was no other way into the valley. When they arrived at the bottom, it was very obvious that careful stone mining had been occurring here for a long time. The exposed rock had been ground into flat layers and slabs chiseled out. But the giants made for their huge scrap pile at the far end of the valley. Here they loaded five enormous bags — each with the black stones. Rolf explained how they mined the blackys and that these were just scraps. As far as she could tell, here was an unlimited supply of this unusual stone. On a whim, she asked, "Rolf, if I wanted to build my castle from this stone, could you mine it for me for gold in return?"

"Gold? Yes, yes, yes. Treasure!" She saw a gleam not only in Rolf's eyes, but also in all of his friends as well.

On their way back, she said to Jon, "Ukko was right. This stone may make one terrific castle. I think we have come to the right place indeed!" Jon imagined images of such a castle; impressive, he thought.

He added, "But its walls have to be highly polished. Then, you'd have a spectacular castle indeed!" She squeezed him as they walked arm in arm back to the cave. When they arrived back at the caverns, they found the outside area totally soaked with water. Mandy was just finishing up a major cleaning effort.

"Hundreds of animals in a confined space for long periods of time equals a really big mess, not to mention the odor," she explained while replacing the stopper on Alison's decanter of water. She had just finished hosing out the large cavern section in which the caravan was staying. She'd effectively hosed the mess down the mountain side.

Jon and Alison grinned and teased her, "Glad we missed this party!"

"Oh no, next time you get latrine duty, Jon," she ribbed him back. They all laughed. Alison's water supply also provided the caravan its water supply for there was a distinct lack of much water here in this high cavern complex nestled in the tall mountains of Hell's Gate, Desolation Range.

The remainder of the afternoon, Alison, Jon and May worked on just how to best handle the sulfur mine of the Vyndocians. From examining the mental images the giants had from working in the mine, Jon knew its location and what it looked like. He described it as more of an open air surface dig, in that a lot of material from the surface had been removed exposing the layer of sulfur. Because of the extensive dust and fumes from the raw sulfur, none of the people from the city had wanted to mine it. By using the giants, they hoped to get a large volume per worker. From the view point of the giants, he had an estimate of its diameter. The pit, as it was referred to, was about four hundred feet across and now about one hundred feet below the surface. And from Jon's point of view, perfect for a fire.

The real problem was how to ignite it on a massive scale and not endanger themselves in the process. Alison suggested that they use a simple approach, tossing burning lantern oil. Jon was immediately reminded of Molotov cocktails, but wisely didn't mention it so he didn't have to explain the term and of what gasoline consisted. She explained that they only needed to get the oil spread over as large an area as possible. Once the oil was spread, she could cast a rudimentary ignition spell that any beginning wizard would know. Jon complimented her, "I like it, it is totally simple. Nothing can go wrong."

"Of course, Jon, something could go wrong," she corrected him. "But the real problem is getting a hold of that much extra lantern oil. The caravan does not have much excess. It's not like we can go to town and buy some. Perhaps the giants have some they could spare." After a thorough examination of the caravan and the giants, they had only about one gallon of extra oil which just was not enough. The plan called for a massive mine-wide blaze. It had to be extensive in scale to avoid the Vyndocian efforts to put out the fire.

This time, Mandy had the solution. "In a pine forest, the worst thing you can do is to accidentally let your fire pit spark nearby pine needles. If you mix a little oil with a large mound of dry needles, you will get a big fire very fast. I know, I've seen them." So the late afternoon was spend collecting bags of pine needles from the groves somewhat lower on the mountain side.

While leading the collecting party, Mandy also took time to use the Eyes of the Eagle that Jon had given her some time ago, the binoculars. She really needed to know what actions and reactions the cavalry were taking when they discovered the caravan had just disappeared. When they reached a section that offered a clear view of the distant foothills, she paused to search the horizon. It would be hard to hide an entire army of cavalry, especially if they were on the move. She occasionally caught glimpses of riders crisscrossing the main east-west track that the caravan had used. It appeared some were even backtracking in case the caravan had retreated.

It was not until they collecting party was finished and heading back to the cavern complex that she finally spied the main cavalry group which she figured was the one that Mat said was to the south of their position when they were at the cross roads. The rising dust cloud was unmistakable. Hundreds of riders were galloping northward, perhaps twenty miles from the cross roads. Evidentially, the general had changed his mind and was now pressing toward the caravan's last known position. She sighed, at least they would not now be facing the pincher attack that Mat discovered they were attempting execute. That would have really been a total overwhelm of the small caravan with an army attacking from either side. One army was more than sufficient. Still, at this point in time, two armies lay between them and the only wagon passage in this area through the Hell's Gate Desolation Range.

She had chatted with Rolf about the possibility of other passages through the mountains or if there were another pass that the wagons could manage. But there were none. It was through Deadman's Pass or go back out onto the Lost Steppes and head south or north looking for another way across these tall, granite mountains. Neither of these could the caravan afford to do with the supplies they currently had and with the armies of Vyndoc chasing them. They could not stay here hiding in Rolf's caverns for much longer. Sooner or later, riders would come here seeking them out. And she knew that if the caravan were caught here, there was almost no hope of escape. And the friendly giants would also be badly hurt. Walking back up the steep rocky canyon floor to the caverns, she realized that this trip was the most challenging one she had ever led. And she was very troubled because, as yet, she could see no real avenue of escape.

When they arrived at the giant's cave, the smell of freshly baked bread swamped their sense of smell. William had been at it again, only this time using the massive ovens of the giants! He greeted Mandy as she arrived with a smiling face and two large, warm loaves in his hands. "You have to try these, my love. Just perfect. Such ovens these giants have. Why one can bake vast quantities most easily!" Her moody look dissolved into a wide grin. Here was a man untroubled by whatever circumstances in which he found himself; he always found a way to brighten life with a fresh loaf of delicious bread!

"William, whatever am I going to do with you?" she jested, wolfing down a quarter of the first loaf.

"Marry me," he teased back.

She poked him playfully in the ribs, "You might get more than you bargained for!" And both laughed. She did not need to tell him how frustrated she felt about just how to get the caravan over these mountains without another massive battle. Instead, he merely got her to relax and enjoy life a bit. His philosophy was "something will turn up if you only give it time."

And what turned up was quite unexpected by everyone, including the giants. Just as dinner was being served all around with every wagon getting its own loaf of William's bread, a look out signaled the approach of strangers. Mandy bolted for the cave entrance, beating all of the others there. But many others were right behind her, including Rolf and Raul. One of Raul's guardsmen had raised the alarm.

Defensive postures were taken rapidly. The giants manned their boulder piles, ready to toss hundred pound boulders down on the enemy. All eyes were upon the bend in the path from which they had originally arrived. While the path generally headed in a north-south direction, it curved westward as it entered the narrow canyon and upwards to the barrier wall and caverns of the giants. Soon small figures could be seen stumping along leading small ponies. The small men all had relatively long beards for their size. "Well I'll be, dwarves," exclaimed Mandy as all of the sudden sense of dire emergency eroded. Everyone relaxed visibly.

Twelve dwarves, panting with exertion, slowly made their way up the steep canyon path. Rolf stood at the entrance in the newly rebuild blacky's barrier wall awaiting his new visitors. When they were ten feet away, the lead dwarf stopped and, in an out of breath, deep voice said, "Hail Rolf, Lord of the Giants, Hail and Well Met Indeed. I am Draken, son of Dathor, grandson of Nain Anzulbizar, the Great Lord of the Mountain Dwarves!" He bowed so low that his grey beard touched the grey stone of the ground beneath his feet. Rolf smiled as he now recognized his old acquaintance that he had not seen for several years.

"Hail Draken, me no see you for long time! Come, we eating now. You eat too. Tell Rolf lots of news." The invitation brought noticeable wide grins to all of the dwarves; they had been on relatively meager rations for the better part of a week. Mandy watched the two friends shake hands; it was a startling contrast in size. Draken was a little over three feet tall while Rolf was at least twelve feet. Draken actually shook one of the giant's fingers; Rolf's hand was huge compared to the dwarf's.

As the dwarves marched inside the cave complex, Tessa greeted them too. "Where are your manners, Rolf? Draken's men need to wash up; then eat." She looked down at the little man and ordered, "You wash, then talk and eat." And she ushered the little folk straight into a small side chamber that served as their restroom. Meanwhile, the others went back to their dinners. While the dwarves were washing the road from themselves, Rolf had Mandy and her friends bring their plates into the large common room where Tessa rapidly setup eating arrangements for the smaller folk. She evidently had done this before because she wasted no motions putting some furniture on their sides to serve as stepping stones for the dwarves to climb up to the table. She used some of Tog's old stone blocks as seat risers. So in less than ten minutes, when the dwarves filed out of the restroom, Tessa had a table full of food, Mandy and her friends situated on one side, a long row of stone blocks for the dwarves, and places set for her and Rolf. Mandy and Alison complimented her on setting up the table so fast. She replied, "Me have much experience with wee folk. Me know what to do." But she did have a pleased look on her face.

One by one the line of dwarves marched up to the table, climbed up the makeshift steps and onto the bench and down the line of stone blocks. Soon all twelve were seated at the table across from the humans with the two giants at either end of the table. Rolf ordered, "You eats first, then talks. Me knows you hungry. Dwarves always hungry." They needed no second request and helped themselves.

Jon was surprised at just how much they ate. He'd expected because of their smaller stature they'd eat less. When they had finished their first round, Draken proceeded to introduce his traveling companions one by one. Jon then introduced all of his friends.

With the requisite dwarven formalities out of the way, Draken began talking seriously. "This is not a social visit, Rolf. I bear an urgent message from my father, Dathor, Lord of Hell's Gate Bastion. Our main entrance way to the outside world has come under attack by Vyndocian cavalry."

"Better explain to Mandy," Rolf interrupted, "she no understand entrance way." Indeed none of the humans had any idea what he was talking about.

"We are mountain dwarves. We live under the mountains," he said emphasizing the word "under." "Our underground city is the finest in all Hell's Gate, ruled by my father, Lord Dathor, son of Nain. We have always maintained an entrance way into our realm for trade with you surface dwellers. We are the finest miners, finest metalworkers, and finest gem cutters in all the land." He was anything but modest.

"As I was saying, the entrance way, called 'The Golden Way,' has come under assault by the Vyndocian cavalry. They have brought powerful wizards and high priests with them. Now, our stone fortresses guard and protect 'The Golden Way' from all intruders and has done so since it was built nearly a three hundred years ago. However, these evil mages used some devilry upon us. Vast sections of our vast barricades of granite somehow turned into mud! And the cavalry then breached our outer defenses. However, they have yet to gain access to the passageways that lead to our city, for the Iron Doors of Gothos were shut and barred. These are doors that are three feet thick, solid iron, set on massive hinges which penetrate into deep bedrock. Their mud spells have yet to weaken them."

"Me know, me see great doors once. Really big, giant can walk through and not bend head," Rolf added. "So doors keep bad riders out. No troubles."

"Plenty troubles, Rolf," Draken protested, "we are under siege! When we left, the evil mages sworn to melt massive amounts of rock around the doors, sealing the doors shut. If that should happen, it will take a major feat of dwarven engineering to get the doors working unobstructed again. But we have other ways, secret ways, in and out. Our scouts reported that a whole garrison of cavalry has arrived. We believe that they intend to force entry into our underground domain and loot it. So Lord Dathor has sent me to get help. We need an army of giants to come help us push these nasty horsemen out of Hell's Gate. In about two weeks, the first snowfall should arrive here in the high country. That will force the cavalry to retreat or risk having their horses slip and slide down the mountain side to their doom."

"Messages have already been sent via the eagles to Nain, asking for assistance. The reply was encouraging. While Nain was apparently not at his place, Thorm, his lieutenant, said that ten legions of dwarves would begin the march on foot to our defense. But they will not arrive for another two months. He said that he could speak for Nain and that he sent a message to Vyndoc saying that if one hair was harmed on Dathor's head, Nain would remove Vyndoc city from the map." Draken was getting excited and prone to slight exaggeration. He went on, "The sight of ten legions marching into battle is wonderful to behold. A legion is about one hundred dwarves. First, ranks of archers loosen a rain of deadly arrows; many riders fall on each volley. Those that charge are met by ranks of pike men who step forward, plant their pikes and skewer both beasts and men. Then, they fall back and the hammer and swords take out the remainder. Glorious to behold."

"Our only problem is to somehow hold on until help arrives," he explained but suddenly realized that, if the dwarves were this powerful, why would they need any help. He wondered if perhaps he had over done it a bit.

"Rolf fight some riders; Rolf cannot fight whole army," he replied dolefully.

Mandy took this opportunity to say, "Draken, we may have some information for you about all this. We are in it too. But first, this Nain Anzulbizar fellow you have been talking about. Is he about so tall?" she gestured, "with full beard and an excellent sword maker? Travels with a couple friends and a gnome?"

"Yes, yes. That is Nain Anzulbizar!" he replied excitedly. "You know Nain?"

"Well, yes. We all stayed with him in a mine they were digging nearly six weeks ago now or there abouts. He was across the Lost Steppes just north of Freetown from where we have journeyed. I think he is going to make me a special bastard sword," she replied. Since Draken had not seen his grandfather in many years, Mandy had to take the next ten minutes to tell him all about their chance meeting with him. And then she had to explain all of the recent events in Freetown followed by a complete account of the caravan's journey thus far. Of course, the dwarves insisted on hearing every detail of the glorious combat twice. She finished by sharing what Mat had learned, that indeed a garrison of cavalry had headed toward the dwarves. She did not tell him that a second garrison was also in the vicinity of that first one.

Alison felt troubled. "In a way, maybe we are directly responsible for you dwarves being attacked. It would seem that the Vyndocians are after us and Jon and the caravan. Perhaps, the entire attack on your people is to prevent us from receiving any sort of aid and assistance from you folks. And if that is so, then we must come to your aid!" Of course, she shared Mandy's concern, that they could not even protect this caravan wholly, let alone go to the rescue of the dwarves. But if they were responsible for the dwarves' plight, then she had to at least try.

"But this will have to wait until tomorrow, Draken," Jon insisted. "Tonight, we must raid Vyndoc and put a sulfur mine out of commission to stop them from inventing a terrible weapon of such destructive power that it could literally blow your iron doors off their hinges. Trust me, I am not from this world and in my world this weapon is a horrible one. We must put an end to its development. Or no one in this land will be safe any longer."

This, of course, generated further conversation. Jon found that, like Nain, these dwarves loved to discuss things far into the night. At last, the adventurers had to excuse themselves so they could get ready for their midnight assault on Vyndoc.

When the party was alone at their wagons and preparing for their night's adventure, Alison commented, "You know, we really must visit these dwarves. They must somehow be important to us. Otherwise why would the Vyndocians attack them? Surely they have also traded with these dwarves. You don't kill your weapon smith without a compelling reason."

"If nothing else," Darless added, "my curiosity is aroused. I now want to know what is so darn important about these mountain dwarves. They live north of pass, as far as we can tell. In all likelihood, the caravan would never have found them. So why? What is it that the Vyndocians don't want us to have access to? I'd sure like to know!" The others completely agreed with her. Something was going on and they did not know what.

Meanwhile they prepared for the attack. This time, Jon would provide the transport. Alison, Darless, Mat and May would accompany him. Mandy was to remain here guarding the caravan just in case. Mandy fretted that the dwarves might have been followed. If so, perhaps the giant's cave might be attacked. Besides, she still had the picture book and could get to Vyndoc in an instant should the need arise.

When the midnight hour approached, all of the dwarves turned out to watch the party depart and bid them good luck. Rolf and Tessa also watched, though they had to admit that there was nearly nothing to actually see. The group, holding onto various sacks, just held hands. Jon said take a step forward. In unison they all did and simply vanished. This, of course, impressed the dwarves who insisted on knowing how Jon did this. Tessa tried to explain how she had been rescued and brought home this way, but this only confused the dwarves further. Then, they all went to bed. All except Mandy, who sat in the common room with a lantern staring at the picture of Vyndoc in the magical book. She would not sleep until they had all returned.

Shortly, William quietly joined her. He sat down beside her and put his strong arm around her, though saying nothing. She rested her head on his shoulder. After a while, he said, "This place is very defensible. And if anyone does get past the barrier wall, I will simply send them home at once."

Mandy smiled at him, "I was actually counting on that, William! I've never been in charge of such an indefensible group as this one. It is really frustrating. What do they want with us anyway?"

"Who knows," he replied. "Perhaps we may never know." And they sat there leaning on each other for another hour, waiting.

Jon had carefully viewed the giant's mental images of their experiences with the sulfur mine. Thus, he has a clear concept of just where to go. The mine was due east of the city about a mile. He formed the idea of just having arrived beside its eastern rim and was there bringing the others along with him. It was quite dark, as expected. The brilliant stars faintly illuminated the vast pit in front of them. The distinct odor of sulfur assaulted their nostrils almost at once. The sulfur mine was really a vast strip mine. The giants had moved a great quantity of overlying earth to expose a wide expanse of the sulfur layer.

They took a minute to get their bearings and accustom their eyes to the night time illumination. Darless surveyed the horizon for people but found none whose body heat she could see. Jon, Alison and May began unpacking their incendiary supplies. "No guards are nearby that I can see," Darless whispered and then helped the others get the supplies ready.

Once they had the oil and pine needles ready for the disbursement phase, Alison wondered, "Golly, the mine is so vast and we have such a small amount here. I wonder if it will be enough to really do the job. We probably will not get a second chance if they discover that the fire is not a natural event."

"If there are any high priests here, and I am sure there must be, they will surely use divination methods to find the source of the fire," commented Darless rather pessimistically.

"What do you mean by divination methods?" asked Jon who did not understand this interesting new facet.

"When a priest wants some information that is not normally known, they pray to their gods, Morrigan in this case, and if the gods so wish, they can inform them, assuming that the deity actually knows the answers," she explained.

"So we really do need this to look more like a natural occurrence to confuse the issue," Jon commented more to himself than to Darless. He was thinking about natural fires. "You know out west where I come from, lightning starts a lot of fires. Could we manage a lightning strike? Er, not likely, the sky is beautifully clear." He thought some more and muttered, "Once a cow kicked over a lantern and started a fire that nearly burned an entire city down. But no cows here."

"No, but there is some faint light on the other side of the mine close to the town," offered Darless. "If it is a lantern, maybe we could use it somehow."

"Well, let's spread the mixture throughout the mine and end up over by that light," Alison suggested. "Darless and I will use our magical skills and fly out over the mine dropping the oil and needle mixture down on the sulfur. You two hike on over to the light, but be very careful. We don't know what is down in the pit or if there is a guard house or guards."

And so the two mages began flying over the pit dropping the oil and pine needles at periodic locations. It took them about fifteen minutes to complete the task. Jon and May began the trek around the rim. But because of the loose piles of dirt and rock, the going was tough with no light. Finally, in frustration, Jon took her hand and just stepped them near the location of the light. May took it from there. "You stay here and I'll check it out," she ordered. Jon obeyed and crouched down as much out of sight as he could and yet still see what was going on.

Within five minutes, May returned as silently as she had left. "There are two guards in the shack. The light is indeed a lantern hanging on a hook just outside the door. As near as I can tell, they are playing a card game. Now what? We wait?" Jon whispered affirmatively.

Soon, the two flying wizards swooped over Jon and May and landed. May repeated what she had found and everyone began to figure out a way to make the fire look like it began of natural causes. "I've got it," May whispered. "Alison, give me about three minutes to get in the right location. Then, you fly to the lantern. Bang on the wall hard, throw the lantern on the ground so that it breaks and the oils spills and catches fire. Then fly out over the pit and circle back here and then let lose all the fire starting spells."

"But surely the guards will come charging out and see me and see the fire and put it out before I get back here and really torch it," her sister protested.

"Oh no they won't," May argued. "They will see a large elk thrashing about, knocking the lantern off and breaking it and diving into the pit with its feet on fire."

Alison wanted to ask just how come the guards would see that but refrained as she remembered that May practiced illusionary magics which were of an altogether different nature than the magics she practiced. "Okay, let's do it," she whispered. And May quietly stole off into the darkness once more. She needed to be facing the shack's door so that she would have a direct line of sight of the guards when they came busting out. Once in position, she began a rather lengthy chant. This was not an easy spell to conjure; it took planning and skill. But May had been using this spell for years now back in Freetown. People see what they think they see, was her motto. She just helped them see what they think they see, or rather twisted it slightly.

Soon Alison's flying form came around the cabin and very visible in the dim light. She flew hard into the side of the cabin giving it a resounding thump. It nearly knocked the lantern off! She then took the lantern and threw it on the ground near the edge of the pit. The oil leaked and caught fire, a bright narrow line of flames seeping down into the pit. The door burst open and the two men gasped audibly. She swooped over the pit and turned sharply left and quickly landed out of sight of the men who were tramping on the burning oil and cursing. Quickly she and Darless began shooting simple fire starting spells down into the pit at various locations. It was hit or miss, since the oil and needle mixture was spread widely about the mine floor. Some sparks did nothing, while others ignited the oil and needles. Together, they shot nearly twenty of these elementary apprentice spells. Small fires now dotted the mine floor below them.

They heard the guard curse and swear and try to figure out what to do. One of the guards then said in a rather distant voice, "Let's go get help." The other whole-heartedly agreed and both men began running toward the town. A minute later, May appeared beside Alison once more.

"Gosh, you sacred me, I didn't hear you coming!" Alison said a bit dismayed.

"You weren't supposed to hear me come, silly. Now is that enough fire to do the job?" she asked.

Jon replied, "Nope, it is going to need a lot of help, actually. Now what?"

"Time for a little help, then," Darless muttered and began chanting. Jon knew exactly what she had in mind, though not by reading her mind. He'd heard both wizards using this chant on many occasions. In seconds two large balls of fire exploded on the mine's floor, then another two and another pair. Now the central portion of the mine really began burning heavily. The sulfur turned the flames very yellowish. Billowing clouds of a horrid smelling odor rose up from the inferno at the center of the pit.

"That ought to do it," Jon acknowledged. "Now what? There goes the fire alarm in the city!" Indeed, loud distant noises bespoke of people taking action to the sudden fire. Jon hoped that they did not have a fire truck, but then quickly realized this was not Urbana. "We'd better move back from the rim," he suggested. The flames were getting rather hot, to say nothing of the asphyxiating smoke billowing up from the fire. This was what actually saved their lives, though they did not know it at the time. Also, they also did not see a tall man with a cloven foot standing about a half mile from them, who was watching their every action since they first arrived here.

None needed any further encouragement to move way back from the rim. They had gone about a thousand yards when a tremendous explosion violently shook the very ground they were walking on! What Jon could not have known was that the inventors had been storing a large quantity of both ingredients in barrels to one side at the bottom of the mine. Indeed, the workers had stockpiled over a hundred barrels of the invented mixture ready for future use and experimentation. When the fire ignited one barrel, its explosion ignited the remaining ninety-nine barrels in one massive explosion that flash ignited all of the sulfur that was exposed.

The concussion knocked the four completely off their feet, landing solidly on their faces, momentarily stunning them. Debris and flaming bits flew high into the nighttime sky, illuminating the city in an eerie yellow light. "Let's get out of here!" cried Alison frantically trying to keep her long hair from catching fire. Darless and May likewise were covering their long hair as the flaming debris rained down on them.

"Grab my hand!" yelled Jon. As soon as he felt all three grab a hold of him, he stepped rapidly into the common room of the giant's startling Mandy and William. They brought remnants of the horrid sulfurous burn odor with them, it permeated their clothes. It was on their skin and in their hair.

"Am I burning?" cried Alison, frantically patting her hair. The other women were doing the same.

"Gosh you all stink really badly. No, nothing is smoldering that I can see," Mandy replied. "You startled us. I take it you were successful?"

None of the three women were convinced that they were not burning until William and Jon looked them over as well and after they looked each other over.

Satisfied that her hair was not burning, Alison finally answered, "Yes, but something happened. There was an explosion. And it rained fire on us. We were nearly burned to a crisp! What the heck happened, Jon? Sulfur does not do that. It just burns with a smelly smoke."

Jon replied, "I think that the inventors actually helped us. My guess is that they had some of their explosive mixture stored down there and it caught fire and did its thing. You see what I meant by it being a very nasty weapon. What would have happened to your castle doors if that had hit them?"

Her eyes opened wide as she grasped what Jon was suggesting, "What doors would be the result! With that much power, gaping holes could be punched into walls! I have to hand it to you, Jon; you certainly were right about this thing.

Golly, if they perfect that as a weapon, nothing I know of could withstand such a blast!"

"They would eventually rule all the land," added Darless, "and no one could stop them. That is scary. Do you think we actually stopped them?"

"Only time will tell," Jon admitted. "But that fire must certainly be a terrific setback. We can only hope that it forces them to direct their efforts in some other direction. Say, we need a bath right now. I stink badly!"

Mandy retrieved Alison's water decanter and effectively hosed them down. Their clothes were covered with tiny burn holes where the flaming debris landed on them. Still later, they washed their clothes because May wanted to keep them as a souvenir of this night. Even after a lather and a makeshift shower, their noses still smelled burning sulfur. However, as the hour was very late, they were too tired to care and went to bed as they were. And by the next morning, their sense of smell was back to normal.

The adventurers had no idea of the impact their fire had on Vyndoc. The entire city was engulfed in noxious fumes forcing the evacuation of one third of the town nearest the mine. All activities in the entire city came to a halt for three days and did not really get back to normal for a week. And the populace as a whole were so outraged over the fire and noxious fumes, that all further research of this type was permanently halted by official edicts.

The only clue that the adventurers had of the scale of the fire came the next morning when their lookouts pointed out a strange dark cloud on the distant horizon in the direction of the city of Vyndoc.

Instead, their attention now turned to the dwarves and how to help them. "If our caravan's passage here has somehow caused the Vyndocians to suddenly turn on the dwarves so as to somehow impact our caravan, then I feel it is our duty to go and see what we can do to assist the dwarves," Alison declared before anyone else could espouse their views.

"As much as I agree with you," Mandy replied, "we still have the welfare of the caravan to look after. If we all go off to help the dwarves and then something bad should happen to the caravan members because of our absence here, I'd, I'd, well, it would be really awful."

"Ah, but don't forget," Darless countered, "these people already chose to leave Freetown knowing full well the inherent dangers and without our protection. As a group, they have never requested our direct aid. So legally we are under no obligation to them. We've been helping them out and with luck, many will want to help Alison build a new town and castle complex. But don't get me wrong," she hastily added as Alison began to protest, "I am not suggesting that we throw them to the wolves. I'm just saying that they knew or suspected what they were getting into when they began this trip. And to that degree we are not responsible for their safety."

"Well, one thing is for sure," declared Mandy, "we *must* get them out of here and back on the trail. Cooped up like this with all the animals and people in the same space is becoming a nightmare. And there is no way to safely continue the journey with two armies right nearby searching for us." She paused a minute and added "Besides, I am absolutely amazed that their high priests have not prayed to Morrigan for assistance in locating us!" The silence was total; no one had any ideas or even suggestions. Mandy had precisely stated what everyone held as a certainty. They had to get going but to go was to be subject to attack from two garrisons, perhaps as many as a thousand cavalry. Stalemate.

"'cuse me," Tessa's voice broke in on their glum thoughts. "You want all these peoples on big pass trail — not down at crossroads? You want fast way to dwarves?"

"Yes, Tessa," Alison explained, "we need to get the caravan on up into the mountains on to the Deadman's Pass trail, safely beyond the reach of these Vyndocian horsemen while the rest of us need to get to the dwarven city as fast as possible. But there is no way to do that."

"Maybe, me knows a way. Me ask Rolf. Me be back," she said, her eyes bright and full of hope. She too wanted the hundreds of horses out of her cave for altogether different reasons. Quickly she went to find Rolf. Shortly, they heard the two giants discussing something just out of earshot. Then, both giants came into the common room. Tessa had a look of victory on her face but Rolf looked concerned.

"Me used to have big mines here. Passages go to lower part of pass very close to dwarves city; we used to trade ore for treasures. No more ore long time ago, though. Me close

495

entrances. Me can open 'em again; lead wagons," Rolf explained.

At once, Alison got out her crude map and Rolf pointed out where they were now, about twenty-five miles south and ten east of the crossroads. He pointed out where the dwarven city was located, some fifty miles north of the crossroads. Then, he made a guess at where the abandoned tunnel intersected the great east-west road as it climbed steadily into the Deadman's Pass.

"That's it!" Mandy exclaimed. "The caravan would be way beyond the cavalry into the narrow track passing through the mountains. We could probably safely let Raul and his men lead them onward for a few days until we caught back up with them again."

"I'll go with them as insurance," William added, "It's what Reylona asked me to do."

"Great, William," she replied. "With you along with them, I would feel much more comfortable about leaving them." They smiled at each other.

"Draken, he know shortcut from tunnel to city," Rolf added trying to be helpful. "Cut much time off getting there."

"That settles it," Mandy declared. "Let's get this show on the road as soon as possible. Rolf, you get the tunnel ready. I'll get the wagons hitched. Wait a minute," she suddenly realized they would be traveling down a mine shaft. "We'll need lights on each wagon. Is the tunnel high enough for the horses and wide enough?"

"Me make it so me can stand up in it," Rolf answered, "but need light. Go in one line, long line. Me go first. Move rocks out of way of wagons."

It was agreed and each went into action. This was what Mandy preferred, action, to sitting around. She had already sat cooped up in a cave far too long for her taste. And the caravan folks also were elated that a way had been found for them to escape the cavalry and get on with the journey, though none had any idea what travel would be like in the mountains. Yet, most were very eager to get into them and explore. Their escape from Freetown now had turned into something resembling a vacation trip if it were not for all of the attacks.

With Raul and his men's help, she got each wagon ready to form a long line. She explained that they were going to go through a tunnel complex in single file. Each wagon had to supply its own lantern light for the horses and the drivers to see. Each driver was ordered to maintain a ten foot distance from the wagon in front of them. She did not want anyone getting lost, taking a wrong turn or crashing into the rear of a stopped wagon. In an hour everyone was ready.

Rolf removed a huge stone from the old mine entrance which was here in the cavern and had his pair of lanterns going, one in each hand. He strapped a huge pick that must have weighed at least a hundred pounds onto his back. "Me ready. We go now?" he asked.

And they were off. Mandy rode beside the giant. On horseback, she could finally see eye to eye with the big man. He grinned when he observed that detail too. Darless followed behind them along with the dozen dwarves and their ponies. Jon and Alison stayed behind. She wanted to wash out the cavern one last time. The horses had created quite a mess and she did not want Tessa to have to deal with it. Jon stayed with her. It took nearly a half hour for the last wagon to finally get its chance to enter the dark tunnel. Jon took their two horses into the tunnel and Alison got out her magical water decanter. Soon the gushing waters were washing all traces of their stay out the front door and down the mountainside. That took her another half hour to fully accomplish.

Just as she finished, one of the other giants came rushing in from his guard position high on the rim of the canyon outside. "Bad men coming! Bad men coming!" he yelled.

"Quick, Tessa, shut up this tunnel entrance. They are likely going to want to question you about where we are. Now you can safely say without lying that we are not here. We have left and you have no idea where we are because you really won't know exactly where we are." And she gave the giant woman a hug around her huge leg. "Thanks, you've saved our lives!"

Tessa beamed, "You good giant friend. Okay, me shut it. Then me no know where you are. Bye." And as Alison stepped into the tunnel and mounted her horse in the almost total darkness, Tessa rolled a number of bounders back into place, sealing them inside. Indeed in a short while she was explaining she did not know where peoples were and was convincing for the Vyndocians' assumed giants were really stupid because of their speech patterns.

Total darkness encompassed Jon and Alison when the last boulder completely closed the abandoned mine tunnel. The mage spoke a command word and a light globe appeared on top of her wizard's staff, illuminating the tunnel. They began to follow the obvious trail to catch up to the rear of the long line which she estimated to be at least a mile long, what with the necessity to also lead along all of the newly acquired war horses. The walls were rough cut grey granite and solid. The floor was covered in dust or dirt a half inch thick, from horseback she could not tell which. The ceiling was a little over twelve feet high, more than enough to ride horseback. However, once the tunnel began to delve deeply into the mountain, its width narrowed to perhaps ten feet at best.

Dangling spider webs hug from the ceiling, ripped loose from their moorings by the previous folks. Jon secretly was glad he was not in the lead. He disliked spiders and the awful feeling he always had whenever he accidentally ran into a large spider web, usually in the fall. Occasionally, small side passages opened on either side but only dark depths could be discerned as they rode by them. Most could not support the passage of their wagons.

The air was dry and stale, but breathable. Jon noticed the faint odor of something, but he just could not place that smell, something like a musty leather. The temperature was cool. Indeed it was a uniform fifty-five degrees and Jon found that he needed to don a jacket from his saddle bag. And after an hour, they finally caught up to the rear wagon which was going significantly slower than they were.

"I've never been this far underground before," Jon explained to Alison. "I can almost feel the immense pressure of the whole mountain above us. Is it dangerous in these deep mines?"

"Yes, very ominous. Hope no one is claustrophobic! I hadn't thought of that aspect," she replied keeping an eye on the wagon in front of them. "How dangerous? I don't really know. Abandoned mines are not a good place to wander around inside. This one has no shoring supports to keep the roof up. See those rock piles off to the side there? I expect some bits of ceiling have come down. Probably Mandy and

Rolf are busy way up front clearing it out of the way. Maybe that is why we are going so slowly."

"Since both ends of the tunnel were sealed, according to Rolf, I don't think we have to worry about any wild animals being inside, you know, like bears and such," she talked on. "Whoa, there." She suddenly reigned in her horse. The wagon in front of them had stopped.

"Bet they are removing debris," Jon surmised. And he was right. The giants had not used this tunnel in about fifteen years. They abandoned the mine when the ore veins played out. After a minute or so, they moved on again. Monotony was setting in. This would be a long day of travel indeed.

And it was. Twelve hours later and none too soon for everyone, Rolf opened up a stone barrier that was blocking the exit. And out into the evening twilight and fresh air came the mile long line of wagons.

Here the track they had been following now followed the bottom of a narrow u-shaped canyon generally continuously rising in altitude. Patches of grass grew near a bubbling stream about four feet wide that flowed down the middle of the canyon. Huge boulders dotted the valley floor and intermittent patches of pine trees stretched skyward. Here the Deadman's Pass trail could support only wagons in single file. However, for camping purposes, they could be crowded together.

Mandy had Raul and his men set up camp right here. And they set about the lengthy task of maneuvering each wagon as it appeared from the tunnel into some semblance of order. The camp actually spread over about a quarter of a mile of canyon floor. Since Mandy was terribly worried about the Vyndocians discovering their location, she ordered no campfires tonight. Supper would be cold rations. And indeed the late September mountain night air was very chilly. No one had proper winter clothing and bundled up as best they could to ward off the cold. She knew that they had to get across these mountains before the first snowfall or real survival problems would befall one and all. She also knew that the first snowfall of the season was not far off. Both Rolf and the dwarves had told her so. The only detail that Mandy neglected to ask about was why it was called Deadman's Pass. And perhaps, considering all that she had to worry about, it was best that she did not know this detail.

From Rolf and the dwarves, she estimated that the shortcut under the mountain had placed caravan about twenty miles up the pass track and an additional thirty miles from the crossroads. If they had any luck at all, the caravan would now be more than a day's ride from the cavalry hordes that threatened them. Raul was very cheerful now because defense of the caravan was now possible in this narrow canyon land. They could use wagons to effectively block charging horsemen and present only a very narrow area of vulnerability. The sides of the u-shaped canyon rose rather sharply to several hundred feet above them. "You needn't worry about us now," Raul declared. "In this country, we can hold out reasonably well, especially if William is with us. And with all these extra war horses hitched up to the wagons, why we should make good time and not wear the animals down doing it."

"Thanks for the vote of confidence, Raul," Mandy grinned at him while eating a bit of cold supper along with Darless and the dwarves. The dwarves were insisting on traveling more miles yet this evening. Rolf was also eating a leg of deer he had brought with him along with a couple of loaves of William's bread.

"Say, me have idea," he mumbled and took a drink to wash the bread down. He had been watching the wagons slowly file out of the tunnel and get directed on up the canyon track and into the camp area. "Me can make sure horsemen can't come up this track after you."

"How? If you could, we all would be very grateful indeed! One major worry would be completely gone!" she asked.

"Me know trail. Down there a bit," he pointed back toward the steppes, "track narrows. Me could put boulder walls there. Only giant can move them. Me wait some days and then remove them. You safe then."

"Why that is positively brilliant!" she declared. "Then we can be almost certain that the cavalry cannot reach the caravan while we are off helping the dwarves. Rolf, you are a genius," and she gave his leg a hug. The big man smiled down at her. He saw a lot of Tessa in her and his thoughts went longingly back home to his cavern.

Finally, just as they finished eating, Alison and Jon appeared from the tunnel's mouth. "Over here," yelled Mandy and the two dismounted, stretched and joined them. Mandy shoved some food their way and began to bring them up to date on the situation. They both groaned when they heard that they would soon be moving out following the dwarves, but cheered up when they heard Rolf's plan to block the trail. "So eat fast. We should leave in ten minutes. The dwarves believe that we can make their fortress by tomorrow night if we go another spell tonight before it gets too dark. There is a bit of moon for a while." Both groaned again.

Soon the party said their farewells to the others in the caravan. Thea and William both got last minute advice and suggestions. And then they were off, with the dwarves in the lead this time for they were in very familiar lands.

The party of twelve dwarves and six humans traveled slowly. It was now too dark to safely ride. The smaller stature of the little men resulted in a shorter stride. Thus, the humans found the pace more leisurely. About a mile down the trail toward the crossroads, the canyon widened a bit. Here the dwarves turned left and headed toward the steeply rising walls. Hidden behind a dense grove of trees, a very narrow spur canyon met this main one. Unless one knew this passage was here, it was easily missed. Plus, the thick trees made forward progress in the near dark tough and slow, with many a curse, as limbs snapped back into unsuspecting faces. At long last, they entered the narrow canyon that the dwarves called Wolf Wash. Apparently sometime in the distant past, a party of travelers who took this trail by mistake were wiped out by a pack of wolves. The dwarves had come upon their remains and the name had stuck ever since. It was easy to see how a party could be ambushed in such a narrow confined space.

The ground here was rocky but a very narrow track had been kept clear by the dwarves for their use. In the dim light, it was hard to see, let alone stay, on that path. Stumbling became common place as they walked along. They dared not risk lantern lights which could easily give their location away to the enemy spies. Only when the moon light failed utterly did the dwarves halt for the night. They just stopped in the middle of nowhere and said "Here we camp."

Mandy looked about as did Alison. If they tried, they might be able to stand two abreast. The rocky ground looked completely uninviting. Jon groaned again, too tired to protest. "Ah this is ridiculous. We cannot camp here," Alison protested.

"Just find a spot by a tree and curl up," suggested Draken sourly and in a nasally voice. He did not like it any better. But it was too dark to see. In fact he could not see his hand in front of his face, which is why he stopped. He had just smashed his nose into a boulder but had said nothing about it.

"Ah what a life without a wizard!" declared Alison. She grabbed her staff which was strapped on her horse and chanted briefly. Suddenly, a pair of golden doors appeared at her feet.

"Hallelujah!" cried Jon. "Thank you!"

"Fabulous idea," pronounced Darless, a note of real relief in her voice.

"Terrific as always," Mandy declared. "Wish I could do that one. Sometime, maybe you could make me some scrolls with that spell. I'd even pay you for them," she teased.

"What is it?" asked Mat and May in unison. They had never seen such an inviting portico and doors.

The dwarves stood spellbound wondering what these doors were and how they got there and where they led. "Okay fellow, we go inside my mansion for the night. Lead the horses and ponies in with yourselves," Alison explained. Jon, Darless and Mandy went inside at once. Mat and May walked in very slowly looking at every detail. The dwarves followed them in single file, their eyes looking all about as they walked in through the ornate pillars and doors. Once inside, splendor greeted them. It looked much like a palace. They left the horses and ponies in the entrance way after taking care of them for the night.

Alison gave them on a short tour of the mansion, showing them the bathroom and dining area and the main living room. She explained that any of the food and drink that they found inside was not real. Thus, you actually ate whatever you brought in with you. The dwarves, of course, had to touch and examine everything from the walls to the vast pile of cushions in the living room. They all happily slept on a mountain of pillows that night. They would have a story to tell their children at bedtime after this night.

The six adventurers made the small dining room their bedroom for the night. It was close quarters, but they felt better this way than sleeping out in the main room surrounded by all of the dwarves. Jon and Alison lay close to each other, snuggling. Mandy lay next to them and Darless next to the ranger. Mat and May, next to her.

Mandy finally relaxed totally. "Gosh, I didn't realize what a strain leading this caravan is having on me."

"Yes, but you are doing a terrific job of it," Alison mused. "I don't know what we would do without you!"

"Thanks, but right now, you know, I see you two lying there and I suddenly really miss William. And that is strange," she added.

"How so?" wondered Darless.

"He is a nice fellow," May complimented.

"Why, I have never ever missed a man before, that's why," she replied solemnly. "Could I be in love? Alison, what do you think? You are in love with Jon here. Am I becoming love-struck?"

"Could be," she dreamily replied, "he is really nice and you two do seem to hit it off really well. It's just that you two are so very different."

"I think you two complement each other very well," Darless broke in. "There is something in that, unless you wanted a fighter like yourself."

"No, one fighter in the family is enough," Mandy replied with a sigh. "I've never met a fighter who knew how to treat a woman. They have such egos, you know. I'd end up stomping on it whether I tried not to or not. William is very different," she said dreamily.

"I'd just like to find a man," Darless sighed, "one who really wants me as I am. But I'm resigned to being an old maid. What human is going to want an alu-demon for a wife?"

Her last pronouncement irked Jon. He spoke for the first time, "Darless, you want to find a man who wants you for you, one for whom your body form is irrelevant."

"Yes, but isn't a pretty face and shapely body sexy to you men?" protested Alison. "Men always go silly around me when I'm dressed up. Doesn't a sexy body have something to do with the attraction?"

Jon decided to philosophize a bit. "Well, as I see it, there are two things at play here. One is pure animal attraction, lust. The other is deep love, admiration and respect. The first is shallow and fleeting, the second may last all eternity for all I know," he answered. "But you know, there is nothing wrong with a little animal lust along with love," he playfully teased Alison and gave her a tighter snuggle. She poked him with an elbow and then returned his hug. After a pause, he added, "I've often wondered if 'sexiness' is not more a matter of how a person feels about themself than how they look."

"Well, what about us?" interjected May. "We're doomed. Mat and I are so close that we often think the same thought at the same time. How can we ever find a lover? We've talked and talked about it. We've even tried to go our separate ways on dates. But it never works. We each know what the other is doing, feeling. It gets so confusing at times."

"No kidding!" broke in Mat. "Once May and I went out on separate dates to different parts of the city. She ended up getting kissed, of course, and I sensed it and she, likewise. Just think what would happen if either of us really went all the way, you know, and did it."

"It's most embarrassing and impossible to explain to your date," May continued seamlessly. "So Darless, your problems are much easier to solve than ours."

"I'm sure that there are other twins out there in the world like yourselves," Darless thought. "It is just a matter of locating them. But even so, how would you know if a pair of twins were the right ones for you? I just don't get this love thing at all well. I appreciate it. My dad and I were very close. But I've never been in love that I know of."

"Some marry without any love in it," Alison offered. "I've seen it happen lots of times; some marry for sex, some for money, some for power and position. Sometimes it works out, other times it brings only misery to both parties. I think that Jon is right, you need to both admire and respect the other person. I also think that Mandy is right. You start to know when you feel a bit empty when the other person is not around." She snuggled a bit tighter with Jon, and he, her.

Darless was silent for a minute. "Well, this is going to sound awfully funny, promise you won't laugh at me. But the only men I feel that way about are Jon here and your paladin friend, Sir Thomas. I just cannot stop thinking about him. You know back there at your castle, he treated me with respect and as an equal in many way, especially in front of his men. Plenty of men have been after my body, like the evil mage, Kagor. But maybe all paladins are like that, you know, treating women with respect."

"Sir Thomas!" exclaimed Alison sitting up and looking over at Darless. "Why I never would have guessed that you had a thing for him!"

"I know it is impossible. I represent the very thing he is sworn to exterminate, demons," a note of hopelessness was in her voice. Fortunately, it was fairly dark here inside the mansion; Alison had only left on a few night lights. No one could see a single tear well up in her eye and drip down the side of her face.

"Again I say, Darless," Jon inserted his opinion, "any man worthy of you would find your body form totally irrelevant."

"Besides, most people cannot even tell you are a bit different," May encouraged. "Jeesh, I sure am tired. I didn't realize so much horse riding would tire me out this much." And she yawned heavily. And the six slowly fell into a peaceful night's sleep. Dawn came much too quickly.

Chapter 19 The Confrontation

At first light, the dwarves were up and making breakfast even though there was no outside windows to tell them the sun was up. They were used to living far underground; actually seeing the sun was a rare sight.

The others rose and cleaned up and joined them. "A good day's march should put us at the Golden Gates, the entrance to our underground world," Draken proclaimed. "Of course, you should see the view from the Eagle's Nest which is nearby. You can see all the way from the Dead Marshes to the beautiful Maiden's Pond, a crystal clear, blue pond just outside our entrance where the Silver Springs bursts forth from far underground into this world above. Spectacular, indeed." He talked on and on about the sights.

Jon could have listened for hours, but Mandy broke in, "Well, then, let's get going." She was eager to get into action. And so they saddled their horses and ponies and led them out of the wide doors into the sunlight, boulder lined track they had left the night before. Everyone watched as the mansion just disappeared when Alison spoke the proper word of command. Then, they were off as before, dwarves leading the way up the narrow canyon floor.

As they traveled, Mandy caught sight of several mountain sheep. There were plenty of elk tracks here on their trail. The ranger felt a definite relief that wildlife were becoming more plentiful. The barren steppes was so unlike the terrain that she loved, woodland forests. By midday, just as the track turned westward once again, the dwaves took another turn up a canyon that led on northward, Dry Gulch.

There was no water to be found anywhere in this canyon which was even narrower than the one they left behind. The floor had a much steeper grade than Wolf Wash but the sides were significantly lower, some twenty feet above the floor. In a few places, they had to dismount and lead the horses up particularly steep slopes. Nevertheless, they still made good progress and by dinner time, Mandy estimated that they had covered at least thirty miles and were several thousand feet high.

"Behold the Eagle's Nest," Draken suddenly exclaimed and pulled to a halt.

"Where's the eagle," asked Jon looking about, but seeing nothing but the low canyon walls.

"Leave the horses here, and follow me," the dwarf leader ordered, giving his pony to one of his fellows. "Even if all of the world is being attacked, you should first gaze upon the world from the Eagle's Nest. This way," and he began climbing up the right side of the canyon toward a large grey granite peak. The others scrambled up behind him. It was only a twenty-five foot climb to the top.

At the top the sight was indeed spectacular. The very top was hollowed out into a bowl shape by the elements and was about twenty feet in diameter. At the eastern edge, the mountain fell away in a sheer cliff some three thousand feet down! Nothing blocked their view to the east and north and south. To the south, the grey-green Dead Marshes stood out dark among the rolling hills. The pencil thin line of the great east-west road and crossroads where they had met the giant was visible. As their eyes swept across the view heading northward, the hills grew steeper and more rounded. Then to the north lay a vast plain in the shape of a V. The entrance to the dwarven underground city lay at its point. On the northern edge of the valley was an oval pool, the Maiden's Pond.

A stiff up-thrusting wind blew on their faces as they peered out at the world from the Eagle's Nest. No one said a word. It was so incredibly inspiring that they just stared for quite some time, trying to take it all in.

Finally, Mandy spoke, "There are some places in this world that are just totally awe-inspiring. Here the hands of the gods have been at work!" The stared at the view for nearly a half an hour until Mandy added, "Look, you can see the two Vyndocian armies. There and there," she pointed out a mass of horsemen east of the Maiden's Pond and another somewhat below their position here in the Eagle's Nest.

"Yes, below us is the main entrance path that comes from the crossroads. See, just beyond it is the Barrier Teeth, that little black set of hills. They are not really teeth, but the small cliffs look rather like that when coming from the south.

Horses can only pass through the Barrier Teeth on a narrow track right below us. Otherwise, they have to ride east some twenty miles to get around them. It looks like one army has already done so. It does not bode well for us! We should hurry," Draken urged, a bit of fear in his voice.

"If they should attack, won't your people just go underground and shut the entrance doors behind them?" asked Mandy while they slipped and skidded back down the hill to the horses and the waiting dwarves.

"Yes, and then we may be trapped out here!" he huffed and puffed, hurrying as fast as he could safely go down the steep slope. "When we left, there a garrison of my clan were holding the Barrier Teeth. I fear for their safety. Let's hurry."

The canyon crested just a few feet from where they had stopped. Then it pitched sharply down, winding this way and that. Jon, May and Mat now found out the one thing they hated about horseback riding, going down lengthy, steep grades, mile after mile! It was the scariest three hours Jon had ever had on horseback. At every step, he swore that he would just fall on over the horse's head! The three clung to the saddle horns like glue, forcing themselves to stay in the saddle. It was with immense relief that they finally landed on the main road way here in the valley they had seen from so far above hours ago.

They arrived onto the main roadway built and maintained by the dwarves. From the Barrier Teeth to the Golden Gates, they constructed a stone roadbed cut into the side of the mountain. An engineering marvel, the roadway itself was smooth and slowly rose about one thousand feet from the Barrier Teeth to their underground entrance. The opposite side of the roadbed had barbican stones evenly spaced to prevent wagon accidents, for beyond its edge, the roadway dropped several hundred feet to the plains below. The steep trail they had just come down joined the road at a junction.

From their viewpoint, looking back toward the tunnel entrance was a harmonious arc of elevated roadway curving around the face of the steeply rising mountain wall. To the south, it curved out of sight in the distance. However, hundreds of dwarves clad in chain mail and some plate mail were scampering in both directions. "Ho what's up," Draken called out to one sergeant who was heading back toward the underground tunnel.

Puffing, he cried out, "Lord Draken, woe has befallen us. Your father, Lord Dathor has fallen defending the Teeth. Valiant was his fall, though. He has been carried back to the tunnel entrance, but there is little hope. You should make all haste to get to him. The line still holds, though."

"Dower indeed is this day if Lord Dathor has fallen!" sourly replied his son, Draken. "Come, we must hasten to his side at once." He bravely contain his grief and shock until he had his pony running full speed down the roadway toward the entrance. The others followed right behind him. The clip-clop of hooves echoed along the road. Dwarves on foot, mechanically moved out of the way. Jon noticed that most of those heading back toward the tunnel entrance were wounded, while those heading out toward the Teeth were fresh replacements. He wondered what they were going to do when the other arm of the cavalry rode straight up to tunnel entrance from the Maiden's Pond. Perhaps they did not know that the Vyndocians had out flanked them.

The Golden Gates were another dwarven marvel. Here at their entrance, the sheer rock face rose nearly vertical for a thousand feet. Neatly carved in the precise center of the base of the cliff was a twenty foot tall pair of doors, each ten feet wide. These were the thickest doors that Jon had ever seen, nearly three feet thick, constructed of heavy iron. Both were open. In front of the doors, a huge canopy had hastily been erected providing some shelter. This served as their emergency first aid center. Hundreds of dwarves lay on blankets upon the ground. Several doctors, Jon assumed, were attending the wounded. Nearby were a large mound of bodies which were covered completely by blood soaked blankets. Jon assumed these were those who had given their lives.

"Over here," yelled someone and Draken quickly dismounted. Everyone else did likewise. Several of the other dwarves took the reins so that the six could follow Draken. They meandered carefully around the wounded and soon arrived beside Draken who was kneeling holding onto his father's hand.

The elder dwarf had sustained mortal wounds. Swords had punctured his rib cage in several places. Two great slashes on his arms continued to bleed through the hastily applied bandages. Lord Dathor still lived, but not for much longer. Though conscious and recognizing his son, he could not speak because of the seepage of blood. He blinked his eyes in recognition and tried to say that Draken was now in charge, but could only make gurgling sounds. The doctor in attendance, actually a priest of the clan, softly told Draken, "We've done all that we can do for him. His time has come."

"I say it hasn't," interrupted Jon. "I've had just about enough of these Vyndocians and their slaughter of people!" He raised his hand and said, "In the name of Ukko, come to me." To everyone's surprise, his walking stick which was secured to the saddle bags of his horse, instantly appeared in his hand. "That's better. Now in the name of Ukko," and he gently touched the dwarven ruler. A yellowish glow appeared over his whole body. He coughed and coughed.

And then sat up and coughed up more blood and hollered, "A drink, a drink, will someone fetch me a drink!" And a further coughing spell ensued. A startled nurse quickly brought him a flagon of water and the dwarf gargled and washed blood out of his mouth. Then he looked around. "Have I been taken to Valhalla? I swore I saw the face and hand of Ukko touch me! This does not look like Valhalla to me. Are you all dead too?" He looked at the strange humans and then his son and the others about him.

"No, I brought you back from near death, my lord," Jon stated. "I, we all need you here still. How are you feeling?"

A most surprised look appeared on his face. His hands felt for the two arm wounds and found nothing but blood soaked rags which he discarded at once. He felt his chest gently and finding nothing, he fairly pounded on it. "I have no wounds! Though I still feel very weak. Who are you?" he asked staring wide-eyed directly at Jon.

"I am called Saint Jon Brown, the Redeemer, so named by Ukko. This is ranger Mandy Blackthorn, Lord of Blackthorn Castle, mages Alison d'Ambrose and Darless Holy Paladins of Ukko, and May and Mat d'Ambrose Holy Children of Ukko, recently from Freetown. We have come to help put an end to the Vyndocian treachery." He heard hushed whispers from many dwarves around him but could not tell if that was good or bad.

"Ah, your help is most graciously accepted!" Lord Dathor replied. "Are you then a very high priest of Ukko? Can you help save more of my fallen companions?"

"Er, no. I am really just a musician, really. But that is a long story. "Ukko has blessed me with this stick which can heal a limited few. But we all here can perform a good deal of healing. But there is so little time. From high above in the Eagle's Nest, we saw one army moving this way down by the Maiden's Pond. They should be here by morning."

"Curses," he spat, "but then I knew it would only be a matter of time before they came around the long way. At least the Teeth still holds." While he talked, he continued to feel his body where his wounds had been. "Am I really healed? I can find no traces. But I am so very weak," he added.

"Yes, no wounds, but you did lose a lot of blood. It will take some time for a full recovery," Jon explained. "In the meantime, I can still save a few more of those closest to death. Then, we can all set about the task of healing what we can of the others. So you choose, whom am I to try to save from Death's Door?" It looked like there were hundreds to choose from and he certainly did not want to have to make that choice.

The old man let out a chuckle, grimacing as though he expected his wounds to pain him, but they did not. "You leave the choice of life or death in my hands. Now that is a wise man! Learn from him, Draken. Here someone help me up. Who's in dire need?" Quickly his priest helped him stand and survey the fallen.

"Ah, save Beothar there," he pointed. "That man took a thrust aimed at me when I was down. And Jonas the Black, there, he fought valiantly by my side. And Jasper, good old Jasper, took down ten of them, he did." And so it went. As one was pointed out, Jon spoke his command words and touched the dwarf. Each time, a yellowish glow enshrouded the dwarf and restored life. He was able to rescue five others before the stick failed.

Now the others went quickly to work. Mat and May, using their newly acquired healing skills, each helped four others to get back on the road to recovery and then helped with the bandaging of many others. Alison, who had no such skills, helped her brother and sister as she could, administering additional first aid. Jon, Darless and Mandy used their healing skills as much as they could and between them another fifty dwarves found themselves well on the road to recovery.

By now it was getting dark. The quarter moon provided some illumination shining through patchy high cirrus clouds. Lord Dathor has eaten some, rested and recovered enough to sit in on a war council with his four field commanders. Draken was at his right hand for he was given the task of relaying orders while his father recovered. As soon as the six had finished treating the wounded as best they could, Lord Dathor motioned for them to attend.

"We are planning our next defensive positions," he announced. "If you have any suggestions, I'll listen."

"Well, your right flank is not holdable and will result in the total cutoff of all men holding the Teeth," Mandy observed. "Just as soon as the cavalry charges this position from their gathering place at Maiden's Pond, all those you have holding the Teeth will be cutoff, thus weakening your position here."

"Hum, I've thought about that," he replied thoughtfully. "But if I pull those defenders back, then there is no real defensive position between the Teeth and here. That would allow the second army to assault us on the right while they come at us from the front. Is that not even worse?"

"Aye, that is true," Mandy conceded. "I'm afraid that I do not know the territory here. Is the roadway about the same from the Teeth to where we came down that steep trail as it is the rest of the way here?"

"Yes, it is much the same. We cut it from the sheer sides of this mountain wall. It's nearly twenty-five miles long. Just beyond the Teeth, it is raised at least two hundred feet from the valley floor and slowly slopes down until it reaches the plain's floor here," outlined Commander Stone Fist, an older dwarf with a streak of silver in his long hair and beard.

Just then the sounds of a cantering set of pony hooves broke the stillness of the night. An aide arrived from the Teeth are in great haste. "The Teeth are about to be breached!" exclaimed the messenger as he hopped off of his pony.

"Calm down, corporal," Commander Stone Fist ordered. "Just tell us the facts."

The aide was a young dwarf on his first assignment. The commander's words did not put him at ease, but he managed to speak less hastily. "They have brought up two massive battering rams. By now, they will have smashed through our barbicans and may be charging for us even as I speak!"

"Ill news indeed," the commander acknowledged, but then added, "And when did you see this happening and how long have you taken to get back here with the news?" This was, of course, the leveling question.

"Ah, well it was before dinnertime. And I did ride as fast as possible to get here," he added encouragingly, suddenly realizing that his news was already five hours old and totally out of date. He did not hear thundering cavalry on the road behind him either, for that matter. He shuffled his feet and looked at the dark ground.

"And what were the standing orders to the defenders should the enemy break through our lines?" the commander asked.

"Scramble and ramble, sir!" came the instant reply. He perked up having gotten the reply perfect.

"They are not likely to attack us at night," interjected Mandy. "It puts them at a distinct disadvantage trying to fight from horseback in the dark. But what is this scramble thing?"

Commander Stone Fist smiled at his own cleverness, "If we were breached, the men were to disperse in all directions and make for the higher elevations of the mountains and regroup at prearranged locations and head for the safety of the underground." He did not elaborate and was obviously hedging his explanations, unwilling to divulge unnecessary information. "So you are probably right, they won't attack in the night. But if they have busted through, then we may find them right here at our side as the other army arrives from the Maiden's Pond."

Now it was Alison who interrupted. "You know, I have been thinking about all this. What would happen if a large section of the roadway collapsed? There is no other way to get here except by that road, correct?"

"Yes, the only other way is back around the Teeth as the army down by Maiden's Pond have done. But we built the roadway so that it would not collapse," protested the commander. "I helped oversee some of its construction. It is very well engineered."

"Okay then. Here's my idea. I believe that Darless and I can actually destroy a section, say twenty-five feet of it. Then, there is no way they can pass. If we can do so, do I have your permission to try it?" she asked politely. She had no intention of causing such destruction of their engineering marvel without their full permission.

This time, Lord Dathor himself answered, "Absolutely, do anything you can to stop them. It will be hard enough to fight one army, let alone a second on our flank. Get going! I hope it isn't too late already."

The six left the conference and held their own. "What do you have in mind?" Mandy asked before anyone else got a chance.

"Well, I intend to teach them a lesson; what goes around, comes around," Alison replied. "I have the spell that turns rock into mud; it's the same one that they have been using on the giants; quite probably, the same spell that was used to partially level Castle d'Ambrose as well. And Darless can use a disintegrate beam to help out. Between the two spells, we should be able to make a section totally impassable."

"Ah, that would be a good tactical move," Mandy mused, "It will keep them from joining armies and even out our chances a bit. Good idea."

"Yes, but how are you going to get there?" May interjected. "The information is hours old; the cavalry could be half way here already."

"I'll teleport Darless and me there, several hundred feet above the Teeth area. We can use our rings of flying to maneuver as needed and the rings of invisibility too," she added as an afterthought. "There is nothing to worry about. We will be perfectly safe. We are just going to breech the roadway and hurry back." While the others were not totally convinced that this would be either easy or safe, no one else had any better ideas.

Jon gave her a farewell hug and whispered in her ear, "Hurry back, love, I'll keep the blankets warm for you." And he gave her a warm, loving kiss. But she could sense that he was a bit uneasy with this arrangement. However, if they were going to be a couple, she had to have her freedom to do those actions she desired. Alison thought this was as good a time to test Jon a bit. Needless to say, she pleased with his acceptance. "Holler if you need anything and I'll step in the reinforcements," Jon added.

Her sister and brother also gave her a hug. And Jon gave Darless a loving hug too. Mandy just shook their hands bidding them to use extreme caution. The ranger was very ill at ease with this plan for it put the party's top wizards next to the enemy with no backup and no help. But she could think of no better plan.

The two wizards made last minute preparations, including donning a pair of rings each. Holding their staffs in their opposite hands while holding onto each other, Alison spoke a command word and they disappeared. Jon sensed Mandy's uneasiness as soon as the mages had left. "Let's stay close til they get back," Jon said, "I told Alison and Darless to contact me if they need anything. I'll step us all there in a instant if they holler."

"Well, why didn't you say so in the first place!" she replied a bit haughtily. "I was really worried about their safety, so close to the enemy and all." She visibly relaxed, "Say how about seeing if there is any tea to be had anywhere around here." The four went in search of some refreshment.

They had just finished their tea when the mages reappeared as suddenly as they left, only this time they arrived in the air and floated down to the ground near where the foursome were relaxing. "Hi, glad you are back. All go okay?" Mandy got the first words out before anyone else had a chance.

"Just fine," replied Alison as she set foot back on the ground and cancelled her spell. "Any chance of a cup for two tired wizards?" Her friends were sitting on some blankets and leaning on their saddles out in the open under the stars and moonlight near the entrance to the underground city. Before them numerous campfires of the dwarves flickered reddish light like fireflies in the night. They had purposely setup an extravagant number of campfires to confuse enemy spies into believing that there were more dwarves here than were actually present. It did look impressive.

While the girls settled themselves, Jon brought out a pair of cups for the new arrivals and poured for them. "Well, it went exactly as planned. The barrier at the Teeth has indeed fallen. Most of the dwarves have dispersed with many trekking down the road towards us. The cavalry had only advanced a short way. Camping is not an option along the road itself beyond the Teeth. So they took enough to completely hold the road and called it a night. So our task was easy. About a mile on down the road from their furthest outpost, I melted the bedrock and roadway into mud, turning it into a steep downward slope. Darless disintegrated another chunk. So now only a mountain climber could get past that break. Horses can neither cross nor go down to this plain we are on. They have no choice but to come around the long way as the other garrison has done, down by that pond."

The two gracefully accepted the applause from the others on a job well done. "Now I can sleep better," Mandy declared. "Tomorrow we face only one army at a time. Our flank is secure. What a relief. I'd better go relay the information. Back in a bit." And she went in search of the dwarven leaders.

"The only drawback to all this," Darless added, "is that we have exhausted our spells for today. No mansion tonight. We sleep under the stars."

"Well, it is rather romantic," Jon teased, snuggling Alison who gave him an elbow first in jest and then a kiss. And it was not long before they all drifted off into slumber. It is noted here that all six awoke with numerous aches and pains from sleeping on the solid rock surface.

At first light, everyone was up and active stretching and rubbing out aching limbs. With no visible signs of the enemy's advance, breakfast was made and eaten solemnly for the day grew dark and grey. The first storm of the fall season chose this day to make its appearance felt. Somber dwarves scuttled in all directions about the broad, sloping plains just outside the cavernous doors to their underground realm, intent upon their last minute preparations for the coming cavalry charge. No one spoke much. Words sounded loud and harsh here on the eve of a momentous battle.

Alison, Darless, and May spent an hour discussing various spell options, preparing their wizard staffs and setting May up with more offensive spell casting means. Mat also prepared himself for the coming battle by sitting on a blanket and meditating the morning hours. Jon, feeling rather out of place, wandered about checking on the healing dwarves that he had helped the day before.

Mandy, on the other hand, hated all this waiting. Not knowing what was going on with the enemy was making her furious. After telling herself to "think" several times, she got a bright idea. She borrowed a magical ring from Alison and retrieved her "Eyes of the Eagle," the pair of binoculars, that Jon had given her many months ago. She carefully spoke the ring's command word and began rising up into the air about ten feet from the sheer rock face. Up and up she rose until she estimated that she was about a thousand feet above the ground. Next, she used her Eyes of the Eagles to search for the enemy encampment about five miles distant by the Maiden's Pond.

Although the forms were tiny, she could discern activity and motion. Like the dwarves, the men were preparing for their assault. She did a quick estimate and figured there would be about five hundred cavalry in this vanguard. Next, she pivoted to her right and found the Dragon's Teeth. Sure enough, she could see tiny figures exploring the damaged roadway. And already, she glimpsed vast numbers of cavalry riding hard the long way around the formidable rocky outcropping to join up with those already at the pond. These forces would not figure in today's battle, she concluded, for they had a good day's riding to cover that much ground. She took some comfort in that observation. She made a mental note to praise Alison for her night's accomplishment.

Finally, she began to study the plain on which the battle would surely take place below her. The terrain here was strange and magnificent. The sheer rock face behind her was one of the dominant features. The rugged grey granite mountains formed a V-shaped valley. The dwarves had made their main entrance at the bottom of the V. She noticed a small stream actually seeped out an opening near the base of the mountains on her left flowing downhill feeding the Maiden's Pond. As she was studying this she suddenly grasped a detail that had eluded her initial observations. This whole V-shaped valley was man-made, or more likely dwarven-made. From this altitude, she could see the distinct patterns of carved rock surfaces. They had made the channel for the stream to feed the pond. They had removed any surface features of the plain out to about five miles from the entrance door. This plain was perfectly smooth and sloped steeply downwards. A plan instantly popped into her mind.

She quickly lowered herself back to the ground and began walking out from the great doors and down the sloping plains. It was indeed perfectly smooth rock. Horses would be at a very distinct disadvantage here, slipping and sliding on this surface. There was nothing for their hooves to dig into for support! Now she began to understand the dwarves defense. Work crews were busily moving the large stone barbican blocks that prevented an accidental spill from the long roadway. These three foot tall blocks were placed in a line blocking off the tip of the V point from the sloping valley. The row of barbicans was about a quarter of a mile long. Behind these, the dwarves positioned themselves in an attempt to block the cavalry from gaining the precious gates that led underground. But this would force the cavalry into a tight formation, easy targets for archers who could not miss such a densely packed enemy. The only real problem, she lamented, was an insufficient number of archers.

Lord Dathor, having recovered much of his strength, approached her. "Been strolling our defenses. How do they look to you? Anything we have not thought of?" He was just being polite, for he was certain that they had left nothing to chance. "The hundred archers are positioned well back of the makeshift barrier and will launch many volleys of arrows as the cavalry approach, reducing their numbers. Next, the two hundred pole-armed dwarves move out in front of the stone blocks, planting their weapons against its base. Any charging horses and riders are skewered. They fall back behind the barrier while another two hundred climb on top of the stones and between each bunch, the enemy is attacked both high and low. Any that breech the line face my private guards, some hundred strong here at the very gates." He finished with an air of certainty that all had been well thought out.

"If all goes as planned, you have a good defense. I noticed that this is actually a man-made valley, or should I say dwarven made?" she asked to confirm her suspicions.

"You have the keen eyes of a ranger!" He answered but would say no more.

"Actually, it is rather diabolically to have made this last five miles of approach treacherous for horse travel. Only by slow, careful riding can a horse traverse this grade safely. A cavalry charge is virtually impossible, in my opinion. But we'll see to what extremes these Vyndocians will go. I just wish there were more archers," she replied.

Lord Dathor smiled but again would say nothing more about the making or design of the valley. Instead, he commented, "Looks like a storm is brewing; first of the fall season. May bring heavy snow at the higher elevations."

"Yes, that brings me to what I've been meaning to ask," Mandy cleverly responded. "What if when the attack comes, it is pouring heavily? This rock surface will then become slippery. That should nullify any possibility of a cavalry charge. Even foot soldiers would find the upward climb treacherous."

"Yes, it certainly would, but then there is no way to predict the weather, now is there?" the lord answered. "If Silverbeard smiles upon us, it may rain in time. Then again, it may not."

Mandy smiled, she knew what she had to do. "I can make it rain, perhaps very heavily this time because nature is about to do so anyway. With your permission, I will let it loose as soon as the enemy makes a forward advance. It takes time for my spell to achieve peak efficiency."

Now it was Lord Dathor's turn to be surprised. "You, you can make it rain? I've heard of great druids who can command the elements. I bow to you, Mandy Blackthorn. If you can make it rain, please do so. It will only help us! Since you need to know when they leave the Maiden's Pond, I'll give you the signal." He lowered his voice and pressed his mouth close to her ear as she bend down. "I have a signal spy located high above this sheer cliff, way up in the mountains. He is spying on them. When it is time, you will hear a rock landing out there beyond our defense line. That's his signal they are on the move."

"Great. I had better let the others know to be prepared for wet weather," Mandy replied. Indeed, Lord Dathor also hurried off to spread the news of the impending rain to the dwarves. She went to look for the others.

"Hi Mandy," Jon greeted her as she approached. "I think the wizards are done doing their wizard things. Could you see the enemy from way up there?"

"Yes, those Eyes of the Eagle work great!" she answered with a big smile as the three wizards joined them. "We need to rig for rain. I'm going to make a big downpour when the cavalry begin. That should turn the rocky approach into one slippery steep slope and slow any kind of charge down to a crawl."

"Great!" Alison encouraged. "We have got our most damaging spells prepared. Between the three of us, we should be able to make a dent in the assault. When it starts, I am going to put a protective spell on May. She is the least experienced in combat spell casting. I don't want her getting hurt while she is trying to cast. Jon, you and Mat are going to be needed protecting us from the enemy so we can get our spells off. We've decided that the best position for us would be centrally located just about here, directly in front of the doors to the tunnel. Mat will stand before us and deflect or stop any ground forces from getting to us. Remember, unless these are really stupid generals we are facing, they are going to concentrate all of their forces on eliminating us wizards."

"That goes without saying," Mandy interjected, but quickly realized that the twins and Jon were not experienced in warfare as were Alison and herself. But she could not take back her words and added quickly, "I'll be mobile in front of you. I can cover where needed. Dwarven fighters are a solid bunch, but if breeched, the going will get mighty rough. I would expect that they would retreat back into the tunnel. So if worst comes to worst, be prepared to beat a hasty retreat into their realm."

Jon did not relish another long trip underground so soon. However, before he could grumble, she added in a whisper, "They have a look out perched way up at the top of this sheer cliff, up there in the mountains. He's to signal when they begin their advance by throwing a stone out there somewhere beyond the defensive line. So stay alert." Jon wanted to ask her how she knew that but did not get the chance. Suddenly the dwarves made a commotion off to their right. Someone was coming down the elevated roadway toward them.

"Say, those look like giants," exclaimed Jon. Indeed two dozen huge grey forms were ambling along the roadway not too far away. Each carried several huge bulging bags slung over their shoulders. Whatever they contained, it was heavy. The giants were each slightly bent over as they shuffled along.

When they got closer, everyone recognized Rolf and several others. "Hi Rolf! Good to see you," shouted Jon and they rushed to greet their friend. Lord Dathor and several of his generals were already greeting the new arrivals.

"Hail and well met indeed, oh great giants of Hell's Gate!" exclaimed the dwarf Lord.

Rolf acted as spokesman, "Hello small fellow, stone lovers. Me cannot stand by when me small cousins face menace of horsemen. Me come to aid. Me bring giants. We help. We throw stones at them. Bash them."

The dwarves let loose a volley of cheers and "Here-here's;" all of the giants smiled broadly. As Jon and the others drew closer, they saw the stark contrast. Lord Dathor barely reached Rolf's knee, yet they both were lovers and workers of stone. That, they held in common. After the serious hand shaking between leaders, Lord Dathor assigned stone throwing positions behind the central area. Jon surmised that the dwarf leader chose this position such that the enemy would have to get through all of the giants and Jon's group before they could get to the actual entrance to the underground realm. It made sense.

Once in position, Rolf sat down by his six new friends and they chatted. They found out that the giant both loved a good fight and wanted to obtain some payback for the kidnaping of his wife and son. Twenty-four stone giants definitely added to their defense. And they had not long to wait. Barely a half hour after the giants arrived, a stone landed out beyond the makeshift line of stone barriers. Several dwarf trumpets sounded; dwarves scurried in all directions heading for their assigned positions.

Mandy looked at Lord Dathor behind her; he nodded his agreement. Mandy began her solemn prayers to Reylona. "What she do?" Rolf whispered to Jon.

"The enemy is now on the move here. She is going to cause it to rain like the devil, making the approach up the valley here very slippery. No cavalry charges are likely today," he explained in a whisper. Her prayer did not take long at all, Jon thought.

"There, that should do it, if I am worthy of her grace," Mandy pronounced, satisfied that she had done all that a good priestess ought do. "Now we wait. It should take them some time to get close enough to see clearly."

"How you know you make rain?" Rolf asked her. "Going to rain anyway today. So how you know you did anything? Me curious."

The ranger smiled as she carefully donned various pieces of armor to protect her arms and legs and chest. She never wore any helm; she found them too restrictive and hid her long beautiful hair. "Yes, it will rain today, Rolf. But if Reylona answers my prayer, the rain will be far more than anyone expects. In truth, Rolf, I have never requested a storm when a storm was eminent in the first place. So I'm hoping to see a really big, violent one." Then, satisfied with her armor pieces, she retrieved her short bow and several quivers of arrows from her portable hole and refolded it and tucked into her bosom, its usual resting place. "I'm going to help the archers at the beginning. The more we can take down before the battle closes, the better." She laid one bastard sword beside Jon. "Here, you keep an eye on this one. If I lose one, I will dash here to grab it." With that, she moved up to the very front of the temporary stone barricade, joining the other archers.

Mat stood quietly at the point of his group, located several hundred feet back from the barricades and a hundred feet from the tunnel entrance. Behind him stood Alison with her wizard staff at the ready. Darless with Alison's spare staff stood just back of her on her right while May, holding a pair of magical wands, stood to the left of her younger, more experienced sister. Jon stood alone behind the three of them. He had his walking stick in his right hand.

Behind him some fifty feet was the canvas tent structure that served as the infirmary. Jon noticed that all of the injured dwarves had been transported somewhere inside the dark tunnel out of harm's way. Or was it that the infirmary was being readied for more injured? Perhaps both, he mused. Then it struck him, he realized that every action a dwarf takes has been meticulously calculated to be just the correct action at that time. He now realized that their music also reflected this philosophy as well. Jon remembered a melody line that Nain and his friends had taught him several months ago when they had encountered them while they were on their way to Freetown from Ravenswash. Nain had explained that it was a battle song. Bored with all the waiting, Jon got out his flute.

The low soft sounds of a dreary dirge floated across the entire field before him. Every dwarf instantly recognized it, even if he missed a note or inflection here and there. Smiles and chuckles broke out. With a nod from Lord Dathor, several dwarves left their posts and scurried into the tunnel and reappeared with some drums and stringed instruments. Soon, Jon's plaintive sounds were supported by full accompaniment. And only minute later, the stringed player took the lead, allowing Jon to follow. If they were going to play, they should perform it correctly, insisted Lord Dathor. The lament soon gave way to a rousing march and fighting song. All around the perimeter, dwarves began chanting and clapping in time. Spirits rose to a fervor.

And so it was that the advancing cavalry heard dwarven revelry at their approach. This was rather the opposite of what their leaders had predicted. It was only the first of their miscalculations. By the time the advancing cavalry, some five hundred strong, had climbed to within a mile of the dwarves, great bolts of lightning began arcing through the sky followed by ominous, loud thunderclaps that shook the ground. Their leaders had assured them that the rains would hold off until late afternoon. The riders closed to within a half mile of the battle line when an enormous bolt of lightning struck the right side of the canyon wall, splintering rocks flew in all directions. The thunder was deafening, several horses stumbled and fell from the violent shaking of the ground under hooves. Then the rains came.

Rain fell so thick that one could only see a couple feet ahead. Torrential rains drenched everyone in less than a minute. Then hail the size of golf balls pummeled the entire area, bouncing off of the shields the riders held over their heads. The ground quickly turned white as a layer of ice quickly built up. But since the stone surface pitched steeply down, the ice covering slithered back down the valley toward the Maiden's Pond. Forward progress became totally impossible. Indeed many horses, burdened by the heavy weight of their suits of chain mail, slipped and fell crashing to the ground breaking many riders' legs as well as their own. Mass pandemonium broke out but was witnessed only by those within it.

From their position at the barrier wall line, the defenders could see nothing other than the pummeling, torrential rain and hail. Mandy did indeed cause a storm. Soon it became abundantly clear that they all needed to take shelter and dwarves, giants and humans all rushed for the relative safety of the tent and tunnel. Rolf's comment to Mandy caused her to grin sheepishly. "Me thinks you over did it a bit! Me never see it rain this hard."

She yelled back over the tumultuous noise, "Yes, but we have shelter. They have got to be in serious trouble exposed, out in the open down there. I'd sure hate to be in their position right about now!"

"You can say that again!" Jon yelled playfully back at her. "Of course your storm has silenced my music. But I'd rather have it this way. Think maybe they will give up and retreat?"

She did not get a chance to reply. At that exact moment, a flash of magic appeared in front of them. A tall man with a goat's foot, wearing dark black, plush velvet robes lined with crimson red, and a black goatee appeared before them. He instantly got soaked and moved close to the others just under the sagging tent for cover.

"Dispater!" echoed several voices in unison.

Smiling, he yelled, "None other! Am I in time to watch?" Without waiting for an answer, he complimented, "Mandy, such an effect. I might have guessed you were behind it." He bowed low to her. She, however, did not share his welcome. The arch-devil was about the last person she wanted to see just now. Jon glanced at Mandy and noticed that neither she nor the others were fighting or even feeling his "chill of death." Always before, accompanying his presence, a bone-freezing cold penetrated their bodies. Jon concluded that this was something Dispater could control and use as he saw fit.

The dwarves hastily retreated a good distance from the visitor. However, having no real choice in the matter, Lord Dathor had to move forward to greet this unexpected, unwelcome new arrival. Fearful and anticipating dire consequences with this confrontation with the devil, he tried unsuccessfully to control his shaking legs as he approached the tall man. "Wha, wha, what do you want with us?" he managed to shout out above the thunder, deluging rain, and hail.

"My good dwarf lord, why I want nothing more than to watch the battle unfold," he pronounced charmingly and even nodding in respect to the smaller person. "I promise not to interfere in any way. That is, unless, of course, someone here wants to bargain with their soul," and he chuckled, knowing full well that Jon and the others knew precisely what he meant.

Lord Dathor was taken aback by his statement; he could not determine true intent. "We, we do not want to die for your sport. This is an unwelcome, unasked for battle. We, we did not provoke it. Why, why not go down with the Vyndocians and watch it there? There is sure to, to be, er, chaos and confusion there." Almost as soon as the words left his mouth, he regretted his outburst. He suddenly envisioned the defeated Vyndocians bartering their souls for a victory against the dwarves.

The arch-devil read the dwarf lord's thoughts, "Ah you would have me stay with the Vyndocians and let them trade their souls for success over you, is that it?" He laughed; even Jon had to smile. The befuddled dwarf lord had spoken rashly. "No, my Lord, all I really wish to do is watch. If an event comes to pass as I suspect it might, then I am fully satisfied. And if it doesn't, well that's acceptable to me as well. Truthfully, no one has bartered with me for victory over you dwarves. You may relax on that account. Would it help if I were invisible?"

"Well, perhaps," was all Dathor managed to reply before the raging storm suddenly abated. "What?"

Indeed, the hail stopped and the torrential downpour instantly ceased. The dense grey clouds, which had totally obstructed vision, thinned and disappeared in less than a minute. Below them about a half mile away stood five Vyndocians. Four formed a semi-circle around one man whose arms were outstretched, reaching toward the sky. His rich blue robes hung heavily, fully drenched. His right hand held aloft a staff. It appeared that the storm was being sucked into his staff!

"A high priest!" exclaimed Alison. "It would seem that the others are wizards. Now we are in for it!"

With their view now cleared, the effects of the storm were also quite evident. The orderly forward march of the cavalry regiment was gone. Only a very few stray horsemen still remained standing. Many horses were lying down, unable to rise. Numerous men were also lying on the stone surface, crushed or trampled by men and beasts. For the most part, men and horses were separated, scrambling for safety down near the Maiden's Pond. They had routed. Mandy could see their leaders valiantly attempting to restore order. But she knew this fighting force would not be the same after this day.

The priest lowered his arms and glared up toward the defenders, satisfied that he had absorbed the storm. He then turned and the five walked back down the slope off to the right. They had not been a part of the main cavalry force. Mandy concluded that they had come from the other force that had been cut off by the destruction of the roadway by Alison and Darless the night before. She also knew what this interlude meant. They were regrouping. The main assault was yet to come. The dwarves also realized that the battle had yet to be fought and only responded with small cheers.

Dispater turned to Jon. "That was Hegate Sebastian, Lord High Priest of Morrigan, Council Elder of Vyndoc. He is not a man to be trifled with; I do believe you have rather upset him. And that, young man, is hard to do."

"You know these people, then?" Jon replied. "I have no idea why they are so insistent on attacking us. They have tried to attack us over and over as we traveled the road from Freetown here. Why? I have no clue. What are they after anyway? Do you have any ideas?" Jon doubted that the arch-devil would really answer but he knew that if Dispater chose to answer, it would be the truth, at least the truth as Dispater saw it. The arch-devil was very different than the demon lords who said what they chose which may have nothing at all to do with the truth. He may be thoroughly evil in nature, but Dispater was also highly principled and followed rules of conduct not unlike those of Alison. These two held totally opposite set of values of good and evil, but were amazingly alike in other ways. Both held firmly to their tenants of conduct. Life with Mandy, on the other hand, was never dull or predictable. She, similar to the demon lords, believed that the individual was all important, and that a person did what they wanted to do when they wanted to do it.

"I believe that it is a complex conjunction of many variables," the arch-demon replied thoughtfully. "You have just heard Lord Dathor pronounce that the dwarves have done absolutely nothing to the Vyndocians. Now I ask you, based upon your wisdom as Saint Jon the Redeemer, have you ever seen two combatants who had never, ever done anything to the other?" He paused allowing Jon and the others to think this concept over carefully.

Memories of a childhood scuffle appeared in Jon's mind. He was hitting another kid who was trying to take a toy car away from him. It was kindergarten days. The other boy first asked him politely if he could play with the car for a while. Jon remembered he teased the other boy with a sneering, "No, I got it first." Then the other kid tried to snatch it from his hands and Jon slugged him. "I believe you have a point," Jon finally replied. "But what has this to do with us? I've never even met these people who seem bent upon my or our destruction."

"I ask you, Jon Brown, does it seem reasonable for a regiment of cavalry to just attack in force of their own accord?" replied the devil who refused to give a direct reply. Instead, he wanted Jon to work it out on his own so that there could be no suggestion that he, Dispater, was dispensing information. But a gentle nudge along the right path was not out of bounds.

"Where I come from, such an all-out assault order can only come from the leader, our president. So a safe assumption must be that the ruler of Vyndoc has been ordering the attacks on our caravan," Jon surmised. "But I don't even know who that could be. All I have been able to ascertain is that they are followers of Morrigan."

Dispater smiled, "Ah."

And he would say no more but Jon spied a twinkle in his eyes and his lips smiled. Jon added, "Thanks. We have a saying where I come from. 'A picture is worth a thousand words.'"

"Well, I must be off now. I will return when battle is joined. Til then, I bid you adieu." And before Jon could reply, he snapped his fingers and vanished.

Alison, who was expecting a battle any moment, cried out, "What do you mean? They are not going to attack shortly?"

"No, I think not," surmised Mandy, her sense of tactics kicked in as she explained. "The priest and mages only just arrived. Otherwise, he would have canceled my storm spell as soon as I launched it. So it is safe to assume they just got here. It is also likely they were a part of the force you cut off last night. Remember, it is our guess that it would take one day's hard ride for the cavalry regiment to go the long way around. So they probably used spells to get here as soon as they did. If I were their leader, I would certainly wait for the reinforcements to arrive, doubling their strength. It also allows time for them to regroup and set new plans. So, no, I think Dispater is right. I don't think that we will see any further attacks today. Actually, I think that I would be exploring other assault options, if I were in charge. It is suicide to charge this last mile totally in the open and up this flat, rising valley — uphill and no cover — our archers would have a field day."

"They underestimated the effect of the terrain. I believe their commander today believed that they could gallop uphill and gain hand-to-hand combat before we could launch many volleys of arrows. But they did not grasp the full intent of the dwarven defense. That was a brilliant concept to clean the entire valley floor to bed rock; it makes horse charges nearly impossible," Mandy finished up.

Lord Dathor's face radiated pride, "You indeed have captured the essence of our master designers' plans when we first arrived here three hundred years ago. But I cannot see any other way of taking our entrance here without coming up this valley. Though I do not see any other tactic, I will go consult with my generals." He bowed, gave the stand down orders, and summoned his generals into the underground tunnel for new consultations.

While the dwarven soldiers retreated to their camp sites, Jon and the others walked back to their staging area. "I could use a cup of tea," Jon suggested.

"Wow. Was that really Dispater?" May asked Alison excitedly. She had never seen a devil before now, but she had heard many children's tales. Alison chatted about their previous encounters with him; May and Mat paid close attention. Jon noticed that Mandy seemed troubled and was lagging behind, lost in mental thought. Darless, at her side, was also lost in thought. So Jon lagged a bit to join them.

"Hi," Jon said as she nearly bumped into him, thereby catching her attention.

"Jon, I am very worried. I don't like the sudden turn of events one bit. That high priest in less than a minute turned the entire outcome around. Imagine what he might be able to do with a day's planning!" she added, looking him squarely in the eyes.

"Well, I don't like the appearance of Dispater," interjected Darless. "It is no small matter when demons and devils appear at a skirmish of mortal men. Something rotten is going on. And I hate it when I do not know what is going on!" She stamped her foot hard on the ground and then momentarily regretted the action. "Ouch."

"I'll make you all a tea and we can hold our own council. I'm sure we can figure something out if we try," Jon encouraged. He set about the task of making tea for everyone. It was something he could do. In a few minutes, the water was hot and he made a large pot and had everyone sitting on the stone blocks on which the dwarven archers only minutes before were stationed. From here, sipping their tea, they could stare down the long valley and see the tiny forms of the enemy moving about.

"Okay, then," Darless began, "Number 1, since Dispater is involved, there must be some connection between him, Morrigan, and this battle. Number 2, thus, he has a vested interest. Number 3, I do believe he is anticipating that we will do something beneficial or in same way helpful to him, some plot of his is to bear fruit. Number 4, he was in cahoots with Metrarch which is very, very unlikely possibility, but he was. So Number 5, he is or was trying to achieve some end of his own and is or was using Metrarch to achieve it. Number 6, since he is still with us, and I believe his sole reason for appearing was to let us know just this, that his ultimate goal has not yet been reached. Number 7, since he was unbelievably pleasant, no chill of death even, he expects that we will be doing that something for him, though we do not know what that might be." She paused but could not track this thread of reason any further.

After a long pause, May added, "Number 8, I don't think we need to be concerned with doing his bidding. It is likely just a byproduct of our defending ourselves. So I think that he hopes, expects, or desires that we kill someone, one of the enemies we are to face."

"But if that were the case, why even appear to us?" countered Darless. "He appeared for a reason, something that he thought was so vital that he had to come personally to us. But did he tell us anything?" Everyone tried to recall the conversation but it seemed nothing more than casual talk.

"She's right," added Jon. "He does not appear at random. No, something he said he considers absolutely vital to the successful outcome of his plans or he would not have appeared. But what?" No one had an answer to that one and sipped on their tea in quiet thought.

"Zagroot zounds!" Mandy cursed, breaking the silence and getting everyone's full attention. "I hate to be a pessimist, but I think that we are going to find ourselves in deep trouble in the next attack. Look, they now have four mages to our three. They have a high priest and we have none; I really am not in his league even remotely. The only key defensive point here is that our archers expect to take a heavy toll before the front lines reach hand-to-hand combat. And then how long can these few dwarves and handful of giants hold out against their sheer numbers? To say nothing of the huge number of magical spells they will unleash in an attempt to destroy us! Man, it's grim."

A sobering minute of silence followed. Finally, Jon asked, "Mandy, if you were their commander, how would you launch the next attack?"

"Well, I would do two key things: one, find a way to minimize any losses from archers during the long approach, and two, launch a devastating and relentless magical barrage on the key members, us, in other words. If they take us out, the dwarves should be easy to overwhelm and to force them to retreat into their underground realm. That's why I cursed; we are doomed!"

Another minute of silence ensued broken by the occasional sipping of the still steaming tea. "No, there's one thing that they have not counted upon," Jon replied thoughtfully. "We are a team. We may be out-spelled, if that's the right word to use, but we work together as a single unit. A group is always more powerful than the sum of its members. That's how we will defeat them; teamwork."

"Jon's right," Alison finally spoke. "If we try to cast spells their way, I would expect that they will have one or two mages whose task is solely to absorb or deflect or counter our spells, leaving the others totally free to cast attack spells on us. Dar and I can suck their spells for a time using our staves. But when we do so, we will be unable to attack them. We can only do one thing at a time."

"Well, Mandy and I can provide physical protection from attackers closing to combat," Mat offered. "I can even snatch flying arrows headed your way, though I doubt that Mandy can do that. I swear to not allow a single arrow or sword to reach you. So Mandy and I will stand in front of you and deflect physical things. That's a start."

"And there are a few defensive spells that we can cast on ourselves," Alison added enthusiastically, "that will protect us completely from a few attacks that might get through." It was a hopeful start.

"Ah yes, and don't forget that I can help too," Jon interjected. "Remember the white dragons? Won't these wizards likely to try to fire ball us or freeze us, or whatever you call those spells? I can counter those fairly easily."

"White dragons?" asked May full of curiosity. "You never told me about seeing or fighting dragons! Sis what is this all about?" Alison spent a couple of minutes relating their adventure in obtaining the Theos tree for Lady Ursla. Mandy had shape changed into a Pegasus and had flown them to the area of the trees. Unfortunately, the location was inhabited by a number of white dragons which had given chase and nearly frozen them had it not been for Jon.

"I've learned how to nullify heat and cold over an area," Jon tried to explain. "I create the opposite energy. It is really rather simple."

"Well simple for you maybe, but inconceivable for me," replied May. "Well, I can reserve a few dispel magic type of spells. I am not as powerful as you two are, so I might not be so successful, if the enemy is also powerful. But I will give it my best shot. And I can also try to confuse them. My skills are honed to a city setting, you know, crowd control and such. But they may also prove useful here as well."

"And one other thing, we can communicate by thoughts, mentally, at a far more rapid pace than they can use speech. Just think your thought at me and I'll see that it gets carried out," Jon volunteered.

"And there is one other thing that we have on our side," Mat added. "We have five of us that can perform emergency healing as needed. If our suspicions are correct, they have only the high priest, and he also can only do one thing at a time as well. So we have an advantage there."

Thus, spirits rose as hope rekindled. The five healers spent the remaining hours tending the wounded whom they had helped the previous day. The balance of the day dragged on hour by hour. There were no attacks from the enemy. Though far off in the distance, Mandy, using her Eyes of the Eagle, constantly spied upon their encampment hoping to gain a clue to their strategy for the coming battle. She could see that they were at work on some kind of preparations, but could not discern what.

Meanwhile, dwarves scampered about reinforcing their meager defenses and drilled some contingency plans involving rapid retreat into their dark underground tunnels. The giants took several forays into the mountains in search of more boulders to throw. By the end of the day, each had very large piles of stones to throw arranged in neat piles beside their positions behind the stone blocks the dwarves had placed in an arc before the entrance to their tunnel.

Jon, on the other hand, brooded; he felt out of place, out of time. All about him, the others passed the time profitably. Mandy sharpened her many blades and readied her arrows. Dwarves rushed about sharpening their axes and blades, while others fiddled with their bows. The mages poured over their spell books, deep in concentration, speaking occasionally to each other in hushed voices. Even Mat was busy practicing his martial arts moves and meditating. Though Jon had made his rounds of the injured doing what little he could, that took less than an hour. Over his third cup of tea, he muttered to himself, "I've no real purpose here right now. A fish out of water is the expression I've always heard. I really, really understand that fish right about now!"

So he took a walk around and around the perimeter. On his third circuit, his frustrations and gloom subsided and his mind began thinking, reflecting upon Dispater's words. He was now certain that the devil was trying to tell him something, but what. Then, with no more than a slight hunch to go on, he sought out Lord Dathor and queried with him about the dwarves prior relationship with the Vyndocians. The dwarf was more than willing to list all of their grievances, problems and confusions with these horsemen. Several times, Jon interrupted the verbal tirade with "and how do you know that; who told you that." The same name kept reappearing which Jon thought was most curious. After a half hour, Lord Dathor excused himself and went to another of his council meetings with his generals. Jon paced around and around the perimeter again, pondering what he had learned. He could not make any real sense of it all, save that the dwarves had obviously been cheated out of a good deal of money by the Vyndocians, but hardly a thing worth going to war over.

When the cover of night fell bringing a cold chill of late fall, the dwarves again lit their numerous coal-fired braziers both for warmth and for light. Their greatest concern was a sneak nighttime attack, to be taken by surprise. Although Jon did not know it, one hundred dwarven scouts crawled far out upon the dark, sloping plain. Their eyes could detect or sense the heat of warm bodies; their sole job that long night was to sound the alert should a sneak attack come. None did. The Vyndocians were not fools; they knew the dwarves could see the heat of their bodies in the dark.

Dawn broke dimly; grey clouds rolled in from the west; the first heavy snowfall of the season heading their way. Jon had slept poorly on the stone ground and awoke grumpy. After a good breakfast, Alison and the others prepared their spells and defenses. For Alison and Darless, a great deal of thought lay behind their spell selections for this battle. Never before had these mages faced so formidable a challenge.

As they began their final preparations, Alison explained, "Our objective is to stay alive. If their mages are anything like what we have seen in their cavalry, it's certain that they are going to try every destructive spell they can muster, attempting to kill us any way possible. So our strategy is to avoid destruction. We've drained our staves so that we can absorb as much spell energy as possible."

"Say, I like the sound of that!" commented Jon playfully at last he was out of his doldrums. "I don't want any of us killed or hurt even." Alison poked him in the ribs and smiled at him.

"However, we will have to launch a few attacks," Darless added, "so that they can use up their hopefully few defensive spells."

"That way, we can then use their own energies against them in the end," burst out May with a twinkle in her eye. She clearly saw the total concept.

Jon, however, frowned, "I don't follow what you mean? How can you win? What do you mean? Are they to fight themselves?"

"No, silly," Alison pulled on his shirt and smiled into his eyes. "After they have used most of their assault spells and we have rather soaked up all of that magical energy into our staves, we then volley our attacks back at them using that stored up energy. It's rather like doubling our total strength."

"Ah ha. Brilliant!" exclaimed Jon, finally grasping her plan. "So the trick is to be alive and kicking, so to speak, at the end. Ah, stay alive! Brilliant."

"Excuse me," interjected Mandy. "I need one critical detail clarified. Since I am the closest thing to a 'general' that we have, I know that I can be torn between working flat out to protect all of you and a keen need to assist the dwarves, should things go ill for them. I fear that I might have to make a sudden choice, go to their aid or stay with you."

Darless turned to her at once and said, "Number 1, if their lines fail, two armies can easily overwhelm us. Number 2, therefore, if you see the need to assist them so their lines can hold longer, why by all means do so. The alternative is worse. So just do it when you feel the need is there." The others nodded complete agreement. Mandy's sigh of relief drained the last uncertainty from her mind. Now she was ready for whatever would come.

And come it did. This time, no dwarf signal was needed, for several horns sounded a battle anthem. Then, from several miles away, faint drum cadences carried on the gentle, chilly wind. Hastily, the dwarves, giants and the party took up their defensive positions. Behind the giant arc of relocated roadway barbican stones some thousand feet long, the archers prepared their bows. Each had several quivers of arrows at the ready. A stone giant with a huge pile of stones was paired with every dozen or so archers. Thus, the stone giants with their superior strength were uniformly placed around the defensive arc. In the center of the arc and in front of the tunnel entrance stood the party of adventurers. In front of the wizards stood Mandy, with her bow out and numerous quivers of arrows at the ready, and Mat. Alison positioned herself in the center flanked by Darless on her right and May on her left. Jon stood alone behind her. Then, they watched and waited patiently as the mustered might of Vyndoc steadily climbed up the long slope toward them.

Mandy chanted a brief prayer to Reylona ending with a sweeping gesture that encompassed all of her friends. Jon felt a pleasant glow of comfort spread over his body. "I've blessed you all in the name of Reylona. May you all shoot straight." A chorus of thank you's acknowledged her efforts. She had seldom had the time to cast this particular spell.

The rhythmic pulsing drumming grew ever louder as the enemy trudged closer and closer. When they were about a mile away, Mandy cursed, "Zagroot zounds! Look they have made some kind of mass shield cover to protect them from our arrows. That is an ill omen. I had so hoped the archers would level the numbers."

Indeed, the front-most men were hidden behind a wall of stretched horse hides, evidently made from the horses that died the previous day. Now flights of arrows could not cut down their advance directly. This fact was not lost on the dwarves either, for much muted cursing could be heard from the several hundred bowmen. Mandy stared at the advancing line, there was still time to think, and think she did.

"Do not try to target the front lines," she yelled out to everyone. "Instead, lob the volleys over their heads into the close ranks that follow in their footsteps. While we will not harm the front row, we can still devastate their ranks, lessen their overall numbers," yelled Mandy. Plenty of "ah ha!'s" echoed all around her.

Then, she heard Raul's voice bellow out, "Leave front row to giants. Horse hides cannot stop stones! We throw at shield wall." Mandy smiled; she recognized teamwork in operation. This was a good omen: men, dwarves and giants all working together. She smiled grimly.

She figured the short bow's maximum range was perhaps one hundred eighty yards for a normal shot. However, in this case they intended to shoot at a forty-five degree angle to gain maximum distance, counting on a rain of arrows to do damage. Thus, when the approaching lines reached two hundred twenty yards distant, the arrows and stones began to fly. Each volley sent well over two hundred arrows en mass flying into the compact formation of men. Mandy estimated that the charging enemy would close the gap in about thirty seconds. So the archers' objective was to let fly arrows as fast as they could shoot them. Most of the archers let fly an entire quiver of twenty arrows before it came down to hand to hand combat. The effect of four thousand arrows in that thirty seconds was appalling. Falling men could be seen all along the advancing line. Fully a quarter of their numbers fell in this rain of death.

The enemy's problems were compounded by the giant's stone throwing. Each giant lobbed stones weighing well over twenty pounds straight into the shielded front line. While no arrows pierced this horse hide barrier, the protection was no match for the boulders of the giants. Everywhere the stones landed, the front line collapsed and staggered. Jon guessed that it must be similar to being hit by an incoming cannon ball. Each time a stone hit, one less man staggered back onto their feet.

But these soldiers knew that their doom was at hand if they did not press forward at the fastest possible speed. The longer they took to close to combat, the heavier their losses would be. So they had a vested interest in ignoring the carnage about them, charging steadily forward toward the dwarven line. Indeed in less than a minute the sounds of steel upon steel and bone echoed all about them. Groans and grunts, cries and screams blended into a cacophony of sound. In short, it was mass slaughter, mass mutilation of bodies.

But the chaos of battle was just the backdrop for the real fight. The high priest and his four mages along with several guards positioned themselves about three hundred feet away, just out of effective bow shot range. And as the arrows began flying, they began casting spells at the opposing wizards. Under normal circumstances, these mages would have cast fireballs into the dwarven archers to prevent them from raining deadly arrows upon the advancing footsoldiers. Instead, just as Alison predicted, they focused solely on the mages. The high priest launched the first attack.

Jon felt the air above them begin to crackle and spark. He recognized its effect at once and sent to the others, *I'll take care of this one, it's some kind of fire spell.* Concentrating he mocked up an ice cube and threw it up into the air, and then two, then four, then sixteen, then hordes. He felt the spell detonate and a sizzle of steam enveloped them briefly as the priest's spell fizzled. At the same instant, two separate volleys of magical arrows appeared in front of Alison who spoke a command word and sucked them into her staff. A few seconds after that came a bolt of lightning streaking toward them but was sucked into Darless' staff. May's chanting produced a flight of magical arrows going after the priest, but they seemed to have no effect upon him.

Out of the corner of his eye, Jon spied a shimmering effect and sensed that an invisible Dispater was standing out of harm's way, watching the battle. "This one is a nasty one, get it Darless," shouted Alison. The alu-demon did so. Another ball of fire exploded over their heads, but Jon dissipated that one and more steam arose. Alison absorbed another lightning bolt directed at them while May, using a wand, shot a fireball back at the evil mages, one of which countered it with some kind of dispel magic.

Suddenly, one of the priest's spells got by their defenses. Jon felt himself moving in slow motion. He could not move his feet. Panic swept over him for an instant before Darless counter-spell fired, freeing them all. After two minutes of intense spell casting, it was a stalemate with neither side doing any actual harm to the other. And then the front wave of the dismounted cavalry reached Mandy and Mat's position. Jon watched as Mandy flew from opponent to opponent, a dodge and upswing cut one man down followed by a sweep, feint and down swing felling the next man. Bodies piled up before her. Mat was just as deadly with great circle kicking blows to heads or thrusts of his short sword. "I've got twelve so far," she yelled Mat's way.

"Only eleven, no make that twelve here," he hollered back.

And still the spells continued to rain down upon the wizards. "Jon, take this one, it is a cold spell," Alison ordered. Now in the past, Jon's method of countering these spells had been to mock up or create the illusion of say one ice cube or one blow torch, and then doubling them as fast as he could. But now, he decided to just mock up one huge blast furnace and be done with it. He miscalculated and a huge wall of flames shot skyward rather like a roman candle.

"How'd you do that?" asked a startled May, but there was no time to answer; more incoming spells required instantaneous handling. Darless now launched a lightning bolt from her staff and this one got through knocking one of the mages off his feet, sending him flying backwards several feet. Several magical missiles pierced the party's defenses. Jon and May both took direct hits. Quickly Jon healed himself, musing on the benefit of being hit by these magical arrows which disappear after piercing their bodies, unlike the real ones. Then, he healed up May and was just in time to dissolve another fire spell. Another lightning bolt pierced their defenses and hit Darless squarely in her chest, knocking her off her feet. Jon helped her stagger back to her feet, otherwise unharmed.

"Thanks," she coughed. "Takes more than a lightning bolt to damage an alu-demon. Now where was I?" And she began chanting another spell.

The three minute point in the attack passed. Mandy glanced at the defensive line between parries. The dwarven line was slowly being forced back by sheer numbers. And the party was forced to retreat ten feet. Mandy and Mat had stacked up a large body pile before them. Maneuvering room was scant; blood pools on the ground was making the smooth rock surface exceedingly slippery.

Another of the priest's spells got through their defenses. Suddenly, Jon felt his so weak that he could hardly stand. Mandy stumbled and two blades easily found their mark as she staggered backwards, lost her footing, dropped her sword and fell hitting the ground hard. As the two lunged toward her fallen form for the kill, Mat leaped high into the air between them. Each of his feet connected with the sides of their heads and they fell instantly lifeless to the ground, necks broken.

Darless quickly chanted a counter spell and Jon felt his strength returning. He watched as Mat whirled and kicked other opponents who were trying to close on them. As quickly as he could, Jon helped Mandy up, touching her with his walking stick as he did so. As it made contact, Jon spoke, "All praise to Father Ukko." And the two grievous puncture wounds began to heal nearly as fast as they had come. However, the party had been forced back yet another twenty feet.

Mandy glanced at the defensive lines on either side. It was grim. Nearly half the dwarves were down and the others were in dire need. Any second they would be overrun, in spite of the best efforts of the strong giants who began throwing the enemy soldiers around as if they were sticks. She heard Lord Dathor cry out "Retreat! Retreat! All is lost!"

Retreat my ass! thought May. *I'll show them!* Her thoughts blazed in Jon's wide open mind. She began a long chant. Jon, now keenly attuned to her mind, listened in but understood none of her words. When her spell was complete, she looked out upon the cavalry men to her right. Jon saw that she began imagining terrible beast, slithering, crawling creatures, half man, half snake, poison dripping from their fangs. The spell moved out from her and into the minds of those enemy soldiers closest to her. Instantly they panicked, shrieked in utter terror, arms flailing to keep the hideous snake-like creatures off of them. Several began running in wild abandon back down the valley, discarding weapons and other gear as they fled. Slowly her spell moved outward until it reached its maximum area of effect, some twenty feet from her. Jon was utterly amazed, since this was just an illusion. The snake creatures were not real.

I wonder if I can just move the illusion out a little further? Jon tried a little mental tweak and found the he could easily affect another soldier. And then the next one and then the next one. It was easy; he just reinforced May's spell. He could not look on both directions at the same time, so he just shut his eyes and expanded it both the their right and left. The cavalry line, only seconds from a complete victory, began to disintegrate one man at a time, right down the line. Like dominoes they dropped their weapons and fled shrieking in madness and terror.

"What's going on?" cried Mandy. Everyone looked in all directions, unable to grasp what was happening. Only May and Jon with his eyes closed continued to concentrate, oblivious to the others.

Their high priest and his companions ceased all attacks on the party. They bent their entire efforts toward dispelling this diabolical spell that had turned sudden victory into total defeat in less than thirty seconds. But every attempt at dispelling the magical effects of May and Jon met with total failure. Worse still, Jon had not ceased in expanding the area of coverage. As the madmen flew by their positions, the screaming high priest could not even get their attention. Then the spell hit them full force. Three of the wizards dropped their staffs and fled, fleeing the slithering, twisting terror that threatened to devour them. Only one wizard stood his ground, yelling "Don't believe it! It's just an illusion! It's not real!" No one was left to listen to him.

The high priest chose to stand fast and fight these imaginary demonic creatures. He drew forth his mace and swung wildly this way and that way, attempting to bash these creatures. But as soon as he perceived that he had utterly smashed one snake-man, two others enveloped him. His mage cast a dispel magic spell fully on him to no avail. He then dropped his staff and stood out of the way of the wildly swinging mace. He looked up to the party and signaled his surrender and waited.

From far off in the distance, Jon heard someone calling his name. "Jon! Jon! You can stop it now. They have retreated. You can stop." *Stop?* he thought. *This is incredible. The power I feel surging in me. Wait. What have I done?* And he instantly stopped and opened his eyes to a totally different scene before him from when he had shut them seconds before. May also stopped and cancelled her spell.

"How — how did this happen?" she muttered. "It was only supposed to go out about twenty feet at most. How? It's not possible." She was in complete disbelief and even pinched herself to see if she were alive still and not dreaming.

"Er, sorry May. It was my doing," Jon apologized. "I saw what you were doing and just added to it a wee bit."

"A wee bit?" Darless exclaimed. "A wee bit! My you have a new definition for 'wee' that I have never come across. That was brilliant!"

"Congratulations, sis," exclaimed Alison, who finally found her voice, but only after a slight cough. "You have saved us all. I didn't know you had that much power."

"But I didn't, er don't," she protested. "What did you do, Jon, to my spell? Do you know illusionary magic?"

"No, but I could see the images you were sending to them and just duplicated it over and over and over. Such a power I felt! God! I got carried away with it. Okay. More than a wee bit, Darless. God, I got sucked into my own sense of power over others. It nearly got out of my control. Alison, May, Darless, we gotta talk! I'm terrified of the power over men's minds that I've discovered. What have I become?"

"Not now, Jon," Mandy took charge. "They are surrendering. Dathor, you and the giants look after the wounded. We are going to accept their surrender. Come on you guys." And she marched stately down the slope toward the wizard and priest who had crumpled to the ground utterly exhausted after his fight with the illusionary snake-men.

Quickly, the others fell in line behind her, stepping over and among the fallen warriors. Hundreds of dead, dying and wounded lay all about them. Jon felt sick to his stomach, but said nothing. In a minute they reached the wizard who was now supporting his priest who was gasping for breath.

As Mandy approached the defeated wizard, he spoke first, "This is Hegate Sebastian, Lord High Priest of Morrigan, and I am Mage Thurgood Sandstone, the Elder. We stand defeated here at the moment of what should have been our ultimate triumph. One spell totally undid everything. Never have I seen a spell that could not be dispelled. You realize that we cast ten different dispel spells and none had the slightest effect? How can that be? It was just a mere illusion. It should have been gone on my first attempt or even Hegate's." He looked at Alison first, then seeing confusion on her face, stared at Darless.

Alison knew what was going on in his mind. It was not the loss of battle, not the threat of death or even imprisonment. It was the confusion of not knowing what had happened, the knowledge of why he had failed. That was the sole burning issue in a mage's mind. If she were in his position, she knew that would likely be the uppermost thought she'd have. Why?

"It began as my illusion," May spoke very softly.

"But, Mage Sandstone," Jon added, recovering from the walk across the battlefield, "there is more power in the universe than magical spells. You chose to attack a saint who has spiritual powers beyond even his imagination. Powers that he can create. Yes, it was an illusion. But what started out as a mere spell took on a life of its own and thus could not be dispelled by magic when it ceased to be powered by magical energies."

"Are, are you then a god?" he asked, trying desperately to grasp Jon's meaning and failing.

"No I am not a god nor do I have any desires to be one, to wield that much power," Jon replied, "though today I was sorely tempted. Such slaughter — needless slaughter." Then, turning to the priest, he asked, "Why? Why are you attacking the dwarves? What could they possibly have done to Vyndoc that warrants this slaughter?"

While the mage pondered Jon's words, the Hegate Sebastian replied, "They have stolen from us. Why, the list of crimes is a mile long!"

This, of course, was not the answer Jon had expected. It took him totally by surprise. "What, what do you mean? Lord Dathor has an equally long list of grievances with you folks. Something about not having been paid for the last shipment of weapons and armor. Something is not aligning up here. How do you know that they have stolen from you and how do you know about crimes?"

Hegate was only too glad to have the opportunity to vent his frustrations with the dwarves. He began to recite a litany of grievances. But Jon kept interrupting him, asking how he knew of each grievance, much as he had done with Lord Dathor earlier. "The dwarves produced faulty armor in their last batch they sent us. It was useless. I heard it directly from Red Jordral, our merchant who deals with the dwarves." And on it went, nine out of ten times, the name Red Jordral came up. Jon smiled at the first mention of that name, then grinned broadly and finally broke into a laughing fit which completely interrupted the conversation. "Are you mocking me?" blared Hegate. "I'll not be mocked by anybody!"

"No, no forgive me. I meant no offense, sir," Jon genuinely meant it as he struggled to contain his mirth. "Let me explain this. Bear with me a minute, your highness." He turned and yelled back up to the dwarves, "Lord Dathor. Lord Dathor, please come down here at once!" He saw the leader stand up and walk proudly toward them, stepping over the fallen bodies as if they were mere rocks.

The dwarf leader stretched himself as tall and straight as he could, as befitting a noble conqueror. "Yes, Jon. I see you have the culprit at hand. Do you want me to chop off their heads?" The mage cringed but Hegate spat on the ground in defiance.

"No, no there has been enough blood spilled needlessly and senselessly here today. No, I want you to tell me and Hegate here your list of grievances and from whom you have heard of each of them."

"Hurrumph," he cleared his throat. "Well, tis a mighty list. Where to begin? Ah. We have not been paid for the last shipment of weapons and armor we sent you. They were some of the finest work we have done to date."

Hegate could contain his wrath no longer, "Worthless! They were all utterly worthless. A dart could penetrate that armor."

"Wait a second. Just a second here. Lord Dathor, who told you this?" Jon insisted.

"Why it came from their own merchant himself, Red Jordral. He said the Vyndocians were not going to pay. That it was way over-priced!" he replied, glaring at his vanquished foe.

"And Hegate, who told you that the armor was worthless?" Jon asked so that both men could hear the words.

"Red Jordral," came the thoughtful reply. Both man and dwarf looked at one another suspiciously. Doubt spread across both faces.

Darless spoke up, "Red Jordral. Red Jordral. Do you realize that is an anagram for Lord Jarred, the Demon Lord?" She had been pondering the name. She now realized what Dispater had been hinting at all along. Treachery.

Everyone's mouth dropped, all except Jon and Darless who smiled at each other. "We, we've been had!" exclaimed Hegate. "Duped!"

"And so have we," the startled dwarf added, "it really was the finest armor we have ever made, really. If I ever get my hands on Lord Jarred, I'll throttle him with my bear hands!" He cursed and swore.

"You'll have to wait your turn. I want him first!" exclaimed Hegate, smashing his fist into his hand. "He's cost us and you to, Lord Dathor, the lives of many a good man and dwarf here today. I will personally see to the finding of this 'merchant of chaos' and deal with him! Lord Dathor, you have my word on that." They shook hands to the amazement of all. Hegate added, "You will receive payment within a fortnight for that last shipment, though I do not know where the equipment is now located. It is only fair."

"Come, let us spread the word to those that remain and help each other tend to the wounded. The first snow is due any time now," said Lord Dathor. He turned to Jon, "If you will give us leave, we will now attend to these higher, most urgent matters."

Smiling broadly, Jon commented, "By all means. Let us see to the healing as fast as possible. However, Mr. Sebastian, you highness, if that's the right term of address, I still have some questions for you."

"Reverend Sebastian will do. Yes, my son?" came the reply.

"Why are you folks trying to kill me and my friends?" Jon asked the question he had been dying to ask from the start.

"Nothing against you," he replied calmly. "We do not even know you. Just following orders. Goddess Morrigan ordered us to slay you and all in your party. She does not often tell us why. We just obey. But at this point, we have no further regiments with which to assault you. This folly has cost us four regiments of our best cavalry! So if you will excuse me, we have very urgent business to attend to."

Jon let them both go their ways. The friends just stared at one another in total disbelief. Moments ago, the two sides were arch enemies fighting to wipe the other off of the face of the earth. And now they were acting like good, long time trading partners, as if this devastation had never occurred.

Finally, Alison spoke. "Will someone please tell me what just happened? I simply do not understand this, not even remotely!" Several others vocally agreed with her assessment. This was not how any other battle they had ever been in had ended.

"It's something Dispater said that reminded me of the truth," Jon explained. "In order for any conflict to occur such as this war, it takes an active third party to bring it about. Here, Lord Jarred, the Demon Lord, was inciting both sides to war. And he succeeded in poisoning both sides against the other. Once both sides saw who was the actual source of their conflict, why the conflict evaporated. Pretty darn amazing, if I so say so myself."

Chatting about the events, they turned to walk back uphill to assist in the healing actions, but had not gone far before there was an explosion of magical energies. Out of sky a great horse appeared bearing a woman rider, whose face was blackened and shriveled, her skin tight to the bone. Her face more closely resembled that of a skull with a trace of dried skin covering it, hideously ugly. She bore a red spear in one hand and a yellow one in the other hand. Cries of "Morrigan!" sprung up all around them. Hegate fell onto his knees in worship, fearing the wrath of his goddess for his total failure this day. The dwarves scurried for the shelter of their underground realm. The party turned around to watch her horse float down from the sky and land about fifty feet from them. She was furious. Rage shook her otherwise womanly frame. They watched as she floated up off of the horse and settle gently to the ground, planting both feet defiantly toward them.

"You guys all get back out of the way!" ordered Jon. "Don't interfere. And whatever you do, do not stand behind me — get off to one side or the other!" So vehement was his order, that they obeyed at once, though not without misgivings. Jon could hear Alison mutter, "Oh no, here we go again." Consoling her sudden terror of Morrigan, he sent her, *Not this time! I'm ready for her. Trust me.*

I love you! she sent back, desperately fighting back the tears. If this was the last time she could talk to Jon, she wanted him to know that simple fact. Images of their last encounter with this goddess flooded her mind. She had jumped between Morrigan and Jon as the Goddess threw her spear of death at Jon. At that instant she knew she cared enough for this man to sacrifice her life to save his. "Please, please don't let this happen again," she whispered to herself. Darless' face and upper body was as tense as rock, but she managed to put a supporting arm around her dear friend. Mandy whispered the brief details of their encounter with Morrigan to May and Mat.

Jon faced Morrigan's approach. Off to his left, he detected a slight shimmer. *Must be Dis. Concentrate, Jon or you'll blow it.*

She took a step toward Jon before speaking. "Vaina, er Jon," she faltered, "how dare you?" But Jon missed hearing her remaining words for so strong was that greeting and so solid were her mental pictures that he could not help but see into her mind and was fascinated.

Who is this Vainamoinen character anyway? he placed in Alison's mind. *She has me confused with him.*

A hero, bard, minstrel, sometimes called the Son of the Wind. Rumor has it he is the son of a goddess. He's a really powerful good man. Is that enough? she replied. Jon acknowledged and Alison whispered what Jon was asking to the others, though Mandy and Darless already knew for they were eavesdropping — unquenchable curiosity.

Morrigan was shouting curses, raving like a madman, but quickly she got to her intended tirade's end. "So now I will teach you Vaina, Jon rather, never to meddle in my affairs again! Here's your death!" And she threw both her spears, which were enchanted to never miss their target, straight at Jon. Jon knew this would happen, *You are a predictable old crone.* He stepped forward and was ten feet ahead of the spears which were now ten feet behind him. Both spears, which had never missed before, clanked noisily on the rock surface. Morrigan's eyes opened wide. For once, no words came out of her open mouth.

Jon said in a normal tone of conversational voice, "Morrigan, look at me. Who am I?"

Again, she started to say Vainamoinen but checked herself momentarily and said "The accursed Saint Jon Brown." But Jon saw that she was looking at him through a huge mental picture of some tall, proud fighter, Vainamoinen, he presumed.

"Thank you. Now look at me. Who am I?" Jon repeated, wondering how easily she would start to look at her mental pictures and how she would take to following his commands. He endeavored to be as socially polite as possible, but firm, so as to give her no excuse for not following his commands.

Once again, she started to say Vainamoinen, but caught herself just in time. A puzzled look appeared on her blacken, skull-like face. Jon instantly felt her looking through his eyes back at her. She was just enough curious to know what he was doing or seeing that she took the bait.

Jon again replied politely, "Very good. Now look at me. Who am I?" His command carried the total certainty now that she would indeed follow his orders.

This time, she yawned before answering, somewhat covering up her stumble. This process went on for nearly five minutes before she suddenly had what might be taken for a slight smile and said, "Why you are not Vainamoinen after all are you?"

"Thank you. No I am not. I do not know of this other person. I take it that he did something really bad to you?" Jon replied, ending his process. He had gotten her to look, to differentiate between her mind's pictures and the reality before her. It was a good first step.

He was not quite prepared for the sheer violence of the fresh images that appeared in her mind in response to his simple question. Evidently, these two were arch enemies and it was he that had caused her face to be so disfigured. And Jon also saw why.

She saw at once that no words were needed to answer his question. Her flood of images communicated faster than a thousand words. Though for an instant she regretted not having taken the opportunity to vent her rage at all the things Vainamoinen had done to her.

"I can perhaps help you to heal up your face, if you are willing," Jon offered. He felt that in some small way, doing so might put them on a better level of understanding. He wanted her attacks on them ceased forever, if he could.

She thought for a moment but replied, "I want none of Ukko's healing; I need not your pity. My face works miracles for me. All who gaze on me cannot face me! Well, all except you, that is. No, it works for me. I've grown to rather like it this way. What am I going to do to you? You realize you have destroyed four regiments of my finest cavalry?"

"Remember, that they attacked us first. We did not provoke them in any way. Ours was simply a matter of self-defense. But I agree, we need a way for both of us to save face. Your worshipers are watching our every move," Jon pointed out, though he was not sure which way she would go. On one hand, with everyone watching, she ought to take a powerful, decisive action. But on the other hand, she had made a gross error in judgment or observation. It would not do to set such a bad example.

"Are you suggesting that we should fight it out here and now?" she responded, acutely aware of the circumstances. Indeed, if her face was not all black, a reddish flush would have been observable. She had made a gross error which was ultimately responsible for the death of so many of her own followers. This was perhaps the most important factor she had to considered, if she wanted to remain a goddess. A goddess is only as strong as she has followers. She could ill afford to lose any more.

"No," Jon fumbled for a second. "I'm suggesting that we both say that a mistake has been made and shake hands and go our separate ways. Nothing more. Keep it simple."

"Shake hands with a mortal? Silly egocentric humans!" she commented, but a grin actually formed on her stern lips. "A slight bow will suffice."

Jon did not hesitate but spoke loud enough so that others might hear, "A mistake has been made." And he bowed to her. *The ball is in her court now,* Jon though.

"Yes," she replied in a similar tone. "A mistake has been made. We go our separate ways, but do not let me find you crossing my path again, for I will not be so lenient next time."

In a whisper, Jon said, "Thanks. I offer you this tidbit of information that your high priest just found out. Demon Lord Jarred was behind and totally manufactured this confrontation with the dwarves. I suspect his goal was to either reduce the strength of Vyndoc and/or the dwarves or make you enemies. Take care, he might be trying to take over your lands around here."

She looked at him anew. This was something foreign to her. Here was her enemy or at the very least her antagonist offering her critical information. She managed to say, "Thank you." And nodded to him. Then raising her arms upward, both spears instantly reappeared in her hands. She floated up and onto her horse and both rose skyward. At the last instant, she yelled down to Hegate, "We need to meet at the altar very soon!" And then she disappeared into the grey clouds and was gone.

Jon turned and walked slowly back to his friends. He was totally exhausted, but knew he must keep walking. It would be unseemly if he collapsed onto the ground after such a meeting. He concentrated on each step, cursing the fact that it was now uphill. His friends quickly rushed to his side and cleverly Alison and Mandy put their arms around him to support him. To Jon, walking back up to the tunnel entrance area through the dead, dying, maimed and wounded was sickening and he finally blacked out. He had to rest. He did not see the first large snowflakes falling, melting and mingling in the pools of blood.

Chapter 20 Of Plans and Snow

While Jon slept, the dwarves, though weary, tended their fallen. Nearly one hundred dwarves lay beyond hope. But the count would have been far higher save three things. One, Mat, May, Mandy and Darless tended as many of the most severely wounded as they could. Two, Alison borrowed Jon's walking stick. She remembered the exact words he used to activate it. This mage had keen eyes and ears; little got by her that was of interest to her. She healed fully as many as she could before the device was exhausted and then prayed to Father Ukko to thank him for his aid. Third, Lord Dathor's father arrived, Nain himself, accompanied by three hundred fighters and a score of dwarven priests who were healers themselves.

Still, the casualty list was high. Over two hundred dwarves suffered some kind of wounds. The stone giants fared much better with only a few having taken really grievous wounds. Raul was one of those more severely hurt and was the first one healed by Alison using Jon's stick.

When Jon awoke, he found himself lying on a bed of furs inside a huge underground cavern. Actually, it was only twenty feet from the entrance doors which were now closed except for the watch windows. Ten fires crackled around the rim of the spacious cavern. Numerous oil lamps illuminated this golden-hued hall, the Golden Hall of Tharkan, after the dwarf who first discovered this cavern hundreds of years ago. The ceiling was about fifty feet above Jon. Great arches rose from the floor supporting the dome. Ten side passages, now dark, lay behind him with only the one passage leading to the entrance doors.

"Ah, sleepy head wakes," Rolf's teasing voice greeted Jon's ears. "Here, you have tea and meat. Lady's orders. Rolf must feed you when you wake. Here." And he thrust a mug of warm tea into Jon's hands followed by an entire leg of lamb which was bigger than Jon's head. "Lady's say you eat lots now." This was the stone giant's idea of a lot, Jon thought. But he was hungry, of that he was certain.

"Thanks. How long have I been asleep? Where am I? What's been happening? Man, I *am* hungry!" And he began to bite off a mouthful, finding it actually tasty, he tore into it.

"Hum, ten hours, maybe, me thinks. In Tharken's Golden Hall, just inside tunnel entrance," Rolf began trying to remember all of the questions.

Several bites later with a warming in his stomach, Jon looked around. This chamber was huge, at least three hundred feet square, or roughly so. Hundreds of people were lying on the ground on furs, just like he was. Ever bustling dwarves were tending their wounds. He realized that he was obviously in "sick bay."

"I've gotta get up and help heal these people," Jon suddenly realized and tried to get up but his legs faltered. He was still overly hungry and a bit weak.

"No. Eat first. Lady's orders," Rolf cautioned. "Your lady used your stick to heal Rolf. She be healing others too. Other friends healing too. Nain comes, brings many healers. Lots healing done. You rest; you eat first. Plenty to do later. Snows come. White outside. Pretty."

So Jon relaxed, ate, and felt his strength returning. He looked about and sure enough, he could see many tending the fallen. It was all very orderly. "Well, Rolf, my big friend, how bad were you hurt?"

"Me got it bad, both arms cut deep," winced Rolf, thinking about his injuries that had only a few hours ago gone away completely, thanks to Alison. Jon saw the dried blood all down his front. He had been cut up badly. And an idea formed.

"Say, Rolf, tell me about it. How did it happen? Start at the beginning and tell me," Jon asked. And he listened intently. The stone giant explained that when the dwarves were finally overpowered, he had put himself between them and the enemy, taking on eight men at one time. He had dispatched six of them with his swinging fists before the remaining two got their blades into his shoulders. They had cut him twice each before they shrieked in madness, dropped their weapons and fled the battlefield. Jon could see the residual pain that the attack still had on the stone giant.

"Thanks, Rolf, now let's go through that again. Start in at the beginning and go through it all and leave nothing out.

Tell me what is happening as you go through it," Jon requested.

"But me just told you," he protested slightly.

"Yes, but you still have some pain from it right? The shoulders still carry around some after effects, right?" he answered.

"Hum, yes, still weak in both arms. That's why Lady has me lie down too. Rest, she says," the giant replied.

"Well, trust me, Rolf," Jon answered. "That weakness and pain comes from your mental pictures of the event. We are going to sort of remove them. So let's go over it again, all right?"

"Sure, me tell again. Me do see big picture of it." And he went through the fight again. At the end of it he was becoming a bit angry. Jon thanked him and had him go through it another time, and another. On the fifth recounting, the big man yawned and yawned. Then, he brightened up saying, "Me knew me could not hold back eight men! Me knew it, but me did it anyway." And he began chuckling, which of course, being a giant, it was very loud. Many glanced their way.

"Very well done, Rolf," Jon beamed at his large friend. "How's the shoulders now?"

"Why, why me fit," he exclaimed. "No pain, not weak anymore. You did miracle!"

"No, you did it, Rolf, you did the looking. I just helped you do it," Jon replied. "I think I have a lot of work ahead of me to help all of these wounded."

"Me no understand, but you maybe not wanna help those way over there," he pointed to a bunch of men on the far side of the huge cavern. "Vyndocians. Dwarves actually help them. Me no understand it. First we kill them, then we help them."

"It was all just a very big misunderstanding, Rolf." Jon went on to explain how Lord Jarred had played one side against the other fomenting the entire war. Once both sides had figured out the true cause of their conflict, their differences quickly resolved.

"You be genius to figure that out," Rolf replied, genuinely awed at the deductive powers of Jon. "When snows come hours ago, high-priest man made deal with Dathor to care for worst off men til he gets wagons here in couple weeks. Gives dwarves much more treasure, me thinks."

"I did not get the chance to see if the Demon Lord was behind the attacks on your people, Rolf. No time, but I suspect he may well have been," Jon added. Rolf nodded his agreement.

"Ah you are awake," came the familiar voice of his love, Alison. He turned to see her approaching him, her clothes covered in crusting blood, but a smile shone on her face.

"Good show on using my stick!" Jon replied. "Looks like you have been busy playing nurse. Rolf told me about it. I just ran out his mental pictures of it too. Now Rolf's totally fit once again."

"He be genius, Lady! Cure me too," Rolf beamed. "Me get up and help too now. All fit. You see." And he did so, flexing his powerful arms and waving them all around in the air until she laughed.

"Thanks for looking after Jon for me, Rolf," she said watching him wander off in search of something to do to help out. "I'd give you a great big kiss, Jon, but I don't think you want to get all this icky blood all over you. Time enough for that later. I take it you are now rested and okay?"

"Yes, my dearest, just perfect. It looks like I missed a lot. Rolf says the dwarves are healing some of the Vyndocians?" he asked.

"Yes, seems they are now on good terms with one another. Pretty darn amazing, I'd say. Say, Nain's here too. He brought two dozen of his priest friends. So there has been plenty of healing help for once. All have now been initially tended to. I am just going to clean up. We can all have a bit of a conference in about a half hour. Cya." And she strolled off down one of the side tunnels to the wash room.

"Hey, wait for me. I need to find the bathrooms too," he called out as he scampered after her.

Jon had finished using the latrine and was cleaning up when there was a flash of magical energies behind him. The door shut and Dispater appeared once more. "Greetings, Saint Jon. Now then with the door shut, we cannot be interrupted. I wish a few words with you. Here, this is for you; you have earned this." He handed Jon a large bulging sack.

"What's this?" Jon opened the drawstring and peered inside. He was not prepared for what he saw. Bright flashes of red, green and white light sparkled from hundreds of gemstones, finely cut. "What's this?" he repeated himself.

"You achieved the bought and paid for revenge of Heinz Hollander," he explained.

Jon tried to hand the sack back, "No, I do not want blood money. I do not work for you."

The arch-devil grinned, grasping instantly Jon's considerations. "That's why I barred the door, so we will not be interrupted. Let me begin at the beginning. When you have heard the complete story, then reconsider. It began thirty-nine years ago not too far from here, about twenty miles further north. Heinz was a farmer, a grower of wheat, to be precise. He lived with his young wife and three year-old son on a farmstead that he himself built with his own hands. They lived alone out here in the wilderness, trading grain twice a year with the outside world. Then, one day while he was tending his fields, a stranger rode up to his home. He stopped and headed back to greet this stranger. But within a minute he heard the screams of his wife and son piercing the still air. He sprinted toward them but was still a quarter of a mile off when he saw this stranger dragging his wife and son out of the house, tied them to his horse and rode off toward the east."

"He yelled and screamed but the rider never looked or turned back. When he reached the house, he paused only long enough to get his quarterstaff and continued to run after the rider. He had no horses, only oxen for the plows. After four hours, he caught up with them, or rather the remains. Lying beside the road, with signs of struggle everywhere, he found their bodies. His son had been decapitated; his wife raped, tortured and then killed."

"Grief stricken, he buried their remains and vowed justice would one day be taken. Next, he made a pilgrimage to Vyndoc, there seeking the council of one of priests. In short, he was told that for 100,000 gold pieces, I would personally extract justice. He returned here and neglected forever his farm, turning to mining, alone in these hills. Each year, he returned to Vyndoc to convert the year's ore into these precious stones. For ten years, he thus labored to earn the fee he thought I required. But low, he was deceived by these priests in my name. As you well know, riches are not my fee. He was sent on his way to meet me out in the desert to consummate the deal, when he was waylaid by men sent by these very same priests. However, I found out about the treachery but unfortunately arrived one minute late. I dispatched the robbers at once. And in his dying words, he told me his tale and begged me to fulfill what he thought was the bargain he had made. I swore that I would see it done."

"It has taken me quite a few years to find the identity of the detestable creature who perpetrated this crime. He was the late General Hamid of the Third Royal Regiment of Corsairs. And he was one of the few who actually died from your mind illusion back there. I believe his pointless, wanton destruction of people finally caught up with him. So this bag here is, in fact, untouched by my hands. It represents the efforts of one small man to gain justice in this world. Without the Rule of Law, this world would not be worth visiting, much less living in."

Jon was moved by the story, but he countered, "You realize that if I agree to take this bag, I would only do good things with it, not reinforcing evil?"

"Of course, I have considered that detail," he replied raising his eyebrows. "You see, you and your friends and I are not unalike in so many ways. Yet, I tell you this, how can there be Evil without their having been first Good. Indeed," his voice rose in pitch and animation, "How can you even define Good if there is no Evil? Is it not often said that 'opposites attract?'"

"That's an interesting argument," Jon's mind rapidly explored the possibilities. "One desires to do what is best or right or good. But that immediately presupposes that there is something that is not the best, or wrong or not so good. It would seem to me to be an infinite scale from Ultimate Good to Ultimate Evil. We choose our path between them. Yet, is not happiness and fulfillment dependent upon doing the most good that one is able?"

Dispater roared with a sudden outburst of laughter. "It is always refreshing to speak frankly with you, Saint Jon! But time is pressing and I have other matters to attend to. Ethically, I cannot keep this bag created illegally in my name. That it may do some good to counter its origin is itself in some small way another form of Justice. So I ask you one last time, will you accept the bag with no obligations attached to it whatsoever, to do with however you see fit or not?"

"All right then, I will take it and use it to help better the world," Jon relented but added, "What I do do with it may come back to haunt you."

The arch-devil roared once more, waved his hand and the door flew open revealing a throng of concerned faces trying to "rescue Jon." This time, a ball of flames enveloped him as he departed. The stench of sulfur hung in the air. He displayed a bit of theatrics for the benefit of the dwarves.

"What was that all about, Jon" cried Alison. "We were all afraid some new devilry was at play. Are you all right?"

"I'm fine," Jon said, "it's a long story. Here, love, add this to your treasury. Darless, you just got your college building, I'm sure."

"Never have I had a devil in my caverns!" retorted Nain. "I'll have to consecrate this entire room. Perhaps we should just wall it off, fill it in with debris and forget it."

"Hi Nain, good to see you again," Jon answered. "No, there was no Evil actions done in here. He just wanted to have an uninterrupted conversation. Actually, a great deal of Good was done by a leader of great Evil. And that's an interesting conundrum that I should like to discuss with you when we get the chance. You might say that Dispater came here to do a Good Thing."

His speech had its effect as the panic and fear subsided. "All right then, let us hold a conference," Nain replied, "before anything else happens. There is much that I greatly desire to know of these recent events. And you, Jon, seem to be in the center of them." Without waiting for any possible protest, Nain led them all down a corridor into another room.

Jon found himself in a chamber about twenty feet square. Rich tapestries lined the walls. Golden lanterns hung suspended from the domed ceiling twenty-five feet above them. A huge oak table three inches thick dominated the central portion of the room. Jon saw a wide variety of chairs, some tall, some low. And each person was given a chair to match their height. Jon found when they were all seated, that everyone, no matter their size, was at eye level with the others. It was an interesting arrangement. Nain smiled as he watched Jon's eyes taking in these details.

The fact that all eyes were focused upon him did not intimidate him. Instead, Jon methodically moved his eyes around the room taking in all the ornate details. This was his first experience with Dwarven high culture. The distinctive zig-zag, bright colors motif adorned everything, from walls to tapestries to ornately carved furniture, even to the table setting. After a minute, Jon duplicated the anticipation, the utter expectant silence. "Okay," he grinned sheepishly — Alison caught a glimpse of redness appearing briefly in his cheeks — "all right, I can take a hint. Let's begin at the beginning, the very beginning."

And so Jon began explaining their entire adventure from the Chasme Bug attacks which seemed so long ago. He spoke mainly in generalities, and, of course, mentioned nothing about the actual departure of Metrarch, who was not dead but very much alive. He placed particular emphasis on all of the double crosses between the Demon Lords. Vyndoc, surrounded on three sides by lands controlled by followers of these Abyss demons, surely felt threatened. And in fact, Jon carefully explained how Lord Jarred, disguised as a merchant of Vyndoc calling himself Red Jordral, had been poisoning both the dwarves and the rulers of Vyndoc, spreading lies and falsehoods.

"It is *such* an obvious thing," interrupted Lord Dathor, "but we failed to see it. How could we not have seen his deceit?" Other dwarves echoed his anger. It seemed so obvious, yet they had all missed it completely.

"You saw, heard, and believed what you wanted to hear, if you don't mind me being blunt about it. A person in fear and anger seldom sees what is actually before them. Can you 'reason' with an angry man?" Jon replied. "Don't despair, remember the high Vyndocian lords also fell for the plot and it has cost them dearly. Their loss is ten times or more than yours! I do not doubt that some of their lord's heads will roll as a result! Now as far as Morrigan is concerned and all of these attacks on our caravan, it was all just a misunderstanding. She had me confused in her mind with some other person, one Vainamoinen, of whom I really don't know much of anything about save what Alison has told me a while ago. By killing me, she thought she was killing him. So that's straightened out now. I expect no more attacks from them."

Nain's black eyes blazed into Jon's blue orbs. "While it might be *just* a simple confusion of two people, she *is* a Goddess and you are a human. Her confusion would be more correctly defined as an insanity, or my name isn't Nain! How did you, a human, figure this out and so impact the mind of a Goddess? Now *that is* the real question!"

An awkward silence followed, while Jon formulated a reply that could be understood. "While we were talking, she kept trying to address me as 'Vain...' and would catch herself each time. I just followed that thread so to speak." His reply seemed to satisfy Nain, who began to see that perhaps it was not magic after all.

"Well, I have a question," Mat interjected. "The one thing that I want to know, professionally speaking as a monk, is how did you evade her thrown Spears of Death? From what Alison told us of your earlier encounter with Morrigan, she took a Spear of Death aimed at you. Only by the Grace of Ukko does my sister still live." A chorus of "yes's" came from Jon's friends as well as the dwarves.

This was a tough one. Jon paused for a minute. "When she threw the spear at where I was, a finite amount of time, though small, lapses between her release of the spear and it arriving at where I was at. During that time, I moved myself to a location that the spear had already passed through. The best I can describe it is like getting the idea you have already arrived there and just be there. I've only recently realized that I can do that if I am alert to the incoming projectile."

"Ah ha!" exclaimed Mat, his muscles relaxed. "Now that makes some sense. We monks are trained to make effective use of that small amount of time. We, however, deflect or dodge or catch the projectiles. If you move forward, do you not therefore move through the incoming spear?"

The monk's frame of reference flashed in Jon's mind. He understood the problem with which Mat was wrestling. "No. A dodge or catch is remaining where you are at. Moving forward would indeed just make the projectile arrive into its target sooner. I don't move as such. First I am at this location; then I am at that location. There is no continuity of motion from point A to point B. If there was continuity, I'd be hit. Rather, I am at point A and then when it is safe, I am at point B without the necessity of going continuously through all of the intervening space. You follow me?" A quick glance at the monk's face told him that he did not.

"Can this be learned?" asked Mat. "If so, I would treasure such an ability."

"Perhaps," was Jon's answer. Mat then paid no further attention to the conference. Instead, he took two cups and a knife and began to demonstrate to himself Jon's explanation. Mat realized that such an ability would give him an enormous advantage in any combat. Deflecting a blow was one thing, but to just be elsewhere instantaneously was quite another.

Meanwhile, Jon then got to the appearance of Dispater, the Lord of Hell, and the dwarves and Nain, in particular, strained to hear his every word. Nain was really a very high priest among his clan. The appearance of an arch enemy was of major importance to him. Concentrating fully, Nain marked every word Jon uttered, committing them to memory. In the end, there was considerable discussion among everyone present except Darless and the preoccupied Mat as to whether or not this was "blood money" or an acceptable money or whether there was something sinister in the offering. In the end, no one could find anything sinister in Dispater's unexpected gift, no bargaining with the devil, no strings. Further, Jon's open declaration to Dispater that he would use the money for good by donating it to the building fund for Darless' proposed Mental College convinced even Nain that here was a case of evil actually doing something beneficial to all. Yet, this still troubled him. To this dwarf, a Lord of Evil doing a "good deed" seemed a conundrum of magnitude.

Yet, it was Alison who had the last word in the matter. "You are looking at it all wrong. It is not a matter of good versus evil with Dispater. This time it was a matter of lawfulness versus unethical chaos. By all rights, he was not entitled to this fund. Jon was. He could not keep the gems and still claim to follow the rules. I bet he pondered long about actually doing a good deed, though," and she chuckled. The others then roared with laughter finally fully grasping her explanation. Jon was relieved that his tale was done and that mirth had returned.

"Ah there is one final detail to be undertaken," Nain bellowed, instantly commanding the undivided attention of all the dwarves present. Seriousness reappeared; Jon thought,

Now what? He saw his thought echoed in the eyes of his beloved, Alison.

"Dwarven recompense," was all Nain said. Jon saw Nain's son's eyes dart to the floor; his head bowed. Jon would later describe Dathor's look as "crestfallen."

"Alison, Jon, Mandy, Darless, Mat, May — to say nothing of our giant friends — Rolf beamed — all of you have done the dwarves a great service. Indeed, you probably have saved my son from certain death. Indeed, you gave your assistance freely and uncalled for. You abandoned your own caravan and came here to our aid. Had you not — well, the consequences are mind boggling. We, Dathor, are deeply in your debt. How may we repay you for your aid?" Nain finally asked.

Darless answered first. "We came to your aid just as you would have come to our aid, is that not so, Lord Nain? Your thanks is sufficient." She knew she hit the mark with him. Her flat statement postulated certain future dwarven aid for them at any time should they ever need it. He smiled at her astute political posture, which was indeed a correct one.

"True, if you ever need our aid, gracious Lady of Ukko," Lord Dathor pronounced in as formal a tone as he could muster, "you have only to send word. Dwarves will come to your aid."

"But is there something more tangible that we can do for you?" Nain added. "Some small token of our immense gratitude?"

"Well, Nain," Mandy, who had been mostly silent throughout the proceedings, "I would really like that special balanced bastard sword we were discussing when last we met!" Her beaming grin met his. His eyes twinkled.

After a big smile, he replied, "I had already begun its forging, my pretty ranger. For you, a bastard sword like no other it shall be. And what of you, Jon?"

"Oh, well if you insist," Jon smiled. "I would love to come back here at a later date, once we get the caravan to safety and all that, and learn much about your music, learn to play some of your instruments, learn some of your songs — that is, if a human is allowed to do so."

Nain roared with mirth. Jon could have asked for a king's ransom and received it. He could have asked for an incredible suit of armor or weapons not found in the realms of men. Instead he asked to learn their music! "So be it. You shall have the services of Gloth Everbeard, our master musician, whenever you return!"

"And what do the d'Ambrose's desire?" asked Nain, though he already suspected their answer.

"Well," Alison began with a broad smile on her face, reflecting a lifelong goal that has reached fulfillment, "I have the funds to rebuild Castle d'Ambrose as well as a small connecting village. I need it built to specific specifications, using specific materials that Rolf already knows about, a special type of stone. There is no question that dwarven stonemasons are the world's finest. I should like to hire all the dwarves that can be spared to build my castle. And to build it in record time." She heard stifled gasps from some dwarves; such a request for a free project of that magnitude would sorely task them. She added, knowing full well the final result her words would bring, she knew something of dwarves, "And I am willing to pay triple the usual fees that human masons charge, if the work can be done in three shifts per day." A chorus of "Ahs" spelled relief. To obtain dwarves to construct a castle for a human was a great gift in of itself, rarely done. That they would also receive their expected pay for such made them more than eager to do it at once!

Lord Dathor, stood and said commandingly, "So be it. Let the word go forth that we shall construct Castle d'Ambrose." The official pronouncement was followed by "Here-here's" echoing for the next three minutes. Word spread rapidly and cheers of distant assents resonated from the hallways. Dathor whispered to Alison, "Of course, you have already drawn up some plans. Come back as soon as you can and meet with our architects and planners. We will begin just as soon as you desire."

"You got it. I will be back just as soon as I can," she radiantly replied. The utter joy on her beaming face told Jon just how much this moment meant to his love. She would never forget this day. Even Mat and May were elated. Now they would indeed have a home to return to and a town as well!

But it was Mandy that brought them back to reality. "Now if we may, we really need to return as fast as possible to our caravan. We've been told that an early winter snowstorm has hit the high country. The caravan is not equipped to survive in the cold and snow. I fear that they are in very grave danger. We must get to them as fast as possible." As she spoke, Jon realized only too truly the magnitude of the caravan's plight. High country snows could easily freeze all of them.

Lord Dathor turned to Mandy. "Lethos here will guide you along Route 4. Our distant scouts have an approximate estimate of their current location. He will get you there as fast as possible. However, if your people are not equipped for the deep snows of the mountains, there is little we can do. We have no clothing suitable for big folks, nor boots that would fit, save your children. If all else fails, you can bring them back here underground. But there is one other possibility. I have discussed this with our Scout Force General Ugnagh Bearweather. He tells me that your caravan is not too far from the Hidden Valley Ruins. There are some human inhabitants there that may be able to assist you. Certainly, they can provide warm lodgings. Beyond that, I do not know what else they might be able to provide. However, if you do go there, be extremely cautious. The inhabitants are a bit strange, I am told. Perhaps, dangerous, but not evil."

"Okay, this way! Follow me!" interrupted a taller than average, middle aged (for a dwarf) General Ugnagh. He was dressed in a spotless blue military uniform with tall, highly polished black boots. Gold ornaments dotted his chest. He was a take-charge general as befitting the division he led, those that scouted for information at the edge of their world.

But first, it was time to say farewell, and this took another ten minutes. Finally, another five minutes passed as the party gathered their gear, while dwarves readied their horses. So within fifteen minutes, the party, holding lanterns, accompanied by a half dozen scouts were headed down a dark tunnel. General Ugnagh had changed his uniform to that of a non-descript outdoors man. Leather tunic and matching boots befitting field duty was his common attire while in the field. In fact, had they not known he was the general, there was no outward signs that distinguished him from his five other scouts. The scout motto, he explained as they walked along was: "A Scout sees but is never seen." Jon recalled their earlier trip here and realized that they were undoubted seen and their progress marked by many unseen dwarven eyes. His respect for them increased significantly.

Time passed, though it seemed endless to the travelers. The tunnel road went on and on, crossed occasionally by side tunnels. Periodic skyward air vent shafts let in fresh air that was noticeably colder than the ambient warmth of the tunnel's constant fifty-five degrees. Jon relished the tiny shafts of sunlight that accompanied these shafts. Later on, he noticed that now no light appeared. They had marched from day into night. He had no idea of their speed, direction of travel or distance covered. It was one long solemn march.

However, after a day's travel, an occasional scout would appear as if from nowhere, bringing additional information. They learned that the early winter snowstorm had brought about three feet of snow at the higher elevations. This did not bode well for the caravan's prospects; all had thoughts of frozen fingers and toes, six hundred shivering, freezing people. Their sense of urgency overrode all thought of rest stops. They munched on dried food as they walked.

One of the marvels of dwarven tunnel works lies in the principle that the shortest distance between two points is a straight line. What overland in the mountains would be a long journey full of twists and turns in the path, in a dwarven tunnel runs straight and true. Shortly after nightfall, General Ugnagh called a halt. "We have reached the desired exit point. Here is where I leave you. Once outside, follow the path to your right. Scouts report the caravan is not much more than a couple miles on up the trail. May Silverbeard guide you true." He bowed low.

After many thank you's, he led them to the exit point, a narrow opening disguised by hanging vines. Once outside, looking back, they would not have recognized this entrance, had they not just come through it. "Well, I have now got a much higher respect for the dwarves," declared Mandy as they shivered from the cold, struggled through three feet of snow to mount their horses. "I would have missed that entrance entirely had I been looking for it! Incredible indeed. Come on, we gotta get to the caravan fast. I fear the worst! This is really ugly."

"My kingdom for a parka!" declared Jon.

"You haven't got a kingdom!" retorted Darless playfully. She alone was nearly impervious to the cold; her body was, after all, half-demon. Mat and May, however, accustomed only to the hot desert climate, fared the worst; their teeth chattered noisily within just a few minutes.

"Follow me; single file," commanded Mandy. "Darless, you are the rear guard; Alison, you come after me, just in case we run into trouble — might need a spell or two if you can muster one; Twins, you follow her. Jon, you follow them and keep an eye on them. This can be very tricky riding indeed. Do not stray from the trail I break through the snow pack!" And they were off.

Their physical exhaustion electrified in the chill still air. Jon was only too glad that Mandy took charge; he knew he had not the strength of will to forge ahead just now. And for a while he, losing all sense of time, he mused on how Mandy got her energy, her drive. When all else failed, he knew he could depend on this ranger. Indeed, their lives and all those of the caravan, although they did not know that yet, now lay in her hands.

Chapter 21 Salvation

A soft white blanket three feet deep covered what Mandy assumed was the narrow valley's boulder strewn floor. A faint trickling of water from a buried stream competed with their horses' occasional snorts, spraying the air with a bluish hued mist. Mandy carefully broke trail. It was the most difficult passage she had ever undertaken. With snow nearly up to her horse's belly, it was a challenge to avoid the treacherous, hidden boulders and rocks — anyone of which could snap a horse's leg in an instant. Sweat poured down her cheek. She whispered a prayer of thanks for the nearly full moon whose light she used to her advantage. A dimple or raised mound in the sea of white indicated a boulder beneath. Yes, she was guessing and Mandy hated to be reduced to gambling. Yet there was no other choice.

The others followed single file, careful to duplicate Mandy's path as best they could. Fortunately for the others, their horses had the good sense to follow in Mandy's track without guidance from their riders. Back at the rear, Alison found the going relatively easy; the snow was nicely compacted by the five ahead of her. Instead, she shivered trying to keep warm and to stay alert for any mischief coming at their rear. But she really did not expect any surprises at this time.

It took them an hour to go about a mile. "Finally!" exclaimed Mandy, "Here's the main path and solid evidence the caravan has passed here very recently." In the grey light, all could see the compacted snow, wagon ruts and the occasional manure piles. "The going should be much faster now. How are you holding up?" she asked to those behind her.

"It-t-t's-s-s co-o-o-ld-d!" stammered May bravely.

On they rode into the silent night. As Mandy predicted, they did make much better time following in the caravan's wake. Around midnight, they encountered the trailing wagon. Yet for over a mile before meeting the rear wagon, they knew they had caught up to the others. Red flickering glows lighted the sky and, as they drew even nearer, the sounds of axes chopping wood echoed in the still night.

The caravan had halted for the night, but instead of making a camp, each wagon had pulled up close behind the one in front of it, stretching on for three-quarters of a mile. All horses remained harnessed to the wagons. In fact all of the extra horses Jon had acquired were also hitched which provided a greater pulling power. Every few wagons, a huge bonfire blazed; blanketed people huddled close for warmth. Nary a soul had had any sleep for approaching forty-eight hours for fear of freezing to death in their sleep.

These travelers were totally unequipped for winter and for snow. Their light-weight cloaks, which fended off the desert night chill, provided little warmth. To stay warm, every available bedding blanket had been pressed into service wrapping the shivering folks who huddled forlornly around and staring numbly into the flickering fires. A few hardier men traded turns fetching and chopping more wood until their hands could no longer grip an axe.

Most did not even notice or stir as the six rode on past them. Midway up the line, they finally found Raul and several other guards. One wagon had been moved very close to a rather large fire. As they dismounted, they could see a number of forms heavily blanketed in the wagon's bed. "Thanks be to Ukko that you have finally returned!" hailed a very weary Raul. "We've had a time of it and are in deep trouble, Mandy. We've got six here with frostbite I think; two are near death. We cannot get them warmed up; one fell into a stream yesterday."

Jon, Mat and May began examining the injured with Jon tackling the two that were in the worst shape. Despite their own rattling teeth and shaking hands, the twins laid their hands upon the four that were not near death's door, calling upon Father Ukko for healing warmth. Jon used his staff on the older man who had gotten wet the day before and a woman, bringing them back shivering and shaking into the world of the living. Darless relieved several men and brought cups of hot broth that they had simmering, giving each an infusion of warmth.

Meanwhile, as Raul, Mandy and Alison walked their horses on toward the front of the caravan, he explained, "We ran into a blizzard two days back, kept going on in spite of it. Alison, if it had not been for Thea, your young assistant, we would all be like those six back there or worse. Bless her heart,

Thea's been lighting everyone of these fires each night with her spells. No one has gotten any sleep yet. And tonight has just totally exhausted her. William is looking after her up at the front."

Soon they reached the lead wagon. There was no mistaking it. Beyond them stretched a three-foot wall of snow hiding the trail, a white barrier to travel. William was in lying in the lead wagon. Alison found him snuggled up close to the sleeping form of her young assistant, Thea, trying to keep her warm.

Mandy leaned over William and whispered, "I'm back, my love." She gave him a gentle kiss on his cheek. He roused from semi-sleep, smiled back at her. But the dark rings under his eyes told all. "Back in a minute, dearest," she added. Mandy joined Alison and Raul by the warming fire; now she too was shivering uncontrollably. All her sweat now threatened to evaporate the last warmth from her body. She knew she must get dry by the fire and soon. "We must get these people somewhere warm to sleep!" she said to no one in particular.

"I know," Alison replied. "Darless and I can create several mansions. If people crowd in, I think we can manage to fit seventy-five to a hundred into one. But it takes a mage to be inside and command the doors. So tonight, Mandy, you and May are going to get a wizardry lesson. If we can get four mansion spells going, that will leave only a couple hundred out here." She then explained what her plan was all about to Raul. He noted that some guards, of necessity, must remain to keep the fires going and protect the horses and caravan. They could sleep in shifts.

By the time that Jon, Darless and the twins arrived, Alison had already retrieved several magical scrolls from her portable hole and had one mansion cast, its shimmering portals glimmering in the moonlight. Quickly, she explained what was needed and gave May and Mandy very careful instructions on the mansion command words of operation. Once the two mages were convinced that Mandy and May knew how to operate the portals, Darless took May and Mat back to the other end of the line, pausing partway to cast her mansion spell and instructing the nearby folks to get inside. Finally, she cast a second mansion spell from Alison's scroll and helped May and Mat get shivering folks inside. Those that remained outside would be relieved in about four hours. This way, everyone could get warm and some much needed sleep. At last, she headed back to her mansion, found that it was filled to the brim and entered herself. She thought that the hardest part would be trying to wake in four hours to let replacements out and the others back in.

Mandy and William took many of the guards in their mansion, while Jon and Alison took charge of Thea and many zombie-like townsfolk. For these people, it was the first night's sleep in two days and the first time that they were really warm. As Jon and Alison snuggled up to the still sleeping Thea between them, he whispered, "This is positively brilliant, my dear. I love you!" She smiled back at him, knowing that she had just turned the tide of the potential disaster for one night at least. Sleep came quickly to everyone.

The next morning was filled with exclamations of awe and gratitude. Over and over, the mages were thanked for the unexpected warm housing. Mandy insisted that everyone have a good hot breakfast before breaking camp and trudging on through the heavy snow. This gave Alison some time two discuss magic with her apprentice, Thea. The warm, good night's sleep did wonders for Thea. And awaking to find herself inside a magical mansion brought her boundless enthusiasm back. She had to inspect every corner of the mansion in detail, wondering all the time how soon she could learn to cast such a spell.

"Okay, now it's time for another magic lesson, Thea," Alison began. "I'm really proud of how well you have helped these people. How many fires did you light? Tell me all about it."

Thea needed no coaxing. "Well, by the time we stopped two days ago, all the men's hands were so cold, no one could get a fire going — besides all the wood was wet and green. So I just went around starting fires with my spell." She faltered a bit, uncertain of just how to explain her problem. "I cast the fire starting spell about fifty times two nights ago and around thirty last night before I fainted and fell asleep." Alison's eyes opened wide as did her mouth, but no words came out. Thea knew something was very wrong and hastily added, "I know, I, I was only supposed to be able to cast a couple of them. But everyone was so desperate for fire, so I just kept going and going and going." A tear welled and trickled down her right cheek. "I know I am not supposed to be able to do that. But I just know that spell by heart now. Somehow I don't need to learn it proper like, as you told me I should do each morning."

"There now, don't cry, Thea. You did nothing wrong, really. I've heard of mages with exceptional abilities that can do what you did. Actually, Thea, you can do something that even I cannot do with all my experience. Both you and Jon never cease to amaze me. And no harm is done. There is very little that could go wrong with that fire starting spell except a fizzle and that did not seem to happen. Just be careful with the more powerful spells. I knew a wizard once who did not pay close attention to his transmutation spell and when he transformed back into human form from his rat body, he ended up with a rather large rat tail hanging out his rear." Thea stared at her in disbelief. Was she teasing her? Alison's stern eyes told her no. The apprentice burst out laughing.

"A real rat's tail? Honestly? Now that would be a sight to behold!" she replied between chuckles.

"Not if it were your tail," Alison grinned back. "Everyone would see your goofy magic. But seriously, I think you are more comfortable with fire based spells. So let's teach you how to cast a proper ball of fire upon enemies."

Thea's eyes opened wide. "You mean a real fireball spell? Wow!" Thus, the lesson began in earnest, and everyone got to witness Thea's first real fireball. She exploded it over the unbroken, snow covered trail before them, melting all the snow in a thirty-foot radius. Onlookers clapped and cheered her spell, rooting her on. After all, it had been Thea, and Thea alone, that had provided them their evening fires for the last two days. Her position had increased enormously among the caravan folks.

During this time, Mandy and Raul held a conference. He explained how they had been breaking the trail for the last two days. Twenty-five riders basically trampled down the snow ahead of the lead wagon. It was excruciatingly slow progress, he commented, "Mandy, at this rate, we will never make it through the mountains. We are getting low on supplies and feed for the horses. All it takes is one more snow and even the horses will not be able to go forward. In spite of the mansions, we are likely doomed. Many of my guards speak of it in hushed voices when they think I am not listening. But really, I think it is on everyone's mind, though unspoken."

"Raul, you have done a terrific job so far. Things have gone about as bad as I reared when I saw the snow coming. I've been worrying constantly. I had a feeling things were going really bad for you. I got us here just as fast as possible. But there is some hope. The dwarves said that we can seek shelter in the Hidden Valley Ruins not too far from here. I have directions, only they don't mean much with everything covered in snow." She watched relief pour from his troubled face; he even managed a smile, which was something for this veteran campaigner. She asked him, although she already knew what she should do independent of his answer, "Do you think we should explain where we are heading to the caravan folks?" She knew it was important for him to be asked; the guards were, after all, his men and under his leadership.

He said carefully, "Though on the surface of it, the name Hidden Valley Ruins does not sound too hopeful, it will give them an immediate focus — a goal that we can reach soon. That alone will help everyone focus." And so the word spread throughout the caravan that today they would be making camp at the Hidden Valley Ruins where two humans dwelled. For hours speculation ran rampant about this mysterious destination, as the caravan made its slow forward progress. Would they find any comfort in a ruin? What kind of ruins? Who were these mountain people that could live in this desolation, this cold and snow. In the end, none of their wildest imaginings that day proved true.

Mandy and Raul forged about a half mile ahead of the twenty guards who continued to use their horses to trample down the snow for the caravan wagons. It was about one in the afternoon when Mandy found the side turnoff trail and, about a half hour later, when she stopped and dismounted. Before her was a very strange sight. This side valley had steeply rising walls, a V-shaped canyon. While the snow cover had only shown an occasional sign of life, a deer track here, a rabbit's there, at this location the ground signs were plain and ominous. Even Raul saw them though he did not recognize them. He asked, "What made all those tracks? A big animal for sure!"

"Bear. From the signs, many, many bears. Or perhaps only a few bears on a well-traveled path. This is not a good sign, my friend. Our war horses will stand before a bear, but those from town will likely bolt in terror. Yet the signs are most confusing. They both come and go, and come and go. I don't know what to make of it. However, there is no choice but to go forward. Well, at least our passage will hide these bear prints. I don't want to cause panic just yet." And so they mounted and rode on up this narrow valley but only for a short distance. Around the next curve, they halted again. Before them was a pair of ancient, iron gates which showed signs of a recent repair, though the new workmanship was rather crudely done. Mandy observed that the bear tracks went up to the gates and also led away from the gates.

"Perhaps the bears only get this far and the gates stopped them," offered Raul hopefully.

"This is even stranger, Raul," Mandy commented, "Look, the gates are fastened from this side. Shouldn't the gates be locked from the other side?"

"Mighty weird," came his calm reply. "It's like someone wants to lock whomever or whatever is inside this valley inside this valley! Strange doors."

They dismounted. It took both of them to unlatch and open the doors. The heavy snow layer had already been compacted or shoveled away from the doors so that the doors actually opened properly. They were expected, evidently. Remarkably, just inside the gates, only a few inches of snow lay on the ground. Mandy dutifully pointed out that the steep, tall sides of this north-south valley kept heavier snow from accumulating on the valley floor. Both were relieved to see only human footprints in the snow. No bear tracks could be seen inside the gates, though Mandy was alert for them all of the rest of the way. She saw only the footprints of at least two humans, a large and a smaller one. "Look Raul, their strides were different. Perhaps our benefactors are male and female. That would make sense, way out here in nowhere."

About a thousand feet inside the doors, they spied a black ore seam streaking skyward, a coal seam. "Recently worked," noted Raul. Indeed, there were pick axes and poles and baskets neatly stacked nearby. From the depth cut into this exposed seam of anthracite, its coal had been mined for many years.

"Coal means heat," grinned Mandy. Raul returned an even broader smile and his eyes light up, expectant of a warm bed for a change.

"I do not like cold mountain winters, I've decided," he added. He then beckoned to one of his guards who had arrived near the gate. Raul gave instructions that after the last wagon had entered, the gates were to be shut and fastened. He and Mandy continued their ride on up the narrow valley.

Around the next bend, the narrow trail opened up into a wide, sheltered valley, about five hundred feet across. The final remains of a vast summer's garden could be still be seen. About a thousand yards further into the valley, a strange collection of stone buildings caught their attention. Smoke rose from several chimneys, a most welcome sign. But even stranger, to the right of the buildings, was an immense stone ruins carved into the depths of the sheer cliffs. Great stone pillars carved from the bedrock announced some great entrance hallway leading far underground. The architecture was unlike anything that Mandy had ever seen. It certainly was not dwarfish in nature. And even more surprising were the columns of black smoke belching from escape holes high up the sheer cliff walls. They rode on gazing from the ruins to the buildings, but seeing no one.

When they were about fifty feet from the closest stone building, a door opened and out came two figures heavily bundled up in immense furs. Both wore black fur boots, hats and coats. They looked very warm indeed. It was obvious that they knew how to stay warm in this climate. Oh what Mandy would give for just such an outfit!

"Hail, friends," Mandy called out as she dismounted and tried to not shiver so badly. "Lord Dathor, the dwarven lord, told us that we might find shelter here for our caravan which has gotten caught in the snow storm. I am Mandy Blackthorn, Ranger of Reylona, and this is the Caravan Master, Raul. My other companions will be here shortly. Ah here they come now." Indeed, not wanting to be left out, her friends came galloping up from the rear. Mandy continued the introductions as they dismounted.

"Here are the mages Alison d'Ambrose and Darless. This is Saint Jon Brown. And these are the twins, May and Mat d'Ambrose." All of her friends were wrapped in bedding blankets, trying to stay somewhat warm. Mandy saw their eyes drooling over the warm, black fur of these denizens of the Hidden Valley Ruins.

Their hosts smiled and shook hands one by one. "We are Jake," began the tall man in a basso voice full of restrained power. He stood about six-foot four-inches tall. Beneath the bulging furs, Mandy assumed that he was also broad shouldered, but not much else could be discerned, save his piercing, coal black eyes.

"And Jennifer Newcastle," the woman finished with no hesitation. Though smaller in stature, she was only slightly less broad with equally piercing black eyes full of life.

"Brother and sister," added Jake, answering their obvious unspoken question. Indeed, everyone including Jon kept glancing from Jake to Jennifer and back again. "We have been expecting you."

"Thraxanndiur, a neighboring dwarf," Jennifer continued without a pause.

"Told us of your plight and coming," Jake went on.

"We are a bit unsure how we will manage so many of you," Jennifer picked up from him.

"But we'll figure it out," Jake finished the thought. "Your leaders are welcome to stay in our home complex."

"But you have so many! So we've tried to fix up the Old Ruins to accommodate all of the wagons," Jennifer added. "We've gotten the old fireplaces burning, but with all of the windows long gone,"

"It's liable to be a bit drafty. Do you really have six hundred people?" asked Jake.

During this short time span, Mat and May stared at each other in disbelief. Alison's mouth opened as if to say something, but no words came out. Likewise, Mandy and Darless. Jon's comment said it all, "Deja vous." These two talked just like May and Mat. They had to be an unusual set of twins as well. It was plainly obvious that they each knew the other's thoughts. For the first time in their thirty-some years, the twins felt emotionally excited. Here were others similar to themselves. Their hearts beat rapidly as they simultaneously recalled Ukko's words to them. Both wondered if these could be their potential mates.

"Well, yes," Mandy resumed her composure and take charge attitude. "None of us are equipped for this cold. Our plan to be across these mountains before winter came has obviously failed miserably. We are forever in your debt. We are cold, but all of the travelers are healthy. We cured the frostbite cases last night. Should we lead the horses and wagons and all into big circle out here?"

"Wow," exclaimed Jennifer, though no one was exactly sure what had impressed her. "Er no, the Old Ruins is actually quite"

"Huge," Jake finished her sentence. "Just drive the horses and wagons and all right on inside the stone guardians."

"Follow us," added Jennifer as they both turned to walk toward the two, hundred foot tall statues. Between the stone guardians, carved like a pair of juggernauts with one hand pointing to the door and the other holding a globe, stood a huge pair of iron doors, slightly ajar. At one time, an ornamental bias relief upon these doors once greeted visitors. But now, the ages had rusted the images. "We've lit many of the old fireplaces,"

"So it should be fairly warm by now," finished Jake. "There is, of course, only one small problem,"

"We do not have the food resources to feed this many people," Jennifer added to his thought. "We keep only enough for our meager needs."

"But we do have some we can sell you," Jake explained. "I'm afraid that we are not equipped to feed horses."

"We don't have any, anymore," she added. Jon thought that he detected a note of sorrow or grief in her voice. He sensed a fleeting mental image of the two turning their horses loose to fend for themselves. He wondered why they would free their only means of travel stuck here so high in the mountains.

As they entered the doors, spacious caverns hewn from the solid rock greeted them. "Who made this?" asked Mandy genuinely awed by the huge expanse. "This does not look dwarven make." No indeed, the motif was square entirely plain, devoid of ornamentation. Everything was precisely square, rooms, walls, doorways, and support pillars of the original bedrock that remained — all was square within a tiny fraction of an inch — quite a remarkable engineering feat. There were even tables and chairs carved out of the floor. The drawback of the stone furniture, besides being hard to sit upon, was no possibility of rearranging the pieces; they were carved in-place, in situ, according to some master plan.

What a dreary place, mused Darless to herself. ***Plainness*** *taken to its utter extremity.*

But it was substantially warmer inside the caverns. For that, everyone was grateful beyond belief. Jennifer continued, "We are Provisioners by trade. We make Healthy Traveler Rations. Perhaps you have heard of them? Sold mostly to adventurers who need to travel light; one week's staples weighs only a few pounds."

"No! Really?" exclaimed Alison, her eyes lighted up. "HTR's, as we call them, are absolutely the very best rations. Some of my other friends and I have used them extensively for the last ten years. I just want to tell you that your HTR's are just fantastic indeed. Thanks for making them. You could charge twice what you do for them." Unfortunately, none of her other companions had ever heard of these rations. Although blushing noticeably at this unexpected compliment, Jennifer's eyes sparkled with pride in her products.

"We grow everything here in this valley," Jake acknowledged. "And we also make winter coats, boots and gloves. They are sold down in Tannersville. That's where we are originally from, about two hundred miles as the trail goes."

Recovering her composure, Jennifer explained further, "You see, quite by accident, we can sell you a lot of rations and winter garb. Each fall, traders from Tannersville journey here to us and purchase our year's production, paying in some needed staples for us as well as money."

"But something dreadful has happened this year," Jake's tone expressed deep concern, "the traders have not come at all. They are weeks over due. Now that the snows have come, I fear that they could not get here by wagon even if they tried."

"So we are stuck with nearly a thousand of these rations and fifty-five dozen sets of winter apparel," Jennifer explained. "We'll give you a bargain price on the lot. If only you have some salt; we are dangerously low on salt."

"I'm sure that I can get you all the salt you can possibly use," Alison replied. "Let's see, the rations come to about what, five thousand gold coins?"

"Oh no!" exclaimed Jake in dismay. "We only get one gold coin per ration."

"The traders do mark up the product substantially, we hear," Jennifer expanded further. "They have to pay wagoners to come here and get them and so on. I guess it covers their expenses and profit too. The winter gear is in all sizes from children to large adults. We usually get thirty gold pieces per dozen."

"Well, I think you are being exploited, taken advantage of," Alison huffily said. "We must pay you a fair price, after all, we are desperate for warm clothing."

"I hate to interrupt, but here come the wagons," broke in Mandy. The lead wagon, driven by William, arrived just outside the iron doors. Mandy motioned for him to drive on in.

"You sure you want the wagons and horses inside here?" he hollered, rather confused, and so the organized chaos began. For the next hour, wagons entered through the doors and were directed to various side chambers. Horses were unharnessed and led to yet another chamber which had six windows or rather outside openings — the windows, of course, were long gone. Here the horses were fed and rubbed down. The coal fires that Jake had stoked furnished reasonable heat to keep them warm.

The tired travelers established their camps with a dozen groups per chamber on the average. In all, they filled nearly two dozen of these inner-connected chambers. Yet only a small percentage of available chambers were actually used. Jon could not believe the size of the ruins; Jake told him that there were two hundred twenty-five chambers in all. Everyone was nearly identical in size and shape.

Two of the chambers held the Newcastle's neatly wrapped goods ready to be loaded onto the trader's supply wagons which had never arrived. When the folks in one chamber had their wagons setup for the night, Alison led them into the first of the two chambers. Here she and Jennifer doled out the HTRs, the iron rations. Each wagon received three weeks' worth of food per person. These rations consisted of dried or dehydrated foods, a healthy mixture of vegetables, meats, nuts, cheese, berries, fruits, and grains. One only needed to add water and then cook or warm them, the idea being that an adventurer could always find water. So the weight of the food was drastically reduced by the drying process. Obviously, the fixing of these rations had occupied a great deal of the Newcastle's time throughout the year. Alison insisted on giving them two gold pieces per ration, or about two thousand coins. If she had had to purchase these rations in a town, she fully expected to pay five thousand. So this mage figured not only did she have a great bargain, but also more honestly recompensed the Newcastle's for their labors.

Once the food had been handled, next Alison and Jennifer tackled the stacks of winter clothing. This proved a challenge indeed. Each bundle contained a dozen sets in various sizes. Jennifer explained that usually one storekeeper would take one or two bundles to sell to various customers. So they had tried to make each bundle a respective mixture of needed sizes. Things were further complicated because of the different furs used in the apparels. Some were made from rabbit, in several colors. Some were of fox and similar creatures. Some were from black bear. And a very, very few were from ermine and mink, exquisitely done, and of course, very expensive.

Just as soon as Alison laid eyes on these, she exclaimed, "Oh my! I just have to have these!" She bought all the ermine and mink sets, giving each of her friends a "present" for the Winter Solstice which was still six weeks away. The rest of the afternoon was spent in matching a person with the right sized winter garb, or as near as they could, for they soon ran out of the more common sized garments. No one complained, though, the idea of warmth outweighed all other considerations. Most of the folks insisted on paying for their new found clothing, either all or in part. So Alison ended up only having to come up with about five hundred gold coins, mostly for the expensive ermine she just had to have.

She had just finished counting out the coins when Jake arrived. Alison could not help but notice the stern tone in his voice as he said, "Jen, it's that time."

Alison watched as the joyful, excited face of her host darken visibly. Jennifer commented, "Sorry, I completely lost track of time, Jake." Turning to the mage, she explained, "Okay, I don't have much time, Alison, so here are the rules. You all are welcome to stay the night in our cottage outside. Help yourselves to anything you need. Do not look for us during the night. We will speak with you in the morning light. There is one other vitally important rule." Here, her voice grew stern and somber, quite unlike her joyful mood all afternoon. "Under *no* circumstances whatsoever should anyone go outside the gates during the night; *never* ever open the gates when it is dark outside. You must promise me this. None of you will go beyond the gates after dark, promise me!"

"Sure, we always try to follow our host's wishes," Alison replied, "You have my word none will go beyond the gates at night. But can you tell me why?"

"No, not really," Jake answered gruffly as Jennifer merely stared at the floor, trying to hide the tears forming in her eyes. "It is dangerous out there. Many black bears and wild beasts call these desolate mountains their home. We do not want anything ill to happen to you." Perhaps for city-dwellers, his explanation might make sense, Alison thought to herself.

Without another word, both hastily made their exit, leaving behind the numerous sacks of their newly acquired gold still sitting on the stone table. "What was that all about?" asked Mandy, who along with Jon had just entered the chamber and overheard the parting words. Without waiting for an answer, she quickly brought Alison up to date on her activities, "Jake has spent all afternoon showing the men both where and how to dig for coal to stoke the fires. Would you believe that that coal vein is for real? It provides cheap heat for cold winters. They have everything here."

Jon, however, spoke the obvious, "She was crying when she left here. I could sense grief radiating from her as we walked in here." So Alison explained what they had said and what she had promised. "Why?" was Jon's comment.

Mandy's reply was expected, "Of course, we will stay inside, but I've personally never ever had the slightest bit of trouble from wild animals, not even bears. Yet that might explain all of the bear tracks that I saw when I first got to the gates — dozens of them coming up to the gates and leaving the gates. I saw no signs of bear once we were on this side of the gates, though, and no clawing marks of bears trying to get in. I found it all very strange then, and I still do!"

"I don't know what to make of this either," Alison agreed, "It took me by surprise, and I don't feel right sleeping inside someone else's home when they are not around. Where could they possibly have to do at night?"

"Me either," added Jon. "We have everything we need in William's wagon. I vote we all stay here with the rest of the caravan. Perhaps it can be a night of music and songs. It has been some time since everyone had some relaxation, some merrymaking."

"I agree, Jon," put in Mandy. "It will definitely lift their spirits. Besides, just now, I have no idea how the caravan is going to be able to make any further progress through these mountains with all this snow, clothes or no clothes. It will give me time to think." And they all headed back to William and the wagons.

William had been busy. When they arrived, they found the stone table all laid out for a formal banquet. Heady aromas from hundreds of cooking pots filled all of the chambers kindling a ravenous appetite in everyone. "Wow, William! This is really terrific! A man after my own heart," Mandy smiled partly in jest, but partly from a profound joy in the thoughtfulness of this man. She gave him a big hug and a warm kiss.

"'Pologies, folks, no time to bake any bread," William finally spoke as the others gathered around the table. "Tomorrow I'll see about that. But for tonight, a feast for m'lady and friends. I figured you've all earned it! Have a seat. Mind you, stone's none too comfortable." He received a chorus of "Thank you's."

Over a warm dinner of peas, potatoes and rabbit, they discussed the day's events and relayed all that had happened during the defense of the dwarves. At Alison's insistence, Thea joined her and Jon, Mat, May, Darless, Mandy and William for dinner. The lowly apprentice felt a surge of pride at being asked to dine at the hero's table. She listened with eager ears at all of the tales of combat, though admittedly she was horrified at the enormity of the battle they had fought. Inwardly, Thea wondered if she would ever find that much courage. When the discussion centered around Jon's confrontation with the Goddess of War, Morrigan, and the arch-devil Dispater, her heart skipped a beat. She cringed and shrank into as small a form as possible; she knew she was less than a helpless pawn in the presence of gods and goddesses.

Alison spotted her distress and spoke reassuringly, "Thea, don't worry. I've been adventuring for more than a dozen years; we all have, except for Jon here. I still remember how, on my first few adventures, the fighters had their hands full just trying to protect me, to keep me alive long enough for me to cast my few spells. For the first few years, I was utterly dependent upon them for my life. I am eternally grateful for all the aid the Holy Paladin, Sir Thomas, bestowed upon me. If it weren't for him, I would have been dead many times over during those first few years!"

"Really?" Thea's eyes opened wide. Never had she given a thought to how Alison had become so powerful a mage. She had always seen her as the greatest mage she had ever seen or heard of — that Alison had begun much as she had never crossed her mind until now.

"Yes," Alison continued, "I began with just a single spell enabling me to cause those of weaker minds to fall into a deep sleep — a most useful spell at times. I'd cast it and that was all I could do. The rest was up to Sir Thomas, Slik, and the others. In time, I learned more, just as you will." She put her arm around Thea and gave her a motherly hug. Unbidden, the thought of her hugging her own daughter with Jon beaming at them came into her mind. She smiled, *Time enough for that joy yet*. She found that image not unenjoyable for the first time in her life. She smiled toward Jon who picked up her mental image; he grinned back at her.

Finally, the discussion turned to their hosts, the Newcastle twins. It wasn't long before May asked Alison, "Say, do you believe in love at first sight?" Everyone instantly roared with laughter; May's face turned red as a beet; Mat's as well, though no one noticed him, for which he was grateful.

"Forgive us," Alison finally manage to get out, "We didn't mean to embarrass you so. It is just that that thought has been on all of our minds, I'm sure, from the first moment they introduced themselves."

Jon added quickly, "Like two peas from the same pod — that was my immediate reaction the second I heard them speak. Other than you two, they are the only others I have ever known that are so connected with each other. I admit, I have been wondering if you two would find them attractive and all that. I think we all though probably thought pretty much the same thing." The embarrassment left both twins just as fast as it had arrived. Both realized that they were not being ridiculed or mocked.

"But to answer your question, sis," Alison went on, "I just don't know. Jon and I fell in love, but not on the first meeting. When I first met Jon, I had him pegged as a thief of one of our books or worse. So I am not one to ask."

"William's been my village's baker for years," Mandy couldn't help but add her opinion, "and I never even noticed him before, until back there in Freetown. That's rather the opposite of love at first sight."

"Well, with m'Lady here," William added in his own defense, "I always thought she was completely out of my league — her being the Lord of the Blackthorn Castle."

Not to be left out, Jon said, "I find that love is a combination of admiration and respect for each other. For me, I found it easy for me to admire Alison immediately, just as I did Mandy and Darless. In a very short time, mutual respect has grown out of communication. We share many of the same values." He faltered a bit confused by his own explanation, "Hum, but so it has with Darless and Mandy. Logically, I could easily have married any of the three."

The three giggled, and Mandy teased, "Ah so now you want to marry all three of us, is that it?" Jon fumbled for words but did not become embarrassed as he would have only a few months earlier.

"I think the word you are searching for, Jon, is 'soul mate'," Alison offered.

He brightened up, "Yes, that's it exactly, soul mates. But none of this is helping you, is it?" Jon noticed the twins were now completely confused.

"You mean, like Mat and I are?" asked May frowning. "We cannot marry each other!"

"No, you have the rare sibling bond of soul mates," Jon tried to explain his way out of the entangled mess into which he had gotten himself. "How could you both ever be truly happy married to soul mates who were themselves not soul mates? Am I right?"

"Precisely," Mat spoke at last, "that is it exactly. We could never be content with mates who were not as ourselves. It could not possibly work out."

Darless, who had been very quiet until now, finally spoke up. "So it seems no one here can speak of 'love at first sight'. Well, I can. It has happened to me only once. I once met this handsome, virile gorgeous hunk of a fellow. I looked deep into his eyes and felt my hearth miss a beat. But there is always the other side. In this case, it is utterly impossible for him to ever under any circumstances be in love with me. So it was doomed from the onset. I just let it be." She sighed.

"Who was he?" asked Alison, Jon and Mandy almost in unison. Never before had they heard any of this from Darless. It took them by surprise; it was so unexpected.

Darless, looking at the ground, answered meekly, "For both our sakes, I will never name him. And no, it is not you, Jon," she looked up and grinned at him. He felt relief at that pronouncement. Hurting Darless was the last thing Jon would ever want to do. "So I say, the answer is yes, there can be love at first sight, but remember it must flow both ways."

"Now that does make sense," May sighed in relief. The built-up tension of the twins blew off like dandelion's seeds in a wind.

"Say, I'd better get the musicians gathered if we are going to have some festivities tonight," Jon suddenly remembered his evening's intention. "Come on Alison, let's go get some celebrations going." As the two got up to go, Thea got up as well and tugged lightly on Alison's sleeve.

In a low whisper, Thea asked her, "I've never been much interested in the men I've ever seen. I find them mostly crude beasts. Does that mean there is something wrong with me?"

"Heaven's no," Jon, who could not help hearing her, replied, "I find your description rather accurate myself!"

"Good reply, Jon," Alison smiled, "You took the words I would have said. One thing you must know, Thea, all men are different from each other; all are unique, like the grains of sand in the desert. But some of them you may find are more to your liking. And one day, I'm sure you will find that special man, the love of your life. And if my own experience is of any worth, it may happen when you least expect it to occur! At least it did with me." She gave Jon a knowing nudge. He did likewise as the gloom vanished from Thea's face and mind.

"Then I shall not expect it and be surprised when it comes," she gaily pronounced and skipped off to find her parents.

For the next three hours, music and song filled the chambers, echoing off the bare stone walls. Warm shelter, warm clothing and plenty of hot food completely altered everyone's view point of their fate, at least temporarily. All save one. Mandy thought, *Let them make merry tonight. But tomorrow is quite another picture. We are in the middle of high mountains at the very start of winter. The situation could not be much worse.* She wandered in search of Raul and together they discussed how difficult it had been to get the wagons this far through the deep snow cover.

"I've no experience with this cold winter weather," Raul explained. "I'm at a complete loss of ideas. I trust you have traveled through mountains in the winter?"

"I hate to burst your hope, Raul, but no," she replied sternly. "I have done quite a bit of winter travel, but the terrain was flat and the snows not deep. This is quite another matter entirely. I am extremely worried about the down slope side of this trip. Climbing up is one matter, but I am having nightmares about wagons sliding down into the horses and all then plunging over cliffs and the like. How do we keep the wagons from skidding off on their own? No, admittedly, I am very worried indeed. Worst case scenario, we could be stranded here until the spring snow melt."

He did not like the sound of that any better than she did. "I'll think of something," Mandy added in a vain attempt to cheer him up. For once, she almost did not believe her own words. "I think I will take a stroll and do some thinking. Night, Raul." And so Mandy donned her new winter furs and went outside into the cold night.

The moon was full, she noted, casting its cold, frigid beams across the white valley. The stone buildings which the Newcastle's called home looked dark and desolate. No lights were on, though smoke could be seen curling into the sky, like a pale ghost. *It is lonely out here,* she though. *No people. Who would want to live such a life devoid of all company?* The more she thought about the Newcastle twins, the odder their situation seemed to her. *They do not look like hermits. Yet, a hermit's life they lead. Strange.* She strolled aimlessly, deep in thought.

After a time, Mandy found herself standing before the entrance gates to the valley. Both were shut tight, latched from the opposite side. This prevented her from opening them to leave the valley. Suddenly, she just had to see what was on the other side. Present Mandy with a locked door and she found it utterly irresistible not to open the door and see what lay beyond. She had always been this way. A childhood memory came back to her unbidden. One time her father had locked the door to his bedroom one night. Her curiosity was such that she just had to see what was going on. That was the first time she had ever picked a lock. Mandy grinned, her first picked lock resulted in her seeing her father in bed with one of the kitchen staff.

She knew what she had to do. Quickly and quietly, she scaled the wall near the gates. At the top, she looked down at the outside world. All seemed as she had expected. The snow had been compacted by the passage of hundreds of horses and wagons. But wait. Her keen eyes picked out fresh bear footprints leading from the gates back down the trail they had originally come! These tracks were on top of the hoof indentations! One was obviously a large bear, the other somewhat smaller. *Strange indeed,* thought Mandy. *How do I read this riddle?*

She eased herself back down to the ground and ambled back toward the cliff-side chambers, all the while pondering this strange turn of events. By the time she got back inside the warmth of the chambers, the music was dying down. It was about midnight. So she headed to William's wagon and some sleep. He was already asleep so she curled up beside him. He mumbled something and put his arm around her. And so she fell asleep, dreaming of bears along with slipping, sliding wagons pummeling down steep cliffs.

The next day broke bright, clear and cold. The utter stillness of this isolated valley actually enforced its silence upon the caravan folks as they arose at the crack of dawn. By the time Jon stirred and got up, the many coal fires had been stoked and the aroma of breakfast greeted his nostrils. But there was hardly a sound, save cooking. "Morn'n William," Jon spoke aloud, hearing his voice echoing off of the walls. "Thanks for doing the cooking. I'm starving."

William grinned and whispered back, "My pleasure; help yourself. The others have already eaten, sleepyhead. Today's going to be bakin' day. I've a craving for pumpernickel, but I don't suppose I'm going to find any molasses around here though."

Jon sat down beside Mandy who was drinking a final cup of tea. She'd already finished the pancakes and meat; Jon was not sure what kind of meat it actually was and did not wish to ask. Between mouthfuls, he asked, "Where's everybody? And why's everyone whispering?"

The sour look on Mandy's face at once told Jon that she did not sleep at all well. She replied in a soft voice, "Alison, Darless and Thea are off practicing magic spells. I think they are teaching Thea how to cast some more spells. Mat and May went in search of our hosts who are not apparently up as yet. And no, I had nightmares of caravan wagons slipping and sliding off of steep cliffs and bears eating us alive." After a pause, she added, "This place gives me the creeps. Everyone feels it; it's so utterly quiet. The only sound is the babbling of the creek out there that runs the length of this valley."

Mumbling between eating, Jon persisted, "I didn't know you had nightmares. Wonder what caused it?"

"Oh probably the bear tracks I saw last night," she sighed. Yes, her attention was still on those tracks. She took another sip of her tea and told Jon what she had seen last night by the gate wondering what he might make of it.

"Hum, where I come from, bears hibernate through the winter, unless they are polar bears; those are the kinds that live in the Arctic, the land of eternal ice and snow," Jon muttered absentmindedly between bites. "Guess the bears around here are different."

"Zagroot zounds!" exclaimed Mandy, her bubbling enthusiasm rushing in once more, in a flash driving out her doldrums. "That's it! Bears should be hibernating this time of year. There should be no bear tracks at all. That was what has been gnawing at me all this time. They should not be here.

How silly of me to have not thought of that myself; and I call myself a 'ranger'. Ha! Thanks, Jon."

Just then, Jon saw several men bundled up in their new warm firs heading outside. "Hey, where are they going?" he asked.

"For coal," came the reply. "Remember that exposed coal vein we saw near the gates yesterday? Seems that you just go pick out some more fuel for fires when you need it. We're letting the men do that work. It's a rather dirty job, I imagine. Besides, I got bigger problems to worry about, like what do we do now, as well as the bear riddle. Bears where there should be no bears; a gate that locks backwards; stern warnings not to venture beyond the gate at night. Makes a strange set of circumstances, doesn't it. And this place — a giant city carved in bedrock in the middle of nowhere — totally deserted for ages. I wonder who used to live here and why they left."

Jon grinned and took a sip of his tea; he'd put away as much food as he dared and was leaning back listening to her. He teased her playfully, "I'd say you have way too many questions and far too few answers."

Before she could reply, Mat and May bounced in and up to the stone table. Their faces had a youthful, radiant glow and not from exertion. "They are up and have asked us all in for a tea and chat; come on!"

Though Jon really did not need to ask, he was feeling playful this morning. "Who's up?"

"Jake," giggled May.

"And Jennifer," Mat added, eyes aglow.

"Okay, I do have a lot of questions to ask them about how to get over these mountains," Mandy replied. As she got up, she placed both of her hands, palms down on the stone table. It was a bit difficult maneuvering into and out of these fixed, stone seats. As her hands made full contact with the table top, a grey misty appeared before her.

She saw dozens of families going about routine, daily tasks. Great lanterns illuminated the room. Tapestries depicting great hunting scenes adorned the walls. But it was the people on which her attention primarily focused. They were short, stoutly built, akin to dwarves. But their kindly faces looked very different from anything Mandy had ever seen. They were squarish in shape with overly large, perpetually smiling mouths, pudgy noses and deep-set black eyes. Suddenly, without warning, a massive ball of flames swept through the room. Terrified people screamed in flaming agony. Mandy caught a glimpse of a red dragon flying by, going from window to window launching a blast of flames into each. Once the flames dies down, she watched as the dragon walked into the room and began to eat his dinner. Mandy shrieked and collapsed.

Jon caught her before she hit the hard stone; he had seen something was very wrong with her and had made mental contact just before she received the repulsive shock.

Immediately, William, Mat and May came to his assistance and help him get her into the wagon and onto a makeshift bed. "What happened to her? A fit or something? Is she alright?" May's voice was full of concern.

"I've never seen anything like this happen to her before," Jon muttered, feeling for her vital signs. William passed an awful smelling bottle before her nose and one whiff brought her around.

"How awful! What happened? Where am I?" Mandy muttered confused to find herself lying inside the wagon staring up at all the concerned faces.

Jon answered her, "I sensed something was wrong and made mental contact just before you fainted. I think you just wanted to get away from those images. Did that event happen to you in the past?" Jon was ready to help her get through the trauma of the hideous incident.

"No, I'm okay. That wasn't me. Those were the people who built this place; I'll stake my life on it," she was starting to make sense of her vision. She told the others what she had seen. "This place has a pretty traumatic, terrifying emotional residue about it. No wonder we all feel so subdued. These people were roasted alive for the dinner of a red dragon!"

Suddenly the magnitude of what had just happened to her intruded into her consciousness. "Zagroot zounds! You realize that I just picked up on the ancient, emotional trauma housed in here?"

"That's incredible!" May interrupted. "How do you do it? Can you teach me how to do that?"

Mandy laughed in an attempt to shrug off this rather unsettling experience. "That was frightening, actually. I don't even know how I do it yet. Let me learn how to control this new skill and see how to use it. Maybe then I can. Right now, I have no idea. It just happened. It's never happened before; of that I am certain. The vividness of it, wow! I could feel their terror and burning pain. It was horrid." After a pause, she added, "Well now, Jon, I have the answer to one of the burning questions — pun intended." Both laughed. Then, they all put on their winter coats and headed to the cottage of Jake and Jennifer. It was about midmorning.

Their stone cottage had also been built in antiquity by the same people who carved the caverns. It showed signs of disrepair. The Newcastle's had done their best to repair what they could, but neither of them was a stonemason or a metal worker. As the party filed in the front metal door, Jennifer pleaded, "Please ignore the mess. We almost never have any guests. Our house is really our workshop."

That was an understatement. Several rooms were piled high with drying fruits and meats — all in various states of dehydration. These were the very last of the season. Another room held piles of furs of all kinds as well as sewing equipment. "Here's where we make most of the clothes," she explained. "We spend most of the winter days sewing."

Jake added, "And in the summertime, we concentrate on growing and foraging." Indeed, it seemed every conceivable location, every manner of chest, table, and shelving overflowed with projects.

"You certainly don't lack for something to do way out here," Alison teased playfully. She was impressed with the labor-intensive projects and their sheer volume. The Newcastles cleaned out some space in the actual kitchen around the table and brought in chairs and boxes for their guests. (They had only four chairs in the house.) The tea kettle boiled furiously on the hearth. The aromas wafting through the house were heady.

"What kind of tea do you all want?" Jennifer inquired. She was about to routinely make tea but then realized her guests may not like her choice.

That was all it took to interest Jon. "Oh boy. What kinds do you have?" And he allowed Jennifer to lead him to a cupboard brimming with over twenty kinds. "These all sound good. How about this one?" he said sniffing it. "It smells a bit smokey."

"Ah now that is an interesting one," Jennifer replied. "Smokey Black, it's called. Rather good flavor and a very different aroma." And so Smokey Black it was all around. Soon everyone was chatting merrily.

Mandy inquired first about travel through these mountain in the winter, explaining the caravan's awful time with the drifted-over trail. Jake answered her worst fears, "About the only travelers this time of year come by sleigh or donkey cart. Otherwise, I've no idea how you can get the wagons through the pass." In short, Mandy was beginning to really fear that the caravan may be stranded here for the entire winter!

"We get so few visitors here, please tell us about where you come from? Where you are headed? And all about any adventures you might have had? We heard rumors from the dwarves that you were involved in some kind of war and are great heroes," Jennifer asked with rounded eyes and a pleading look that no one could ignore. And so two hours passed as the companions told them much of their recent adventures. Jake and Jennifer asked many questions and proved eager listeners.

Around noon, just as Jennifer volunteered to make some lunch for everyone, Jake interrupted, "We have a new visitor entering the gates. I'd best go see who it is."

"How do you know that?" inquired Jon who had heard nothing out of the ordinary. Mandy also looked baffled; her neck was not tingling, so no danger.

He grinned and pointed to his ears, "We've got keen ears. I heard jingle bells of a harness. Back in a bit." He grabbed his fur coat by the door and was out in a flash. Meanwhile, the ladies all helped Jennifer set up the table for lunch. Jon found another box for the supposed new guest, just in case.

Right in the middle of setting a plate of meat on the table, Jennifer suddenly remarked, "Oh it's Rufus." Everyone stared at her and she became a bit self-conscious, a twinge of red flushed in her cheeks. "Jake just told me. We are close, you know. We know what each other is thinking most of the time."

And then the door opened and in came Jake and another very small person behind him.

After taking off their furs and hanging them on pegs by the doorway, Jake and his guest joined the others in the kitchen. "Let me present Rufus Quickenbroadbeam, Inventor Extraordinary."

"At your service," bowed low the little man. He was, in fact, a gnome. Rufus was all of thirty inches tall weighing nearly thirty-five pounds. A long brown beard touched his belt. His hair was long and matted down from an extended period of being under his hat. But it was the colors of his clothing that amazed everyone except Mandy, who had had dealings with several gnomes near Blackthorn Castle. Every color in the rainbow was visible in zigs and zags and swirls. It was almost a hypnotic pattern! "Yes, I am an inventor. I create very useful things!" He pulled a device out of his pocket. "I see that it is time for lunch. Here we have the portable eating utensil. Just pull this lever here and presto, a fork; and this one extracts the spoon portion. I never go anywhere without my eating gizmo."

Jennifer and Jake began laughing, "He is always trying to sell everyone he meets some of his inventions. If you let him, he will talk like that for hours until you buy something just to shut him up!"

"Ah my dear," Rufus feigned, "haven't I always provided you with many remarkable, useful items?" Both knew very well that he had and on many occasions.

While they were eating lunch, Jake asked Rufus, "How come you are back so soon. You left for town only two weeks ago. You could not even have gotten out of the mountains in that time. What happened?"

"Ah, now here's a tale for you!" he said excitedly, while still munching on a bit of bread dipped in honey. "I only got as far as the plains. Do not look for your trader friends to arrive this year; maybe never. They are all dead or wish they were so."

Shock spread across the faces of both Jennifer and Jake. "What happened to them?" she said; her voice bespeaking dread.

"Hobgoblins, that's what. Thousands of them. More that I have ever seen in my life, that's what!" Rufus declared. "I figure they all come from northern Hoar Frost." He added for the benefit of the new folks, "That's the mountainous area farther north of here. It's like every hobgoblin from the Northern Lost Steppes to the Hoar Frost have come swarming over onto our plains. I bet folks in Tannersville are in real trouble. About a week ago now, as I and my trusty Amos, that's my donkey who pulls my cart-sleigh, reached the edge of the plains, we spied smoke and a commotion. I parked Amos in a side passage and snuck up on the action. I spied the burning remains of what was probably your trader's wagons on their way here, Jen. Looted completely. Dead men lying all about. Hobgoblins were dancing and whooping it up in a victory celebration. At night, I snuck about trying to see if there was a way around this war party. But the whole plains for miles in all directions were filled with fireflies, the campfires of the hobgoblins. Hundreds of them. Almost like they were lying in wait for someone or something. Ah well, no use trying to get around them, so I headed back here to let you know you are also in trouble. No winter supplies will be forthcoming from Tannersville this year. We are all just going to have to tighten our belts, so to speak." He finally finished, satisfied that he had relayed all of the news.

During the silence that followed, Rufus suddenly remembered something. "Hey, Jen, I managed to pilfer something for you. I left it in the wagon. Back in a second!" And be scampered out of the room and out the door like a rabbit. He returned in less than a minute carrying a heavy sack, for him. He proudly walked up to Jen and said, "My dear lady, Rufus here snatched a precious bag of salt for you from the hobgoblins." He gave her a ten pound sack of salt.

"Why thank you, my little man," she said genuinely happy. "We are really very low on salt. This will tide us over a while. I guess we shall have to see what we can buy from the dwarves. Too bad you could not get to Tannersville, Rufus. I know you had a whole bunch of inventions to sell and supplies to purchase. Are you going to be wanting for something? You just let us know and we'll do our best to help out."

"Honey, lard, and smokeweed — I'm all out," he replied hopefully.

Jake answered, "We have all the honey and lard you could want, but I am afraid we've no tobacco."

"Most kind of you. I figured you had no weed; never did see any around here," Rufus replied smiling.

Turning to the others, Jennifer explained, "Rufus is our nearest neighbor; he lives in a cave complex about ten miles northeast of here. We always help each other out. Thanks for the salt."

There was a tone of seriousness in his voice as Jake asked, "The evil creatures didn't see you did they? You weren't followed?"

"Nope. A gnome is only seen when he wants to be seen," he replied, bragging a bit in front of these strangers.

Jennifer added playfully, "Rufus is something of an illusionist and a thief. So watch your pockets and purses when he is around."

Inspired, May spoke a few words to Rufus in a language no one else understood. He replied in the same language. Immediately afterwards, his very important look vanished from his face. She said to the others, "I'm an illusionist too. We just figured out that I am a somewhat more skilled in the arts than he is, much to his dismay." Everyone laughed.

"Rufus, you be careful around those twins there, they are *the* Twins from Freetown," Jennifer playfully chided him. Evidently the fame and skills of the Twins had spread far and wide.

Rufus became very excited, "Are you really *the* Twins, *those* twins? Really?" They nodded. He came and shook each of their hands heartily, "Most pleased to meet you indeed!" And so the conversation took another twisting turn.

It was late afternoon before they broke up. As they were saying their thanks and byes, Mandy mentally sent Jon, *Have you noticed that we did all the talking? We know almost no more about our hosts than we did before we came I here today. Strange.*

Jon sent back, *Now that you mention it, yes. They always seemed to sidestep our questions, if that's the right word.*

As Jon was shaking Jennifer's hand in farewell, he asked off-handedly, "Say Jennifer, don't the bears around here usually hibernate during the winter? We keep seeing bear tracks is why I ask."

Her hand reactively tightened its grip on his hand. Both Jake and Jennifer flushed. It was Jake who replied, "Yes, most of the bears around here are probably hibernating by now. But do be careful, not all of them are."

They are hiding something! Mandy sent Jon as they walked the short distance back to the Old Ruins.

Or perhaps they are just not saying something that is vital. Jon sent back. *I sense both of them are withholding something about bears from us.*

She sent back as they entered the iron doors to the underground chambers, *If we are going to be stuck here all winter, we'd better find out what!* The aroma of freshly baked bread clobbered everyone's nostrils as they entered. "William's been baking!" exclaimed Mandy. "Get ready for some 'real' bread!"

Indeed he had. Ten loaves were cooling and another five were baking and another five lay rising near his commandeered hearth. "Bread for m'Lady?" he proudly asked as she entered. She didn't answer, but rather ran up to him, gave him a hearty hug and a prolonged kiss. "Only a small sample for you all just now; don't want to spoil you appetite for supper, now do we?" he teased the others. Needless to say, one loaf quickly disappeared.

Rufus soon appeared leading his donkey cart or sleigh, since it currently had runners. Mandy watched him wondering how it would slide on the bare stone floors. At the main entrance to the caverns, the gnome stopped and pulled four levers in turn. The snow skids retracted, leaving the wheels touching ground once more. Smiling at the observant ranger, he led his faithful donkey and cart inside. Rufus parked his cart near William's wagon.

Of course, Mandy's immediate comment was, "How does that work anyway, Rufus?" Pleased that one of his inventions had caught her eye, the gnome diligently explained its construction and operation. Mandy's comment was simply, "I wonder if we can put skids on all of our wagons?" She went in search of Raul to discuss the possibility.

Jon now found himself momentarily alone with the gnome; the others were about on errands. Seeing this opportunity, Rufus whispered to him, "You'd best not say anything about bears around the Newcastles. They are sensitive about them." That was all Jon could get out of him; subject closed. Of course, it only confirmed Jon's earlier conclusions.

"Say, you don't mind if I display my wares, my inventions, to your caravan folks, do you? Some of them might be interested in making a small purchase," Rufus politely asked.

"Sure go ahead," Jon smiled. "Just don't make a pest of yourself. I take it you also wanted to sell stuff in Tannersville. I'm not sure if these folks are going to be very interested, but you can give it a try." Delighted, Rufus began with the other wagons in this chamber. Jon grabbed a loaf of William's bread and dashed off for the Newcastle's cottage. His purpose was two-fold. He wanted to make amends for any possible affront or embarrassment which he had earlier caused and he had just thought of a burning question that he wanted to ask Jake.

He knocked on their door. Jake answered, "Back so soon?"

"Present for you and Jennifer — one of William's freshly baked loaves of bread," Jon replied, handing him the loaf. Jennifer had come up behind him and took it instead of Jake. "Williams is Mandy's boyfriend," he added as an afterthought.

"Come on in, if you want," Jake said, as he perceived Jon did not leave once Jennifer had the loaf.

"Thanks, Jake. I did have one question that occurred to me while I was talking to Rufus a moment ago. It's about the origin of these hobgoblin creatures. I've never seen one plus I am not familiar with these lands. Can you make me a sketch of how all these nearby lands fit together? We came from Freetown nearly due east of here. Where's Hoar Frost and these creatures and where's Tannersville? We've only got the vaguest, sketchiest of maps."

"Sure thing," Jake sounded relieved. Jon noticed that for a moment he was on edge; Jon's earlier sudden questions about the bears plainly still bothered him. "We don't have any real maps, but I can sketch the general lay of things. Come on into the kitchen. I'll get something with which to sketch." In the kitchen, Jennifer was cleaning up the dishes from the all of her visitors.

Shortly, Jake entered and laid out a parchment and began drawing and explaining. "Here's Desolation; it goes nearly due north and south. This area here where you are at is also called Hell's Gate because of the sharp, angular, high peaks, through which travel is always difficult. Further north of here, say about a hundred miles or so, the peak elevation begins to drop off, just as it does about two hundred miles to the south of here. Way over here is Freetown and over here is Tannersville," Jake explained. Indeed, Jake had placed Tannersville about one-third the total distance that Freetown was from the Desolation Range and slightly north. "Once out of these mountains, it is an easy week's journey there."

"Now, way up north here lies the region we call the Northern Hoar Frost. It is always very cold up there and the mountains are really only rugged hills. It is a land of misery where few venture. The hobgoblins are the primary denizens of that area which is another reason few go there," Jake continued.

"Oh my goodness!" Jon interrupted him for he suddenly saw a connection, one that he wished with all his heart was not. As Jake drew, he mentally reflected upon Metrarch's maps that he had seen showing the deployment of the various Demon Lords' followers and armies. The lands just to the east of Desolation Range had been labeled 'Lord Jarred's Lands' on the map. There was nothing else on the map all the way up to the Hoar Frost region. "By chance, do you know if the demon Lord Jarred is worshiped in that area?"

"Well, yes," Jake mused, "I think so, along with their hobgoblin goddess as well. Is that important?"

"Jake, Jennifer," Jon began in an apologetic tone, "I am very sorry but I fear that we have brought the doom of Lord Jarred down upon you. It is no accident that the hobgoblins are swarming in masses on the plains where the mountain trail finally leaves Desolation. I'll bet anything that Lord Jarred has ordered them there in an attempt to ambush me and the caravan. At the Council several months ago, I really upset him badly. I'm certain he is seeking revenge on me and my friends. I'm so sorry that your livelihood has inadvertently been impacted by all this. Please forgive me."

"No apologies are needed, Jon," Jennifer said. "You could not have known nor could you really have done anything about it. Traders are always aware of the dangers of long distance travel — robbers, bandits, evil creatures — to say nothing of natural disasters. But I am a bit worried about your safety."

Jake continued that thought, "If you follow Deadman's Pass here on through Desolation and arrive on the plains, then according to Rufus, you must fight your way through thousands of the nasty hobgoblins. However, if you stay here all winter, and you are welcome too, I suspect that eventually the hobgoblin hordes will come marching into these mountains looking for you. Our valley is somewhat defensible, but not from thousands of them. I think we have —"

"A big problem," Jennifer finished the thought. "Tonight, Jake and I will take a little reconnoitering trip and see what is about out there." Expecting a very worried look from her, Jon was surprised to see her eyes were bright with relief. Curious, he thought.

"Thanks, I had better go tell the others of this bad news. Oh wait, one more question, please. Why is it called Deadman's Pass?"

The both laughed and said together, "You don't want to know!" He left it at that. Jon hurriedly took his leave, taking Jake's parchment sketch with him to show the others.

He found Mandy and Raul by William's wagon accompanied by several caravan men whom Jon recognized as blacksmiths. All had a downcast tone. Mandy looked up when Jon arrived and said somberly, "Well, making skids for all the wagons is a possibility. Our blacksmiths can make them. But the bad news is that it will take at least a month to get them all ready to travel. We may be stuck here a long time."

The blacksmiths took their leave. Just as soon as they were out of hearing range, Jon said, "I hate to add to your disappointment, but we've got an even bigger problem coming our way, if we stay!" Quickly, he outlined what he had just learned about the hobgoblins and their likely connection to Lord Jarred.

"Zagroot zounds!" exclaimed Mandy. "I've had about enough of all this. Why cannot I just lead a nice caravan on a nice, safe, road home?" She really looked frustrated.

William had just come up and had heard it all, "Because my love, you'd be incredibly bored on such a trip."

She glared up at him for an instant and then burst out laughing. All of her tension evaporated.

"You are absolutely right, dear! I'd be so bored that I would have to invent some kind of problems." And she laughed until her sides ached.

Alison, Darless, and Thea arrived in time to hear her laughter. "What's this all about?" the demure Mage asked. They had been teaching Thea a dozen magical spells and the apprentice had learned them quite easily. Both Alison and Darless were amazed with Thea's progress. Jon explained the situation once more. And just as he finished, May and Mat arrived and so he had to tell it yet another time.

"Well, now what do we do?" asked May, completely baffled by this new, unexpected turn of events.

"I guess we can always return back to Freetown and try another route," Mat offered. It was the only answer he could imagine.

Ever the practical one, Mandy decided, "Tonight, Jon, you arrange for a dance to help folks relax. For you all, it will help take your mind off of these pressing matters. Sometimes the solution will just pop into your head this way. Tomorrow, we'll see if we have any other ideas besides returning back to Freetown." The others agreed. Everyone then pitched in to help William fix supper for all.

After the dinner dishes were done, Jon went in search of his fellow musicians to arrange the dance. The others set about notifying all of the caravan folks scattered about in these many chambers. May and Mat went to invite the Newcastles, but returned downcast. It was fully dark outside and their new friends were not in their cottage nor anywhere around the grounds.

Jon came back to get his flute and other instruments. One look at the faces of the twins told him the Newcastles were not home, but he asked May about it anyway. For an instant, Jon recalled the unexpected, excited gleam in Jennifer's eyes when she mentioned they would take a reconnoitering trip tonight. He mused on its significance but soon forgot about it as he headed off to direct the musicians.

Indeed, the dance took everyone's mind off of heavier matters. This was more like what life was meant to be; people felt more comfortable and confident with this small measure of normalcy in their lives. And by ten p.m., the dance ended; sleep slowly overcame the best of the dancers. All would get a really good night's sleep tonight.

That is, all except Mandy. Just as Jon was about to turn in, she led him by the hand to a corner. Whispering she said, "I aim to do a little reconnoitering of my own tonight. This bear thing has me both puzzled and worried. I aim to get to the bottom of it."

"Please, don't upset our hosts," countered Jon. "We really need their help; and besides, look at the doom we are potentially bringing down upon their heads with all these hobgoblins running about wreaking havoc."

"I will be very discreet, I promise," and she gave him a hug and kiss. She already had her fur clothes on and was off before Jon could say anything further. She just wanted one of her friends to know what she was up to, just in case something went very wrong.

Jon soon fell soundly asleep. Mandy carefully crept up to the locked gates. This time, she concentrated mentally, using her innate powers to transform her body. A small bat fluttered its wings where she had just stood. The bat flew to the top of the gate and perched itself on one of the pillars supporting the giant hinges. Sure enough, she spied fresh bear tracks leaving the gate. She noted some of these newer prints had overlain those from the night before. The bat grinned and waited patiently, dozing.

Twilight rose pale in the eastern sky as two large black bears ambled slowly up to the gates. The bat's eyes fluttered and opened wide. The bears stood before the gate listening intently to the silence. Confident that the way was clear, they waited as the sky turned pinkish. Mandy watched the bear forms slowly transform back into the nude forms of Jake and Jennifer. Quickly, they dove for their clothes carefully hidden from view. Mandy had missed that detail the night before. Once fully dressed, they looped a thin rope over the door bars, opened the doors, and entered their valley. Using the rope, they lowered the bars that locked the doors, retrieving the rope. After glancing about to make sure no one was about, they hastily headed for their stone cottage. Neither noticed a bat fluttering past them and in through one of the open windows in the ruins. Mandy knew their secret now, but it would have to wait a bit. She was very tired. She snuggled in beside William and fell into a sound sleep.

This morning, Mandy was the last to get up for obvious reasons. When she finally got up and ate, she called the others aside. "I know what the Newcastle's problem or illness rather actually is. All of our help is likely needed. As Jon said last night, we need to be very discreet and careful of their feelings about this. Come on, let's go see what we all can do for them."

Mandy had made her desired effect on her friends. She would say no more about it nor how she had discovered their secret. So once more, around ten, Jon, Alison, May, Mat, Darless and Mandy stood outside the Newcastle's stone cottage knocking on the door. "Come on in," Jake said.

"We were expecting you," Jennifer finished the thought. "We did a little hiking last night and found no trace of any hobgoblins for at least the next twenty miles of trail."

"We also set a few ambushes for the unwary just in case," Jake finished as Jennifer poured a round of tea for everyone. She thoroughly enjoyed the company. This desolate life had a price they had to pay.

"Thanks," replied Mandy. "But that is not why we are here today. Please don't get upset with me but I have discovered what it is that you have been hiding from us." The smiles vanished from both Newcastle's faces; an uneasiness replaced it. "Do you remember that little bat upon the gate post this early morning as you arrived at the gate?" The uneasiness turned into looks of shock. "That was me," Mandy continued. Explaining now for her friend's benefit, Mandy went on, "Yes, two black bears wandered up to the gates, rested a bit and turned into the Newcastles." She did not mention the part about rapidly donning their clothes for Jennifer's sake. "My guess is that you have a disease called lycanthropy, am I not correct?" Mandy finished confident of her conclusion.

Shock turned into fear. "Please don't kill us!" begged a terrified Jennifer.

"We mean you no harm," added Jake, now clutching his sister to protect her in any way he could. His eyes darted from person to person like a caged animal, fearful of their intent.

"We have no such intention of hurting you or telling anyone else about your condition," Mandy answered. "Please come have a seat and tell us your story. How did you get it? How long have you had it?" Now things fell into place. Mandy realized why the Newcastles were living out here in the Old Ruins as hermits. "I hope we can help you," she added as an afterthought.

Timidly, both sat down facing the others; Jake still had an arm around his sister. He would protect her with his life if need be. "It's — it's all my fault," he floundered for words. "Ten years ago, I was out hunting and killed a bear and got a bit cut and scratched up in the process. At that time, we lived in Tannersville. Our parents had passed away and we inherited dad's general store. I fancied myself something of a hunter and had gone off alone on a little trip. It took a week to get back and to get my wounds properly cleaned and healed up. By then, it was too late; I was infected. Around the times of the full moon, at night, I turn into a black bear. At first, I tried to keep it from Jennifer, but nothing is a secret between us. She found out almost at once. She was supportive of me. I'd sneak out of and back into town as the change occurred."

"I kept trying to find a cure," Jennifer continued their story. "In the end, the only answer I could find was that a high priest, if paid sufficiently, could perform such a cure. We tried to save enough money to pay for a cure, really we did. But just as we almost had it paid for, I accidently got scratched by Jake and I came down with it too."

"See it is all my fault," Jake moaned. He'd lived all these years knowing that it was he who had infected his own sister with this terrible disease. "We both knew that there was no way we could ever afford two cures. So we sold our store and used our savings to buy sufficient supplies to be able to survive in the wilderness."

"And we left Tannersville behind forever," Jennifer continued. "We figured Desolation was a good place to hide out. Here we could not infect others and also be left alone to our misery. It was quite by accident that we stumbled onto these ruins."

"This place makes an excellent home for us," Jake picked up their story. "It is out of the way; no one comes here; we can live life, such as it is for us."

"Only Rufus and a few dwarves know of our disease," Jennifer added, "and they have been most understanding and helpful, making our desolate lives a bit better. To make matters worse, you all arrived, six hundred people. We were petrified when the dwarf told us of your coming. But when we heard that you all were freezing to death,"

"Well, we couldn't let that happen," Jake finished her thought. Everyone now started to talk at once, asking for details on this and that, complimenting them on how well they made the best of it all. Mandy had to explain to Jon what the disease was for he had no idea what they were talking about.

Mandy took charge once more. "Okay, now folks, the question is how do we go about curing them. I guess this is mostly in my domain or sort of. I am not a high priestess, but a ranger. However, I do have priestess healing abilities. I think I might be able to perform a cure disease prayer spell on them. Do you all think that would do it?" The next ten minutes were filled with a sharing of information on lycanthrope curing. Alison had run across werewolves once and Father Johnas had healed one small boy using a priestly spell which she assumed was a disease curing one. May and Mat offered to "lay their hands" upon both of them, but Darless pointed out that their gifts from Father Ukko were more for healing wounds, not diseases. Both looked crestfallen.

In the end, it was Jon who found the answer, though not at once. He asked, "May I touch you and probe your bodies mentally to see if I can see what is wrong?" He explained how he, Mandy and Darless could heal damaged cells.

"Does it hurt?" asked Jennifer.

Darless answered, "No, it is more like being totally intimate with another person." A huge smile formed on her face as she recalled the times she and Jon had had such contact. "It is about as close as two people can get to one another."

So Jon placed his hands on Jennifer's arm and sent his awareness, his consciousness into her arm, her body. He made solid contact with her and she him. He felt her grace, her love of life flow into him; both smiled. Then, he made contact with another living organism. Reactively, he let go of her arm and jumped backwards. "Whoa! What was that?" he exclaimed.

"Whatever that was, it was nasty. There is some other life form completely pervading her body!"

Jennifer whispered to Jake, "His touch was almost like what we share, a union. It was beautiful while it lasted."

Darless wondered, "If we all concentrated together, could we not drive this other life form out of their bodies?" And so another round of discussion ensued. Darless, to gain firsthand information, touched Jake. She explained that she was really an alu-demon which took the Newcastles by complete surprise. She was forced to give a fifteen minute summary of her life and travails. "So I do understand your predicament fully; it is somewhat similar to my own fate, though for mine, there is no cure. Do you mind, Jake, if an alu-demon probes your body?"

He didn't and she did. What Jon might find totally repulsive and could not easily confront, she could for Darless, the alu-demon, had seen far worse, the worst the Abyss had to offer. She could confront it. And she did, though Jon did see her face grimace up in revulsion but she did not back off. After fifteen minutes, she broke the connection, commenting, "Jon's right; there is a foreign life force within his body. More discussion followed.

"Can I ask you a question, Mandy?" Jennifer finally interrupted.

She looked up, "Sure anything."

"How can a ranger become a bat? I — we did see you there, but at the time, all I thought was how odd to see a bat sitting on the gate post," she asked timidly, but full of curiosity since Mandy could somehow change her body form, not unlike their disease. "You don't have the disease yourself, do you?"

"No, I'm perfectly healthy," Mandy chuckled, "It is one of my mental abilities that I have always had since I was a little girl. I can change my body's form into just about anything as long as it is no smaller than that rather large bat. I was a bit worried you would realize that the bat was the largest bat you had ever seen. About the largest creature I can change into is a Pegasus, a flying horse — that is my specialty. I love being a Pegasus!" And so the discussion continued for another hour.

Jon got up and stretched and looked around and looked at Jake and Jennifer deep in discussion with the others. He felt rather outside the situation at the moment and so just observed everyone. Suddenly a fact that had not been considered appeared blatantly obvious to him. "Wait a minute, everyone," he called out.

Into the ensuing hush, he said solemnly, "Jennifer, can I have another look? I think that there is something more to all this. I want to see, please?" She nodded her assent and Jon again took hold of Jennifer's hand and concentrated, enveloping all of her this time. Then, for a moment, he was her and she was he. Her eyes opened wide! Jake's eyes did likewise; for he was so intimately connected with his sister, and, thus, now was also Jon, who was also Jake. Satisfied of his observation, Jon moved back out and dropped the contact.

Jennifer's comment said it all, "Are you a god? That was unbelievable; that was *so* intimate!"

Jon blushed, "Yes, I know." Darless, Mandy, and Alison just smiled; they knew exactly how she felt. "Okay, we are indeed missing something significant. I'm not sure how to explain it but bear with me," he smiled, adding, "Pun intended." Everyone chuckled, relieving some tensions.

"Imagine, for a moment, that you just got bit and contracted the disease. In such a case, the correct action would indeed be cure the disease." He paused as they nodded their complete agreement, though none could guess where he was headed. This statement was rather obvious.

"Now consider their situation. They have lived with this transformation into bears for many, many years. It has become a part of their makeup. They have found uses for the transformation; they have used it to their advantage, am I not right, Jake?"

He fumbled briefly but agreed, "Well, yes. You saw that we have no animal traps around and yet we produce all of these winter apparel made from furs. A bear catches many animals rather easily, so to speak."

"And a few times, we used our bear forms to protect our lives from thieves and highwaymen," Jennifer appended. "We have really come to depend a good deal on our bear forms, now that you point it out. It is rather obvious that we have and do at this point. What choice have or had we?"

"None, none at all," Jon agreed. "Do you all see where this is heading? If we suddenly cure them of the disease, we also are robbing them of something that has become a significant part of them as well. For example, Mandy, what would your life be if you could not transform your body into other life forms?"

She grimaced, "It'd be awful. Honestly, I don't know how I do it; and I don't see why others cannot do it. After all many wizards can shape change as they desire; some even make magical potions so anyone could do it. Ah, I see your point, Jon. If we cure their disease, we are also robbing them of what has become a part of themselves. So what do we do?"

Jon suggested, "Well, it has now become more like a curse than a disease. There really is another life force trying to control them which is evil in nature. If we can get rid of the curse, perhaps then they can change into bears when and where they so desire. In other words, let's see if we can get it under their complete control."

"Ah a remove curse — now that we can all do!" Alison stated emphatically. "I can, Darless can, and May can also. How about you, Mandy?"

"Nope, curses are way out of my line; I heal. Sorry," she replied.

May now had visions of being the one who saved Jake and how grateful and indebted he would be to her. She shook her head no. *I want him to want me because I am me, not because of something I did for him.* "I've only recently learned how to cast that spell, so I am certain that Alison or Darless would have the greater chance of success," she volunteered rather meekly.

Jon thought for a moment before he spoke, "I believe my walking stick from Ukko can also remove curses, but I have not yet read my owner's manual on how to do it. So if it is alright with you ladies, I'll keep that as a last resort and go study my manual if your attempt fails. Is that okay with you?" Of course, they all agreed.

Turning to Jennifer and Jake, Jon said, "Okay, then it is up to you. Do you want us to try to remove the curse portion and see if we can then help you with the getting the shape changing thing under your control or should we go for the all-out curing of the disease? It's your call."

"But we don't have the means to repay you for this," protested Jake.

"We could not even afford paying for one of us," Jennifer added. "How could we ever repay you?"

"You already have," Jon replied. "by offering our caravan sanctuary and winter clothes and food in our time of need. We would have all frozen to death out there without you. Further, it is highly likely that by our coming this way, we have brought the doom of the hobgoblins down upon you as well. So it is more like we who owe you both whatever we can do." After a pause, he added glancing at Alison, "Besides, I think that everyone of us here would do it for you just because you need it and for no other reason. What kind of a person would stand by and do nothing to help out another in need when it is a trivial matter for them to come to their assistance? It's not like attempting a cure is going to cost us anything except our pride if we fail."

"Well put, Jon," Alison added, "It is our pleasure to give it a try; you owe us nothing except to continue to help out others in need as you can. So, which will it be, the curse or the cure?"

The two looked at each other. Minutes ago, they were afraid for their lives and now their long sought cure was potentially at hand. Jake was the first to answer; his tone was serious but thoughtful. "So long ago now, we prayed for a cure. But now after living with this curse, dealing with it," he paused.

Jennifer continued; the same lingering doubt in her voice, "It has, as you say, become a part of us, how we live and deal with life. Do you really think that we could control this shape-changing?" She looked directly at Mandy who, always optimistic, nodded affirmative. Her gaze turned to Jon; he was not so optimistic.

"Well, I really am out of my league, so to speak, in such matters. But, if it does not work out for the best, we can then try curing the disease as well. I'll just need a little time to read up on how to make my walking stick do its thing. Shouldn't take very long to figure it out," he tried to sound as hopeful as possible without making a promise he could not keep.

"Then, we should like to try to get rid of the curse, the evil thing that dwells in our bodies," she sighed in relief taking hold of Jake's hand. "What are we to do?"

"Great!" Alison took charge now that their cure was in her hands. "You make a fresh pot of tea while we wizards go prepare our incantations. We should not be more than an hour getting ready. Keep Jon, Mandy, and Mat company." Turning to her friends, she added, "Okay, come on, we've got some spell preparations to make!" She, Darless, and May quickly left the stone cottage and returned to their wagon, discussing their plans along the way.

"This is an awesome thing that you are doing for us, you know," Jennifer commented to Jon as they went about making tea in her kitchen. "Never in a thousand years would I have predicted that total strangers would come to my house and cure us!"

Jon chuckled, "And never in a thousand years would I have predicted that were-creatures even existed. I always thought they were just a figment of someone's over-active imagination. So we are even."

"I'm really getting excited about getting cured," Jennifer confided, "To be normal again, to be able to be around people and just be ourselves without having to hide our dark secret, that's almost too good to be true!"

Jon smiled and then had an idea, "And you know that there is one young man who has taken a fancy to you, you know, he has his eye on you." And just to make sure she understood fully his implications, he hastily added, "And also there is one young lady who has her eye on your brother too." Jon was playing cupid, well at least he wanted to test the waters for the twin's sake.

She blushed, straightened her hair instinctively, and whispered, "Really? I dared not hope for that! Mat's a handsome man and I just know May is right for Jake. But you really think there is hope for us?" She hastily explained, "We've tried to look cold and disinterested to them, you know because of our disease. But if we get cured, you think they will still be interested in us, really?"

Jon whispered, "May was asking me about love at first sight, even. I think they are crazy about you two! But don't tell them I told you so. You four are like four peas in a pod, as we say back home."

A bit later, while they were all relaxing and awaiting the mages' return, Mandy began to query the Newcastles on what they knew about the Old Ruins. Jake told her that the ruins are still pretty much like they found them. They had fixed up this cottage portion substantially, making it more livable. The underground chambers were full of debris and dust. It had taken them a couple years to sweep clean most of the chambers near the entrance. They used them primarily for storage of finished products and for temporary storage of produce. "Two of us cannot handle all the stuff that ripens at nearly the same time, so we store some in the dark, cool chambers until we can get to them," Jake explained.

"How far underground do they go?" Mandy asked out of curiosity.

"Oh, I'd say your people are using about half of the chambers that we have explored," Jennifer replied. "But we've never looked in all of them, no reason to do so." And so they chatted.

Within the hour, the three mages returned, confident and ready. "Now here's what we are going to do," explained Alison. "We want you two to stand beside each other really close to each other. We are going to cast three remove curse spells simultaneously from three directions. Mandy can you first cast your 'bless spell' in this area so it effects all of us? I want to ensure the best possible chance for a good outcome."

"With pleasure," Mandy replied. It took her only a few seconds to perform the holy ritual to Reylona, once she had gotten her holy symbol out.

"Thanks, Mandy. Now I want you and Jon to be very observant of what happens to these evil life forces after we cast the spells. Make sure they depart out of here," Alison explained. The three mages took up their positions forming an equilateral triangle around the Newcastles.

Jon listened to their melodious, unison chanting. Evidently, he noted, they had rehearsed their casting. He smiled as he suddenly grasped Alison's actual plan. May had just learned the spell a short while before and had never actually cast it. On her own, she might have failed. Further, while just Alison's spell alone might have been totally sufficient to remove the curse and drive the evil out of their bodies, by having May involved and working in unison, even if May's did not work, no one would ever know. It was now a team effort and May was part of the team. Alison had arranged matters so that May did something of immense value to the person she had fallen in love with. Romantic indeed, he thought. He felt a surge of pride in Alison, his Alison.

Then the spells went off. Jon perceived a greenish glow encase the twins. It sparkled, and twisted and intertwined their bodies, permeating them. The twin's bodies groaned in an agony but not theirs. Jon watched as two black forms shot upwards out of the twin's heads. Jon caught a glimpse of Mandy's head arcing upwards, following the path on out of the roof. Mandy lowered her eyes and met Jon's who were also lowering. Both nodded to each other. And Mandy spoke, "Yes, that blew them right out the roof! They were blackish in color, some kind of beings, pretty degraded, if you ask me." Jon nodded agreement.

"How do you feel?" asked Alison.

"I — I feel so light, so free," Jennifer began.

"But we cannot find the right words to explain," Jake finished. "We are no longer fighting something continuously. I think it has worked!"

From the corner of his eye, Jon caught a glimpse of May's face. She was beaming, positively radiant! Jon created a mental picture of a huge red rose and placed it inside Alison's head. Suddenly, Alison looked curiously over towards Jon. He smiled and wiggled his eyebrows at her and blew her a kiss. She returned it.

"Okay, now comes the hard part," Mandy took charge once more. "We got to get the shape changing under your control."

Both Jennifer and Jake became embarrassed at the same instant. At once, Mandy realized its cause. They had always been naked when they changed form so that their clothes were not shredded. So Mandy hastily added, "Now the rest of you, outside. Go take a short walk. This is between them and me. If we need anything, I'll give a holler." She watched the redness subside from the twins. The others quickly left, leaving Mandy and the Newcastle twins alone.

Once outside, May and Mat were bubbling with excitement. "Oh I do hope they can master it and finally be themselves and be okay!" blurted May.

"That was a really fine thing you mages did," Jon replied. "I was proud of you three. Yes, I think they are now in the best of hands with Mandy. It'll probably just take some time. Let's go for a stroll." And so they strolled around the snow covered gardens and orchard, noting the compose piles of last year's plants. It had turned out to be a fine day indeed, Jon thought to himself.

Suddenly, Darless called out, "Everyone, get under cover fast. Hide. There are a number of ill birds heading our way. Probably spies of the enemy. Hide!" Indeed, far off in the west, a small flock of dark birds were flying their way, swerving first to the right and then to the left as if in search of something or someone. They were some distance from the stone cabin, no time to get to it. The Old Ruins was even farther away. A small outbuilding was the nearest refuge, so they all dashed to it and hastily entered and shut the door. A distinctive foul odor brought them to attention and Alison quickly created a very dim magical light. They were in a meat drying house. All about them hung carcasses of various animals drying out. "How apropos," Darless muttered.

"How do you know those are spies of Lord Jarred?" whispered May, her voice full of concern.

"I don't really. But the flock is behaving unnaturally. Remember all the ravens that Metrarch's followers had back at the castle? It is a reasonable supposition," the alu-demon announced. "At least they will not see a caravan, if that is what they are looking for."

"Won't all of the smoke rising from the chimneys of the Old Ruins be a give-away?" asked Alison.

"Maybe and maybe not," she replied. "Perhaps they do not know these ruins exist. Perhaps they do not know about the local villages in this area. So we are probably safe for a few more days until they fail to find the caravan on the main trail. We are going to have to do something and soon." Jon did not like the sound of that. He had no ideas whatsoever; he hoped that Mandy would come up with something. She usually did.

A short while later, they heard the sounds of some wild animals sniffing just outside the door of the outbuilding they were inside. Alison opened the door to take a peak and there stood two black bears! As she watched, the bears changed form and became Jennifer and Jake, fully clothed. "We did it!" they cried aloud for joy in unison. Mandy was walking along some distance behind them, rather like a proud mother or teacher whose children had just given a good performance of their lessons.

Everyone hugged everyone else in joy and happiness. Mandy explained that it only took a short while to get the twins used to controlling their change. It was now second nature to them to form into a bear at will. Congratulations flew in all directions.

"But why were you all crammed into the meat house?" Jake finally asked. "We came out looking for you and could not find you. So we changed into bears; as a bear, we have a very keen sense of smell, you see."

"And we tracked you here," Jennifer added.

Darless described the flock of birds that had passed by a short while ago. Fortunately, they were gone by the time Mandy and the twins had come outside in search of the others. This turn of events did put a damper on their celebrations somewhat. However, it is noted here that Jake and May and Mat and Jennifer were left alone by the others for some time. And both Newcastles were very animated, full of life — life had been given back to them.

While the two sets of twins were off together getting closely acquainted, Jon, Alison, Darless and Mandy returned to their wagon in the Old Ruins to confer on what was to be done next.

The results of the conference were less than pleasing to one and all. They were in unfamiliar territory with no detailed maps, though they expected Jake or Jennifer could assist if only they knew what to ask. That Lord Jarred was still after them was highly likely what with the swarm of hobgoblins and the flock of birds. They could not stay here indefinitely; they would be trapped like rats in a cage or worse still like the original makers were in the distant, unrecorded past. Mandy made the only real suggestion that offered the faintest possibility of hope. Perhaps the snows had melted a bit or perhaps the depth of the snow fall had lessened the further along the pass. Thus, they decided to make a small foray on down Deadman's Pass to see for themselves if conditions improved farther they went.

Bundled up against the cold in their new furs, they set out on horseback. Mandy took the lead along with Jake who enjoyed being on horseback after so many years of total abstinence. Jon and Alison followed behind them, then came Darless and May, with Mat and Jennifer bringing up the rear. At the gate, Jake showed them a clever, easy way to open the gates from the inside. They headed back to the main trail, which was reached in short order; the snow had been compacted by the caravan two days before.

At the junction with the main trail, Mandy paused and surveyed the scene. Deep bear tracks and those made by Rufus and his donkey cart were clearly visible heading further westward. The snow was still very deep, nearly up to the horses' bellies which made the going slow and awkward. An hour later they had gone perhaps another five miles, climbing, twisting ever upwards. The panting horses had to be rested. The late afternoon sun hung ominously above the distant peaks, a warning that darkness came early in this country. They dismounted and spread out. To the south a small stream babbled noisily from the slowly melting snows.

Alison and Darless trudged up the narrow valley for a closer look. It was strenuous; the snow was still three feet deep. The view, however, was spectacular. Neither had been in the high country in wintertime and they decided to make the most of it.

Mandy and Jon took care of the horses, while the two sets of love-struck twins chatted gaily. Jake and Jennifer pointed out distant sights while May and Mat took it all in; they had never seen snow or been in the high country before and they made an eager, attentive, appreciative audience.

On the other hand, Mandy glared at the snow; she was in an ill humor. Obviously the situation was not improving. Suddenly, the hair on her neck prickled. *Jon, someone is spying on us. I can sense it,* she mentally sent to him. Slowly, without calling attention to herself, she pulled out her short bow from its case upon her saddle and notched an arrow, all the while keeping the bow hidden from view behind her horse.

Jake and Jennifer both stopped mid-sentence; they also had developed keen senses as bears. "You three stay here and act like nothing is going on; I'm going to warn Mandy and Jon," whispered Jake. He knew Jennifer had also detected the presence. He slowly ambled over to Jon and Mandy and arrived just as she had an arrow notched. He pretended to pet the horse.

"We are being followed by someone in that direction," Jake nodded back the way they had come. "It's the same person we smelled last night. We tried to find him, but could never see him. We never forget a smell. It was like he was invisible or something. Odd."

"Yes, I know we are being watched," the ranger whispered back. "The hairs on my neck never lie. Be on your guard. I suspect treachery." Of course, Jon would have said "but you always expect treachery" but there was no time. For at that instant several things occurred simultaneously.

A man, ill-clad for this weather, suddenly became visible as he fired a heavy crossbow aimed straight at Jon's head. He was about fifty feet from them. In a split second, the quarrel would skewer Jon's forehead. Jake defensively ducked as did Mandy. Even so, had they been the target, both would have been hit. Jon, on the other hand, having learned how to dodge Morrigan's spears of death, attempted to do the same thing here. He stepped forward. However, the distance was so close and the time interval so short, he was not entirely successful. The quarrel grazed his forehead and thunked noisily into a stunted oak tree trunk behind him.

Before the attacker could retreat or disappear once more, Mandy rose up and let fly an arrow. The man saw it coming and cleverly knocked it out of harm's way, much as Mat had done in the battle with the Vyndocians. However, it was Darless who scored the direct hit. She had seen Jake move over to Mandy's side, saw Mandy armed with her bow, knew something terrible was amiss, and prepared her spell in advance. In the same instant as Jon moved forward and Mandy returned fire, she let loose her wrath, a disintegrate spell. As Mandy, Jake and Jon watched him dodge her arrow, they saw an energy beam fly beside them and a neat one inch hole appear in their opponent's forehead. Light shown briefly through the opening. The man slowly collapsed onto the ground. The total time of the encounter was two seconds.

Immediately everyone began yelling at once and heading toward the man, on the lookout for others. But they saw no others. As Jon moved forward, blood and something blackish dripped down his forehead. "Looks like I was not fast enough this time. I got hit," he said, but a strange wooziness came over him. He staggered and swayed. "Something —

something — I don't feel so well." He felt his legs melt like butter and watched in slow motion as the soft, white snow came rapidly up to his face. Then it was dark, but he could hear distant voices talking above him.

Mandy was the first to reach his side. "He's been poisoned!" she screamed aloud. Quickly she ministered first aid. It was only a scratch, but the quarrel had been dipped in a fast acting poison so that only a scratch was needed to bring on death! She knew she had to hurry and fumbled for her holy symbol of Reylona hung inside her fur clothing. Ripping it out, she began chanting a prayer to her goddess. Alison and the others gathered around her, as she knelt beside the semi-conscious Jon. Alison put on a brave face; she knew that Mandy knew what she was doing and motioned for the others to be quiet. After about a minute's prayer, Mandy still holding her holy symbol in one hand, placed her other hand on Jon's forehead and spoke her prayer's command. Jon moaned and relaxed. The blackness in his head slowly dissolved; sunlight appeared once more.

"Oh my head. What happened?" he muttered, trying to sit up. "It was only a scratch."

"Poison quarrel," Mandy replied, putting her holy symbol safely back against her bosom once more. "You had a lucky call there. Another few minutes and your body would have died. Strong poison, fast acting too. Let's see that quarrel," and she walked back to the tree. "Yes, it is dripping still. Everyone, do not touch it! Oh yes," she added, "very nice shot Darless." The alu-demon grinned.

"Who is or was he anyway?" asked Alison. "Why would he be trying to kill Jon?" That was the question everyone had, including Jon, who mumbled "I'm only a musician" once more to deaf ears.

"Number 1, he was invisible," replied Darless. "Number 2, he was following us. Number 3, he uses poison and attacks sneakily. Number 4, he easily dodged Mandy's arrow. Number 5, my guess is that he is another assassin."

"In that case, we need to be extra careful when examining what remains of him," Mandy ordered.

"Absolutely," Mat added. "You all stay here; this is a job for May and myself. Keep a lookout for any others that might be with him." No one argued with his request, for they all knew firsthand just how dangerous handling the possessions of an assassin could be. Memories of the attempt on Metrarch's life came unbidden into their minds.

The twins trudged through the snow up to the fallen man. Using extreme caution, they began systematically examining him and his gear. Beside him in the snow was a half empty vial containing more of the black liquid. The others watched the Twins perform a very careful, yet thorough search. In about a half hour, May came trudging back holding a scrap of paper.

"We found the usual traveling gear; he's alone and on foot carrying a good deal of rations. He has the usual weapons one would expect to see an adventurer carry and several vials of liquids and a couple rings. But we did find this," she held out a small piece of parchment. "We cannot read it. Perhaps it is significant. Can any of you read it?" She passed it to Darless who looked and shook her head passing it on to the others. It was in a strange language she had never seen. None had, for that matter.

"Well, I hate not knowing what it says," Alison declared, stamping her foot into the snow defiantly. "Let's see, I should be able figure this one out." She chanted for a minute and cast a spell onto the parchment and herself. She read aloud.

Sigmund,

Confirmation. One dead Saint Jon Brown — two hundred thousand gold coins.

Jarred

"That's all it says, gang. Lord Jarred strikes again. Now he is using assassins!"

"Doesn't he ever give up?" protested Jon a bit dismayed.

"Jeesh , you are worth a lot of money," teased Darless. Everyone laughed as tensions eased.

Jake rejoined them. "What should we do with his body? He has a lot of dangerous items on his person. Should we bury him?"

"Ah, wait a minute," Darless interjected. "Number 6, he is from the assassins. Number 7, undoubtedly, his passage and activities are being monitored by who knows who. Number 8, if we bury him or loot him, the observers are going to know that we got him instead. Thus, Number 9, they will know that he was on to us, caught up with us and so on. Number 10, as soon as they see that hole in his head, they are going to know all about this encounter; it's a dead giveaway. Pardon the pun!"

"What if it looked like he died of 'natural' causes?" ventured Jennifer. "Wouldn't that tend to throw them off the scent? Or at least delay them?"

"Absolutely," replied the alu-demon who liked the idea. "But how do we disguise that hole in his head. One look and any wizard will know he was hit with a disintegrate beam."

"Leave that to us," grinned Jake. "Come on sis, let's do our thing." Before their eyes, the twins slowly shape-changed. Two large black bears appeared where the twins had stood. Together they lopped lazily over the snow up to the fallen assassin. The larger bear, Jake, opened his huge mouth and closed it violently over the dead man's head, crushing it and mashing it. Jennifer made long sweeping tear marks across the dead man's chest. Both then trampled the area sufficiently and tore up some of the surrounding ground for good measure. Satisfied, they loped back covering up all traces of human footprints and resumed their human forms once more. "How's that?" Jake proudly asked, though from the amazed looks, he need not have asked.

"Perfect!" Darless commented. "Just perfect! Remind me never to tangle with bears!"

Jennifer smiled meekly, "Bears are at the top of the food chain out here in the wild, but it is going to be dark very soon now. We had better head back at once."

They returned back to the relative safety of the Old Ruins arriving in time for supper though well after dark. They were tired, concerned, and defeated. There was really no hope in trying to move the caravan down the main trail through the mountains.

They found William had the dinner table already laid and was keeping dinner warm awaiting their return. Rufus was with him and helping out. The gnome was even more loquacious than normal. While they were eating, he said to Jon, "I am forever in your debt for letting me demonstrate my inventions to your people. I have now sold the entire lot! So I do not have to make the journey to Tannersville after all. My purse is heavy for the winter! Thank you. Thank you."

"My pleasure," Jon grinned, he could not help himself. Rufus had that personality that defied any other reaction.

"Would you permit me one small question, though" he asked. Without waiting for permission, which was his trademark, he went right on, "Why are you all so downcast? So somber? It has been a beautiful winter's day. And there is no snow in the immediate future, well at least not tonight anyway," he added hastily. "I've consulted my weather-o-meter; it dips when stormy weather approaches, you know."

Jon explained their plight. They had to get out of the mountains and down to the plains and probably into or around Tannersville to get home, that they were essentially trapped here, that the hobgoblins were really lying in wait to ambush them, and that assassins were also on their trail. Jon sighed, "You see, we are rapidly running out of options."

The gnome pulled his beard in thought, his eyes twinkling with excitement. "Let me see if I understand you right. You want a way to easily get all these folks and their wagons safely to the plains below and unseen by anyone or anything. Am I right?"

"That would be ideal!" Mandy interjected before Jon could reply. She'd been listening to the gnome's conversation. "But it is not possible, as far as I can see," she added somberly.

Rufus grinned from ear to ear, "All right then. I have a deal for you. You purchase my weather-o-meter device and I will show you a way you can reach the plains below without anyone seeing you. It'll probably take you several days of traveling, mind you. But absolutely secret it is." Now he had everyone's full attention, including the Newcastles.

"Rufus!" scolded Jennifer, "None of your tricks now; these people are serious."

He feigned taking offense at her words, "When have I tricked anyone?" He added hastily, thinking better of it, "No, don't answer that. I am serious. Even you don't know about my secret way. Do we have a deal?" he asked Jon.

"Okay, okay. How much do you want for your weather-o-meter?" Jon asked, expecting an exorbitant sum.

"About ten gold pieces will do nicely," Rufus replied eagerly. "It's got some rather expensive parts in it. Liquid silver, for one thing. Here, I'll fetch it for you." He went to his wagon and shortly returned with a small hand-held device, proudly displaying it to Jon. The gnome then spent ten minutes instructing Jon it its operation and care.

Suddenly, Jon realized what it was. "It's a barometer, that's what it is, Rufus. You've invented a barometer. I know how they work. An engineering friend of mine back home once went on at length about how they work. Monitors barometric pressure." Jon soon found out that he should have kept his observation to himself. For Rufus proceeded to ply him with endless questions about barometers for the next hour! There was no shutting him up until Alison, totally frustrated with the conversation suddenly plopped a small pouch with the twenty gold coins in it on the table beside the gnome. That shut him up; he grabbed it and counted the coins silently.

"Okay, now that you have our funds," Alison took advantage of the moment of silence and quickly changed the topic, "how about telling us just how you plan to get us out of here?"

Drawing himself up to his full height, he declared, "I, like the Newcastles, make use of what I can find. I make my dwelling in another of these old ruins, as they know, about ten miles from here. It is a much smaller place, probably a guard post or outpost. But what no one but me knows is that there is an natural underground passage way leading from my rear storage room all the way down to the plains. It comes out about ten miles north of where the main trail comes out. And no one but me knows about it. It is big enough for the wagons; I know, I've taken my cart through it any number of times, especially in bad weather. See?" he smirked at Jennifer, remembering her rebuke.

"Wait a minute, Rufus," Alison interrupted. "If we take the caravan to your place, we will be putting you in imminent danger from the hobgoblin horde. Just as soon as the evil birds spot the trail and us, they will swarm down upon you."

"Not if we go the back way to my place and go during a snow storm. That will hide all traces of your passage!" Rufus beamed with his own cleverness; after all he was the master inventor.

"Brilliant!" exclaimed Mandy. "Rufus, you have just saved us all! Now all we need to know is when is it going to snow again."

Rufus laughed once more, "Jon can now tell us." He pointed to Jon's newly acquired weather-o-meter. Everyone roared with laughter, including Rufus. This gnome had a mind of a genius, Jon thought. For the next half hour, everyone talked of just how to carry out the move. In a lull in the conversation, Rufus quietly asked, "Will Jen and Jake be going away with you?" A note of sadness could be discerned in his voice. "I will miss my dear friends, that I will."

Jennifer and Jake flushed and did not know what to say or how to reply. They had not been asked to come with the others although they were now hopelessly in love with the d'Ambrose twins. Nothing had been vocalized. It was an awkward moment for all, until May spoke out.

Looking right at Jake, May proclaimed, "Mat and I have been looking for you two all of our lives! Now that we have found you two,"

"There's no way we are going to let you two go!" finished Mat. "You are welcome to come with us. Indeed, Jennifer," Mat got quickly down on one knee at her side, "will you marry me?"

Not to be outdone, Jake dashed to May's side, got down on one knee and added, "Only if you, May will marry me!" The other two chorused in unison "Yes, of course!" Instantly everyone was congratulating the two sets of twins. Alison and Darless had to keep wiping the tears of joy trickling down their faces. Jon hugged Alison and found his eyes were wet as well.

Mandy just gave William a long loving kiss. Quietly, she whispered to him, "How about it, handsome, will you marry me, knowing that I am a Ranger first and foremost, with all my faults and preoccupations?"

He kissed her back and whispered back to her, "Do you have to ask? Of course, My Lady. But are you *sure* you will be happy with just a humble baker for a husband? I'm no fighter; never will be. I just want to bake."

Kissing him back, she whispered, "Of course, dear, or I would not have asked. Shall we announce it?" He bashfully nodded.

"Ahem," William cleared his throat. "I have another announcement to make if you will all be quiet just a bit." A hush fell at once. "Mandy and I are also going to be married, though what she sees in a humble baker I do not know. But I'm the proudest man alive and the luckiest!" Once more congratulations flew right and left. Alison and Darless found that their shirt sleeves were really soaked in tears, Jon sheepishly also had a very damp sleeve.

When the celebration died down a bit, Darless spoke up, "Hey, I have a great idea." With everyone's full attention, she offered, "Why don't we all get married together in one big celebration in the spring when the flowers return? It would be spectacular indeed!" Suddenly, she realized her gaff. By her phrasing, she had accidentally included herself in the wedding party.

Jon saw the alu-demon's instant blush. He knew that Darless seldom, if ever, blushed. Very little embarrassed Darless due to her unfortunate childhood and upbringing. Quickly, he replayed her speech in his mind and picked up her goof. He remembered just how much Darless had wanted a man to marry for so long. Still, he couldn't resist teasing her just a bit, so he mentally placed into her mind, *So who's the luck fellow you have picked out?* She blushed even more, but fortunately, everyone was commenting on what a terrific idea that was, no one else detected her goof but Jon and he had the kindness not to voice it aloud.

She teased back, *You'll never know!*

But in that instant, trying to withhold whom she had come to love from Jon, he caught a fleeting image of the silver clad man and Jon recognized him. He smiled and said nothing. He fully understood her plight now, her unfortunate situation. He sent back, *It's better to have loved than never to have felt it.*

Jon detected a little sigh as she sent back, *Yes, I know that now, but it still hurts. Thanks for not saying anything.*

And so the evening passed with blissful plans of weddings and springtime echoing off of the bare stone walls of the chamber underground. What a day of contrasts, Jon noted to himself and found himself wondering when it would snow again.

Chapter 22 Plight on the Plains

Billowing clouds announced the arrival of the next day. Jon's weather-o-meter was falling, a winter storm was coming. Hastily, the two sets of twins spent the day going through their belongings deciding what to take and what to give away and what to leave behind. William's wagon had ample room for much of their more valuable items. Some of their equipment, such as gardening tools and sewing gear was stowed in several other wagons which yet had plenty of space available.

Mandy and Raul took the time to personally inspect every wagon in the party guaranteeing that all was in good repair, that the occupants had plenty of rations and water, and that each wagon carried either some firewood or coal for campfires. Notable was the fact that not one wagon was found low on coal; these travelers had spent their time wisely mining the coal, laying in a good supply for their journey ahead.

Following Mandy's orders, Jon led a party of strong men to cut down a fair number of pine trees and make a large number of torches. They would be traveling underground for several days, and Mandy wanted every wagon to have some form of emergency lighting available. By the end of the day, the work party had delivered several torches to each of the wagons.

The one commodity the caravan sorely lacked was lantern oil. Lanterns were the favorite means of nighttime illumination. The mages devised their own scheme to provide light. Alison, Darless, and Thea went down to the small stream that ran through the middle of the valley and collected two hundred small stones. They spent the remainder of the day casting light spells onto them. In the evening, they affixed the light emitting stones to the top of torches to serve as wagon lights. True, Alison figured they needed at least another hundred or more for everyone to have one, but it was a start anyway.

At dinner, Jennifer, looking exhausted, commented, "I never realized just how much junk one accumulates over time!" They had had quite a time deciding what to do with everything. In the end, they followed Rufus' advice. They left what they did not want in the stone cottage so if anyone came by, the cottage would look mostly inhabited.

While they were relaxing with their after-dinner tea, Rufus came inside excitedly announcing, "It's starting to snow. Tonight's the night. How soon can we leave?" He wasted no time getting to the point.

By seven in the evening, the caravan began to roll once more. This time, Rufus and Mandy led the way, heading on up the Newcastle's valley opposite the entrance gates. Here the snow was not so deep and progress was relatively swift for some time. Near the head of the valley, Rufus veered off to the left following a narrow tract on the windward side of the valley. Here the winds had blown most of the earlier snowfall away. However, the snowflakes now began to fall much harder, making visibility poor in the dim light provided by the light stones that the wizards had made. So Mandy called upon her skills and prayed for a delay in the storm's intensity. Her goddess answered her prayers and the snow fall dwindled.

Along this narrow, winding trail, progress was intentionally slow. Mandy feared for the safety of the wagons over such terrain. She spread the guards out along the more difficult passages so they could provide guidance to the drivers. When the finally reached the crest, they discovered deep snow on the downward side and progress became painfully slow once more as paths had to be trampled down to allow the wagons to pass. It promised to be a very long night indeed. And it was.

Fortunately, Rufus's underground home, another set of ancient ruins, was only four miles further down. Yet it took six hours to get from the crest to his home. By day, his ruins might have been spectacular, a stone guard outpost chiseled into the very mountain side. But by night, the weary travelers barely noted it. One wagon followed the next right on inside Rufus's entrance, past his living quarters and on through his laboratory and right through his secret door that opened up into a vast underground, natural cavern. In this portion, Rufus had installed many oil lanterns. He often came here to work on his inventions or to test them. So while it was indeed underground, the lighting offered a sense of cheer to the travelers as they pulled in and made a close camp about a quarter of a mile within his caverns.

Just outside the gnome's doorway, Mandy stood silently watching each wagon as it lumbered up and moved on inside. She was waiting for the last wagon to get inside to safety. Rufus joined her and together they watched the last ten wagons roll by. "Finally," muttered a very tired Mandy. And she began her prayers once more. Within minutes, the blizzard began in earnest. So strong were the winds and so heavy the snow, one could not see two feet in front of oneself. She was glad they did not have to be out in it.

"That ought to hide all traces," Rufus proclaimed. "You are a mighty wizard yourself, Mandy Blackthorn."

"No," she corrected him, "not much of a wizard. But my goddess does answer my prayers. It is she who is helping out with the weather tonight, my good gnome. Let's get inside. I'm freezing just looking at it snow out there!" They went back inside. Rufus then unhitched his cart but led his donkey on inside the underground caverns. Once they were inside, he pulled a pair of levers and his mechanical walls silently slid shut. Anyone who visited his home, his ruins, would only see what appeared to be a rock wall. By the time they had gotten to the head of the caravan, Raul had most of the lights covered. Only a dim illumination remained. No one needed a second order to get some sleep that night.

The blizzard raged in its full fury all the next day blasting pounding snow against unyielding rock and gnarled trees, their branches forced back from the fury. But deep underground, the sleeping party was aware only of a deep silence and darkness. Only the occasional sounds of milling horses broke the stillness. And it was cool; the temperature was a constant chill. The caravan folks, glad for the warm fur clothing, snuggled with their family members and friends in the wagons. No guards were needed.

Mandy rose refreshed though she knew not whether it was day or night. As far as she was concerned, in here it did not really matter. She was awake and hungry, so it was time to rise. She lit some of Rufus's lanterns and undid some of the covers of the light stones the wizards had conjured, spreading a dim morning aura to the chamber. Soon others were rising as well. Due to the confined space, they dared not risk numerable campfires for cooking. So leftovers had to do.

While the others ate and prepared for the day's drive, Mandy had a look ahead at where they were headed. Jon, feeling a bit bored with no chores to do, joined her. They were in a large natural cavern but here and there, someone had mined or excavated narrow ways allowing passage of even the largest of their wagons. However, the ceiling was irregular and of insufficient height to allow for the riding of horses. So it would be a long walk for those not in the wagons. The floor, while also uneven, sloped gradually downward. Small stones littered the floor. The larger boulders had been moved off to the sides. The signs of contact with men were quite visible even to the untrained eye.

"There are occasional pools," said the gnome who had ambled up behind them totally silently. Both whirled around, startled by his voice. He ignored that and continued, "So water will not be a problem. I usually camp around a pool when I use this way."

"Are we likely to encounter any dangerous creatures?" queried Mandy thinking about all the possibilities.

"Nope. Not even rats. Some spiders though," came the quiet reply from Rufus.

"Say, how about veins of gold and silver," Jon suddenly asked, thinking of mines, "Or gems even?"

"Well, yes," he said haltingly, choosing his words carefully. "If you know where to look, you can find some traces of precious metals. I don't believe there is sufficient quantity to actually work this as a mine, though. But I have gotten a bit of gold for some of my inventions, when that is needed. Gems are a little out of my line. I do have a cousin who is a gems-smith, though. I've never really been interested in them. You cannot make much with them except pretty baubles for which I have no use."

Jon realized that Rufus would continue talking, so he said, "Very good, Rufus. I understand."

For once, the gnome looked at him, ceased talking, and smiled. He, Rufus, had actually been heard. From this point forward, the gnome took a particular liking to this human man, though he knew not why.

Then they were off on their journey once more. Mandy and Rufus led the way, followed by the rest of their party, each leading two horses. William followed with their wagon. For safety's sake, Mandy and Raul spread the twenty-five guards out uniformly amongst the wagons, mostly to help out as needed. Alison, Darless, and Thea spent the first few hours riding in the wagon preparing more of the stone lights. They created another fifty between them. And Thea proudly walked back down the long line of wagons, handing them out.

Now their progress was slow primarily because of the dim illumination. Mandy was unfamiliar with the route and decided to err on the side of caution. Besides, many had to walk and so it was a walking pace that she set. Within a few hours, the novelty of the cavern or tunnel wore off, and Jon found himself bored once more as did many others. To break the monotony, he began to collect pretty rocks that he passed by or saw off to the sides. Soon others began doing the same.

The only noteworthy event occurred about five hours into the day's march. From somewhere behind them, a commotion arose, forcing a temporary halt to the column. Mandy and the others rushed back to see what the trouble was. She feared the worst, a wagon had broken a wheel or a horse had stumbled and broken a leg. Instead, they found a throng of people scouring the floor picking up and discarding stones. "What's all the commotion about?" asked Mandy, a bit irked at the situation. "Master Smyth has found a gemstone" someone ventured to say. Indeed, many were looking all about for more, bringing possible stones back to the gems-smith for his appraisal. Already, ten gems had been located which was causing quite a stir.

To bring order, Mandy yelled, "Okay, everyone. We don't stop. We must keep moving; we've a very long way to go underground. So keep moving. Those that want to look for gems, okay, but please just collect them and put them in a bag. Bring them to Master Smyth tonight when we stop for dinner. Don't hold up the caravan. That's an order!" And so the column began moving once more, but at least fifty people scampered about continuing their search. As she headed back to the front, she wondered how soon these seekers would decide that they needed to be in the very front to get first looks at the rocks. "Zagroot zounds," she muttered to herself.

The rest of the day was wholly uneventful. When Mandy felt tired, she called a halt as they entered a particularly large chamber area in which outside water trickled into a small pool at its center. The water was clear and cold, but had a definite mineral taste. While not the best drinking water, it would suffice.

Here the ceiling rose to some thirty feet above them, so she decided to risk making campfires and a hot meal. The familiarity of a warm fire and the mundane task of dinner did much to ease the concerns of many about being so far underground.

When Master Smyth turned in for the night, he had verified the finding of several hundred gemstones. Most were of small value, but several, when cut might be worth as much as a hundred gold pieces. As word of this spread among the caravan folks, it did much to raise their spirits and desire to travel onwards in search of more. Some described it as finding money just lying on the ground. At least it kept their interest off of other matters, and for that Mandy was grateful. Inwardly, she worried what might happen if someone became claustrophobic and caused a panic. But then it was her job to worry about such things.

Little else can be said of their five day journey underground, though no day ever came here. Jon had indeed found several gems but soon became bored with that game. He could not remember ever being so bored. If only they had really good lighting, then the scenery might be interesting for a time. He decided he really did not like living underground.

It was actually late afternoon of the fifth day of travel when Mandy first saw a faint light ahead of them. As she walked along, it grew progressively brighter and larger. They neared the exit of the tunnel complex. Rufus was right. There were no real side passages along the way that were longer than a few hundred feet. It would have been impossible to get lost.

The exit was cleverly concealed in a narrow twisting canyon that led out onto the plains. The area for miles around was desolate; no villages or hamlets or farmsteads could be seen for miles. However, if Rufus's account was correct, then there were thousands of hobgoblins scattered over the plains before them. Due to the lateness of the day, Mandy decided it was best to camp within the tunnel yet another night and make their run across the plains at first light.

Therefore, over supper, she conducted a war council to plan how best to face the next days battle which surely must come. Much depended upon where the masses of the vile creatures were located in relation to their proposed path across the plains. If they had any luck, they would be far from them and actually escape without any confrontation at all. If they had the worst luck, they would run smack into the main mass of hobgoblins and would be easily outnumbered ten to one. With such a wide spectrum of possibilities, making a solid battle plan was indeed difficult.

Few had ever seen a hobgoblin. So Mandy described them this way, "They are taller than men and stronger and heavier, but they cannot run as fast as we can. We may be able to outrun them, especially with horses. However, the slow moving wagons are another story. They are tribal in nature, highly organized, especially in combat. Many wear bits of leather armor into combat, but they are as easy to kill as an ordinary man. That gives us a chance. They have various group leaders, just as we do, but more importantly, they follow orders at all times. They will be difficult to route. If they attack in numbers as I suspect they may, the hobgoblins will not be a push over. Oh yes, they love to dine on human flesh; expect no mercy from them. They are altogether evil creatures. I hate them. And one final caution, I tend to go berserk when doing battle with hobgoblins. One of you might have to assume temporary command if I do."

It was a sobering speech and silence followed her last words. Still digesting her summary, an idea formed in Jon's mind, "Mandy, are they subject to illusions? You know, like those May launched upon the Vyndocian cavalry and that I expanded. Could we try something like that?"

Mandy didn't hesitate, "They sure can be. May and you can provide close-in wagon protection. If they actually get near the moving wagons, you two let loose what you can to drive them off. The last thing we want is to have the entire caravan halted; we'd be sitting ducks in that case."

"You are going to need more than just two protecting the flanks," Alison observed. "I'll get Thea setup with magical wands; she will be able to do a good deal of damage to any that close to the wagons. I'd like to keep Darless and me freed up so we can best use our powerful, wide area spells and help out wherever needed. Also, let's position Mat and the Newcastles in their bear forms near the center of the caravan as well. That would make six strong counter measures if we cannot hold them off."

"Right, Raul, you and your guards will ride point in a V-shape, cutting a passage through any hobgoblin lines for the wagons that follow. I think we should position the wagons at least six abreast and in close formation — any more and it will be hard to move rapidly from side to side if we need to in a pinch," Mandy added.

"What about using the Force Walls tactic once more?" Darless tossed out for discussion. "We could affix them to the sides of wagons to provide a barrier wall. We could not cast enough to cover the entire flanks, but certainly those near the front. The only real problem is that we would have to cast them tonight so that we could be fully armed with offensive spells tomorrow. I'd hate to not have access to all of my more powerful spells during the combat."

After some discussion, that idea was tabled. The Force Walls would have to be cast here inside the tunnel and of necessity would have their height severely restricted. Plus the organization problems of getting the right wagons into the right positions once they moved out of the tunnel in the daylight would slow them down. It was assumed that speed was paramount once they became visible upon the plains.

Raul also had an idea. "Since we need to get the wagons into formation just as fast as possible and since right now they are strung out in a line nearly a mile long, I've thought of a way to maintain some forward progress and still get them in positions. I'll go down the line tonight, giving each wagon a number, from one to six, counting as I go. Then, I tell them that just as soon as they exit the tunnel, they are to race with all possible speed into the growing formation ahead of them. One's are on the left, six on the far right. As long as the lead wagons go at a walk pace, the others should be able to move into their positions rapidly. Once the last wagon has reached its position, then the whole caravan can move out as fast as we dare. One of my guards can follow the last one out and ride swiftly to the front to let us know when to launch into high gear."

"Terrific!" Mandy complimented him, as did the others.

Jon had one final question that lingered in his mind. "Say, what about the three hundred or so war horses we now have? Are they going to be hitched up to the wagons as they were in the snow fields or are they going to be led as they are now in the tunnel? I ask, because perhaps I can control them and use them to attack those that get too close to the wagons." This led to a good deal of discussion. In the end, they made the decision to hitch them to the wagons for extra pulling power and thus extra speed over a longer distance. None could predict how far they would have to travel to leave the hobgoblins behind and reach relative safety. It was at least two hundred miles to the edge of Alison's known world ahead, the safe area of Banner's Tower.

They broke up into smaller groups to prepare themselves for the coming day. Jon had very little to do, so he wandered amongst those who were making their preparations. He watched as Mandy gave her stallion a good rub down, closely inspected each hoof, and fed him a little extra. "I think I shall opt for a little armor in this battle," she muttered mostly to herself. Jon watched as she rummaged about in her portable hole, throwing out various bits and pieces. She saw that Jon and William were watching her every move. "Okay guys, I'm going to don a light chain mail top. No peaking." She took off most of her outer clothes, slipping the clinking chain mail over her head onto her chest. She tied her belt around her waist thereby affixing the mail into place. "It's a bit heavy and confining, guys, but since I may go berserk, I don't want to worry too much about taking weapon hits."

"Well, I've just the thing for that!" Alison's voice surprised them. She had just walked up and had overheard that last. "I've got a special spell I'm going to cast upon you which will totally nullify about the first dozen blows you take before it wears off. That should give you a bit of an edge at the onset."

"Wow! That's cool," Mandy exclaimed. "Is that one of the new spells you've acquired?"

"Yes, but it is a really high level spell, so I can only do a limited number of people. I'm doing you, Darless, and myself.

That way, we wizards will not initially be troubled by surprise attacks and can concentrate on protecting the caravan," she explained. "Now hold still a minute." And she began chanting her spell. Jon loved the alto sound of her voice speaking the unknown words. It was almost like music.

When she finished, she touched Mandy who felt a little energy flow over her body. "Say, how soon does it wear off?" she asked.

Alison grinned, "The thirteenth blow that hits you will indeed hit you. You are now rather like a cat with twelve lives," she jested. Everyone laughed and Alison went back to her group of wizards to continue their preparations.

Mandy next fastened some armor pieces to her upper arms, her forearms and her thighs. She walked about testing her flexibility and the fit and adjusted several. Finally, she put her fur coat and hat back on to stay warm until the battle. Next, she fastened two quivers of arrows to her saddle, tied a long pointed knife to each leg. Finally, she strapped two bastard swords in their sheaths across her back and tested their pull. She could pull with either hand. Satisfied, she said, "Okay, I'm ready. Let's go get some tea." Jon and William smiled. Each took one of her arms and together they strolled off to get some.

While they were sipping, an excited Rufus joined them. "You'll never guess what May has done for me nor what Alison had given me!" He paused for dramatic effect and continued talking just as fast as he could. "May said that after the caravan leaves the tunnel, your trail will lead a blind man back to my secret way here. So she has cast a permanent spell over the entrance. It now looks like the rest of the side of the foothills here! Amazing. She said it will not ever go away. Alison has given me a scroll spell to cast once you are all about a mile way. She says it will create a huge gust of wind that will obliterate all of your tracks for quite some distance. That would make it double hard for anyone to then track back and find my entrance. Now isn't that just super ingenious?" He finally had to pause for breath.

After agreeing with him and shaking his hand, they four headed for the entrance. From inside it looked no different, but when they stepped outside into the night and looked back, they saw only more hillside. The tunnel had vanished. It took some nerve to walk through what appeared to be ground to regain entrance to the tunnel. They were most impressed indeed. They found Alison waiting for them. "You like it?" she teased. "May's idea was positively brilliant, don't you think?" This, of course, led to quite a discussion about the illusion. And then it was time to sleep, if one could, here on the verge of a battle.

Mandy had everyone roused in the twilight before dawn. They had an hour to eat a light breakfast and make their final preparations. Alison, Darless, May, and Mat donned their white tunics with the huge blue cross, symbols of the Holy Paladins of Ukko. Jon gave Alison a loving kiss as she mounted and prepared to leave. She would be at the very point with Darless and Mandy and Raul, while he had to stay well back with the wagons, providing whatever assistance he could for the caravan folks and for his other friends. He carried his trusty walking stick in his right hand so that it was always at the ready to save a life. With a simple "Giddy up" from Mandy, the large party began to move out of the underground tunnel and out onto the reddish plains now covered with a light dusting of snow. Mandy was glad that the heavy snows stayed up high in the Desolation Range. Most of the guards followed them. William in wagon number 1, began moving and soon came out into the light of early morning, the southeasterly rising sun casting long shadows to his left. He twisted around to view the Desolation range behind him, white, snow covered peaks rising skyward. He was very glad to be down here on the plains at last.

The guards motioned him into his position as other wagons came up beside him. He turned again to watch as more wagons moved in behind him, keeping at least twenty-five foot distance from his rear. When they started moving fast, if a wagon should break a wheel, that distance would be barely enough for an alert driver to avoid running into the disabled wagon. In the end, it took only thirty minutes for the last wagon to get into position, a rather remarkable coordinated effort indeed.

On horseback, from his position near the middle of the pack, Jon could see the entire caravan. Up front, Mandy led the way with a wizard to either side. Raul was behind her and the guards formed a trailing V-shape behind him. William and the lead row of wagons were near the center of the V. And then he watched as the last, lone guardsman came galloping up and into position. In a way, it was fascinating to watch. Mandy set a trotting pace and the wagons, which were slowly moving in waves, increased their speed to match. Shortly, the wave hit where he and the others were and they too began to trot. Jon hated trotting. He bounced and bumped around the saddle. He hoped that Mandy would pick up the pace just a bit. Eventually, she did so gradually but not for the reason Jon had.

He scanned the horizon ahead of them looking for the hobgoblins. Far off to the south and east of their position, he could see many tendrils of smoke from campfires nearly gone out. A breath of hope filled his heart. The enemy was probably a good twenty miles distant. With their path of southeast, they should be able to out distance them without even a fight. Perhaps, he thought, they might not even be spotted.

In fact they were not spotted for over twenty miles. *Outlying guard position ahead*, Mandy placed into his mind, bringing back the fear of a fight. Jon could see about a dozen tall hobgoblins ahead and to their right. Though the caravan was moving a good clip, a half dozen of them began running to overtake them; the remaining ones began beating the alarm on a set of hide covered drums. Ordinarily, Jon would have been keenly interested in their musical pattern. But just now, it sounded ominous. The six fairly rapidly closed the distance. Jon watched as Mandy let fly a volley of arrows. She controlled her horse with her knees while shooting to the side from her saddle. He was amazed at her skill and prowess. Two collapsed with an arrow in their foreheads. The remaining four dropped back a respectful distance, just out of short bow range.

You are darn good! he sent her.

Thanks, but they are on to us now, I'm afraid. Now the chase begins. We should be able to outrun them thanks to our head start, she sent back.

The caravan was now due east of the main concentration of hobgoblins who were arrayed around the point where the main trail, Deadman's Pass, which traversed the Desolation Range finally reached and opened up onto these plains. Jon estimated that the main hobgoblin masses were now slightly less than twenty miles due east of them.

Even if they all ran as fast as they could, he felt confident that the caravan could not be overtaken by this hobgoblin horde. And ordinarily, that would indeed have been the situation.

They rode on for another ten minutes. However, the distant sound of drums grew as the alarm was spread far across the plains. Jon kept a watchful eye over his left shoulder where he though he saw a darkness grow. There, thousands of hobgoblins rose and prepared for battle, though he could not see them, just a slight darkness from the masses at this distance. Good thing these plains are so utterly flat, he though. Ahead, the plains appeared completely empty save occasional scrub brush. Jon wondered how long the horses could maintain this fast pace. Eventually, they would have to slow down which would give the enemy time to close the distance. Still, it looked very hopeful.

Then it happened. As Jon was gazing westward at the dim darkness of the far horizon, suddenly there was a huge flash of energy of some kind and the entire black hue was gone. "Zagroot zounds!" yelled Mandy at the top of her voice, pulling his attention to the front. Ahead of them, perhaps just two miles was the huge hobgoblin army, hastily forming ranks preparing for battle.

"How can this be?" screamed Alison. "It is no illusion, I don't think."

No illusion; probably a gate spell is my guess, Darless calmly sent mentally to all her friends. *And that would imply some very powerful person or persons are with them,* she added.

If we run into that mass, no matter how many we slay, they will surely form a barrier to halt our forward progress! Mandy mentally and hastily sent to her friends. *I was rather startled by their sudden unexpected appearance,* she added. Jon detected the trace of embarrassment at having yelled out her surprise instead of using their mental abilities.

The enemy line stretched now for a mile on either side of their forward line. Mandy knew that they could not charge straight into that mass, so she altered direction to her right aiming for the enemy's left flank positions. Jon saw that it was an attempt to bypass as many of the hobgoblins as possible. However, it was only marginally successful. As Jon watched, the entire line of the creatures began running to their left countering somewhat Mandy's action. But they were not making any attempt to close the distance.

They were about a mile from the front lines when another sudden gigantic flash of magical energies flared in their direction. Jon perceived a yellow beam arcing from somewhere in the rear of the hobgoblins ahead of them. The beam headed straight for Darless, who was just to the right of Mandy. *Incoming,* was all Darless had time to send mentally before the yellow beam struck her in the chest. Motion seemed to stop for Jon. He saw the energy connect with his friend in her chest, saw it ricochet off of her and hit the ground far to the caravan's left side, saw her knocked physically completely out of her saddle landing with an awkward thump on the ground, and heard a deafening explosion the energy beam as it hit the ground. Dirt and debris flew into the air showering him and those around him.

Thankfully, the alu-demon was riding a light war horse. For the instant its rider left the saddle, it came to a halt, awaiting her return. Jon darted between the wagons and was the first to reach her, fearing the worst. Mandy had slowed the pace trying to grasp what had happened. Jon jumped off his horse and saw Darless moving. He put his arms around her helped her sit up. "Are you okay?" he cried out to her.

She nodded and took deep gasps for breath. "Just got the wind knocked out of me," she answered shortly. And Jon helped her stand. It took her a minute to regain control of her body.

"That was the most powerful lightning bolt I have ever seen!" she finally said. "Look at that hole in the ground." Jon turned and saw that where it had hit there was now a crater some twenty feet across and all of ten feet deep.

"I saw it coming, a yellow beam, saw it hit you. How come you are not dead?" Jon gushed out his thoughts rather out of control.

"They picked on the wrong person!" declared Darless. "I'm rather resistant to magical effects. Bet you forgot that little detail," she teased him, regaining her composure. "Come on, we are being left behind." Sure enough the last of the wagons passed by them. Quickly they remounted and galloped back into their former positions.

Now they were so close to the front line of the enemy that Jon could make out their ugly shapes. Mandy sent her final mental message to all her friend, *Whatever we do, try to keep the caravan moving. If we are forced to stop totally, we are doomed by their sheer numbers. So do what you have to do to keep everybody moving somehow.* Jon relayed her message verbally to both the Newcastles and the Twins and Thea who looked very pale. Jon felt a twinge of pity for Thea, this was her first pitched battle and it did not look at all hopeful.

Jon tried to comfort them a bit saying, "Remember, if anyone gets badly hurt, let me know and I'll use my Ukko's stick on you to heal you up." Thea smiled, but the color did not return to her face.

Another distant explosion brought their attention back to the front. Alison had begun launching long distance balls of fire. From the area of each detonation no hobgoblin ever arose. This was encouraging, but she only had a limited number she could cast. For an moment, Jon dreamed of having a Gatling gun like in the old westerns. He shook that fancy off as Darless also began launching her balls of fire as well. Jon noticed that they were concentrating their efforts at blasting a hole in the line for the caravan to pass through, if possible.

Soon they were passing through the area of the first fireballs. Dead creatures littered the ground as more came swarming from both sides of the caravan. Their progress was slowed to a fast walk as the wagons had to maneuver around all of the dead carcasses. This, of course, allowed the enemy to close to combat distance.

But the closure was not without a price. Jon watched Mandy shoot all of her arrows. Nearly everyone found their mark, but twenty dead hobgoblins out of a thousand was insignificant. Finally, it was time to defend the flanks. Thea began launching her few available fireball spells slowing down the waves of creatures hitting their right flank. Meanwhile, May began putting up heavy illusions of monster-sized bears to their left side. "It's working," Jon called out encouragingly, "They are staying their distance." With the illusion up, she then began shooting magical missiles at those who dared to challenge the illusionary bears. For a short time, the flanks held.

The hobgoblins were not stupid and soon found an opening, their rear. No one was covering the trailing wagons. "We've got the rear", yelled Jake. Jon watched as Jennifer and Jake began running at full speed to the rear. He watched entranced as their moving forms gradually turned into large black bears momentarily frightening the horses they passed. They tore into the evil creatures who were beginning to attack the terrified drivers in the last row. A hobgoblin is no match for an infuriated black bear. The twins wreaked havoc on them, tearing limbs from bodies, crushing skulls. Theirs was a very bloody battle and the hobgoblins beat a hasty retreat. After several minutes, they changed tactics, attempting to kill the bears with volleys of arrows. The twins took a few hits until they utilized the rear wagons for protective cover.

"I'm out of spells and the wands are exhausted," yelled May a trace of panic in her voice.

"Me too," screamed Thea, "What do I do now?" The young teenager was now completely at a loss. She felt suddenly very useless; despair began to overwhelm her. Jon had to think fast.

"May and Mat, you defend with swords on Thea's side. I'll cover May's side myself. Thea, you come here in the middle and watch everyone. Let me know if any get hurt so bad that they need immediate healing from me." That was all it took. In chaos, the order became their stable datum around which to focus their efforts. May drew her sword and dashed into combat. Mat, forsaking any weapon, preferred his martial arts, took down two that were closing from each side of him. Jon got a glimpse of Mat jumping into the air striking each hobgoblin with a simultaneous flying kicks and extended fist strikes to their necks. Both fell lifeless to the ground, necks broken. *Mat can hold his own!* he thought to himself. Now he had to act fast on his side for, once the illusion wore off, the hobgoblins were once again closing all along his side.

Jon concentrated and mocked up a huge fifty foot tall bear and had it begin attacking the closest enemy. However, the attack was really a mind blast from Jon. *Oops. That was a bit too much.* The heads of the first he attacked literally exploded. So he lowered the amount of energy he sent with each attack. Naturally, the hobgoblins began to test their new opponent, the bear. Jon played along with them, having his image recoil somewhat from a spear thrust and arrow hits. But always he had the bear seem to attack back at them. Now he had the proper amount of energy to expend and they either died outright or fled raving mad from the battlefield. "So far so good," he thought.

Thea did her best to try to watch in all directions. "Mandy's being pulled off her horse. She's being crushed underneath a pile of hobgoblins. Now, she's stabbing them with her knives. Now she's back on her feet. She's got her big sword out. They are falling like flies around her. Each swing fells another one. I think she has gone berserk now. Alison is still blasting away at concentrations of them. So is Darless. May and Mat are doing okay. No, May's taken a hit; no, make that two cuts. She's bleeding. Jake's doing okay. Jennifer has a lot of arrows protruding from her. I think she is slowing down. You might get ready to go help her. Yes, Jon, she's fallen down. Hurry!"

Without thinking, Jon stepped himself from his position and arrived at her fallen bear form and touched her with his walking stick saying the proper words. Energy flashed and the arrows flew out of her body. She struggled to her feet. "I guess I am healed up, but I feel a little weak yet," she managed to say. Then she was back into the fray. Jon mentally stepped back Thea's side and renewed his bear illusion once more. This was tiring work, but he grimly kept at it.

"Mandy is definitely berserk. She's is swinging wildly charging into their ranks killing anything she can reach. Alison is now using magical missiles on those that get too close. I think she is trying to help Mandy out. The pile of dead hobgoblins are acting as a barrier keeping the other hobgoblins from charging the front. The guards are holding their own at the very front. Oh no, May's taken a really bad hit. Jon, she needs help right now," came Thea's report.

"You are doing a terrific job, Thea, keep it up. Back shortly," Jon attempted to validate her good reporting as he mentally stepped to the side of May and mind blasted the three that were attempting to finish her off. Then, he used his walking stick of Ukko to heal her. "Okay, you are fixed up. You are doing a good job. They still have not reached the actual wagons."

May managed to flash him a smile. True enough, through their combined efforts, the caravan proper so far had been spared any significant damage. She resumed her challenge of the nearest hobgoblins. Jon glanced at Mat. Seeing that he still looked in fairly good shape, he then stepped back to Thea.

"Mandy's just killed another couple dozen; they just fell over dead like yours do. Oh no, someone's blasted her with a spell. It's knocked her off her feet, she's flying backwards at least fifty feet. She's landed on a pile of dead hobgoblins. She's alive, she's struggling to her feet, she looks dazed. Now she's charging forward again," dutifully reported Thea. Suddenly another huge explosion from the front lines blasted in Jon's ears. Thea was almost crying, "It's Alison, she's been blasted from her horse, she's flying through the air toward us. She's going to crash into a wagon!" Jon turned to look. He saw his love flying in a large arc toward the wagon nearest him; she didn't seem to be responding. Jon acted. He mentally stepped to a point just before her and when he arrived, his arms grabbed her and just as she was going to come crashing onto the wagon, he stepped to Thea's side still holding the unconscious Alison.

Tears streamed down Thea's face as she felt for a pulse. Alison's face and chest were blackened from a severe magical detonation; she was indeed badly burned and unconscious. Jon did not hesitate but again used his walking stick from Ukko. Before Thea's eyes, the burned flesh healed to a healthy pink! She stirred. Thea gave Jon a tight hug and kiss, "Oh thank you!"

"What's this, kissing my man?" Alison managed a very small tease. Thea flushed and immediately explained Jon's spectacular catch. "You'll have to tell me all about it later. There must be one really powerful magician somewhere. But we just cannot see any men about anywhere. Darless and I are totally baffled. If we don't stop him fast, we are all done for. Rats, I've lost my staff." She gave Jon a hurried kiss and rushed forward looking for her staff.

"Jon, look out!" Thea cried. During this lapse of time from his side, the hobgoblins had broken through the bear illusion and were swarming onto the sides of the wagons. William was fighting one off by hitting him with a frying pan.

Jon began to mind blast them in an arc, beginning with those around William and moving toward the rear. Within a minute, the hobgoblins that remained beat a hasty retreat once more.

I've found him. Lord Jarred is doing these devastating spells. He is in the rear using the form of a hobgoblin. I'm going to take him out personally! Darless sent to all her friends.

Thea reported, her voice now full of conflicting emotions, "Darless is flying over the heads of the hobgoblins. She's heading toward their rear. Dozens of arrows are bouncing off of her. How can that be?" Thea realized she was forgetting the others, and added, "Alison has her staff back but is using it to beat the hobgoblins. She and all the guards are standing together in a small clump entirely surrounded now. Looks bad. Oh no! Mandy's down. They are piling on top of her! Body parts are exploding, but I don't see her anymore. Oh Jon, do something. Oh no, May and Mat are both in trouble. This is the end, I know it. Jake and Jennifer look like pin cushions; both are barely moving! Do something! Oh no, no, no! Alison has taken a club to her head; she is falling down. Do something, please," she pleaded nearly hysterical.

In his mind, Jon screamed, *I cannot be in all these places at the same time! Help! If we ever needed a miracle, now is the time.* To Thea, he ordered, "See my bear?" She meekly said she did. "Okay, you keep it attacking like I had it doing. Use your mind to will it to do things." She began to protest that she had no idea how to do it. "Just do it!" Jon ordered. He took a deep breath and began to make his rounds. His only idea was to make the circuit healing each just as fast as he possibly could, beginning with the bear twins. He made the jump to the bears and rapidly healed them with his stick; that took thirty seconds, he judged. He jumped to the other twins, but unfortunately they were not close to each other; it required two separate jumps to heal them; another minute had elapsed. He jumped for Alison, homing in on her mind because he could not see her. He landed in the middle of fallen bodies, twisting and spraining his ankle severely. Another thirty seconds and Alison staggered to her feet, fending off incessant blows from the hobgoblins. She shot her last missile spell to protect Jon as he prepared for the next jump to rescue Mandy.

This time, Jon had no choice but to home in on Mandy's mind for she was so far out in front of their leading edge he could not see her. He again landed amid fallen bodies spraining the other ankle as well. He ignored the pain as best he could and tried to find his dear friend. But all he saw was a huge pile of dead. She must be under them all, he surmised. "If I can just find a piece of her body, an arm or leg," he muttered to himself. His ankles protested and Jon found himself falling to his knees. Slowly, he began moving carcasses out of the way, probing for Mandy. They were heavy and the task more suitable for a strong man. Jon groaned under the strain, but doggedly kept at it, knowing that her life was in his hands. A couple of hobgoblins saw him and came at him. He looked at them and just blasted away, mindless of the overkill. He was getting frantic.

The end is near. Go on. Save yourself. Jump back to the safety of your world. These words came unbidden into his mind.

Jon recognized their sender at once. Jon grimaced and sent back, *That may be what you would do Lord Jarred. But thank the gods I am not you! Never. I will save my friend! Then, I am coming for you!*

Jon felt Lord Jarred begin to make contact with him to continue the conversation, but it suddenly broke off, just as suddenly as it had begun. Evidently, the Demon Lord had other matters to handle. Jon continued looking for Mandy. He heard a lone trumpet sound in the distance. Then another and another. "Must be sounding the victory call," Jon muttered under his breath. "Well, we are not finished just yet! At last!" He found the unmistakable leg of a woman. Quickly, he touched his stick to her leg and spoke the command phrase. The leg stirred. Jon struggled to move more bodies off of the pile. His own strength was ebbing. Jon knew that he had once again pushed his mental abilities beyond their limits, but he had to free her or she would just suffocate under the dead.

Meanwhile, Lord Jarred did indeed have a sudden new problem, the alu-demon. Darless had spotted him and in her rage, she flew straight toward him as fast as she could go, heedless of all other things. Darless knew that unless Jarred was disposed of on this plane soon, all she held dear in life would be utterly destroyed. No one else had seen through his disguise, only she. No one else, save maybe Alison and Jon, could possibly get to him. She knew that neither had the strength or capabilities of defeating a Demon Lord. She might not be able to either, for that matter, but she would die trying.

Just as Lord Jarred was bandying his victory words with Jon to torment him before the final kill, she smashed headlong into his body, knocking him backwards. They fell onto the ground locked in a demonic struggle. His fists smashed into her chest, while she dug her fists into his face, and clawed and tore at his flesh. It was the wildest brawl that anyone had ever seen. Under normal circumstances, Lord Jarred, a Demon Lord, should have been able to best an alu-demon fairly easily, but not now, not under these circumstances. He had already exhausted all of his most powerful spells, including his wish spell, which he had used to move his entire army to block and overtake the caravan.

He had not counted on her ferocity, her steel determination, her utter lack of her own sense of self-preservation. Darless had only one thought in her mind, his destruction. They rolled over the ground gnawing, tearing, beating on each other. Then, both managed to regain their feet, but Darless was the quicker. She grabbed both his arms and gave a tremendous jerk backward, adding to it by using her mind similar to the way she thought Jon must do when he stepped into another space. Though she did not really know how Jon did it, she imagined herself doing it. And that extra was just enough. Both Lord Jarred's arms were ripped from their sockets and Darless fell backwards holding the lifeless stumps. He shrieked in pain and terror; such had never happened to him; such should never happen to him — he, Lord Jarred. Yet he was not utterly helpless! He tried to kick at the prone alu-demon, but she rolled out of his way and regained her footing. Now fire blazed from her eyes as she stalked toward him.

"Leave this plane immediately or die on this plane!" she shrieked. She did not even wait for a reply. She grabbed his head and wrenched it from his body. Instantly, all traces of the body of Lord Jarred vanished utterly. She was holding empty space in her hand. "Guess you died," she muttered. Only then she turned to find out what was making all that trumpeting noise. "Oh gods! Another army to fight! As if this one is not enough!" But then she took a closer look. What she saw sent shivers down her spine, white flags with blue crosses, the holy flags of paladins of Ukko. Then, her legs failed her and she fell to the ground. Her body ached terribly. She had been fighting at the end with two broken legs and several cracked ribs. She had not even noticed it before so strong was her intention to defeat the demon. She lowered her head and used what little remained of her strength to begin the healing process.

None in her party had seen her valiant fight and victory over Lord Jarred. But another had. Sunlight shone bright off his suit of polished steel as his heavy war horse charged forward, lance pointed ready to skewer the nearest hobgoblin. Indeed, Sir Thomas was charging to the rescue. He had raised an army of some five hundred fighters and had only just arrived in search of Alison and the caravan, just as the Air Maiden, Fruella, had instructed him to do. It was Sir Thomas who bore witness to Darless' victory over Lord Jarred. He witnessed something that even he could not do, the shredding of a demon's body by sheer physical force. That he was impressed was an understatement.

As soon as Sir Thomas spied the distant battle, he signaled for continuous trumpeting and an all-out charge. Five hundred cavalrymen galloped at break neck speed into the battle. Jon looked up to see charging horsemen attacking hobgoblins all about him. So he relaxed and continued to move the fallen bodies off of Mandy. One rider pulled up beside him. "Can I be of service?" Jon recognized that voice. It was Lonnie! A burst of joy filled his heart.

"Mandy. Mandy's under here somewhere. Help me get these off of her," he called out. "Are we ever glad to see you! We were nearly done for here." As Lonnie quickly heaved bodies right and left, Jon suddenly realized just how tired and weak he really was. Help, though unexpected, had arrived. So he relaxed, sighed, and fell forward onto the pile of bodies and passed out from total exhaustion. He did not feel the strong arm that picked him up and gently set him down nearby. He did not feel the surge of healing energy from the paladin's hand as he touched him. He did not hear Mandy's gulp for air and statement, "It's about time; I nearly suffocated a second time under that pile. Oh. It's you. Where'd you come from?

What happened to Jon? I thought he was here healing me? Oh. It's gotten very confusing all of a sudden."

Helping her regain her feet, he proudly replied, "We are following the advice of Fruella, the Air Maiden that we rescued. She told us to raise an army and head here. We are only just in time, but Sir Thomas will explain it all after we get things put to rights here. Jon's passed out. Is it safe to move him?"

"He's probably just sleeping. He often over does it and pays this price. We can move him, but to where?" she looked about at the hundreds of dead hobgoblins.

Lonnie took charge, signaling to their supply and rescue wagons, which had been some distance behind the main force. Soon, strong arms lifted the slumbering Jon into a wagon and began the tedious drive toward the caravan. Any direct path was hopelessly filled with carcasses of the fallen. Mandy climbed aboard the wagon, though healed of wounds, she was near total exhaustion as well. She fell asleep beside Jon.

Meanwhile, the charging cavalry flew across the battlefield chasing after the routing hobgoblins who were now running north as fast as they could go. Within five minutes, a great silence came over the plains; all combat was finished. Thea, alone of the companions who was still fresh, took charge, ordering wagons be prepared to allow Mat, May, Jennifer, and Jake a time of rest to recover from their exhaustion. One look at the gratitude from their eyes told her she was doing the right thing. And all four also fell into a deep sleep, all traces of the adrenalin rush was gone; fatigue took its place. She had just tucked them in when Alison, looking a bit dazed herself half walked — half staggered up to her. "Ah, good idea, Thea. Jon's with Mandy, I think. I cannot find Darless. I'm going to rest up a bit. See if you can find Darless. Wake me if she is in trouble." And she, with the aid of her assistant, climbed into the wagon beside her sister and closed her weary eyes. One sigh and she was sleeping as well.

Thea headed to the front of the caravan in search of Jon, Mandy, and Darless. Raul, nursing many wounds, pointed her in the right direction. "They are out there, see by that wagon." And so she headed out to meet the slowly approaching wagon accompanied by a tall rider in gleaming armor. From this distance, he looked a handsome fellow. She noted that he too wore the banner of a paladin of Ukko. "Hail there," she called out, trying not to stumble unseemly over the dead bodies all around her. "I'm Thea, Mage Alison's apprentice. I'm looking for Jon, Mandy, and Darless. Have you seen them? I'm to see to their needs, on orders of Mage Alison." *There, that should be formal enough*, she thought to herself.

The young lad, in a grand manner dismounted, bowed low to her, saying also formally, "Hail and well met, Apprentice Thea! I am Lonnie, Holy Paladin of Ukko here to rescue you. Jon and Mandy are both doing well but are exhausted and sleeping in the wagon. So you need not fear for them. They are in good hands. As for Darless, I have seen her not. Where was she last at?"

He talks so fine, she thought, a*nd what a handsome face. And his eyes, oh my.* Her eyes met his and then she quickly lowered them to the ground. "Alison said far out here somewhere. I guess I should go look for her."

"Tis not safe just yet. Permit me to accompany you. Darless may be in dire need, for thus far, I have seen none but the dead all around," Lonnie replied gallantly. "Please, fair maiden, sit and ride upon my horse. I will lead you in the search. I fear not all the fallen are yet dead; one may try to wreak some vile treachery upon you as we walk among the fallen." He offered her his hand and helped her into the saddle.

Thea did not refuse and hopped up easily onto his horse. "Thank you noble Lonnie. Oh, you can see so much better from up here. I think that way is right. It's the direction towards which I last saw her flying." She chatted on about the battle. "After I had used up all my spells and drained the last charges from all the wands Alison loaned me, Jon had me watch everyone and tell him when he had to go and heal one of the fallen." And on she talked explaining everything to this fine lad as fast as she could talk and still look ahead for Darless.

Lonnie enjoyed her company immensely; she was like a breath of fresh air, as far as he was concerned. He took an instant fancy to her. Within a couple minutes, Lonnie saw the kneeling form of his leader ahead in the distance. He interrupted her gracefully, "Ahead is Sir Thomas, our leader and a very high holy paladin of Ukko indeed. He is helping someone, I believe, or he would have never stopped his charge

into battle. Perhaps he has found Darless. Let's hurry up."
Thus, they came upon Sir Thomas and Darless.

Prior to their arrival, Sir Thomas, from far off, saw the
alu-demon's battle with the Demon Lord and her ultimate
victory. He watched as she afterwards collapsed and leaned
forward, full of hurt. He forsook his forward charge and rode
to her side. He dropped his lance and dismounted at her side.
She was indeed in need, though not dire. Her clothing was torn
and tattered, yet the white tunic with the plain blue cross was
undamaged, though soiled with blood. Indeed, she was
covered from head to foot in drying blood. She was deep in
concentration, using the last of her strength to attempt some
healing of her legs, for she could no longer stand on them. Her
crushed and battered ribs could wait. Then, unbidden, she felt
his hands gently rest upon her shoulder; strong hands,
powerful hands. And then the unmistakable healing energy of
that can only come from Ukko spread outward from his hands,
pervading her aching body. She sighed in relief and raised her
head.

Her eyes met those of Sir Thomas. "It's you!" she
exclaimed and her face flushed crimson. Oh how she had
yearned for this man, how her heart had been aching just to
see him once more. And here he was. She fumbled for words.
"My legs, they are broken. And I've got crushed ribs. Otherwise
I am okay. I can't stand anymore. Thank you Sir Thomas for
your timely aid. We all nearly perished in this battle."

She could not notice that his eyes bore down upon her
in an intense gaze. "Ah then," he said in his deep bass voice,
"Let me see what I can do about the legs then." He uttered a
holy prayer to Ukko. His hands touched her legs bringing a
soothing healing energy to them, easing her pain. "There, that
is all I can do for you. I am afraid that your legs remain
broken, but the pain should be less. Honored Mage, pray let
me take you to Father Johnas, our high priest. He can fully
heal you, for you are more than worthy of such!" Without
waiting for an answer, he picked her up as if she weighed but a
feather and gently sat her upon his silver, heavy war horse. He
signaled the supply wagons and slowly led her toward them.

Upon reaching the wagon, he called out, "Father
Johnas, quickly here. She is in need of much healing for she
has fought with and defeated the Demon Lord himself!"

Darless was completely unused to so much personal attention. Usually, it was up to her to help herself, or perhaps one of her dear friends. But weak as she now was, she had no choice. She watched as a tall, older man dressed in the finest priestly robes she had ever seen, climbed out of the wagon and came to her. Sir Thomas gently lifted her off the horse and sat her on the snowy plains. Father Johnas began chanting and she relaxed completely for it was much like Jon's holy music she'd often heard him play. Then a golden glow of energy surged throughout her entire body. Wherever it flowed, all pain, all hurt, all damage in that location was gone. In later days she tried to explain it to Jon; how it was so very different than the healing from his stick or his mind. It had a special holiness about; that was the best way she could describe it.

"There now, my dear," the high priest of Ukko said when he had finished, "you are now fully healed in body. Yet I can do nothing for your exhaustion, I fear, only time, rest and food will handle that. Please, ride in my wagon to yonder caravan. That will free our leader, Sir Thomas, to do his work more effectively."

"Thank you, Holy Father," Darless humbly said. "I can stand once more and my breathing comes easier. But you are right. I am beat. I gave it my all and then some." He helped her into the wagon.

"Head for the front of the caravan," Sir Thomas ordered. To Darless, he added, "My Dearest Lady, we shall speak more fully later. First, I must see to all of the others." He galloped off toward the caravan and toward one of his men leading another on his horse coming toward him, Lonnie and Thea.

"Hail, Sir Thomas," Lonnie called out when they were close enough. "Everyone is okay back at the caravan. I've Apprentice Mage Thea here with me. Under Mage Alison's orders, we are seeking word of Darless; she is still unaccounted for and may be in dire need of aid."

"Ah, that is better news that I'd hoped for, Sir Lonnie. Rest assured Darless is fully recovered. I saw to her needs, which were great. Take Thea to Johnas; let her ride back with My Lady Darless. And come with me. We've much yet to do on this battle field." Quickly, Lonnie took Thea to Darless and galloped off after Sir Thomas.

"Are the others all right?" was Darless' first words to Thea.

And so Thea once again began to recount the valiant defense of the wagons. She did not see Father Johnas listening to her every word, smiling to himself. Soon Darless drifted into sleep, listening to the excited, though comforting, words of Thea. "Darn, she's asleep!" commented Thea, somewhat at a loss.

"Come sit up here with me," Father Johnas spoke softly. "Tell me more about the happenings here. I am particularly interested in all these tunics of Ukko. Apparently, there are more holy paladins of Ukko here than are in many towns I have passed through. So Thea eagerly began her tale once more. He listened intently.

Sir Thomas lost no time in producing order on the battlefield. He sent out a small rear guard on all sides to make sure none of the hobgoblins returned to slit their throats while they slept. He ordered all of the fallen to be counted, searched and stripped of weapons. A great pit was dug in the plains and all of the dead were placed within it and the dirt mounded high. The burial mound was indeed huge, rising fifty feet from the level of the plains. When the burial detail was finished, Sir Thomas proclaimed that hereafter, this mound was to be called Ula Boca, the Black Mound, in the tongue of the hobgoblins.

The final count: Mandy in single combat had killed one hundred thirty-two. The mages had slain two hundred and forty-two. Another hundred and twenty perished around the wagons proper, including the sides and rear. The arriving cavalry accounted for another eighty. Over five hundred hobgoblins perished that day, nearly half of those that Lord Jarred had transported to this location. Sir Thomas estimated that more than double those numbers still lurked to the east and north of the caravan. It is noted here that his was a gross underestimate, but it was of no consequence.

In the process of the search, the wizard's staves along with Mandy's weapons were found and brought back to their wagons. Once the southern area had been cleared of the fallen, Sir Thomas had the caravan travel about a half mile out into a fresh, unsoiled area of the plains. It would not do to camp amid this despoiled area where the great battle occurred.

During this time, Father Johnas and six of his assistants tended the many lesser wounds of Raul and the guards and those few caravan folks who had been injured. In short, as the sun set that day, order and normalcy had been returned to the caravan.

Fearing no evil, Sir Thomas ordered huge bonfires to be lite. For the first time in days, everyone could cook a warm, hot meal. Admittedly, finding sufficient brushwood in these semi-arid plains was quite a task. But he had the man power available. And the caravan folks all pitched in to help in any way possible.

And as the sun sank, one by one the sleeping companions awoke to the familiar smells of cooking food and crackling fires. However, each was caked with dried filth from the battle. Alison came to their rescue. She got out her decanter of water and in its gushing flow, they bathed and cleaned up. Though not a proper bath, it did wash off the filth and refreshed their spirits. Clothed in new garments, the companions rejoined the others around the bonfire and dinner.

Needless to say, they all ate heartily first. Talk came second, when William served the after-dinner tea. "Let me begin," Sir Thomas began, "for ours is a short tale. It began when we arrived too late to do battle at the ruined tower. I must admit, Alison, that you were right and I was wrong. I arrived too late. My heart sank to the vilest pits when I saw your nearly lifeless form being gated to the very depths of the Abyss! And then I beheld a wonder I had not expected. My Lady, Mage Darless, heedless of her peril, literally dove, much like a swan, into the gate to rescue you! That alone gave me much to ponder." His eyes focused upon Darless. Both Jon and Alison noticed that for the rest of the evening his eyes never strayed but a moment from her. Jon wondered.

"Then, in my agony and despair, I was comforted by the Air Maiden, Fruella. She told me to ride fast and raise an army to do battle with a great evil host. She commanded we come here to these desolate plains predicting that you would need our assistance most gravely. And all praise be to Ukko, I heeded her words which were most true. I fear I came not a moment too soon. I wonder now how different it may have been had we not tarried so long? But be that as it may, that is all of our tale. Excepting one small detail, Alison, there seem to be a rather large number of dwarves around your castle ruins. Something about building a new castle? I have only one question that must be answered." He paused for dramatic effect, for he considered this to be of the utmost importance. "If my eyes do not deceive me, many of you, including yourself, Mage Alison, now wear the banner of a Holy Paladin of Ukko. How came this to be? What does it mean?" His eyes still gazed only upon Darless.

Alison spoke first. "Sir Thomas, ever are we in your debt. As always, you seem doomed to come to the aid of your mage." Both chuckled at the private joke they shared for she had been the wizard of Sir Thomas's adventuring party for many years. She began her fledgling career with him; and he had, of necessity, had to look to her well-being. "But ours is a long story. Let me begin by introducing my twin brother and sister. Here are May and May d'Ambrose." They stood up for all to see. "We also have rescued another brother, but he had been held in prison in the Abyss for all these long years. His body was near death and his mind was gone. Currently he is under the care of Lady Ursala of Hollybine Woods. And yes, May and Mat were anointed as Holy Children of Ukko by Father Ukko's hand himself. As were Darless and I similarly anointed by his hands as Holy Paladins of Ukko. But how we came to be in his presence is a part of this long tale."

At this point, comments, congratulations, cheers, and other exclamations and praises arose from all quarters. Fully five minutes passed before she could continue their tale. She explained how they had been gated to the Abyss and placed great emphasis on all that Darless had done to protect them all while they were there. She also noticed Sir Thomas's eyes open wide at this. Then she explained the dealings with Metrarch and Dispater and the bargain that had resulted in her brother being returned to her. She dwelled at length on the situation in Freetown or Twins Town, going to lengths to show all that May and Mat had done there.

May and Mat were asked to tell much of their life there and their dealings with the Church of Ukko. Then, came the startling discovery of the early history of the town and the protection of Ukko and how they discovered its location and how it operated. Mandy described in detail the events of preventing the assassination of Metrarch, though she did not reveal that he, in fact, had faked his own death.

Then, Jon described the defense of Freetown against the invading, warring armies of the Demon Lords. But when he got to their meeting with Father Ukko, he let Alison describe it fully. Indeed, she had to repeat it several times for Sir Thomas and Father Johnas kept asking for more details. For them, meeting their God in person was the highest possible honor of which they had yet to personally achieve, and here they were in the midst of a whole group that Ukko had taken unto him personally. If Sir Thomas had been impressed with them before, it was nothing to his reverence now. He continued to stare at Darless all the while, as if he could not believe what he was seeing and hearing. His own God had knighted her, an alu-demon, and yet he had seen her single handedly slay a Demon Lord using only her hands, a feat he had not yet achieved, though he secretly longed to do so.

After spending a full hour going over and over their visit with Father Ukko, Mandy took up the tale of the caravan. As she expected, the warriors with Sir Thomas all wanted complete details of their seemingly unsurmountable battles with the Vyndocian hordes. They asked many, many questions about her tactics and overall strategy. For the first time ever, Mandy had an appreciative audience that was keenly interested in the same things she was. She relished the limelight and thoroughly enjoyed answering their many questions about the battles.

Alison then took up the tale with the helping of the stone giants and later the dwarves. Again, Jon had to explain all about his part in unraveling the battle and his contest with Morrigan. At this point, Father Johnas, himself, asked Jon many questions about her and what he had done and how the principles of the third party to the conflict operated. Jon could see that Father Johnas was learning something from him in these matters.

Then William told of their plight in the early winter storm that dumped three feet of snow upon their trail through the Desolation Range. Mandy finished up by relating the rescue by Jake and Jennifer. Although she did not mention their disease, she did explain that they were shape-changers who preferred the forms of great black bears. Finally, Thea explained the current battle for she alone had had the most complete view of all of the action.

But it was Darless, who all evening had not said a word, who was called upon to relate what she had done to Lord Jarred. In a quiet voice, she described what she had done. Jon's comment was, "Darless, that was unbelievable. You have my eternal thanks for doing that!" She got a huge round of applause and many, many compliments. There were many in this rescue party who would have given anything to have battled a demon lord, Sir Thomas not the least.

She added for Jon's benefit, "Lord Jarred was only defeated on this plane of existence. He is not dead, but forced back into the Abyss. He cannot return to this plane in any form for fifty years. So we may count on a respite from him, thankfully."

By now, it was midnight, and one by one, everyone turned in for the night. This night everyone in the entire caravan slept in complete peace, fearing no harm, fearing not the rising of day. They had an army to protect them. For the first time in months, Mandy fully relaxed and had a very deep sleep.

As Jon snuggled in with Alison, he kissed her lovingly and whispered to her, "Did you notice how neither Darless nor Sir Thomas could keep their eyes off of each other all night long? You don't suppose that they?" He did not finish his sentence for she poked him playfully.

"How could I? It was like they were glued to each other. You don't suppose?" She paused and then added, "Nah, how could he? He is so prejudiced against demons." And so they fell asleep together and slept more soundly than they had for a very long time.

It was one in the morning as Sir Tomas stoked the failing bonfire. He was still up, though he need not be, for there were plenty of competent guards on duty. He could not sleep. His mind raced this way and that, while his heart leaned yet another. He stared at the dying embers. Darless silently walked up beside him. He could not help it; a big smile instantly appeared on his face. She had changed into a sleeping gown and had wrapped herself in a blanket for it was winter here on the plains, though nowhere near as cold as it had been in the high mountains. She hesitated a moment and then gently placed her right hand upon his shoulder as he knelt beside the fire.

He responded by putting his hand over hers. They each looked deep into the other's eyes. Finally, he spoke, "My Lady, something has happened to me since we last chatted beside a fire much like this outside the ruins of Castle d'Ambrose so long ago." He faltered, embarrassment rose in him.

"Yes?" she encouraged him, not daring to hope, yet wanting with all her heart.

"I've, I've, I've really missed you." *There I've said it and it didn't hurt,* he thought to himself. "I mean, I've really missed you!" He paused and explained, "When I saw you heedless of your own life dive into the gate to the Abyss to aid Alison and the others, something happened to me in that instant. Since that night, I just cannot get you out of my mind. I see you in my dreams. I look at a campfire and see you that night. I look out over the green hills and see you riding off. I look down a hallway and every person I see reminds me of you." He hesitated once more. Until now, he had not uttered a word of this to a living sole. If she should tell others about his obvious infatuation with her, but no, he trusted her.

So absorbed in himself and trying to communicate what was obviously hard for him to do, he entirely missed Darless' reaction. Her eyes opened wide in near disbelief. She gazed longingly at him but dared not yet say a word. She had had many sexual dealings with men and knew not to interrupt them until they had said what was on their minds. She waited as patiently as she could, even though she wanted to gush out her similar feelings for him.

Now he started down a new train of thought attempting to justify his actions. "Remember our conversation about love we had that night outside Alison's place? We agreed that love consists of a total admiration for the other coupled with a deep, complete respect for them. My Lady Darless, I, Sir Thomas, have both for you! I believe that I am wholly, completely, hopelessly in love with you. If it would not offend thee, would you permit me to most formally court you?"

Darless felt that her heart would explode. "Sir Thomas, I too must be fair to you. For quite some time now, I have had similar thoughts of you, fantasizing about you and me being wedded. In truth, my heart yearns for you. I know we are very different people with very different moral codes and out looks on life. Yet you have my admiration and respect as well. It would appear that I am just as madly in love with you as you are with me!" she grinned rather sheepishly.

"However, before I let fantasy approach reality, I have a few questions I must ask of you." She paused, noticed he was waiting expectantly and so said, "Number 1, do you want to have children, perhaps many?"

"Most definitely! Sons, daughters, both. Oh, I see what you mean," he suddenly realized the full implications. Their children would be one-quarter demon, inheriting from Darless' mother's side.

"Then that leads to Number 2, are you prepared to fully support those mix-breed, so to speak, children, to nurture them, help them surmount the bias and prejudice of this world?" she asked watching even his body language as he answered.

"Of that I am certain because I have learned that it is the spirit, the being, that really determines whether or not they are good or evil, demon or man. You have taught me that; it was a hard learned lesson, I might add," he replied humbly.

"That is good," she went on, "Number 3, suppose that we were living in a large building with some of our dearest friends in other rooms. Suppose further that there was a huge fire and that I and our children had been overcome by smoke, as had many of our friends, and suppose further that you had not. Whom would you rescue first?"

Sir Thomas hesitated not. "I have two arms and am strong. I would get you and the children to safety first and then go back for our friends. That's an easy one, I cannot imagine life without you and the children."

A great peace flooded all through Darless' body, a peace she had never known before. But she had one final doubt, "Number 4, would you trust me with the children's safety no matter what the circumstances might be? Trust me implicitly without demanding complete explanations beforehand?"

"Well, I must admit that Alison has taught me a thing or two about that. Yes, I would. If you say something is the way to proceed, then I support you. Look, haven't I already proven that I sometimes make the wrong choices? You all were totally correct about the Chasme Bugs. I went charging all over the countryside and ended up arriving where you were and arriving too late to matter. My children are vital to me, so yes I trust you totally, perhaps even more than I do myself."

Her huge smile reflected in the third quarter moonlight, "Number 5, then Sir Thomas, you may most definitely court me. But please do hurry up! I long to hold you and kiss you and hug you and." She did not get to finish, for he leaned over, put his strong arms around her, and kissed her as gently as a rose pedal. She returned the flow even more strongly. Her passions flowed free at long, long last. Not since her childhood with her father had she felt such an outpouring of love.

Then, they took a long walk, arm in arm, all around the outer most edge of the encampment. They chatted about their lives, sharing events each held dearest. "You know, there is one thing that you have got to teach me how to do," she begged him. "You have got to teach me how to handle a sword of some kind. After that last battle yesterday with Jarred, I know I need some kind of backup weapon when I run out of spells!"

"Consider it done," he replied proudly, "for if there is one thing that I am a master of it is swords — all kinds!" She gave him a hug. As they walked, sleep overcame both of them. He invited her to sleep beside him out here under the stars. For several weeks now, he had slept on the ground staring up at the stars, always thinking about her. She did not hesitate for even a second! They slept soundly with the joy of eternal happiness flooding their whole beingness. They also did not awake at first light.

Alison, always a light sleeper and early riser, found them as the ruddy rays of dawn sprang over the whitened plains. Her eyes opened wide; she rushed to wake Jon. "Wake up. Come on. You have got to see this!" She kept pulling on him until he roused and got up. Throwing this fur coat over his shoulders, he hasten after her. Mandy, who had only now just arisen, stretching and yawning, followed them, full of curiosity. Alison stopped a fair distance from the sleeping forms. Darless lay snuggled, cradled in Sir Thomas's arms; their sleeping faces radiated a happiness never before seen in either of them by these companions.

Quietly they slipped away before speaking. "Isn't that incredible?" Alison whispered. "Who'd of thought those two would make a pair? They are *so* different. I'd never have matched them up."

"Love is blind, it is said," Mandy whispered back, "but I never believed that. I agree with you, they are so different, but then so are William and I or you and Jon, for that matter. I wonder how long that has been going on? I never suspected anything was going on between them."

Jon, who had been sheepishly silent, finally whispered, "I did, but I swore I would not reveal it. I did not know until yesterday how Sir Thomas felt toward Darless. Did you notice that he could not keep his eyes off of her from the moment they met yesterday? I think it is just great that they both are enamored of each other. After all that Darless has been through, she deserves only the very best, in my opinion." Alison kissed him. Together the three went in search of breakfast.

The love struck pair did not rise until midmorning. Jon observed that Sir Thomas appeared a bit bashful, until holding onto Darless' arm, he got everyone's attention and proclaimed, "I, we, just want everyone to know that I, Sir Thomas, am formally courting My Lady Darless." If he intended to say more, no one knew for at that, cheers and congratulations flowed from everyone.

"Then we can all get married together this spring," May proclaimed, "five couples together! Won't that be something to tell our children and grandchildren about?" Jon watched a slight blush rapidly appear on both Sir Thomas's and Darless' faces. Broad smiles quickly replaced it as each gave the other a gentle hug.

Darless pretended to be a bit taken aback, "Well, I don't know about the spring." She paused for dramatic effect before adding, "I don't know if I can wait that long!" Everyone roared with laughter.

Then, it was time for the business at hand. Although the paladin was the leader of the rescuing cavalry, he asked Alison and Mandy where they leading the caravan. Alison explained that she was not only rebuilding Castle d'Ambrose but also building an entire town. Most of the caravan folks greatly desired to live in the new town. These people before had placed their faith and trust in the Twins. After their experiences on this journey, they could think of no better "protector" than the d'Ambrose family and their friends. Thus, the holy paladin found that the caravan was actually heading back to the castle ruins. Because there was no place for these people to live once they got there just yet, Alison explained that she planned to put them up at her expense in the nearby villages and castles.

Sir Thomas was most impressed at the keen leadership Alison demonstrated, worthy of a holy paladin, he thought, but reminded himself that Ukko had now so appointed her, a mage, not a fighter. He was humbled; his stable datum that Holy Paladins of Ukko were great warriors had been dashed by Ukko himself. He knew that he still had much to learn or perhaps relearn.

However, it was Mandy's next idea that won the day, "What I wouldn't give for a real hot bath! Can we make for the nearest town, please?" she pleaded to Sir Thomas. Not only did her friends cheer her, but also the townsfolk standing nearby whooped and yelled their complete agreement. Thus, a town with baths became the next priority. "Sir Thomas, I hereby give command of this caravan to you. Never in all my days have I so welcomed a change in leadership!"

Sir Thomas roared with laughter. He tried to jest, "Here we have this female ranger of the woods who has just performed a task that even I, experienced as I am, would be ill-prepared to accomplish, giving *up* command? Against herculean obstacles, yet with almost no casualties, this ranger has brought the caravan to safety. When I say that I am impressed, I mean it. I tip my helm to you, Ranger Blackthorn"" And he did so. Thus it was that Sir Thomas took over the command, leading his cavalry and the caravan northeast to Tannersville; they arrived in four days without mishap and without events of note.

Chapter 23 Home at Last

The caravan rested and re-supplied in Tannersville. This took another four days to complete. And yes, everyone, including all six hundred plus caravan members found time for a hot bath, compliments of Alison. Mandy and Darless both spent a half of a day soaking, cleansing themselves of the filth from the journey.

Jennifer and Jake spent time visiting their old haunts that still remained, for it had been over ten years since they had last set foot in their hometown. They enjoyed showing the d'Ambrose twins the sights and where they had lived and played as children.

Jon, of course, found several music shops and acquired another six instruments to complement those he already had.

Meanwhile, the future brides went shopping for wedding gowns, but, after four days of searching, had not found exactly what they wanted. Alison was all for great elegance and finery, while others preferred a more subtle approach. In the end, they decided that first they ought to plan the wedding before acquiring the gowns. They all laughed with relief when Mandy pointed out that normally, the bride's parents did most of such planning; and they, to a person, had a distinct lack of parents at hand. None, in fact. Mandy also noted that none of them had actually been to a wedding nor had a hand in planning one. "No wonder we are having so much trouble!" she declared. So it was Darless and her methodical nature that took charge. As usual, she enumerated a rather long list of things to find out and to do to prepare for that exciting day, sometime as yet unspecified in the spring. Her idea of bringing Lady Ursala in on the planning, as she was the nearest thing to a mother to them, was willingly accepted by all.

Now heavily laden with supplies and new clothes, refreshed in spirits, the caravan resumed its westward journey on the fifth day since the great battle on the plains. Ten uneventful days passed before they reached Banner's Towers on the edge of the Greenway, a vast grasslands stretching for leagues to the east. Needless to say, the desert dwellers were tremendously impressed with all this grass, even though it was winter time.

Another week and they reached Fitzgerald Castle at the north edge of the Brown Hills. They were nearly home. Another five days found them at La Fontaine resting at the northern edge of the Lockwood Forest. Three more days through the forest, which Mandy found delightful even though it was winter, and they arrived at Edgeway, located at the southern edge of the forest. Here Alison intended to have one third of the caravan folks spend the rest of the winter, for the d'Ambrose ruins lay only a long day's journey to the south. Another third Alison planned to spend the winter in Jascar Mines, located about day's journey south of the ruins just at the northern edge of the dark Druse Wood. The remaining third, she hoped, could winter over in Stonefist Castle located immediately west of the ruins at the edge of the small mountain range, the Rolling Hills, that began there.

Two days were thus spent in acquiring housing for the third that would remain behind here in La Fontaine. Following Sir Thomas's advice, riders went forth directly to the other two towns to prearrange lodgings. Lonnie was appointed to lead another third of the caravan directly from La Fontaine to Stonefist Castle. Thea accompanied her parents so she might see where they were going to stay at this castle. Lonnie promised to bring her back to Alison after the others were settled.

It is also noted here, that as they passed through these areas, many of the cavalry Sir Thomas had acquired departed as their homes, villages, and towns drew near. Thus, when they left La Fontaine and headed south to the ruins, only one third of the caravan came with them, those destined to winter over in Jascar Mines, and one hundred and fifty of the cavalry.

On the twentieth of November, Alison and her brother and sister finally arrived home at long last. Only a little snow covered the grasslands, and that was patchy, but May and Mat had never seen the devastation of their castle. During that horrible night so long ago, they had used their picture books to escape the crumbling walls. So it was shocking for them to see the huge pile of rubble. The castle was totally destroyed, not a wall still stood. They were silent in their shock and grief and memories for quite some time.

Suspecting this would happen, Jon and Darless were both close beside the Twins as they crested the last hill and the ruins became visible. Based upon all that they had learned about the ways of the mind, they began running May and Mat through their memories of that awful night until the terrible mental images lost their force and command over them.

On the other hand, Alison hardly recognized the place. Fully a hundred mountain dwarves were busy with the initial stages of construction. The head engineer, Thraxton Ironlegs, greeted her. "Hail Mage Alison d'Ambrose. As specified, the work has already begun. We have much to discuss as soon as possible."

Tears of joy trickling down her cheeks, she answered, "Hail Master Engineer. This is a sight I have yearned for all my life! Many heartfelt thanks for starting in the middle of the winter! Let me see to the housing of my guests and then I am all yours."

He lowered his head, feet pawed the ground like an impatient horse, and fumbled about for the right way to put this. "Er, there is something you must know before you go into your dungeon entrance. Forgive me if I have indeed made the wrong choice."

"Whatever are you talking about?" she asked dismayed and completely clueless.

"Well, Great Mage, as specified, we have begun to reuse the better stone that remains from the old castle. It was even as you suggested, we did find the remains of some fallen people. We have carefully placed them as best we could in a line against the south wall of your tunnel entrance. We did not know what better thing to do. We assume you wish to examine them and bury them after your customs of which we know not."

"Excellent, Master Engineer," she replied; it was as she had feared, many of the castle defenders had been buried in the collapse. Always her fear was that she would find the bones of her father or mother or siblings. Visions of her nightmares of seeing her mother and father crushed to death under tons of falling stonework came unbidden back into her mind.

Sir Thomas led the remaining cavalry and caravan on past the ruins and new construction, heading due south to Jascar Mines. William pulled his wagon up beside the entrance to the tunnel and waited patiently. Jon and Darless were still busy with the Twins and the Newcastles were nearby watching and listening and learning from them. So it fell upon Mandy to accompany Alison into the tunnel to see firsthand the remains. The gravity of the situation this ranger knew full well; she gave Alison her full support.

Just inside the entrance lay the remains of a dozen people. Skulls and bones were all that remained, some showing gnawing marks of field mice. Alison stared at them unsure what to do now that they had been found. "Now what?" she asked to herself. "I've got to try to identify them. I've just *got* to know if they are my relatives or not. But how?" Tears streamed down her face; she had no idea at all how to proceed.

"Ah, don't worry, Alison," Mandy tried to lighten her burden, "You've got me! And you know, maybe there is something I can contribute. Let me see." And she knelt beside the first neatly arrainged pile of bones. She put her hand on its skull and concentrated. Darkness swarmed about her; she heard yells and screams; orders barked; men rushing this way and that; sounds of combat and then the heavy, crushing weight of stone falling on him. She had seen the image of his last traumatic moments that still lingered impressed into the bone. She let go of it and daylight replaced the darkness. "This one," she said haltingly, for the experience of seeing the lingering physic residue, still shook her emotionally, "this one was a guard."

"Oh, thank you!" exclaimed Alison. "So you can tell. You are the answer to my prayers! Please continue if you are able to; just don't over do it like Jon does."

Mandy flashed a smiled and went to the next one, and then the next. She had just finished with the last one when Jon and Darless brought a now relaxed and cheerful pair of twins into the entrance along with William who stood silently at the rear. "Nope, Alison," pronounced Mandy, "all of these were guardsmen. None are your relatives. Of that I am quite sure." Alison gave her a huge hug.

"Oh, come on in," Alison's composure returned once she knew these were not her parents, "Mandy has just identified the remains of some of dad's guards that died here that night. I shall see that they get a proper burial soon. So do come on in and see what I have fixed up. It's not much, but quite comfortable until we get our new houses built this spring." May and Mat began chatting gaily as their childhood memories, long forgotten, came back to them of running and playing in these dungeon hallways.

Mandy thought that it would be a bit crowded for the six of them, but doable. She joined William and put her arm lovingly around them. "Neat isn't it," she said, "seeing them reunited and happy once again."

"Yes indeed," he whispered back, "but I've got tears blocking up my nose." She looked him squarely in the face, saw wet lines streaking down either cheek, smiled lovingly, and gave him a hug.

Jon felt a little awkward, so he quietly said, "I'll leave you two love-birds alone. I'm going outside and see what all the dwarves have been doing."

An hour later, after Alison had shown the two sets of twins all of the details of their new temporary home, including how to remove the bags over the permanent light stones, she went outside to find Jon and to inspect the new construction. She found Jon watching the industrious dwarves.

The Master Engineer, upon seeing Alison return, hastened to her. "As you can see, we have made some slight changes in the plans. First, the location you specified was ill-suited which is why we are proceeding with the construction on this hillock. One of the reasons the original castle fell was poor footings in loose soil. A pox on that designer, the fool. We have found good bedrock and are proceeding well. The footings are in place. Miners are nearly half done with the 'special underground excavations' — exactly according to your specifications. I admit that is a very wise design feature. There must always be secret ways out." Alison complimented him on everything. His fears evaporated and excitedly explained all their works to date.

They had, as expected, been able to make use of some remaining stonework for the footings of the great wall that was to surround the entire town. Already on one side, the ground had been excavated and the footings laid. It stretched nearly a mile in length to the west. As planned, her town walls were to be square in nature and a mile long. The castle proper was to stand at the northwestern corner. Already, Jon could see where the entrance guard houses were to be located.

Thraxton continued, "We expect Nain himself to arrive any day now. He has left word that he wants to see Mandy when he comes. You'll see to it that she is still here? I understand that she lives elsewhere." Alison agreed to tell her. "Okay, Nain will, of course, want to see you too. And I believe that he has a surprise in store for you as well," he teased. He knew full well what and how Nain would arrive and why, but would say nothing, fearing to spoil his liege's surprise. "And finally, we need to know fairly soon what the plans for the alu-demon's college building are and specifically where it is to be located — because of the footing, you see." Hence, Alison went to find Darless, leaving Jon to watch the busy dwarves.

One thing he noted was that the dwarves had already built themselves a sort of home. Deep within the soft earth, resting upon the now exposed bedrock, old stones from the fallen castle had been hastily arranged to form a shelter block house. Smoke came from a cleverly designed makeshift chimney. Jon hiked down the embankment to get a closer look at this newly build blockhouse. As he got there, the door opened and out came a young dwarf wearing an apron. "Hail sir, Zender, at your service," he bowed low.

"Hi, I'm Jon, Jon Brown," he replied, trying to mimic the dwarf's bow.

"Ah, the Great Mage's fiancé," he recognized him now, "the musician. We have something in common, Jon, though it is not all this infernal cooking. You see, I am considered too young to work on the actual construction; I'm only fifty-five. So I am relegated to being the chief cook and bed maker. But really, I am a musician myself. I've heard that you want to learn dwarven songs? Is that right?"

"You betcha!" exclaimed Jon. This was more to his liking. He could watch the construction and learn dwarven music which totally fascinated him. It was so dark, so inspiring, so unlike any he had ever heard. Jon just knew that he and Zender were going to become close friends!

That evening as the companions finished dinner in the now rather crowed dining room of Alison's, she said, "Okay, tonight, I have an urgent job for all of you. I'm told that Nain himself will be here any day, and we must be prepared. It is a very high honor indeed to have the mountain dwarves build our castle. In all such matters, they must be paid. Further, I am having them build it as fast as possible. That means they are working three shifts each day, and that means triple wages must be paid."

"Where are we ever going to get that much money," cried May a bit startled by this talk of what must be a vast sum.

"Ah yes," Alison went on, "it is precisely one and a half million gold coins, in fact. Which brings me to the urgent job with which I need your help." She moved over to the side wall, uttered her command word to open her secret treasury room. "Da ta!" she exclaimed. The door opened revealing her treasury room. The last time Jon had seen it, Alison had a small treasury stacked over in one corner. Most of the room was her workshop. But now, the entire room was filled with gold coins and the occasional bag of gems. There were many exclamations of complete disbelief.

"Some of this is your share, Mandy, Jon, Darless. So we need to divvy up your shares and, most importantly, count out into a pile in the hallway one and a half million of these coins for the dwarves.

"Just put my share with yours," Jon said quietly. "I've no need for all this."

"I'm using my share to build my College," Darless stated. "So let's just leave mine here too and whatever is left over from construction costs I can use to furnish it and such."

"Well, I don't need this vast a sum either," declared Mandy, "but I could use some of it to fix up Castle Blackthorn and improve conditions in my village. So can I have say about two hundred thousand coins at the most. The rest, let's put in on the castle construction."

"Thanks, each of you. There is going to be lots left over. So really, guys, anytime you need any funds, just ask. I'll hold it in reserve here for you, but come on, we have a mammoth task before us, counting out this huge a sum! I hope none has a weak back!" Alison teased.

Jon faked a moan, "Oh my aching back. Perhaps, I should go find Zender and practice music making." She poked him and everyone laughed and then set about the task.

It was no small task either, but when they were done, aided by some nifty magical spells that Darless thought up to make the matter easier to accomplish, a huge stack neatly lined the entire tunnel entrance, ready for the dwarves to take home with them. Jon wondered how they could manage to carry such a huge weight but he would soon find out, much to his surprise.

When they had finished, the workroom appeared a room once again. Several hundred thousand gold coins and a sprinkling of silver and some others yet remained, stacked neatly against the southern wall. Now their attention turned to the gems. All told, there were now well over one thousand of them in various sizes and types. Some, Mat explained, were exceedingly valuable, but most, he thought were worth between ten and a hundred gold coins. Still, it was a significant amount. Tired and exhausted by the labor of handling such a weight in gold, they all slept very soundly that night. It is also to be noted her that they now appreciated living in the dungeon because the noise of the third shift construction could only barely be heard this far underground.

Nain arrived around noon the next day in a rather spectacular way. Darless and Alison were outside discussing the placement for the College when a huge flash of magical energies appeared upon the hill above the new location of the castle and town. A golden disk about ten feet in diameter appeared midair and floated to the ground and seemingly merged with it. Then, a yellow beam appeared arcing from high in the sky beaming down until it touched the disk. "A gate spell," cried Darless aloud. "Someone is using a gate spell!"

Once the yellow beam connected with the golden disk, Nain suddenly appeared carrying a large bundle. As he stepped off the disk, other dwarves appeared behind him also hastily leaving the disk for even more were appearing. In fact, fifty dwarves had gated here with Nain. Many were fighters, well-armed.

"Greetings, one and all," Nain called out. "Glad to see you made it here safe and sound. Though we did have word of your successful passage through the Desolation Range and hobgoblins. I say, was that really Lord Jarred that you dispatched, Darless?"

"How could you possibly know that?" she exclaimed a bit startled. Did all the world now know she had killed a Demon Lord?

Nain's eyes twinkled and he smiled just to confuse her further. "No, actually, we heard through the grapevine from a little gnome friend of yours. Seems he saw the whole thing from a mountain top using what he calls his far-seeing-glasses; makes far things look big and up close, he says. Be that as it may, is it true?"

Thus, Darless had to recount again what she and the others had done that day. When she had finished, it was obvious to everyone that Nain, a high priest among his people, was not satisfied with her explanation. "I doubt your words not," he said, "but clarify a detail for me. You are strong, yes. But by the time of the attack on Lord Jarred, were you not physically exhausted from all your previous combat?"

"Well, yes I was indeed," she agreed, not seeing what point he was attempting to make.

"And did you not say that during the fight with Jarred, both your legs were broken along with many ribs?" he asked.

"Yes, when I was finished, I could no longer stand, and it was very hard to breathe," now she was beginning to follow where he was heading. She had been there briefly before in her thoughts, but had found no answer and forgotten it all.

"Then answer me this," Nain finally made his point, "how then did you have the physical strength to rip, as you say, his arms and his head off his body? Surely that takes a very great strength indeed. I know, I am a very strong dwarf but even I cannot do such a feat." This was indeed that point of her tale that he did not understand. Jon wondered how he had missed this detail, but then priests, he thought were supposed to be wise.

Darless thought for a minute before speaking. Attempting to put this into words that could be understood was difficult. Even she did not fully grasp how she had done what she had done. "Well I remember grabbing onto his arms. I was on the ground at the time, yes, I could no longer easily stand, legs were broken. I jerked hard once on them. I think I realized at that instant that if I could pull his arms off, the combat would be over. Jon, I've been meaning to ask you about this, only I keep forgetting to. It was like I knew I did not have the strength to do it with my body, but I recalled sort of how I imagine Jon does his thing of mentally stepping to another place. So I got the idea I was about three feet behind where I was kneeling. Then, I was there holding on to his flopping, dangling arms. I did the same thing with his head when I grabbed a hold of it."

"By golly, Darless," Jon exclaimed excitedly, "you've figured out how to do it like I do it! Only you forgot to bring the rest of Jarred's body along with you. You must remember to will the rest of the person along with you. I've never tried to only will just their arms. The instantaneous motion would surely rip limb from body. So that's how you did it. Congratulations!"

Nain was still not totally satisfied, so Jon drew him a sketch in the loose dirt. "First you are here and then in the next instant you decide you are here. See? If you only decide to bring the arms, there is no time for the other to respond. I think it is like what happens to a wizard who is teleporting and arrived say too low and materializes underground. There is no time left to do anything about it." Relating it to teleportation satisfied Nain; to that he could relate.

"Ah then, I believe I finally understand!" Nain then turned his attention to Mandy. He said most formally, "Ranger Mandy Blackthorn, I hereby present you with Zond." He unwrapped the package he was carrying to reveal a bastard sword in a jeweled case. Mandy was speechless and stared at the marvelous sword as Nain continued. "It was forged by my own hand and crafted for you and for you alone. It will give you that speed advantage that we discussed so many months ago. That it is a worthy blade, let it hereby be known that it withstood four magical enchantment levels! Its edge will cut through ordinary steel. I know, I tested it by cutting through a two-handed sword. Yet this may be your biggest problem with it, for it cuts through most anything. So be careful in practice or you will destroy your opponent's weapon," he jested.

Mandy got down on one knee and accepted this royal gift. She knew no words sufficient to thank him and so just said, "Thank you, Nain. I don't know what to say. I am honored beyond words."

"Ah you have more than earned it," he replied, "you saved my son from his own foolishness and early demise. It is a token of my gratitude."

Turning to Alison, he said, "For you, I have something that will interest you and be of great benefit in the near future. As you can see, I arrived here by using a gate spell. But what you may not realize is that while one end of the gate is here, the other end is near the special black stone. The gate remains here permanently here until the construction is finished. Need I elaborate?"

Alison took a moment to fully grasp the total significance. Jon knew that she had suddenly duplicated the true importance for her mouth fell open and no words came out for a brief time. Finally, she managed to utter, "That will mean getting all that stone here will be easy and swift. No long caravans bearing stone."

"Yes, that alone will cut nearly six months off the construction time," replied the dwarf. "I figured that is the least I can do for all you have done for my kinsmen, all unasked for. But yet there is one other surprise that I have for you, but it is for your ears alone. Come hither." She walked up close to his side and bent low to hear his whispers.

"Those silver streaks within the blackys as Rolf calls them — well, I have identified what it is. Mithril, my lady, mithril. That is why those rocks were unaffected by the rock to mud spells of the Vyndocians." Alison eyes opened wide; her jaw dropped for a moment.

But she quickly recovered. She whispered back, "I had a strong feeling that that was what it might just be. I am getting a royal castle and town indeed!"

Then, Alison spoke in her normal voice for the others to hear, "I'm doubly honored, doubly blessed then," she replied. "For dwarves, the world's best stonemasons, are building my castle and town and now going to build it in record time!"

"Well, there is the small matter of recompense," Nain added in a low voice.

"Ah yes," she quickly replied, glad that they had done the sorting last night, only just in time. "Do not fear, one and a half million lies neatly stacked in the dungeon tunnel ready for you. If you will follow me?" she added.

"One million only," Nain corrected her. "The gate is cutting the cost by a third." Nain followed by the other fifty men he brought along went to examine the funds. Needless to say, it took the dwarves the remainder of that day and far into the night to get it all carried to the golden disk and gated back into the Desolation range. Once the transportation process had begun, Nain toured the site and chatted with his friends while his helpers labored with all the gold.

In the late afternoon, he watched as Mandy took her first practice session with Zond. "This is a fantastically well-made blade!" she exclaimed as she practiced. Nain beamed proudly; few had the skill with weapons that he had.

"Oops," she exclaimed as her swing connected with her dueling partner's long sword which was promptly cut in half. Shortly after that came another "Oops!" from Mandy. Her blow had just cut a corner off of an entrance stone to Alison's tunnel. "Zagroot zounds! This can cut through stone! Nain, you are incredible!"

"So is the one who wields Zond," and his eyes twinkled as he raised his eyebrows in a tease. She leaned over and gave him a kiss. "Bahhh," he exclaimed in mock protest, but inwardly, he enjoyed her attention. *A mighty fine human woman indeed,* he thought to himself.

I know! And a mighty handsome dwarven man indeed, came suddenly into his mind. Mandy had read his thought and countered. He flushed red and pretended to clear his throat.

Thus the day passed enjoyed by all. When the last of the gold had been gated back to the mountains, Nain said his farewells, promising to come and visit as regularly as time and events would permit. He too then stepped onto the golden disk; the energies flashed and he was gone.

As they all stood by watching him go, "Alison suddenly said, "Oh no!"

"What's the matter, love," asked Jon a bit concerned that something important had been forgotten.

"I just realized that now we have to move all that gold back into the treasury room! Perhaps one of you strong fellows would take it all to towns and exchange it for gems?" she teased.

"Sure thing," exclaimed Mat. After a pause, he added, "But can we do it a little at a time? That is one heavy pile of gold!" Everyone laughed and headed into the tunnel to move it out of sight back into the secret workroom.

The next day, Mandy and William prepared to depart for their homeland and Blackthorn Castle. She explained, "I now know how our lands connect and we can get home overland, but that will take way too long. So I guess we'll just use the picture book." She showed William the valuable, magical book page that opened near their land. He recognized Blackthorn Castle at once.

"Wait a minute," Mandy exclaimed. "You've all never seen my castle. Why don't you all come home with us and visit our place for a few days? The dwarves have everything under control. It's a perfect time to come visit me, though I have no idea what the condition of the castle will be in, I've been gone for so long."

"Yes, let's do, Alison," urged Jon. All this time and he had never seen her castle, and he found himself really wanting to see it firsthand. Alison and Darless wanted to see it as well and took very little convincing. However, the two sets of Twins declined, saying that they all had had enough traveling for the moment. All they wanted to do was stay in one place, one that preferably was not moving!

Then came the problem of transporting her two hundred thousand coins. This they solved my putting much of it into their three portable holes. When they were ready, Mandy questioned, "Okay, now how do we get there? By book, by teleport, or by Jon?"

"Oh come on!" exclaimed Jon, grabbing hold of Mandy's and Alison's hands. "You two grab hold of William and Darless."

"But I don't know what to do," protested William a bit frightened by this unexpected move.

"Nothing to it," Jon said, "Just step forward and the next step, ah, here we are, you see the castle." And true enough, there they were, standing before Mandy's castle, looming large with its black stonework impressively before them.

"Ieee," exclaimed William, as he fell flat on the ground. Hastily, he picked himself up and dusted off the dust and bit of snow. "Watch that first step there," he added, "It is a big one!" Everyone roared with laughter.

They stood near the entrance gatehouse. A small moat surrounded the castle and a wide dirt road led from its gatehouse up to them and then on behind them. "The village lies behind us, see," Mandy pointed. Sure enough, while a dark oak forest surrounded all the land for a hundred miles around, some two hundred feet behind them, buildings could be seen. Jon marveled because he recognized the architecture as mediaeval British tutor style.

These were great oak trees, though bare here in winter, they still rose to an impressive height. Their girths were so great that Jon could not put his arms around them. The forest stopped only at the edge of the moat, though some great bows stretched across the water and high castle walls.

Mandy noted Jon noticing that detail. "I know, if we are besieged here, the enemy can breech the walls by climbing over the branches. But the trees are so beautiful, I haven't the heart to cut off their branches."

Mandy took William by the arm, "Come on, love, you have rarely been inside. You are soon to be a 'lord' of the castle; you should see what you are getting yourself into."

"I don't know about this," he said. "I've only been inside a few times and then only in the great hall for the equinox feast. Are you sure I'll be accepted? I don't know anything about castles or their operation or anything. I just make bread."

"You'll do fine," Mandy convinced him. "My staff run the place with no need of help. So all you need do is bake bread, if that's all you want to do, but I hope you want to do a little more with me, especially at nighttime," she teased. He flushed and gave her a little squeeze on her rear.

As they walked up toward the gatehouse, a gong from a tower high above them began a regular pattern. "Someone has spied me," proclaimed Mandy. A man in chain mail came rushing out of the gatehouse.

"Greetings, Lady. Welcome back. It has been quite a while and we've had no word about you. Forgive us for not having everything prepared for your arrival," he was being polite and practical at the same time.

Mandy introduced her friends, "John here is the daytime gateman, in charge of permitting actual entry to the castle grounds." He bowed to her guests. "Oh yes, John, from now on, William here is to be granted total access, for we are to be wed this spring!" Jon watched as her words sunk in.

A huge smile formed, "Well, it's about time. Congratulations indeed! William, the Baker, who would have thought he'd be the one to win your heart! I just lost ten coins on that one."

"What do you mean?" Mandy toyed with him. She knew darn well that all sorts of wagers had been made over the years as to who she would marry. Red faced, he explained what she already knew. Then she led them in past the gatehouse. She pointed out the arrow slits all around. No one could safely gain unauthorized access, at least not easily.

Once inside the massive walls, they crossed the wide open grounds that served many purposes, including sword practice arena. Before them rose the large stone main house in which Mandy had lived her whole life. A man and woman rushed out to meet them.

"Ah here's Martha and Matthew, they actually run the daily operations of the castle, you know, all the mundane things. Without them, this place would go to pot in a day!" She introduced the husband and wife team to her friends and again told them about William.

"Oh my. Oh my," exclaimed Martha as tears gushed out. "We'd almost given up hope you would ever find someone. Congratulations, My Lady. And you too, Master William. So went the joyful reunion.

Mandy gave them the grand tour of the castle which took over two hours to see in its entirety. Alison and Jon were making notes of its good points for discussion with the dwarves on her castle. In fact, they got a rather large number of ideas. The most significant one was that Alison had no real idea of castle defenses and how they should ideally be established. Mandy promised to return and help them get it designed correctly.

When they had seen everything, Jon commented to Mandy, "You were right. Your castle is really terrific, beautiful and functional and well-maintained. The others that I was so impressed with before pale to yours."

"Really, you all should see it in the spring or summer or fall. We are smack in the middle of the Gnarled Oak Forest. So when the flowers and trees are out, it is always cool and refreshing here. It is a true pleasure to go for a walk in the woods! I love it dearly. That's why I stay here," she added. Jon tried to imagine what it would look like in the spring, but he realized he needed to come back and see. He vowed to do so.

"Let's walk down to the village and see William's shop," offered Mandy. "You know that is the one detail that's wrong here and I aim to spend some of this new funds repairing this. You are doing it right."

"Sure, let's," answered Alison, "but what are we doing right?"

"Notice my village is hundreds of feet away. If enemies come, the villagers have to leave everything behind and rush to get inside the gates before they shut," explained the seasoned Ranger. "You are making the town walls and defending castle as one unit. That is defensively far superior."

As they entered the village, which was home to several hundred people, Jon marveled at how all the homes, tutor in nature, were built around the giant, stately oak trees. Indeed the road twisted and turned moving around the trees. The original designer was loathed to fell a single tree. The village blended with nature, or was at one with nature. This fact was not lost on Alison, Jon nor Darless.

Townsfolk were going about their daily lives. Smoke rose from various chimneys. Children were playing the roadway; there were no fences separating homes. Only an occasional wagon moved slowly on the streets, no one seemed in any hurry, save the children playing. Suddenly one spied William and called out to the other, "William's back! William's back. Cookie time!" At least thirty children from those just able to walk to those in their early teens swarmed around William. The older ones backed off and became more formal when they saw Mandy, their Liege Lady, but Mandy would have none of that, "Keep on playing, kids."

"Kids," William knelt down on one knee, "I got to bake them first. Maybe tomorrow it will be cookie day." They cheered and ran off to tell their parents the news. He explained that he always had a cookie for the kids and they had come to expect it; he loved doing it.

"I didn't realize you had such a way with children!" exclaimed Mandy, hugging him. "How could I have missed so obvious a thing?"

"Cause you were always off fighting the bad guys, protecting others," he replied confidently, and that was the truth of the matter. She seldom had time to stroll in her own village.

"Here's my house, my bakery," he said as they stopped by another house, almost indistinguishable from all the others, save for the giant loaf of bread carved from wood that hung over his door. He led them inside. Jon noticed the door had no lock. William noticed Jon noticing that too and said, "No need for a lock. I've nothing of value, only cookies." He grinned.

Jon realized in that instant just how similar William and he were. Both were quite content to bake bread for others or make music for others. Neither had any higher aspirations in life for doing what was life for them. A man doing what he truly wants to do is a happy man indeed, Jon mused.

The first floor of William's two story house was very different that most of the surrounding homes. He had converted the whole first floor into a bakery shop. One room held vast stores of ingredients. The kitchen held four ovens and a huge oak work table. The dining room housed the purchasing and sampling area, while his living room held the finished products. "I won't show you the upstairs because it is a mess. I had to leave in such a great hurry when I got Reylona's message that it's a really big mess."

After the tour, they ambled around the village. Word of Mandy's coming marriage to William spread like wildfire among the villagers. So everywhere they went, her villagers stopped them to wish them the best. Indeed, these simple townsfolk were proud that one of their own had captured the heart of their Liege Lady. Many had feared some outsider would come and take over things. Now those unfounded fears evaporated for William was one of them.

At dinner time, they ate in Mandy's Great Hall. Jon stared at the sights barely eating. The room was done in mahogany and done spectacularly. It was magnificent, he thought, done with excellent taste. It also boasted a musician's stage. Mandy noticed Jon noticing the stage. "Oh, I almost forgot." She clapped her hands three times and a side door opened and in rushed four musicians with lutes, guitars and a flute like instrument. They mounted the stairs to the stage and took their positions. One then said, "Your desires, My Lady?"

"Romantic music, Guy. William and I are betrothed. So are Jon and Alison here and Darless is too, though her fiancé is away on other matters at the moment." As they played, Jon ached to get up on stage and join them. Mandy knew that, she was teasing him, and Jon knew that she was too, but that did not lessen the fact that he wanted to play as well.

Darless brought him back to the table by commenting, "I think that the walls of the College should be wood, rather like this room, don't you Jon?" He could only agree; it was beautiful and very relaxing in here.

Over after-dinner tea, Mandy advised Alison, "You know the most important thing about running a castle is to hire only the best, most competent staff. Without Martha and Matthew, this place would soon be a shambles. They always know the right way to do something and just what needs to be done and when. You should start looking for such people right now even before the town and castle are finished." The questions and answers flowed until it was late.

The main house had four stories above ground and several below. The Great Hall was on the second floor. The servant's quarters were in the basement along with the food storage and preparation rooms. The guest quarters were on the third floor and the Lord and Lady's quarters on the fourth. They spent the night in the guest rooms. There were ten in number, each huge in size and done in a different style and color scheme. All were elegant and cozy. It was in the blue room that Alison and Jon spent the night, her call. Mandy and her staff had excellent taste and quality, she noted, but Alison tended to luxurious items, the exotic as well. She wore ermine when others chose fox or rabbit. Both kept you snug and warm, but the ermine made the difference in visual impact.

So in truth, Mandy was right in getting them to visit her right now, for Alison and Jon learned just how much they had yet to learn about castles and castle life. Alison told her so and thanked her too.

The next day, over tea just after breakfast, Alison suddenly realized they had completely forgotten her brother. "Oh good grief! We forgot Lenny. I do hope Lady Ursla has healed his body. We really must go to her at once!" All felt a bit downhearted about having totally forgetting about him.

"Yet, his plight is almost unconfrontable," suggested Jon, "that alone makes it altogether too easy for us to put him out of our minds, our plans." His words rang true.

So Darless made mental contact with the druid, letting her know that they were on their way. The three said their farewells, promising to return soon, and Jon stepped the three straight to the door of Lady Ursla's cottage deep within Hollybine Woods. They found her waiting for them at her door, tea cup in hand.

"Good morning," she greeted them, "It certainly has been a long time." There was the hint of offense in her tone. Alison had dumped her brother off on the druid and then disappeared for several months without a word. Jon sensed this and relayed it to Alison, who really did not need Jon's words, she was fully aware of what had transpired.

Once inside and seated with a proper cup of tea, Alison began, "I am truly sorry that it took so long for us to return. I feel we owe you a full accounting." Therefore, she spent the next two hours relaying the highlights of what had happened. Unbeknownst to Alison, much of what she told the druid, this high priestess already knew from her druid contacts in the area of Freetown. However, she also felt that she was owed a full explanation from Alison. She also asked many questions. Frequently, Jon observed her eyebrows raise, indicating she was impressed.

However, when Alison relayed Darless' fight and victory over Lord Jarred, Lady Ursla could contain herself no longer. "Oh daughter, you could have been killed! But I'm so proud of you!" She hugged her tightly for several minutes. "I'd had heard rumors, so it's true then. You are indeed a demon slayer!"

When the full accounting was finished, Lady Ursla spoke formally to Alison, "Indeed, Mage, you have fulfilled your part of the bargain. You have restored the balance. I thank you."

"But wait, Lady Ursla," protested Alison, "to this day, I do not know to what or where I was supposed to return the balance too! I'd fully come here today expecting to be scolded for not have done it sooner."

"Why, my dear, to Freetown, that's where. You did it with grace and style, worthy of a Great Druid, I might add."

"Oh," the mage commented to herself. "Oh, well, you need not have worried about that. There was no way I could not have done something for that town." The Great Druid merely smiled and gave no indication one way or the other if she always knew that.

Now it was Darless' turn. "Mother, I have some other news for you. You already know that Jon and Alison are getting married. But also her brother and sister, the twins, are going to get married at the same time as is Mandy and William, the baker." She paused as the druid nodded, not yet seeing the point. "And so am I. I've found him!"

The Great Druid's eyes opened wider than Jon could imagine. "To whom?" she asked sternly. "And do you truly love him? What about the racial barrier? Has that been considered?" Jon knew that she was very concerned that Darless not get emotionally hurt.

"Yes and yes. To Sir Thomas le Bonnaire, the Holy Paladin of Ukko," gushed Darless. It felt so wonderful, so free, to just be able to say out loud to others what she had long held inside.

"Oh my goodness," the dignified older woman replied, "that is exceedingly good news, then. In many, many ways." Jon could see her mind racing over the unlimited possibilities that a familiar connection to a Holy Paladin of Ukko could bring. "That is, my dear, a very wise choice, very. Come here." She hugged her for some time.

When they separated, Darless continued, "And, ah, that brings us to a problem that I thought you might be able to help us solve."

"Ah ha, then there is a catch," replied the Great Druid, half-heartedly.

"Well, yes. Usually, the parents of the bride make all the arrangements, you know, plan the big day, and all that. In our cases, none of us have any parents. And when we all went shopping in Tannersville, we discovered none of us have any idea about how to do it! Then, I thought of you. You are the closest thing any of us have to a mother, you being the wife of my father. Would you please, please, help us plan this thing? All of us want to be married in a single ceremony. Please?"

"Daughter mine," the Great Druid pronounced, "a child's wedding day is supposed to be the happiest, nicest day of her life. What mother would not help? Yes, yes I most certainly will. But you all have to help me, for I know not all your customs and tastes."

Alison found herself also hugging the Great Druid along with Darless. Even Jon offered her his heartfelt thanks. The three women chatted gaily for some time.

"The first thing you must do is set the date and the place," explained the druid, "for all else flows from that. But come, we are forgetting your brother in all this excitement."

"Oh, yes, how is he doing?" Alison asked suddenly deadly serious once more, fearing the worst.

"Both good and bad," she replied. "It has turned out as I thought it might. I have restored his health, his body. But his mind is another matter. Come with me and visit him. I have done all that I can for him. The rest is up to you." She led them out her backdoor and into her gardens now grey with the coming of winter. Yet it was still reasonably warm here in Hollybine Woods. There sitting by himself was her brother, staring at the dried plants. His body was fully healed; indeed he looked healthy and fit. But Alison also noticed that two of the druid's lions lay a short distance from him, watching over him, least anything ill befall him.

Alison's heart sunk at the sight. "He just sits there?" was all she could manage to say.

"Yes, he follows orders, if you are pleasant about them. If you are forceful or angry with him, he breaks into terror fits," came the diagnosis. "It is all mental now and in your hands." No one spoke further.

Jon broke the silence, "Thank you for healing him. I believe Darless and I can help him now. Come on Alison, let's get him safely home. It's time." They said their farewells for just a while. Darless promised to return very soon, but she was committed to helping out as she could. The druid fully understood.

This time, Alison teleported the small group home to the ruins of her castle, for Jon was unsure how Lenny would respond to Jon's mode of travel. Though they arrived at dusk, Jon did observe that Lenny recognized his home. Jon though that there was some hope yet for Lenny.

676

The dismay of May and Mat upon seeing their brother was great indeed, but they valiantly said nothing within hearing distance of Lenny. "Don't worry too much yet," Jon consoled the twins. "Darless and I are going to try our mental approaches with him. We may yet get him back."

And the next morning, Jon and Darless began their work on Lenny. They had him in what used to be a dungeon cell, but was now a guest room. "Where do we begin?" Jon wondered.

"Let's both take a look at what he is looking at right now," suggested Darless. They reached out and entered his mind, saw what he saw. It was more horrible than anything Jon could ever have imagined. So horrid it was, that he was momentarily sent reeling out of contact with Lenny and fell to the floor, bumping his head. Darless helped him back up. "I figured this would be a bit much for you to handle, Jon. Remember, I was raised in the Abyss. I've seen it all. Jon, give me this patient. Let me handle him."

At first, Jon was only too willing to give her the responsibility alone, but then he thought better of it. "Okay, but I am going to monitor it all as best I can. I should, must, have to be able to confront this evil. It is just going to be a bit rough. So you have the patient, but I am going to watch and learn."

"Thanks," she replied, "And do offer any suggestions as they arise. Or if I screw something up, let me know at once."

He willingly agreed. "You know, this is about the worst possible case imaginable. If you, or we can get him back in control of his mind, get this horror erased from controlling him, why you should be able to handle anything that comes your way in the College." Darless agreed with him completely. Slowly, ever so slowly, she reentered his mind to scout and decide where to begin.

After a time, she noticed in one small corner of his mind, he was looking at a picture of himself playing with a ball running around the corridors of this castle before it was destroyed. *Good a place to begin as any*, she sent Jon. He agreed.

"Okay, Lenny," Darless began. "I want you to return to that time when you were young and were playing with the red ball and running about these halls. Yes, that time there. Yes.

Now I want you to go through what happened there and tell me all about it as you do so."

Lenny was slow, but he uttered his first words in a dozen years. "My ball. My ball. Fun. I have fun." Thus it began. Jon knew that this man would have to run through an enormous amount of evil events, horrors beyond horrors done to his body, to him. But it was a good start. It would take time.

She ran him through this time many times, noticing each time, he volunteered more details, more of the sights and sounds that he had experienced at that time. Finally, he even chuckled and smiled. Darless ended off at this point.

They left him lying on the bed, smiling for the first time in twenty years. Alison was awaiting them anxiously in the kitchen area. May and Mat were also with her. "Well?" she blurted out as soon as Jon and Darless walked into the kitchen. "Did we hear him laugh just then?"

Darless grinned, "You certainly did. The first session went without a hitch. Some progress, although very slight, has been made. Jon's technique appears to work well on him. Don't get too excited, though," she added noticing the expectancy of Alison. "We only ran a time he had fun playing with a ball as a child. This process is going to take a very long time with him. But it does seem to be working and workable. You will be seeing a lot of me in the foreseeable future," she teased.

"Anything, anything you want, you got!" exclaimed Alison. "I owe you so much I don't know how to repay you."

"You already did," answered the alu-demon, knowing full well that that would shock her.

"What?" exclaimed Alison in dismay. "What have I done?"

Darless spoke very quietly, "You gave me Sir Thomas." She said no more. Nor could Alison get her to elaborate, merely leaving her to ponder her words. Darless left and went for a walk outside to get some fresh air.

Alison looked hopelessly at Jon. "Don't look at me," he said. "I've no idea what she meant." But he began to try to figure it out for himself.

They looked at each other and thought for a half hour before Alison cried out, "This is maddening. What does she mean?"

"Maybe we need to interpret her literally?" suggested Jon. So they both thought and reasoned some more.

"Oh I get it," Alison finally called out. "It is literally meant. For years Sir Thomas has been trying to court me and I was not interested, never gave him leave to do so. So by my action, I made it possible for him to be available for her and him to fall in love. Darn, that's not a sufficient reward for all her aid! I feel I need to directly do something for her."

Jon thought for a moment, "Hon, let it be just now. There may yet come a time when you can reciprocate, return the aid." Alison could accept that.

"Okay, I will say no more, but remember, Jon, I owe her and am determined to repay her."

"I wouldn't be marrying you if I thought you wouldn't be," he lovingly teased her. She responded with a loving kiss.

The next day, Sir Thomas returned from his trip to Jascar Mines. Immediately, Darless rushed to his side and together they took a very long stroll around the grounds. She first let him report on the proper resettlement of the remaining third of the caravan folks. It had gone very well for them. When he had finished, she brought him up to date on the recent events. Finally, she took him to see Lenny, who at least now looked up at the people who entered his room. Though he did smile when he saw either Darless or Jon.

Sir Thomas was speechless. He could find no words to say for a long while. Tears, he wiped from his eyes several times. At last, upon seeing Jon again, he managed to utter, "You are indeed Saint Jon Brown, the Redeemer!" He emphasized the last word. "If in life, I can in any way assist you, do not hesitate to ask, any time, any place."

Careful, Jon! Alison, who overheard the paladin's vow, sent to Jon. *He's pledging you his highest level of support; only to Ukko does he have a higher pledge.*

Trying to be as formal as he could, Jon answered, "In Ukko's name I accept your most worthy support. And accept my heartfelt thanks for your aid." His speech seemed to please the paladin. Alison, moving to his side, gave him a reassuring hug, so he relaxed a bit. He wondered if this man ever just relaxed and enjoyed himself.

Over dinner that evening, Darless brought up a final piece of unfinished business, one which under the present circumstances, she would be hard-pressed to fulfill. "There yet remains another matter. If you will recall, I promised Metrarch that I would see to it that all of those people that he injured or the relatives of those slain by his Chasme horde would be recompensed financially." She paused, giving them time to recall before she continued. "In this matter, I am rather ill-suited to perform it. Number 1, my first immediate duty is to help the recovery of Lenny. I cannot be away from him for any extended period of time. Number 2, I do not even know precisely how many citizens of these lands were killed or injured. Number 3, even so, I suspect that they might not accept money from an alu-demon. Number 4, I feel strongly that they should get their financial assistance as soon as possible. Some may be in great need, now that it is winter. So I am open to suggestions on how best to handle this situation."

"I'm sorry, Darless," Jon muttered, "I had totally forgotten about that pledge. You are right on four, some may really be in need since it is winter."

Sir Thomas cleared his throat, "Ah, hem. I believe I may be of assistance in this matter," he began formally. "My Love is correct; some may not desire to accept money from an alu-demon, but they would take it from a Holy Paladin of Ukko. If you recall, it was my party that had the most news of the damage caused by the demon horde as they passed through these lands. So who better than I to accept this duty? Besides, it would be a dangerous mission carrying that amount of money about the lands, you know, brigands and thieves and all."

Everyone thanked him for accepting this obligation, but he was not through talking. "There remains one small detail. If we say the money comes from Metrarch, then many questions will be asked. Many that are best left unanswered. Indeed, some may refuse recompense from demons. So what shall we say to them? That is the question."

There was much talk on this point. Certainly Alison and Sir Thomas wanted to tell as much of the truth as possible, without compromising Metrarch. In the end, it was Jon who had the last word. Having thought it through, he suggested this speech:

"The perpetrator of this crime against humanity has seen the errors of his ways. While nothing can resurrect those that were killed or ease the pain and suffering of those who were wounded or those whose lives were so severely impacted by the loss or injury of a loved one, he, nevertheless, wishes to make some recompense. I, Sir Thomas, Holy Paladin of Ukko, have been charged with seeing that you are in some small way compensated for your loss. Please accept this in the spirit in which it was intended. Use it to better your life and those of others. If you refuse these funds, then I am charged to make it as a donation to a public charity of my choice in your town, presented in honor of the name of the victim."

"Absolutely perfect!" cried Sir Thomas. "Are you sure you are not also a Holy Paladin of Ukko?"

Jon grinned, "Nope, not even his musician. Now that would be something, to be the Holy Musician of Ukko." He intended it as a jest, but it took them a minute to realize he was just teasing. Then they all laughed, Sir Thomas, most hardily.

Next came the problem of how to transport such a sum. This, Sir Thomas readily handled. Using William's wagon, he transported a vast loads of gold to nearby towns, trading for gems. It took him a week to accomplish the conversion. It is noted here for the record, that with each load of gold, before he transported it, he cast spells upon it to determine that no evil radiated from said coins. None ever did, much to his amazement. Once he had it converted into gems, he and his band loaded up on supplies. To accomplish this task, he expected to be gone at least three weeks, perhaps more. He and Darless said their farewells and he promised to return just as soon as he could. Their parting kiss, he would long remember.

The short winter days passed by uneventfully. The dwarves were busy with the construction. Soon great slabs of the black basalt stone with the tiny swirls of mithril embedded within them began to arrive. The outer walls consisted of two layers of these huge stones. Sandwiched between each was a magical wall of force cast by either Alison or Darless. The outer walls were ten feet thick, but unknown to others, a wall of force lay five feet back of the outer walls, right in the middle. Each outer surface had been highly polished by Rolf's stone giants and shone brightly in the sun, reflecting its rays. This castle was going to be spectacular in appearance incredibly difficult to destroy by any means.

Thus, the mage's time was spent working in close consort with the dwarven engineers. She became involved with its construction every step of the way, learning much in the process.

Darless traveled often back to Hollybine Wood to visit with Lady Ursla, planning the big day. Yet always, by dark she returned back to her patient. Indeed, with Lenny, it was slow going. Yet each day, one more nasty incident from the Abyss days of Lenny had its force over him erased. But there were so many, many of them. Lenny was definitely a long term project. Still, Jon's technique — the technique on which she intended to build her College — was working. Jon pointed out that as time went on, they were handling rougher, nastier incidents. So both remained hopeful of the final outcome. Jon found that it was far easier for him this way because he only had to confront a little bit of nastiness each day, not wallow in all that the Abyss had to offer.

Then came one special day, hereafter known as the turning point for Lenny. After the session was over, Darless brought Lenny to the supper table where they all were gathered. When Lenny sat down, he looked all around and said to everyone's total surprise, "Hi Alison, May, Mat." That was all he said, but Alison and May began crying for joy. Even Jon and Mat could not keep the tears away. Darless beamed with pride in her patient.

During this time, Sir Thomas had arrived having visited the Chasme damaged towns north of here. He was resting the horses for a couple days before beginning the more lengthier southern leg of his visits, and he too witnessed this turning point. He took his love aside and said, with tears flowing down his face, "You are the greatest person I have ever known!" He hugged her for a very long time.

The wedding date that was finally agreed upon by all was May Day, the first of May. The location took longer to resolve. After much discussion, they decided to do it at Blackthorn Castle. There were many reasons for this choice, not the least of which was that Lady Ursla would certainly enjoy the woods. Preparations began in earnest.

The months went by swiftly. The town walls were completed. The construction of the castle proper and the many stone homes commenced at a rapid pace. With the coming of spring, many of the townsfolk were able to move into their new homes and begin life anew, helping to make this a wonderful town in which to live. Henry continued to make daily progress, his sanity was slowly being restored. In short, these were happy, joyous times for everyone. And to one and all, the future look bright, full of happiness and joy.

There is but one final footnote to relate and that concerns Mandy Blackthorn and William Conners. It happened one evening shortly after Alison had left to go to Lady Ursla to fetch Henry. The two were lying in her master bedroom basking in each other's love. Both spied a shimmering white light dancing before them. They only had time to rise when the familiar form of Reylona appeared before them. Both lowered their eyes in reverence to her.

"Arise my most honored children. I have come to personally thank you both. William, you have once again proven my faith in you. What would you wish for your reward, my son?" she asked. Her radiance was such that he found it hard to gaze directly upon her face.

"Nothing Reylona, for I already have more than any man could want. I have the love of Mandy," he replied humbly, but completely truthful. There was nothing in this world he desired but the love of her.

"Come, William, surely there is something that I can give as a token of my eternal gratitude," she prodded.

William held steadfast. "Then my gift to you, dear child is two-fold. First, I tell you this. You will indeed have many lovely children to care for and to love and to cherish." This, of course, brought a great smile to both his and Mandy's faces. It was comforting, to say the least, knowing a tad bit the future held in store. She continued, "Second, is this." She gently touched her index finger to his forehead. Strange energies flowed from her through him. A dark corner of his mind opened as the light of Reylona pierced its darkness. That corner would never return to darkness again. She then said, "Mandy and Saint Jon can help you master your new abilities."

William had no idea what she was talking about, but thanked her anyway.

"And now my dear Mandy, what would you ask of me? You, who have proven yourself the most worthy of all my rangers?"

"Nothing, my lady," Mandy replied truly humbled and honored. "You have always answered my prayers, even in the darkest of times. What more could I ask for?"

Then, Reylona said, "Father Ukko has opened more of your mind to you. Of that I know. However, you will be making good use of that in the very near future to help your friends. Their path is long and dangerous still. So my gift to you, hardy ranger, is this." A ring appeared on one of Mandy's fingers. She felt it fuse to her flesh. She was startled to say the least.

Reylona continued. "My ring is attuned to you and you alone. It is a ring of three wishes, for you may have need of them in the days to come. Use them wisely and only when no other course is available to you. Until the three wishes have been used, the ring will never leave your body; it is inseparable from you, though now it becomes invisible."

Mandy glanced at her finger. True enough, the ring was now nowhere to be seen. Yet she could feel its presence, a warm tingling around her finger. Tears flowed down her cheeks uncontrollably; words failed her utterly.

Then, Reylona bless both of her children and gave each one of them a kiss on their forehead. "Until later," she said and disappeared. Within a second, the white energy field also vanished, leaving the two shocked and speechless for quite some time.

Mandy was so overcome that she could only cry on William's shoulder. "I'm so glad you are here. Hold me," she blubbered. She could not recall when the last time someone was there to comfort and support her when she so desperately needed it. She had had only her pillow.

I know, I know. There, there honey. It's all right. She did say we would have many fine children, William thought. But before he could vocalize his words, a startled Mandy pulled away from him a bit and stared at him, eyes wide open, though wet.

You can now do it too, she sent him. Now it was his turn for shock; his eyes opened wide.

Instantly, the magnitude of Reylona's gift to William was understood by both. Now both leaned on the other and cried out of joy for quite some time. *I — I don't know how to do this exactly! Help!* he send to her.

That's why you got me, silly. I'll show you how and all that. Don't fret, she replied. They embraced for a long time. *God, I do love you so!* she sent him.

Not half as much as I love you! he retorted.

Oh yeh? she teased back. So she threw a pillow at him, but he found that he already knew her intention to do so and thus had plenty of time to duck. He then threw another back her way but she knew his intention and just parried it. They laughed in recognition and dove for each other's embrace once more. Their life had just taken a momentous leap forward. He imagined a red rose and put it into her mind. Mandy found that she could even smell its fragrance! *Where have you been all my life?* she implored him.

Oh, just down the road a bit, he teased back. Both broke out into a fit of laughter.

The End.

Other Books by Vic Broquard

Without Warning (fantasy)

The Trident Series: (fantasy)
>Volume 1 The Trident and the Book
>Volume 3 The Trident and the Scepter
>Volume3 The Trident and the Resurrection

The Adventures of Elizabeth Stanton Series: (science fiction)
>Volume 1 The Evolution of the Path
>Volume 2 The Great Messiah
>Volume 3 Of Kings and Queens and Troubadours
>Volume 4 Chaos in the Aftermath
>Volume 5 Power Plays
>Volume 6 Age of Exploration
>Volume 7 Abducted
>Volume 8 The Emperor and Empress
>Volume 9 A Job Worth Doing
>Volume 10 Degradation
>Volume 11 The Second Crusade
>Volume 12 When Worlds Collide
>Volume 13 Dark Ages

The Lindsey Barron Series: (fantasy)
>Volume 1 The Rod of the Apocalypse
>Volume 2 The Board of Governors
>Volume 3 The Crown of Moses
>Volume 4 Dominus for President
>Volume 5 The National Health Care Program
>Volume 6 States Justice
>Volume 7 Cross and Double-cross

Zoran Chronicles Series: (fantasy)
>Volume 1 A Dragon in Our Town
>Volume 2 Dragons, Power, Courts, and War

Planet of the Orange-red Sun Series: (science fiction)
>Volume 1 When Kingdoms Fall
>Volume 2 Dark Ages

The Return of the Wizards: Twelve Companions – The Making of Wizards (fantasy)

www.ingramcontent.com/pod-product-compliance
Lightning Source LLC
Chambersburg PA
CBHW050837030726
47503CB00007BA/2205